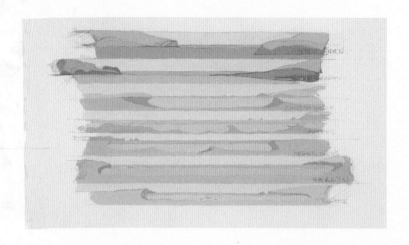

D0185197

AS A GOD MIGHT BE

Neil Griffiths

First published in 2017
by Dodo Ink, an imprint of
Dodo Publishing Co Ltd
Flat 5, 21 Silverlands, Buxton SK17 6QH
www.dodoink.com

A CIP record for this book is available from the British Library

Text design and typesetting: Tetragon, London
Cover design: Jon Grey
Copy-editor: Lynn Curtis
Proofreaders: Sarah Terry and Jayne White
Endpaper image: 'Seven Bays' © Pen Furneaux

ISBN 978-0-9935758-4-6

Printed and bound in Great Britain by TJ International
Trecerus Industrial Estate, Padstow, Cornwall PL28 8RW.

The novel is dedicated to the memory of

JOANNA GALLAGHER
11 June 1970–19 March 2010

&

PEN NEWKEY-BURDEN
8 July 1970–11 June 2015

&

RICHARD MACAULEY
19 November 1934–19 November 2016

CONTENTS

BOOK ONE · NEW TESTAMENT

Part One · Grace

Let There Be   13
Deus Absconditus   71
Laughter   115
Eschatology   143

Part Two · Love I

Wilderness   155
Tribes   178
Lilith   209
In the Cool of the Day   228

Part Three · Love II

The Ark   233
Publican   243
Intertestimental   252
Lazarus   258

Part Four · Thou Shalt Not I

The Four Gospels I   277
Confession   297
Sin   312
Apocalypse   325
The Accuser   332
The Four Gospels II   347

BOOK TWO · OLD TESTAMENT

Part One · Thou Shalt Not II

Tetragrammaton   393
Terry   409
Cell   428
Mutiny   446

Part Two · Forgiveness

Home   461
Visiting   473
Family of Love   488
Apocrypha   538
Miracle   549

Part Three · Love III

Death   559
Death in Life   568
Sermon on the Beach   581

Book One

NEW TESTAMENT

'Here I am'

Abraham

PART ONE

Grace

LET THERE BE

'You must wager,
it is not optional,
you are embarked.'

PASCAL, PENSÉES

I

He built a house and next to it a church. He had never
worked with his hands before and new skills were needed,
a great arc of learning: distribution of load, local geology,
the ebb and flow of team morale. Within days his intention to build
alone, by an act of will, had become a shared enterprise, a job of
work. There were no miracles. It would cost lives.

By the end of summer little of the original vision remained, yet
the buildings were up: a patchwork of accidents, others' persuasion,
the inspiration of materials. To look from the ridge, down the slope
of rough grass, and against the blue backdrop of a Mannerist sky,
was to see an artwork, a home and church as utterance of something
beyond themselves. This was never his intention. His vision had
been of a modest house for his family and a place of gathering for
a small, imagined congregation. Yet it had become something with
which others identified and declared representative of something
they could not explain.

He chose the spot by instinct, his car abandoned on the side of
the road. Striding across fields, he wondered whether only the sea
would stop him. But then a thousand paces before the cliff's edge,
he reared up and his body became stiff, a new alertness within him.
'Right here,' he said, and with his arms extended to their widest,
turned on the spot, creating, or so it seemed, a centrifugal force that
gathered in the landscape: the give of the ground, the blue of the sky,
the fall of waves on the beach, and finally, on his lips, the minerality
in the air. Back in London he claimed the moisture on the breeze

tasted like Fino sherry. He ran with a clever set and was kindly and not so kindly mocked.

On the second day, he marked out his plot and squared it off with small piles of stones. The distance from the back door of the house to the west door of the church was calculated with largish strides (his leg raised at the marching angle of a tin soldier), and from that moment on, this patch of land was to remain wild and tussocky, any wearing away to be the work of ministering footfalls, the hurrying over the rough and ancient land connecting him to primal dreads. At night he envisioned only lighted windows to show him the way, and if the buildings were dark, the moon and starlight were to be enough. He remembered a darkness from childhood, like heavy fabric around him, and walking with his hand before him as if searching for the parting in a curtain.

Separating the two buildings was the west wind. During days of storm, walking from house to church felt precarious, as if close by the world had a sheer edge, as it did. Sometimes he was blown onto one leg like a tightrope walker trying to regain his balance. A deep cleft in the cliff funnelled the wind into an arrow, its point tipped with a sharp coldness from the deep sea. At its strongest it carried the final crash of the waves on the shore and the close clacking of large pebbles—a heavy, menacing sound. There was also a higher note, and with its echo—so impossible on the featureless land—a desperate music was created, or a last and missed warning. Yet when he tried to listen in, nothing was discernible. By that point he feared they had all been right: he was afflicted.

On the first evenings when he lay down on the rough ground, his weight on the sun-warmed grass formed a soft bed. During the long dusk he recited Andrew Marvell's mower poems, an act of concentration, of willed recall: he had never quite known them by heart. He slept in his clothes beneath an alpaca blanket, his hands clasped under his cheek. Some nights he woke to rain falling on his face, yet returned easily to sleep, the heat of his body burning away the damp on his cheeks. With each predawn drop in temperature he sat up, the grass cold and damp with dew, and yearned for something beyond the warmth of his London bed, his partner, the hot halo of his children's presence. It was a yearning to be rid of something, and yet he was already empty enough. He had read that desolation was a journey into turmoil and hopelessness, a cutting off of oneself from others. Was this not what he was doing? Others had said as much. How could he argue? He was sleeping in a field close to the edge of a cliff. He tried to listen to himself but heard only a dull reverberation, neither whisper nor scream, and like the wind, it carried no message. In that way it was a comfort.

Early mornings were always smeared with sun: a bright deep liquid orange. From nine o'clock the air was nakedly bright, a translucence, and for hours at a time he sat back, supported by his arms, legs crossed at the ankles, face upturned. There was no rush to accomplish anything, no schedule had been set, and dawn now seemed a different age, a nightmare from a long time ago, something he'd read about.

Afternoons were spent at the top of a steep grassy bank under the shade of a single oak. The tree was old and heavy, its lowest branches thickset and curved to the ground. He read large books on church-building, fetched from the car. Facsimile plans of Rheims, Amiens, Chartres; Protestant churches from the paintings of Pieter Saenredam; and a photographic history of the English parish church. He made lengthy notes. In a separate book, with thicker paper, he tried to draw exact representations of what he saw in his head, keen to respect a tradition he hoped would provide a sense of continuity. His initial visions were of a house and church like old boats, or aspects of boatmen's shanties: walls of weathered timber, small windows, patches and daubs of bright paint, buildings that would rattle and shake in the wind yet gain from this a strength and rightfulness of place. There were memories from childhood of a boat run ashore and a desire to make a home in it, or a camp made under an old upturned skiff, supported by driftwood. At times he found himself dreaming of a cube of steel and glass, where for those who wished it, or believed it to be true, God's gaze might have a clear view. He tried to draw freely, to use these images as a spur, his hand to be led. When he rubbed out, he did so concentratedly, and brushed the mistakes off into the grass. He was neither artist nor architect, and the visionary, he soon came to realize, doesn't necessarily have a steady or reliable hand.

In the early evenings the landscape took on a hazy aspect. The bank of grass cooled quickly. The oak became a pattern of packed shadows and silhouette, and when night finally fell, its canopy became a bouffant shape on the dark horizon.

During the day he was not always aware of the edge of the cliff and beneath it the rough toil of the sea, yet at dusk this edge seemed closer, the drop greater, and the water below a desperate place to be. Like dawn, there were moments at dusk when he felt a terrible loneliness and feared something essential in him was precariously placed. For the first week he saw no one.

2

It took from June to late August to complete both buildings. Help came from people who first stopped to watch and then found themselves forced to step in as he swayed with materials too long or too heavy for one man to carry, running down the slope to take whatever end or edge needed support. Under the weight of the material, in a breathless voice, he introduced himself—Proctor McCullough—and gave directions as to where things should go. Some stayed only to assist in the one task; others lingered a couple of hours; a few returned day after day as if it were a job of work. Those who chose to remain on the ridge watched and judged him, an unusual man in their midst. Those able to study him more closely were surprised that he made jokes, was easy of manner, and claimed ignorance in everything he was trying to do. He worked with the laces of his boots untied, the tongues out. Dressed in different tones of denim he looked like an American of the plains, confident with livestock, the materials needed to contain great spaces. But this wasn't the case: he peered at timber, at the simplest of tools; the instructions on packets baffled him. He looked both older and younger than his forty-four years. Days in the sun had given his face a weather-beaten look, a depth of colour, and labour had made him lean. They noticed he used his upper arms to wipe perspiration from his brow. When the wind was up, he held his hair away from his eyes. At times they thought he must be an actor researching a part for a film, a rural drama, yet when he spoke it was his hands that caught their attention, as if he might be a conductor of music. Neither fine nor delicate, nor particularly dexterous, he used them to shape in the air the things he was going to build. A few found themselves mesmerized as he tried to give form to the invisible and disclose how his vision might be made real. It wasn't the first time he was taken for someone who might be believed in.

After a week he was left with a group of regulars, all under twenty-five years old. He spoke with candour about himself. He lived in London, with his partner and their twins; his work, a kind of market research, was at present confidential. Other questions were asked. Where was his Bible? He responded that he had many, and that not all were the Bible. He further confused them with other responses to questions they believed had only two possible answers. He tried to explain himself more fully, with reference to medieval and modern theology, and they listened as best they could over the keening of the circular saw or the suddenness of split stone filling the air. If there was a strong breeze it was as if he were just mouthing the words. At times, when he couldn't hear what they were saying, he tried to provide answers to questions he had spent months asking himself.

By the end of the second week there were three boys and a girl left: Rich, Nathaniel, Terry and Rebecca. At seventeen, Rich was the youngest, the son of a jobbing gardener. He had long straight black hair and strands of leather looped and tied around his wrists. He liked to dress in black, the logos of guitar bands on his T-shirts faded to indiscernible patterns. Terry, the oldest, was an amiable drifter. He had the smile of a sage and spoke with a quiet, amused Essex accent. His hair had matted into dreadlocks and his partial beard was twisted into thin strands and threaded through enamel beads that clicked when he spoke. Nathaniel lived closest, in the local manor house, his family well known to the others.

The boys helped out longest and seemed to enjoy interrogating McCullough. From his narrative each seemed to take something they wanted. Only Rebecca refused to take him seriously, and chided him for a vanity that she made clear would be his downfall. She didn't claim clairvoyance, only to be sensible and clear-thinking. Much of the day she sat in the grass, halfway up the bank, smoking cigarettes, occasionally a joint, her long fingers combing through her abundant curly hair in search of split ends. He gave her work to do as if she were not special, not beautiful in a way that made his heart stop and his enterprise seem pointless.

A generator was bought and via smartphones music was played. It was only Rich who seemed to have strong preferences. Now and again McCullough insisted on Bach, especially at dusk, which in August never seemed to arrive.

At around seven o'clock each evening, after they'd all drunk a can of beer or cider cooled in a small fridge, he was left alone. Invitations to join them in the pub, the chippy, or Nathaniel's for a little supper with his parents, were refused. He denied even Rebecca, her body cantilevered against his weight as she tried to pull him up by the wrist. 'You'll like my mum, I promise,' she said more than once. Over their shoulders they watched him pace around the site, phone to his ear, his free hand describing work that had been done. At times, it was noted, he would throw the phone to the ground.

3

It was morning and he was at the top of the ridge, standing under the oak. He had been gone a week. The sky was blue, the sun rare in its blaze. On the ground was a layer of sap, and the soles of his boots picked up rotting twigs. The canopy created a shadow that was complete and the air was damp and chilly. In other weather, it would feel snug, welcoming, creaturely. But today, lit up by the sun's glare, the world beyond promised a kind of bliss. He knew the composition of light was just packets of particles moving at great speed, yet it beckoned him out, reminding him the pagans weren't wrong when they felt the sun god spoke kindly.

He stepped out and took a deep breath, held it for a moment, and then let it go. Beyond the field and the footpath, maize was the height of a man, with leaves the shape of stiff green flames. On the stone and flint churned up in the fallow fields sunlight was like fresh oil paint on canvas, a deep and viscous glint. A mile away there was a small building, its slate roof collapsed. It was like a detail from a rural scene, a pre-industrial age. Yet next to it a new tractor was parked, the glass cabin and red metallic paint reflecting the glare of the sun with the sharpness of abstraction, the machine age. Further inland, the fields became an uneven and skewed pattern, the rise and fall of the land not permitting what man would have exact and square. The horizon was the start of the moor, its springy nap somehow visible, soft and unbroken—the beginning of a different world.

Below were Rebecca, Terry and Rich. A few metres away, Nathaniel. McCullough announced himself with a cough and made his way down the slope, his boots unlaced. At the bottom, as the land flattened, there was a small fire, fluttering and pale, surrounded by white rocks. It needed constant feeding with handfuls of long dry grass and then thin timber offcuts. Keeping it alive had become a symbol of the team's will and persistence, their Olympic flame. At that moment Terry was on his haunches, poking it with a thin stick peeled of its bark. He liked to assess, to judge, and make good calls. Suffocating the fire was a failure that pissed him off for an hour. From his haunches he got down on all fours, elbows out, back concave, eyes level with the fire. He blew over it with long gentle breaths. Small flames started up and quickly withdrew; grass was added from his fingertips like parsley over a salad. It crackled and was eaten up in seconds. Rebecca watched, cross-legged, her hands in her lap, turning a ring on her finger. Lying on his side, his head propped up by his hand, a blade of grass in his mouth, Rich was talking over his shoulder to Nathaniel, who was sitting on a makeshift stool of stone and timber, dressed as usual for a casual afternoon in a country pub: pink polo shirt, khaki trousers, heavy-soled brogues.

McCullough joined them without fuss, shaking hands only with Nathaniel, who stood up with his hand out. Driving from the motorway to the site McCullough had had an idea. There were so many abandoned buildings, old cottages and huts, and much of what they required for the exterior of the two buildings might be found there: shingle, slate, stone.

'Surely where possible these things should be foraged for, reclaimed, upcycled?'

'You mean just steal it?' Rich sat up. He was wearing a black thrash metal T-shirt and faded black jeans; in his hands he held taut a long narrow triangle of blue and white material, his bandana. He was readying himself to put it on; it was always an awkward job tying a knot at the back of the head, fingers blind. On occasion Rebecca would assist. The ease with which she circled him, tucking in his hair to make it neat, always caused him to blush. He was waiting on a place at agricultural college with no intention of going. Farms were for losers, apparently. He wanted to work in a bar in Exeter, or even Bristol.

McCullough laughed. 'It's not stealing. Think of it as salvage.'

'Your honour.' Terry was sharp and watchful. His face was inexpressive, and yet there was a gleam of underused intelligence in his eyes, the presence of an interesting interior world. That his view from this world was largely negative was revealed by the sarcasm in his laughter. Statements of fact were scornfully dismissed. His drifting was an expression of his mission not to participate. Every day he wore the same clothes, mostly unwashed, his jeans sagging and fallen in the seat and requiring a hitch-up every minute or so over his narrow hips. There was a lot of scratching at his scalp through the dreadlocks. Each morning he arrived with two packs of strong lager hanging from his fingers. He turned down most offers of food. He liked to discuss conspiracy and corruption in the real world; there were forces at large only he and a few others seemed to know about. He claimed to read biographies of great men: Bismarck, Trotsky, Oppenheimer. He liked greatness reassessed. Early on he was open about what he was not willing to discuss: 'Let's you and me stay away from the God conversation, Mac.' Each day he left a little earlier than the others.

Terry continued: 'Everyone knows stuff has value the moment some cunt wants it. It's basic economics. Supply and demand.'

This was too simplistic for Nathaniel and he stiffened. He judged Terry by his accent, his obvious lack of schooling, his swearing. He seemed embarrassed on McCullough's behalf. He stood up to make his point: wide-waisted, with big thighs, his genitals always created a soft round bulge in his trousers. Everyone looked at him. Terry didn't like to be contradicted, least of all by Nathaniel.

McCullough offered a thought. 'Is it that we've got enough problems, whatever the economics?'

Nathaniel sensed he was being placated and didn't like it. 'I just think it's more complicated than supply and demand.' He looked at the ground; the top of his head revealed the start of a bald patch. 'And isn't what we're doing here different?' Then as if to reset his dignity: 'My dad says we'll get moved on sooner or later.'

Terry sniffed and grinned; the crevices between his teeth were brown with little raised sugary spikes the colour of nicotine, tea, ale. 'Hee-hee.' His laughter could also be sweet and charming.

Rich pulled the knot of his bandana tight at the back of his head and then went about tucking his hair in around the sides, adjusting the line over his forehead. It was a complicated business.

McCullough turned to Nathaniel. 'You make a good point. I can't pretend I decided on this place by orthodox means, but I've checked the legal position. This is common land. And while there is a covenant stating no fixed building can be erected here, going back further, there is permission for a church and dwelling for a pastor, if no trees are cut down or crops seeded or land enclosed. Plus, at one point during the Commonwealth, a radical sect sought to build here. There is no evidence they were prevented.'

Everything he said was partially true, but he knew it could be contested. He took off his jacket and looked around. They had worked well while he'd been away, mostly at what suited them. Whether anything had moved forward he couldn't tell.

'Where have you been?' Rebecca said, looking up at McCullough. Her legs were out now, at length, her skirt brought up past her knees. There was something about the straight legs and the gentle forward curve of her back that was like a dancer at rest, with always some stretching work to be done. It made McCullough think of the small of her back, the tension there. Her feet were bare and brown, her toes fidgety, as if she had just removed shoes and socks.

He wanted to say London, to see the twins, Holly, meetings at work, the start of fieldwork for an important project for the government—the facts. But during that time something more fundamental had happened. His visions had become more intense, impossible to set aside as epiphenomena, or symptoms of something organic. He was being presented with a rent in the world's fabric and needed to make himself available for a gift that might be passed through. Similar sensations had been felt before but without the same promise of transformation. Now, after each vision, he found himself possessed of a new kind of strength, open to deeper meaning, capable of subtler discernment. An orthodox religious interpretation was straightforward: he was being gifted small packets of grace, and by slow accumulation God's presence was building up within him, irresistibly. Whether or not he believed this wasn't the point. He feared open-hearted acceptance might change him in a way that would separate him from all that he loved. Yet it was foolish to fight. The day before he'd experienced such an inflow of light, it was like waves of lava sucked back over the lip of an erupting volcano, filling the earth to bursting. It didn't matter that his capacity was limited: the source was infinitely giving and expected him to be infinitely open. A new kind of inwardness needed to be created and he was to become a receiving thing, a vessel.

So there were two answers to Rebecca's question. One involved the irresistible gift of grace and intimations of the eternal; the other was much simpler. He went with that one.

'I've been home.'

The site was now strewn with deliveries. Dusty bags of sand and cement were stacked on timber pallets. Samples of stone had been sent in reinforced boxes: local limestone and Portland stone, grey granite, pale travertine. Lifting the corners of thick opaque sheets of white plastic, Nathaniel revealed the steel mesh that would reinforce the concrete base. Big brown envelopes containing timber samples were opened for him: cedar, larch, English oak, walnut.

'Are you rich?' This was Rebecca, trailing behind a little. The question required them all to turn around and wait for the answer.

He paused. 'I have a good job.'

Terry grinned.

Rebecca continued, 'What all this costs . . . you know you could give it away? Save some lives in Africa. Little children.'

He knew this was true.

'So *how* much is this costing?' Rich could be bold and then look a little nervy, but he liked to be wowed.

'I don't know,' McCullough said, but then felt it was wrong to keep things from them; they had, at least for now, committed to the project. 'I have . . . the budget is . . . maybe . . . a hundred thousand pounds.'

'Fuck!' Rich *was* wowed, and he turned to the others, his eyes wide.

'A lot of lives, Mac.' Rebecca knew such teasing was unfair, unanswerable.

'I know.'

Taught from an early age that talking about money was vulgar, Nathaniel wanted to keep the conversation vaguer. 'Is it a second mortgage? That's what people do.' He paused. 'I'm told.'

'I sold some equity in my business.'

'Your confidential work?' This was Terry's area of interest.

McCullough felt impatient. 'Enough, enough. We're here to build . . . a church.' Said out loud like this it sounded ridiculous, and in that moment he doubted everything about the endeavour.

'And your gaff,' added Terry, pointing to the smaller rectangle of stones.

'Yes, my "gaff".' Was that how they should refer to it?

'Are you planning on being a trendy vicar?'

Rebecca didn't flirt, she liked to deaden what was around her, as if her beauty, which had about it a liveliness, an abundance—she was all hips, bust, a mass of dark untrammelled hair—needed a counterbalance. When she saw him study her, she curled her lip mockingly. He turned back to Terry.

'I don't think my partner will live in a vicarage. I rather like "manse". It means "dwelling" . . . from Latin originally.'

'I thought it was Scottish?' Nathaniel wasn't disagreeing but rather trying to participate at a level of knowledge he believed only he and McCullough possessed. His brows were knitted in concentration.

'Yes, but it is used elsewhere. America.'

They all took this in as if it should have some significance, but found it had none.

Terry produced his leather pouch of tobacco and started rolling a cigarette. 'Sooner or later you're going to have to come clean.'

It was difficult to know what he was referring to but McCullough imagined Terry believed there was an ulterior motive somewhere; there had to be.

'Yeah . . .' Rich decided he agreed but wasn't entirely sure with what.

Back on his haunches, Terry lit his cigarette with a twig placed in the fire for a couple of seconds. He stayed squatting.

'Come clean?' asked McCullough.

'All this.' Terry's hand now gestured blindly over the site behind him.

'I've told you everything.' Had he taken for granted that these four young people had chosen to trust him and believed he was being was open and honest, as far as he was able to be, knowing so little himself? It would be heartbreaking if they thought they were being misled.

There was a pause. 'So it's not the Illuminati, then?' Terry grinned, as if a denial would be the ultimate proof.

McCullough found he had nothing to say. That this enterprise might be misconstrued in such a way had never occurred to him. The Illuminati! That was so childish. He had hoped that in this instance at least Terry might drop his cynicism and set aside his default position that everything was a con. McCullough felt naive and embarrassed. What reason did Terry have to believe what they were doing was authentic, or that he, McCullough, was to be trusted?

Terry bounced up from his squat. 'Don't worry about it, boss. Maybe you don't even know yourself.'

Nathaniel handed McCullough an envelope. 'Soil survey.'

There was a cross-section drawing of the earth beneath them. Analysis showed that just over a metre down there was a layer of sand. Apparently sand of a certain depth and density was deemed firm enough to build on—to build a church on. It didn't require a rock.

They were now faced with the first of many new decisions: whether to remove the earth themselves or bring in machinery.

'What do we do with it?' Nathaniel was immediately practical. The others were thinking about the effort involved—it would take days.

'Cliff.' A neat and perfect spilling gesture was made by Terry. 'Just wash it away.'

They all looked the hundred metres to the cliff's edge.

The volume to be displaced seemed too much, as if tipping it over a cliff was breaking a natural law. Yet removing it with machinery, dumping it into skip after skip to be driven away, was surely against the spirit of the enterprise. At least tipping it over the cliff was giving the land back to the sea, which was going to happen sooner or later.

'Rebecca?'

She shrugged and skewed her mouth: she would only do as much as she wanted and the fate of this particular volume of earth was beyond her level of caring.

They stood looking over the two plots, marked out with piles of stone at the corners and at five-pace intervals.

'Just over a metre down.' McCullough gave them an idea of the depth with his hands, from his thighs to above his head. 'More maybe.'

Rich said, 'If one of us dies, we can just be left there. Buried under the church.' No one was sure whether he was being ironic or not. He tended not to be.

'It'll be unconsecrated ground.' Nathaniel often missed the tone of a conversation completely.

The meaning behind this response wasn't clear to Rich so he just said, 'Like I give a shit.'

'No one's going to die,' McCullough stated as though it should be obvious to all.

Then Rich added with a sigh, 'My dad says I'm afraid of hard work.'

McCullough studied the boy for a moment, recognizing when someone felt compelled to explain themselves, to unburden.

'Does he know what you're doing here?'

'It's hardly hard work.'

'It is now.'

Terry dropped his rollie to the ground. 'So it's agreed. Bit of manual labour is good for the soul, right, Mac?'

'If only I knew.'

'Your heart up to it?' Rebecca was standing a little way away from the group. There was never any inflection in what she said, as if she understood that the words alone were enough if your timing was good. McCullough feigned a heart attack in slow motion, hand gripping the left side of his chest. She shook her head, embarrassed on his behalf.

A roster was created, with half-hourly shifts of digging, carrying, unloading. They all liked to watch the spill of loose earth from clifftop to the waves below. It was a knack, the upturning of the wheelbarrow, to lift and angle it away from the body and then tip. There was a risk, a kind of brinkmanship, in taking the wheel as close as possible to the edge. But the pleasure of a pure, even, uninterrupted sliding off was worth it. The dirt, in its long, stretching descent, was like a shadow in the air. Then on hitting the water it was gone, as if dispersed on impact rather than disappearing below. No build-up was formed, no rump gathered above the water. The coastline would remain unchanged.

Rebecca worked as hard as the others, on the second day turning up in cut-off jeans and a black singlet. She cared about dirt on her face; anywhere else on her body she was like the others, streaked and caked. Like McCullough, she used her upper arms to wipe sweat from her face, and the mixture of perspiration on her arm and dirt in the air left dark marks smeared across her forehead, over her cheeks and nose. She kept a small mirror in her back pocket to check. McCullough felt moved whenever her forehead was streaked and she was unaware of it. She'd asked to be told immediately. When he spotted something, he'd merely indicate with a little circular movement of a finger at the same place on his own face. She'd then bend so she could use the bottom of her singlet to wipe it off, after which she'd always ask, 'Is it gone?' And he'd nod or point again, directing her more accurately. They seldom chatted.

Only Rich made no demands on him, except to talk about music, certain bands he assumed McCullough was old enough to have listened to at the time. 'It's amazing, isn't it, that Led Zeppelin weren't rated back then, not by the critics anyway, and look at them now—greatest band ever.' McCullough took Rich through a timeline of music and placed his own formative years at the first emergence of Goths, with whom he'd briefly identified. Rich had opinions on what made a good horror film and talked McCullough through his DVD collection. With a mixture of thrill and wariness, he asked about London. At one point he stopped digging and looked up. 'You must think we're so lame down here.'

McCullough laughed and then wondered whether this was also Rebecca's fear, the reason she challenged him.

'It hadn't occurred to me to judge you.'

'Is that you being all Christian?'

He laughed again. 'I don't know what to say to that.'

Rich paused. 'I know we're lame.'

'You're not lame. And thinking other people think you are can become a vicious circle.' McCullough stood upright, hands resting on the handle of the spade. 'You're imagining what imaginary people think about you. And to think about you, these imaginary people have to think about the person imagining them. And my guess is that somewhere along this imaginary chain, someone gets it wrong.'

'But I was asking what *you* think about us. You're not imaginary.' There was a note of hurt in the boy's voice.

'And I'm telling you—you're not lame.'

'I guess.' Rich turned over a red worm with his boot. 'I'll think I'll run it by Terry later.'

McCullough took a moment and then asked, 'Tell me, does Terry ever go to the pub with you lot? I mean, he always seems to leave before you three.'

'He's got to get home to his mum. She's got—you know.' Rich spiralled a finger at his temple. 'Alzheimer's. He has to feed her, get her into bed. Sometimes he has to find her first.'

This required a second or two. 'Every day?' McCullough asked.

Rich's response was baffling. 'Yeah, why not?'

'But I didn't think he was even from around here?'

'He's been all over.'

Rebecca wandered up and surveyed the work so far—a roughly shaped rectangle of dirt and mud, red chalky stone—no sign of sand. 'I don't think we're going to get on *Grand Designs*.' She started to roll a cigarette, and then looking at McCullough, asked: 'Why isn't your family here?'

This wasn't a conversation Rich was interested in so he decided to swap jobs and joined Terry unloading the wheelbarrows; Nathaniel was digging in a corner of the plot.

There was no good answer. There was so much space for the twins to roam. Down between the cleft in the cliffs the sea was shallow and calm; on the beach there were shells to collect, ammonites and flints. Along the bottom of the cliffs small sea life was trapped in the rock pools. And then there was his son's favourite beach activity: running back and forth along the shore, trying to anticipate which waves would surge up and over his feet.

But it wasn't about the twins. It was Holly.

'It's complicated.'

'I bet.' Rebecca was undeterred. 'Do you still love your wife?' It was easily asked.

He laughed. 'Partner. And yes.'

Under her fringe Rebecca's eyes glittered. 'Why do these boys think you're so great?'

He laughed again. 'They just want to build a house.'

'And a church.'

'Well, it's something to build.' His upper back, between his shoulder blades, itched, and he scratched the area, hand over his shoulder, elbow pointing to the sky. He'd never really laboured before, unless he counted moving house and a bit of gardening in the summer, and there was a quality of tiredness he'd always known he was missing out on. Life was so seldom about differences of degree.

'Are you just trying to escape London, all the dirt and sin? Is it as boring as that?'

'Tell me, Rebecca, why do you come here every day?'

She shrugged. When she got bored she often sat in the long grass marked off for the path from house to church. It seemed churlish to ask her to move. She could amuse herself for hours by looking into her small mirror, as if her face occupied her in ways that didn't seem entirely, or at least not straightforwardly, vain.

At the end of each day, the work had just about moved on and they would spend a few minutes standing in a row, surveying what had been achieved. On the first evening Terry had remarked, 'It's not much, but it's something,' and from that moment on this became the thing to be said whenever the opportunity arose, which was often. Somehow Rich's timing was always the best. Perhaps because they least expected wit from him.

In a week and a half they were done. Two rectangles a metre deep had been dug.

4

Then it rained for a week and work was slow. For long stretches of time they sat under the oak, coats over their shoulders. The ground was damp and cold, the air chill. Terry, sitting cross-legged, made little circular indentations in the earth to hold his beer can. Rebecca preferred to stand or lean against the tree. When boredom made them hungry, Rich wandered to the village and returned with pasties and cakes in wet and greasy paper bags; he seemed to have the greatest need for food, as if he were still growing. Only Nathaniel didn't mind being out in the rain, and worked on until it became like hard slanting pellets, impossible to see through. When the rain stopped the air held the moisture until it began to rain again. They felt the damp beneath their skin. McCullough joked that country rain induced fevers and that recovery required plenty of bed rest, and even then it would probably still end in death, especially if you were in love. Rebecca asked, 'Who's in love?' as if only fools could be.

There were long periods of silence, the rain taking all their attention. After the first few hours the land was defeated, unable to resist, the ground unrecognizable, the whole site awash. Rich and Nathaniel were content to chat about sport—the Premier League, Rugby Union. On the third day, Terry decided it was time for McCullough to be more precise about his views. He circled the group, the tree, can of beer in hand, throwing out questions. McCullough was tempted to believe Terry was looking to catch him out in some way, as others had tried to do in London.

Rich joined in, emboldened by something: 'It's like you always avoid giving a straight answer.'

'There is no straight answer, Rich. I'm not even sure there are any straight questions.'

Rebecca laughed; she was standing, arms folded, bottom against the tree trunk. 'A lot of people around here go to church. Are you planning on them defecting?'

There was an easy way to avoid explaining what he himself didn't understand and that was to pause and just wait for the next question.

Rich asked: 'Are you "born-again"?'

Followed by Nathaniel: 'There was an historical Jesus, wasn't there?'

Bless him.

Looking to answer them all, McCullough said, 'You're not alone. My friends in London think I'm mad. They're worried about me. Well, not worried so much as "concerned".' Rich laughed. 'They think I need help. I've said no more to them, explained no more to them, than I have to you. Not even to my partner.'

'Holly?' Why Rebecca wanted to clarify this, he didn't know.

Terry interrupted: 'Anyone want a rollie?' Only Rebecca smoked, and she shook her head. Then his attention was back on McCullough. 'Go on.'

'There's nothing else to say. I want to build a church—is that not explanation enough?'

'We're helping you—what does that say about us?' Rich picked the wet fabric of his T-shirt off his shoulders, pinching it away from his torso.

'You are nice people.'

'I think I'm going to vomit.' Rebecca walked once around the trunk of the tree, letting her fingers glide over the deep vertical runnels in the bark. 'I asked my mum what I should ask you, to—you know—get at the truth. She's a little bit intrigued, I have to say. She's not religious, but her parents were. *Seriously*. Anyway, she said, "Ask him whether he believes in the risen Christ. Does he believe the tomb was empty or not?"'

A gust of wind released drops of rain from the leaves, and there was a cold heavy fall on their heads and down their backs. It was miserable under there.

McCullough smiled. 'Now that's a question.'

'So?' asked Terry.

'First you're assuming I'm a Christian. But what does that actually mean?'

'Here we go,' Rebecca sighed.

'There are a lot of different types of Christians. Some don't necessarily even believe in God, but regard themselves as culturally Christian. Or morally Christian. Maybe it's a fudge—I don't know. But it is still true, and important. We need to remember none of us comes at this from a vacuum. Also you have to bear in mind another thing: in many ways we're living in a post-religious country. To all intents and purposes we are a secular state, and the current intellectual trends are towards atheism and materialism. I say this only because it has a bearing on anyone who wants to talk seriously about God. Now, bundle these things up: cultural Christianity, a secular society and materialism . . . What kind of battle is someone in for if they want to announce an authentic interest in the existence of God?'

Rich noticed crumbs on his T-shirt, brushed them off and looked up. 'So are you saying you believe in God or not?'

Terry: 'Can I remind you, you are building a church.'

'But am I?'

Terry liked this and hee-hee'd.

'Just answer the question.' Rebecca was chewing at the nail of her little finger.

'Which one: existence of God or risen Christ?'

'Are they not the same thing?'

'Clever. We have a theologian among us.'

'So patronizing.' It was said under her breath, with a shake of her head.

McCullough squared his shoulders. 'We might as well tackle the risen Christ, it's a bit easier—more concrete. But first, can I ascertain that you all understand what is being asked?' Their nods of assent were hardly eager. 'And whether anyone here believes in the literal Biblical version: that Jesus, after he died on the cross, was placed in a tomb, that a stone was rolled against the opening and three days later the stone was found to have been rolled back and the tomb was empty; and that later Jesus was seen and believed to have risen from the dead?'

'Not me,' Terry was quick to say.

'Nor me,' Rich agreed.

Nathaniel paused and said, 'Don't tell my mum.'

Rebecca walked once more around the tree before she said, 'You don't get my vote.'

'I haven't asked for it.'

She slid a tablet of gum from its packet and popped it in her mouth. 'Anyone?'

Rich took some; he always did. Then, as he chewed, he said, 'You're avoiding the question again. Rebecca's mum doesn't care what we think.' He was good at being persistent.

'OK. There are a number of ways of looking at this.'

'Loser!' Rebecca shook her head.

He needed to ignore her. 'Do I believe a real man, Nathaniel's historical Jesus, died and was then resurrected, as Christians understand it, and left the tomb on his own two feet, alive once more after being dead for three days?' He paused. 'No.'

Nathaniel felt on safe ground here. 'That means you're not a Christian.'

'But do I believe, as it is written in the New Testament, that the tomb where he was buried was found empty and Jesus walked again among the living? Yes.'

'This is nuts.' The ring pull of Terry's can was like an explosion relative to all the other sounds under the tree.

'Wait—I haven't finished. You have to ask yourselves something: is what I am actually saying that what's written in the New Testament is a metaphor?'

Rebecca again, in a sing-song voice: 'Cop out.'

'Hold on. If something is a metaphor, does that mean it isn't true?' McCullough could sense Terry's excitement and held up his hand to be allowed to finish. 'Could it be that this metaphor, amongst others in the New Testament, reveals a different kind of truth? In the sense that if you read it as a factual narrative to be rejected *and* as a metaphor to be accepted, you allow yourself a kind of cognitive dissonance—believing two opposing things at once—and that another deeper version of what is true is reached, one that cannot be arrived at by making a straight choice. By which I mean we do not abide by the law of the excluded middle, a necessary truth—something either/or, with nothing possible in between.

'So, to answer your mother's question, Rebecca: I believe it to be possible that the tomb was both empty and not empty at the same time.'

'As I said, nuts! Fucking nuts.' Terry offered the can of beer round; only Rich took a slug.

'So you don't believe Jesus is the Son of God, our Saviour?' Nathaniel was frowning, concentrating hard.

'That's not quite the point I'm trying to make.'

'But you've said nothing.' Rebecca kept on with her revolutions of the tree trunk, although her gaze didn't seem to break from McCullough. 'Nothing that makes any sense. And I don't think you have answered my mum's question. And she won't like that.'

'How about if I said: if you go to Jerusalem now, you'll find the tomb empty? And that the tomb has always been and will always be empty?'

Rebecca smiled with wry, disparaging amusement.

Rich tucked his long straight hair behind his ears. 'Just answer the question: do you believe in God?'

McCullough took a moment. 'OK. How about this? We're building a church, and that does suggest I must believe in something. But it must be obvious that I don't believe in the God taught in Sunday school, the God I imagine is referred to at least now and again in your local church—so I cannot be called a Christian in any normative sense, Nat's mum's sense. But not being a Christian obviously doesn't mean I therefore can't believe in a god. I could believe in Allah or Brahman. But as I'm not a Muslim or a Hindu or an adherent of any other religion or sect—does *that* mean I can't believe in God? If the answer is yes, it would mean belonging to a religion or sect was the condition of possibility. Which is nonsense. And before you ask, and in fairness to myself, neither am I looking to concoct some new notion of a supreme being.'

Rebecca had stopped wandering around the tree. 'You mean we're not going to be a cult then?' Her smirk was like a teenage daughter's: clever, heartless, not without warmth.

He had wondered when someone might allude to such a thing. He laughed.

Terry's eyes flashed darkly. 'We'd make a shit cult.'

Rich looked at Nathaniel and said, 'He still hasn't told us whether he believes in God or not, am I right?'

Nathaniel looked at McCullough. 'Are you just saying you're agnostic?'

'No, Nat—I'm really not saying that.'

5

Next day, under a shimmering sun, the grass soaked and knotted, the earth moist and giving, they worked hard to make up time. Nathaniel stuck close to McCullough. He talked about his parents and his three elder brothers. Was it normal to feel so different from your family, to be treated as if you were different? Did other families behave that way? There was in Nathaniel an honest spirit of enquiry. He wasn't interested in the underlying meaning of things; he wanted explanations, clarification: how he was to act and what he should expect from others. He approached emotions and psychological states like work on the site. He relied on them to behave with the same exactness as physical laws. He even made notes with a small pencil on a wad of paper; some things McCullough said were worth getting down verbatim, apparently, and he raised his hand when he needed more time to keep up. On the whole, McCullough found him good company, if a little earnest, and over time realized he could be appealingly self-deprecating in a way that made them both laugh aloud a beat after Nathaniel said something disparaging about himself. The boy wasn't mistaken in thinking that they had a connection.

Great oak beams arrived, a bright yellow-white; the colour, they assumed, of the inner flesh of the oak on the ridge. Bundles of larch and cedar cladding were thrown off the back of a truck and piled together. Blocks of local Portland stone the size of plinths for military heroes came aboard a truck with a mini crane attached. Fixed to the cab, the cantilevering arm picked up pallets from the back, and after the swing of the load died away, moved them over the side and rested them on the ground. There was always a little plosive of dust between pallet and material as the weight settled. The team stood in a line watching, the sun on their necks.

Three delivery guys, wearing thick gloves, were efficient with the rusting equipment. Their hand signals to the man in the cab had the deftness of close-up magic. When they stopped for a break they sat in a row on the back of the truck, bunched up together, legs swinging. They smoked in silence. One poked at his phone, eyes squinting against the sunlight. Cigarettes were finished simultaneously and flicked away with no interest in where they might fall, then with shuffles of their rears the men were off the back of the truck and at work. Nathaniel decided to break ranks and help. At first the men were unsure what to do with him, but then took him through the process in detail, discovering in the telling a renewed feel for the levers, the material being lifted, the jeopardy of the work—things they'd forgotten a long time ago. The boss, seated in the crane cab, leaned a little to the right and looked at them in the wing mirror, shaking his head. When all the materials had been unloaded, covered in plastic sheeting and tied down, Nathaniel returned to join the spectators.

'Beautiful timber, Mac.'

'I chose the oak like Stradivarius, tapping every tree. Each plank is a note in the scale of C minor. Beethoven's favourite key.'

Terry's eyes narrowed. 'Bollocks.'

McCullough laughed. 'Nice idea, though.' He then tried to explain how the materials were going to be assembled, pointing to the piles of timber and stone, and then to the rectangles of concrete poured in two days before.

'Think Portland stone around the bottom, to waist height, then glazing, the oak as columns, and the larch and cedar on the roof, over time turning the colour of silver.'

They couldn't quite see it. To them the concrete slabs seemed, in their simple naked flatness, to forswear any promise of scale or majesty.

'There was a phase in English church-building called the "beauty of holiness".'

Rich was unimpressed. 'You just want to avoid it looking like a scout hut.'

McCullough pictured the exteriors of his local churches, and felt even a God endowed with that paradoxical mix of omnipotence and personhood would find something forbidding and uninviting about them. Perhaps that was why congregations were 'dwindling', if even God couldn't face going in. Was it specious to identify this as a problem? His instinct told him incipient faith was vulnerable to small things. He tried to imagine how it might feel to be desperately in search of something and enter one of these places for the first time. Was it wrong to expect space and light to play its part in spiritual recovery? If one lived and worked, as so many did these days, behind glass, what did it suggest about God's love when its physical expression was so gloomy? A kind of parsimony?

He knew this to be a particularly British experience. The Catholic churches of Latin Europe were full of tokens of mystery, abundant in painting and sculpture. The Protestant churches of North Europe, even when simple to the point of austerity, were nevertheless bright and light, ideal for silent contemplation of the ineffability of the divine. Five hundred years of the national character at work might have shaped the various British places of worship, but what did that mean to a modern congregation when there had been a paradigm shift in the national experience of place? The values of the Church might be eternal, but technology meant the built world was being conceived anew. And this wasn't merely a question of fashion: who would want to return to damp and cramped darkness? Hadn't someone once said: people who live behind glass will be happier people? Space and light were good for the soul.

Terry stood, hitched up his jeans, scratched his cheek and looked at McCullough. The older man was staring over the plot in a trance-like state. Terry glanced at the others and nodded at them to check it out. They all studied him. Even Rebecca, for a moment, seemed without judgment.

'So what do you see, Mac?' Terry nudged him.

There was a pause while McCullough returned to them with a slight refocusing of his eyes. 'When the sun's out the church should seem like pure light, like liquid. It should almost disappear.'

Rich thought only of the other buildings he knew made of glass and said, 'Like a greenhouse?'

'Thank you, Rich. Scout hut, greenhouse . . . two things we need to avoid it looking like.'

'What about the inside?' A rare straight question from Rebecca.

What he could see was a wondrous emptiness, a spilling-out and saving space infinitely larger than its cubic volume. What would find its way in there, he didn't know—he wasn't against ornamentation, graven images. But of what? He turned to Rebecca. 'Some very important decisions will need to be made.'

She looked over the concrete plot. 'Pews are uncomfortable. You need to do something about that.'

'Nightmare on your arse,' Terry added.

McCullough looked at them both. 'So no pews then.'

6

It was a hot day. He stood with his hands in his pockets, his shirt fully open. He had stubble on his chin, rough as splinters; there were wood shavings in his hair. Next to him stood Rebecca wearing a long skirt with wide circular bands of colour—red, ochre, black—and her usual black singlet. She had whipped off Rich's bandana and wore it herself.

'Are you sure you have a real job?' she asked.

'I do.'

'Then why aren't you there?'

'Because I'm here.'

'You're not what people want in a leader.'

What could he say: he *was* a leader? If humans could be judged empirically, he tended to leadership. But that was in business, where decision-making had been replaced by endless meetings, and he got bored easily and people turned to the bored for decisions. That was one of his jokes, often mistaken for insight, which of course in a way it was. But now, as always, there was nothing he could say that she wouldn't think ridiculous. When she was in this mood he tried to avoid her, but it couldn't be denied that his sight lines were always drawn to her body. They both knew this.

'Have you come here to save us?'

'Save you from what?'

She shrugged and stirred a tray of mortar with a long stick. She'd become their expert in wet materials. Consistency was Rebecca's thing.

Terry came down the slope, sidestepping, cans of beer in each hand raised high for balance.

'What you doing about Building Control? They'll tear it down if they haven't passed everything. I mean everything. They'll make us dig all that up—just to prove the foundations are deep enough. They're cunts like that.'

Rebecca tutted at him, a rare thing. Was she intimating this kind of project didn't need permission from Building Control? She glanced quickly at McCullough, aware she might have confessed to

been in the job long enough to know saving souls was the least of it.

McCullough continued, 'I've talked to ministers. I have asked for a kind of refuge, in the sense of an open-minded welcome. What I've found is a kind of rectitude that helps no one. It's never judgmental, of course, but it fails to offer what I think is central: we should be set free by love to find our way to ourselves through God. I mean, if I was putting it in Christian terms.'

'Yes, well—we often fail, but we do try. And you're right, some of us are not very good at getting the Christian proclamation in the right order.'

The older man, his shirt buttons open top and bottom, looked around, pondering. 'Will you seek consecration of the building from the Church?' Unaccountably he put air commas around 'the Church'.

'I cannot declare any allegiance. I've read the Thirty-nine Articles and can't claim to believe in many of them.'

'Few of us can.'

McCullough took a deep breath. 'Isn't that a cop out?' He had to face it: ardour in middle age had the seriousness of the young radical and the same lack of humour.

Geoffrey needed to reconfigure his face. He raised his chin and pouted a little, an expression McCullough decided all vicars learned to adopt when faced with potentially unpleasant confrontations. It was followed by a tight smile and a narrowing of his eyes, as if he wished to show a level of concentration equal to whatever might be coming, even if he wasn't going to listen. It was clear to McCullough he was close to being judged a troublemaker.

'I'm sorry, I *really* don't want to seem rude, but you must believe in the spirit of the meaning otherwise you couldn't do the work. It's important because it's a distinguishing factor.'

The two men stood there for a moment, then Geoffrey gestured around the site. 'You say you're building a church yet you don't believe there will be any common ground with the nation's Church?'

'I'm building on common ground, Reverend, if you'll forgive the . . . is it a pun? I also don't believe in an established Church, Reverend.'

'Geoffrey. Please call me Geoffrey. Not Geoff, I'm afraid, or at least not in front of my wife.' He laughed; domestic life was a source of amusement to him. There was a pause. 'You don't believe in a lot of things, it seems.'

'Maybe. I don't know. Probably.' McCullough stopped. 'Or all of the above. I'm sorry. I promise I'm not being deliberately obtuse. Ask this lot.' Both men looked around and found four expressionless faces looking back at them. 'And I do appreciate your interest, and would love at some point to talk to you, when I feel more on top of things. Most people think I'm having a breakdown.' He realized his eyes were rimmed with moisture. 'I am in need of some patient understanding.'

Geoffrey gripped McCullough's upper arm. 'Of course. Let's not assume what you are doing doesn't come from God. Expressions of God come in many shapes.'

'Then can we leave it at that?'

'So you do admit to a belief in God, at least?' If it were possible to go away with something definitive, Geoffrey was going to do it.

'I admire your persistence. But I take the question so seriously, most of the time I feel silence is the only answer. And yet I realize that that helps no one, especially me. Half the time, I feel I'm going to explode. You have no idea how much reading I've done in the last few months—I've been in a kind of fury. I vacillate from believing everything I read to believing nothing. There seems to be theological writing inspired more by the Devil than by God. All the total depravity stuff and the good we're capable of only proceeding from God. Luckily I found a friend in Pelagius, only to discover he was declared a heretic. And then there is Molinism, which is about as far away from the Anglican Church in terms of orthodoxy . . . but it works for me, as much as I understand it. But as much as I feel affinity with some things, as you know, it's all nonsense in terms of the felt presence of God.' He felt everything he'd been thinking about for months skidding out his mouth.

'Do you read the Bible?'

'Yes, I have read the Bible. But like Marcion, I'd trim it down a bit, then add in Shakespeare, Whitman, Dostoevsky to give it back some physical heft.' McCullough laughed. It was the longest he'd spoken about these things in his life.

The old man reeled a little. Faced with such a teeming mind, an adequate response was impossible. 'Interesting.'

'Look, I don't want to seem like someone who's read everything and believes nothing . . .'

'You're searching.'

McCullough paused; drew in breath. 'I'm being found.'

This required thought from Geoffrey. 'Found, you say?'

A minute passed. The others stood waiting, watching, lips turned in to prevent themselves from laughing.

'I suspect people more powerful than I am are going to stand in your way, so I'm not going to.'

McCullough felt great relief and said, 'Thank you. Thank you.'

It wasn't the end of the meeting: for a while they spoke about the view across the fields to the moors, the dip in the land that hid the village and Geoffrey's church; his other parishes—he had three, and not contiguous, he complained.

McCullough showed him around the site, once again sketching a picture with his hands of what he hoped would be built. With the chortle of a large man, Geoffrey asked whether he was using cubits as the unit of measurement. McCullough laughed. 'If the Old Testament didn't give precise measurements for almost everything, it would be half the length.'

'Considerably less than a cubit,' Geoffrey added.

McCullough smiled, but he was beginning to be embarrassed by the others, who were following them at a distance, now unable to do anything to prevent themselves from laughing.

7

Work began on the frame of the ground floor of the house. If they were to raise the beams themselves others would be required to pitch in, friends from the village. Rebecca, Nathaniel and Rich set off to recruit them. By mid-afternoon there were five more people on site. It was difficult work, a well-coordinated summoning of effort on a single count. Some fled. Mid-afternoon, McCullough had to break up a fight between Terry and a man named Alan, who from the moment he turned up joked that everything was a 'satisfactory bodge'. The fight lasted seconds. No one seemed to see it in real time. Terry's fists were fast and sharp, and Alan was on the ground, mouth bleeding, teeth pink. McCullough blamed himself. He knew that after four cans Terry was easy to offend. On most days he let Terry drift away at this stage, do his own thing; it was no use coaxing him to participate. But today everyone was required.

Alan left with a finger shoved between his top teeth and cheek, feeling for movement. Terry sat down on a pile of large travertine tiles. His smile, when people caught his gaze, was sarcastic, nasty; they were all fools.

Rich explained to McCullough: 'There are times when Terry just looks for a fight. He's known for it.'

'Tell me more . . . ' Too much talk about people made Rich uncomfortable, but McCullough pressed him. 'Go on, Rich. I need to understand.'

'If he got beat up more, you'd think he enjoyed the punishment. But he frightens most people round here. Rebecca says he's too wired—you know . . . super tense.'

Rebecca was right. It was apparent in his body; there was no fat on Terry, there was stiffness in his gait.

McCullough went over to him.

'You all right?'

'Cool.'

'What happened?'

'When?'

'Oh, I don't know. At breakfast.'

Terry laughed; in the back of his throat there seemed to be an accumulation of dark smoke, a residue of lager.

McCullough risked sitting down. Terry made room.

'I don't even know how old you are, Terry.'

'Ah.'

'Or where you are from.'

'That's easy. A shithole. Can't you tell?'

'What about a girlfriend?' He sounded like an uncle doing his best with a nephew.

'Have to fight 'em off.'

Terry's gaze concentrated on the horizon and yet at the same time seemed directed inwards. He was angry, amused, bored, sobering up.

Later that day they worked together on the corner of the timber frame. Now and again Terry took the peg McCullough was sanding and finished it himself. Terry's fingers were bone slender, pale and nimble, articulate. As he worked he narrowed his eyes to avoid the smoke from his roll-up. Each peg was examined against the sunlight. He never appeared satisfied.

McCullough spoke first. 'I want you to promise me something, Terry. Please don't fight with Nathaniel, whatever happens.'

'Tell him not to be a cunt, then.'

'More than anyone here, he's looking for a bit of—you know—guidance.'

'Fuck off, Mac. You won't save me that way.'

McCullough felt stupid. Would he have said such a thing a year ago? Was this what people called pastoral care? It was no more than banal advice—help yourself by helping others. He was embarrassed and yet couldn't think of any way to rescue himself—any attempt at self-ridicule would only make it worse. Terry didn't like to be pandered to. McCullough changed the subject to Rebecca. 'Why do you think she comes here every day?'

'What else is there to do? She's filling in time before she goes to Cambridge.' Terry paused. 'Her mum went there.' It was important that McCullough understood only a fool believed in pure merit. McCullough realized, with this new information about Rebecca, how little anyone talked about themselves, except for Nathaniel.

'What's she doing?'

'Maths. She's a numbers girl.'

McCullough took a moment. 'Have you known her long?'

Terry looked up and handed back a peg. 'We went out a while. A year or so back.'

Two surprises. A rare personal detail from Terry. And Rebecca and Terry. The latter shouldn't be so surprising. How perversely exotic he must have seemed to Rebecca after the kind of boys who would have pursued her.

'But it didn't last?'

'What do you think?'

The finished peg was pushed in by hand, after which it was hammered in with a rubber-headed mallet. The fit, as was always the case with Terry, was important, and he was delighted when there was no movement or give, and when he stroked the timber with his fingertips and the finish was flush.

He patted McCullough's upper arm. 'Don't worry about it, Mac. We've all clocked how you look at Rebs. It's why we don't think you're queer.'

This unsettled him. 'People around here haven't seen how I clock Rebecca because I don't. Not in that way.'

'Then you must be a queer. Can't beat a bit of logic.' Hee-hee. All residual brooding and irritation was gone.

'Funny.'

'Don't worry. She's used to it.' Terry patted McCullough again.

'Trust me, Terry.' McCullough started on another peg; it was in his hands for a minute before Terry took it from him.

'So now we're getting all matey—what's your story? Your missus find someone else? You dying?'

McCullough sensed any answer, whatever it might be, would not be judged.

'None of the above.'

Terry examined the peg, turning it in his fingers and bouncing it on his palm, and declared it good. Then, after looking over the timber frame of the house, a quarter completed, he added, 'I like what you're doing here. I approve.'

Had the fight made him more open, willing to be kind, as fights can do, creating a mix of embarrassment and a need not to be judged an animal?

'Thank you.'

'I mean . . . a house and church. Who does that these days?'

'A member of the Illuminati?'

'Hee-hee.'

Nathaniel had joined them. 'Do you actually know why you're doing this?' It was awkwardly asked, like a pre-approved question— from his mother or father.

McCullough laughed. 'You're right, Nathaniel. "The heart has reasons that reason cannot fathom."'

Terry added, 'Your honour.' Nathaniel ignored him. The peg was ready and pushed into its hole and clunked at with the mallet, McCullough and Terry taking turns. Between times, Terry hitched up his jeans, fallen below his hips, and front-tucked in his T-shirt. When the peg was in he wandered off. He was attractively bow-legged, a caricature of a gunslinger.

Nathaniel leaned on the upright. He was in many ways the most masculine of the males, no fashionable androgyny in his clothes or manner. Rich was pretty, with a long fringe always in his eyes; and McCullough imagined that he himself must contain a residue at least of the pale, skinny youth he'd once been. Yet Nathaniel, with his thick chinos and pink polo shirt, his big thighs and bunched-up phallus, was, when left alone with McCullough, almost flirtatious. In this moment, he circled the beam, one hand trailing, as a young girl might do around the upright of a summer house, smiling as he appeared in front of McCullough, only to draw himself away.

Feeling a little embarrassed, McCullough asked, 'How's life at home?'

This focused Nathaniel. At the end of the summer he was expected to start the second year of a Modern History degree and he didn't want to. This had been discussed before. Nathaniel's argument to his parents was weak: he was twenty; it was his life.

Nathaniel sighed.

'No progress, then?'

'They say . . .' He shook his head; it was too incredible to con-template. 'We have this house in Putney. They say they will live there and I will live with them. That's the threat. What are they going to do—walk me to uni?' He paused. 'Did I tell you when I got into

UCL I heard my father on the phone saying something like "That's number four sorted".'

'I don't think he sees you as a number; it's just shorthand.'

'What's wrong with "Nat's off to uni", sounding proud?'

'I'm sure he is.'

Nathaniel pondered. 'What did you do when you were my age?'

It had been discovered that McCullough had chosen less orthodox paths in life for someone who claimed to work for the government, the BBC, other big organizations.

'It's difficult.'

'You didn't do what your parents said?'

'It started early. My disobedience. It makes a difference. It sets a pattern.'

'Actually . . .' Nathaniel hesitated. 'They're blaming you.' There was something in his eyes, a glittering, as if he wanted to gauge his ability to cause a reaction in McCullough.

'Me!'

'It's not fair, I know. But they're not fair. It's because you're not talking me out of it. In their world you're either a good influence or a bad influence.'

'Tell them: my view is that you can always go back to university. Two years of misery is pointless. There are a million graduates these days—personality and strength of purpose are the determining factors in getting a good job, as they are generally in life.'

'So you think I should leave, whatever they threaten?'

'I didn't say that. I'm merely pointing out some facts, as much as there are facts when it comes to people's lives. You need to make an informed decision. And going to university at your age is a little old-world.'

'I want to be an actor.' It was said quickly, like the confession of some minor crime.

McCullough could find no immediate response, and after a beat managed only: 'Acting? That's interesting . . .' as a kind of fill-in while he waited for something more encouraging to come to mind. He knew what the boy wanted, and that was instant support, an unconditional acceptance that this was a good idea, the right decision.

In McCullough, Nathaniel believed he had found a will of greater strength than anything his family might muster; after all, he had chosen to build a house and church on a clifftop, with no experience and no notion of what he was doing. Nathaniel had transmuted what to others seemed an example of arrogance, foolhardiness, mental imbalance, into the act of a great maverick—who better to take his side against his family?

McCullough wanted to laugh, but stopped himself. Instead he said, 'Sorry, Nat. I didn't have you down for an actor. My fault. We make assumptions. I should know better.'

'You don't believe I can do it?' This was the crucial question. His parents had always regarded his potential talent as irrelevant. McCullough, however, would tell him the truth. Except Nathaniel had mistakenly bound together honesty with unconditional support and constructed an understandable but false syllogism in his head: McCullough was honest; honesty was good; good was being supported.

McCullough's nose itched and he cleared dirt out by pinching at his nostrils and rubbing. Always uncomfortable with making proclamations beginning with the word 'life', he had recently found himself explaining away most hardship or misunderstanding in just that way, and here he was about to do it again to a twenty-year-old. Was there some unavoidable connection between platitudes and pastoral care?

'Life isn't really about what other people believe.'

'So what is it about, then?' It was supposed to be a cutting response, but while there was a sharpness in his tone and he tried a sneer, Nathaniel's eyes betrayed him: he was still seeking guidance.

'I want to say, people do what they want to do; they find a way to do what they want. But I don't know how that helps you.'

'Do you believe I really want to be an actor?'

There was the impulse to laugh again; Nathaniel had become almost comically grave.

'I believe you believe you want to, and that's all we've got to go on. Also, I am a great believer in catastrophic life mistakes. If anything reveals us to ourselves it's things going wrong at that level.' McCullough tried a smile, but there was nothing reciprocal from Nathaniel, just focus. 'Your parents don't want you to do this because they have no idea where to put the safety net. And my guess is they have a different view on the merits of catastrophe.'

Nathaniel nodded. This was the beginning of something he could work with; he was undeterred by the irony.

McCullough went on, 'That doesn't mean, if you explain it like that, they will give in. What underpins their position is the defence of what they believe in. Look, if you try to address what might be their more unconscious concerns you may be able . . . '

'What?' Nathaniel needed the solution made clear, especially as McCullough appeared to be suggesting that he address something that neither he nor his parents might be aware of. It was at this point that McCullough noticed a red light on Nathaniel's phone.

'Recording me is no solution.'

8

'So do you reckon yourself a mystic?' Terry's face was scrunched up after a slug of extra-strong lager, as if he hated the taste.

'Mysticism is a technical term in theology, in the sense that it means something fairly definite. For argument's sake, let's just say my experiences, whatever they mean, are very intense and sit outside the mainstream.'

'That's a mystic in my book.' He offered the can of lager to McCullough. 'Come on. You know you want to.'

The two of them had worked until dusk, the others gone hours before, and were now sitting at the top of the bank. McCullough assumed Terry's mother must have help from elsewhere, but knew to enquire was to risk censure for intrusion, and perhaps Terry never returning. He suspected Terry would reject any notion of being defined by good deeds. He was a man who didn't like to be misconstrued. Whether or not that gave him a kind of integrity, McCullough didn't know. It was in his nature to read in the drinking, conspiracy theories, even the anger, a storing away of pain, and that gave the younger man a dignity of sorts.

As the sun disappeared, Terry's head began to droop with the heaviness of drink. His stomach churned. He belched. He apologized with a flash of scorn across his face. He didn't like to apologize or to be seen like this.

After choosing the timber for tomorrow and marking it, he set off, waving goodbye without turning around, stumbling over the tussocks of grass, swaying backwards a couple of times as he walked up the slope. At the top, he paused to roll and light a cigarette, the tiniest of breezes fanning out the flame. He cast aside the lighter. McCullough felt saddened and wanted to help, but what could he do—run up the slope, find the lighter, steady the boy so he could get his cigarette lit? He tried to imagine what Terry's mind might be like at these times. It was easy to hear a tragi-comic rant, everything around him sworn at, the classic drunk's reaction to the obdurate world. But it was impossible to know for sure, and it was this that was at the centre of McCullough's sadness. Terry found solace in being unreachable by others, and the drink separated him from himself, leaving him doubly alone. For some this was the definition of hell.

The site always seemed different at night. Silhouette and shadow created its own architecture, giving everything a strange and mysterious extension, a hazy doubleness. He found himself walking around the buildings as if he'd found himself in an alternate reality, moonlit and blue, and was challenged to judge what was real. The timber frame of the house, fixed and robust in the day, became little more than a dark geometric sketch on paper. Whereas its shadow self seemed a construction of permanence, a configuration of black monoliths that would be marvelled at for a millennia. Buckets, of which there were many, and moved around all day long, became solid objects, and their position on the ground a fixed pattern that might be discerned from a distance. The piles of stones he'd originally used to mark out the footprint of the building, now strewn around, seemed to lose density, as if they were filled with ash.

He dozed for an hour, a blanket over his feet, and then awoke as if it were morning. There was soft breeze across his face. The air was salty. He stood up and looked across the cliffs. There was no horizon, just the moon against a mute and infinite darkness. After his eyes adjusted, and the stars became visible, the sky was an illumined blue, the work of a realist painter, a perfectionist.

He walked down the gully between the cliffs and across the stone and shale, bright and brittle under his boots. At the water's edge, he looked out over the shifting sea and felt within himself its furthest reaches, and sensed what it must be like to be out there alone, with no sight of land. He sat down and picked up a flat smooth grey stone, and with his weaker arm skimmed it over the water. He heard one plop, then silence, no echo. The gentle withdrawing of the waves over the pebbles was like the crinkling of tissue paper. The breeze brought no sound with it. He imagined the site, a few hundred metres behind him, and it seemed an absurdity, a defilement. What sensible argument could he make for doing this? Was he just being stubborn in not admitting that what was happening to him was little more than a drawn-out conversion experience, and it was only an overweening sense of his own specialness that prevented him joining a congregation close to his home? Hadn't he read enough theological and mystical writing to know that, if he wanted to, he could make sense of what he was experiencing in a language that people like Geoffrey Guffie would welcome? Maybe that was what the old reverend wanted from him: his humbling. There was nothing new or unique in what he was going through and the vicar must have come across such arrogant fellows before—sooner or later it would be understood that a religion of one was not only nonsense, but an insult to those others who subsumed themselves into a spiritual unity. McCullough also knew that if he did commit to a local church, it would make it easier for Holly and his friends. They could merely refer to his new beliefs as they did to others they knew who went to church, mosque or synagogue.

Yet would this not be, in its own way, a kind of blasphemy? Didn't the strength of his experiences prevent him from being just another communicant in a church where he would be in only meagre accord? To narrow down what he was going through and to settle for a single variant of such a thinly sliced religion would be an act of bad faith—surely no one gained when an individual's relationship with the divine was reduced to its commonest elements? He couldn't see how conformity made any sense. To conform was to reject what was plainly happening uniquely to him. To proceed with the grand plan, whatever it might confirm in others—mainly their long-held suspicion about his egocentricity—was the only honest way forward. But what was the grand plan? Build a clifftop church and then hurry away back to London when it was finished? Or was he to remain and become a spiritual guide of some kind? He didn't know; he didn't want to know. It was why he must remain focused on the church, the home next to it: a purely material and physical activity.

Had he been a painter, or a musician or a poet, what was happening to him would no doubt find expression in an artwork, and appear less strange, an acceptable manifestation of spiritual exploration, part of a broader creative journey. But without those gifts, what was he to do? Maybe this was why he was undertaking something so obvious, so unimaginative. Yet it seemed right. What remained within him, when the vast inner space became clear, was a vision of a small church next to a small family house, below a ridge with an oak on it, near the sea. That was it.

McCullough stood up and looked to the sky, now translucent and starlit, and, compared to the churning sea, imperturbable. He found it difficult to move. He felt no sense of being transfixed, just that he was aware of himself as both a fixed point in the landscape and a self wanting to be free from the lineaments of his body, a gentle pulse of being pushing against his insides and vibrating outward, a tiny juddering of waves emanating in concentric circles like a stone dropped in water. There was nothing to see, of course, only waves at his feet, withdrawing across the stones, froth bunching around his boots, darkening the leather, dampening his socks. It was his cold feet that broke his trance and brought him back to himself—no more than a man standing a little hunched from the damp chill of the night, a mobile phone vibrating in his pocket.

9

Early on Rebecca had pronounced that none of them were sexy, she didn't know why she came here every day—as if that were ever a good reason. On really hot days she wore cut-down jeans, a black bikini top and walking boots on her feet, her hair piled up on her head in a high helter-skelter, a thick timber peg anchoring it in place. After weeks in the sun her skin was bright, redolent with health, a burnish just beneath its surface. On her iPhone, she had The Band, Neil Young, Van Morrison—her mother's favourite music, she explained, and then shrugged. With sweat on her forehead, she seemed to have about her the heat of the roadhouse, of a southern sun. McCullough said this, innocently enough. She rolled her eyes. He responded dryly: 'Of course, you've heard that before. What a bore I am,' knowing she hadn't; the dismissal had been reflex. She brushed away at her knees—there was a little dirt and they bore pinkish impressions of grass.

'Don't spoil the music for me.'

'How can I do that?'

She shrugged.

'Tell me.'

'Just let me enjoy it.'

'Yes, you're right.' And she was. He had connected her body to this music because there was a connection to be made, but it was unfair to place her at the mercy of what that might mean. He had learned that women of great natural beauty were forever carrying the burden of imposed meaning. Perhaps this was why she'd chosen Terry for a brief time. He sensed they might still fuck now and again.

'My mum's interested in you. She's got another question.' Her hands were half in her pockets. 'She wants to know if you were born religious.'

Her phrasing was awkward because she wasn't hugely interested.

McCullough paused, rocked on his heels. 'Not really. My parents weren't religious, if that's what she means.'

She regarded him.

'Anything else?' He took off his stiff gloves.

'She wonders why I'm here.'

'I think we all do.'

'That's what I hate.'

He tried to imagine her mother and found nothing came to mind. An eyeball itched and he placed his thumb into the socket and pressed. There was dirt, which he cleared away, like sleep.

'I don't come here because of you.' For the first time she appeared unsure of her utterance, wondering to herself whether this dismissal might be more of a question to which she had no suitable or convincing answer.

'I don't believe you come here because of me, but then neither do I believe you would come here if you swapped me for just anyone.' He smiled; he was on firmer ground. There were ways of being playful he understood.

'So you do think you're special. I knew it.'

'It's not that simple.'

'It's always simple. Men are so vain.'

'Pathetic too, I suspect.'

'Vain and pathetic.'

'Am I pathetic?'

'There's still time.'

'So just vain?'

She skewed her mouth and looked at him. 'You're not an idiot.'

'Thank you. What else am I *not*?' He continued to smile, not mockingly, but taking pleasure in her inner struggle.

'Nothing, I'm afraid. That's it.' She shifted her hair around, her hands high and drooping into its fullness. After manoeuvring her curls into place, she secured them by driving in the peg. Her armpits were clean-shaven, whitened with deodorant. For a few moments, with her voice a little strained, she worked on tucking away the long strands hanging loose around her face. 'Why don't you think I went travelling after school? Everyone else did. Answer me that.'

'I don't know.' He didn't know where to look. She would walk away if she detected anything on his face, especially sincerity.

'No idea?' There was no teasing note in her voice, but from the tail of her eye she studied him.

'Maybe. I don't know.'

'Tell me what you think.'

He saw no harm. Perhaps the insight would be helpful to her. 'You knew however far you went, you'd still be there. We can't leave ourselves behind.' It was half a joke, half the terrible truth for everyone.

She ignored him. 'There are loads of reasons, and all of them make me a terrible person.' There was a pause while she finished tidying her hair. 'And guess what? I don't care. The only good reason for not going travelling I could think of was that I didn't want to bore anyone with all the tedious stories people come back with. But really, I just couldn't bear the thought of doing what everyone else was doing. It made me want to vomit. Whenever someone was going on about it, I almost doubled up with stomach cramps. You think I'm joking; I'm not. I felt physically sick. Everywhere they said they were going, made me think: I know exactly what's going to happen; I can just see it—the jungle, the white-water rafting, "Oh, it was so cool", the "local" drink, even the awful khaki shorts and white singlets they'd all be wearing. And as for trekking from temple to temple . . .'

She caught herself and laughed. 'Now I suppose that *is* ironic.' She shook her head in disbelief. 'But that's not the worst of it. When girls at school told me where they planned to go, you know what I did? I laughed in their faces. There's no better way of making people realize you despise them than by laughing in their faces. They thought I was going mad. I had to see the school counsellor. He was a bit shocked, I can tell you. I said to him: "Come on, don't you hate eager schoolgirls? Or do you want to fuck them?" Session over.'

She looked up at McCullough. 'I just couldn't stand the fact that they really believed they were going to have such a great time. Even after I laughed in their faces, they still said: "Come on, Rebs—it will be really cool. The jungle, the beer, the temples, and the dope, the dancing." And you know what—it *will* be cool. They're right. For them. But I would hate it. I'd want to ruin it for them. I'd really make sure they all knew what a big cliché they were. That's what I worked out. That's what I'd do if I went. How terrible is that? Their great time is such a big bore to me that I won't be happy unless it becomes a big bore for them.'

She stopped. She was amused and glowing, an ironic energy flowing through her. It was the confession of a truth that she believed would be with her for the rest of her life.

What could he say? That he understood?

'But you're going to go to university?'

Wrong response. Rebecca snorted. He really didn't get it. If he'd got it, he would have remained silent and not asked such a boring question. Did he think she was asking for advice, a solution? She looked at him with disdain, a mocking smile. He represented another failure in others to live up to her standards. It took McCullough a moment or two to realize that he was witnessing a kind of sophisticated tantrum. He had long believed that the tantrum was a display of existential will and was to be taken seriously. The father of two six-year-olds, he had experienced many classic versions, and had learned that when there is nothing you can do to placate a child, it is because the child knows that anything that might release them from their rage will be a compromise, and somehow they know— what gifts humans possess!—that all compromise is a kind of death. Rebecca might not be crying and thrashing about, but she was demanding something with the whole of her being. She wanted silence, a mirroring nothingness, because she alone understood that the facts could not be altered: here was a truth about herself, about herself in the world, and that was it, and in not accepting this he was killing off a small part of her.

All that was left to him was to say was what he believed to be true: 'You really are a most extraordinary person.'

She smiled warmly for a moment, as if she accepted what he'd said was meant kindly. She then sucked in one cheek. 'You should meet my mum. You'd love her. And she'd love you.' There was a small laugh and a shake of her head. 'God, you and my mum! Maybe it really would have been more fun in darkest Peru.'

He laughed. 'Is your mum at all like you?'

'She thinks she is. But she's more like you.'

'How so?'

'Vain. Not an idiot. But pathetic.'

'So I'm pathetic now?'

She didn't answer; just shrugged. Offending him so boldly was not her style.

He added, 'I suppose it's a change. Most people call me mad these days.'

10

There was a man at the top of the ridge carrying a briefcase fattened with paperwork that caused him to compensate for the heaviness by leaning a little to the left. He spanned his free hand over his brow. Yes, they were down there. He disappeared for ten minutes and then returned with his shoes changed for Wellington boots, a fluorescent vest over his suit jacket, and on his head a yellow hard hat.

Down below, Terry said, 'Uh-oh.' Rebecca looked to McCullough for a moment, quick to conceal her worry, and then returned to her mortar, squatting low, skirt tucked between her legs, brown knees shiny in the sun. Nathaniel stepped closer to McCullough as if about to confer with him, but said nothing. Rich, noticing the man a beat later than everyone else, shouted, 'Hey, look!' and pointed. Everyone sensed this man might end what they were doing.

McCullough slapped his hands together and removed his gloves, dropping them to the ground. 'There is nothing to worry about.' He wore a watch from the 1960s; its face was a dull silver, the black leather strap dusty. He looked at it. The face came into focus. The second hand seemed to slow down as it clicked around, as if disclosing time as a pressing force, resisting measurement. It was almost 9.30. The date was wrong.

He made his way up the hill, trotting the last few metres, the laces of his work boots undone. He felt able, muscular, and physically present in ways that were new to him.

The team watched as McCullough shook hands with the visitor and led him, with a hand at his back, to the shade of the oak tree. The man was young, in his early thirties, with a long thin head, pale hair, steel-framed glasses. Standing side by side, they looked down at the site. Hands deep in his pockets, McCullough listened to what he was being told. Each statement made by the man was accompanied by the pointing of his finger and shaking of his head. A height was indicated by a flat hand, palm down, and a low cutting-off point was shown with a slash of the air.

McCullough released his hands from his pockets to intervene, to describe something. He was now practised at this, each movement refined to a precision that meant even quite subtle ornamentations might be made visible to the imagination. Within seconds the man looked stunned by what he was being asked to assess. McCullough laughed. Yet after a little while, with McCullough pointing to the invisible sea, the wide sky, the furthest fields, the man was seen to jiggle his head from side to side as if willing to admit there might be something in what he was being told. McCullough pressed on, at one point seemingly using his hands to accompany the rhyme 'Here's the church, and here's the steeple, open the door and here's all the people', at which point the other man clutched his chin with his hand and skewed his mouth in thought. Maybe there was a solution.

For a short period they both rocked back and forth on their heels, each contemplating something they assumed the other man could see. Finally, taking up the briefcase in his arms, the man rummaged around in it for something buried deep inside. A large calculator was produced. They both stood over it, the screen difficult to see; it was too dark under the oak, but beyond it the sun was too bright. After something was explained, this time the man using his hands to show what he meant, McCullough borrowed a pen and wrote on the back of his hand, then on his palm. What he'd written was then checked over and corrected by the man, taking his pen back and writing on McCullough's hand. The calculator was replaced in the briefcase. McCullough invited the man to sit down, and they walked out into the sun.

It wasn't long before McCullough's hands returned to describing something else, but this time his palms were first pressing against his chest, and then his fingertips were at his temples. He seemed to be saying that you will only understand what I am doing if you can imagine the buildings from the inside out: their meaning first; existence second. He turned to the man. Do you see? The visitor nodded with no appearance of confidence.

On the site, the members of the team looked at one another: were they themselves victims of a kind of trick, because it seemed as if the newcomer had moved from wishing to obstruct them to obediently following McCullough in whatever he said?

Fifteen minutes later, the man stood up, brushed grass from the seat of his trousers and replaced his hat. McCullough stayed where he was for a moment and then flipped himself into a standing position like an athlete preparing for a race. The two men shook hands and parted.

At its steepest the ridge was almost concave with subsidence, the exposed earth after days of sun a dry mix of crumbling clay and sand and red stone. McCullough would usually walk straight down, sidestepping where the earth tended to fall away. But this time he walked around the ridge as if it were a spiral leading him down to the centre of the site; the others needed to turn on the spot to follow his progress, shielding their eyes or dropping sunglasses down from their foreheads to make him out against the sun.

It was Terry who spoke first, calling out: 'He were council, right? Building or Planning? What did he say? Are we shut down? I'm surprised there was no Old Bill.'

Nathaniel shook his head at Terry, almost admonishing him. 'Just wait.' Terry's face went cold: he didn't like being told what to do.

Upturning a bucket, Rebecca sat down, bundling her skirt between her thighs; one strap of her singlet slipped off her shoulder. Her feet were bare and grey with dry cement; to her ankles she was like an aboriginal. She added her opinion: 'Maybe they'll take pity on us. We're clearly just a bunch of retards playing in a sandpit with bits of wood. I mean, is this how normal people want to spend their summer?' Her face was pinched, nose wrinkled, as she peered through the sunlight beyond the other three to the descending figure of McCullough. Most days she found time to remark that they were like infants allowed to play with adult things. Wandering the site she often picked up a bit of timber and said 'Can I break this?'

Nearing them, he began to explain: 'As I've said, and as the vicar also pointed out, this is common land, with rights to build certain dwellings in perpetuity. But there are limitations. Building regs change.'

'Is he going to make us dig it all up?' This was Rich.

'No—he will take the depth of our foundations on trust. He's allowed to use a little discretion.' He showed them his hand and palm, the notes he'd taken. 'These are the basics we must follow. Mostly environmental.'

'Then we're fucked.' Terry threw down his spirit level. McCullough thought he saw beneath the narrow yellow glass the bubble right itself—were they really building on land that was true?

Rebecca looked up at him, shielding her eyes. 'Did you pray or something?'

His laugh was easy. 'No.'

'Then what?'

Nathaniel stepped forward. 'Come on, Mac—he's not just going to leave us alone.'

Rebecca gave McCullough a direct look, her hand in a chevron shape above her eyes. 'Maybe it's a miracle.'

Was this the moment when they all wanted to be made to believe that what they were doing was really possible?

'Think of it more as a mystery.'

Terry was having none of it. 'And that's it? No way!'

McCullough took a deep breath before he replied. 'OK. I *do* need to insure everyone. Myself included. And you might need to sign waivers. But that's not his area—it was more advice. Certified electricians and plumbers will have to be used. There is a lot of paperwork required at the end, and he will need to sign it off before the building is used by the public, if it ever comes to that.' He sensed Rebecca's disappointment. It seemed she really did want it to be a mystery.

For the rest of the day they worked without true effort, dispirited. Jobs that would usually have been finished quickly were undertaken with a dull patience. McCullough received sly glances, mostly eyes flicked to him for a second or two, in a narrow, hard stare, then flicked away. He was supposed to see; he was meant to feel their mood. He sensed collective anger building up. Declaring only the need for insurance and certified tradesmen, followed by a vague promise of a mystery, wasn't enough. The boys also glanced at Rebecca: after all, it was she who'd made them believe something genuinely miraculous might be at work, if only for a second. Her belief in the world as a set of straight or crooked acts made any nod to the uncanny an important admission. Maybe she was colluding with McCullough. They'd noticed that when the two of them spoke together, rather than facing one another, they stood side by side as if surveying something, a vista none of the others could see. Terry once explained McCullough was just trying not to look at her tits. It was agreed this was probably part of it, but there was something else: he and Rebecca seldom chatted; it was all so clipped and tense between them. Maybe behind these short interactions there was the passing of some sort of code. And wasn't it odd that only she was working at her usual pace, oblivious to their tacit agreement to 'go slow'?

The meeting was called for six o'clock, and included Rich making an excursion to the village for beer, cider, packets of crisps, and a Ripple for Rebecca. While they waited for him to return they sat in a semicircle halfway up the ridge where the grass was warm and deep, McCullough just one among them. The progress they had made was undeniable. Corner posts of both buildings were up; the ground-floor frame of the house was almost complete. When extra help fled, it had taken all five of them working together to heave up, steady and slot into position the largest beams. Nathaniel had proved they could do and always took the most weight on his shoulders. It wasn't, as the others joked, a kind of vanity, but honest toil and could be measured by the result: the beams were up and in.

Terry removed his boots to reveal bone-white skin and black-ened and shapeless toenails.

'Cricket balls,' he explained.

The real mystery was this boy, thought McCullough. He shook his head and smiled. 'Batsman or bowler?'

'Bit of wrist spin. Taught myself from a book.'

'Field position?'

'Slips.' It was said as if no other position were possible. McCullough supposed it was the evidence of his toes.

'You don't play now?'

The assumption irritated Terry. 'Why not?'

'He's really good.' This was Rebecca, face turned to the sun. Was this why she went out with him, the rarity of a quality wrist spinner?

'I'd like to watch you play.'

'When's the next home match, Rebs?'

'Probably two weeks.'

'I'm a reserve.' Nathaniel had stood up. He mimed a backward defensive shot, elbow high in the air.

'You're a batsman?'

'He makes up the numbers.'

Terry returned to his feet, the desperate state of his toenails, the layers of compacted hair coming apart, the ends frayed and fringed. McCullough found he possessed a wincing fascination with the level of disgustingness before him.

'I think they've had it, Terry.'

'Nothing the rubber mallet can't sort out.'

Nathaniel was still concentrating on his cricket shots and tried an 'air' cut. 'Think Moeen Ali.' Pause. 'I'm nothing like that.'

Terry laughed, a rare moment of friendliness between the two of them. 'Think of a number eleven who can't bowl.'

The general mood was lifted with this chatter, but it was short-term—they were waiting for Rich. There was a looming sense of the serious discussion to come.

The approach to the site from the village was from behind the ridge, a straight line north-east from the oak across a field, but when Rich appeared he came directly from the north, from the road.

Raising his shopping bags, he called, 'Got a lift.'

Provisions were shared out. Rich dumped a can of cider in the grass in front of Rebecca.

'Do you drink cider in the pub?' McCullough wasn't sure why he asked this, except perhaps that they were in the West Country, and it seemed like a relevant question. Rich and Nathaniel also had cider; Terry had gone for an extra-strong lager.

'Usually. They stopped serving snakebites. It was making us all mental.' Rebecca popped the tab. 'Those were the days.'

McCullough opened his can of beer and stood up. He positioned himself in front of the semicircle. He felt like the commander of a troop of soldiers, reduced to four, but still with a mission to complete. They looked up at him, cans in their laps.

'So, speech time.' He paused and took a slug of his beer while he looked at them. 'First, your youth depresses me.'

He expected a laugh, an ice-breaking laugh, but there was nothing, just young faces bemused—youth does not project itself forward and see the great tragedy of middle age and laugh at it in advance; why would it? Steadying himself, he placed his hands in his pockets and brought his shoulders in. He felt like a teacher who'd taken his class outside for a lesson.

'I detect frustration. The man from the council—my explanation.'

He waited, but it didn't seem as though anyone was about to chip in. Nathaniel, sitting squarely on his bottom, pulled in his body slightly, a reflex against further disappointment. Then Rich's hand went up, bent over his head, palm facing the sky.

'Yes?'

'We're not idiots.'

'No, of course not.' There was silence. McCullough bent down and pulled up some grass; it required a tug and the sound was like the ripping apart of material. Once the dirt fell away the roots looked like bean sprouts, white and fresh.

'OK. So, what do you want to know?'

His sitting position now almost a ball, muscles tight, the fabric of his chinos stretched, Nathaniel made his first contribution, a burst of emotion he seemed unable to control. 'You're not so great. We don't think you're so great.'

The others tensed up, and looked at one another, as if to say, 'Where did that come from?' Rebecca poked her head forward to peer at Nathaniel, who was at the end of the row. She appeared to make no judgment. Without ceasing to pick at his feet, Terry chuckled to himself. Rich's hand went up again.

'So if we're not idiots ... we have a right to know.'

'Yes. I asked you: what do you want to know?'

It was usually only boredom that pushed Rebecca to rescue someone, and then she usually made sure an inflection in her voice underlined her lack of interest, but in this instance she seemed to want to help out. 'I think the boys are worried it's really all over and that you're keeping it from them.'

Nathaniel knew he'd embarrassed himself; there was a new set to his chin. 'So it is all over. Fallen at the first hurdle. Didn't take much, did it?'

McCullough wondered whether there was in Nathaniel's expression, the cocky set of his chin, the attempt at a sneer in his voice, an element of performance. Surely he hadn't picked this moment to display his acting talents?

McCullough laughed and said, 'Steady on, Marlon,' following it with a wink. It was a mistake. Nathaniel's acting dream hadn't been shared with others, and whilst this one allusion didn't give anything away, all he saw and heard was condescension, his dream used as a put-down. He sprang up and rushed McCullough, driving his head hard into the older man's chest. The angle of the slope meant that for a couple of seconds they were both airborne, bonded together in flight. The impact with the ground tore them apart, McCullough landing hard on his back, his head hitting the ground a split second later than the rest of him, a juddering thud felt by everyone. All breath left his body. With more initial momentum, Nathaniel continued on and down the slope. For a moment it looked like he was going to tumble over and roll all the way to the wall of the church, but somehow he managed to stay upright, and after a second or two of almost comical rebalancing, his left leg in the air, his hands outstretched, he turned around. He was in shock, pale and trembling, close to tears. He stared at McCullough, halfway up the slope, lying at a thirty-five-degree angle, head lower than his feet.

Terry stood up with slow, reluctant limbs; this sort of thing was always a chore to sort out. He pointed at Nathaniel: 'You stay there, you twat.' Then, moving over to the prone man, bent over, hands on his knees. 'You all right?'

McCullough tried to make out Terry's face, but couldn't focus; everything was a glistening blur in the evening sunlight.

Rich and Rebecca came over, occluding the sun, and he tried to focus on them instead. He felt like a man on a hospital trolley slowly coming to, trying to make sense of his surroundings, expecting to find loved ones. Rich removed his bandana, as if out of respect.

He was asked again if he was OK. He wanted to answer something but a bitter burn from some bile-like substance had filled his throat. Where was Nathaniel? Just before McCullough went over he'd seen the hurt and betrayal in the boy's eyes. How embarrassed he must now be. McCullough tried to angle his head backwards to find him, but it meant looking into the low sun and seeing only the thick movement of silhouettes. He thought he heard the sounds of a second tussle, this time between Nathaniel and Terry, and then Rich getting involved. He wasn't sure—even his hearing lacked focus, his ears drumming to the dull beat of his heart. He closed his eyes. Under his lids the sun made perfect flashing spots of gold and red and a terrible rumbling pressed at the backs of his eyes. He couldn't remember passing out.

When his eyes opened again, he was in the shade of bodies and faces peering down at him. He heard Rich saying, 'He's not dead,' and behind him Terry, say, 'Come on, Mac. He just jumped you. You London boys are stronger than this,' and then gurgle with laughter.

McCullough's hand came up; it was all he could move. 'Like I said, I'm old.'

The nearest head moved in and blocked out more light. It was Rich again, peering down at him. 'So you OK?'

Rebecca answered, 'He's OK,' and stood up. McCullough felt the swish of her skirt over his forearm. Rich leaned in even closer, a great looming set of eyes, nose and mouth. 'You wear contacts?'

'No.'

'Good.'

It hurt to laugh; his stomach muscles were in spasm and his lungs still burned as if they had been scraped out and filled with concrete.

'Let's get you up.' Terry's bandy frame stepped into view, and his long thin limbs, always awkward in appearance, set themselves to take the dead weight of McCullough's body. His cool, bloodless hands dug their way under McCullough's armpits. There was an easy strength in Terry, especially in this manoeuvre: he understood the intimacy of post-fight contact and was well practised. Rich stepped aside, and Rebecca, watching from a few feet back, pulled mildly skewed faces, mirroring Terry's effort with an absent-mindedness that suggested the last vestiges of her childhood were still with her.

As he lifted McCullough, Terry said in a tight voice, 'I expected to see God come down and cradle you mid-flight and set you down safely on the grass.'

Rich added, 'Yeah, and send Nathaniel down to hell!'

'Well, he has gone back to Kingsford.' This was Rebecca speaking, tonelessly, as she turned and wandered into the centre of the site, to where her large soft shoulder bag was placed in the grass. She squatted down and rummaged. She found some lip balm and paused to apply it, then her hands were back in the bag.

McCullough was on his feet now, his stomach muscles and lungs aching dully, and the slow mechanics of his laboured breathing visible under his shirt.

Rebecca returned and said, 'Here.' She was offering him a strong mint, pushed out from the pack.

Terry opened a can of Special Brew and offered it to him. 'Medicinal.'

McCullough took both, although they remained untouched.

'Did he seem upset?'

Terry said, 'He'll get over it.'

'I should find him.'

Rebecca said, 'We think he loves you.' She was interested in his reaction.

'He doesn't love me.' It was snappish; they were being childish, frivolous.

Rebecca twisted at the hips and feigned coyness. 'But we all love you, Mac. Didn't you know: you're our saviour.'

'Very funny.'

There was another pause; then: 'Are you disappointed in your disciples?'

'Stop it, Rebecca. I'm worried about Nat.'

'Shall we call him Judas?' Rebecca had fixed him with her gaze. It seemed that now everything was calmer, and he was fully conscious, she wanted him to know what had happened was his fault, and prodding him for a reaction was her attempt to make him understand this. He stared back; he wasn't giving in to stupid games. She raised an eyebrow.

'Fuck off, Rebecca.'

'Ladies!' Terry picked up an off-cut of timber and lobbed it into the distance. 'There's a summer's worth of labouring here.'

'We need Nat,' said Rich, taking off his bandana and pulling the coiled fabric taut in his hands. 'Don't we?' He looked at McCullough first, then Rebecca.

'You're the loser, Mac,' Rebecca said, her lips curled in a smile. She would play by any rules she chose.

'I'm not entirely sure why you used the definite article. Is it perhaps because up until this point you've regarded someone else as a loser? You should reflect on this.' He wanted to undermine her: she was a beginner and he was years past any interest in psychological games. There was a momentary glimpse of something uncertain behind her eyes.

'Shall we call it a day?' His whole body was beginning to ache; it was as if his bones were releasing toxins; there was a soreness in his bloodstream. 'I can't take much more today.'

Rebecca rose to this. Her face, her neck, her bust. There was no anger, but the assumption of a new supremacy. He'd learn now: she really didn't care what she destroyed. She bent over him and laughed in his face.

11

He was alone on the ridge, sitting cross-legged, a posture of defeat. On some molecular level his body was still juddering, waves of energy emanating from his centre, carrying the dull ache into his organs and muscles. Bent over her bag, Rebecca had been efficient in packing up. When her bra strap fell from her shoulder she was lazy in her blind repositioning of it. It was a small thing, but McCullough recognized from this that she would not return. It was unlikely the others would be back either. Rich was disconsolate but not particularly troubled. Terry, sitting on the slope, can of lager between his legs, watched the proceedings with an amused and knowing smile; he'd already moved on. He had waited for the others, unusually for him, and then they'd all left together.

It was over then, because within an hour he had driven two of them away. Perhaps, after all, they had wanted what they had asked not to be true: for the coming of Building Control to signal the end. It was easy to believe. Who would allow such a thing to be built on a clifftop? Or, more fundamentally: what type of man would want to build a church in this way? He wasn't prepared to blame himself. He'd required nothing from them and made no promises. It was basic human stuff that had gone wrong. Nathaniel had flown at him for good reason. He hadn't recognized the level of loyalty required, the special treatment Nathaniel had decided was due to him in front of the others.

And then there was Rebecca. What might he be guilty of there? Outwardly, of course, he had done nothing. But inwardly, each time she took him on, he'd been charmed, and she was too clever not to recognize this, and that meant every exchange had become a game. It didn't matter that he was no longer a man for whom an attractive woman was always the centre of things; it was enough that he'd once been this man and that she recognized, in the involuntary glittering in his eyes when he looked at her, a residue of this. At Rebecca's age matters of degree were not important. It was boring; *he* was boring. It wasn't even that he'd let her down. Her frustration was with more than him; he'd just been more proof.

They left without saying goodbye; he was on the phone, first to work, and then to Holly. Standing in the middle of the plot, the height of the ridge meant they disappeared within seconds, as if over the edge of the world. He wasn't even sure he saw them go, but he'd seen it many times: their hands in pockets, bodies angled forward, weight in the upper body driving them upwards, trudge, trudge, trudge. They had walked these fields for years, and they were efficient at it, muscle memory deep. They were at home on this land. It had been a back garden to them, and through memories of childhood they retained a sense of ownership. It was a quaint thought, he knew, but three of them had built on this land before him, sometimes real things—camps and tree houses—but most often imaginary worlds. They would resist this fanciful theory, all 'growed up' as they were, but maybe it was this that had kept them coming back each day: they were partly believers because they themselves had once believed, and as much as their muscle memory knew how to trudge over this land, their minds were also open to this land being transformed. Perhaps this was why, finally, it had to end. The coming of Building Control really did break the spell.

He knew what this felt like: he'd grown up with fields at the back of his house and remembered endless summers of play. That was the problem with acts of the mind: with only a little imagination, all before him looked like the true beginnings of a house and church. But in reality, it all looked like nothing.

DEUS ABSCONDITUS

'One keeps forgetting to go right down to the foundations.
One doesn't put the question marks deep enough down.'

LUDWIG WITTGENSTEIN

Two months earlier

I

'How do you propose to do all this? You live a life of the mind.'

McCullough was eating dinner with friends. Holly was sitting opposite him; she had refused wine all evening. Upstairs, the twins were asleep with other young children.

McCullough replied that it could be done, even if he didn't know how: he'd had visions of its completion.

'And you're going to do it alone?'

He supposed he must. He imagined somehow that it would be made possible; something would happen when he could not lift what needed to be lifted. 'Perhaps all it will take is an act of will.'

'No miracles then?'

'No.' Unless one didn't believe the impossible could be achieved by an act of will, then lifting materials too heavy for one man would seem like a miracle.

Simon drew a pen from his inside pocket and, stretching out the fabric of a white linen napkin, sketched an equation in blue; he had to drag the nib of the biro against the weave of the material to make the marks; the ink was thick and bright and there was a little bleed in the numbers.

'God's mathematics,' he said. 'The impossible is impossible.'

Simon was the kindest of his friends, a scientist, and open to almost anything without making a judgment. Pale and gentle and slow-moving, he seemed, compared to most people, to be without ego. He lived alone, tidily; ate with his dinner on his knees while catching up with the most unexpected TV shows, and played chess through the night on Facebook. For a long time McCullough had thought him saintly.

Looking around the table at his friends, McCullough said, 'For a moment I want you all to think this is not impossible.'

Heads nodded; heads shook. All evening they had called him mad, seriously, half-seriously and not seriously at all. Gregory, often made irritable by too much red wine, declared any sudden belief in God, if indeed this was what it was, as symptomatic of something else, and with McCullough here, surely something much darker.

Gregory had the bearing of a butcher, his biceps pressed at the fabric of his shirt; he had big fleshy red hands. He was a personal growth trainer for so-called 'high-value individuals'. It was work that embarrassed him; he'd wanted to be a professional athlete. McCullough didn't respond directly, yet he did try to explain that any discussion of whether he was mad or not was futile; the only credible position was one of not-knowing. It was too gnomic a statement for Gregory and it didn't wash generally. His friends were men and women of reason, or had become so. Reason simplified things and yielded more, or so it seemed—certainly they had come to believe that the irrational helped no one.

'OK. I want you to hold two ideas in your head. That I can do this, and that I can't. Now which are you most compelled by?' McCullough picked up Simon's linen napkin and held it before him. Without any apparent effort on his part it was torn in half and became two sets of numbers, letters and symbols that now had no meaning.

'Oh, no, a miracle!' McCullough said jokingly, though he wasn't entirely sure how this had happened.

'You can be such an arse, Mac.' Gregory slurped at his wine; he tended to be a little piggish over dinner, another of his butcherly ways. 'You've just taken the middle-class aspiration of "I want to move to the country" or "I want to do something with my hands", and made it fantastically self-aggrandizing. Because that's what it is: a phenomenally self-aggrandizing version of moving to the country and/or making artisan furniture. Really, it's just another example of white flight, except that you're using God as an excuse.'

Simon had reached over for his napkin and laid out the two sides before him, placing them together; it took some fine adjustments to line up the equation. He then folded his arms over it.

'But I'm going to build a church!' McCullough's broad smile was a provocation. He understood that without any comprehensible motive it must seem like the flimsiest of projects, the most absurd enterprise. Indeed, that was how he himself felt about it. For the longest time he'd tried to convince himself that all that was required to fulfil his mission was an act of imagination—to build a church in his mind. But he soon discovered that even thinking about it made him want to vomit, as if to build a church in this way was still to build a church, and that sooner or later he would no longer have the space to contain it, and a great emptying out would be required. Emptying out. A manifestation. He feared being left with nothing.

Marvin, whose own nature was also a constant challenge to his friends, looked across the table and asked Holly what she made of all this, could she help them out? Was McCullough mad? How did *she* feel? 'Are you going to be his first follower?' He tended to end such interrogations with a gently ironic demand. 'The truth, now.' It had always been Marvin's way to press for candour, what he called 'dinner-party best practice'. All the years that McCullough had known him he had been socially mischievous, yet always claimed that his insistence on honesty would benefit them all. He'd once said, 'Doesn't the truth make us unassailable?' At the time people around him were in tears.

'Don't be a prick.' Their host, Lucien, didn't like Marvin. For the sake of 'candour' he had explained early on: 'Lawyers don't like artists. At least this lawyer doesn't.' Holly was also a lawyer. Lucien had once admitted to McCullough—whether for the sake of candour or not, McCullough didn't know—that he was smitten with Holly, and this was the reason, McCullough supposed, that he had stepped in, having noticed her reluctance to comment.

'I just want to help. I'm an enabler,' Marvin added.

Lucien leaned back and switched on a lamp. Marvin swivelled towards the window and lit a cigarette. He blew smoke out of the side of his mouth and it drifted upwards out of the open sash. The night air was warm; from outside the new lamplight looked like a benevolence.

Holly had grown to like Marvin and forgive him for most things, yet she still rose from the table, saying, 'I don't know. I really don't know,' as if not quite hearing the question. She stacked the dinner plates to take them through to the kitchen.

McCullough said, 'It's not about followers. That would be easy.'

There was some space between the table and the fireplace and Lucien pushed his chair back. He was tall, long-limbed, in tight spaces all elbows and knees. Even when he had plenty of room he liked to sit in easy knots, leaning forward, elbow on his knees, one foot in its shiny black shoe tucked behind his calf. He'd just been made QC and deputy head of chambers; this was a delayed celebration. His career path had been marked by a lack of interest in the feelings of colleagues and an incongruous sentimentality towards his clients. He had a desire to seem brilliant in manner as much as substance, which he deemed was a given. He'd taken out into the real world something of St John's High Table, with its undercurrent of intellectual spite and patrician impatience, and the real world loved him for it. Beyond chambers he was always to be found with a wine glass in his hand, often paused before his lips. Over-large teeth gave him a wonderful smile. He said he liked McCullough because he was amusing. Candour again.

'Charisma is not a choice. McCullough has always had acolytes.'

'Some things are beyond our control.' Jane had been silent for a while and was searching for an in; she had made up for Holly's lack of drinking. She was there to meet Gregory, intrigued by his job, having declared to Holly, 'I need someone positive in my life.' She was, however, more taken with Marvin, who, in contrast to Gregory, believed life was based on one choice, authenticity or annihilation, and in that moment Jane decided what she needed more than positivity was greater authenticity, and from that everything would flow. Her two children were upstairs asleep in the same room as the twins.

Marvin tipped his chair forward and stubbed out his cigarette on a plate. 'Of course. You will be his first, Jane. Follower, I mean.' He'd stated jokingly, within five minutes of meeting her, that she was in love with McCullough, laying the blame firmly with his friend. Hadn't she known McCullough liked to seduce women with intellectual flattery while at the same time charmingly deprecating their actual world view? It was a neat trick. Jane was doubly wowed. Gregory appeared to have some grease on his chin.

If McCullough rocked back in his chair, he would see Holly in the kitchen, standing by the drainer, her hands released from the stack of plates, fingers still splayed as if the plates might topple. She did not want to return to the table: Marvin's questions were the right ones, but she had no answers; she had no idea what she thought or felt. Just that evening, as they were getting ready, she'd admitted her inability to grasp the meaning of any of the things he described was having a deadening effect inside her. At her lowest she found herself hating him and regretting their lives together.

Along the mantelpiece children's birthday cards, wedding invitations, christenings, were interleaved. Another lamp went on. McCullough poured himself more wine, his fist around the neck of the bottle, the two different densities of glass clinking. Across the table, Maria, Lucien's wife, picked off the petals of a purple tulip, tore them into vertical strips and dropped them from her fingertips; they fell slowly, rockingly, and then lay inert on and around her plate, like shallow skiffs. The table no longer had defined place settings; it was a mess; they tended to be relaxed in one another's homes. It was Friday.

'Don't fuck your life up, Mac. You've got so much. Think about Holly. The twins.' Maria glared at him, then found her smile, which she flashed reflexively, but without warmth; she was an attractive woman, once notably so, and her skin gleamed. Her hair was a thick, smooth chestnut colour, and as she sat there, leaning on her hand, she clutched a bunch of it in her fist. She liked to feign focused intelligence before men; it was her look, a kind of shtick. McCullough waited, knowing there would be more; she enjoyed admonishing him. Since the births of her three boys, one upstairs asleep, two in the family room watching a film, Maria—once described among her circle as 'bloody good fun'—had become humourless and irritable. It had been noted she was oddly sardonic towards her children and it was wondered whether she really loved them. McCullough especially disliked her attitude to men. She reckoned them all to be boys still at heart. What she would have made of her husband's need for regular sex with young trainee barristers, usually in the gents of the pubs around chambers, McCullough didn't know. Lucien himself excused his behaviour by saying that without such straightforward rutting at least once a week, he would be peevish all weekend. McCullough feared Maria might agree.

'It'll be fine, Maria,' he said; it was recognized and accepted that neither of them had any patience with the other.

She wanted more, however, something sensible she could take to Holly for comfort, but they were all distracted by Gregory helping himself to whisky and saying, 'It's not only Mac who's been making radical relocation decisions. I've been thinking of moving to France. I'm almost fifty, and bored out of my mind. What better way to solve that than by moving to France and spending the rest of my days doing nothing. I want to do nothing under preposterously high ceilings, where the paintwork is peeling, the odd window broken, while sharing my food with mice.' He tucked his hand beneath the table to feed imaginary mice. Jane, drunkenly, found something interesting in this and swivelled in her chair; her fist supporting her chin.

'Wouldn't you need company?'

His big arms rose, his shoulders rolled forward, his chest broadened—the outward mechanics of a great indulgent sigh. 'I'm imagining French milkmaids.'

Simon laughed. He drank only tap water and his glass often stayed full.

Lucien said he felt no such need to leave London, but he did want much of London to leave. There was an indignity, he said, in being expected to retain an interest in youth culture beyond the age of forty. Surely it wasn't right to feel prematurely old because he'd chosen not to listen to Kanye West—genius or not. 'I have more in common with those ancient West Indian gentlemen one sees on the Tube, dressed in a suit and tie and hat and burgundy cardigan, even in the summer, for whom dignity of bearing must have been all they had when they arrived, and have continued to show an impressive steadfastness in retaining it. I quite fancy spending time in their clubs, drinking rum and playing dominoes. Talk isn't cheap, I suspect—which again would make a change.' One of Lucien's long arms was raised above his head and his hand gripped the mantelpiece behind him. He wore his father's wristwatch.

Marvin offered his glass for a top-up of wine. 'Well, I'm sure they'd be delighted to have you.'

'Thank you, Marvin.'

'You're welcome.'

A third lamp was turned on, and the table's disarray became more evident. Maria stood to tidy it. Simon slipped the two sides of his equation into his pocket. The light from outside was noticeably dim. They awaited the promised cheese.

McCullough had drifted away from the conversation and was staring at his half-full wine glass, at the brownish tinge to the surface of the wine when tipped at an angle. His business had won a new project, their first for the government, and he'd been in meetings all day. The proposal had taken him a month to write, with little help from his business partner, Jim, who initially refused to sign the Official Secrets Act and so was unable to see any of the supporting documents. McCullough looked around the table and wondered how each of his friends might respond to the scenario he was being asked to research: the psychology of public behaviour during a biological attack in London. That afternoon at the Ministry of Defence he'd been asked what insights he might share at this point, given his previous work in 'catastrophe'. He'd answered honestly. In the first instance, there would be an atavistic residue of shared horror, of fellow feeling, but he would not be surprised to find that over time others' suffering would become burdensome for many people. As nation, a society, we'd lost patience with such concern and tended to pass it on as 'share', 'like', or 'retweet'. After all, who, nowadays, had the time for close listening and nuanced response? At this point, Jim had kicked him under the desk. He'd gone off message, and not for the first time in recent weeks.

Was this really the case—suffering had become wearisome, a burden? His friends' attitude towards his recent experiences might be taken as evidence in support of this. Declaring him mad or dismissing what he was going through as a midlife crisis hardly displayed the emotional attentiveness expected of old friendships. McCullough had self-diagnosed a succession of fugue states, or more precisely a bifurcation of his self, where one self was in a perpetual fugue state while the other looked on. He experienced life as if he were peering at bright objects at the bottom of a shallow pool, only to find upon reaching in that the water was impossibly deep. But rather than actual suffering, what he felt was terrible powerlessness: if he were required to save or rescue something essential in his life, he'd remain trapped behind this infinite transparency and could do nothing.

When Holly returned to the table, she came with a response, an explanation of sorts. She stood behind McCullough and rested her hands on the back of his chair. Her smile was brave.

'I've been expecting as much. He is forty-four, we have two young children, both difficult in their own ways. Each day at work his clients require him to imagine the next catastrophe that might hit them.' She paused; one hand went to McCullough's shoulder. 'At some point he would find his own.'

Everyone laughed except McCullough. He knew without looking that Holly's eyes were rimmed with tears.

'I shouldn't even be surprised it's taken this shape. Hasn't he always been a reactionary of sorts?'

Holly took hold of his other shoulder too, and McCullough gripped both her hands. 'I don't understand what that means,' he said. 'Unless you are suggesting I don't always fully embrace change.' It was Holly who had worked out that his nature, outwardly habitual, was really quite flexible, new habits easily adopted.

'He thinks he's like Blake.' She said it ruefully, yet with a little admiration.

'From *Blake's 7*?' asked Simon.

'Blake Edwards?' asked Marvin.

'Only the crumbliest, Blakiest chocolate?' Jane blurted out, and then sat back in her chair, not entirely sure why she'd said it.

McCullough dropped a shoulder, twisted his neck and skewed his gaze upward at Holly. 'Blake and his wife sat in their garden, naked, imagining they were in Eden; he was rightly suspicious of the impact of the Industrial Revolution on the nature of man. Can't we just say of some reactionaries that they are merely super-radical, an epoch in advance?'

Even when he was joking, Holly found his self-assessments difficult to take, especially in company; he had always been unashamed of his abilities. She slid her hands out from under his and moved around the table to sit down. Maria left to collect the cheese. Port glasses were placed on the table by Lucien. Jane was now staring at Marvin, chin on her fist again; her expression seemed to say, 'So, who are you—you mysterious man?' It was brazenly flirtatious. Lucien raised his eyebrows. Being taken in by Marvin was a personality flaw. Marvin tended to feel the same.

'Marvin has a son in Australia,' Maria threw in, returning with the cheese, talking to Jane's blind side.

'Yes, I am a person with a son in Australia.' Legs crossed away from the table, blowing smoke out of the window, he was really only available to them in quarter-profile.

'That's a long way,' Jane said.

'It is.'

'You don't like to talk about it?'

'What is there to say?'

'When did you last see him?'

'A week ago.'

'Oh.' Nothing too tragic, then.

Holly put her hand on Jane's arm. 'He's really a lovely boy.'

Simon started to make little cheese sandwiches with water biscuits. It was a thing he did. He liked the give of the cheese under the two brittle surfaces when pressed between thumb and finger. If the countervailing forces of up-and-downward pressure were too great and slightly differently exerted, there was a mini-explosion, a centripetal fanning out of cheese and hard crumbs. To the onlooker it looked like Simon was clicking his fingers with a mini-sandwich between them. He had once drawn the equation for this energy event in the air. It was remarkably long and he wasn't entirely sure he'd got it right, rubbing out sections in mid-air. They were expected to follow. If the mini-sandwiches didn't break up, they were eaten whole, distorting his speech.

'I'm thinking of taking time off to look for a site,' McCullough said.

Knowing he also planned to build a family home, Maria focused on this. 'Are you going, Holly? What about the twins?'

'No. We're not invited, are we, Mac?'

The white tablecloth before him had the darkly pale shapes of ingrained wine stains. He looked up. 'What can I say? You haven't been too keen . . .'

'Do you know where you're heading, Mac—or are you waiting for divine inspiration?' There was perspiration on Gregory's forehead; he'd turned his cuffs back; his fists were balled together on the table. They reminded McCullough of a knuckle of pork he'd once been served for lunch in Prague; he'd been alone and had eaten it all with a bottle of cheap Czech wine. In between mouthfuls he'd read Kafka's long letter to his father.

'It's a nice thought. Being led somewhere, through all those country lanes.' Lucien wasn't without a romantic side.

'You'll need to learn to drive first, darling,' Maria said. It was a fact worth pointing out, if only to remind the group that two of the five males at the table couldn't drive, Simon being the other one. What always made the subject more amusing was that Lucien only had to lean back to locate framed photographs of himself at the helm of various tractors, and only a little further away, a large photo of him pretending to drive a tank.

Gregory asked, 'Are you taking the Audi?' The substance of the question was understood—Holly and McCullough owned two cars—but his reason for asking it mystified everyone.

Jane looked around at their faces. 'I think he'll do it.'

Marvin hadn't been entirely wrong in his assessment of her affections. But it wasn't love she felt for McCullough; there was just something, to her mind, intrinsically moving about such ambition.

Marvin was quick to comment, 'Self-build isn't a trope for self-help.'

'Has anyone read *Walden?*' McCullough asked, but was ignored.

'This is never going to happen, Mac.' With the heel of his hand Gregory rubbed at a drop of port that had landed on his shirt. 'Admit it.'

Maria eyed Marvin's cigarette packet. 'Let him have his thing.' She didn't care if she contradicted herself; she found Gregory brutish and wondered why he was there.

'Yes, I'll grow out of it, I'm sure.'

'Now, now,' Lucien said.

'The thing is . . .' At first Maria's appeal was to Lucien, but then to the whole table. 'I mean no one's even bothered to ask him if he believes in God.'

There was now port on Gregory's chin, and he tried to locate it with his thick tongue. 'Personally I am all for the New Atheists. A most amusing bunch. I believe in the Hubble Telescope. Isn't that right, Simon?'

Simon looked up while running his finger around the circumference of his water biscuit and Roquefort sandwich. 'If you don't publish primary research that isn't subject to peer review, you can say anything you like.' There was relevance in there somewhere.

Jane's head swivelled around to face McCullough, her fist now a pivot for her chin. '*Do* you?' Her drunkenness has something attractively melting about it.

Holly placed her hand over Jane's other hand; complex messages of tact were sent.

'It's a simple question.' Maria cradled her wine glass at her chest and shook back her hair; she disliked her husband's insistence on port with cheese. Her first bottle of red wine was open by mid-afternoon.

Cigarette packet held between his thumb and forefinger, Marvin judged height and trajectory so it would make it over the table without hitting anything; and with his mouth drawn down in an attempt for genuine accuracy, gently threw it in front of Maria. 'Go on, girl—you know you want to.'

Maria flicked the packet of cigarettes away. 'Stop trying to protect your friend.'

McCullough held up his hand. 'Wait.' He looked at Lucien. 'Permission to speak with latitude?'

Sage nod. 'Permission granted.'

'The question is inadmissible. No meaningful answer can be given.'

'Ha!' Maria looked around the table—she'd won something, surely.

Gregory vigorously scratched the back of his hand, then his exposed chest; there was a crackling sound. 'Funny but not really good enough, Mac. You have to give us something.'

'I'm not entirely sure he does,' Lucien pointed out.

'Maybe he doesn't know himself.' Maria offered this as a deep insight; she was proud of herself.

There were looks exchanged between Holly and McCullough that no one could decipher, but guesses were made. McCullough was unashamed by displays of sudden bad behaviour and Holly was warning him now wasn't the time.

He turned to Simon. 'Please, Si, ask them to define their terms.'

'Everyone. Please define your terms.'

A boy child appeared, dressed only in pyjama bottoms, worn below his hips; his ribcage was visible, almost like an X-ray, his stomach smoothly concave.

'I'm going to bed. Alfie's staying up.' He crossed his arms, turned and was gone.

'Good night, Kieran,' Maria called. 'No kiss for Mum?' As she heard footsteps thumping up the stairs, she added too loudly: 'See if I care.' It was meant to be funny. Her laugh was embarrassed, shrill. Lucien grimaced.

'Not sure we're going to produce a Proust.' He'd read Modern Languages. His dissertation had been on Combray as a stifling prison, the pollen of the abundant hawthorn the cause of Proust's asthma. He had been awarded a double first.

'I wouldn't want to.' Maria was snappish because they hadn't laughed with her. 'Our children are self-reliant.'

'Anyone read *Self-Reliance*?' McCullough asked.

'Where were we?' Once again turned towards the window, Marvin winked at Maria and nodded at his cigarette packet.

'Yes, Mac—where were we?' Gregory sat forward, elbows now on the table, fists balled together.

Holly stood up. 'I'm going to check on the twins.' She disentangled her silver bracelets and shook out her wrists. 'Then we should think about going.'

'Is it perverse that we're all meeting again tomorrow?' Lucien raised his port glass. 'Staying with the Proust allusion, I would hate to think we're like Madame Verdurin's "little clan". Each age has its own version of vulgarity.'

Like her husband's, Maria's neck was long, and tended to strain and flush when she was tense, becoming blotchy.

McCullough looked at her and then Lucien. 'It's only when we're here that we're certain of not being vulgar.'

Maria covered her neck with one hand. 'I want to know about Mac and God.'

'All right. All right.'

'Careful, Mac.' Marvin didn't even bother turning his face to the room; he was now almost as relaxed as it was possible to be for someone whose antennae for mischief were always alert. He tended to smoke with his chin up, cigarette always at one side of his mouth. It hadn't been lost on the others that the antipathy between Lucien and Marvin was based on an odd mirroring effect when they encountered each other. They both saw versions of themselves they found deplorable.

'Why's he got to be careful, Marvin?' Maria sat up a little primly, although she wanted to suggest that by defending his friend, it was Marvin who was taking things too seriously.

When in conflict with McCullough, Maria was a prime target for Marvin's social mischief, as if somehow McCullough stripped her wiring and left her exposed—it was an obvious assumption that if they fucked it would be electric. Marvin had even said so once.

'No reason. Difficult subject, that's all.'

Impatience got the better of her. 'Difficult? Really? To go to church on Sunday? What about marriage—you and Holly aren't married, surely if you believe in God that's ...' If she could amass a number of arguments she might win twice: be seen to be clever *and* make McCullough look a fool.

To him the first question was irrelevant, the second foolish. He decided to challenge her. '"Surely that's ..." what? A sin? You're going with that as an argument: a belief in God makes our relationship sinful?'

Lucien tended not to come to the defence of his wife in these situations, but whenever he did so Maria reacted as if he were opening up a new front of attack against her. Tonight, he set about opening another bottle of port.

On the other side of the table, there was something about Jane that only Simon had noticed: she had moved her chair closer to Gregory and had slid her arm under his and was now resting her head on his bicep. Simon raised his eyebrows at this, puzzled over how it had happened without comment. He rather liked Jane and had earlier wondered whether, through Holly, he might ask her out for a walk or a cup of tea. Gregory didn't appear to have noticed, or else had just taken it for granted, as if his bicep was a natural place of rest. With his free hand he flicked the fallen tulips petals over the table. 'Just answer her question, Mac. Do you actually believe in God or not?'

'Jesus—you're supposed to be educated people. You should know such a question is meaningless. Unless, God forbid, you think I am to answer in terms of a man in the sky with a grey beard, who is receptive to our requests for intercession, and makes judgments about our actions and what is to happen to us after—you know—we die.'

'Neatly put.' Lucien liked such summing up. Clarity and sarcasm were what he was required to deliver most days in court.

Holly returned from checking on the twins. 'Please tell me it's sorted.' She halted when she saw the side of Jane's head resting on Gregory's arm. 'Jane?'

Without moving, she explained, 'I'm a little drunk and he's comfortable. I will be leaving with you guys, don't worry.'

'Shame!' Gregory laughed. Simon took in a deep breath. Holly noticed and smiled at him. There was a moment of silence, and then, sitting down, she said coolly, 'Why don't you tell them what you told me.'

McCullough stared at her. 'Please, Holly—'

'Cross-examine him, Lucien—do your thang.' Unaccountably, Gregory was now chewing a tulip leaf, dealing with its bitter taste.

'"Thang"—really, Gregory?' Lucien mock shivered. 'Anyway—if he is to be cross-examined, he will need to be examined first. Due process and all that.'

'That's what I'm doing . . .' Maria had covered Holly's hand.

'I think you'll find that's Marvin.'

'OK, OK,' McCullough said. 'If you think this is somehow necessary . . .'

'Actually, please . . . can you . . . ?' Maria gestured for McCullough to wait a moment. She wanted everyone to concentrate and Lucien had just stood to top up the glasses of those drinking port, his long body bending at the waist over the length of the table, and Simon had pulled the cheese board closer to himself and was trying to cut delicate, almost transparently thin, slices of the Manchego. He noticed everyone looking at him. 'I want it to melt.' His early cheese-sandwich experiment had made a mess, and with a straight stiff hand he corralled the crumbs off the edge of the table, letting them fall into the palm of the other. He then funnelled the crumbs out of a loose fist onto his plate. 'I'm ready.'

'Thank you, Simon.' Maria smiled, and turned to McCullough. 'You were saying.'

McCullough's willingness to pause, allowing her to prepare the table for his answer, had warmed Maria towards what he was about to say. She now no longer wished him to fail, but, as though he had been invited by her for this specific moment, the very opposite—she wanted him to dazzle.

McCullough had dreaded this moment for months. He drew a slip of paper out of his inside pocket. 'I have a little something prepared.'

The laughter around the table was genuine. He snapped open the folded notepaper with a rapid up and down movement of his eyebrows. More laughter. A short passage was flashed at them. No laughter—it was time to get on with it.

He needed to take a deep breath. If he didn't deliver this quickly, he likely wouldn't finish. He looked at Holly. Scratched his ear. Took a gulp of wine.

'Before I begin—a word on pronouns. I've used "He" and "Him" for God. "It" didn't feel right, and if I'd used "She" you'd be distracted by that choice. What can I say . . . the whole enterprise is intrinsically problematic in terms of language . . .'

'Get. On. With. It.' This was said by more than one voice. Maria smiled, pleased by the unity they were displaying.

'OK. OK. Here goes.' McCullough laid the piece of paper before him; the words were blurry and there was a slight breaking up of the letters that crossed the folds.

'This is what I think. Or what I thought. Something.' He used his finger beneath the words to make sure he read them without mistake.

'"God is the transcendent Other for whom creation, what we know as life, is a gratuitous act of love, a dispossession of a portion of His infinite creativity given over to our thriving. It is a gift from His infinite excess. That we can know Him at all is because of the possibility of this excess within us, which we experience as love, art, great feats of the mind. Our bounty is Him."'

Maria: 'Fuck.'

Jane to Holly: 'I love Mac. You're so lucky.'

Lucien: 'Say again?'

McCullough felt sick and embarrassed and exposed. 'Our bounty is Him.' Did he really write that? What could he possibly mean? He wanted to push himself away from the table and leave, to search for a cleansing mouthful of fresh air, wintry and honest, redeeming, hot in his chest. But outside, the air was full of the promise of spring, of the simple bounty of physical life.

Gregory sat back, surprising Jane, and said, 'That's bollocks and you know it. What's that got to do with anything anyone thinks about God? It's a cop out. You can't build a church based on that. No one will come.'

The impulse to flee was soon replaced by sadness; a formless, sickening sadness. There was something irrevocable about his confession, yet he knew it meant nothing—it was just a string of clever words given torque by a slickness of delivery, a gift he possessed. He wanted to cry, to sob, and be held by Holly, squashed between the twins, and give himself to everything loving around him—*his* bounty. Perhaps that's all it would take to slip through the infinite transparency back into the world. All he needed to do was focus on his family, turn sideways, draw his body up, and slip around. But it was impossible. There was no narrow passageway, however determined he was and slender he became. You cannot disbelieve what you believe. There is no choice. He was committed. Indeed, with a half-filled glass of wine in his hand, he felt the separating field was greater than it had been even moments ago, the transparency deeper, more solid. He shouldn't have said anything; what a fool he was. What a stupid fucking fool.

Holly looked around the table and then at him. She paused. 'I'm not sure you're being entirely honest, are you, Mac?'

2

No one talked much in the car. The four children were asleep in the two sets of back seats; Holly was between the twins, stroking their hair. Jane was in the passenger seat next to McCullough. Although she claimed not to have fallen asleep on Gregory's arm, she was worried she'd missed something. When they parked across the road from her house there was a moment of silence, as if something disastrous had happened, and each of them had to face the rest of the night alone. McCullough helped carry in one of her children. Neither twin woke up on the two-minute journey home nor when being transferred from car to bed; instead they lolled in their parents' arms as if their heads contained a revolving weight. Placed carefully into bed, they kept their shape on the cool mattresses. Drawing up their duvets gave McCullough comfort. He noted in silence something he and Holly had often mentioned: that each child's innermost character was apparent when asleep.

Holly made mint tea and set the cup on his bedside table. He took off his watch and placed it on the chest of drawers. The bed was unmade from the morning and he straightened it. They had lived together for eleven years and the routine at bedtime was fixed. There was little talk—that was a morning thing now, as was sex, when it happened. They had a large bed with an expensive mattress so neither was disturbed by the other during the night. Each read underneath their own bedside light, and had learned to sleep with the other's light on. In most weather Holly started the night in pyjamas and socks but by morning was naked. McCullough wore pyjama bottoms. Tonight, he looked down at his stomach, at the newish band of flesh around his waist, the soft covering of dark hair with growth patterns that seemed to obey different currents. He'd once described middle age as the time when the body's transformations and discolorations happened *to* you and not by choice, but you still recognized yourself; old age, he surmised, didn't even allow for the latter. He now divided life into two parts, not allowing for a middle section at all. The first was when the mind and body were in alignment, physical and mental growth co-extensive; and the second when any feeling of youth was an illusion because the body was *prima facie* evidence of where exactly you were in respect to death. Which was where he positioned himself at the moment. The cusp, he believed, had been a few months back.

Holly stood by the side of the bed. She was in white cotton pyjamas. Dark underwear was visible; she had her period. He felt this put her at a disadvantage, but then he was standing in baggy pyjama bottoms with fat around his middle.

'You didn't tell them everything. Why not?' She had a novel in her hand.

'I don't want to talk about it.'

'Why not?'

'Because I feel terrible. I should never have said anything. I feel foolish and stupid.'

When he'd first confessed to fearing he'd been approached by God, she'd accused him of being a child of enthusiasms. As insults go it wasn't a terrible condemnation of character, but it was aimed to belittle what he was experiencing by reminding him of his long-past Romantic inclination to be open to such notions, rather meanly referring to a phase in his life she'd only heard about from *him*.

But these days their arguments rapidly reached a point where Holly felt everything he said was a judgment on her, on the family. 'We're clearly not enough for you. Just admit it.' Demanding that he confess this was the nearest she got to high emotionalism.

The accusation was difficult to counter: to prove that his love and commitment to his family were not diminished he had to talk about a largeness of capacity, to set himself apart from others for whom these things were enough. It meant periods of silence that he accepted must seem like unwillingness to face the issue.

Holly stayed standing by her side of the bed. It was a kind of protest.

'We need to sort it out, Mac. You need to decide what you want. I wouldn't care if you were willing to admit it's a midlife crisis.'

'You're not being fair. Have you thought about why people go through midlife crises and whether it's applicable to me?'

'But it's you and not others who are going through this.'

'And you are the one calling it a midlife crisis without thinking about whether . . . I don't know.'

It was easy to lose track of what the other was actually saying, what was meant.

'It's not just me. Everyone *is*.'

'Everyone isn't. What about Simon?'

'You ripped up his thing . . .'

'I didn't rip it; it came apart in my hands.'

'Mac, listen to yourself. Please.'

'I'm not saying anything other than it came apart in my hands.'

Holly softened. 'Everyone's worried. I'm worried.'

'That's because everyone thinks I'm having some kind of break-down. But what if I'm not?'

She didn't reply. She'd grown tired of saying *If it's not a break-down, then what is it?*

McCullough continued: 'How do you expect me to prove this isn't a midlife crisis? You know better than anyone it's impossible to prove a negative. And it's doubly impossible to prove *what* it is, because whatever I say will sound ridiculous. It will sound like at best a midlife crisis, at worst full-on madness. And then we're back to me trying to prove a negative again. Please, just trust me: I'm not mad. I haven't gone mad.'

He saw a flicker of sympathy in her. Holly regarded double binds as one of life's great traps. But it wasn't so much the logic he needed her to set aside, but to accept something that might be beyond her immediate ken. However, suggesting this tended not to wash; it judged her to be narrower than him, and that wasn't fair.

He sat on the bed, quarter-profile, one knee up, looking down into his lap, the fly of his pyjamas open. He found the inertness of his genitals dispiriting; there was no sense of hidden potency. Maybe it was all about this—a flaccid cock. He closed the gap and looked at Holly. Her black underwear was like a shadow beneath her pyjamas.

'What are we *actually* arguing about?'

'You, Mac. You. And what all this means for us as a family.'

He looked at her, narrowed his eyes; he was exhausted. 'But what's going to change? I mean, fundamentally?'

Holly remained standing. 'God, you're so frustrating. You say *you've* changed fundamentally.'

'Yes . . . And no.'

'You can't say that! It's not fair. You've either changed or you haven't.'

'Can we not deepen? And that be fundamental, but not—I don't know—essential?'

'Fundamental . . . essential . . . You've changed, and I'm scared.'

Early on in their relationship, when their love for each other was a subject for analysis and dissection (did it differ from other attachments in their pasts?), he wondered aloud about its gener-osity, its longevity. Yes, it felt different . . . deeper in a way neither of them had encountered before. But did it have the capacity to endure a long life together? In short, what could Holly take and still love him? She had asked for specifics: 'What do you mean? If you were unfaithful or you became sick, for instance?' Sickness had split up her parents. She stated: 'Unfaithfulness apart, I think I can cope with most things.' His response was prescient: 'Love is only tested by things we can't cope with.' Had he been truly prescient, he might have asked, 'What about a life-changing moment with God at its heart?' Would she have shrugged it off as nothing compared to unfaithfulness and true sickness? But now he wondered whether she would prefer him organically ill, or in love with another woman, eventualities she'd considered. Instead he'd decided to sell a part of his business and use the proceeds to build a church as an expression of God, of whom he maintained he had no understanding, or even definite belief in. What could she say?

'I don't believe I'm different in kind, but maybe in degree.'

She shook her head. It was a stock phrase, one he used with clients. 'I want you to see someone. I want you to get help. You owe me that.'

He didn't respond, and this last request felt like the final exchange of the night. Holly moved to the door and listened for stirrings in the twins' bedroom. 'All quiet.'

'Good. Let's hope they sleep past seven.'

Together they plumped the pillows and sat on the bed, backs to each other. Holly removed her watch and dumped it on her bedside table. They shifted themselves onto the bed and opened their books. Holly was making her way through Zola's *Les Rougon-Macquart* series—one every few months. She'd reached *La Bête humaine*, but was finding the details about trains somewhat dull. She liked to read on her side, turned away from him; some nights she wore reading glasses, depending on whether or not she remembered to bring them upstairs with her. He remained sitting up, reading glasses on the end of his nose. He was halfway through volume three of a five-volume critical biography of Dostoevsky. It was disappointing; he wanted more enthusiasm for the Russian's genius, a deeper sense of the man. After the first volume, the biography read like lists of literary journals, their failure, the inevitable debts, and then relatively straightforward interpretations of the novels. He hadn't known that the first part of *The Idiot* was written over a few days in Italy; but he couldn't forgive the biographer for not expressing any great wonder at this, and not exploring what drives a writer to conceive the first scene in Nastasya's apartment, where the collective self-abasement reaches such a desperate and comic pitch that the reader is offered a kind of apotheosis, bearing witness to what only God usually knows of a man.

Within minutes, Holly turned off her light and got under the duvet, tugging a little, pulling it over his raised knees. She was quickly asleep. He read for another twenty minutes and then closed the book and took off his reading glasses. It was necessary to reach over the alarm clock to place both down safely. He switched off the bedside light, turned on his side and looked across to the window. The blind was not completely down, its long base resting at a fifteen-degree angle to the sill, propped up at one end by a Lego construction of a small spacecraft built out of white and blue bricks. The streetlamp outside produced a pale yellow light, and every few minutes car headlamps shone through and created expanding and contracting scalene triangles across the walls and ceiling, withdrawing into a single point exactly in the corner of the room.

Over the last few weeks, whenever McCullough switched off his bedside light and turned over to sleep, he experienced a sense of physical embodiment that was new to him. It lasted only a few seconds, a minute at most, but in that time he felt vividly present. There was no overflow or loss of self, just the sensation of being perfectly contained, as if he were neatly and compactly pressed up against the edges of his body and making gentle contact with the world, like a hand pressed against the thinnest of material. It was a reciprocal experience, with all things in the world seemingly giving of themselves equally, to their very edges. He didn't believe anything particularly mystical was going on, just that for some reason, at these particular moments, the world seemed full and explicit in its there-ness, and there was no need to concern himself about its existence, its objectivity. It was as if the transparency that separated him from the world became active and volitional, and chose to withdraw for a few seconds, revealing in its wake a new clarity.

He remembered something similar happening years ago. For a few days in his early twenties he'd had the sensation of being blown apart, his body shattering into fragments, each piece small beyond imagination, and spreading across the universe. He continued to work, eat, drink, sleep, but this was not how he experienced himself. He was an onlooker, beside himself almost, like he'd shifted slightly out of alignment. At one moment he wondered whether he was in fact dead, and this was what death was: both a great dispersal across the universe and a witness to oneself carrying on in life. It didn't make much sense.

There had followed a month of teetering on the brink of euphoria. Persuaded to see a doctor, he was sent for tests. No organic illness was found. And then it had passed. That had been twenty-three years ago. He had to accept that if there were similarities between then and now, then perhaps Holly was right, and he needed to see someone. There was new technology these days. A diagnosis might be offered.

He stared at the worn and burnished corner of his bedside table, the dull gleam of the radiator, the glossy sill of the window, and the darkness of night lifted to a dawn-like grey by the bright white duvet cover. He heard a noise, a thump and then rattle, probably the bear holding maracas falling off the bed of one of the twins. The bedroom door was wide open. To watch them sleep was to see bodies in shapes reined in at adulthood, as if the ego is most present in infant slumber. Pearl was an extravagant sleeper, her arms flung above her head, her torso twisted. She often chattered through the night, arguing with friends, her mother. Walter slept with a mute contentedness, as if he understood that sleep was an opportunity for kind of supreme withdrawal and the stillness on his face suggested a depth of repose few reach. Their sleep was as different as their behaviour in waking life, and watching them felt like wearing spectacles with a different lens for each eye. He'd quickly learned it was a mistake to train the wrong lens on the wrong child. To watch Walter with any expectation of encountering Pearl's liveliness was to see a withdrawn child;

but to watch Walter as himself was to see a wonderful inner light generated from a mysterious calm. It was for this reason that he'd questioned the quickness of his son's autism referral and diagnosis.

It seemed to McCullough that much of what was assumed from his son's behaviour indicated little more than a lack of imagination on the part of the beholder, with scant regard for the margins of allowable difference. Indeed, the autistic disorder spectrum itself was no longer a linear measure, but a matrix which acted as a catch-all net for any behaviour that wasn't bordering on dull. The diagnosis, as an indication of the difficulty Walter might face in his future, was made easier by his being a handsome boy and easy to love, a beguiling and appealing child rather than unreachable and emotionless, lacking affect. McCullough was less fascinated by Walter's mysteriousness than he was by what kind of mystery the world was to Walter, or if it was a mystery at all. There were times when it seemed to both parents that the boy's world view was the clearest of them all, and that his experience of being in the world was unencumbered by all the things that mysteriously encumbered everyone else.

Holly's earliest interpretation of the true nature of McCullough's condition was that he was over-empathizing with Walter, and that he had pushed himself into an imagined version of his son's world and mistaken that for seeing the world anew. It might have all been based on the love he felt for his son, but as she pointed out, love was generally a distorting lens. He couldn't deny that he felt a different kind of love for Walter than he did for Pearl, and that he sometimes believed Walter was a kind of angel. He'd even been open enough to confess he felt changed by his son. Holly understood this; it was the same for her. But she was always quick to say: 'What about our daughter? She needs you just as much.'

It was true; Pearl's oppositional nature was equal in force, if outwardly projected, to her brother's inwardness. Seldom content as a bystander in the world, she wanted to take part and be noticed. People had great significance for her. With a gift for mimicry and a preternatural talent for subtle facial expressions, she seemed to ironize almost everything she said or heard. Sarcasm had come early.

She had a devastating glance. At school she learned to sign with a deaf boy and was equally expressive. All forms of communication were essential to her, but she had no instinct for compromise. She would throw herself to the floor and threaten to kill herself. This was aged four.

McCullough suspected life would be difficult for them both and felt a sense of guilt, as if some ancient judgment, handed down to him, would be visited on his children. When he'd come across the quote from Heraclitus: 'A man's character is his fate', nothing before had seemed so true. This was why he stared at the children so much, and had done since their birth: as if he might decipher on their smooth unblemished skin their character and hence their fate.

Maybe Holly was right: he should see someone. There were clearly issues to confront besides his belief that he was awaiting a directive from God. But then Holly regarded herself as equal to these other problems—it was the God question she wanted examined. But how do you choose a therapist based on such a thing? If the therapist did not believe in the possibility of the transcendent, wouldn't he/she just say the same things as Holly and his friends? *Yes, I know it feels real, but it's about something else.* And yet if he/she were open to the possibility of the transcendent, would Holly be satisfied? Another double bind: atheist therapist—you're ill. Theist therapist? It's very possible you're ill and just possible you're not. Of course, there was a third diagnosis: it was also conceivable that what he was experiencing was true and he was mentally unwell for other reasons. Or he'd become mentally ill as a result of the truth of the visions. How was anyone to know which was the case? In this instance, just being another human, whatever one's levels of empathy and insight, wasn't going to be enough. Any true judgment would require the therapist to be God. A big ask. How had the world survived so long without this access to the truth in others? Wasn't this kind of notion of loneliness and isolation the modern conception of hell? That we don't think this, that we still believe, against all the evidence, that we might reach someone when it is most needed, might just be an indication of God's uniting essence. It was something to think about, but he doubted it would convince anyone. Especially not Holly. He needed to remember that when seeking a diagnosis for Walter she was led by her instinct to trust those who displayed caring and kindness on seeing him, as if the response to him in the first instance was the crucial criterion; expertise was secondary. He had to presume it was would be the same for him.

3

On Monday, McCullough took to the streets seeking answers, wandering the city in the hope that he might be drawn somewhere, a hand might guide him. The wretchedness he felt after his confession at the dinner table had kept him in bed all Saturday and he was no better on Sunday. Holly was right: it was time that the full extent of what he believed was expressed aloud to a disinterested party and he listened closely to what was said back. He accepted setting out to be understood was always a dangerous mission and didn't expect much more than blanket incomprehension. In a way this would be a victory; at least it would mirror his own thinking. Yet wasn't it arrogant to assume there were not men and women out there who would listen with patience and understanding, whatever their likely perception of his condition?

His first encounter was with a young Anglican minister. He welcomed McCullough with an eagerness that augured well. Morning service had finished and he was at a loss as to what to do before setting up the lunch tables for the food bank visitors. Within ten minutes vivid lines of concern were concertinaing across his brow. Moments later he was manifestly cross. McCullough's story was 'technically' heretical, blasphemous to many, and would not be welcomed by the congregation he hoped to build. McCullough admitted his intensity might be a little *de trop*, unseemly even, but he was really just after guidance, and would take any suggestions for further reading. Scripture was sufficient, he was told. The only actual guidance he was given was a soft hand at his back, moving him down the aisle and out on to the church steps, where he was ushered away like a nuisance parishioner on a Sunday morning.

The therapist recommended by Lucien was located in a mews house behind Harley Street. A handsome man in his mid-fifties, with a perfectly domed forehead, he wore tailored tweeds, including a waistcoat, and a white shirt open at the collar. McCullough was directed to lie down on a deeply upholstered green velvet couch. Within five minutes he heard a stifled yawn and a single word being written on a notepad. Just short of the hour he was offered an evening session three times a week, and the confident claim that, with regular attendance, positive results could be expected in two to three years. What these positive results might be the therapist refused to be drawn on.

He called Simon. If he were to complete the trinity of soul, mind and body, McCullough needed to consult a scientist next; he was nothing if not ecumenical. Late afternoon he met a consultant neurologist, an Irish woman ten years younger than himself. Her position was refreshingly clear: if neuroscience eventually located God in the brain, she for one would not be surprised—*everything's in there*. It was the one miracle that gave her pause for thought, if that wasn't a contradiction. She agreed to give him an fMRI scan, a procedure he found strangely calming. No abnormalities were detected. After which they spent an hour peering at a collection of dissected human brains that looked to McCullough like large, thinly sliced porcini mushrooms. At the end of the session he was happy to bequeath his own brain to the institute.

After each encounter he'd wanted to call Holly and ask if he might come home, as if she had given him an ultimatum: seek help or don't return. But it had been his decision; she thought he was at work.

The following day McCullough set off again, but with little optimism. He was wearing a suit and a tie, and had spent time in the morning shining his shoes, a yearly chore. He remained, however, unshaven—four days' growth prickled under his fingers as he pinched at the skin around his Adam's apple. He'd spent time in front of the mirror working on his hair, looking to achieve something specific, based on the assumption that this aspect of his appearance, being so close to his head, might be the way the state of his mind was judged. After yesterday he wanted to take back control. When Holly passed him in the bathroom she declared his vanity had always been rather attractive, but she felt sure God didn't feel the same way.

The late spring sun was warm, but a sharp breeze carried a penetrating chill. The world seemed bright and clean, without any dirt in its corners. There was blossom on the trees, in the air; shallow drifts had built up against walls. It looked wonderfully artificial, a decoration dreamed up as a celebration of spring that had now become a civic tradition, like Christmas lights. McCullough imagined delicate fingers creating each leaf from the thinnest paper, then lightly gluing them to thousands of branches to create a look of abundance, and then, when the slightest breeze released them into the air, of marvellous transience. He felt a little like fallen blossom himself, contingent and set adrift.

From invisible distances the air crackled with sound, recognizable as refuse collection, street works, the construction of buildings—the sounds of work undertaken by people who seemed to exist in another world. The Thames seemed alive with activity, as if it had returned to a previous incarnation, when it was the city's great artery. He stopped and looked at the grey-blue water, somehow solid-looking, as if it were more impermeable membrane than liquid. He walked on. Even though he took this route often and had a destination, he feared that today he must look like a man without purpose, or at least have the appearance of a man distracted by thoughts in which he could find no sense. He felt conspicuous to passers-by, as if some vibrant, nervous energy marked him out. How often had he seen the afflicted striding along the streets, their psychic state somehow thrown beyond themselves, a desperate aura of tics and shudders and pointless urgency? Was that what Holly and his friends now saw in his behaviour? Yesterday's encounters were a confirmation, if he needed it, that what he was experiencing made little sense to others, and it was plain he was having no luck making sense of it himself. This would have consequences. People were sent mad by conundrums that yielded nothing for years on end. Perhaps madness was just this: the need to solve a puzzle, to reconcile an unexpected detail, but finding oneself always one number, one figure, letter, data point out. And right now he knew no breakthrough or reconciliation loomed. As revelations went—if that was what they were—they seemed to promise the opposite. Nothing concrete would be disclosed; no returning from a high place with tablets of stone or verses for recitation awaited him.

Yet it made no sense to be given access—or a promise of access—to something so fundamental and not be permitted to comprehend its meaning. Wasn't meaning what it was all supposed to be about? All he had to hold on to was an assumption that the visions, as obscure as they were, must emanate from a wellspring of clarity, and it was not always going to be like grasping a beam of light in the hope that it might contain either something of its source or something of that which it falls upon. In fact, even light would be something. Wasn't it always present at the beginning? Only the other day he'd read that the ancient Hebrew of God's first words was more casual enquiry than great command, as if God were merely trying out the extent of His creative powers. Rather than 'Let there be light', it might be translated as 'Light?' But in this instance the mood was irrelevant, He still began with light and not just because He needed to see what He was doing. Then there was the Big Bang: surely that must have produced some kind of light, even if it was only as indeterminate energy. Yet most of McCullough's visions were dark and shadowy, and all movement was without form. To give them their full due, they seemed to take place in an ontologically impossible nothingness, a not-there nothing-there-ness. When he tried to imagine this (non-) place, it made him think of the somewhere into which the universe was said to be expanding, a kind of margin of nothingness, but perhaps containing light after all—uncreated light.

He passed the red-brick wall of Lambeth Palace and stopped at the doors. The previous incumbent had been a man who McCullough believed would be sympathetic to his needs. A shared love of Dostoevsky might allow for the conversation to start in an unorthodox place, side-stepping God for a moment. There was the Russian's most puzzling statement about his own faith: if someone were to prove to him that Christ was outside the truth, and it was really the case that the truth lay outside Christ, then he would choose to stay with Christ rather than with the truth. It wasn't Dostoevsky's choice that mattered to McCullough but the proposition itself; a knot of felt meaning, an intuition beyond reason or logic, a choice he imagined would be incomprehensible to most. But Dr Williams was no longer Archbishop, and McCullough didn't know what the current fellow felt about such conundrums. He suspected that he was a more conventional believer and Christ as synonymous with the Truth was an ineluctable part of his faith. Maybe that was all it took—to capitalize the T; problem over. Or maybe these days we could just set aside the Truth altogether; it was after all a tricky concept in a relativist world, of language games, fake news, the probabilistic theories of quantum physics. In that way, Dostoevsky was visionary—he just didn't foresee there would come a time when truth in whatever form might cease to exist. Either way, he knew that knocking on the door of the palace and asking to see the new incumbent on the off-chance he was available, might, if referred to later as evidence of madness, prove conclusive. At best, it would suggest a disturbing grandiosity.

McCullough walked further on, found a bench in the sun and sat down. He looked at his emails, shielding his phone's screen from the light. There was nothing of consequence. A short note from Holly's father, about a biography of Adam Smith he'd just finished reading. Edward was a man who knew his own mind. The God question had been answered for him way before the New Atheists. His start point was Spinoza and the radical enlightenment; his end point, Marx and Nietzsche. But, perhaps most importantly, he was honest enough to confess to having no spiritual aptitude, which meant when looking for answers he was predisposed to the rational, which of course didn't preclude the existence of God, merely his own inability to apprehend him. McCullough should have headed straight to Edward yesterday morning. Holly would regard her father's credentials as being perfect for the task, the older man's love for McCullough no small part of that.

The office was on the top floor of a building midway along the Strand. McCullough was announced by a secretary named Pamela.

Edward was a big man, with large round shoulders and a large head; his hair was white and lustrously curly. For ten years, he had been paralysed him from the feet up by multiple sclerosis and he moved around in a high-seated electric wheelchair, feet and knees turned in. One hand was now badly affected and seemed to cling to his stomach like a hard-shelled sea creature, pale and cold-blooded. His other hand was relatively flexible but juddery in its movement. He had a deep voice, and his rare notes of emotion over his illness were most often ironic, as if he couldn't quite decide whether his condition was one of choice or not. Sometimes he blamed his intake of coffee; at other times, that having possessed a doom-laden mindset for much of his life he'd finally been delivered of the catastrophe he'd been expecting. Strange positions to adopt for a man who still declared himself a Marxist with a big-hearted nostalgia for post-war Labour politics. But then he regarded himself as something of an economic apostate; he was now on the board of directors of a subsidiary of an international bank. At seventy, forced retirement was looming. A matter of weeks away. He wanted his illness to play no part in his departure. He was toughing it out.

Today Edward sat hunched in his wheelchair in a hazy pool of sunlight, motes of dust moving around him in unorganized patterns. He was patriarchal in his mass and stillness, as if his manner would be the same if he were not ill—large of bearing, deliberate of movement. When there was little or no business to attend to he dozed, claiming an empty, contented mind. McCullough whispered his name. There was a pause, then a large hand was raised from his lap and flapped him in. The electric wheelchair turned on the spot with soft pneumatic urges to its mechanical parts. Edward's jacket was bunched around his middle and his tie knot was loose and lower than it should be; his fly was partly undone.

'Ah, Proctor—come in. Come in.' There was a pause as his pale eyes roamed over McCullough. 'You look shattered, old boy. Sit down.' More flapping of the hand. 'Do you want coffee? Pamela!' His bellow had been fine-tuned: these days he couldn't afford not to be heard.

McCullough pulled out a chair from in front of the desk, angled it towards Edward, and sat down. 'How are you?'

'I do OK, I do OK.' His grin was clear in its meaning: he was continuing to get away with something, as we all are. What he was getting away with was a complicated matter, probably hidden from him, but then he was the son of railway signalman, a grammar-school boy and a socialist, now working for a bank—so something was not as it should be.

'How are you?'

'I've just cancelled a meeting with a curate.'

'I'm sure it would only have been good in parts.' Edward's teeth weren't great; his smile was that of a boy with too much cheek. 'The vicar in our village, a young man—Michael—we joke that neither of us is entirely sure what he believes in.'

'This one, yesterday, was very gentle. Almost aggressively so. He seemed oddly insubstantial under his vestments. Ghostly.'

'Thin blood.'

For a moment, McCullough wondered what it must be like to spend one's days in a church; he supposed thin blood, even cold blood, might be an advantage.

'I'm taking it for granted that Holly has told you about my recent . . . experiences?'

'Yes, but I'm not clear on the details. She wasn't very forthcoming. I note you haven't mentioned it on previous visits.'

McCullough crossed his legs. 'I was fairly sure you wouldn't approve.'

'That all depends on my mood. Which depends on the spasms. Today I'm relatively free.'

'You're feeling generous?'

'I suspect anything I say is going to be much the same as everyone else has told you—it's a midlife crisis. That said, I don't think becoming religious will do you much harm, if that's what you're worried about.'

'I hadn't got that far. Or at least . . . '

Pamela brought in coffee; Edward's was served in a transparent plastic mug with a large handle, and she helped his fingers find their way in. She also tucked a linen napkin into his collar for spills. These days he tended to slurp.

'You know, I blame this stuff.'

'I know.'

Edward added, 'Good things happen to bad people; bad things happen to good people. And from this we surmise that we cannot know God's plan.'

'I haven't got that far.'

'Perhaps God is punishing me for turning to the dark side. I wish I were a wicked person to whom good things happen—what luck that is in life!'

'God doesn't punish.' He had got this far—maybe.

'That'll be a hard sell.'

McCullough stood up and looked out of the window. Below, if he tilted his head, he could see Embankment Gardens. All the benches were taken; people were sitting on the grass, on walls, drinking coffee, smoking, reading. Two young men played ping-pong on a fixed table. McCullough recalled there was a statue of Sir Arthur Sullivan down there, a rather appealing naked maiden at his feet. River life was calm and the water dark grey; its currents seemed cold, remorseless. At the South Bank, an LED display scrolled through details of something, but resisted being read in the sun, however hard McCullough squinted.

'I have no sense of what it means to be religious. No family history. Until six months ago my only reference points to Christianity, apart from churches as a tourist, were from Dostoevsky, and various irreverent but warm-hearted comedies on TV.'

'Your parents weren't religious?' Edward often asked questions he'd asked before under different circumstances, on the understanding that whilst the answer was unlikely to have changed, a new context might deliver extra insight.

'No. Not in any meaningful sense, although I got the feeling my dad wanted something to be out there, but more to blame than anything else.'

'So it's not really latent religious feelings you're talking about, is it?'

'If only.'

Edward drank his coffee, relying very much on his lips to suck it up and pass it back into his mouth.

'I don't imagine Holly's very patient, is she?' There was that grin again. This time, however, Edward was sharing his understanding of his daughter—McCullough was unlikely to be getting away with anything. Edward accepted his daughter's love for McCullough would be generous, but her tolerance of anything mystical would be slight.

'It's difficult.'

'Maybe you'll marry her. Which means that from my point of view it can't be all bad.'

They both laughed. It was an old-world consideration for Edward—his daughter's reputation as an unmarried mother.

'She'd never accept it on those terms.'

There was a brief silence and McCullough sat back down.

Edward's hand jumped up, as if to indicate he was about to speak, but it was not always the case. There was a pause. Then with a faux bluffness to his voice, he said, 'Now listen here, what I've discovered through my middle-class adult life is that we are largely happier without too much idle consideration of these matters, and if God did anything for man, he made him toil so he couldn't think too much. Something for which this atheist is eternally grateful.'

McCullough answered with a 'Hear, hear,' then after a short pause changed the subject to one that always interested the older man. 'We're busier than ever at work.'

'Maybe God's showing his pleasure in your new-found faith.'

McCullough stood up again. He didn't feel particularly fidgety but his body refused to be still. 'I need to get used to that.' He picked up a paperweight made by Holly when she was a little girl—a tiny guinea pig eating an even tinier carrot. 'That whatever the true nature of this crisis I am going through, almost everything that happens to me, almost everything I say, there is a stock joke, mostly about reward and punishment.'

'Can't be too precious, old boy.'

McCullough crossed to the small bookcase where Edward kept his *Boswell's Diaries*. 'Which is interesting in itself. Because it's almost like saying: whatever you do, don't be too serious. We're a flippant people now.'

'We've talked about this.' Edward had a deep and abiding and much-thought-about love for a certain aspect of the English sensibility: namely practical, unsentimental, no-fuss reasoning. At times his ideological passions were undone by his admiration for the political smarts of the British ruling class. Whilst as a young man he might have wanted a revolution, he was now thankful others had known how to avoid one. He also admitted that his tendency to romanticize the British working class was based more on literary works and his own father's decency than anything else.

McCullough squatted to read the Boswell titles. He'd only read the London volume; few books had given him more pleasure. Would he ever read the others? A few weekends ago it had been decided that he and Holly would take all her father's books when the multiple sclerosis finally put him in a care home.

'I have a feeling I'm going to be a little serious for a while,' McCullough stated.

'You're a serious chap.'

'Thank you.'

'Do you want more coffee?' Edward's hand flapped at his side like a dolphin's fin.

'No, thank you.'

The sun went in and the large window became dull, the office cold. McCullough sat behind the desk and swivelled in the seat. 'What do you actually do in here?'

'If you mean in the seat—nothing.'

McCullough moved the blotting square, tidied its alignment with the desk edge.

'These days I mostly dictate.'

'What?'

'Policy documents.' It was said wryly, followed by a chesty laugh. 'Do you know, when I look back on my life, I sometimes think the only thing I've really achieved is the skill to write a good policy document.'

'Few can say that.'

As often happened, a spasm in Edward's leg lifted his knee, and as his foot came back down it slipped off the metal rest.

'Will you put my foot back, please?'

It was a fascinating manoeuvre, its replacement. The leg's resistance seemed an act of individual will; it pushed against the upward movement that was necessary to slide the foot back, and there was always the small surprise that paralysis caused such stiffness, that the limbs weren't flaccid, empty of purpose.

'There's your good deed for the day.'

'You see. Another joke.'

As he was about to stand, McCullough felt that had Edward had any real freedom of movement in his arms, he might have placed a hand on McCullough's shoulder in a show of sympathy. Instead he said mischievously, 'Have you met our chairman? A Scot. Now there's a proper atheist—and a serious race for you. The Scots.'

The sun emerged across the river and light returned to the room.

McCullough stood up and looked out. 'I think it's as hard to judge who is a real atheist as it is to judge who properly believes in God.'

'Is there a wrong way to believe in God?'

'I find most atheists are not so sure what they believe when it comes down to signing up to pure biological determinism.'

'I've always suspected my lack of imagination has let me down when it comes to matters beyond the rational.'

McCullough was distracted. 'I can't help but think that to believe in God—if He exists—the individual has to do a lot of work. Very little grace is involved. First but not least, you've got to get yourself down in the abyss, and that's a long way down—it's the abyss after all—and you only get there by asking yourself what if, what if, and yet, and yet, until you have no answers left, nothing. At which point I suspect most people stop. I mean what comes after nothing? Wittgenstein said: "Every time I see a foundation, I feel the need to slip another one underneath it." I'm like that with nothingness. There's always more of it. I suppose that's the one thing of which I'm sure: when the answers stop, you've just begun. It begins with nothingness. It's here you make your first choice.' McCullough shrugged; it was as simple and as complicated as that.

'Is that what you did?' There was concern in Edward's voice, a rare moment when he seemed to believe that an individual could be genuine in his seriousness and spiritual hard work.

'Ironically, it seems I'm blessed with a quicker route. Although I go the other route as well—as a kind of due diligence.'

'Hah!' Edward was amused. 'But that means you must believe—I mean unequivocally.'

'Unless I'm mad, of course.'

'But surely you know the difference?'

'Perhaps only in the way a madman does.'

'But you've devised this other way?'

'It's the only way to shut up the atheists or Church types at dinner.'

'God will not be pleased.'

'No, I suspect not.'

'Do you want to speak to Michael, our local man? Or does he have to pass your authenticity test first?'

'Actually, that whole Anglican thing—that they don't really believe in God. I was thinking the other day, that isn't true—I mean of course it's not true—but it's not true on a profound level. What it means to believe in God is so cluttered by expectations that simply being attuned to a "still quiet voice" is not enough somehow, and therefore the most authentic experience of God is doubted. How awful is that?'

'Is that what you hear? A still quiet voice?'

'I hear nothing. What I *fear* is a more awesome encounter. Abrahamic.'

'Don't try and sacrifice Walter, will you?'

'A part of me thinks all this stems from him. One of the more hokey specialists we saw said he was here to heal me. I didn't say anything because I'd already felt something like that.'

'You always were a fanciful chap.'

'Serious and fanciful—no wonder God sought me out.'

And they left it at that. Their parting handshake was always awkward because the older man's right hand was the sea creature clinging to his stomach, and his left hand was not entirely under his control, and once raised needed to be grabbed at. They often had to be happy with a rather flimsy stroke of the fingertips.

In the lift McCullough stared at his feet as if some answer might be found in the reflected gloss of his shoes. What did looking at one's feet mean? A reminder that whilst our footing may seem firm, we are not rooted? He always felt a tendency to turn his toes up or to rock back on his heels like a police constable. Might that mean something? How must Edward feel, always separated from the ground, always in a sitting position, feet up on a platform? At night he was taken by a hoist across the room to his bed. These days there was never any contact with the ground. The lightness he must feel or the dizzying state of suspension was probably as wrongly inferred as the supposed emptiness of his limbs. There were times when McCullough and Holly had to adjust him in his seat and he felt twice the usual weight of a man his size. When he'd fallen out of his chair once at home, it had taken two ambulance men to replace him.

The lift doors opened at the ground floor. The doors out to the Strand were blasted with sunlight. McCullough looked at his phone: a text from Jim.

A meeting with the Home Secretary has been scheduled for 5pm. I judge him to be an arse.

4

Home was chaos. Before he opened the front door, he heard three competing voices. Walter was having a hyperactive episode. His sister, probably only moments ago wondering how much fun might be extracted from this, had taken him over the edge and was now pleading innocence. Holly was still in moderating mode: 'Please, you two. Just let me—'

McCullough's key in the door and actual appearance made little difference. His son's mania was at the stage that alternated between laughter and tears: the excited, fun side making him seem almost drunk with overstimulation, the tears indicating the inevitable crash. Right now he was flopped over Holly, arms flailing at his sister, crying and laughing. Both parents had wondered what it must be like to be trapped in such euphoria, when the laughter was too intense to be an indicator of pleasure. Pearl, on the other hand, didn't care—Walter was a perfect audience. She only had to say one nonsense word and he would drop down laughing, often adding his own element of play-acting: squealing, rolling his eyes, letting his tongue loll, because he wanted her to continue, to take him higher. But this act of complicity relied on Pearl. If she decided she didn't want to play any more, or she thought he was to blame for some earlier unfairness, there were ways to goad him into a rage that had no pantomime about it. A teasing look behind their mother's back would produce a reaction beyond anyone's control. If his laughter was an opportunity for perpetual fun, his anger was a different kind of game, because she would then have to be protected from his lashing out, which gave her new angles of sight for a victory smirk, raising the level of intensity even further. It was noticed early on in their young lives that she had a very high tolerance for pain: her brother could grab her hair and pull hard and it seemed up to her whether she wanted to drive him madder by displaying no reaction at all or to cry out in terrible pain, only the next moment to announce it didn't really hurt. It was a performance of masterly control, and at times elicited a kind of awe from her parents.

Today was not one of the happier versions: Walter was reeling around the hallway, oscillating between laughter and tears; Pearl was banished to the stairs for teasing him about something that had happened at school. She was not afraid of being cast as the villain. Holly looked exhausted. She had texted McCullough that she'd be late home from work due to the sudden detention of a vulnerable client. Jane had picked the children up from school, something Walter always found difficult—he didn't like surprises and it tended to unsettle him for the evening.

Holly was determined to be fair. Long before Walter's official diagnosis she had decided that Pearl's behaviour—both intrinsic to herself and as a reaction to Walter—needed equal levels of understanding: she was six years old and was going to demand attention. All parenting books said that to a child of her age bad attention was better than no attention, which meant that it wasn't really bad attention, according to Holly. And attention must be value-free, otherwise it was something else. The stress and upset she felt when she couldn't reach her son made her offer him the next best thing: a physical presence to envelop him if he wanted, as he often both did and did not want at the same time, which made him seem like a creature that was attached to her yet wrestling to become free.

To stop things escalating Holly often had to send Pearl upstairs, or at least away, which she knew would only make things worse on a different level, because Pearl would start to describe aloud exactly what she believed was going on: 'You only care about Walter; I'm upset, too. But you don't care about that.' At which point Holly had to risk letting go of Walter, hold her daughter by the shoulders and plead for understanding and permission to attend to her brother, giving Walter the opportunity to become hyper again and start jumping on her back, thus distracting her from showing Pearl the attention required to convince her to do the grown-up thing and leave Mummy to calm her brother down, which resulted in Pearl searching for another way to continue the emotional bartering: 'I'm not a grown-up. That's not fair.' Which was where they were when McCullough walked in.

First he pulled Walter off Holly's back and slung him over his shoulder. Then he glared at Pearl: wasn't it just this weekend they'd talked about her not goading her brother? After which he snapped at Holly, 'Break the cycle, remember.'

Holly was unimpressed. This was what he did: issue edicts or remind her of edicts she hadn't necessarily agreed to. She was also alert to the bias of empathy father showed son when things were out of control. McCullough himself wasn't sure how much he empathized with Walter at these moments, but he knew any appeal to his son was pointless and an act of misdirection was needed. It was easy enough to accomplish, but it required breaking all the parenting rules. Surprise him with a treat. But what signal did that send to his sister? How was she to make sense of her own behaviour resulting in sanctions and her brother's in a treat? McCullough felt unfairness was going to be her burden. To make fairness his and Holly's burden would produce bigger problems in the long run. But Holly didn't buy it. She accused McCullough of favouritism.

McCullough turned his glare at Pearl into a smile. Her fierce independence and even fiercer intelligence made her an object of wonder as well as awe. But wonder and awe weren't love. He didn't particularly worry about this—he and Pearl would find their own way to a relationship, and surely everything in the twins' lives didn't have to run in parallel. Did it matter if his love for Pearl was more complicated than his love for Walter? Complicated love had its own rewards. Holly, however, was worried and felt wounded every time McCullough showed his impatience to their daughter. She could see something in his eyes: judgment, irritation, dislike. He accepted his emotions were easily read and might seem unkind, but explained they were just momentary, pantomime-like, not dissimilar to their daughter's.

Two hours later, McCullough and Holly were on the sofa. In the intervening time Holly had put the twins to bed while McCullough wrote up his notes from the afternoon's meeting. He'd talked the Home Office into a methodology that he wasn't sure would work, Jim was convinced wouldn't work, but which they both had promised would provide genuine insight.

Holly wanted to talk about Pearl. 'You need to spend more time with her.'

'I will. I promise.'

'She just wants a reaction. You know that.'

'I know.'

'She picks up on how you feel.'

'I know.'

'I don't want you two to have a bad relationship.'

'We won't. I promise.'

Sometimes it all seemed like too much and he wondered whether he'd made a mistake in becoming a father. But then he knew that if he were to go upstairs and look at them asleep, he might read their shapes under the small duvets as if they were hieroglyphs and discern much, and his love would bloom as it did every time he took a moment to watch them as they went about being the human beings they were in this world.

'I'll take her to see a film on Saturday, to the Kids Club. Just me and her.'

'She'd like that.'

The TV was on; the start of episode one of season four of *Breaking Bad* had been paused. McCullough sipped from a large glass of red wine, Holly from a large cup of herbal tea.

After a long silence, he looked over at her and raised his eyebrows. 'This is the life.'

'For you.' It was meant kindly.

'I saw your dad today.'

'He called. Said you looked tired. Did you see anyone else?'

What had Edward said? McCullough pictured the poor curate from yesterday. 'If you're asking have I sought some advice, then yes, I have.' He sensed Holly's relief.

'What did they say? What did you say?'

'Well, what "they" think is that I'm heretical and/or mad, and/or—wait for it—experiencing epiphenomena due to some basic neural malfunction.'

'How do you feel?'

'All of the above.'

Holly pushed his feet with her feet. 'As long as I don't have to take the children to a mental home and explain their dad thinks he's Jesus Christ.'

'What about Moses?'

'OK, maybe it's the mental home bit I don't want.'

'We live here.'

'Very funny.' She looked at him. For the first time in a long while he felt warmth from her, a desire to soften herself towards him. 'I can't worry about you as well as Walt.'

'You don't have to.'

'Our lives are hard enough.'

'I didn't say anything.'

'I know you.'

'Then you should know I'm responsible and reliable.'

'Yes, you are, in your own way.'

'According to my lights.'

'If that's how you want to put it.'

'I think we need to accept that. It doesn't mean I'm not those things.'

'But that's what I have to do with Walt. I can't spend my life trying to read between the lines and hope we're all going to be happy. That he's going to be happy. And that you're happy.'

'You're not responsible for me.'

'But I am.'

Was this true? He knew she cared about his happiness, that she understood that, just like their son, he was vulnerable to obsessions and the world easily darkened for him. Perhaps this had engendered a new sense of care for him, a little part of him now blurred with Walter. If this was true it wasn't good for their relationship; they often talked about husbands treated as boys, often naughty but adorable boys, by wives keen to be mothers to the world; this was usually after seeing Maria and Lucien.

Breaking Bad was watched in concentrated and intense silence with only one interruption from Pearl, appearing in her pyjamas and needing a drink, and then they got ready for bed. They used the same electric toothbrush; it had become a habit. Holly brushed her teeth while on the lavatory, making McCullough wait to use both, a source of much irritation. He had taken to using a moisturizer; it felt cold and bright on his skin, awakening nerve endings. In the mirror he glared at the remnants of a face he'd prepared to present to a world of orthodoxy. It seemed silly now to have prepared at all; it was unlike him to hide like that and not offer himself up in all his honesty and error.

Maybe he should go back to see the curate now, face bright and shining, dressed in his pyjama bottoms. After all, the accusation of heresy only occurred after he'd tried to explain what he was experiencing in precise theological terms. Had he been vaguer—more truthful, more desperate—about what was actually happening, he might have been welcomed as another lost soul God was trying to gather up. But that was the problem. While everything remained

vague, inchoate, and impossible to articulate, there was little doubt
that what he was experiencing was a more extraordinary calling.
From the doorway Holly watched him, and then offered over the
toothbrush.

In the bedroom there was a short discussion as to how wide
to have the window open. There was no perfect aperture that
would provide fresh air (for Holly) but not deliver a draught (over
McCullough). Outside, the sound of traffic on the main road was
airy, distant, all journeys long.

Holly climbed in next to McCullough and laid her hand on his
chest. She smiled. He smiled back.

'We'll be all right, won't we, Mac?' She seemed content that
something meaningful had been achieved.

McCullough thought about it for a moment, then said, 'We'll
be all right.'

Holly curled her fingers so her nails bit into his skin. Both of
them liked the remnant of erotic meaning behind this. It was enough
for tonight.

The following day McCullough left early, compelled from the
moment he awoke to get into his car and drive. He was gone for
three weeks.

LAUGHTER

'Theology after breakfast sticks to the eye.'

WALLACE STEVENS,
LES PLUS BELLES PAGES

Terry turned up at McCullough's house early in the morning, and, using the brass anchor, knocked hard, sharply, displaying no awareness of the time of day or proximity of other dwellings. When McCullough opened the door, Terry said, 'You look like shit,' and stepped inside. McCullough wanted to embrace him, to cry.

It had been three weeks since his return from the site. After the team had left he had stayed on two more days. He hadn't expected to see them again but waited anyway. On the first day he tried to clear up, dragging things here and there, dropping them near where they were supposed to go. On the second day he kicked bits of stone and slung timber around indiscriminately. Driving home, he'd been stopped for speeding. When asked for a reason, he offered the only one he could think of: if I don't get home to my family soon I'm going to die. The police officer was amused and asked whether a man so close to death should be driving. McCullough explained that spiritual death posed no risk to other drivers. 'No, but ninety-eight miles per hour does.' It was a fair point.

At home he'd broken down, Holly and the twins standing before him. Pearl looked embarrassed and glanced up at her mother. Walter had a small, highly complex Lego plane in fidgety fingers and tried to show his dad how it worked, as if his father had not been gone three weeks and was not on his knees crying. Holly was cool with him; he'd broken promises to return and now here he was, clothes covered in mud and cement, his nails black.

As if he really had been away on holiday, Pearl asked to see pictures on his phone. They sat together on the edge of the sofa, her small bottom pressed high into his thigh. She scrolled through the photographs with swipes of a sticky finger. Leaning away, he used the back of his hand to wipe clear the snot from under his nose, and his forefinger to flick his cheeks free from tears. Pearl said nothing looked like a church, nothing looked like a house—where were they going to live? He tried to explain, as he had done to those who had now given up on him, how what was shaped on the ground would be shaped in the air. The people in the pictures interested her more. He answered her questions as best he could. How had Holly explained his absence, his failure to turn up each day? After the photos were finished, Pearl wanted to move away, but she let herself be hugged by him and he rested her chin on his shoulder so he could grab her more tightly. In front of his eyes the bright blue, red and yellow of Lego bricks rose before him. 'See, this goes like . . . and this here, to make it fly. There are boosters.' He tried to clutch at his son, bring both children in, but Walter strained back, not to get away but because he wanted to concentrate on his model, focus on the intricacies he'd created and explain them. Holly said she needed to prepare dinner.

He spent four days in bed. It felt like jet lag, his body commanded to sleep, eyes heavy in a way that was irresistible. The blinds were opened during the day and he shifted the bed across the room so he might lie in the sun. When Holly sat on the side and said, 'What are we going to do?' he spoke of rejuvenation, a new start, but then turned over to sleep.

Then there was work. Couriers came to the door with packages, endless iterations of documents he'd written weeks ago, amended by Jim. He read in bed, making small refinements, sitting up like a recovering patient in a private room.

When he was able, he went back to the office. Twelve-hour days. He hired facilities, supervised recruitment, implemented a methodology that seemed like madness. After the first day of interviews, he was challenged by the civil servants watching from behind the glass, saying the whole process was too emotionally charged. What did they expect, McCullough had to ask? The narrative that participants were responding to included their impotence when confronted by a slow and terrible death; and even more terribly, to imagine and describe their feelings and potential behaviour when the death was that of a loved one. After a day in the field McCullough hired a security guard to stand outside the room: there was a risk that some people would express themselves with violence. But mostly they left in tears, bereft, hollowed out, asking themselves deeper questions than ever about the world they were living in—a by-product of the methodology, not the objective.

At the weekend the family visited Edward at his home near Cambridge. In the large house McCullough found a spot in the sun and read and dozed, read and dozed again. Edward did not interrogate him; no jokes were made. It was a sombre time.

And then at six o'clock on a Saturday morning Terry arrived, a canvas holdall at his feet, a beer can in his hand.

In the sitting room, in the promising morning light, they sat opposite each other, drinking tea from large mugs. Terry scanned the room, his fierce but friendly eyes taking in the paintings on the walls, family photographs, the many artefacts displayed on shelves. He wasn't wearing socks, just his old red Converse plimsolls, only one with laces. His pale ankles were filthy.

'Nice gaff.'

'Thank you.'

Since his return from the site McCullough had been picking at a piece of skin around his thumbnail; the pain was tightly located, exquisitely needling; it gave him something to concentrate on. 'How is everyone?'

'Not very impressed with you fucking off.'

McCullough smiled. 'No faith, I guess.'

'You got your family to think of.' It was said lightly, as if it went without saying. Many miles from home, Terry seemed less watchful and self-protected. Maybe it was the early morning, a night without sleep.

'True.'

'Did you think we was your family down there?'

'No.'

'I think Nat did.' The smile was sly, a 'gotcha'.

'How is he?'

'Rich went round there.'

'And?'

'He was a bit embarrassed; he knew he'd been a cunt.'

'I should have gone to see him.'

'Don't worry about it. Him and Rich have been down to the site and tidied everything up. Everything's under control.'

McCullough pictured the place tidied, but imagined it still must look like a terrible act of hubris, a ruin.

'That's kind.' There was a pause. From the shape of the fabric of the holdall at Terry's feet—jutting corners where there should only be soft spreading folds—there appeared to be a number of books inside. 'What about you?'

'Me?'

'Yes.'

'I've been doing some reading.'

'I can see.'

'Spent some time in the library, as you do. You order stuff and you get it in a day. I like a good database.' Hee-hee . . .

McCullough smiled.

'I had no idea there were so many effing translations of the Bible. I imagined there was just a couple—you know: *the* one and then the one for daft buggers.'

'It's a learning curve.'

'At first I thought, why bother? Then I had a proper read. It started off pretty much what I expected: "Let there be light", Adam and Eve, Abraham and his kid, Joseph, Moses. After that it's some full-on boring shit about the tabernacle—I'm glad you weren't so picky about that shit.' McCullough laughed. 'Then . . . it's a whole load of bloodletting and genocide. I mean proper: go in there and fill your boots. After which it gets seriously fucking repetitive and I can't say I didn't skip a few pages or a hundred. Then it gets a bit more interesting—a bit Zen. After that there is the whole intermission thing. Time for ice cream. Then it's Jesus and all the stuff on posters outside churches. But the genocide: I thought God was supposed to be loving and merciful?'

'Picking and choosing has always been the way with scripture. Someone once said that the whole of the Bible, from the jealous and vengeful Yahweh to the benevolent, loving father, is the story of God learning how to be God.' McCullough pointed to the holdall. 'Not full of Bibles, I hope.'

'When you hitch—take something to read, that's my advice.' It was an automatic response; there was no break in Terry's train of thought. 'But when you get into it, while it might be boring as hell—I mean John Grisham don't have anything to be worried about.'

'I think the competitive set was more your Philistines and Canaanites.'

Terry laughed. 'Yeah. Fuck them.'

'I believe that was the general sentiment at the time.'

'But, please, *some* consistency—we're talking about God!'

'An early church father edited down the whole of scripture to some of John and a bit of Paul. Dismissed the whole of the Old Testament as the story of a demiurge—a kind of sub-God. To him the real God, the God of Love, first reveals Himself through Jesus; everything up to then was just a preparation, a prequel. It's called the Marcion Bible. Personally, I wouldn't include much of John at all, and would include whole books of the Old Testament—the Zen stuff. I suppose the ironic thing about Yahweh is that he is a great original—the first single God. But he's too human, too capricious; he continues to behave like previous gods. The difference is the notion of singularity, not the quality of the relationship. We needed to wait for the Greek notion of unknowableness before we even had a way to think about a truly transcendent God, which was to allow something not to make sense, if you see what I mean. And that really does change the quality of our relationship—God's incompatibility with our cognitive resources.' McCullough took a mouthful of cold tea and imagined Terry in the local library, his concentration flowing, his mind open, his natural scepticism leading to suspicion, his suspicion leading to deeper, more engaged reading. He wasn't surprised, then, by Terry's next words.

'There is this geezer Reimarus . . .'

McCullough laughed again. Twice now in a few minutes; it had been a while since that had happened.

'It's fucking great! Explodes it all. The stuff about miracles is the dog's bollocks. He was too afraid to publish his work in his lifetime. It was suppressed until well after he croaked. They even did it back then.'

'You'll find back then suppression of thought was the norm. Suppression in plain sight.' McCullough then asked, 'Why are you here, Terry?'

'We was all in the pub last night . . . ' And one thing led to another, seemed to be the point.

'None of you know where I live.'

Terry paused and scanned the room again, now made brighter and larger-seeming by the encroaching sunlight.

'Maybe it's a miracle.' Hee-hee. He placed his teacup on the floor blindly and started to roll a cigarette. All his visible skin was dark from nature, as if he were an itinerant who slept out every night.

'Maybe.'

'Do you believe in miracles?' There was a slight smirk on Terry's face: did he believe the answer would give the older man away? McCullough had seen this before, usually when Terry was drunk, as if in drunkenness he felt he possessed insight others were blind to, and knew just the right questions to reveal whatever ignorance or hypocrisy he wanted to expose. His expression could be unpleasant. Scornful. Sneering. But not this morning.

In the pause before McCullough answered the younger man winked. He also possessed other, kindlier, insights.

McCullough asked for more precision. 'Biblical miracles? God's or Jesus's?'

'Are they miracles if they come from God?' Terry laid the cigarette on his thigh.

'Good point. If Jesus was the Son of God: are his miracles?'

'Touché, sir.'

'Perhaps signs and wonders is better.'

Terry straightened the rolled cigarette, then turned it at a right angle to the side of his leg. 'That's one of the things I noticed: there are a lot of miracles at the beginning of the Bible, then they sort of fade out, and then Jesus comes along and it's miracle after miracle. That's all he does—perform a miracle, preach, miracle, miracle, have a wander, preach, miracle, miracle. It's more miracle than preaching. He's a busy man.' Terry paused and spun the thin rollie on his knee. 'It's interesting. You know me, I don't believe anything I read, but I started to think, when people say: "Where's the proof—you know—where's the proof of God?" you could say: "Look at all the miracles."'

McCullough smiled.

'I know, I know, but hold your horses. You could say: look at Jesus. Look at all the miracles he did. Just like the regular Bible bashers might say. Now I know most people laugh at that. Most people think the miracle stuff is made up. Jesus might have been real, but all the miracle stuff is nonsense. Or if you were feeling generous you could say, right, if you want to use miracles as some kind of proof, then this batch were so long ago, if God wants us to believe in Him—why doesn't He do some now? That's fair enough, right? But when I was reading the Jesus miracle stuff, I found myself thinking: this isn't so long ago. Two thousand years is nothing compared to how fucking old the universe is. So if you're going to use that argument—those miracles was a long time ago—you could also say that if something happened yesterday in, say, like, Iceland, "That's a long way away". I mean it's just a different part of the space-time continuum, right? So for all this "Why doesn't God just show Himself?" to actually work, everyone would have to see him, and everyone would have to see him doing the same thing at the same time. Imagine what that would have to be. A great hand in the sky? An old beardy cunt pushing his face out between the clouds? Anything like fire and brimstone—that'd just be explained away as a natural phenomenon.'

Terry broke off for half a second, his mind racing ahead of his examples. 'Now you reckon I was convinced by Reimarus. Well,

I was and I wasn't. That's the great thing about being me—everything sends me the other way. This is what I reckon: if we're going to think about what a miracle might be, the Jesus stuff in the Bible is sort of on the money. Raising the dead, feeding people, walking on water. So I say: what if it's true? That for a short time there was a whole bunch of miracles? It wasn't so long ago. To be honest, it doesn't even have to have anything to do with God, does it? Could be just some geezer with the gift of miracles. One guy.'

'Signs and wonders . . .'

'The whole "signs" thing has been a bit disproved though, hasn't it? Sign of what? There was no end of the world or shit like that. I mean people have stayed up all night waiting for the end, only to go for a fry-up in the morning. I like "wonders".' Terry burped and turned the cigarette perpendicular to his knee, the tips of his dark fingers gently manoeuvring the bright white paper, a crinkle of tobacco in the air.

'I agree.'

Terry nodded as if mulling over McCullough's agreement—it wasn't necessarily to be trusted. He then looked up to the ceiling, the moulding around the light.

'Where your little 'uns?'

'It's early.'

'I thought all kids got up at the crack of dawn. That's why parents are so fucked.'

'Ours buck the trend.'

'What about your missus?'

'Likewise, asleep.'

There was a pause. A stirring above. A soft quick pounding of floorboards. A shout of 'Mummy' from Pearl.

'So they do exist.'

'They do.'

Terry sucked the rollie through pursed lips like someone might a cigar. 'Are you coming back down?'

'Is that why you're here?'

'As I said, we were talking in the pub.'

'A church might not be the best thing.'

'For what?'

Indeed, for what. 'An expression.'

Terry scratched at his chest, then deep into the roots of his great flattened dreadlocks.

'Come on, Terry. You've got to admit, it's a bit bloody obvious. Feel God; build a church. If you wanted scriptural authority for such an enterprise—beyond tabernacles and temples—I'm not sure you'd find it; quite the reverse, in fact. The word "church" is just a broad translation of *ecclesia*—assembly or congregation—something I'm most definitely not after. And no one builds a church for it to remain empty.'

Terry placed his rollie between his lips and brought out his lighter. 'Do you mind? I'll smoke it in the garden if you do.' The lighter was withdrawn from his rollie as a new thought occurred. '"On this rock I will build my church." One of us would have to be called "Cliff" though, right?'

'That's funny.'

'Yeah—made it up in the pub. As you can see, I've got quite into it.' The elision of the last two words made them sound like a little seesaw of vowels. 'Even Rebecca's bored of me. And she's listened to me go on about some stuff, I can tell you.'

'Ah, Rebecca.'

'Don't tell me you haven't been thinking about *her*.'

'I've given you all some thought.'

'I bet you didn't think I'd turn up here . . . an expert.' Terry grinned. His foot jerked a little and he toed over the empty can of beer; the clatter sounded doubly hollow on the wooden floor. 'Oops.' He righted it.

There was a pause and another scan around the room. He squinted at photos on the mantel, at the books at eye level. 'But if you don't mind, I'd like to get your thoughts on a few things.'

'I'm not sure I'm the best person to ask. I suspect you'll get more sense out of Mr Guffie.'

Terry sat back, cigarette in mouth, lighter flicked on and off as if he was tempting himself to light it, but he was just fiddling while he mused.

'Who's looking after your mum?' McCullough asked.

'Neighbour.' It was said quickly to end the enquiry, then he stood up. 'Show us the way.'

For a moment McCullough looked up at Terry, standing in his sitting room, and wondered what he was being asked.

'To the effing garden.'

Holly appeared in the doorway in her dressing gown, worn slippers, her hair a mess, glasses at the end of her nose, used teacups in one hand.

'Hello.'

Terry stepped forward, hand out, bending over a little, shoulders hunched. 'Terry. I was helping Mac here on the big project.'

Holly removed her glasses and blindly put them into the pocket of her dressing down. 'Would you like some tea?'

'He's just going into the garden, to have a cigarette.'

With a hand on his shoulder, McCullough guided Terry into the kitchen, through the folding doors, which he opened fully, then over the decking, onto the grass and into a patch of early sun; the ground was cold and the grass damp under his bare feet.

Pearl appeared in outgrown pyjamas. She looked up at Terry and said, 'I've seen a picture of you on my daddy's phone.' Terry smiled and she noticed the state of his teeth and glanced at her dad, eyes wide and enquiring.

'Do you want to go in and tell Mummy we will have that cup of tea?'

She didn't appear to want to and stayed where she was, studying Terry from head to foot. The more she understood that his dishevelment was a complete look, the more she realized that here was an entirely new kind of grown-up who seemed to reject most of the things she was told were important: clean teeth, brushed hair, washed hands. When she spotted the beads in his thin beard, she stroked her own chin, as if to feel what it must be like.

'Is your brother up?'

'Don't know.'

'Do you want to go and find out?'

Pearl looked at Terry. 'Is that girl here?'

Terry laughed. McCullough placed a hand on his daughter's head and pivoted her a hundred and eighty degrees. 'Inside, you.'

Sensing she wasn't going to get any more answers, Pearl scratched her tummy just above the waistband of her pyjama bottoms, turned around and went into the kitchen, calling for her mother.

Breakfast was eaten at their long oak table in the kitchen, one end disappearing into the pale misty light of the weekend morning. Walter said hello to Terry when asked to do so, but without making eye contact, and shouldered away his sister as she tried to whisper to him all the stuff he should look at, a small finger pointing. He remained quiet at the table, although hummed while he ate, and was then off, his departure from the room fast enough for the others to fear for a moment he might actually have disappeared. McCullough and Holly both called into the empty space: 'What do you say?' But he was gone. Pearl explained for Terry: 'He's supposed to ask, "May I leave the table?" but he never does.' Then she added, 'I don't either.' And again, as if mesmerized by the beads in Terry's beard, she stared at them and tickled her own chin.

Holly placed her hand over McCullough's and addressed Terry. 'He was in a terrible state when he returned.'

'That was Nat's fault for attacking him. He was being a cock.' Pause. 'Nat was.' The last statement was to make clear any confusion about who was the cock; the inappropriate language didn't concern him.

Holly was aghast and removed her hand from McCullough's, twisting around so she could stare at him. 'You didn't tell me that.'

'It was nothing.'

'Nothing?' She looked over at Terry. 'Were you there?'

He shifted in his seat, scratched at his hair, dirty nails digging in. 'Nat just lost it. Not much of a sense of humour. Likes attention. A bit of a patronizing cu— ... twat.' The list was meant to explain something precise about why stuff like this happened and why it didn't matter. 'We all reckon he's in love with Mac.'

Pearl glared at her mother. Holly turned to McCullough. 'This doesn't make any of it easier to understand.'

'Nathaniel and I had . . . I don't know. I misread his sensitivity. It's my fault.'

Nothing was said for a moment; Terry smiled at Pearl. His teeth seemed sticky with the sweetness of something dark, like liquorice. On the inside of the window a bumblebee dully thumped at the glass. The early-morning sun created a balloon of milk-white light. Most of the time only the droning of the bumblebee could be heard.

Holly sat back in her chair and smiled without warmth at Terry. 'What do you think about what Mac's doing?'

'Down *there?* He's not doing much right now.'

McCullough glanced at Holly without really seeing her. Did she feel that she needed to defend their family from his excesses, and in order to do so should cross-examine Terry? He felt pity for them all.

'I heard you talking about miracles earlier.'

'It'll be a bloody miracle if it gets built.'

The lack of reaction from Holly made Terry uncomfortable. His usual easy laugh stuttered and failed. He looked around the kitchen and must have seen signs of opulence new to him: foodstuffs that usually came in packets in thick resealable glass or ceramic jars; copper pans hung from the ceiling; a hundred bottles of wine were stacked in what was once a large fireplace. He started to itch more—chest, lower back, different parts of his head. The scratching of his dreadlocks gave off the satisfying sound of matting being clawed at.

'Let's not talk about it, Holly—Terry must be tired.'

Holly stood up and began to clear the table. She placed a sheet of paper and coloured pencils in front of Pearl, who started to draw without a beat: first a house, then a sun, a large cat, then a little girl not unlike herself in broad terms—reddish-brown hair, freckles, blue eyes. McCullough went to the kitchen door and called out to Walter: 'Are you OK up there?' There was no response. 'Give me one minute, Terry.'

'Help get him dressed, please,' Holly said.

She started to empty the cereal bowls into the bin. Terry watched Pearl colour in the green hills of her picture with uncontrolled shading and rough smears of her fingertips, and then blow away the sticky residue on the paper across the table. After a minute or so Terry repeated his compliment about their house. 'Nice gaff, Mrs Mac.'

Holly thanked him and began to cry. She hid it well: rinsing the bowls, opening the dishwasher, sorting cutlery with extra care. It took her a minute or so to find a smile and turn around. 'What has he said to you about all this?'

Pearl, hunched over her drawing, added, 'My mummy means God.'

Terry laughed and Holly found a moment to wipe her face with a dishcloth. She wanted to cry again. 'Darling, why don't you go and have your television time?'

The child was savvy enough to know she was being bought and that there must be a reason for this worth discovering, but the pull of TV was too strong.

Holly filled the kettle. 'I feel so mean-spirited. That's what this has done to me. It's as if I'm trying to catch him out.' But she repeated her question anyway. 'What has he said to you . . . about all this?'

'I don't understand.'

'Has he told you why he's doing it? I mean, how he feels?'

Terry felt empowered by Pearl. 'About God?'

She tensed up. That word. It had never held any meaning for her. Most of her adult life she had always believed it had no *intrinsic* meaning at all. Yet it now seemed to possess a property that created a physical reaction in her, as if despite its dull, thudding sound it had taken on sharpness and nicked at her skin. At its very mention she immediately found herself arguing with McCullough in her head, always—finally—damning him with the same insult: whatever he believed, whatever he thought he believed, if he attributed it to God, a god, it was silly. Yes—'silly'—as if she were speaking to a child. It was hateful of her. Patronizing and mean. But it wasn't dishonest. It came from a final reckoning with herself; it was what she ultimately believed. She did think it was childish, and it was in her nature to be true to her position. There were times when she was open to discussions as to *why* people believe in God, what it said about us

as human beings. And in that sense, she couldn't discern any fundamental difference between whatever it was that McCullough seemed
to believe and the occasional Sunday morning visitor keen to leave
a leaflet with bullet-pointed statements about God's existence and
his work here on earth.

She smiled at Terry. 'Yes.'

'Not much. Quite a lot about, you know—'

She tried not to snap. 'No, I don't know.'

Terry tugged at his thin beard. 'Stuff being true and not true at
the same time.'

'That sounds like him.'

'I don't think he believes Jesus is the Son of God.'

Holly laughed and wiped away a tear of relief. 'Well, that's good
to know.'

The kettle had clicked off a moment or two ago and she clicked
it back on. 'Are you religious, Terry?'

'Me, no. Although I've been doing a bit of me own research—
you know—since Mac . . .' He couldn't think how to finish his
sentence without saying 'fucked off', so he changed tack. 'I read a lot.
You name it. I like a big book.'

But Holly wasn't listening. 'I heard you talking about miracles?'

'I was just saying that in the beginning of the Bible . . .' He
paused.

'What?'

He'd felt on firmer ground with McCullough. 'Have you read
the Bible?'

'No.'

'Well, it's not what you think. I thought it was all love thy neighbour. Church poster stuff. There's a lot of blood-letting and genocide.'

'Sounds lovely.'

'That's what I thought.' He skewed his lips. 'Can I go out into
the garden for a smoke, please?'

Finally, Holly laughed. This boy was nothing to be afraid of. She
smiled at him. 'Of course, sweetheart.'

She watched him rise from the table and for a moment thought
she saw in Terry a grown-up Walter, a dishevelled young man,

without interest in clean teeth or hair, slightly odd in his manner, but in his own way straightforward. It made her want to cry again. But she resisted. It was easy to project Walter's difference into the future and be moved by it, and yet the only thing she was certain of about her son was the impossibility of forecasting what his life might be like. All that could be known from his current behaviour was that he would find aspects of the world interesting in a way that the rest of the world wouldn't quite share and he would never quite understand why. McCullough had said their job was to help him seem different in degree, not in kind. This had frightened her. She couldn't bear to think of Walter being isolated and lonely because of the perceptions of others. She felt sick with sadness.

Through the large window, Holly could see Terry, bow-legged, standing in the centre of the garden. She hated herself for having been hardened to him. She tightened her dressing gown and went out with a mug of tea.

'I noticed you put in a few more sugars than is usual,' she said.

'Jamaican sweet, it's called.'

'I didn't know that.'

Terry grinned; the sugar's work was impressive.

'You should brush your teeth, Terry.' It was the pleading of a mother. 'When did you last see a dentist?'

Terry revealed his teeth in full, the way a chimp might. 'I find dentists just make stuff up.'

Holly wasn't sure how to react: she was amused by his quaint 'I find' and shocked at his belief that a dentist might make anything up.

He added, 'It's the government's fault.'

She wondered what it must be like to kiss him. She had been a keen smoker herself until ten years ago and maintained it was vanity rather than fear of death that had made her stop. Mostly the smell of smoke in her hair.

There was a pause and Holly put her face up to the sun. Her feet were bare in the grass.

Terry sniffed hard with one side of his nose, nostril rising and opening wide like the aperture of some strange horn. Phlegm was loosened at the back of his throat and then swallowed. 'You should come down to the site. Bring the little ones.'

'Tell me what you think, Terry. You've come up all this way. What's going on? Why's he doing it? What's going to happen?'

'A lot of questions there.'

'Please.'

He shrugged. 'I don't know.'

Above their heads a sash window rose and McCullough leaned out. 'How did you actually get here, Terry?'

'Magic carpet, mate. All the way up the M4.'

'You hitched all night? You must be exhausted. Do you want to lie down?'

'You're all right. Just wanted a chat really. I'll be off soon.'

Holly gently clasped his arm. 'You should take a nap.'

Instead he chose to watch cartoons with the twins.

McCullough and Holly sat at the kitchen table, a pot of coffee between them, the newspaper, delivered on Saturdays, still wrapped in its cellophane, the iPad cover closed, radio off, phones on charge. Holly's arms were stretched over the table, her hands clasping McCullough's. She was used to him being available and open to her; he had never been a man to withdraw or hide. But even now, having hold of him, she felt he was turned away. Everything she said glanced off him, as if he were slighter than he ever had been, positioned at an angle, pulling himself up to create a narrower target. Except it wasn't quite that, because he was there, facing her, hands warm, eyes willing. Part of her wanted to climb over the table and grab him, try and grasp some central part of him, pull it round and set it straight. But she knew that that wouldn't work either . . . he wasn't present enough to be grabbed. She accepted that what was happening to him wasn't his choice, he wasn't doing it on purpose, but it frightened her that it seemed beyond his control. Which meant she felt it was up to her to fix things, and this made her angry. *Had* made her angry. This morning had changed that.

Terry provided a new perspective: this man before her was fully real to other people, and one of them had hitched miles to see him, and not as a demigod or charismatic but for the reasons she herself had felt drawn to him thirteen years ago: as someone who came at life with a force of concentration that made most others seem partial in their attentiveness. She knew that over the years other women had been attracted to him for similar reasons, but she'd assumed that beyond show—and he could be showy—this aspect of him was now diminished for the obvious reasons: age, work, general energy levels, a narrowing of life with a young family. Something similar was happening to herself.

Yet Terry, that boy in the sitting room laughing at *Tom and Jerry* with Walter and Pearl, had made her feel that McCullough remained as distinct as ever, the equal to himself thirteen years ago. And this was why she had hold of him: she wanted to feel it again, to see it again, displayed for her. In holding his hands she was asking him to send her signals that he hadn't defected and wasn't now sharing his true self only with others.

'We need to do something, Mac.'

He didn't know what to say. All relationships went through periods of unhappiness—a desperate solution wasn't to be rushed through. Part of him believed this was the case; it wasn't dishonest. But he didn't want to offer this up as some kind of excuse, because Holly believed what was happening was serious, dangerous, and that there was the possibility of failure, a permanent end. Only last night she had said that sometimes she felt everything they had together as a family was being shaken around in an open box and she feared he might be flung out, that part of him wanted to be flung out—he was allowing himself a kind of weightlessness in order to achieve it. Whereas she was desperately trying to keep them all in, holding onto everyone. He'd said he understood, but insisted it wasn't an open box, and so he couldn't be flung out, and while she was right to sense he was floating, he was still in there with them. She asked how he could know that. They'd gone to bed in silence.

He smiled. 'I don't know what we can do. What will help.'

'Talk to someone.'

'That was your answer before. And I did.'

'Maybe now we both need to.'

'We need some kind of détente. An *entente cordiale*.' It was half-flippant, but he believed it. He noticed her tense up. She felt blamed.

'This isn't easy for me,' she said. 'You assume I'm in the wrong.'

'I don't.'

'You say that. But you do. You can't understand why I'm not more accepting.'

'What have I asked you to accept? *I* don't understand half the time.'

'This is the bit that's so unfair. You make it sound like nothing, and that denies me the right to be worried. But it's not nothing. You sold part of your business, you spend weeks away, you come back a mess. That's not nothing.'

He removed his hands from hers and poured them both coffee. 'You're right.'

Advice she received from friends was kind but unimaginative: they needed time away together, without the children. It was true, but neither of them felt that the twins could be left with anyone quite yet, especially not Walter. Whether this was just an act of avoidance neither could say. To make them feel better they'd discussed going to Vienna. Jokingly Holly said, 'No churches,' but she found she meant it. If there were churches, religious history, he wouldn't be with her. Yet where was there, no more than two hours by plane, without churches? Nothing was booked.

She looked at him. 'If I find someone good, who I think you'll accept—will you agree to see them?'

'Yes. Of course.'

The relief she felt was immense; a cool, bright lightness appeared in her stomach, and what she'd accepted as an almost permanent feeling of sickness drained away. She had to fight a welling up of tears.

Ten minutes later, McCullough sat down next to Terry on the sofa, the twins sitting on the floor far too close to the TV, faces leaning into the screen, as if their eyesight was bad. He ordered them back. The channel announced a day of non-stop *Looney Tunes*, and as each cartoon played itself out, Walter laughed with a beguiling straightforwardness. Terry snorted his appreciation. Pearl kept looking back over her shoulder at him.

'I don't want you three to get too excited, but the plan for the rest of the day is lunch and then a walk on the common.'

No one spoke. The Road Runner was on one of his curving runs, seen from a great distance, a few shrubs and cactuses to represent the desert. Wile E. Coyote was waiting at the top of a mountain with a very elaborate set of scales and boulders.

Without taking his eyes off the TV, Terry said, 'You coming back down then?'

'I've got to work out what I'm doing.'

'You're building a home for your family. And a church.'

McCullough gestured around the sitting room. 'I've done that here. Apart from the church.'

'Think of it as a nice little place in the country. With a church.' Terry laughed; he was enjoying his own persistence. There was the sound of a thick liquid-like substance being displaced in his lungs. He then coughed to settle it down.

McCullough sat forward. 'Most people think I'm mad, and I don't mean in the—you know—it's just a mad thing to do, but that I'm having a serious breakdown. That I'm delusional.'

'Yeah, but you're not dangerous.' It was meant to be genuinely helpful. Something to consider on any tick list.

'No. No one's said that. Yet.'

'You know me, Mac—I don't care what you do.'

'Except you hitched all the way up here.'

Terry pushed himself up from the sofa like an old man. 'Is it all right to have a can in front of the . . .' He motioned with his head to the children.

'Of course. But you haven't slept or eaten anything.'

'I'm fasting. I'm a holy man now. Next week you might find me shaving the top of me head.'

Studying Terry at that moment, McCullough felt the boy was made of a different substance from himself, something leaner, tauter; but as he moved, he walked stiffly, as if there was some distant pain he was ignoring, a poison somewhere. There was also a dryness about him: his skin was papery in places, under his eyes, around his fingernails. Drinking was the cause of most of this. Whether his intelligence was similarly affected it was difficult to know. Certainly his mind didn't seem blunted. He was alert to levels of possible meaning, offered insights that seemed to provide both clarity and an endorsement of life's great mysteries, even if that wasn't his intention. He possessed a kind of Negative Capability, although McCullough sensed there were certainties that were unavailable to others.

The holdall was in the corner and Terry retrieved a warm can of strong lager from one end and held it away from himself to open it. Pearl turned to discover what the source of the sound was and then went back to the TV.

Holly came in with two small plates of carrot sticks and placed them in front of the children. She noticed Terry glance at them. 'Would you like a carrot, Terry?'

He thought for a moment and then said, 'I could do a carrot.'

'Do you want me to cut it up?' Holly managed to make this a joke, whilst allowing Terry the option.

'Straight out of the ground for me.'

What Holly brought in seemed to have a naked yet somehow artificial luminosity after they had all pictured a carrot covered in fresh mud. Even the crunch seemed a little over-clean.

Bugs Bunny was on the TV.

They all watched cartoons for fifteen minutes, Holly perched on the arm of the sofa. When McCullough ordered the TV off, Walter refused to accept this, having registered his sister was watching TV when he came in. He was allowed five minutes more. Pearl went back to drawing at the kitchen table, hunched over her sheets of A4 as if taking an exam. McCullough took a work call. Excusing himself, hand over the phone, he explained to Terry, 'We're struggling with intimations of the apocalypse—how people might react.' And then went upstairs.

After the carrot Terry had gone to the fridge himself and taken out a stick of celery. Holly was preparing lunch.

'Mac says you're a lawyer.'

'A solicitor. Asylum.'

'You meet people who've been tortured?'

'Yes.'

'Do you reckon we torture in this country? They say we don't, but the Yanks do, and we pretty much follow them.'

'I think we probably go up to the line of what most reasonable people would call torture, but I'm not sure we step over it.'

'Yeah, but who says where the line is?'

'I think it is the man on the Clapham omnibus. Which is a way of saying: what would most ordinary people think?'

'Most ordinary people would bring back hanging.'

'Maybe it's what a judge thinks the man on the Clapham omnibus would think, if he could be trusted to be reasonable.' She'd wanted it to sound jokey, not patronizing. She wasn't sure that it had. Nor as friendly as she'd have liked.

Terry bit off some celery with his back teeth and chewed with his mouth open; a pale green juice was created and sluiced around. 'So it's what a judge thinks?'

'Often, yes.' Holly sat on the table and put her bare feet on the bench. 'You'll find they're a pretty liberal bunch.'

'I'm always up in front of the magistrate.'

'What for?'

'Got a bit of a temper.'

'Have you been to prison?'

'A couple of times. Three months, six months. It's all right. You could be my brief next time.'

'I'm an immigration solicitor.'

'Not many immigrants down there.'

'I know.'

There was a brief pause, a crunching of celery.

'So what you going to do—if he ever finishes it? Make tea for the old ladies? There are a lot of old ladies down there. And they don't like immigrants.'

'Maybe Mac will make them see the light.'

'I don't think anyone'll turn up. They all go to the church in the village.'

She looked at him, the pale, almost translucent celery in his hand, its fibres teased out of the hard ridges and hanging off the end, glistening like dew on threads of cotton. 'Do you understand why he's doing it, Terry? I mean really.' There was a new pleading in her voice, as if she understood they were entering a sudden and brief intimacy and it must be exploited. It didn't matter that she'd asked him this same question, or a variant of it, only an hour ago, in the same way that it didn't matter that she'd asked herself the same question in every variant possible a hundred times before—to stop asking was to presume there was no answer, and she didn't believe that.

Terry looked at her. 'God told him?'

'Do you believe that?'

'What, God said, "Hey, Mac, build me a church"?' He shook his head. 'Nah.' Definitive as far as he was concerned.

Holly wanted to trust this boy, if only at this moment and on this subject. 'Then *what*?'

'Maybe he just got a feeling.'

'But that's not enough.'

'A big feeling.'

'However big.'

'What about all the patriarchs and prophets?'

'What about them? They didn't live in a semi-detached Victorian house in Wandsworth.'

'Maybe don't think of what he's doing as building a church.'

'Then what is he doing?'

'I don't know. What he calls it: an expression. Hey, I'm just the foreman.' Terry laughed. 'Not even that.'

She felt let down, and hardened herself against him slightly. 'You're here for a reason.'

McCullough came down the stairs, still on the phone. '*You* know the fucking difference—I write a report and no one reads it; we do it in PowerPoint and everyone falls asleep. Personally, I'd write it in heroic couplets if I could.' There was a pause and he laughed. 'OK. See you Monday.' He clicked off and tossed the phone on the sofa while passing the sitting room.

'I'm now beginning to understand why governments never get anything done,' he said. 'They ask you to explore the impossible and then want simple-minded fucking answers! Actually, they don't want answers—they want actual solutions, which they'll ignore because they won't permit them to be labelled "solutions" but dressed down as "possible suggestions". This morning Jim—my business partner—has had the Home Office onto him, trying to track me down. On a Saturday. We're only midway through and they want to know—even before we're committed to *anything*—what's the top line? The headlines. Really? Quarter of a million quid, a month-plus to go, and they want to know, just in case the event we're researching actually *happens*: what should they do? The headline is that you should have commissioned the research earlier, you moron.'

Sitting on the table, Holly swivelled her bottom to face McCullough and then swivelled back towards Terry. 'You'll get used to this.'

'What?'

'Ask him what this is all about.'

'What's this all about?'

'Nonsense. I mean not entirely nonsense. Actually, this time not nonsense at all. I've been waiting for a project like this for years.'

'Good timing, then.'

Holly looked tired; the usual light in her eyes had dimmed. McCullough could see the diminishing of happiness in her.

When he first met her, she had been guileless and with a pre-disposition for fun. She was, as he often said, invariably 'sunny'. He'd fallen in love with her almost immediately, within a matter of days. It had taken her longer, but that was to be expected. That it had happened at all, he regarded as a miracle. For the first two years she'd refused to commit to anything beyond friendship and the occasional drunken fuck, and he'd resigned himself to look elsewhere. But then one day she called him from work and matter-of-factly declared herself in love with him, and they moved in together. Now, thirteen years later, he knew she was still the same person because he saw how she was with her friends. That their relationship had changed was inevitable, and while both would agree that over the years their love had deepened, it was cruel that such a deepening meant they were less playful than they used to be, less independently generous with each other. If they were honest, part of the best of each other was now played out beyond the relationship. Was this the case with all couples? He suspected it was. Was it possible to retrieve their earlier selves? He suspected not. Did that matter? He had no idea. It sometimes felt that his love for Holly was a large smooth stone that was impossible to lose but easy to set aside, overlooking how extraordinary an object it was. To remember, he needed to pick it up more often, but his hands were full with other things much of the time.

And then there was the nightmare he'd been having ever since they moved in together. The narrative was always different, the story the same. Holly no longer loved him. He regarded the level of his despair in the dream as directly proportionate to his love for her in waking life. The cold hard fact of the loss of her was unbearable, a crushing pain, bewildering, panicky, sickening. She made it clear she wasn't to be persuaded because love isn't biddable or summonable out of nothing, and she felt nothing for him; her version of the large smooth stone was irretrievably lost. When he woke he'd recall standing before her, hands held out imploringly, as if he had something else to offer her, a replacement for her missing stone, but his hands were always empty, and he knew that no matter what he said or did, his love could not be constituted outside himself, created into something and passed over. So she just looked at his empty hands.

It didn't worry him that he was having these dreams almost nightly now. He didn't believe that her love for him was more vulnerable to loss or breakage at this moment—that would be to doubt it on some ontological level, and he didn't. But he feared if something didn't happen to guide them through this, they would lose contact with those aspects of each other that kept them a close loving couple, and they'd soon become, like many of their friends, a partnership connected only through the children, and mostly through the children's needs rather than the intrinsic pleasure of being a family—the very thing Holly was desperate to preserve. So he let her sarcasm pass and joined her sitting on the table, their sides touching, his hand on her knee.

Terry wiped his fingers on the legs of his trousers. 'I should be off.'

McCullough laughed. 'Got somewhere important to be?'

'You know me, Mac.'

'Stay the night.'

'You forget my old mum.'

'Then let me give you money for the train.'

'You can give me the money but I'll still hitch.'

Holly hopped off the table and turned on the oven. 'I don't think I've seen a hitchhiker in years.' She returned to the table.

'We're a dying breed.'

'You've got all those books.'

'I didn't say I was going to walk.'

'You've got to get to the motorway.'

The beads in Terry's beard clicked as he shook his head. It was another moment when he seemed to be in possession of a piece of information that had been denied everyone else. Given his outward appearance it was difficult to believe that it was good information, but whatever it was, McCullough hoped it was worth the sacrifice of his teeth and other aspects of personal hygiene.

He laughed. 'You are marvellously unencumbered, Terry. Even with a very large bag of books.'

'Yeah, 'cause a bag of books is a burden, right?'

'Well, they possess physical properties that tend to make them so, especially in volume.'

'It's a bag of books, Mac.'

'Let me drive you to the motorway.'

Holly looked around at him. They were sitting so close together that she had to pull back slightly to bring him into focus. 'You will come back?'

'Of course I'll come back.'

Terry wiped his hands on his T-shirt. 'Well, while you two sort this out, I think I might go and watch a bit of telly.' He grinned, hitched up his jeans and left the room.

Nothing was said for two minutes. It was as though all that could be managed was breathing. Even focusing on what was passing through their own minds was impossible, such was the pressure and dullness of their thoughts. There was actually a point when they both wondered if they might just sit there forever if there had not been the children to consider. Finally, Holly found the energy to slap McCullough's knee and smile.

'He's a strange boy.'

'He is indeed. Hard to call him adorable, but . . .'

'It's terrible. Anyone I meet these days who's not—you know, completely normal, I think: is this how Walter is going to turn out? And that's not right because Terry—as long as he's happy—is a wonderful boy.'

'Apart from the teeth.'

'Apart from the teeth. But it's like suddenly when your child might not conform—conformity seems a lot more attractive. More attractive than it should. I love him so much . . .'

'Terry or Walter?'

Holly laughed. 'I can't quite accept wanting something ordinary for him when we know how wonderful he is. And I'm not thinking he's wonderful only in our home and somehow expecting him not to be wonderful out of it . . . We should just want the best for him, shouldn't we? Is Terry happy?'

McCullough covered Holly's hand with his. 'My guess is that Walter's going to find life harder than most some of the time and easier than most a little less of the time. But he has no bigger advantage than the fact he's a happy child, which he gets from you.' He believed this deeply and it gave him pleasure to say it. The moment the twins were born both parents enjoyed tracing and mapping the provenance of their children's traits, especially those that seemed to be derived from their own parents, as if that generation were possessors of certain undiluted characteristics. It was usually where they laid the blame for any extreme behaviour. This was McCullough's way of exonerating Pearl, making it clear that he believed the Ideal of Wilfulness was to be found in Holly's mother. Holly countered with McCullough's father's ability to find women slavish to the cult of his personality. Certainly there could be no way of knowing at this point whether Walter possessed any gifts for choosing or being chosen by women, except that he appeared to be handsomer than his father, if not quite as strikingly handsome as his grandfather. What both parents agreed upon was that Walter possessed many of McCullough's more banal traits: a need for structure, routine, the dependability of others. Indeed it was noted early on that McCullough seemed to possess a diluted version of Walter's characteristics, as if the inheritance had worked the other way. In most aspects of behaviour, Walter had become the benchmark, the purest version.

Lunch was eaten outside under a blazing sun: a bright broad slab of heat. Terry helped Holly with the garden umbrella as McCullough made hard-boiled eggs, demanded at the last moment by the children.

McCullough and Holly wore sunglasses and felt oddly awkward and conspicuous in them, as if insisting on unnecessary glamour. Terry didn't eat anything beyond a couple of slices of cucumber, but drank two cans of beer to McCullough's one. He was interested in the neighbours, chuckling at anything that sounded gossipy. At one point, after noticing Pearl's eyes alight on the beads in his beard, he let her feel them, her tiny fingers tickling them so they clinked. She was then allowed a pull on his thickest dreadlock, which she didn't believe was real hair and therefore not joined to his head. McCullough said it was a dead cat's tail, which made it even more fascinating. Walter played with Lego Star Wars minifigures and their tiny weapons, now and again giving Terry a catalogue-accurate summary of which mini-figures went with which set, the price on Amazon, eBay, his local toy shop—all delivered breathlessly, head down, but with the odd glance up to make sure of Terry's attention. McCullough and Holly stopped eating and added their own lines of commentary in the hope that some context might make their son's intensity seem more normal; they knew they were doing this and didn't want to, but couldn't stop themselves.

After lunch Terry was persuaded to accept a lift to the motorway. In the hall he offered his hand to Holly. She took it and then pulled him in for a hug, and felt unexpectedly moved by his frailty; he accepted the prolonged moment with a rearing stiffness in his shoulders. He then ruffled the hair of the twins and shook his chin to click his beads together. McCullough said that when Pearl was older she could have beads in her beard, which elicited from his daughter a closed-mouthed 'Da-*ddy*' and a stamp of her small foot.

In the car, Terry refused to wear the seat belt and asked McCullough to stop at an off-licence. They talked briefly, but mainly McCullough listened to Terry outlining his thoughts on whether Jesus would have been considered a terrorist these days. A fundamentalist. Likely to be taken out by a drone.

At the first motorway service station on the M4, McCullough leaned across to open the door for Terry, who seemed baffled by the lack of any obvious handle. He was clutching his holdall in his lap. For a moment they sat in silence.

'Why did you come up here, Terry?' McCullough asked.

First there was the chuckle, then a cough, then finally, a black-toothed grin. 'Ah, Mac, don't you know? Just doing God's work. Just doing God's work.'

ESCHATOLOGY

'Art will save the world.'

DOSTOEVSKY, *THE IDIOT*

The new project at work made McCullough think of Last Days. There was nothing in his visions that suggested the Apocalypse was due, yet between meetings he found himself reading the *Book of Revelations* as if something might be discovered there. There was a deep tonal dissonance from the rest of the New Testament. To his mind, the early Church Fathers who had lobbied for its inclusion did so as an act of fearmongering, of control, and with it took the first steps to creating the power structure of the Church, the Magisterium. Other, more kindly, works had been rejected. That said, McCullough did accept the notion of an End Time, but for him this was the moment when human consciousness perished rather than any final reckoning. What particularly unsettled him was the thought that with the death of consciousness all humankind's great artworks would be left unapprehended. A small matter to some, yes (especially if one didn't care for great artworks), but he had long carried with him an image of a paperback copy of *Anna Karenina* left on a seat on an empty train in an empty world, and the sadness he'd felt, although not overwhelming, presented him with an unworked-through grief, a sense of loss that was metaphysically troubling.

Not that he believed humankind would disappear so suddenly, evaporated in an instant, taken up in some kind of rapture—there would be no high-concept ending. But there would come a time when there would be no one left to read *Anna Karenina*. Why he'd chosen this novel he didn't know, there were many others he loved more. Why he was affected was easier to understand. For the longest time he'd believed that artworks represented something essential and enduring in human life, and through them our contingency in the universe was overthrown. It was his only real argument against the neo-Darwinians; that this aspect of human flourishing was more than a meaningless by-product of fitness adaptation. That many biologists believed that human contingency was underscored by the notion that if time were rewound and played back again we were an improbable outcome, seemed to him a pointless thought experiment, a way of denying life from a position of manifest existence. Indeed, the probability of human life was in fact high, if not certain, especially if the materialists were right and we are just the result of a causal nexus going back to the Big Bang. He supposed we could wind back all the way to the Big Bang and cancel that, and then ask ourselves about the probability of human life, but what was the point of that? That we are here is the only game in town.

McCullough pondered these things at work, sitting by a window, a week after Terry's visit. It was late afternoon. It was hot and the windows were open. The passing buses seemed close to failure, too heavy for the intensity of the heat, the work of a modern city; new models were already an anachronism and something altogether dif-ferent needed to be invented. On the corner a bicycle painted white and chained to the railings registered a death: an Eastern European student unused to riding on the left; a lorry with poor sight lines. It would be removed in a day or so. Across the wide street a great construction project had flattened buildings and then dug deep into the earth, five storeys down. Work was slow-going. When the floodlights came on at night it was like a film set; something colossal had been located beneath the earth. All day men came up from the face in small vehicles. He liked to watch the cranes and strained to see the men in the cabins powering levers to raise and swing the loads. It still amazed him that the great tall arms didn't snap, as it still amazed him 747s left the ground. It wasn't in his nature to intuit physical laws.

Over the years McCullough had spent a lot of his time at this big window, especially in summer. To cope with long working days in central London in the heat an attitude of languor was required. Similarly, the nature of his work required an almost aristocratic detachment if he was to manage its demands. But these days he could muster neither. The heat made him uncomfortable, stiff in his clothes, palpably embodied, and the work made him nervy and fidgety, often producing an out-of-body experience. Before the current project, work had come to feel like a tired performance, creating the sensation of both inhabiting a character and watching himself doing it. He played at being hesitant and uncertain when he was mostly certain and sure. When clients distrusted easy solutions, he gave them complexity, making the simple sound more nuanced and finessed than it was, often by using the words 'nuance' and 'finesse'. He had formed a habit of fluttering his fingers when describing something precise. Some clients feared it was a trick of misdirection, as if on some level he really was performing a sinister type of magic. Maybe he was; he simply didn't know any more.

Jim, his business partner, was not so easily transfixed. He never really stopped moving. He wore his coat in all weathers, as if ready for a quick exit. There was about him the energy of a man enjoyably perplexed, who knew he possessed all the mental resources to sort things out, but didn't want to because to be baffled was one of life's great joys. He seldom sat down but tended to stand in the office's communal areas, legs apart, back arched, one hand rammed into his hair. As a teenager he learned the whole of *Hamlet* for fun, and his stance had something of a mid-twentieth-century interpretation of the Dane—grand, posturing, exclamatory. He knew hundreds of poems by heart and enjoyed reciting them with varying degrees of relevance to the situation. In general conversation he was a great enunciator, in the hope that clarity of diction somehow ironized what he said. Which it did, much to the annoyance of their clients.

McCullough and Jim had known each other for twenty-five years. Their initial contact had the quality of romance. They met over the phone, and didn't set eyes on each other until they'd formed an intimate friendship, largely based around a love of early-nineteenth-century music and mid-twentieth-century novels. What astonished most people, including a great many clients, was that between them they managed to run a profitable business. It was accepted Jim must be flaky because of his physical mannerisms, and that McCullough must be a professional liability because, as one client said, he had an 'unfiltered' personality. Their initial idea was to become consultants on catastrophe—futurology at its most pessimistic. The idea wasn't as original as it had sounded at the time. Futures traders made billions on the basis that catastrophe was a moveable feast and large corporations had small teams planning for terrible 'what ifs'. But there was no independent agency that analyzed behaviour during these events and helped businesses plan better resolution strategies. Asking people how they might behave around some future catastrophe took great skill, for the most part because people themselves didn't know, or grossly overstated their predisposition for calmness or panic, their bravery or cowardice. Yet for successful future planning, being able to predict this behaviour was a small step to managing disasters when they occurred. Their small client base included corporations, broadcasters, and now the government.

The newest project was of a different order of magnitude to anything they'd undertaken before. With this one commission they'd moved into what McCullough called 'Atrociology'. Jim had been sceptical to the point of obstructive. It would require all their time, as well as extra resources, and to actually deliver on the objectives was going to be so analysis-heavy it was less prediction and more experiential guesswork. Despite appearances Jim was a numbers man at heart. But then McCullough had always believed that what they offered was less quantifiable than they promised, and McCullough was inclined to promise a lot. Jim often shook his head in meetings. Never more so than during the briefing meeting with the Home Secretary. It hadn't helped their working relationship that only a day later, McCullough had disappeared in search of some sacred ground on which to build a church.

'Mac?' Jim was in the middle of the office. They'd finished interviewing for the day and he had seen the clients out, accompanying them in the lifts and through the lobby and on to the street, paranoid that if he didn't see them go, they might hide somewhere and catch him breaking the Official Secrets Act and he'd be in prison within hours. Prison was Jim's rational fear. A place you couldn't leave on a whim.

Today it had been McCullough's turn to observe the interviews, to sit behind the two-way mirror and scrutinize every verbal and non-verbal clue, to interpret and judge. What was this man or woman willing to do when their life or the lives of loved ones were at risk? What level of independent agency were they capable of; how far might they disobey instructions to achieve what they wanted? It was well documented that those who broke the rules during catastrophes had a greater chance of survival.

One of the research objectives was to learn how to identify these people. The difficulty was that they often didn't know themselves who they were, so you couldn't recruit them in advance; it was an existential discovery in the face of a disaster. Part of the research methodology therefore was to somehow reveal this behaviour. Each interview lasted an hour and a half: thirty minutes of narrative, the rest for reaction and discussion. During the last hour, the basic fact was repeated every few minutes: you will die and there is nothing you can do about it. Or: your daughter is going to die and there is nothing you can do about it. It was emotionally draining. It felt immoral. A kind of psychological torture. The scenario itself had been handed to them by specialists who had 'war-gamed' every detail and they were instructed to read it out exactly as written, without undue emphasis or nuance, except where there were blanks, at which point they should drop in the relevant personal details—'your son Ben', 'your wife Caroline'. Two people had vomited; one woman sat silent, impassive, and wet herself. Others had walked out.

So far they had discovered only two people with a gift for seeing the opportunity for survival. The civil servants scribbled down every-thing they said and passed the notes over their shoulders to more senior colleagues sitting at the back in the dark.

Now a summary had to be written, and neither McCullough nor Jim could think of anything to say.

'Yes, Jim?'

The pause was recognizable.

'"What a piece of work is a man, how noble in reason, how infinite in faculties, in form and moving how express and admirable, in action how like an angel, in apprehension how like a god. The beauty of the world! The paragon of animals. And yet to me, what is this quintessence of dust . . ."'

To recite from memory was a kind of magic, almost shamanistic, and it bewitched McCullough. Weeks ago when he'd been able to summon up Marvell's mower poems himself, he'd felt a wonder pass through him and experienced a wholeness he couldn't recall encountering before.

'Ah, but Jim, maybe we aren't just dust.'

'Speak for yourself. I'm just happy to be the quintessence of something. Now, tell me: what are we going to do? I've learned nothing except that people love the people they love and we've scared them into post-traumatic stress disorder. It's almost negligent. I'm a kindly fellow.'

Jim liked to panic. Or rather to act out panic. Yet it was unnecessary, because along with all his other gifts, Jim knew how to get things done, although it was never clear to McCullough when he did any actual work. Maybe it was also not clear to Jim, hence the panic. McCullough himself was more dogged. During orthodox working hours he sat at a desk, laptop open, typing away, printing up, marking up, redrafting.

Jim joined him at the window. 'Any ideas what we're going to say?'

'With our noble reason and infinite faculties we'll survive this?'

'That should do it. Great. I'll head home then.'

'What do you think we should say?'

'This is your project. I told you it was impossible.'

'So you really have nothing?'

'Genuinely, my blood runs cold thinking about it.'

'It's a necessary piece of work.'

McCullough looked up at Jim, who at six foot four was a few inches taller and as with some tall men seemed taller than that.

'Don't worry, I'll come up with something.'

'I don't think blaming Thatcher is going to have much traction here. Or Freud.'

Jim stepped away from the window to take up his thinking pose.

McCullough smiled. 'You say that. But . . .'

'Yes?'

'Maybe we're approaching this from entirely the wrong angle. The wrong side of the barricade, if you will.'

'Pray tell.'

McCullough patted him on the shoulder and went to his desk.

'I'll write something up and send it to you.'

Jim tended to read everything on his phone now and text back his thoughts. He liked to stand at a bar, coat on, sport on a nearby TV. He was seldom home before midnight; he lived in Oxford with his wife and two boys. At the weekend he was a committed husband and father. Yet even then his coat remained on.

'Then I'll go. No point hanging around here, unless you're going to transfigure or something. That'd be a laugh.'

At his desk, a Word document open, his chair pushed back, his legs crossed at the ankles, McCullough continued to ponder. A first sentence was needed, a simple and plain observation from which everything else might follow. It was unlikely to come to him this way, a blank page before him, his desk a mess, but as on many other occasions he seemed unable to give up trying, and sat there as if one day he might produce work as he believed others produced work.

After an hour he looked in the fridge for a cold drink and found a bottle of beer. A tiny miracle. There was no bottle opener. The Lord giveth and the Lord taketh away. With eyebrows raised, he placed the crenellated rim of the bottle top on the edge of his desk and, after a few tentative slams with the heel of his hand, managed to remove the bottle top and with it a strip of veneer from the edge of the desk. Some miracles were messy. He returned to the window.

It was still bright outside, but down at the site the floods were on, as if activated by a timer. A few men were securing the great gates with large chains that had the heft and curvature of pythons. Given the scale of the project, McCullough wondered why a team didn't work through the night. He supposed that was a good thing, for the workers, for the few local residents, but he found he rather liked the idea of working underground at night, emerging each morning into the day. The freshness and the cool of the air. The uncomplicated benevolence of the sun. He was reminded of Aesop's story about the wind and sun. Who set the challenge he couldn't remember, but it was simple enough. Who of the two of them might rid a person of their clothes? The wind's show of strength was no match for a free gift of warmth. He liked to think he'd used both on the clifftop, but it still hadn't worked. Since returning he'd ceased to believe he had attempted to build a real church. Once again it was little more than an imaginary three-dimensional shape set against a generic landscape—today for some reason a box of light in a wood of silver birches. 'Ark' was the Hebrew word for box. Noah didn't build a ship but a box. A box to rise upon the flooding waters.

McCullough accepted that he was unlikely to be given an intimation of a great flood—after all, he was experiencing something altogether different: an inundation of the soul, or at least the creation of a space for such an inundation. Thinking back to what he'd left behind on the clifftop, a box would have been easier and more fitting: the simplest expression of what was within him deposited outside. Yet even that came with a risk. In extending himself outward he feared being separated from some elemental aspect of his being, or more scarily, having transplanted this pocket of space into the world, he'd find himself trapped within it by some extraordinary inversion of space and proportion. But they hadn't reached that stage. All they'd done was dig and create space in the earth, laid foundations, erected a few pillars. Whether the space above it would become fully enclosed remained to be seen.

Maybe that was why he'd not returned. Creating space was fine, but trying to reify it in concrete and steel was something else. When it came to God, to enclose was wrong. Was it not actually trying to trap God? We build and we contain. We build gloriously and we contain gloriously. The glory might go to God, but we expect a little reflected back. On its deepest level, to build a church was to reduce God to our own dimensions, to contain Him, and at the same time raise ourselves up. Vanity of vanities . . . all is vanity.

The site below his office window was now empty—a vast expanse of broken land and heavy machinery. The relief patterns of caterpillar tracks were like the fossilized remains of gigantic invertebrates. There was a small cabin with a light on. McCullough imagined a man inside reading a newspaper; but there was a satellite dish on the roof so a TV was probably on. He felt the dirt on the man's fingers. Since returning from the clifftop he hadn't used his hands beyond typing, peeling and chopping vegetables, tickling the twins. He felt the new strength in his hands atrophying.

In his pocket, his mobile vibrated. It was Holly. Cereal needed picking up. Milk. Chocolate, if he wanted any. The children were in bed, a rare occurrence at such an early hour. He liked to be back before they were asleep and, if it were possible, just at that moment when being read to had created in them a warmth and heaviness that was irresistible. At these times even his sudden appearance wasn't enough to pull them away from the warm, soft sides of Holly. Walter tended not even to look up. Pearl might pull a wry face to make sure he knew not to double-guess anything she might be feeling, and especially not to assume she was all snug and comfy like a baby. For some reason this made him think of Terry, a boy without worldly comfort, dragging his canvas holdall of books from the car to the grassy kerb of the slip road, into a stranger's car, to a home McCullough couldn't really imagine but he felt certain lacked the soft landing he hoped his children would always feel.

What would Terry make of all this: exploring the potential behaviour of the general public in the face of a mass terrorist attack? He'd suspect a conspiracy of some sort, at first. Something duplicitous. The government colluding with some other more mysterious power. But it would engage him, that was certain. Would he intuit the answers that eluded McCullough? He felt strongly the boy might know something; his instincts were so differently calibrated. It was a romantic notion, but it seemed a fair assumption—an instinct of his own. Maybe he should consult Terry? Bring him in. Were they not free to interview whomever they wanted, as long as the Official Secrets Act was signed, which he doubted Terry would do? It amused McCullough to imagine what his clients would make of Terry. Government policy influenced by an alcoholic loner with a predisposition to see conspiracy everywhere? As it was they found McCullough himself difficult to stomach. At the formal awarding of the commission, he sensed two civil servants figuratively holding their noses. There was something slightly vulgar about this choice of work: catastrophe, atrocity, plumbing the depths of ordinary people and their tawdry lives. He had little doubt they would class him and Terry as closer than they would themselves and McCullough, despite the superficial similarities—suits, shiny shoes, slickness of language. Were they right to do so? From their perspective it would be regarded as a terrible insult. For McCullough, it was a comfort.

PART TWO

Love I

WILDERNESS

'A sojourner have I become in a foreign land.'

MOSES, EXODUS

McCullough sat between the four of them, on a narrow bench, at a small square table cramped with pint glasses. A window behind him was open to a full car park, then a road, beyond which a village green was lush and bright in the evening light. In its centre, a cricket square was roped off, grass cut and rolled to a dry dun colour. At the far side, there were three oak trees, trunks dark and striated with vertical shadows; each canopy, set against the sky, was like a dark cloud fixed to a thick stem. It was just past seven o'clock.

He had come across Rich first, walking along a narrow lane. He pulled up alongside him, grit spinning off the tyres. Rich didn't recognize him at first, leaning in the open window on folded arms, eager to be asked directions. But after a double take he pulled back and said, 'You! Cool,' and walked around the front of the car and climbed in.

The drive from London took place in a pocket of time to which he had no access. At the door Holly had protested; she'd even come to the car and knocked on the window and pleaded with him not to go. All he remembered was his hand on the ignition key and that was it. From that point on—nothing. Disconnected from linear time, whatever thought came into his head drifted away in an instant, as if his mind itself were blinking and a new world existed after every shutter release of his eyes. It was all very peculiar.

Rich had focused him. Once the boy was in the car, it was McCullough's heart that seemed beyond his control. He was moved by seeing his young friend, in that moment representative of all four of them.

Strapped in and seat pushed back, Rich began to direct him somewhere with inconclusive swishes of one hand, while with the other he texted first Nathaniel and then Rebecca. He showed the message to McCullough, the small screen held in front of his face, requiring him to flick his eyes from screen to road to avoid driving into a hedge. The text read: *Macs back! Off to Dogs.*

In the seven minutes it took to arrive at the pub neither Nat nor Rebecca responded, but as McCullough pulled into the car park Rebecca was there waiting, sitting on a makeshift bench of a timber plank and two red plastic crates; she sat like a teenage boy, shoulders hunched, elbows on knees, smoking. As the tyres pressed over the broken tarmac and gravel, she stood and dusted down her behind; she was wearing dark blue jeans very low on her hips, a white singlet, flip-flops, and carrying a light blue cotton jacket. She let herself be kissed on each cheek.

Nathaniel arrived as they were standing at the bar, Rich with McCullough's debit card sticking out between two fingers, trying to attract the bartender's attention. Nathaniel stood stiffly, pink polo shirt tucked in his chinos, widening his waist still further. Rebecca jabbed McCullough in the side and said, 'Kiss and make up.' McCullough offered his hand. Nathaniel paused before taking it, as if he wanted to be certain McCullough appreciated the gravity of the situation—he wasn't to be fobbed off with empty gestures. Two weeks on, the betrayal was still keenly felt. McCullough disguised his irritation: the boy had been elected stooge by a family of wits and bullies, and that meant wherever possible he needed his moods to be taken with especial seriousness. Eventually, Nathaniel took hold of the offered hand, but claimed he was unsure whether he was staying for a drink.

There were no free tables. The space by the bar was narrow and every few moments they had to bunch together to let people past. It was a proximity they'd never before experienced; so often at the site they had to shout to one another to be heard, and sitting together on the ridge always allowed for a person-sized space between them. On the other side of the pub, through a lattice window, there was a small wedding party. Flashes of bright yellow fabric crossed the glass like intense shots of sunlight. Occasionally large men in grey tails—big bellies, big chests, big beards—passed through the bar area. Rebecca judged them harshly and curled her lip when she was looked at. They tended to have the confidence or stupidity to let their gaze linger on her without shame.

'Everyone been good then?' McCullough tried to inflect the question with gentle irony.

For a second no one spoke, then Rich said, 'My friend fell off his motorbike.'

'I'm sorry to hear that.'

'He was tanked up.'

Rebecca smiled. 'Terry says you have a pretty wife.' She had her thumbs hooked into the waistband of her jeans, pulling them down a little and revealing a soft brown stomach.

'Yes, of course, my surprise visit from Terry.'

Rich leaned against the bar, jutting his elbows back for extra support. 'He's been reading the Bible.'

'So I hear.'

And that was it for three minutes, as one, two, then three pints—lager, cider, ale—were ordered, and then lined up by the bartender, his big arms craning the glasses over the pumps, unperturbed by liquid slopping over the rims. McCullough looked faux beseechingly at Nathaniel. 'Let me buy you one, Nat?'

Rich answered for Nat, or rather bypassed any answer, saying, 'Get him one, Jeff,' and motioned to Nathaniel. Jeff studied Nathaniel for a moment and said, 'Bitter, right?'

McCullough wasn't paying attention: Rebecca was bending over, scratching an insect bite just above her ankle. Her singlet had dropped open at the neck. Her bra was olive green with a tiny off-white satin bow at the centre. He also noticed, next to Rebecca's flip-flops, Nathaniel's big brogues splayed at a slightly idiotic ten to two. He looked up and addressed the boy directly.

'How's the site? Terry said you and—'

'Fine. Yes. Good.' It was said a little sharply, and yet he had to fight a revealing smile, pleased to be the first to provide an update. 'Pretty secure, I'd say.' Delivering this piece of information loosened

Nathaniel's shoulders and chest a little, widening him further at the hips. His shoes were now at almost three-forty-five. A pint was placed next to him by Rich.

A table became free by an open window, four empty pint glasses pushed together in the centre, the apertures in the shape of a four-leaf clover. McCullough was invited to slide in first. Rich picked up the empty glasses with one hand and deposited them on the bar. 'See. I'm a natural.' He then budged up Rebecca and everyone moved around. The benches were narrow and uncomfortable; the small loose cushions were useless and set aside along the windowsill.

There was silence as they sipped their drinks and took stock. For a second or two Rebecca stared at McCullough, her chin on her fist. 'I'd love to see you get smashed off your face,' she said, adding, as a kind of justification, 'Do you have any idea how fucking boring it is down here?' She sat back with defeated weariness and dropped her hands to her lap. Her shoulders were dark with an almost subcutaneous glow, and the curls of her hair were like large knots in dark wood. She often ran her hands through it from front to back, fingers splayed, lifting it up from her scalp. It was as if her hair was heavy and tangled in its depths and her head needed relief.

Nathaniel said, 'So are you staying down here? Are we carrying—'

McCullough interrupted him. 'Forgive me, but I really don't know what I'm doing here. I'm not popular at home right now, I know that much.' And to further distance himself from the question, he looked around and added, 'Maybe I should open a pub. Is it not also a place of gathering?'

Nathaniel grunted; he disliked unclear answers, ironic withdrawals, especially when statements seemed to be saying two things at once. 'Terry said you might not want to carry on.'

'I'm waiting for instructions.' It was a kind of honesty; he wasn't lying. But he was quick to qualify: '"Fearing" might be more correct.' He smiled at Nat, requesting forbearance.

Under his breath, as if to demonstrate his willingness to make sense of it, Nathaniel repeated, 'Fearing . . .' It didn't make sense.

McCullough studied the three of them in turn. They seemed pensive, as if waiting for him to explain something. He felt like a father announcing an inevitable divorce to his grown-up children. They'd all moved on, but still, it was their mum and dad.

'What can I say? It all made sense a few weeks ago and now everything feels so . . .' He looked at his hands; his skin appeared old and dry, and in this light, a sickly pale yellow. 'Everything just lacks substance. Quiddity. It's like when you say the same word over and over again; not only does it lose its meaning, it starts to sound ridiculous and just a pointless noise. It's pretty much how everything feels to me at the moment. I need to stop going over stuff and let the world gather back its meaning.'

He paused and looked at them; no one else seemed ready to speak. 'I once read somewhere that if we were the size of microbes this table would look like a cloud, a massive hazy porous shape. That's what everything feels like to me at the moment. As if the whole world is dispersing. Building a church must have felt like a way to put everything back together, provide some glue. But now even that's dispersing. That's the scary part. I feel like I'm more aware of the space between everything than the actual physical stuff itself. I sometimes wonder whether I can even handle solid material. If I pick up this glass it will be like trying to hold on to water, that my hand will just pass through it. Does that make sense?'

Rebecca smiled. 'I *really* would like to see you off your face.' And then, as through by some unified inner command, they all looked around to watch the door open and Terry enter, dragging with him his holdall, its soft bulging middle caught by the door's closing.

Rebecca seemed relieved to see him. Terry pulled the holdall free. Rich welcomed him. Having been the first to meet McCullough, he'd elected himself unofficial host for the evening.

'Welcome back, Your Grace.' The holdall was dropped to the floor and with a foot shoved under the table.

Rich eased himself out and swivelled an empty chair from the adjacent table for Terry.

'Couldn't keep away, then?' McCullough said.

'Missing you.'

'Made it up with Nat here?'

McCullough glanced over at him. 'Nat's been very generous.'

'No more handbags at dawn, then?'

It was clear Nathaniel was never going to like Terry: to his mind there was something fundamentally wrong with Terry's ease in company—it wasn't earned or learned, and that went against everything Nathaniel stood for.

A glass of whisky was placed before Terry, and Rich shuffled himself back into his seat.

'I met him on the road.'

Terry listened, but was busy with his hands beneath the table, unzipping his holdall, his eyes roaming as if they were searching inside the bag. Then, to a well-rehearsed cough by Rebecca, Terry yanked back the ring pull on a can of beer.

Answering the unasked question, he explained, 'I can't drink the Mexican piss in here.'

Rebecca added: 'They know. As long as he buys something. Hence the whisky.'

Head low, eyes level with the table's edge, Terry took a slug of beer. 'Have I missed anything? Can't take decisions without us all here.'

Rebecca placed her pint glass back on the table. 'You haven't missed much.'

Someone caught her attention, a woman passing behind Terry. She tensed up and McCullough followed her gaze. From behind his hand Terry said, 'Her old girl.' McCullough was surprised by his own reaction. He felt embarrassment on Rebecca's behalf, as if it had been his own mother in the pub; but he was also curious to see the woman. She was gone, though, the glass door banging shut.

McCullough decided to tease. 'Was she checking up on you?'

Rebecca scowled. 'Checking up on you, most likely.'

'Do you live far from here?'

Rich, whose general ebullience seemed limitless this evening, gave a surreptitious point out of the window, just a curled finger jabbing. With a little swivel, McCullough looked out of the window and saw Rebecca's mother walking across the darkening village green.

Her hair was the same as her daughter's but for a few strands of silver. Without turning around he said, 'She might be you from here.'

'Gross.'

'Why?' But he supposed he knew why.

Two pint glasses were empty, Rich's and Nat's, and pushed into the centre of the table as if making a point.

'Do you want another, you two?'

With a couple of big gulps Rebecca finished hers. 'And for me.' Terry knocked back his whisky. 'And me.'

McCullough had over half a pint left.

Rich extricated himself from between bench and table and lifted the glasses with the same simple claw-like grip of fingers and thumb.

'So why you back?' Terry remained hunched down even when he wasn't taking sips from the can between his feet. 'You surprised when I turned up?'

'It was nice to see you. You made quite an impression.'

'How's work? They still on at you?'

How might Terry feel if he'd known he'd been the initial inspiration for this return?

Nathaniel took in a big breath and tried to reposition himself at the table; his big thighs and bottom were uncomfortable on the narrow bench. 'My dad's a senior civil servant. Foreign Office.'

'Really?' McCullough supposed Nathaniel knew why this was relevant.

'I asked him about you.'

'It's unlikely he's heard of me.'

'He hadn't.'

Drinks arrived. Rich leaned over Terry to settle the glasses on the table. There was something natural about his body, his balance, with full glasses. McCullough felt inclined to say something encouraging. 'You're good at this, Rich. You should go to New York, where bartending is an art.'

'I saw this ad for bar work in Exeter.'

Rebecca rolled in her lips to stop herself smiling. 'Bless.'

'Easy stages,' McCullough added.

Bottoms shuffled up to let Rich back in on the bench.

Terry was again eye-level with the edge of the table. There was something wonderfully conspiratorial about this, as if what he wanted to discuss was so secretive that part of him thought he should whisper it under the table. But then after a quick slurp he sat back up. 'Come on, Mac—spill the beans: what exactly do you do? We might even be able to help. We're the three wise men, and Rebs.'

Rebecca punched him on the upper arm. 'Arse.'

Was this boy possessed of genuine clairvoyance?

McCullough took a gulp from his pint and sat forward. 'I might be persuaded to open up a little.'

But then Terry was on his feet, the suddenness of his movement rattling the table a little, pushing McCullough back. 'Good, but it'll need to wait.'

Also standing, Rebecca announced, 'Fag break. He wants to be able to concentrate.'

'And you?'

She paused. 'I'm here, aren't I?'

Nathaniel sat back down, a little further in, taking up half the space left by Rebecca. Rich was at the bar, ordering a second pint for McCullough. Outside the window Terry and Rebecca were lighting their rollies.

'They don't say anything when they're out there, just stand there smoking. Did you used to smoke?'

'I did. With relish. What about you?'

'At school. A bit.'

'A bit?'

'I played a lot of sport.'

Like the reverse action of a fairground grabbing arm, Rich lowered McCullough's pint over the other glasses and onto the table with his fingertips.

Terry and Rebecca soon returned and took their places. Terry knocked back the whisky, and winked at Rich to order him another. Then, rubbing his dry hands together, he said, 'Come on then, Mac. Give us a few secrets of the crown.'

He needed to avoid looking at Rebecca; she would feign boredom even if she wasn't bored.

'OK. Here we go. This is what I do. At least this is what I've been doing for the past couple of months. Let's imagine a Tuesday evening. Say six-thirty. In London. What's going on?'

Rich sipped the top off his pint. 'Not sure that's a job, Mac.'

'Bear with me. Just answer the question.'

'Lots of things.'

Below the table, Terry's arm was searching blindly for his beer, but his eyes were focused on McCullough.

'How many people will be in, let's say, a two-mile radius of the City or the West End? Canary Wharf?'

Only Rich was playing. 'Millions.'

'He's some kind of demographer.' This was Nathaniel.

'Not really, but a good guess. Let's say it's two million. On average. Now let's think about what might be going on that could swell that number. It's a Tuesday and two London football clubs are in the Champions League. Maybe there's been some kind of financial crisis and that sector is staying late. There's a band playing at the O2. Anything else?'

Rebecca took in a breath. 'Film premiere?'

'Good. You'll see why in a moment. Anything more? We're thinking about people being in central London, why there might be more than usual.'

'Nice weather.' Rebecca again.

'Means what?'

'You know . . .' She shrugged.

'People stay in town longer after work,' McCullough encouraged her. 'Other people go into town for a drink. What does that mean?'

'Streets are more crowded.'

'That's one thing.'

Terry was smiling, swilling the whisky under his nose; the black and caramel stickiness on his teeth seemed thicker.

'Come on, Terry, pitch in.'

'You're supposed to be telling us.'

'Nathaniel?'

'Trains and Tubes will be full. Capacity is stretched—generally.'

'Good. But think about people—what have we got here?'

'Football fans, drunk people, kids at a concert.' With her thumb Rebecca counted off each with a flick of a finger.

To praise her risked another rolling of her eyes.

'And?'

Terry smiled. 'Terrorists.'

'Let's consider the worst possible attack.'

'Dirty bomb.' Again, Terry.

'No.'

'Two dirty bombs?' Nathaniel adjusted his crotch, his big thighs rocking the table. Everyone steadied their drink.

'Twice as bad, yes, but not as bad as, say, a biological device—smallpox, anthrax, or a lethal variant of avian flu.'

'You have to work out how many it will kill?' Rich asked.

'No—that's for other people, and the numbers can be quite precise. My job is to explore how all those people, now caught in London, are going to behave during the attack, and what their families are going to do if the police, the army, have to contain the area, create a *cordon sanitaire*. Is it possible to predict the behaviour of a certain set of people if London falls victim to a biological or chemical attack?'

'Brilliant.' Terry loved this, as if he'd finally received proof the government had plans it didn't want him to know about. 'They've got to decide . . . Fuck! This is brilliant. You've got to . . .' He was shaking his head in disbelief.

McCullough continued: 'If they suspect a biological device, there will be a massive containment exercise. The army and police will move in and won't let people leave or enter. Now in theory, in the abstract, we'd all agree that this would be best for the nation. But to really plan for it, we have to know something about how the people directly affected will behave. In this instance, my job is to talk people through scenarios they can relate to: what if you or your loved ones are caught within the zone? I have to try and reveal the possibilities of reaction. Including unknown unknowns, as they say. "Your age group wasn't in our sample set. If you misbehave they'll just shoot you." I'm joking, of course.'

No one laughed.

'So anyway, you're in a pub or bar after a couple of pints, just like now, and you feel fine and someone says there has been a terrorist attack. What's the first thing you do?'

Rich: 'Check your phone.'

'It's down. No signal. Same for other people. Police have sequestered all the bandwidth.'

Nathaniel: 'That happened on 7.7.'

'Do you believe it?'

Rebecca: 'Why not?'

Terry: 'You'd want confirmation.'

'So no one panics?'

'Not yet.' Rich nodded.

'There's probably a TV on in the pub. There's a newsflash—no details, just something has happened. So you can't ignore it now. But you're OK. No one's dying around you. Just means getting home will be more inconvenient than usual. What do you do? Probably nothing. Not until you feel it's serious. Maybe you go outside and stroll around, listening to people. Everyone's a bit jittery, but that's about it. Some people even play it down and go back in the pub, order another drink; and the pubs are still serving so it can't be that bad. Maybe the TV is now reporting more details—still only speculation; after all, it's only been ten minutes. But they do say it might be a dirty bomb and there might be radiation in the air. Or it might be a biological attack and there is a chance of contamination. You can't help but feel a tremor of fear. If it's true . . . But you look around. The streets are full. Life is as vivid in the sun as it always is. You start to wander towards the Tube. You do notice people are talking to one another a little more urgently now. Someone says the Tube is closed. And the train stations. Someone else says they are erecting barricades. You don't believe the barricades part—that's too much. But you do start to listen more closely to strangers' conversations.

'The first Tube station you reach, the gates are shut. You look for someone to ask about how you might get home. Behind you—overconfident, overdramatic—a man says the bridges over the Thames have been closed and the army is north of Oxford Street. You think: how can one person know *both* things? But something has definitely happened. You're beginning to feel worried. A bit panicked even. Then someone walks past, saying: "Get over the Thames and you're fine." McCullough looked at them a little breathlessly. 'So what do you do?'

'I go.' Rich was earnest in his assessment.

Nathaniel didn't want to commit.

'Ask a policeman,' was Rebecca's input—a joke; but Terry was too involved to get it, adding his own conspiratorial flavour, 'They're in on it, too . . .'

'In on what?' McCullough asked. Terry didn't know.

'Is that it?' Rich looked around the table; he wanted more. Zombies, perhaps.

'No, of course not. You make your way down to the Embankment; you don't run, but your pace is quick, maybe a jog. You're beginning to assess things around you: people, what they're saying, details, contradictions. And then you're there . . . for a moment you think you can see . . . Fucking hell! The army is on Waterloo Bridge erecting a barricade. You can't believe it. For an instant, you don't. It's too surreal. But then maybe it's just a checkpoint or something—to catch the people who did it. Then someone says there are police officers with machine guns, like at the airport. Eventually you get onto the bridge and it's all true. You hear a megaphone. You attune your ears. "You're inside an exclusion zone and won't be let through." Then: "People who try to cross the bridge will be shot."'

'Never happen. It's not how it works,' Nathaniel pitched in finally.

'How does it work, then?' Terry wanted the posh boy to explain. 'You don't think Her Majesty's army will shoot her subjects?'

'There are operations for these sorts of things.' It wasn't much of a defence from Nathaniel.

Terry looked at McCullough, dipped down and took a sip of his warm beer. 'This is for real—right? This is what you do?'

'This is my current project. Now let's switch the optic. Imagine you're the parents of a thirteen-year-old, who's in town for something—a school trip, the cinema, a musical with her best friend and her parents. And it's your child behind the cordon, not you. Or imagine being the parents of young children and you're on a rare night out—you're there, and the children are at home with a babysitter.'

'It's fucking emotional chaos.' The gleam in Terry's eyes disturbed McCullough.

'I still don't understand what you do?' For the first time Rebecca seemed interested in clarity and not setting him a trap.

'I've got to make people believe this is happening to them, and from their reaction create a picture of how they might behave. In this case the respondents—that's the people we interview—had to believe that if something like this were to happen there really is going to be a line, a very distinct line, with the possibility, even the probability, of death on one side and life on the other. And to do that I am given a narrative—not quite like the one I've just put to you, but similar—and then based on what I know about their life, tailor it as much as I can so they can really picture themselves in this scenario. Let's remember a biological strike might leave hundreds, if not thousands, dead and many more the carriers of a killer virus. So if that happens, a massive quarantine has to be set up, separating everyone who might be infected or carrying whatever it is, until some massive vaccination programme takes place. It may be hours; it may be days.'

'Fuck.' Rich was shocked. He was picturing something. Probably horror movie-derived.

'It's going to happen,' Terry acknowledged. He didn't want to approve of the government in any way, but he also didn't want to take away from the credibility of what McCullough was saying.

'And it's not just that side of the line. What about people who might try and break over from the safe side? It's more difficult for the security forces to deal with these people.'

Terry: 'It's easy to shoot the infected. Fuck.'

Nathaniel remained unconvinced. 'How do you know people are telling the truth?'

McCullough took a sip of his pint. 'You get them to believe and then you watch them. It's a job for noticers. Then it's a judgment call. Is this a true indication of future behaviour? It's qualitative research on an indicative quantitative scale. We interviewed over two hundred people. You're just looking for clues. Someone might tell you something you couldn't predict. So you watch, think, judge.'

'Why do they get *you* to do this?' Rebecca didn't like his last statement; she didn't want to feel scrutinized.

McCullough laughed. 'Because in my proposal I managed to persuade the client that as an agency we were experienced in understanding how people behaved in states of despair. In fact, I persuaded them that there is a further state beyond despair. That people will feel desperate hardly takes a genius of human insight.'

'Is that what you are?' Rebecca didn't like this at all.

McCullough ignored her.

'Let's visualize it. You're on one side of a barrier—maybe it comprises tanks, soldiers, razor wire and—I don't know—men with dogs, and between you and another barrier is a hundred metres of no-man's-land, and on the other side of that other barrier there is someone you love, someone you love so much you would trade places with them in a second.

'You can see them and they are screaming at you, screaming for you to help them. And that's all you want to do. Except you can't because you're being prevented. The reality is that there is an immovable object before you and you are not an unstoppable force. Worse, you're an impotent, useless, exhausted force. Even to move a little nearer risks arrest and being taken away, permanently, and you know that would seem to your loved one that you'd abandoned them. They wouldn't know what had happened. Just one minute you're there, the next you're gone. Think about it—the frustration, the desperation, the inadequacy you feel. You are facing a direct contradiction to something you've believed your whole life. That if it came to it, if you needed to, you'd be able to find the strength to save the person you love—that you somehow possess a reserve of strength for that very moment. Because on some level that's what we believe. We believe that when there is a person in our life that we love that much we will be able overcome the impossible.' He paused.

'Only those who have been present when they have lost someone learn otherwise.'

'How did people react?' Again, Rich was the only one following McCullough without an agenda.

'First the absolute nature of the separation comes as a shock, so much so that you don't believe it, or don't want to believe it. If it takes time to accept the army will shoot its own citizens, then it takes longer to accept that you cannot love a person enough to save them, that the world won't finally give in to you. It's not even shock. It's incomprehension. Wordless, expressionless incomprehension. Because if the world doesn't give in, your son or daughter is going to die, or your lover or your mother. You look around for help, for understanding. Someone to see sense. But the soldiers will not listen to you. They have their orders. It's like they're the ones responsible. And you can't understand why they won't make an exception, just for you. You make your case: "See that child over there, that thirteen-year-old child crying—just let them through, please." You even offer a justification: "They weren't even supposed to be here tonight. There was a spare ticket." (At this point you don't care about anyone else; your love is deep, not wide.) But they just turn away. You don't give up. Instinct tells you there is someone who will help—someone will listen and do something, bend the rules. But you find no one. No one to beseech, to entreat, to beg.

'So what do you do? You pray. Of course you do. You want a miracle. You need something to happen outside the laws of nature. You look across the bridge, the hundred metres or so, and you pray that the distance will shrink, that somehow it will become nothing—this no-man's-land dividing you and your loved one will become like the narrowest point of an egg timer, width and distance squeezed to a single spot; and when no one is looking they can jump over to you, before everything expands back and the world returns to normal. You can see it in your head. That's all it takes . . . All that is necessary for everything to be good again is this collapse of space. This tiny part of the universe to obey you. Why can't it? You feel like time is obeying new rules, slowing down and speeding up in ways you've never experienced before. This gives you reason to believe: the world doesn't always have to operate as expected. Aren't Time and Space part of the same principle? It just needs you to make it happen. And it's not just you praying for this; not just your will that is being summoned to alter the physical world. On the other side of the other barricade, your loved one is thinking the same thing, willing the same thing. Something impossible to be made possible. But then you realize: if it's going to happen, it's not going to happen for everyone. To think of it happening for everyone is to know it won't happen at all, so you realize that for it to happen for you—you must be special. You must be singled out. But how's that possible? You need to tell yourself there must be a difference between what you feel for your loved one and what others feel. Your love must have more strength.

'And while all this is going on in your head, you are screaming across the space that you'll *do* something, you will think of *something*. They must trust you. But your loved one isn't really listening, because all they want is for that something to happen in that moment, and they can't understand why they are still there, why you haven't done something already—didn't you promise them once that, no matter what, you wouldn't let anything happen to them? But now that time has come, you're failing them. You're on the side of life, you're on the side of potentiality, action, potency—and they are on the side of death. They've been told as much. It's been made clear: a bomb has been detonated, a deadly strain of SARS, anthrax, Ebola—take your pick—has been released, and you might be infected or contaminated. You can't go anywhere.

'But you look around and everyone's still alive. There must be hundreds of thousands of people trapped; surely you're not all going to die? So despite what you're being told, at least for a moment, life is still on your side. Maybe you'll be lucky. Aren't some people just immune to these things? Surely that's going to be you. You feel fine after all. Strength and confidence surge. But then maybe this immunity will only last for so long; more exposure will mean . . . This is the worst moment of all. A feeling of hope. Once again it relies on that other person. If only they can do something now, or in the next few moments, it will be OK. They've made things better before, haven't they? You *do* trust them. So you scream: "Do something, Mum—please, do something." But instead of your mother appearing from behind the barricade to come and save you, there is nothing, nothing . . .'

'This is torture.' Rebecca said it. He wasn't sure whether she meant the actual situation or that he should make someone go through this.

'Sounds quite cool to me.' Rich was rather wide-eyed by this point.

'It's called atrociology.'

McCullough let that float for a moment.

'How do you think *we'd* react?' This was Rich again.

'I have no idea, Rich.'

'So what did people do?' Nathaniel wasn't as sceptical now, but he wanted proof of process.

'I have to be honest, I haven't given you the exact scenario because it's confidential.'

Terry was irritated, slumping back, smirking a little at McCullough.

'You don't want me banged up, do you? I've signed the Official Secrets Act—it's a big deal. But as I said, we add people's names, their sons' and daughters' names. We use pictures. But if you have to know, mostly they cried. Some got angry, of course. We were mainly there to identify those who would do something unexpected. What that might be. The old Black Swan. Something that falls outside the basic prediction models.'

Terry put his can of beer on the table; a hollow sound signalled it was empty. He was nudged by Rich and placed it back on the floor. 'Whether we'd obey in the end or rebel?'

'Must be pretty grim to get smallpox.' There was an inch of cider left in Rebecca's glass and she rolled the bottom in ellipses over the table, watching the cider slosh around. Had she imagined herself stuck behind that line, her mother on the other side? Her tone was never rich with sentiment and he doubted it ever would be, but he sensed an aspect of feeling which was new. He looked to the door, and then out of the window, to where he had glimpsed her mother.

Beneath the table a new can was opened without the cover of Rebecca's cough, and Terry sucked up some of the warm strong lager. Rich gathered up the empty glasses and, after pausing for Rebecca to finish hers, went to the bar.

'So they will have heard of you at the MoD?' There was in Nathaniel's use of the acronym a need to control a little of the conversation, to demonstrate he had a privileged access point, rather than to respond directly to what had been said. With a hotline to Whitehall, it was important that the others didn't think he was wowed by anything said by McCullough. He had chosen his most serious and collusive face.

'Yes, Nathaniel. But to check up on me would be to let them know I've just contravened the Official Secrets Act.'

Terry 'hee-hee'd', took another suck of his beer, and knocked back a third whisky the minute it was placed on the table by Rich.

There was a long moment of silence as they all took a sip off the top of their new pints. The silence was heavy, a bloated beer silence. McCullough had always disliked pubs, especially sitting around a table like this, cramped and leggy. They always felt to him like somewhere one went to register boredom with life, to locate one's life in a place consonant with that boredom, the only piquancy on offer the salt-and-piss atmosphere. But there was also something very male about the pub, a place where men came to drink and be silent, which he rather liked.

He was the first to speak. 'Maybe you are the Four Horsemen of the Apocalypse.' He laughed.

Rebecca was quick: 'Who does that make you?'

Rich thought this was extra funny, although he wasn't quite sure why. Next to him Terry sniffed, for a moment unable to focus his thoughts, but after a few seconds he said, '*Revelations* was added into the Bible late. Big arguments about it. Yeah?' He paused and his eyes narrowed. He wanted to say something more exact, more profound. There were facts he'd learned; insight he'd gained. But the third whisky had fogged him a little.

Rebecca repeated herself: 'Come on, who are you?'

'Yeah?' Nathaniel joined in, smiling, but was glared at by Rebecca, who didn't like support, especially from Nathaniel.

McCullough stared at her. 'I was just joking. I looked at the four of you and—'

'There are no such things as jokes.' Her mood had become dark.

'Why did the chicken cross the road?'

Rich laughed, this time because McCullough had bested Rebecca with the oldest and stupidest joke.

Her face showing nothing but contempt, Rebecca said, 'Because he'd just killed his father and fucked his mother.'

The table top jiggled from Rich's knees bouncing up and down. 'You people crack me up.'

There was nothing to be done; Rebecca was a tactical genius. And she was right, there were no such things as jokes: meaning could always be drawn, and in grouping the four of them together he had separated himself and by implication made himself . . . what? God? What was there to say: she was right and he was sorry. He felt drunk, far from home, separated from unconditional acts of kindness or love. The only thing that was keeping him from breaking down was Rebecca herself. She was radiant with scorn, her beauty enhanced by it, given purpose. This wasn't the first time he'd seen it.

Out of nowhere, Nathaniel said, 'No one believes in God these days.'

Terry was up, swaying a little, tobacco pouch in his hand. 'Fuck off, Nat.' He offered his hand to Rebecca, who stood and waited for Rich to shuffle out so she could wriggle free of the table.

McCullough was left with Nathaniel and Rich, both staring at him, one wishing to be entertained, the other indulged. He had nothing to say.

Nathaniel sat back. 'I know it's a dumb book and everything, but in *The Da Vinci Code* . . .'

'Yeah, I read that.' Rich was keen to join in; he seemed a little hyper. It was an odd friendship. But then Rich was a lovely and generous boy and Nathaniel liked uncomplicated people, and so they tended to endorse each other's moments of wisdom.

After a couple of minutes the other two returned. The fresh air had increased Terry's drunkenness. He stumbled before he reached the table and glared at those around who noticed. He pulled his shoulders back as he yanked up the front and back of his jeans, the contortions of a street drunk, someone to avoid. Something or nothing had pushed him beyond good-natured drunkenness. When he sat down his grin was a false one, and his eyes, which were always fierce, now seemed just mocking.

'Politicians are cunts. Lying cunts.'

Rebecca rolled her eyes. 'Here we go.'

Nathaniel turned away, his disdain visible. Terry noticed but said nothing. The heavy silence was broken by a loud sniff—one of Terry's nostrils opening wide.

'Maybe I'm getting soft. All that "turn the other cheek and love thy neighbour". Nat's a lucky boy.' His glare was directed at McCullough. He seemed in pain; he winced and sucked air in through his teeth, drew the edge of his hand across his stomach as if slicing it open. 'Cheap fucking whisky; burns your guts.'

All their glasses were empty. Through the window the sky was darkening. At ground level there was a hovering mist, giving the village green a mythical cast, as if at night it was reclaimed by the nearby moors. All the roads were quiet. When cars did pass through, they were more a shape of sound than a material presence.

After a wink between Rich and the bartender, it was announced that a lock-in might be in the offing. Rebecca shook her head; she understood the dynamics of the evening and this one was close to over. Nathaniel wasn't interested either and stood up. He looked down at Mac. 'Should we turn up tomorrow or not? What's happening?'

McCullough pushed out his bottom lip and gently nodded, committing without committing, which was how he felt about the whole enterprise. Terry was bent over, hand digging around in his holdall, tail of his eye on Nathaniel.

'You chippin', you old cunt?' There was no response from Nathaniel. 'Because before you go, *you old cunt*, I'd like to know what's in this for you? I mean, we're a bunch of . . . desperadoes.'

There was a hee-hee, but his eyes scowled and his smile was set with hatred.

'I think Nathaniel is probably a . . . desperado . . . in his own way, Terry. In his own home.' McCullough regretted speaking up. Why intervene? It didn't matter that it was true, although 'desperado' was pushing it. Terry would now mock him: appeasement was for losers.

Nathaniel stood up. His unusual brand of vanity meant that in the first instance he was pleased with McCullough's intervention, but then decided it was a kind of brush-off, as if he weren't able to speak for himself. And although Terry might unnerve him, he felt a sense of superiority that reduced Terry to little more than an irritation, not something he needed protecting from.

'I like to work hard.' It was presented as a virtue. One to be instilled in people.

Still low to the table, Terry glared inwards. 'Donkey.'

Intervening again was more reflex than moral. 'Come on now, Terry.' Then to Nathaniel: 'We all work hard.'

A large man in his early thirties, wearing rented grey tails half a size too small, with a large beard, a beer belly and powerful thighs, pushed himself between the bar and the table, his lower half pressing against Terry's back for a moment. Had he been drinking from a full pint the pressure would have been enough to make him spill some. For Terry that hypothetical appeared to have happened in reality. McCullough heard Rebecca mutter, 'Fuck.'

In this mood, it wasn't in Terry's nature to move quickly; his temper was slow and needed stoking. The man apologized but was oblivious to any real offence given.

Terry didn't move, just said in a clear half-tone, 'You're all right, you fat cunt.' It was meant to be heard—just. A kind of test. What were this man's antennae like?

The man stopped as if to reflect on what had been said, to let it seep through the beer in his brain.

Half up, McCullough made motions with his hands as if to say: we are in a sensitive place at this table right now, just let it go.

Rebecca was focused on Terry, glaring at him with the eyes of a mother who doesn't want to be made to get cross. Warning eyes. They were wonderfully vivid, almost comically stern.

The man looked down at Terry; he wasn't interested. The bottom button of his shirt was open and his stomach was pressing through, a hairy navel at its centre.

'Bet you're pleased to be back.' This was Rich.

Nathaniel had zoned out, as if he couldn't quite deal with what was going on. He'd only stayed so he could say a more formal good-bye to McCullough. From over the table, McCullough offered his hand. It was taken with a flicker of irritation: he hadn't bothered to come out from his place.

Terry stood, pulled his holdall out from under the table and dumped it on top. It looked like a fat black slug. The cheap whisky was still burning his insides and making him scowl. He was drunk and in pain.

But he had a finger raised: he wanted to speak. To any onlooker he was just an old-fashioned drunk, swaying a little, yet confident that what he had to say was essential to solve one of the world's many great problems. 'History is written by the winners, Mac. It was the same back then. And you know what—Jesus wasn't one of the winners. Mad, isn't it? Jesus wasn't one of the fucking winners and his name is on every church around the world, a billion fucking followers. So we could call him a winner. But he isn't, is he? Because he well and truly lost. Almost every one of those billion fuckers are wrong about him. Because—wait for it—the loss was the thing in the first place. And they don't get that. Every day the loss is the thing.'

'You're a desperado and theological genius, Terry.' He knew it was a mistake as he said it. But he'd set a precedent that evening of appeasement and protection, and he wanted Terry to know he was also there for him.

The contempt was amused, but still contempt. 'Fuck off, you patronizing cunt. Come on, Rebs—let's get out of here. I don't know why we waste our fucking time.'

Rich shrugged for McCullough's benefit; he'd seen this before. Rebecca shook her head and said, without worrying Terry might hear, 'Ignore him.' She didn't like to be cornered into easing tension, but Terry's body was flexing itself and McCullough's perceived insult was burrowing down into his limbs, where its full meaning would be finally, wrongly, decoded.

After a moment Terry tried to pull himself together as proof that he was clear-thinking, that he'd got it right: it had been an insult, and it was entirely his decision what to do about it. He began to laugh; his brown teeth were now the colour of whisky, receding gums exposing the roots. Somehow the laugh had made him looser, agile; he even managed a few warm-up boxing moves, head down, shoulders hunched. 'Fucking hell, Mac—what the fuck does it say if I give you a slap? After that faggot Nat knocked you over? You've only been down here a couple of hours. We're all supposed to love you. We all *do* love you. Don't we, Rich? Don't we, Rebs? OK—they won't admit it. But I will. I love you, Mac. So don't worry—you're all right. No slap tonight. Not unless you want to strip off and have a little go out on the green. Bit of old bare-knuckle.' More of the air-boxing, but the energy suddenly drained away. 'Nah—you're all right. You've got to forgive me, haven't you? And you've got to love me, too. And I don't mean 'cause I'm lovable deep down, but because you've just got to. Otherwise you're just like all those other billion twats.'

McCullough wanted to say something. To agree. But another cramp in Terry's gut brought on a new wave of drunkenness, as if all that sudden movement had quickened his metabolism, dizzying him. He reached for the bar to prop himself upright. The embarrassment was quickly felt and the scowl returned. He scanned the room, judging the silence, assessing who was watching him from the tail of their eyes. He shook his head. The world was worth nothing but his contempt. With a bent finger, he jabbed at McCullough's chest. 'Love and forgiveness. Give me a fucking break.'

TRIBES

'Thou sealest up the sum,
full of wisdom, and perfect in beauty.'

ＥＺＥＫＩＥＬ

I

What he saw at dawn was what he'd left at dusk weeks before: a building site. He had hoped that through fresh eyes it might look like something in a state of becoming, or even a remnant of something that could not be erased completely, and from which he might build anew. But there was nothing inspiring about large sheets of blue plastic tethered down with timber pegs. Raising an edge of one of the coverings with the toe of his boot, he saw building materials, naked and dusty, ordered weeks ago.

He'd slept in his car, refusing an offer of the sofa at Rich's—his parents away. Rebecca had not returned to the pub after insisting Terry leave and guiding him out and home.

From the pub to the site, McCullough had driven at speed, headlights on full beam, an intrusion in the darkness, ready to catch and pin something against the blackness of the high hedgerows. In the middle of the night, his skin chilled with sweat, he'd called Holly. She refused to discuss anything. He'd abandoned them; how else was she to understand what he was doing when she'd pleaded for him to stay? He knew it was true, but what could he do? He felt compelled. She hung up. He wondered whether this was what it felt like to be tested. It wasn't much, considering the woes of the world, but in the dark and cold, unhappy as he was, what else was he to think?

The sun's rise was slow. McCullough got out of the car and stretched. The warmth came in bursts, as if the sun's rays fixed on him for a moment and then fell away, but there were no clouds in the sky. The dawn light remained low to the ground and speckled, as if somehow taken up and contained in the dew. To wake himself more fully he walked down to the beach, his boots unlaced, ankles turning on the pebbles as they slipped into spaces between themselves and settled under his feet; there was a grinding sound, the slightest of echoes off the cliffs. The tide was out, and after walking twenty metres he came to sand. Across the sea's soft ripples the sun stitched a glistening thread. On some days the water was like this for hours, calm and delicately lustrous. Most days, however, it was as he remembered the English sea from childhood—grey and cold, and without appeal. He shivered; sweat from the night felt like a lacquer on his skin. He was a poor swimmer.

Rich, then Nathaniel, then Rebecca, and then Terry arrived and set about the work they enjoyed. He spent the first hour with Nathaniel, going over the stocks of materials and making notes. With Terry, the quality of the work from before the break in the build was inspected, as if they might learn something in hindsight and take it forward. Rich, he noticed, was staring at Rebecca as she squatted, skirt bundled up and rucked in, making tea. When she handed McCullough a mug she said, 'How long do you think we'll last this time?' It was good-humoured, but she took it for granted there would be a disagreement that would end things, this time forever.

'I'll do my best to behave.'

'My mum seemed to think you looked an interesting fellow.'

'I hope you set her straight.'

'Dead straight.' And with the upper part of her arm, she knocked into him. A josh. What had happened?

With the plastic sheeting taken up, the timber and stone slabs shone in the mid-morning sun; in the stubborn afternoon light their paleness became a shimmering, as if they possessed an energy of their own.

It was decided, no one was sure by whom, to place oak beams horizontally along the stone base, to create a layering effect. Carrying the beams was always a team effort and even Terry was prepared to take instructions from Nathaniel. He did express his disappointment at the impossibility of a flush edge between stone and timber; he wasn't interested in the soft lines created by organic materials.

'It's like fake olde worlde,' he said and shook his head. 'We can do better than that.'

Rich was in favour of the rough edges and screwed up his mouth as he assessed the imprecise fit, his lips mirroring the join.

'It won't look like that with all the glazing,' McCullough assured Terry, as he set about marking out the wide path that separated house and church again; over the weeks away, the grass was back to being untrammelled and plump, and he was determined it would stay that way.

When McCullough said the idea of another floor in the house exhausted him, Nathaniel called out, 'Can't live in a bungalow!' His public-school accent was exaggerated, as if 'bungalow' was a word he might never have said aloud before.

McCullough saw Rebecca stiffen, which was noticed by Terry, who looked at Rich.

Rich looked confused. 'I live in a bungalow.'

Nathaniel didn't know how to respond. He placed his hand on his wide hips and thrust his pelvis a little forward. The others were careful not to laugh. It was the first day, after all.

At seven o'clock, sitting on the top of the right, they shared the last of Terry's cans of beer, and he and Rebecca shared a joint. They all had their legs stretched out and crossed at the ankles. McCullough asked himself whether it would be wrong to think of them as his family, as four grown-up children? But what of his family at home? Was a man allowed two families if no law was broken? He supposed the church might become a home for another, larger, more complex family, whether or not that was his intention. Holly had asked—although she had never quite put it like this—how, if he was failing his real family, could he be there for others? He'd said he'd always believed that good fortune in the widest sense should not be reserved for those one loved. Indeed, the condition of the possibility of love, as he understood it, was that one must offer it beyond one's scope for direct love. It didn't answer her question.

Rebecca lay back, but kept her head up, covering her eyes from the early-evening sun. When she spoke her words caught a little in her throat. 'Not coming to the pub tonight, Mac?'

'Is that all you guys do?'

'No,' Rich said, standing up and pulling his bandana around his neck. 'We work for you.'

'Good point. So then you retire to the pub like good artisans?'

'We do,' Terry confirmed.

'What about you, Nat?'

'One of my brothers is home.'

'Which one?' Rebecca asked, twisting her head a little to glance in his direction. She then lay back completely and looked up into the sky.

'Stephen.'

McCullough thought he heard Rebecca say 'dick' under her breath, but was distracted by his mobile phone vibrating. He wanted them all gone so he might talk freely to Holly. A peek at the screen revealed it was Marvin calling him. There was also a missed call from Simon. He stood and looked down the slope. The small fire was out, a flat indistinct circle of silver-grey ashes. The half-built walls of both buildings were moving into silhouette. Nathaniel and Rich had pulled the plastic sheeting across all the timber and secured it down; Terry and Rebecca had tidied up the tools. Throughout the day he'd noticed the chat between them was muted, more considerate than before, especially from Rebecca. Terry had been ruminative, and didn't look well, but still laughed now and again. In the sagging pockets of his sagging jeans he carried a small pocket Bible. It seemed odd not to mention it, but McCullough decided not to; it might be regarded as permission for the others to comment. Calm and considerate could quickly become prickly.

As they all rose to stretch before gathering their things, McCullough faced them and asked about proper wages. It was only right. What did they want? There were blank stares and raised eyebrows, and eyes shunted away.

'If you can't decide, I propose a kind of honesty tin. I put money in, you take it out according to what you think you are owed.'

Rich managed a 'Cool'. Terry made his almost Pavlovian reaction to any offer: 'You're all right.' And Rebecca said, in a mock posh girl's voice, 'I could so do with a new frock, darling.'

Nathaniel looked at the ground and then up. 'My father won-dered when you might mention money.' His meaning was difficult to discern. There was a rare touch of sarcasm but to whom it was directed, his father or McCullough, no one was sure.

'Well, it will be in the car, on the back seat.'

Rebecca said, 'So who's going to wander over there first?'

She was helping him, he assumed: making clear to him that what he'd thought was a good idea wouldn't work. 'OK, I'll work some-thing out. But you're going to be paid, whether you like it or not.' It was supposed to be jokey, but no one laughed; they had tuned out as if the bell had gone in class at the end of the day.

McCullough called out, 'I'll see you all tomorrow, then?'

Rebecca remained playful. 'Maybe you will; maybe you won't.'

'I'll be back,' Nat confirmed without enthusiasm.

Terry put two fingers to his forehead and shot himself. What that meant, McCullough decided he'd never know.

And then they were no more than a group of stragglers wander-ing over the fields, friends leaving a festival.

He looked at his phone again. Marvin and Simon. No Holly. He pressed the button for 'home'. It took a while but Holly finally answered. There was screaming close by.

'I can't talk now, Mac.'

'When?'

'I don't know. Can't you hear them?'

It didn't matter who ended the call; the button had been pressed and he'd been shut out, as if he'd interrupted something he was no longer a part of. Despair was close. A shadow that followed him.

He walked over to the cliff's edge. The tide was in, and the waves were an indiscriminate crashing force. He held the phone into the air to see if there was a signal. He called Marvin. There was no answer. Simon's number went straight to voicemail. He looked at Lucien's name. They seldom called each other, always struggling to find things to talk about on the phone, as if the caller had crossed a line of intimacy. Meeting up was quite different: they laughed a lot, more so than they did with most of their friends. But even then there were lines that weren't often crossed: Lucien liked to talk about

Holly, but conversations about Maria were avoided. Whilst Lucien had never declared he was in love with Holly, the interest and joy he derived from talking about her was in itself a kind of confession. It was what made Lucien so oddly configured. For all his aristocratic detachment, his chortling irony, he was unguarded and guileless in his expression of deep feelings for the partner of one of his best friends. What Holly thought of it all was difficult to determine. She denied it was love, yet was more tender towards him than she would normally be to a man like Lucien. And so, in the end, to call Lucien and ask for advice about Holly seemed hurtful.

He sat down, legs over the cliff's edge, and looked out to sea. It was an odd thing having nothing to do, to sit back and be still, and for his field of vision to be empty of small things. It was an experience that should not feel so unfamiliar; he was a natural gazer. He narrowed his eyes and looked at the horizon, a long soft line, an indeterminate divide that promised a place one might cross and vanish from the world. It had always seemed wrong to him that the world didn't have an edge, that there wasn't that final choice to leave in such a way. But of course, the world did have an edge, and people were stepping off it every day.

To the west, the sun was resting on the hills, held up in its descent, as if waiting for its burning rim to slice its way back into the earth. Behind him the moon was present, a grey shield of patient, undemonstrative, quiet light. Whether or not he'd made a mistake in building this church—whether or not he was guilty of a terrible cliché—no one could fault him on the location.

2

The next morning, McCullough was crouching down by the fire, shielding a match flame from the breeze, touching it to the corner of a piece of newspaper, when he heard their voices. They were at a distance, laughing. The breeze caught and carried away anything that might be intelligible. He felt like running up the bank and hitting the ground before the ridge, to peer over it like a cowboy. Yet he waited at the fire, pushing at wood shavings with a twig. There was something cowboy-ish in this, so he felt as if he'd satisfied a part of his need to be seen in this way, as an outdoorsman. When they came over the ridge he stood and laughed: Marvin was unchanged from London, dressed in soft black cotton, expensive retro trainers, small round sunglasses. Simon was dressed, as McCullough presumed he often was, for hard trekking, although no one had seen him dressed this way before.

'We tracked you down,' Marvin said, surveying the place with amusement.

'Welcome,' was all McCullough could think to say.

Simon trudged down first. 'It was Marvin's idea. Is this local limestone?'

'Yes, Portland stone.'

Marvin called down, 'You haven't got very far.'

'No. We're working at a disadvantage.'

'What's that, then?'

'No one knows what they're doing?'

Simon pointed. 'Is this oak?'

'Yes.'

Marvin descended, a little more gingerly than Simon, although he was physically robust enough. 'We stayed in the village. Shared a room. Simon played chess all night.'

'Not *all* night.'

'Where are your labourers?'

'What time is it?'

'Nine.'

Simon pointed to the concrete base. 'What is this—a mixture of sand and cement?'

'Yes.'

'How far down?'

'A metre or so. To sand.'

'Sand? Interesting.'

Marvin was not diverted by the details. He had come down from London to make real something he couldn't quite imagine from his house in Notting Hill. He wasn't there to judge, nor was he there to help. His only baggage was his cigarettes. Simon had a backpack and had already produced from it a laptop with a durable cover.

'Simon seems to think you need his genius.'

'I probably do.'

'He's a gift from God.'

'I've long thought that.'

Conversations about him in his presence never troubled Simon and he wandered the site with his laptop open and held in one hand, supported by his lower arm; his glasses were pushed up on to his forehead. 'I have some software . . . but I'm going to need quite a lot of information.'

'You will need to wait for the others.'

Marvin called from inside the church walls, 'And how's Holly taking all this?'

'She thinks she's been abandoned. That I've abandoned her.'

'You have. I've been doing a little research. It's not unusual for conversion experiences to break up relationships.'

'It will be fine.'

'You don't know that.'

'You're right, I don't. I will make it fine.'

'Does Holly know this?'

'I've promised her.'

'Does she believe you?'

'I hope so.'

'You mean you hope she has faith in you?'

'Yes.'

'It's a very high-risk strategy.'

'What else would you suggest?'

'There isn't anything—that's the point.'

In his own way Marvin was merciless, yet he was never hard or abrasive. He'd had a bullying father, a terrifying man, and the fabric of his emotional life had been stretched thin early on. Then in his twenties something negatively transformative had happened and it was as if he'd taken a large pair of garment scissors and set about himself, like a psychopath might a victim. What was left were scraps. That he wanted to stitch everything together was evidenced by his twenty-year stint with the same therapist. That he might never do so was evidenced by his twenty-year stint with the same therapist. And yet despite all this he possessed deep levels of empathy, and managed without betraying himself, and without imposing himself, to be present and interested and thought-provoking to just the right extent to keep everyone's integrity intact. And then there was that other side to him. Appearing to call over to Simon, he said to McCullough, 'Simon reckons he's in love with Jane.'

Without looking up, Simon said, 'I am.' The agreement was a disappointment to Marvin.

'When did this happen?'

'It's been brewing,' called Simon.

'Based on that evening? That was quite an evening. She was pretty drunk. Not that it means anything. I love Jane.'

'I've called Gregory and he seems fine with it.'

'I don't know how that plan was hatched—he's wrong for her. He's wrong for anyone.'

'Gregory only likes hookers.' Whether or not this was true, Marvin said it as if it were. Then added, 'It's why we're down here. Nothing to do with you. Simon needs some guidance.'

From over the brow of the ridge, under the shadow of the oak, Nathaniel and Rich arrived bearing sausage rolls, visible through the grease-soaked paper bags. McCullough made the introductions. Nathaniel behaved impeccably, with a straight and clear 'how d'you do'. Rich appeared never to have been introduced to anyone before, and ignored them both, wandering over to the low wall, where he laid a paper napkin out on his thigh and ate his sausage roll. Next was Rebecca, in her low jeans, black singlet and flip-flops. McCullough glanced at Marvin, who took her in with a side bite of his lower lip. If Simon noticed her beyond being just another person, he didn't show it.

Rebecca spoke first. 'So you're Mac's friends? Interesting.'

Passing by and dropping the base of a tape measure to the ground like a yo-yo, Nathaniel, apparently feeling freer in the presence of more adults, said, 'We all work here.'

Marvin looked down at himself. His clothes were better suited to walking around a pool in LA answering calls, his word on all matters accepted as visionary.

McCullough said, 'Don't worry—we'll find you something to do.' And then asked the others, 'Where's Terry?'

They didn't know.

Simon conferred with Nathaniel, who gave him information from a small notebook, which Simon entered with one hand into the computer still cradled in his arm. Rich stopped by to peer in, but then moved on. Settling herself in the large rectangle of forbidden grass, Rebecca smoked a cigarette, sitting cross-legged.

'I look forward to you explaining her to Holly.' There was such joy in this for Marvin—the marvellous folly of it. McCullough should have known. It didn't matter what he said now: in Marvin's mind, this girl was central to everything.

Simon proved useful. There were many calculations that needed to be made; he researched stress levels, load differentials, environmental regulations. Marvin's contribution was to repeat the phrase 'Think Swedish' whenever a supplier was required. Whenever they believed they had the highest specification, a supplier in Sweden increased the standard. Marvin was happy to make the calls.

Terry appeared before lunch. He was unfazed by the new arrivals. When Simon required McCullough to assist him in measuring the square meterage of the interior of the church, Terry asked if he might help; he'd done little since he arrived except get the fire going again and drink a can of beer.

As they stood together in the quarter-built structure, a hot fierce sun on them, Terry was pale, dry-mouthed, and his eyes lacked the inner focus that McCullough now took for granted, the easeful certainty. He held one end of the tape measure against a horizontal beam. The other hand yanked up his jeans, the small Bible in a baggy back pocket creating visible gravitational pull.

'Still reading the Bible?'

'I hate the fucking thing.'

'There are good reasons to.'

'They just don't do anything to hide the fucking joins. It's designed to drive people like me mad.' There was a laugh but it was joyless. 'We're sold this one big fucking idea, right? There is only one God. That's what the Jews gave to the world, right? That was their big idea. But the God in the Bible . . . the "God" who created the world . . . was a "we", right? Not a He or a fucking "it", an effing "we".'

One day McCullough would understand why 'effing' was used in a sentence that had already included a 'fucking'.

'And it's in "Our" image'? Not "His" image.'

'Yes.'

'Then with Abraham, who I like, the trusting old twat, God's more than one—a whole bunch of God-knows-what turn up outside his tent. But then we're in the desert with Moses and everything changes. It's hard-core one-God stuff. We're even told Moses actually *sees* God. Moses sees the Lord's *back* as He passes by. The one and only time . . .'

It wasn't clear where Terry was heading with this. He wasn't manic, but he nervously wiped away the sticky dryness from his mouth and wasn't going to be stopped. The pain in his guts from two nights ago hadn't gone away.

McCullough offered: 'I think it's twice—Moses sees God passing by, and then later it's implied he sees Him again when he emerges from the Holy of Holies, his face shining.'

'And then no one else. Not even Jesus, his son.'

'Maybe especially not Jesus.'

'Correct.' It was an odd response. 'I don't reckon Jesus is much bothered about God, actually. He's not scared of Him, anyway. He's not in "awe" of Him. Why would he be, if he's God Himself . . . but then he didn't always know that, did he? It dawns on him. Actually I don't even think it dawns on him—that's part of his—you know—charm: he doesn't worry about that stuff; he's too busy.' Terry paused and refocused his eyes. 'Part of me thinks Jesus is supposed to replace God—I mean, entirely. I know all Christians think that anyway . . . I mean not like that exactly, but you know what I mean. And why not? If you want to get really into it, you could say God had pretty much failed. He got so distant and confused, and there were so many fucking laws, it was clear most people were just going through the motions, and then doing whatever they wanted. And then there's everyone else with no proper God, although you could say, us lot here, the druids, we were doing our own thing quite happily. But that's not my point. The Old Testament God had failed. And He knew it better than anyone, obviously, with the whole omniscience thing.'

McCullough laughed.

'So He tries another approach. Not all angry and pissed off, or a whole new set of laws, but as a humble, wandering fella. Which is really interesting. Because God's now a man, right, and therefore it must be more possible for us to measure up, because a man is easier to follow than all those laws. On the surface—smart move. Except it ain't, because he's an *impossible* example, right? And an impossible, perfect example is worse than a bunch of laws, because laws are easy to ignore; no one really cares about laws, or if you do, you're not thinking for yourself—you're just a slave. That's why I've always known laws are bullshit. "I'm a good cunt, I follow the law."' The last word was given a 'spooky' tone to lend it fake mystery. 'No, you're just a cunt like the rest of us. But Jesus . . . he's just a man. It doesn't matter if he's also the Son of God—he's a man first, in this world; the choices he makes are his choices, in this world. OK, he sets the bar impossibly high; he's not a compromiser. But actually— you see—'high' is not right; it's the wrong way to think about it. It's something else. And you know how I know that?' Unusually for Terry, he waited for a response.

'No.' McCullough really had no clue.

'Think about it: if Yahweh is all "do as I say", you'd expect Jesus, as the man version, to be all: "do as I do"; but it's not. He's like . . . Look into your own hearts. That's all he wants from us. *Look into your own hearts*! God hasn't made it easier; He's just made it a whole lot harder. Genius.'

And that was it. Terry stood there, still, mute, gently distracted, fingers flicking the beads in his thin beard, as if he'd been just thinking this stuff through, without great energy or passion. But beneath the surface he was trembling and holding his gut. For a moment

McCullough feared the boy would vomit. After a couple of seconds Terry shook himself free from whatever was moving through him and laughed—*hee-hee*—as if he'd just been having a little mischievous fun—clever stuff, yes, but fun nonetheless.

McCullough's reaction was first paternal: he wanted the boy to eat something, to drink some water, rid himself of the white crud on his lips and the corners of his mouth. But any instruction to do this would be ignored, so he added his own thoughts, for what they were worth, knowing full well Terry tended not to be interested in other people's opinions, likely as they were to be compromised by some agenda, even if they didn't know it.

'You're right. If I'm honest, it's what makes me a Christian in the broadest sense . . . or the narrowest sense; who knows? I realize this sounds so vague as to be meaningless, but I've always thought the Jesus of the Gospels is asking us to do nothing more than think hard about what it might mean to be good and loving and then choose to do that. He just wants us to be free to choose that. To make it a free choice. Not a law.'

Busy pulling up his sagging jeans, Terry had slightly tuned out. But then he turned back to McCullough. 'Mmmm. Except you're not free to love me, are you, Mac? So you've still got some way to go. When you are, let me know and I'll follow you.' Terry's eyes lingered on the older man, musing on him, making assessments. There was a rare plain honesty in his expression. Then, as usual, he laughed. 'Take it from me, Mac. You just don't get it. I wish you did, but you don't. You should go home.'

For the next ten minutes, Terry sat on a slab of stone nearby and called out the dimensions to Simon up on the hill. It was McCullough's turn to look pale, as if he might vomit. What did Terry mean, he wasn't free to love him? The sweat from his brow disguised the few tears he shed. If that was really the case, even now, what was he doing here? What about all the hurt he'd caused?

Mid-afternoon, McCullough was sitting on his own, halfway up the ridge, answering texts from work. Rebecca trudged up to join him. 'Rich keeps looking at me.'

'I've noticed.'

She raised an eyebrow, implying it was a little bit of a bore.

'Don't worry.'

She didn't sit down. 'Your friend Marvin is a bit scary.'

'He is.'

'The other one is nice.'

'He is.'

She drifted away. Were they becoming friends? She seemed less inclined to challenge him, to find him foolish, to turn on him. But that could change. The only constant was the coherence of her beauty and this drew McCullough to her, wherever she was. As much as the church was meant to be a gathering point, so was Rebecca. It didn't matter how much activity there was, or from where or what distance he was looking, his gaze was pulled to her, found focus, and everything else became a blur. She possessed a kind of charisma, a gift to create lines of attention in physical space and alter the way others saw the world. The few other times he'd experienced this he'd felt something emergent between himself and that person, something that couldn't be explained by the natural sciences, nor by anything other than a kind of acceptance that, like love, certain states of being created mystifying connections between people. It didn't matter that sometimes it only happened one-way—music doesn't care about its effect on the listener. McCullough was half convinced Rebecca felt something similar when she looked at him, if on a massively reduced scale. Either way, she produced in him something profound he couldn't articulate, and at times it took his breath away.

Marvin noticed. How could he miss it; he'd been looking for it from the moment she appeared.

The two old friends walked to the cliff's edge. There was little convergence in what they discussed: McCullough talked about strength, Marvin about weakness.

'If she offers herself, you will fuck her.'

'First, she won't offer herself, and in a parallel first, I won't.'

'Ye of little faith, or whatever it is. She will and you will. It's meant to be.'

'I can see why you think that.'

'I *know* you can. Look at her.' Marvin laughed.

'She's half my age.'

'She is ahistorical. Timeless. Trans-temporal.'

'She's eighteen.'

'Poor Holly.'

'No, not "Poor Holly". Just trust me on this.'

'Isn't that what you've been saying to Holly?'

'Yes.'

'Get you anywhere?'

'Doesn't mean it's not true.'

Marvin used the toe of his trainers to find stones among the grass and shuffle them off the cliff, never looking over to see how and where they landed. He lit a cigarette.

'They taste horrible in all this fresh air. You bloody do-gooders.' He was aware of the non-sequitur.

'How long do you plan to stay?'

'I have no idea. Longer now I know about the girl.'

'Give it a break.'

'I don't think you realize . . . if anything is going to make me take notice of what's happening to you, it's her. She's a gift. I'm not entirely sure she really exists.'

'Trust me, she does. I've seen her mother.'

'Ah. And what is she like?'

'It was from a distance.'

The half-smoked cigarette was flicked out into the air above the cliff and brought back on the breeze, hitting Marvin on the side of the arm. A small brown burn mark was left on the fabric of his jacket.

'That's a bit annoying. Do you think God just punished me for being a shit?'

'If only that were possible.'

'I think God loves me.'

'I'm sure He does. More than most.'

'More than most other people love me, or more than He loves most other people?'

McCullough laughed. 'Let me speak for myself: *I* love you.'

'You love everyone.'

'I do, it's true.'

'I was only joking.'

'So was I.'

They returned to the site. Terry was slurping beer, inspecting the squareness of the holes where more uprights were to be placed. Nathaniel was next to him, tape measure pulled out and fixed to the correct length. They seldom worked together. The newcomers were having an effect. McCullough noticed Terry contentedly deferring to Simon, as if he assumed that a calculation made on a computer was going to increase the neatness of any fit. 'He's got all the gear,' was his only comment, but whether he meant laptop or outdoor clothing, it wasn't clear.

Five people were needed to carry the beams, seven to raise them. As before, Nathaniel took much of the weight and instructed others where to stand, where to place their hands, and when to brace themselves. Rebecca was awkward, her body unable to find the right shapes to fit herself in. She didn't appear overly conscious of the difference, but was always first to step back, as if afraid she was getting in the way. Marvin eventually discarded his jacket, and, the oldest of them, became second only to Nathaniel in using every part of his body to hold the beam steady, at times looking as if he was entirely wrapped around it. With the strain of the work evident, McCullough said, 'I'd like to remind both Marvin and Simon we are middle-aged men unused to this kind of work. Be careful.'

It took the whole afternoon, but by six o'clock the eight beams of the east side of the church were in place. The building now looked like an old and ruined temple, the roof long gone.

Rich said, 'It's not much, but it's something.'

Nathaniel tidied up the site, directing Rich to do certain things, which the younger boy didn't seem to mind. Standing next to McCullough, Terry arranged the three black silk bookmarks in his small Bible.

'Here's another little insight. All the anti-gay stuff—that's mostly at the beginning. And then at the end. In between the faggots are left alone.'

'Nicely put.'

'But this is my thought: it's only when things are being set up you get all the "don't suck cock" stuff. The whole new world of the Hebrews, right, as they wander across the desert, and then Paulus/Saulus, as he tries to build Christianity. It's like they fear it. The moment someone has to start laying down the law, it's no fornication and thou shalt not suck cock.'

McCullough laughed. 'You should do your own translation.'

'I'm serious.'

'I know.'

'It gets on my tits.'

'Mine too.'

'I'd like to go through the whole book stripping out all the nonsense.'

'We're back to picking and choosing.'

'The whole "love thy neighbour" thing, which has become so fucking central. It's a lie when people say it means love everyone. It means what it says: love your neighbour, the people in the tents around you, and then we might survive as a people living in the desert.'

'Isn't that why Jesus is so important? He takes that local stuff and makes it universal? It's what we were talking about earlier. It's much more serious when we have to love people we don't know or don't understand. To love freely means two things. It means without judgment and without parcelling it out according to our particular taste.'

'Like you with me and Rebs. We all have favourites.' He was flicking absently through the thousands of tissue-thin pages.

'It's not a law. It's an aim. I'm falling short.'

'Least you ain't a liar.'

The small black Bible was held up; it looked like a chunk of lead. 'So shall I throw it in the fire?'

'Don't you dare!'

'I never see you read it.'

'There are other things to read, to my mind of equal importance. There is no literal word of God. Or if there is, it's in other places as well, maybe more so. Read Dostoevsky, listen to late Beethoven, look at the paintings of Marc Rothko. Religion is an expression of something of which ownership is not possible.'

'Do you believe in *anything?*'

'You know, Terry, this is the first time I've heard you ask a question where I'm not sure you know the answer before asking it.' McCullough looked at him directly.

'Just remember, Mac—no sucking cock, all right?'

An hour later, McCullough was joined halfway up the ridge by his old friends. Sitting down either side of him, they both groaned—it had been a hard day on the body.

'How do you think it's going? Is it what you'd envisioned?' Simon asked.

'What I want is an impossibility. I know that now.'

'You're no builder, that's for sure,' Marvin made clear.

'It's not that. I'm naive and I should know better.'

'I think it's going to look great.' Simon squinted down the bank. He wasn't one for sunglasses.

'I want a structure that will move people to contemplate something other than all the obvious stuff. Thinking we are experiencing some kind of transcendence is easy—we humans are good at that. It's happening in Ibiza every night of the week. But a real sense of Otherness, to be confronted with a sense of something and only be able to define it as Other, that's something else.

'The most convincing examples of this, in terms of creating a location, are the landscapes in *Paradise Lost*. First, the place Satan and his hordes fall to after the great battle in heaven; and then that mysterious inter-zone Satan travels through before he gets to earth. It's a miracle of description really, because Milton creates places that don't exist—not at all—and yet somehow we recognize them. Which I suppose defines Otherness.'

Marvin tried to spring to his feet, but his body had stiffened in the few minutes he had been sitting down. 'Today has been an object lesson on the limitations of age.'

'It gets better. Easier. Do you oldsters need to call it a day?'

'Please, sir.'

Simon was mulling over something, his head cocked slightly, as if an acute angle of sight was required for something.

'What you need is Pascal's mystical hexagon.'

McCullough sat up; that sounded like something . . . 'Please, explain.'

'Of course, I have no idea why it's referred to as mystical. I just remember it from geometry class. It's a conics thing.'

'Conics. Cool.' This was Marvin; it was difficult to know what he felt about geometry, but he tended to enjoy the esoteric.

Simon tried to draw what he remembered from geometry class in the air, as much for himself as the others. It appeared to be a circle with a hexagon inside it, corners flush to the circumference, then lines extended, then a longer line across the intersections. 'It tells us something—not sure what.'

A pencil and paper were called for. Nathaniel trotted up and handed McCullough an A4 pad. The top sheet was smudged with fingerprints, a cup stain, the body of a small dead insect.

As best he could, Simon drew an illustration. It took a couple of attempts; the extensions of the sides of the hexagon went beyond the edge of the paper before they intersected.

'Not all that mystical,' Marvin said, taking away the pad.

'The equation would mystify you.'

'I dare say.'

McCullough stood and shouted across the site: 'Stop! Everyone . . . stop. Up here.'

He didn't tend to call sudden halts. The remaining three workers looked at one another before they decided to obey and wander up.

When they were all at the top of the slope, McCullough grabbed the pad from Marvin and announced: 'We're doing this. We're doing this now.'

Nathaniel had watched the rough sketch being made and stated the obvious: 'That's a circle, we've got a rectangle.' He pointed to the church. 'I don't think it will work.'

'We create a circle inside—'

'A conic,' Simon clarified.

'And then a hexagon inside that, right? That's fine, isn't it?' McCullough added, his hands in the air, tentatively finding angles, tilting his head to find possibilities in what he now saw. 'But the hexagon can't be flat, not if we want the bisecting beam to come out of the land and disappear into the sky.'

Simon took back the pad and turned it, trying to think through what a three-dimensional version might look like. 'I can't see how that won't work.'

McCullough felt euphoric. 'This is perfect. Fucking perfect! *This* is what we're going to build.'

His enthusiasm wasn't infectious; it was the end of the day and everyone was tired ... and wasn't it mad to completely rethink and make super-complex something they'd barely managed when things were super-simple: two rectangles, each with four walls and a roof?

'Simon, can you find some illustrations on the Internet? Or do we need to get something mocked up? It must be straightforward, surely. It's just a set of dimensions, calculations. The rest is just—I don't know—labour.'

It was Rebecca's turn to hold the piece of paper. 'I'm shit at geometry.'

In between McCullough and Rebecca, Simon assured them all, 'Basic computing can take care of most of this.'

'Sure you've got the spare dough? What about the children's education?' Terry was the only one not desperately trying to grab and look at the drawing.

Simon had stepped closer to the soft run-off of the ridge. 'You'll need a theodolite.'

Terry perked up at this. 'Now we're talking. And God's in there somewhere—Theo. You'll like that, Mac. Or maybe it was just designed by some cunt called Theo.'

Rich liked this.

'Are you sure, Mac?' Rebecca regarded him with concern; they'd never seen him quite like this, almost ecstatic. Unlike them he'd been mostly stable in his moods.

'Absolutely. It's the answer.' He looked back at the piece of paper.

'It *could* look fucking stupid.' Terry opened a can of beer. It wasn't pessimism; he just needed McCullough to accept the potential for disaster as well as a miracle.

'That's been a possibility all along.'

'True.'

Marvin was looking on his phone for images of something that might have been built on a similar principle. He found nothing.

'The difficulty,' Simon reiterated, 'will be the angle of the hexagon. I can't quite see it. But I also can't see why it won't work.'

McCullough wasn't listening. Below him, fifty metres away, mapped onto what they'd already built together, there was a vision of something that now excited him. Until that moment everything had been based on decisions that were derived from two rectangles on the ground. But now he saw something that went beyond just stone, glass and steel: an expression of a church, or a church as an artwork, and at the same time something else . . . a deconstruction of a church . . . finally allowing the building to offer up other meanings . . . feelings in response to it from which a sense of Otherness might emerge.

He turned to the others. 'We need to cancel everything that's currently on order. I suspect, for the most part, that we're starting again.'

Later, Rebecca, Rich and Nathaniel went back down to the site to collect their things and potter around, as they tended to do.

Marvin asked, 'Are they slave labour? I mean, are you paying them?'

'I tried. And they are free not to come.'

'But are they, my friend—are they?'

Like Terry and Rebecca, Marvin was there to keep him honest. Did he really need so many people to do this?

'Trust me—they are.'

Simon was feeling buoyant after his day at the site. 'I love them. They're like my PhD students except—you know—human beings.'

'Yes, Simon,' agreed Marvin. 'They are human beings. It is a rare man who starts at first principles these days.'

McCullough stepped forward and called down to the human beings still at work. 'Come on, you lot, there's free beer up here.'

Over the next hour, beer was drunk; joints smoked; Simon finally realized there was a beautiful woman among them; Nathaniel was unusually chatty, perhaps taking up the slack left by Rich, who sat slightly apart and seemed to want to send telepathic messages to Rebecca about feelings he wasn't quite sure he understood. Rebecca asked Simon about his work in London. As it tended to at this stage of the evening, Terry's mood darkened but then brightened again when he discovered Marvin had made his name as a photographer of real-life sex encounters. 'Dogger-in-chief,' he called him, at which point Marvin leaned forward for a handshake and a promise to name his next show exactly that.

The dusk was long and warm, the grass comfortable, and the earth possessed a give their weary bodies needed. McCullough settled back on his arms. Was this how people might spend their time if they came to this church? He hoped so. His own feeling of peacefulness was helped by the presence of his old friends. Put simply: it meant that what was happening down here wasn't a fantasy, a holiday romance with no connection to his real world. But Holly would still judge him harshly. It didn't matter that it was an uncommon peace and that he believed he deserved it; he was still far from her, from the children, and she would be hurt by the fact he was feeling such contentment at all.

Marvin spent his time moving about the group asking each of them about their lives, astute enough to skip Terry. There was nothing he wasn't afraid to ask. Rich and Nathaniel felt privileged that this strange man, cold-eyed and ironic, was taking such an interest in them. McCullough learned much. He'd been more cautious himself and not demanded intimacies that weren't offered. Marvin's enquiries came from an honest fascination, a natural interest in the lives of others, free from judgment. Yet he also tried to set them straight when he felt they were not being honest with themselves. When Rebecca claimed not to miss her father he was happy to say, 'In my estimation that is all you do,' but he went no further—there was no fun to be had in upsetting someone you'd never see again. For him the real joy—perverse and easily misinterpreted—came from being present when true realization dawned. That was the pay-off. In anticipation of such moments Marvin sat with his legs tightly crossed as if he needed the lavatory. It produced a childlike excitement in him to see truth come crashing in. Was this mean-spirited? He sometimes got his timing wrong and inflected a sentence too ironically, and so that might seem the case. But McCullough believed Marvin wanted others to find happiness that wasn't available to him. Indeed, it seemed to McCullough that his happiness derived from others finding happiness, yet somehow not in a way that did him any credit. Marvin was not an evil genius.

The dope made everyone laugh loudly and their voices were bright in the surrounding silence. Simon wasn't used to it and was behaving strangely, his long limbs losing a little of their control, and each joke had him almost spinning on the grass. The others cracked up at this, and they tried to produce even more extreme reactions in him. Rebecca lay on her stomach and rested her chin on her cupped hands, the soles of her feet slapping against her flip-flops. Rich was frowning, and his laughter came a beat after everyone else's. McCullough studied him: when had this happened, this sudden interest in Rebecca? Had he awakened to it? Or had it been just one glance and some chemical reaction had taken place and that was it? Whatever it was, he'd fallen for her, even if he didn't quite know it yet. Poor boy.

The light was now tawny, a glistening sepia, the transition moment from a golden day to a blue night. Only at ground level did any brightness remain, and then that was gone and the grass was cool, even if the earth beneath still retained a little heat. Everyone felt the need to stand, to stretch. On their feet, all felt a little disembodied, limbs heavy. Half in need of genuine support, and half to prolong the fun, they grabbed at one another. It was inevitable that Rich was going to find a way to touch Rebecca and she would break the mood by shoving him off. Which was exactly what happened. But she was quick to remember this was Rich, young, sweet Rich, and she was quick to apologize, and set about adjusting his bandana for him. He looked sullen, peevish. It didn't help that Rebecca was swaying a little before him, stoned, and meltingly sexy. Terry said with unusual lightness and inclusivity, arm outstretched and finger pointing in the direction of the village, 'To the boozer.'

Marvin turned to McCullough, 'You should have told us what fun this double life is.'

Simon, who didn't usually drink, let alone smoke weed, peered directly into McCullough's face and said, 'We'll build this church of yours, Mac. Don't you worry about that.' Then turned to one side and vomited. Before they could attend to him, he was back as if nothing had happened, and added, 'You can count on us.'

Marvin and Simon stayed another four days, until the design for the new build was understood by everyone, and everything necessary was measured and ordered. The great steel hexagon and beams, their lengths and angles, required endless computations so the fit and extensions worked within the confines of the conic that would be set inside the current shape of the church. The circular wall of the conic would prove the most difficult to build and with unusual diligence Marvin researched how this might be done, occasionally apprising Terry of the details when asked. McCullough felt useless, and spent most of the next four days being placed at various points on the site to mark positions. The money he'd set aside for the build was gone. Holly would now notice other money being eaten into. He spent hours making financial calculations in his head, shifting funds from various accounts. They were never going to be broke, but that wasn't really the point. He wasn't asking Holly's permission. Every time he passed Marvin he sensed costs being haggled upwards so orders might be 'expedited'—a word that was now being used more than any other, especially by Simon, Marvin and Nathaniel. 'It's a power word,' Marvin explained. 'It makes us feel powerful to get things "expedited".'

It was Rich who wondered aloud at the leakiness of it all, as he walked around what was already there. The walls were stone on concrete, timber on stone, then stone again, then there would be glass, and nothing in between; wherever you looked there were gaps, fissures, ill-fitting joins.

McCullough explained. 'I want a rough-hewn look. At the moment the lower half reminds me of a Joseph Beuys.'

'You could use felt as insulation?' This was Marvin, who had the look of a post-war twentieth-century German artist.

Simon said, 'We can create something. A silicone or a polymer.'

McCullough pointed at Rebecca. 'She's our wet materials girl. What do you think, Rebecca?'

'What's wattle and daub?' she asked. 'That sounds about right, or at least one of them might be.'

On their last day, Terry turned up late, just before lunch, and looked paler than usual. His stomach was still causing him pain. He peered for a moment at Simon's laptop screen and then went to sit by the fire. 'Vodka—rots the gut.' No one had seen him drink vodka.

Rebecca went over, crouched down and put a hand on his knee. She made him laugh and then there was a cry of pain. 'He'll be all right,' she said when she returned to them. 'Just wish he'd eat. But he never has.'

Simon and Marvin collected fish and chips from the village, and they all ate sitting on the beach. Trainers and socks off, trousers rolled up to his knees, Marvin stood in the shallows with the last of his chips. He was joined by Rebecca, who revealed she wore a bikini top under her T-shirt.

'The French'll want to invade now,' Marvin said.

'I'm not particularly special to the French.'

Later, he whispered to McCullough, 'Keep me away from that girl—she's dangerous.'

'So you're the one who needs to worry?'

'We all do, McCullough—she's come to destroy us.'

Behind them Simon laughed.

McCullough asked, 'So have you actually asked Jane out?'

'No.'

'Where do you want to take her?'

'Kew.'

'Kew!' This was Marvin.

'It's nice.'

McCullough tried to help out. 'It is—yes.'

Marvin didn't understand: it was a garden where you walked around and then had a cup of tea. 'She strikes me as the type of girl who'd like more of a surprise.'

'It surprised you.'

Marvin had to give him that.

An email arrived after lunch. The hexagon and steels would take three weeks to construct. The cost was stratospheric. Maybe he should call Holly—most of their savings would go. But instead he called Jane and asked whether she'd mind receiving a call from Simon. It took her a few moments to place him; she was disappointed it wasn't Marvin, thankful it wasn't Gregory. McCullough said Simon was the best of the three, or four, including Lucien, or all of them, including himself.

Terry didn't leave the fire all afternoon. He said he was reserving his energy for the centrepiece. 'That's where you need a perfect fit.' His stringy, rangy body, so often a resilient type, was letting him down. From time to time, he read from his small pocket Bible, marked a passage, and turned over the corners of the flimsy paper. Occasionally he'd wander over to say something, usually to Rich, sometimes to Marvin. McCullough noticed not even Marvin had the chops to take on Terry's internal world, and instead they talked at length about crypto-currencies.

In the late afternoon Nathaniel's eldest brother, Stephen, appeared at the top of the ridge. He was handsome and tall, and for a man of thirty his skin was attractively weather-beaten. He was dressed in thick corduroy trousers, almost gold in colour, a tweed jacket and what appeared to be the uniform of the male side of the family, a pink polo shirt. Rebecca moved up to McCullough. 'Prepare for a laugh.'

Stephen stood, legs apart, hands on hips, and thrust his not inconsiderable chin into the air. McCullough wasn't sure whether he was doing it on purpose, as a joke. Rebecca nudged him. 'See.'

Stephen began speaking, his voice sonorous and carrying. 'Thought I'd have a look for myself. Nathaniel's never been so pre-occupied. Proper little project you have here. Amazed to find it's common land and you can do such things these days. Which one of you is Mac?' He seemed from a different age, when to bellow was the prerogative of power.

McCullough raised his hand and said, 'I'm Mac.' This was followed by Marvin, a beat later, calling out, 'I'm Mac.' Rebecca was next: 'Me, too,' then Rich and Simon at the same time. Nathaniel was last. Terry wasn't playing.

'Yes. Most amusing. I am Spartacus and all that. I can't understand why no one's objected. We can't very well, of course, because of Nathaniel.'

'Fuck off, Stephen.' This was Rebecca, with no inflection of charm or good humour.

Stephen had evidently decided not to hear her. McCullough didn't laugh—that would come later.

'Why don't you come down and look around?' he asked.

'I can see perfectly well from up here, and I need to go, we have guests.' He looked down at his brother. 'They have arrived, Nat—it wouldn't be good to be late.'

All eyes turned to Nathaniel, whose eyes were turned to the ground.

Stephen paused for a moment. 'Well, I do hope he's of some use.' He walked away.

McCullough crossed over to Nathaniel and said he was shocked, and had never quite appreciated the extent of the—well, you know. He then asked: 'Are they all like that?'

'Stephen's the worst. Then my dad.'

'I don't know what to say.'

'Why else do you think I come here every day?'

'Who are your guests? They sound a big deal.'

'The PM.'

'So no one important, then.'

'Have you any idea what gets talked about when they are all together in private?'

It was Marvin who suggested a local revolution, starting with Stephen up against the wall. He mimed machine-gunning him down. Nathaniel laughed, for once showing a little appreciation of their support.

Rebecca and Simon were sitting side by side on an oak beam, Rebecca following Simon's finger on the screen of the laptop. She had replaced her T-shirt, although it was only Rich's gaze that had made her do so.

McCullough overheard Marvin tell Nathaniel that he had a friend just like his brother, name of Lucien. 'It's a fragile superiority,' he explained. 'But they get under your skin.'

'My brother's made a fortune in the City. Everyone thinks he's marvellous.'

Marvin said, 'I think he's a cunt.'

There was a pause, then Nat said, 'You're the exception that proves the rule.'

Marvin wasn't having that and called out, 'Hands up all those who think Nat's brother's a cunt.'

All hands were casually raised; it was obviously the case and didn't need grand gestures.

'See. You should try that question over dinner. You might be surprised.'

'I don't think it'd be me who'd be surprised.'

'Even better.'

McCullough moved over to Rich, who was incapable of a darkened countenance, but was unhappy enough to be noticed. Out of the four locals he'd been the most spontaneous, but seemed to have become struck by a compulsion McCullough recognized from decades ago: he could do nothing that wasn't aimed at attracting Rebecca's attention. His strategies to find himself close to her were spotted before he himself knew what he was doing. If he played at being remote, she ignored him; if he tried crossness, she was crosser. When on occasion he made her laugh, the fact he wanted more of a reaction irritated her and she stopped laughing. He even tried feigning illness—wasn't she attentive to Terry?—but she sensed it wasn't real. McCullough wanted to explain: she knows what the correct level of interest in her should be and anything beyond that is regarded as ridiculous, foolish, pandering. It was why it made sense that she once went for Terry. Rich said nothing. McCullough changed the subject to music and films.

Marvin swung by for a more candid chat.

'Whatever Mac's saying, it's good advice, but you'll never get the girl.'

'Ignore him, Rich.'

'I'm just saying. Poor boy wants to tear her clothes off. And I bet you're advising honesty, patience, even—'

'Marvin, we are talking about Japanese horror films.'

'You see, Rich, Mac here is a special case. He tends to work on a persistence model, knowing it's only a matter of time before his gifts become apparent and start to transcend the more annoying aspects of his character, of which there are many. Most of us don't have that luxury. No gifts to counteract our slimy, disgusting cravings. So we need other ways to win.' He had Rich's attention. 'They are high-risk and one is never proud after the fact.'

McCullough laughed.

'Ignore Mac; he thinks I'm going to advise something sinister. I'm just going to tell you one thing I wish I'd known at your age: girls like fucking just as much as we boys do. Now, how does that help, you ask? Never for a second try to pretend you're not interested in having sex with them. It makes everything you say seem fake and cowardly, a lie, and also that your cock counts for nothing. They want to be turned on just as much as we do. Don't think I mean go and be all super-masculine—that's worse. But the line, "I'd love to fuck you," don't be afraid of it.'

McCullough made sure Rich understood: 'I don't think Marvin's recommending it as an opening line.'

'Just planting seeds . . . Just planting seeds.'

Rich turned to McCullough. 'I don't know what happened. I just woke up and couldn't stop thinking about her. I think I dreamed about her, and I think in the dream we—you know—did it, and then I woke up. Then when I turned up here it was like it had really happened, and I felt . . . Every time I look at her I feel sick.'

'Accept it as a blessing. It's the one thing I wish I'd done at your age.'

There were spots of rain, although the only clouds were far over the sea. Nathaniel decided it was wise to cover the site as best they could. He'd found a website that sold recovered church flagstones, beautifully smooth with over five hundred years of wear. Ten had just been laid. They were old-world heavy, seemingly impermeable, but apparently needed protection from the weather. Nathaniel and Rich pulled the sheeting across and secured it, and then joined the others under the oak.

'We'll be off soon.' This was Simon, saddened but responsible as always. 'I've left the lab too long. Science needs man just as much as God does.'

The permanent team groaned.

'We can't get Mac's hopes up,' Marvin explained. 'He might start thinking he's the leader of a viable cult.'

McCullough shook his head. 'A "viable" cult?'

'You know what I mean.' Then, 'Do you want us to drop in on Holly—give her an update?'

'Simon, if you'd like to drop by, please do. But do not let this monster near her.'

'Will do, Captain.'

For an hour, they watched the rain lash down, hard and purposeful, the wind turning the raindrops into fields of water that moved through the air in undulating waves. The noise was tremendous, as if over the site there were hundreds of different-sized timpani. But Mother Nature was capable of more than power and rhythm; she was doing great damage, and they feared a signal was being sent. Then the rain stopped and all that was left from its thunderous passing were tracts of grass flattened to smears, standing pools of water, dampness to the skin. Evidence of a sort, but of what had just happened it told you nothing.

They walked to the road, boots and shoes and flip-flops sucked in by the mud. It was hard, ungainly going, knees raised high. Climbing the gate, their feet felt heavier than was imaginable, the mud built up into great thick clods around their shoes. Out on the road they walked as if wearing gravity boots.

By the hire car, hands were shaken, cheeks kissed. Marvin promised to be back, explaining he was only now aware how much he offered in building team morale, and therefore not to return would be immoral—a sin even. Simon merely said he'd exchanged numbers and email addresses with Rebecca—she knew what to do. Terry leaned on the gate, arms folded across the top rung, his forehead resting on his hands.

Marvin announced he was going to drive in his bare feet, and both his and Simon's footwear and socks were removed. Clutching them gingerly, as if mud was a contaminant, McCullough opened the boot and laid them on their sides in the back—the interior velour was immaculate, a glistening deep black. As he closed the boot and the engine started, he realized that he didn't want to go with them, as he'd feared he might, but it remained the case that he was being left behind. There was a chance that both would see Holly and the twins before he did, and this produced a grief he'd not known before—for the living. For the first time in a long while he felt empty, no great force spilling into him. It wasn't in his nature to break down, to fall to the ground and keen, but he felt a weakness in his knees, and knew that if he did stumble, the world would fall away beneath him, and it would all be over. For the first time, he realized what strength this was taking, the great and terrible risk, and how foolish he must seem.

Sitting in the passenger seat, Simon called back to him: 'I'll tell Holly that it's a good thing you're doing. That she shouldn't worry.'

Marvin pressed down on the accelerator and let out the clutch and made sure what gravel and dirt was under the rear wheels filled the damp heavy air. The team waved as a family might when being left by well-loved visitors.

As they headed back to the site, Terry, drunk and in pain, needed support. It was only when McCullough lowered him down next to the black muck of the fire, and asked whether Terry needed anything—to be answered with the customary 'You're all right'—that he realized he could no longer keep quiet.

'Terry, I might be all right, but you're not. Promise me you'll go to the doctor's?'

Terry looked up, expressionless and bored. 'What's he going to tell me that I don't already know?'

LILITH

'She maketh herself coverings of tapestry;
her clothing is silk and purple.'

He was welcomed and brought into a sitting room and given a large glass of white wine, one of three already poured, the chilled bottle standing on a rosewood sideboard. Rebecca sat down on the large sofa, cross-legged, and adjusted her bra-strap. The flat occupied the two top floors of a large Victorian villa with a view over the village green. Off-white blinds were drawn down a quarter-length of the large bay window. There were drawings on the walls, paintings in Fauvist colours, the shapes of Chagall. There was a baby grand, an Erard, the open sheet music a Brahms *Intermezzo*. On a pile on the lid he could make out Ravel, Bartók, Grieg's *Lyric Pieces*.

Rebecca said, 'My mother—Judith—will be down in a moment,' then added cheerfully, 'Were you surprised I invited you? I thought you might miss your friends.'

'That I might be lonely?' McCullough took a sip of wine.

'Would you be distraught if I said it wasn't my idea?'

'Distraught?'

'You know what I mean.'

'Did you object?'

'A bit.'

There was movement above, a creak after a soft stride, then the creak of a stair. 'You two are the same age, I think.'

Judith came in. She was slighter than he remembered.

'I am told I must call you Mac.' She was American. She noticed his surprise. 'What is it?'

'Your accent.'

'I'm from Ohio. Originally. They say you lose your accent if you move somewhere before you are fourteen. I came to the UK when I was twenty-two. Please take a seat.'

Her accent was soft, oboe-ish, dark-toned but not low or husky.

'Thank you for inviting me.'

'You're very welcome.'

She possessed old-world deportment, not particularly apparent in what she said, but there was a composure to her that came from knowing how to behave in any company, to be relaxed so that others might be. She was in a black dress, fitted at the bust, a little flared at the hips; it was knee-length; her tights were black; she was not wearing shoes. There was a languor to her movements that made her seem youthful in a way he couldn't quite pin down. They sat facing each other, three points of a triangle. Judith tucked her legs beneath her. He was the only one with feet on the floor.

'The village is fascinated by you.'

'More the project.'

'No, I think you.' She looked at her daughter. 'Rebecca doesn't tell me much.'

Her daughter was rolling a cigarette. 'I tell you everything. You just think there is more.'

'She doesn't tell me much either,' McCullough said. 'Nor do the others. Except perhaps Nat.' He didn't want Judith to think there were just the two of them down there. Judith smiled. Her eyes were bright, ironic; whether they were flirtatious or not he couldn't make up his mind.

'It seems slightly ridiculous and also terribly private, but I must ask: how is the church-building going?'

'It's mostly ridiculous.'

'Are you comfortable talking about it? I don't want to seem intrusive. I imagine, whatever the motivation is, it's intensely personal.'

Rebecca stirred on the sofa. 'He doesn't know why he's doing it. Do you, Mac?'

'Yes and no. But you're right. Mostly no. Although we've had a bit of a breakthrough.'

'You're married.' It was the gentlest of interrogations.

'No. I have a partner. And twins. Six years old.'

More from Rebecca, filling her mother in. 'They haven't come down. Just his friends.'

A bell went off in the kitchen. Only McCullough seemed to notice.

'Was that nice? Your friends coming down?' She must have mixed with aristocratic types, to whom the rest of the world are really just children. He would say something if she carried on like this.

'Yes.'

'Rebecca is cooking.'

McCullough glanced over at her, raised his eyebrows and sent messages of surprise, teasingly. Judith caught the exchange. He was laying claim to knowing her daughter, at least a little.

'May I ask what?'

Rebecca was flat-toned: 'Tagine. The lamb is old now—it's sheep, really.'

'Mutton.'

There was only one bookcase in the room, wide and tall, painted white, full of twentieth-century American writers in hardback US editions. Rebecca noticed his empty wine glass and offered him hers.

'You're not drinking?'

'Nah.' She lit her roll-up and angled her head to the open window.

Judith unfolded her legs, and after a barely hidden wide-eyed and admonishing stare at her daughter, fetched the bottle and refilled McCullough's glass.

'Rebecca said you think you've had religious visions.'

Her daughter's smile was apologetic, mischievous: what was she going to do, not tell her mum?

'I'm not sure religious is right.'

'Of God, then.'

'Not really of God, even.'

'Rebecca said you wouldn't be uncomfortable talking about it.'

'It's OK.' He felt embarrassed. He was sweating a little, around his cuffs, his groin, his back. He gulped down some wine to cool himself and started to choke. He had to sit up to prevent himself from spluttering wine everywhere. 'I'm sorry.'

'Please, Rebecca, a napkin.'

Off the sofa, into the kitchen and back, moving as if she didn't want to miss a moment of something on TV. There wasn't a television.

'Here.'

He wiped his mouth. 'I'm sorry. I don't know why I'm so embarrassed. It's not something that happens often.'

'You don't have to talk about it, of course.' Judith smiled.

He liked her lower lip, its fullness. She had Rebecca's colouring, but her skin was a little lighter, less exposed to the sun, and there was red in her cheeks, a rose light under the surface, a blush. Her grey hairs were unruly, and separated from the sheen of the rest of her dark brown hair. Only in contrast to Rebecca's, almost wild in its lustrousness, did it seem thin.

'It's all so impossible to describe. That's why there's the church. Or the idea of a church. Which is what I'm aiming for now.'

'But there were visions?'

'Yes. But visions is wrong. What happened . . . or what happens . . . is more a felt thing. There is nothing to see. It's more physical. I feel as if I'm going to be filled with a kind of light, although there is no sense of illumination; it's more tangible, solid. So not really like light at all. It's as if I'm being asked to take the overflow of something.' He paused. 'I suppose it's like I'm a vessel . . . for something. New wine, if you will. New *new* wine. But that's a *post hoc* interpretation. It does seem rather foolish building something when what is needed is space within me. But in the end, I'm not sure it matters: after all, how do you contain boundless light?'

'So it *is* light?'

'Light and dark. It's not reducible to one quality and yet it is not many things. What I do know is . . . it's impossible to articulate. To sum it up and describe. It's a bit like pain in that way.'

Rebecca sneezed. 'Sorry. Hay fever.' She grabbed at McCullough's napkin and wiped her nose. 'Gross, I know.'

There was silence for a moment and Judith pulled herself a little straighter in her armchair; she wanted to be both comfortable and attentive.

'It still happens?'

'Yes.'

'And it's always the same thing? Sorry—tell me if I'm being too intrusive.'

'It's rather refreshing that you've yet to make a joke.'

'Rebecca accuses me of being too serious.'

'You are.' It came from a muffled nose.

Judith seemed unburdened by the need to be overtly ironic. Was that because she was American? It was what people usually thought.

'Again, it's impossible to describe. But it's not all wonder. Loveliness. Who's to say it's not just the manifestations that go with a breakdown? Epiphenomena, I believe they're called.'

'Is that what you believe?'

'I wish it were.'

'But it's not?'

'No. I think I'm being prepared for some kind of authentic encounter with God.' There, he'd said it.

'"Authentic", you say. It presupposes God's existence, that God is there to be authentically encountered. A bold claim.'

'It's all I have.' What did she do, this elegant, delicate, straight American, living with her daughter in a village in the south-west of England?

The earlier downpour had created pools of water on the village green, which were now sodden patches. The warmth of the evening was having a condensing effect and the air was damp and chilly.

'And why down here—building the church, I mean?'

On the sofa, Rebecca unfolded her legs and stretched, her head supported by her hands, her body elongated but still all hips and bust. Her T-shirt was rumpled up, revealing her stomach. She pulled the T-shirt down, stretching the fabric a little. She'd grown used to him noticing.

'One day I just got in my car and drove. From London. I let the traffic decide. Could have been anywhere. But I suppose subconsciously, looking back, it would have been here or the north-east, based on my love of the two coastlines. Then at one point I stopped and walked.'

'Led?'

'No. No. There was just a kind of surplus of energy, which carried me . . . I was quite ecstatic at the time.'

Another bell. 'I think it's ready,' Rebecca said, though without moving.

'We can eat at the table or on our knees. Which would you prefer, Mac?'

'He'd probably prefer the table. He doesn't get to use one much.'

He looked down at himself. Did he appear to others like the vagrant he felt? He'd washed in mineral water; used a strong deodorant.

'Or a chair,' he said. Then, 'I don't even know what day it is.'

Rebecca laughed, and was quickly on her feet. McCullough stood as if out of politeness. Judith was next to him, and took his arm. 'It's Saturday.'

It was a large kitchen, with a sash window at the back. The table was made of thick oak; at one end there was a pile of Saturday newspapers, supplements, on top an open cookbook. Rebecca was quick to lay the table. The plates were stoneware, an ornate pattern in pale green. A bottle of red wine had been decanted. On the counter, the kettle's button was pressed down. Next to it stood a large glass bowl of couscous. The cooker was French-made, a range, Delft blue in colour.

'Do we need knives?' Rebecca asked, the drawer pulled out, forks in one hand. She collected three knives.

At the table, she paused to think through which side of the plates the cutlery went. McCullough liked to watch the mind at work, and Rebecca's was attractively visible. Judith poured the wine. 'It's Bulgarian. A Pinot Noir. Very good. I make the pub keep it.' She handed a glass to McCullough. 'Welcome.'

'Thank you for having me.'

Mother turned to daughter. 'Do you want some, darling?'

Rebecca poured boiling water into the bowl of couscous and covered it with a cloth, then with oven gloves on removed the tagine pot from the oven. Once it was steady on the range top, she removed the chimney-like lid and peered over it, wafting the aroma up with one hand. She waited until the couscous had absorbed all the water, and then brought the food to the table and set it down, turning the edge of pot to achieve something only she could see. The oven glove was discarded on the chair next to her and from a small glass dish she sprinkled almonds over both the couscous and the tagine. How it came to be the case, McCullough didn't know, but he was seated at the head of the table.

Judith stood up and fetched a bowl of salad, with large smooth wooden salad servers lying across the rim. Under the table, a cat weaved between their legs, back arched, then stopped to look up at Rebecca. 'This is Peter,' she said. 'He's mine.'

'Rebecca says you sleep out most nights?'

'I do.'

'Help yourself.'

He did so, self-consciously, as both women studied him, a stranger in their home.

'May I ask what you do, Judith?'

'Wait for it,' said Rebecca.

'Thank you, darling. I'm the professor of poetry.'

'Here? In the village?'

She smiled. His joke was mildly amusing. 'At Exeter. I'm on sabbatical.'

'For what? Or am I being too intrusive?'

'Imagine if I were to refuse to tell you after all you've confessed to me.' She sat very straight-backed in her chair. 'To write a book. On Wallace Stevens.'

McCullough looked at Rebecca. 'You kept this quiet.'

'Wallace Stevens might as well be my dad.'

'He wasn't a good father,' Judith put in. 'Not unlike your own.'

McCullough altered the direction of the conversation. 'How far in are you?'

'I'm really reorganizing and expanding a series of lectures.'

'I know some of *Harmonium*.'

Rebecca sighed, 'Oh, God. Can I go upstairs and watch telly? If you're going to go on about *Wally*.'

'We'll keep Mr Stevens for another time. Tell me about your family, Mac?'

'My partner Holly is an asylum lawyer. We have a boy and a girl. Twins. Our son, Walter, has Asperger's, and is a handful; Pearl is an evil genius and also a handful.'

'Do they miss you?'

'I hope so . . .'

'It must be hard on your wife?'

'Partner. Yes, very. She . . . wishes I would seek help.'

'And you haven't?'

He felt the conversation was deepening his bond with Rebecca, in that none of the others knew any of this detail, not even Terry. Whether she chose to tell them or not, the privilege of being first to know created a new kind of intimacy between them. Was Judith reading his thoughts?

'Sorry, this is very personal, and in front of the workforce too.'

'It's fine.'

'Although your wife might not think so.'

'Partner. No.'

It was all a betrayal. Made worse by its being Saturday night. What would Holly be doing now? By the large clock on the wall it was 8.20. If she was lucky she'd be downstairs, searching for a film to watch, the first moment of the weekend without the noise and presence of the children. It was at these times she said she felt his absence most keenly, a sense of defeat, and confessed that when this happened she tried to accept that this was her life now, the children, her job, her friends (and, yes, with these things listed together it always sounded like a full life), but she refused to let him go, let the family go. When she'd described this to him, she'd done her best not to cry.

Thinking about this released in McCullough a wave of home-sickness that seemed beyond remedy and he wondered who he was, sitting here, eating soft, flaky mutton, drinking a Bulgarian wine, talking to a mother and daughter who seemed in their different ways to indulge him. He didn't feel unhappy in their company, which complicated things.

Judith poured herself a little more wine. 'I like couscous,' she said pronouncing the word with long vowels: coos-coos. A wood pigeon. Then said, 'Rebecca tells me you work for the government, sometimes.'

'It's supposed to be top secret.'

'This is a village, Mac,' Rebecca defended herself. 'We go around telling everyone everything.'

'It's fine.' Then to Judith: 'I have a small business. We help companies prepare for catastrophe. You lose this client, that chief executive . . . there is a war here, a spillage there. We come up with scenarios and then help them prepare for the impact on the brand via the behaviour of employees, perceptions of customers. It's the devil's work.'

'That's not what you told us the other night,' Rebecca pointed out.

'That's because it was a different brief. A new line of work: "atrociology".'

'That's what you called it the other night.'

'Ah, you see—I wasn't lying.'

'It's an ugly word,' Judith said, writing it out with her fingernail on the table. 'Rebecca's father was . . . I mean is . . . an economist. He was quite a bit older than me. He worked for the first Bush administration.'

McCullough turned to Rebecca. 'Do you see your dad?' He hated how that sounded.

'Now and again. He lives in Chicago. He's got a Japanese wife. We don't get along.' The last part was said in a generic American accent.

Hearing Rebecca's mock accent, McCullough realized how anglicized Judith's had become; there was little twang to it, at least not compared to Rebecca's broad impression. It made Judith seem unplaceable, exotic.

'There is no trace of your accent in Rebecca.'

'If there was, she'd get rid of it.'

'That's it. I'm going to watch telly.' She smiled and pushed herself up, slid her rear from the seat, and bending forward from the hips, extricated herself from the table. She was as beautiful and charming as any eighteen-year-old daughter could be. There was no pose or poise to her, just suppleness, youth.

'Ta-ta.'

They were now alone, grown-ups at the table. Judith's fingertips rested around the rim of her glass of wine, her hand arched up, wrist wilted. McCullough's hand was flat to the table, the stem of his glass pressed to the web of skin between forefinger and thumb. It felt as if the evening had been much longer and more wine had been drunk.

'We're free to talk about Wallace Stevens now,' he said.

Judith looked at him and smiled. 'Not tonight. I've been reading him all day.'

'I see you have Brahms on your piano.' With Rebecca gone he was struggling to make conversation. Was it obvious?

'There is a line in Stevens, "Brahms although /His dark familiar, often walked apart".'

'Brahms can feel like that. Although I feel very close to his music, perhaps more so than any other composer's.'

Judith sipped her wine. 'You are an interesting man.'

He was not unused to being seduced. Or played with by intelligent women looking to test him. 'You'll find I'm not possessed of traditional English rectitude, which includes self-deprecation. I am aware of my attractiveness.' It was bold and intended to make her laugh.

Her eyes widened. 'Wow. That's a first.'

'I can only hope God forgives a show-off.'

She laughed at this. 'I suspect He might. That's His job after all. Forgiveness.'

'May I ask you what you believe in, if anything?'

There was a hint more colour in her cheeks. 'We're not big on dessert in this house; all we have is some posh chocolates, I'm afraid.'

She rose from her chair, not unlike her daughter, but more practised after so many academy dinners.

McCullough piled together the used plates and took them to the sink where he set them down on the drainer. Judith sat back down with the same economy of effort with which she had risen. There was something a little prim about the way she smoothed her dress beneath her, old-fashioned. He imagined her as a child, wanting to arrive at the table in silence, politely, unobtrusively. She placed the small box of chocolates between them.

'My father was an army chaplain. He was killed by a soldier on the base. I was ten.'

'I'm sorry.'

'My mother never got over it. Whether she lost her faith or not was irrelevant. She was broken.'

'*You* must have been—'

'I don't know. I brought myself up from that point. And cared for my mother. She died soon after I left home to go to college.'

He wanted to say something but couldn't think what. He was offered a chocolate. Not from the box, but more casually—the chocolate itself. 'Have one of these. Sea salt. Mocha and chilli. Very fashionable.'

He took it. 'So you were brought up . . .'

'More the daughter of an army officer than a chaplain. God was there, of course. I remember thinking of God as stern and unyielding, and Jesus as a forgiving, warm presence. But I don't think I ever really believed in anything, in the way my parents and their friends seemed to. I mean, they *really* believed. To them Jesus was at least as real as you and me, we just couldn't see him. In many ways I was a credulous child. But—'

'You didn't feel it.'

'No. It's hard when deep down your parents think God and Jesus are Americans. I mean, they weren't so stupid as that. But somehow their idea of America and God and Jesus—there it was. A kind of trinity.'

It was difficult to imagine this woman as a child on an army base without resorting to stock images: a large white clapboard house, a tree in the garden, a swing. Her father played by Gregory Peck.

Judith bit into a chocolate, winced a little, and offered the rest to him. 'Not a fan of cherry.' Then she asked, 'Were your parents religious?'

He popped the half-eaten chocolate in his mouth.

'It would make more sense if they were. But not at all. Indifferent for the most part. Although my mother did occasionally evoke God as an exacter of punishment greater than hers. But it was an idle threat. There was a hierarchy. My dad, a policeman, then God.'

Judith laughed, and appeared to wipe away a tear, though it could have been an eyelash.

He went on, 'In my house neither Holly nor I have the temperament to carry through on our threats. Maybe that was why Hell was created. By parents who just couldn't punish their children in this life.'

She laughed again. 'Rebecca was wilful like little girls can be, but she was also strangely serene. I think she understood me more than I did her. I was ignored a lot of the time.' More laughter. The eyelash was still there, bothering her. 'One moment.'

The elegant slipping from her chair again, this time to a mirror on the wall, where she used the tip of her fingernail to dislodge what was troubling her, just inside the rim of her eye. It was very becoming, her concentration on this, his absence in the moment.

'Got it.' She looked at the minute thing. When she turned to him she smiled, as though pleased to find him there, and for a moment regarded him, eyes glittering.

'I could ask you to spend the night. I am in two minds. But not with Rebecca here. And it doesn't look like she is going out.' It was said like that, with her still standing at the mirror.

'I'm flattered. Very.'

'I'm not giving you the opportunity to refuse. Shall I make coffee? Some tea? I have fresh mint.'

Over tea they talked more about Rebecca. McCullough said, 'She's an amazing young woman. Those poor boys.'

'You've met Terry? I feared he might be my son-in-law. I do believe she claimed to love him at one point.'

'He's easy to love, in his own way. I think she must respond to his independence.'

'You mean he doesn't sit outside weeping?'

'You've had a lot of those?'

'Like you wouldn't believe. I sit with them sometimes, comforting them. I think Rebecca sits in here laughing, she has so little empathy.'

'Do you know Rich?'

'I've met him.'

'He's next.'

'Oh, no, and he's such a sweet boy. I don't understand it. Even though I can see, objectively, she's an attractive creature.'

'Maybe it's her creatureliness.'

'Explain.'

'I was just offering it up. I'm not sure what I mean.'

'But you are a man.'

'I am.'

'Then tell me. Why all the crying boys?'

'You know as well as I do.'

'Because she's got a great rack, as they used to say.'

He laughed. 'They think she provides the answer.'

'To what?'

'That's what they'll learn. Or not learn. But the boys who fall for her and sit crying on your doorstep, will be . . .' He paused.

'What? I'm interested.'

'Richer for the heartbreak.'

'What did *you* learn?'

'Oh, many things.' He laughed. The knowledge had been hard won.

'She seems so cold sometimes.'

'It's the nature of a certain kind of wisdom.'

'She's eighteen. Nineteen in a couple of months.'

'She knows we're all desperate and she isn't. It's a kind of wisdom.'

'It sounds desperate to me.'

'She's beautiful, clever, and comes every day to help me, and hang out with a bunch of . . . what? Misfits. She's got a natural talent for mixing concrete—how many women can say that?'

'Are you in love with her?' Judith's expression suggested she hadn't expected to ask it outright.

McCullough thought: There, it has been said. 'No. But I am not invulnerable to her.'

'Maybe you will break her heart.'

Sitting across from each other, the tea in a white pot between them, white china cups, he laughed again. 'Is that what happened to you?'

'Maybe that will be how she's like me.'

'I promise I will not break your daughter's heart. And just in case that sounds fantastically arrogant, I confess that will be everything to do with her and nothing to do with me. There is more chance she will break mine. And I don't mean because I'm in love with her. Men are weak. Weak-hearted. I'm not doing myself any favours here, am I?'

'You're doing fine.'

'I hope you trust me.'

'How would your wife answer that?'

An hour later, Rebecca was called down to say goodbye. She was in a T-shirt and pyjama bottoms. He kissed her on the cheek.

'Your mother has been charming, Rebecca.'

'That's her thing—isn't it, Mother? Charm.'

'I do my best.'

'Thank you for the food and wine, the chair and table.'

'You're welcome.'

Rebecca returned to her bedroom and he heard the opening to Jimi Hendrix's 'Little Wing'.

The cool night air made him feel drunker than he had done all evening. On the street, he could barely remember what had happened, as if it had all been played out in a room into which he now had only a partial view. It was true Judith had propositioned him, playfully but without nonsense, and he'd been given no chance to decline. Then at the door they had kissed lightly, her fingertips to his cheeks, their lips meeting for a moment, just a little, a smudge. Her voice was low and lustrous when she said, 'Thank you,' and then they'd kissed again, this time full on the lips, lingering. A message was passed but it wasn't anything they didn't already know: they liked each other, found each other attractive, and that in itself was worth noting and making clear in a kiss.

Under a street lamp, he looked up. Rebecca was leaning out of a window, smoking. She waved to him and then stubbed out the scrap of rollie on the outside sill and flicked it away.

What was he to take from all this? He might submit, if only vaguely, to something with meaning. But that needn't be anything more than an acceptance that two middle-aged people who were drawn to each other had found a moment irresistible to flirtation but resistible to temptation.

At the top of the road, on the corner of the village green, he looked up at the sky and then beyond to the heavens. He wasn't naïve enough to expect guidance, a lighting of the way, but it was would be just as naïve to deny that new paths were opening up. For the most part he believed he tried to conduct his life with moral seriousness. But it was also true that when life overflowed with choices he tended to question this disposition, and ask himself whether it was self-limiting. How wrong was it to contemplate what meaning might be discerned in Judith's kiss . . . in Judith herself? He knew that beyond the erotic thrill, great spiritual insight was unlikely; history showed that people looking for such things mostly got it wrong— self-indulgence being more preponderant than a willingness to be tough with oneself. But it was also in his nature to believe greater meaning was out there, or a clearer meaning . . . something greater or clearer was attainable . . . and it was unlikely to arrive without causing disturbance or surprise. Hadn't he been open with Judith in a way Holly hadn't permitted? He laughed. Wasn't that the reason most affairs started: 'I feel I can be more open with you'? Oh, dear.

On the edge of the first field, the view before him was an expanse of dark land, vanishing into formlessness, the end or the beginning of the world. Above, the night sky appeared as it should, a perfect dome. The few detached houses that abutted the field had lights on in upstairs windows. The ground beneath his feet was damp and soft. He stopped for a second to summon breath. 'What is it I am supposed to do?' he said aloud. There was the temptation to add 'O Lord'—mostly for effect—but his voice sounded artificial in the empty night air, like an actor with little talent, his lines unsupported by belief, character, the meaning of the words. He felt embarrassed and glanced around as if he someone might be watching him.

Why, he wondered, say anything out loud at all? He wasn't addressing anyone close by, and nothing extra would be achieved by calling out into the darkness. If there was something 'out there' capable of hearing him, his question could just as easily be asked in silence, given that any 'out there' would likely have access to his 'in here'. This much he knew.

The sucking mud from the afternoon rain made each step slow and heavy, and he was forced to stop every so often and shake the clods from his boots. The only question that required an answer was whether he was strong enough to take whatever might be asked of him. Was he competent enough? He wasn't used to anything, however abstract, being so beyond his cognitive abilities that he couldn't make any sense of them whatsoever. Was there even a way to comprehend *nothing making no demands* that at the same time felt like *something compelling* him to act? At present he believed his submission was voluntary—wary but voluntary, but how did he really know? In a moment of candour he'd confessed this to Holly. It was no wonder she was so scared for him. She'd asked him the obvious question: what did he think he was being made to do beyond build a church? He said that at certain times, if he focused keenly enough, there was something at the back of his mind, some message or knowledge stored there . . . just that whenever he readied himself to reach in, it withdrew. He wondered aloud whether it would only become accessible when he was ready to discern its meaning. That everything so far was just a preparation. Half-jokingly he said he rather hoped the message had been already been offered and he'd wandered past and missed it, and he was just living with the consequences of his lack of alertness, his stupidity. Holly hadn't known what to say. It was madness, all of it.

And he understood no more now than he did then. Except that something unknowable was being given material presence. How absurd it was to translate what was happening to him into categories of appearance, shape and colour, position and size—who did that but the artist, or the madman? What was within him was more like the memory of a musical chord, substanceless, and yet somehow filling him with sound. Perhaps what was required of him was subtler attunement, something he wasn't capable of—the church was proof of that.

He was beginning to flounder in the mud, his feet sucked in, legs weakening from the effort. He didn't want any of this. He was just a normal man, with a partner and young children, a job. There were others more deserving, more in need. Others, surely, better prepared.

With every footfall his body was becoming heavier, as if a great weight had been placed at the centre of him, or his heart was the heaviest object in the universe, a collapsed sun. He started to feel dizzy, at moments unsure where he was, as if he'd been awakened in the middle of the night from a deep sleep. He looked down at his feet. His boots were sinking into the mud up to his ankles. With no strength left to release them, he was like a man halted indefinitely by the pull of the earth. From a distance, he must have resembled a life-size sculpture, a statue of a man randomly placed in a field, as they sometimes were at train stations, on rooftops, beaches. He found it difficult to catch his breath and he clutched his chest. The ache was deep, his heart felt like a hard knuckle. He pulled his shirt open; his fingers tore into his skin. He was being punished. Too many questions; too many stupid guesses at the answer. He was a bad choice, if such a thing were possible. A terrible mistake had been made.

A few hundred metres away was the site, his car, the warmth of the sleeping bag on the damp earth. He tried to withdraw a foot, but in that moment he felt himself being struck, beaten from the outside, clubbed. To protect himself he raised his arms, but there was nothing he could do. In the morning there would be bruises. A broken rib. His organs would ache. He tried not to cry out, as if he must endure his punishment in silence, prove his worth. Was this not proof, finally, that what was happening to him wasn't madness, he wasn't making it up—something essential was being wrought from him? It wasn't possible to do this to oneself. He laughed bitterly. He wasn't being prepared for anything; he was being destroyed. New *new* wine indeed. He'd misunderstood everything.

The form of his destruction was clear. It wasn't going to happen in an instant, like a bolt of lightning. It had been happening by attrition these last months, from within and without, although he feared tonight he might be delivered the last fatal blow. He turned his face to the sky. There was no looming storm, no weather cover that might disguise his end. The night was clear and the stars pluckable.

He felt himself directed to his knees. It was in his nature to resist such orders, but he sank down. The damp ground pressed through his jeans. As he made contact with the earth, he felt his back lacerated with a hot cord. His flesh opened up in long wounds and his blood flowed, thick and hot. He placed his forehead to the cool ground, a posture of prayer but also of final submission, his body trembling as if about to go into a fit. What would Judith think of him now? Those two kisses, the irresistible smudge, the lingering promise so sublimely contrived, so grown-up . . .

His guts were loose and slippery inside his belly. Something would soon be expelled. Maybe that was it: he needed further emptying. More space was required. His stomach contracted and he vomited. His bowels opened. The vomit was the tagine, as if undigested. The shit around his thighs was soft, warm, cloying. It was time to give up, give in. To die.

For ten minutes he lay there, staring at the ground, listening to the earth, to distant reverberations, and coughing up more vomit until there was nothing left and his throat burned with bile.

Over time, the blood dried, the shit hardened; his piss was taken in by the ground. He was no more than what constituted a man in his most basic form. He managed to undress, dragging and tearing the filthy clinging fabric from his skin, leaving him naked, his body streaked with mud, shit, blood. Pulling himself along, the thick damp grass wiped him down. To see him from above was to see a desperate creature impelled by an instinct to move across the ground. As a species it was unlikely to survive.

If he made it to the car, there was a three-hour journey home, and then he could fall naked and wretched into Holly's arms, the only person in the world he might give himself up to covered like this and not be judged.

But then what? After he was cleaned up, the caked-on filth run out with the bathwater? Decisions would need to be made. Would the love and sustenance of his family be enough? Or did he need to admit himself to a hospital, a psychiatric ward, and seek a diagnosis?

No doubt there would be tests and scans. No abnormalities in his bloods would be found, of course; no shadows on the plates. Nothing organic was wrong; nothing awry in the brain. What he had wasn't treatable. No doubt the doctors would want to keep him in. Further observation, therapy, drugs. Space and time for recovery. Except there would be no recovery. No cure was possible. After all, what could man do to rid a man of Him?

IN THE COOL OF THE DAY

'One must crush oneself, hacking and hewing away
at oneself to widen the place in which love will want to be'

MARGUERITE PORETE,
*The Mirror of Simple and Annihilated
Souls and Who Remain Only in
Waiting and Desire of Love*

On Monday morning McCullough went to the bank and withdrew fourteen thousand pounds in fifty-pound notes. They were counted out for him, weighed, and then parcelled into five letter-sized envelopes and secured with elastic bands. From the car park, he called Holly. The call lasted three minutes. He spoke matter-of-factly and Holly listened. She was cool and he wanted warmth.

It had taken him a day and a night to recover. Judith seemed a dream from long ago. He struggled to picture her and did not feel any desire to see her, which he'd feared he might.

Only Nathaniel had come by on Sunday. The PM had gone at midnight, apparently, a fleet of cars moving off through the village. His brothers had wandered the house with their chests puffed up to the point where their father felt compelled to say something. For once, Nathaniel was praised for his behaviour in front of those with whom he was often compared unfavourably.

Together they went over the details of works to be completed. When it began to rain they sat in the car and listened to a piano recital of late Schubert on Radio 3. Nathaniel tended not to notice others' moods and McCullough's shaken state didn't register. McCullough asked him to remind Rebecca to get Terry to a doctor. The rain continued to fall all evening and throughout the night. Dawn was overcast and damp, deadly to the spirit.

Would he tell Holly what had happened? He had planned to, but now wondered what words he might use. Any softening of events would likely mean she would believe it was nothing more than his mental state finally pitching him into delirium. Something to be expected. She'd chastise him: did he really want to die in a field? What answer would he give her?

Sitting in the car, he felt heartsick and desperate. All he wanted was to get himself home where human love was enough, doled out in simple acts of kindness. Who would choose to give themselves up to the kind of inpouring and battering he'd experienced, who would be willing to be endlessly raised up and cast down, with no notion of what was expected, when there was the love and warmth of the family home, and where all that was expected was to be present and loving? But it wasn't punishment he'd endured, he knew that now. He'd been singled out, and there is only so much the body can take. It was now up to him to understand in what insignificant way, given his weaknesses, he might be useful, should anything be made clear to him, any meaning finally offered. Maybe he should explain it like that to Holly; he was just making himself available if by chance any insight were handed down. But she'd still insist he was making a radical claim: on some level he was insisting he was 'chosen' and therefore aligning himself with great spiritual leaders, even prophets. But he'd make it plain: as of yet he was possessed of nothing, and he had no plans to endure further punishment. God now had to take him as he found him.

He supposed if he told her the whole truth she'd laugh at him. It didn't take a psychologist to interpret what had happened as an extreme physical manifestation of guilt for his part in the pantomime of seduction at the kitchen table, the two goodbye kisses, the second especially, so full of temptation and promise. And after everything he'd promised her: he was unchanged, there was no threat to the family; she must trust him and bear with him. It was pathetic. He was pathetic. He was on his knees that night because he deserved to be. A foolish and absurd man. A sinner.

PART THREE

Love II

THE ARK

'Seek not, my soul, the life of the immortal ones; but
Enjoy fully the resources that are within your reach.'

PINDAR

'How big is the church now, Daddy?'

Pearl seemed disappointed it was just above head height, even if it was her daddy's head.

'But Uncle Simon had a flash of inspiration and we've had to stop for a while.'

They were returning from the sports club in the afternoon sunshine, Walter concentrating on the sweets his father had bought him. Eating sweets was a serious matter and he was regarded as the family expert. He was unconcerned that he was a quick eater and that his sister took much longer, unless she decided to tease him about having some left when he had none, which she inevitably did.

'When we move there, can I have the biggest bedroom?' It was more of a statement than a question; she needed to know why she might endorse the move when her mother was so equivocal about it.

'Yes, looking out over the sea.'

'Did you hear that, Walter? My bedroom will look over the sea and yours won't.'

Whether he heard what she'd said or not, he understood the tone and his strike was ninja fast. But he had to swing around his father, so little contact was made.

'Maybe you can stay here in our old house with Mummy,' she said.

'What do you mean, stay here with Mummy? What do you mean by that, Pearl?' McCullough pulled them both back; they were close to a junction.

'I don't think she wants to go, Daddy.'

'Is that all?' Was it right to ask this?

Walter leaned against his father. 'I don't want to go. I've got used to it around here. I know where everything is.'

'Wouldn't you like to live in the country?'

'Yes,' he said. 'But not go for long walks.'

'In the country you don't have to go on long walks because you just play outside.'

Pearl tightened one of her bunches. 'I don't want to fall off a cliff. Mummy's worried about that.'

'No one's going to fall off a cliff.'

'How do you know? We might.' It was true insofar as it was always possible, but you didn't hear about it—children falling off cliffs.

'I will build a fence.'

She seemed happy with that. She turned back to Walter. 'How many sweets do you have left?' She seemed content to take the hit, a plimsolled foot swinging around, catching her knee.

McCullough grabbed each child by the nearest hand. 'For God's sake, you two. Please. What am I supposed to do if you goad him and then he hits you, and then you goad him again, and then . . . There comes a point when no one's in the right anymore and you both think you are. I don't know how Mummy's head hasn't exploded.'

Pearl laughed, but Walter just said, 'She knows they're my favourite sweets. That's why she said it.'

There was something so persuasive in his manner; he didn't make an appeal or even look up, and yet it was if something terribly precious had been denied him. It was so straightforward a reaction, it was difficult not to pause and reflect, and find in it a truth. And so McCullough did what he always did and decided Pearl was more in the wrong. After all, without the original tease the first strike would not have happened, and whilst the motivation was probably more complex than a general enjoyment of family drama, it was the inciting incidence and therefore McCullough was not totally wrong in blaming her.

'OK—give me your sweets.'

'What? No! He hit *me*!'

'You teased him.'

'But that's not enough for him to hit me. Hitting's never right.'

Her small hand was now a tight fist, the sweets—tiny gelatine animals—sweating in their plastic wrapping, softening but not really losing their shape or melding together. Her little strong fingers were white with determination. To unpick them was impossible, like untying tightly knotted string—just nowhere to get your fingers in.

'If you don't give them to me, I'll make you give them to your brother.' It was a stupid thing to say. Punitive.

'He hit me and you're going to give him my sweets? No fair.'

They'd picked this up from American television and he hated it. So he shouted, 'Give them to me or I'll ...' What? he wondered. Take away TV time? What had she done that was so terrible she was going to lose her sweets *and* TV time?

'Look ...' A big signal word: compromise was coming, something they all might accept, and therefore, just possibly, allow them all to move on. 'How many sweets have you got left?'

'But, Daddy, he's eaten all his. It doesn't matter how many I have left. I take more time. You know I do.'

'Look ...' It was now his pleading word. '*You* teased him.'

'And he hit me; he kicked me, *in fact.*'

'Because you *teased* him.'

'*Hitting's* worse.'

'There wouldn't be any hitting if there wasn't any teasing.' He was hoping he'd got her here.

'Mummy said he has to learn to control his hitting.'

'And you have to control your teasing.'

'So we're equal. Which means he can't have my sweets.' Pearl was her mother's daughter when it came to this kind of reasoning. And by this point Walter had been diverted by a playing card he'd found on the road and wasn't even listening.

They were now near home, and after they crossed the final junction, Walter would release himself from his father's hand to run the final hundred metres. He'd probably suggest a race to his sister, to which she would happily assent, and in their world everything would be forgotten, unless one of them cheated, in which case by the time McCullough got to the front door there would be kicking and hair-pulling.

Once they were off, he realized that Walter hadn't actually demanded any punishment for Pearl, just that the unfairness be acknowledged. And Pearl, of course, hadn't given up any sweets. There was only one loser. On the face of it this was the case, but he could argue that everyone had lost because nothing had been satisfactorily resolved, no lessons had been learned, and his authority, for what it was worth (and it was worth something as a loving, psychologically astute parent), had been eroded just that little bit, and as an expert in catastrophe, an able metaphysician, and to all intents and purposes a man singled out by God for something more major than a disputation over teasing and hitting (although in its own way this was just another example of a problem that did not have an answer), he should have done better. His laughter was wry, but not without weariness. When he jogged down to the gate to make sure they hadn't run further up the road or started to kill each other, he found them huddled in the porch, Pearl with her fist open, letting Walter choose which sweet he most wanted, and not because he'd won the race, or because she was in the wrong, but just because.

What was he supposed to do but commend her?

'Thank you. That's a nice thing to do. Say thank you, Walter.'

He did. And she smiled at her father. And then Holly was at the door.

'Were you surprised to see Daddy picking you up? Did he buy you sweets? Naughty Daddy.'

At dinner—pasta and pesto, garlic bread, salad, a glass of wine for McCullough—they talked about other clubs Pearl might go to over the summer, and whether Walter fancied another one. He surprised them both by choosing football. His no-nonsense declaration moved McCullough. No interest had been shown before that moment. But the boy seemed certain.

Holly looked at Walter. 'We didn't know you liked football. Of course you can go. I'll put your name down tomorrow.'

'Have you been playing it at playtime, at school?' McCullough said.

'Yes.'

'Do you score any goals?'

'I play defensive midfield.'

How could McCullough have missed this? Surely not by being gone a few weeks. Or exactly that.

'Do you want to play with Daddy in the garden?' This was Holly, keen to make sure Walter understood that what he liked at school might also be enjoyed at home.

Pearl said, 'I want to play.'

Holly glared. 'Walter—do you want to play? You should have said something, darling.'

They were so used to his obsessions—trucks, trains, volcanoes, Lego—that they often thought he was completely open to them when it came to his interests, even when he appeared closed to them in other ways. When McCullough had picked him up from the sports club, he had shown no surprise or particular happiness to see his father. That wasn't exactly right: he'd been pleased to see him, but only in the usual way, based on his father as a consistent bearer of sweets, his little hands digging into McCullough's pockets as reflexively as if he'd never been away.

'Can we get some goalposts?'

'Of course,' Holly said.

'He gets very upset at school when he plays football,' Pearl informed them.

'Does he?' Holly asked. 'Do you? Why?'

'Sometimes they say it's a penalty when it's not.'

'What do you do?'

'He hits out.' Pearl wanted to be the other adult at the table.

'Darling, you mustn't. You have to speak to a teacher.'

Walter kept his head turned down towards his plate, using his fingers to feed the tubes of pasta into his mouth, his fork ignored. 'They're not fair. I get detention.'

'You've never told us this.'

'He gets detention all the time. Because he hits out.'

'Walter—you need to tell us these things.'

McCullough was angry and could already envisage a stand-off between himself and the school. He regarded any hurt suffered by his children as the product of unpunished bullying. His reaction was complexly atavistic: he wanted the perpetrators to suffer, after which he wanted them to learn why what they had done was wrong and become good citizens, so the world his children grew up in was a better place. But in the short term, they must suffer.

'I'll speak to the school, after the summer holidays,' he said.

Holly was clear: 'No, you won't. I have to go in every day—let me handle it.'

'He's not to get detention for behaviour he cannot help. It's like giving a one-legged child a detention for falling over.'

Both children laughed at this and Pearl fell off her chair. 'I've only got one leg.' Crash. Walter thought this was fantastic. 'I've only got one arm.' And he let his face fall into the pasta. By the time he'd raised his head, covered in the glistening pale green of pesto sauce, his metabolism had gone quickly through its many gears and he was on the brink of hysteria. It would only take his sister to mirror him and he'd be lost. Pearl's next move was to hang a leaf of lettuce off her nose and say, 'Look, I've got a lettuce on my nose—you can't give me detention.'

Both parents laughed. How could they not? A six-year-old with bunches in her hair and a lettuce leaf hanging off the end of her nose. Unaccountably, although with a strange unknowable logic, she added 'Moooo'. After that it took over an hour to calm Walter down.

Bedtime went well, with McCullough lying on the floor of the twins' bedroom while Holly read to them. He'd offered to read but they'd chosen Holly out of habit, Walter insisting. The story was about a missing dog, who was somehow very adept at using public transport. Pearl was fidgety, alert to her father being present, occasionally examining a stuffed toy and using it to make unhelpful comments on the story. Walter let his gift for mysterious stillness overtake him. As a treat, Holly read until they were almost asleep, and then as promised McCullough sang them a song—something they still enjoyed.

He waited for Holly to tuck them in, arrange various things, mainly pillows for Walter. He started with 'Ten in a Bed' and finished with 'Ten Little Monkeys Jumping on a Bed'. In the semi-darkness he could sense both children let go and recede into full sleep. Even so, both parents had learned early never to cut a song short. At times, he found himself going into minus numbers, something that gave him a strange satisfaction. Most nights, the moment he moved, Pearl would demand, 'More, Daddy—again!' as if they were as far from sleep as he was. The trick was to just lie there and wait it out. Above him, in his office, he heard his mobile ring.

In the sitting room, her laptop open, Holly said, 'Thank you.'

He stood in the doorway. 'Lucien just called.'

'Lucien?'

'He wants to meet.'

'Now?'

'Yes.'

'But it's . . .' She looked at the clock on the wall. 'It's . . .' It felt late but it wasn't.

'I know.'

'Your first night back . . .'

'I know.'

'And you agreed, just like that. Did you say it was your first night back?'

McCullough leaned against the door frame. 'He never calls. Never asks to meet.'

'You can't see how this is not fair, can you?'

'Of course I can.'

'But I don't think you can. I mean obviously you can because it is unfair—you'd be insane if you didn't realize that. So maybe you really don't care. Is that what you want me to believe? You've been back *a day*. You're not a priest—you have no duty of care. Unless that's why you're doing it.'

He said quietly, 'That's not why I'm doing it.'

'I was looking forward to spending time with you.'

On the coffee table were two glasses of red wine, two small rich chocolate puddings, some salted almonds.

'I've sat here on my own every night since you've been gone. I can't believe you, Mac.'

There was a slight noise from upstairs, or maybe from next door, and they both moved into a mode of stillness that had become second nature. 'It's nothing,' he said. Standing by the door, he felt as if he could cast his hearing, so finely tuned to a child's movement or presence, up the stairs and along the landing to the door of the twins' room and listen in.

'Would it matter? You're going out anyway.'

He moved over to the arm of the sofa and sat down. 'What if I'm back by nine?'

'It's not really the point, is it?'

He looked at her. 'Lucien never calls. He never asks anything of anyone. It's just bad timing.'

'Would he be there for you?'

'That's not the point.'

Holly pulled her legs up and settled down for an evening alone, again. She refused to look at him, but instead scrolled through the TV planner, although he doubted she was taking it in.

'It *is* the point, if you've been away from your family for over two weeks, and he wouldn't do the same for you—that's how you decide whether to go or not.'

She was right, of course, but none of that had occurred to him. He realized she would be upset, but he did feel a sense of duty to Lucien, who was an old friend. If it were possible for Lucien to sound distressed, that's how he had sounded. He'd called from a pub not far away, by the river, and refused to explain what the call was about. 'It's a piece of luck you're back, really,' was all he'd said. McCullough had replied that he wasn't sure Holly was going to see it that way. He'd known it was serious when the mention of her had had no effect.

'What's the matter with him anyway?'

'He didn't say.' Then McCullough added, 'You know I don't want to go, don't you? I want to stay here with you.'

'It seems like it.'

'What do you want me to say?'

'There isn't anything to say. Go to your friend.'

'Don't be like that.'

'Like what? Hurt, upset? That's a bit selfish of you, isn't it? You're going out on your first evening back and you want me to be happy for you. OK, go—have a great time. Say "hi" from me.'

They sat in silence, the remote pointed at the TV, the highlighted band on the planner going up and down. Holly threw it down on the sofa. 'There's nothing on. You might as well go out.'

'Just accept I don't want to go.'

'No. You *do*. Even if you say you don't want to, you do, really. A friend in need and all that.'

She was right, and he felt terrible guilt, yet at the same time he was worried about being late for Lucien. For a moment he hated his friend. Whatever had gone wrong, it would be his own stupid fault.

'I'll be as quick as I can.'

'That's a pointless promise, Mac—you know it is. By the time you get there, have a drink, then another . . .' She paused and picked up the TV remote again. 'Just understand I'm upset, that's all.' She began to cry.

His hands were in his lap, uselessly. She would brush him away if he tried to comfort her and despise him for thinking there was any fix. It would just show he didn't understand. Yet he also knew that she'd be more upset if he didn't make some effort. It was a double bind he deserved, and in no way made her unreasonable. So he moved from the arm of the sofa to the edge of the coffee table and looked at her. She was content for the tears to roll down her cheeks, to make manifest the depth of her sadness.

'I'll make this right.'

She didn't return his look. 'You can't.'

'Don't say that.'

'Just go, Mac. Just go. And don't wake me when you come in, OK? That's the least you can do.'

'I'll be as quick as I can.'

'You might as well take as long as you want. I've been going to bed early since you've been away.'

'But I'm back now.'

'No, you're not, Mac. That's the problem.'

PUBLICAN

'I do not ask you to believe in God, I only ask you not to believe in every thing that is not God'

SIMONE WEIL, *WAITING FOR GOD*

There was something weary in Lucien's bonhomie when McCullough found him in the back room of the pub, sitting on his own at a table for eight. He stood up, a little drunk, his smile weak. On the table were a bottle of red wine, screw top, and a fresh wine glass. He poured his friend a drink. On the occasions when McCullough met him during the week, however much time had elapsed between the working day and their meeting, he was always surprised how high and tight on his neck Lucien's tie remained. He wondered whether it was an affectation: when irritated or bored, Lucien tended to twist his neck a little, as if to create a little give in his collar, suggesting to those around him that, unlike them, he didn't relax until he was behind closed doors. The few times McCullough had been away with Lucien and his family at the weekend, Lucien seldom came indoors, whatever the weather, as if to distinguish being in the country from being in the town.

'So, Lucien. I can guess, or you can tell me.'

'How was I to know she was a devout Catholic?'

'But not devout enough to insist on contraception?'

'Anyway, it's all got very "Brideshead". Have you read it?'

'Yes.'

'I haven't. That's not true.'

Lucien put his head in his hands and scratched at his hairline; his nails were manicured; flakes of dry skin fell to the table.

'I take it for granted that if it's not discussed, everything is fine. This feels like entrapment. I mean, what is she doing having sex like that if she's a Catholic? I know those convent-raised girls, but really . . .'

'What stage are we at?'

'Ha! I like that. First-person plural. You're priceless, Proctor.' Lucien drank back his wine. 'Three months. First scan and all that. You know what I hate about it? It's so banal. Everything from here on in, whatever happens, will be so dull. I can see it all.'

'What about your job?'

'That's the thing—she's being so damned reasonable. She's taking responsibility—'

'I thought you said it felt like entrapment?'

'I was just saying that. She accepts it was half "her stupid fault". She's just not having an abortion. Which I suppose is fair enough.'

'Forgive me, Lucien, but why are you so distraught? I mean *quite* so distraught?'

'That's what I was wondering. I just am. It's not as though I didn't have it coming. I was expecting it. If you can believe it, I have a little savings account for just this eventuality.'

McCullough didn't know what to say and poured more wine into both glasses. 'You're not in love with her, I suppose?'

'No more than I am with Maria.' His laughter was bitter, ironic. 'Well, it's a fact. Do you want to swap?'

'Who's that going to help?'

'Me—you get Maria and the kids, Jo gets her child, and I get Holly.'

'And the twins.'

'You can have them as well.'

'So you just want to live with Holly.'

'Yes, please. Could you ask God to arrange it?'

'I'll do my best.'

There was a moment of quiet. Then after a big glug of wine, Lucien went on: 'I like you, Proctor—you know that. But you're easy to resent. I do wonder, had you not been you, whether I would have called anyone. In fact, I asked myself whether it was *you* making me call and not me *wanting* to call at all, and I started to think: God—is this man my moral compass? Is it somehow him that's making me feel so wretched? Of course, that's after two whole bottles of this dreadful New World piss. If it didn't have a nice load of spice on the finish, I'd have it down for vinegar.'

'Well, if it helps . . . down at the site there is an eighteen-year-old girl who is hypnotically beautiful. I don't think I'd be able to resist—'

'See . . . there you go. "Hypnotically beautiful", "able to resist". I banged this girl in her office, which is a cubicle—a fucking cubicle, with Plexiglas dividing it from other cubicles. It took all of two minutes and I don't think I once looked at her face. She was turned around the other way for one thing. I had my eye on her during her interview. That may even have been why I voted to have her in. So, no . . . your hypnotically irresistible teenager who you haven't fucked—doesn't help. And by the way, just so you know: if you did and told me, I'd go straight to Holly.'

Lucien, face propped up and fists plunged into his cheeks, regarded McCullough wearily.

'No, you wouldn't.'

'Maybe, maybe not.'

'What's going on, Lucien?'

'I've told you.'

'If you'll forgive me playing back much of what's been said to me these past months—this is probably all about something else.'

'Maybe it's boredom.' Lucien's eyes were heavy and tired, but he tried to affect liveliness.

'You aren't happy, that's for sure.'

'I miss happiness—don't you? Remind me: what's it like?'

'I'm fairly sure responsibility isn't in there.'

'Ha!'

'And before you say anything, I'm talking just as much about myself. It might well be that what I'm doing now is a supreme act of irresponsibility, that I'm deluding myself believing everything is suddenly charged with meaning. Think about it.'

'I do. I sit at my desk and think about it. Who gave you the right to suggest that you might have access to something not allowed to the rest of us? Have you no idea how vulnerable we all are, and

I mean *everyone*? You've become a menace, Proctor. Even Maria invokes your name. It doesn't matter how stupid she thinks what you're doing is, it's something based on something and that impresses her. Our poor children. Their father's a QC and his friend is a fanatic, and who's the role model in our house?'

'You have just fucked a pupil.'

'They don't know that!'

Lucien slurped at his wine and refilled his glass. It was left to McCullough to top up his own. It was a mistake to look at his watch.

'Hope you don't do that with your new parishioners.'

He wanted to mention Holly sitting at home, waiting for him— if she was waiting.

'I'm sorry.'

'I know I'm being boorish, Proctor. It's just, right now, I can't think what else to be. Seems easiest. There is something wonderfully indulgent about following cavalier behaviour with boorishness. It's the only thing making me feel any better. Or worse. Which in this instance is better. I do feel guilt, you see. It's just that I'm unwilling to let it in.' He peered into McCullough's eyes. 'Do let me know your thoughts?'

'Well, there are many options.'

'I do like a problem-solver.'

'None of which are meaningful unless you know what you want.'

With a little wine caught at the back of his throat, Lucien said, 'At what point do I get to call you a sanctimonious cunt?' He smiled, but his mood had suddenly darkened. 'This is ridiculous. This is only a problem because we're English. The Latin races have sorted this stuff out. I just need three houses—one for Maria and the boys, one for Jo and the baby, and one for me to get away from them all. Are we all not then happy?'

'Try it.'

'Fuck off, Proctor. Don't be a prick.'

'I mean it. You'll soon learn if you're happy . . . if anyone's getting hurt.'

'You're priceless.' There was a pause; another large gulp of wine. 'Don't you sometimes yearn for a little place of your own? A bed, a few books, a good bistro nearby. A nice big window with good light. Maybe a naked young woman stretched out on clean white sheets— your irresistible eighteen-year-old, for instance? Isn't that what we all want? Men, that is. Women, it seems, would actually choose to have us in their little place. Women want to be with us, have you noticed that? If men were honest we'd admit that the thing we're most scared of—in all of life—is the bloody family holiday. All that forced intimacy. All that play-acting. Except *they're* not play-acting, are they? They're happy. They're in a good mood. Because we're all together. It seems churlish not to play along, but inside we're dying. Inside we're thinking: my idea of a holiday wouldn't include any of you.' He laughed. 'And the young woman stretched out on the white sheets, she'd have to make herself scarce for most of the day. I'm right, aren't I, Proctor?'

Whether Lucien believed himself right or wrong in ultimate terms, in that moment he wanted to be right and for some action to be taken, perhaps even God to intercede and make it so.

'If I may be so bold: you really can't have the girl on the sheets *and* not go on the family holiday.'

Lucien laughed. 'Oh, but that's the point, Proctor. If I have to go on the family holiday, the girl just becomes a distraction, a *divertissement*. No. The choice is all-important. You should understand that.'

'I do. But I thought we were looking for a solution.'

'No, my friend—we're looking for "the answer". I didn't ask just anyone to come here. I chose you. We're going to crack this together. Between us, Proctor, we're going to find a way to happiness. A man's happiness.' Lucien rocked his head back against the wall. 'God, I wish I were gay.'

'That's one way out of it.'

'I mean, what does it matter who is giving the blowjob? In the dark, I mean.'

'OK—I see we're covering all the bases tonight. I'm not sure this suits you, Lucien.'

Without moving his head, Lucien opened his eyes and peered at McCullough, a look he would use daily when he finally became a high court judge. 'Really—you think that's going to work? No,

I'm being self-consciously perverse. I'm going through the gears. I might cry next.'

'I'll stay for that and then go.'

'Do you think there is a chance I might declare that I really and truly love Maria?'

'It's a possibility.'

'Do you remember her, from the old days?'

'I do.'

'Did you fuck her?'

'No.'

'What's happened to her?'

'I don't know. She found having children stressful.'

'Ha! Those poor kids. I should rescue them. Test the Christian love of poor Jo. Tell her I've left Maria and I'm moving in with her, and bringing the kids.'

'I need to go, Lucien.'

'So you don't think we'll solve anything tonight? I thought you were the problem-solver?'

'Real human problems are unsolvable. Otherwise they wouldn't be problems.'

'I like that. That's smart, Proctor. You really don't hear that much these days. It's attractively Stoic, in its way.'

'I see it more as this: that living in crisis is an authentic place to be.'

'I like that less. Bit fucking pompous if you ask me.' There was a brief pause and then Lucien stretched and yawned; his teeth were yellow at the back. 'Shall we have a cigarette outside and call it a day?'

The night was hot and the iron of the railing on which they leaned was warm. The river was at rest. They both stared over to the edge of the water and the dark dull pebbles. There was smashed glass, a can of lager, a shoe. Where water had stagnated there was the spectrum of oil, an odour of eggs.

'I bought a packet, for old times' sake.' Lucien looked at his cigarettes. 'I shall leave them for Maria in a drawer. She will think it's a miracle, I suspect. Or a trap.'

'Has she seen a doctor? It's my guess she just needs antidepressants and she'd be back to her old self.'

Lucien leaned away from McCullough, his eyes bright with surprise. 'A trollop!'

'She got a first, remember. She was a sexy, brilliant woman, with a flair for entertaining and seduction without losing a beat.'

'Did you fuck her?'

'No. Get her to see a doctor. All she has to do is tell him the truth: she's unhappy, stressed out, not her old self.'

'I don't think I could take it—her old self.'

'I'm not thinking of you.'

'She didn't call you; I did.' Lucien flicked his cigarette as far as he could, a metre beyond the passive edge of the water. 'I do wonder whether you've always been a bit of a vicar. You do really seem to care about people—I mean beyond the so-called norm, which is pretty low, I'd say, these days. And you're always full of advice.' He laughed, and then continued, 'Where was I? Oh, yes. You as vicar. I have to say, I'd probably go to church more often if you were there. It would be nice not to have a big softie at the gate.'

'Oh, to be a big softie.'

'Maybe you're right there. Why aren't we big softies?' Lucien looked genuinely devastated.

'Because we aren't, is the best I've got.'

'Oh, fuck, Proctor. That's what I yearn for. Just imagine.'

They were both quiet for a moment. The orange glow of lights in the houses opposite went off every few minutes, followed by fainter light going on upstairs. Across the river, cars on the embankment moved with sleek and collective efficiency as if from another, more modern city.

'I need to go, Lucien.'

'Well, you've been a brick. A lodestone. You are my lodestone.' The night air had made Lucien drunker. His height and long limbs seemed suddenly independent of his long, thin body and not quite attached. McCullough felt the need to loosen his friend's tie; and his cufflinks somehow looked ridiculous; his big bright teeth were too much like a whinnying horse's, as if he was unable to control the muscles of his mouth. It was uncomfortable to watch; Lucien was normally masterful at gauging the impact of his own performance. But he was now drunker than he had been in a long, long time.

'Time to tuck me up in bed. Now to whom should I go? Maria? Jo? Or perhaps you'll take me back to your place so I can be looked after by Holly.'

'You can sleep on our sofa, but I don't think you'll get much sympathy from her.'

'Maybe I'll sneak up in the middle of the night and snuggle in between the two of you.'

'There'll be space, I'm sure.'

'No. I'd better go home. I have three boys who need me.'

'I'll call us a cab.'

For ten minutes they waited, leaning on the iron railing, picking away at its black paint.

In the cab, Lucien lolled heavily on McCullough's shoulder and then laid his head back.

There was a slight cough before he said, 'People don't like you, Proctor—you're just too . . .' And then he was asleep, mouth open. It was a hurtful remark; but it didn't matter. The impulse to release his friend's collar remained.

At Lucien's house, the driver was needed to help pull him out of the cab and stand him upright, so McCullough could get his arm around Lucien's waist and throw one of his friend's arms over his own shoulder, where he could hold it there with his other hand.

The pathway to the front door was short, the bell in easy reach.

Maria was in a dressing gown, a glass of white wine in her hand. 'Sofa' was all she said, and McCullough took her husband inside, carrying his weight and most of his guilt for what looked like a whole evening they'd spent together, actively trying to get into this state.

'I'll sort him out later.' Maria presented her cheek to be kissed. 'Do you want a glass of wine?'

'Thank you, but I can't.'

'No, of course you can't.' She turned to Lucien. 'Terrible thing is: no hangover.'

At the front door, Maria picked a black thread from McCullough's white shirtsleeve. 'How's Holly? Pleased to have you back?'

'I hope so.'

'*I* hope so. Are you sure you wouldn't like some wine? Like Holly, I'm mostly deprived of adult company in the evening.'

'Cab's waiting.'

'I'm not going to ask you what's wrong.'

'No.' McCullough paused. 'How are you doing?'

She laughed. 'Me? I'm a basket case, you know that. Everyone knows it.'

'Go and get yourself some meds, Maria. Give yourself a break.'

'Isn't that what I'm doing?' She raised her glass.

'No.'

'If I do, will you promise to tell me what's happening with Lucien?'

'I'm tempted to accept that deal.' He kissed her. Behind her, the sound of snoring could be heard. Outside, the cab's diesel engine was rumbling, radio on, the football commentary an intrusion into the night air.

When McCullough was at the gate, Maria said, 'Do you feel sorry for the boys? Being brought up in this house?'

He turned. 'No, Maria. Just go the doctor and get some help. Trust me, everything will be fine.'

INTERTESTIMENTAL

'Who is this that darkeneth counsel
by words without knowledge?'

BOOK OF JOB

McCullough and Jim, arms folded, legs out and crossed at the ankles, both in shirt and tie, sat in the anteroom to a large meeting room, a closed laptop on a low table before them. Eyes straight ahead, staring at the blank wall, they waited. The Ministry car had arrived early and the traffic was light. Neither of them was detained for long at the security gates, although a man with a gun was intrigued by Jim's reluctance to take off his large coat; it was twenty-eight degrees outside. McCullough tried to explain: Jim's body didn't respond to ambient temperature in the normal way. Inside the building, a team of young men and women guided them through oak-panelled corridors, briefing them on protocol: who was expected to be present at the meeting, how long they had, how to divide up that time between presentation and questions. A seating plan would be on the table before them if they were unsure who was who and/or the correct way to address them: 'Some will have titles, others complicated military ranks.' Their escorts were used to people who took in information quickly, thoroughly, and without the need to repeat themselves. McCullough and Jim were regarded with suspicion for asking questions and sometimes the same questions.

'Won't "sir" and "ma'am" do?'

'I suppose.'

Jim couldn't resist: 'What about in the voice of Elvis Presley?' Making jokes before a debrief had been a tactic they'd developed early on when they realized too much worrying was having a negative impact on their performance, but sometimes, especially with Jim, they leaked out in front of clients.

A visible jolt affected the young team, something faintly electric passing through them. 'The meeting *cannot* go on longer than an hour—the Secretary of State is flying to Berlin at midday.'

Jim looked at McCullough. 'That should be enough.'

Jim had not wanted to come, and threatened to bail out of the car at a red light. The laptop he carried was a prop: the PowerPoint charts were mostly empty. A week ago, McCullough had promised a Eureka moment, then yesterday, then last night, this morning.

In the anteroom, Jim scanned the corners for hidden cameras. 'For your sake, you'd better have something.'

'I've told you: it's not that I have something, it's rather that I don't have nothing.'

'Which by anyone's calculation means you have something . . .'

'You'd think.'

'Are you sure you're not unwell?'

'No, I'm dwelling in a kind of hinterland or interspace.'

'How the fuck is that relevant?'

'Think about it—the space between the barricades. *Les Barricades Mystérieuses.*'

'That's it? You're going to hum a bit of French baroque?'

'Set the mood.'

Jim uncrossed his legs at the ankles and recrossed them the other way; his arms were tightly folded. 'Just tell me what you're going to lead with?'

'I'm all over the data. I know every corner of it.'

'This is madness.'

'OK. If I get in there and nothing comes to me, I'll say we need more time. This isn't the debrief, remember. It's a pre-debrief. More informal.'

'Tell that to those nitwits.' But there was a realignment of the muscles in Jim's body as he allowed that it was at least a plan.

A period of silence followed. Both of them checked emails on their phones. Jim tweeted, then moments later, on receiving a response, laughed.

A door opened and voices were heard; a meeting breaking up.

'Ready?'

'You are a brave man, Proctor McCullough.'

'Yeah, they burned my namesake at the stake.'

But they weren't called in. A trolley with bevelled cylinders of coffee and hot water was rolled out by a man in a chef's hat; the door was shut behind him.

Sleepiness had overcome McCullough. He'd wanted this project so much, and might argue, despite a lack of concrete findings, that they had done their best work to date on it, but what was there to report? Merely that the nation would be changed forever and suffer a kind of corporate post-traumatic stress disorder on a scale far beyond 9/11, which in its essence happened over a morning, the immediate human terror hidden inside the building, which was why the falling figures had become so central an image. But this scenario, with its visible and physical division, this no-man's-land separating the living from the dying . . . didn't something fundamental change when a nation must shoot its own people for the greater good?

At the start of the interviews, when the respondents were being briefed about the nature of the research, everyone had agreed that a scenario like this should be planned for, and said they understood that there would always be practicalities when dealing with such an atrocity. It wasn't a shock that more than a few people had already accepted their children would live at least some of their lives in a world in which an event like this had taken place, a world entirely different from their own. Maybe that was all he needed to say in the meeting: a broader version of what they were testing was already forming in the collective unconscious, and in that sense it was a psychosocial meme, out there doing its thing, even if people didn't talk about it, or hadn't yet faced it in real life. When McCullough had tried to decode what had been played back to him, what precisely the respondents were seeing in their mind's eye, it seemed to him to be an amalgam of the Twin Towers, Iraq, Syria, apocalyptic movies and the visual persuasiveness of End Times console games. But for all that, it was a genuine fear of an event that went beyond anything imaginable, and would require an acceptance that a phase of human existence was close to passing. Maybe that was also worth spelling out.

An assistant stood before them, a young man. He had a fresh, kind, narrow face. The thick folder he clutched was held before his groin. He introduced himself as Casper.

'Five minutes, gentlemen. The projector is set up.'

McCullough was on his feet, looking for a hand to shake, but Casper needed both to keep the folder where it was.

McCullough said, 'We're going to keep this quite informal.'

'Informal, sir?'

'Yes. I think this debrief was scheduled as informal—so we can bring you up to speed with our thinking.'

'I'm not sure that that is correct, Mr McCullough.'

Jim smiled, eyes shunted away so he didn't laugh; he took a breath and tried to help out. 'Shall we just see where we get to today?'

The young man didn't like this at all—first informal and now inconclusive. He rocked a little on his feet. 'You know who is in there?'

'Yes-ish.'

'The Secretary of State, the Commissioner of the Metropolitan Police, the General—'

Jim interrupted. 'I saw a lot of older men with medals, like in *Dr Strangelove*.' There was no reaction from Casper, which disappointed Jim. He decided to be kind to the young man. 'Look. Don't worry. We do this all the time. They will not want us to be prescriptive. Informality will allow them to take ownership of some very controversial findings.'

The aide took a step back, his folder still protecting his groin. Now they'd added 'controversial'.

'Casper, we're ready.' It was a middle-aged man, impeccably turned out except for a wayward fringe over his eyes that needed a flick from the heel of his hand to smooth it back across his head. McCullough motioned to the younger man that they would follow him in, and turning sideways to the low table, he bent at the knees to pick up their superfluous laptop, although he did intend to have it open before him and press a few buttons now and again.

The meeting room was large, perhaps once an anteroom to a ballroom, with floor-to-ceiling windows, the curtains thick and expensive, edged with gold braid. The sunlight fell in heavy slabs on the long polished table. Some attendees at the end and the far side might be occluded from McCullough's view by the light. Equally, they might not be able to see him. He wasn't sure whether that was good or not. The two men were directed to chairs; the projector hummed; they could feel the heat of the bulb. The occupants' refusal to stand and greet them suggested to McCullough that whatever this research had to say, they didn't want to hear it.

The senior civil servant present at the initial briefings offered them coffee, although he made no indication he would fetch it, and the two bevelled containers were at the far end of the room. The atmosphere was not unusually inhospitable. As consultants they were just one of many groups who cluttered up these people's days, and the expectation that they were going to add anything to the general sum of knowledge was not high. For the most part they were present as an act of political expediency, in case something awful should go wrong. It was due diligence.

Jim leaned over to McCullough and whispered, 'Fuck!'

Before McCullough could respond, the convener of the meeting stood to introduce their guests and outline the project's objectives. He didn't look up, but scanned a single sheet of paper before him, using one long finger to keep his place. There was no inflection in his voice: the hour was merely to be taken up with the next item on the agenda.

McCullough leaned forward, clasped his hands together and smiled. 'Thank you. The purpose of this interim debrief is to inform you of our current thinking at this stage in the project.'

Around the table plumage seemed to retract in some and open in display in others—either way it was a demonstration of annoyance.

Bored more than irritated, the convener drew in his breath. Did these men, one of whom had yet to take off what appeared to be a winter coat, require him to manage the meeting so early in the proceedings? 'Go on.'

The door, which Casper noticed was still ajar, was duly closed.

An hour later it was opened for more refreshments. Assistants panicked and fussed as schedules were pushed back. Two hours later McCullough and Jim were asked to wait outside.

'Well, that went well.' Jim scratched at his cheek.

McCullough had no response but to claw in his toes, let out a long sigh, purse his mouth and wonder what might happen next.

Jim continued, '"It will be epochal", "There will be no disconfirmation"—that's a new one on me.' He was amused, horrified, bewildered, and in need of a drink.

As it happened, they were not called back in. Raised voices were heard behind the closed doors. Casper emerged and informed them that they were to write a short report outlining exactly how they had arrived at their conclusions, with each point evidenced by the relevant data, for delivery by the end of the week. One page would suffice, with an appendix containing transcripts of *all* the interviews. If another meeting was scheduled they would be expected to attend, however inconvenient.

McCullough said, 'Thank you.'

The senior civil servant appeared and said, 'I regard people like you as a menace.'

McCullough stared at him. 'You should meet my wife. In the sense that she thinks I'm a menace. Not that *she's* a menace. Or that you should meet her.'

'You also appear to be an idiot.'

'Probably nearer the truth.'

LAZARUS

'All our lives long, every day and every hour, we are engaged
in the process of accommodating our changed and unchanged selves to changed and unchanged surroundings.'

SAMUEL BUTLER,
THE WAY OF ALL FLESH

I

The drive home on the M11 on a late Sunday afternoon, if
there weren't any tailbacks, lasted one hour and forty-five
minutes and was a classic kind of hell. The twins were not
usually keen to be strapped into the car, but after a visit to their
grandpa's house, it was as if they were being offered a place of freedom, a psychic space in which they might finally express themselves,
and planned to take advantage. Holly accepted this, and for at least
the first ten minutes she would defend their playfulness: they had
spent four hours trying not to tire out Grandpa; of course they
needed to expend a little energy. It was always the same: a game
that began as fun for all four of them, became hysterical fun for just
two of them, then suddenly a point of honour for one of them, and
then a reason for hitting for both of them. This led to crying by one,
laughter from the other, shouting from Holly, followed by louder
shouting from McCullough, who tried volume rather than reason,
which then led to an argument between parents, allowing the twins
a new sense of camaraderie derived from a mutual victory—they
were no longer being told off (indeed, Mummy was telling Daddy
off)—after which they soon found something newly hysterical
to play, beginning the cycle all over again, but this time bypassing
the family-fun stage, and due to their new puffed-up sense of self
(Daddy was silent, and silence was a victory because he'd tried to use
noise to shut them up), tended towards the preternaturally stupid
and inane, even for six-year-olds.

McCullough was therefore pushed to the point where he said to Holly under his breath that any lesser man would turn the car off the road, drive it over a cliff and do them all a favour—a joke which Holly was *never* in the mood for, and somehow made her turn in her seat to face the children and see if reason and special pleading might have some effect, which if it did, would be a small victory for her. But it never did and never was, which was a smallish but worthless victory for McCullough, because by this point the air in the car had taken on a hysteria all of its own and seemed to vibrate with four very different energies, two of which were miserable and negative but somehow not quite enough to cancel out the positive energy of the twins having a fun time.

In his head, McCullough was asking himself, Why, why? It had been his idea to see Edward. A day of family bonding: Holly loved her father; he loved her father; and both imagined her father loved the twins in his own way. But the twins' presence exhausted him, their sheer potentiality drained his tiny reserves of energy. There was something Darwinian in the meeting of surging upwardness and inexorable collapse—only one was going to survive. No one claimed that things would be much different had Edward been fully mobile—the workplace, geopolitics, Western culture were what he liked to talk about; and he wanted his study door closed the moment his daughter or McCullough were inside. But these days the door remained open, parental eyes alert for trouble, minds not fully engaged.

When they arrived Edward was being hoisted from his wheel-chair into a reclining lounger in his study. His carer, Zena, lithe and competent, was dressed in leather trousers, her leather jacket slung over the banister, a powerful motorbike outside. She had been look-ing after Edward for three years. At his office, Edward had declared to McCullough that he'd composed some softly erotic doggerel about her, a woman he seemed unable to call beautiful, but described instead as athletic. The short poems were all based on her whisking him away on her bike to an historic European city. That all she was able to do for him was dress and undress him, help him shower, lift his buttocks to slide the harness under him, made the romance of them running away together touching, poignant, pitiful. What Zena made of these poems—Edward was unashamed of having recited them to her—McCullough couldn't think: he'd never spoken to her at length himself and knew only that she had been divorced twice, had three children, one described by Edward as 'delinquent', and played a lot of sport.

Holly had made lunch at home, and on arrival placed it in the oven to warm. McCullough made coffee. The twins needed to be coaxed into the study to say 'hello', a rare moment when they spoke with their backs straight and their hands at their sides. They visibly slumped when Edward's attempt at grandfatherly humour was to peer over his glasses and say, 'Well, I do hope you two aren't going to be naughty today.' He didn't seem to understand that children were mostly literalists and lived in the moment. McCullough watched them both give the question some thought and decide the chances were that they would be naughty, and so said nothing.

The house was large, sparsely furnished, with expensive objects placed on narrow surfaces. There were many lamps, and the chairs seemed fragile. The television was small, and the few children's films on video often got stuck in the ancient VCR. The garden was off limits after Walter, two years before, had pulled the head off every flower. He'd been uncontainable—the sheer pleasure of the pluck. McCullough had restrained him and brought him inside, but he escaped to finish the job. Edward seldom went outside these days, but the garden remained important to him, and his conversations with the gardener a highlight of his week. He admitted to being a little fanciful in believing that the garden was an expression of his former self, but there it was in vigorous bloom somewhere behind the pale orange curtain half drawn in his study.

Today, Edward had a surprise for his grandchildren. The cleaner had found some marbles. They had been his when he was a boy, and the twins could play with them if they promised not to lose any. Again there was a visible slump in their posture. Both knew it was not a promise they could make. Holly tried to mediate—she would help them find a place where it was impossible to lose them; but even then, they must try to be careful because they were Grandpa's when he was a boy, so were over sixty years old. This sentiment didn't mean much to the twins. All it did was make Edward less inclined to let the marbles go, even for a supervised session. Holly was a little sharp with him: they are only marbles; they don't break. The large black cotton drawstring bag was handed over to two pairs of hands, which struggled with the fickle dispersal of weight as the marbles rolled over each other; it was as if they'd been handed a live fish.

With some help from McCullough the bag was opened. In his keenness Walter turned the bag upside down and the marbles clattered out, a great tumult of clanking runaway balls, white, black and dully flashing. It was too much for Edward and his head drooped. Holly and McCullough were quickly on their knees, their hands like fins, corralling as many as they could onto the rug and back into the bag; the twins just stood there looking down. Messes like this were always baffling to them. It was impossible to determine whether all the marbles had been found, but McCullough decided to confirm they had been, after which Edward raised his head. Holly took the twins into the dining room, moved the furniture aside and showed them how to play. She shut the door behind her.

Half an hour later, back in her father's study, she held his coffee cup to his mouth so he could slurp it down. He drank his coffee all in one go, and proclaimed it good and strong. McCullough wondered how he could enjoy it at all that way.

Holly didn't like to ask her father how he was feeling, but rather tended to ask him general questions and infer from the answers how he felt. These questions were mainly about his work, visitors to the house, what he was reading. He enjoyed talking to her about her own work and was deadly serious about Brexit's impact on social-service provision for EU migrants. He was an active supporter of Amnesty International and had warned Holly that a meaningful part of what would have been her inheritance was allocated that way. There was a brief discussion about McCullough's recent meeting with the government, Edward mostly interested in the characters around the table. In his bookshelves behind him he had the diaries of Richard Crossman, 'Chips' Channon, Tony Benn.

It was only towards the end of the afternoon that the older man said, 'You two don't seem very . . . connected. Holly?'

His daughter was sitting in the armchair opposite him; it was McCullough's turn to stand in the doorway and listen out for the twins.

'Everything is fine, Dad.'

'Really? Proctor?'

'Yes, it's fine.'

'Still building your cathedral?'

There was a pause. 'We're using Pascal's mystical hexagon as a design motif.' Once again, so far from the action, it all seemed a great madness.

'We?'

'Simon is helping. You've met him—the mathematician.'

'You don't seem very impressed, Holly.'

'I don't want to talk about it.'

'You still haven't been down there?'

'You know I haven't.'

McCullough stepped forward. 'It's not really . . .' He stopped because he felt Holly was about to interrupt him, but she didn't.

Edward looked at his daughter. 'You're not the only one perplexed by Proctor's behaviour, but I do think we should give him the benefit of the doubt.'

McCullough saw Holly glance at him. He could read in her expression, inspired by her father's generosity, a willingness to do so, but he could also see her wonder why the instigator of such a unique and unpredictable crisis should be given the benefit of the doubt. At the same time, she realized that there he was in the doorway of her family home, a good friend to her father, keeping an ear open for the children—a good man.

'Maybe when it's all finished.'

'Do you think you'll live there?' It was the important question, directed to McCullough.

'Edward, I have no idea what I'm doing or what's going to happen. At the moment I'm having a *Mastermind* moment—I've started so I'll finish.'

'You're still having the—you know? Visions?' Then, 'I can't remember whether we've discussed Blake. Have you read much Blake?'

'They are never really visions, not like that. But, yes, I still appear to be open to something.' Holly's irritation was tangible. He was surprised she wasn't even more irked by her father's casual attitude to such talk, but suspected this was her way of being generous: she didn't want him to be cut off completely, and if her father was going to understand him, even if it meant going against his natural inclinations, that must be a good thing. Or perhaps she was more forgiving of McCullough in front of her father because, whatever the outcome of *their* relationship, she wanted him to be there for Edward.

'Look, you two, promise me you won't do anything silly. Final.' Edward looked at McCullough; his grey eyes were without warmth or humour. 'I can't pretend to understand what's going on exactly, but I do remember being miserable throughout my forties when I appeared to have everything I wanted. I blamed Thatcher, but I suspect it wasn't *all* her fault.

'And Holly, you're like me, you don't have any patience for the fanciful, at least not to the degree Proctor is being . . . ' He turned back to McCullough. 'When I say "fanciful", you understand, I know what you're feeling feels true to you, but to us it's almost barmy. Anyway—' Back to Holly: 'I think Tolstoy was wrong about unhappy families—they are all the same, it's called being unhappy. But it passes. Unhappiness passes—that should be part of any wedding vows.'

'We're not married, Dad.'

'Shame!'

There was a brief glance from Holly to McCullough. 'He still thinks you might leave me and run off with a floozy.'

'Surely, Edward, without marriage, every day requires a free act of love.'

'Sounds suspiciously hippy-dippy to me.' Edward laughed and his foot slipped off its metal platform. 'Would you put my foot back, please, Holly?'

Holly kneeled before her father, and lifted his foot up. McCullough could see his knees resist, and under the strain Holly's shoulder blades appear under her linen shirt.

'Thank you. I just want you two to be happy. I know that's a silly thing to say, but you do seem very good together—you always have done. And I'm too fond of Proctor here, whatever's going on, to have Holly behave like—'

'Don't say it, Dad.'

'Your mother is stubborn and selfish. Or at least she was. Who knows what life is like for her now? Have you heard from her?'

It was impossible to tell how he felt. Whether he really wanted news.

'A postcard. She seems fine. The same.'

'A mysterious woman. I often wonder how I ended up with such a woman—I tried so very hard to avoid that sort.' And as if Holly wasn't there, as if she'd suddenly been called out by screaming from the other room, he added, 'Holly is nothing like her mother. She's not mysterious.'

'Yes, I am, Dad!' She expressed mock hurt, but it seemed she concurred. Then, 'What's your point?'

'I worry, Holly, about the example we've set. Your mother has set.'

'Don't. I love Mum; she was a very good mother.' It was hesitantly said. She believed being a good mother and a good wife should be judged separately. For the thirty-five years when husband and wife hadn't really needed each other, and Kate was free for most of the day, she'd enjoyed preparing nice food, picking out good wine, recording those rare things on television her husband might enjoy, and, even rarer, they might enjoy together. But after Edward's multiple sclerosis diagnosis, when day by day she was being turned into an underappreciated carer to a man who found it easy to make demands without any real show of appreciation, she had fled. Holly had found her in Brittany, a woman almost beside herself with guilt and relief. She talked of Edward as if he'd been long dead.

'You're right, darling—let's not talk about this.'

McCullough found himself formulating the sentence 'You've got Zena now'—but he didn't say it.

'I'm not like Mum.' This wasn't said directly to either man; Holly's face was upturned, as if to make tears disperse. A prism of light, created by the moisture, floated before her eyes.

'Would you make some more coffee, Proctor?'

Edward needed one more shot of caffeine to get him to the end of the afternoon and the inevitable moment in the day when he needed to give his body up to Zena.

McCullough looked at his watch and listened for the children in the dining room. He heard marbles flicked across the wooden floor, the wobbling rolling, then the shattering sound of the impact, if they were lucky.

'Of course. Then we should think about going.'

In time he withdrew, made the coffee and packed what little they'd brought and loaded it in the car. He looked in on the twins and gave them a five-minute warning, making sure that Walter repeated it back to him. The two of them had, as they sometimes did, decided to be a loving brother and sister, and to play well together. A family of marbles had been created, as well as a school and hospital, and now and again, a war of spectacular devastation. He played with them for the five minutes and then offered them another five or ten before they were to go. They chose ten.

In the study, Holly wrapped her arm around her father for a hug, treating him delicately, despite his bulk. Edward was shy of physical contact, and his hands jerked as if to say 'unnecessary, but thank you'. Time was spent making sure everything was where it should be: phone, glasses, remote control for the radio, the newspaper—something he could still manipulate by dragging his knuckles across the page, using friction to draw the page over. He was a patient man when it came to these manoeuvres and like his daughter he was a precise and methodical reader, so taking a minute or so to turn a page didn't feel unnatural.

The children were presented to say goodbye. The marbles were back in their bag and Pearl placed them on the shelf, cradling up the few marbles dangling off the edge that promised, over time, to pull the whole bag to the floor. Holly set them straight. Edward thanked them again for a lovely lunch and reminded them that Zena would be there soon, so they shouldn't worry. It seemed more for his own benefit, to curtail any worry he might be feeling. To McCullough, he said that he'd be in town only one day this week, probably Friday. McCullough promised to drop by.

Holly gave her father a second hug, this time making sure he felt her, and hoped that whatever messages she wanted to send were received. He gave himself up to it, but there was still impatience—movement was stressful, inconvenient and tiring. McCullough stood with his hands on the shoulders of his children, who were both relieved that here was one person they weren't sent to kiss.

The front door was opened, and Edward called out, as if they were much further away, 'I hope I haven't been too intrusive!'

Holly called back, 'Of course not, Dad.'

And then he reaffirmed, just in case, his voice sounding more relaxed than it had since they arrived, 'Zena will be here soon.'

2

After McCullough had supervised the children's bath, while at the same time checking his emails (replying to those from Casper) and rearranging his diary so he could see Edward on Friday, he fell asleep for an hour. When he awoke, Holly was reading to the children. He went downstairs and scanned the TV listings. He decided they needed something engrossing. There was an award-winning documentary about a Formula One driver, but in that moment he didn't have the generosity to believe it could be that good, given the intrinsic nature of the subject: driving fast cars. He knew he was being simple-minded. It wasn't about speed; it was about the risk of obliteration, and, in this case, the *fact* of obliteration. But still, there would be a lot of fast cars being driven, which he doubted Holly would want to watch. There was a Wes Anderson film they'd both loved but Holly didn't like to watch films twice. McCullough paused the TV at the beginning of a modern Scandinavian horror film. He went into the kitchen and made tea, and while waiting for the kettle to boil, buttered some malt loaf and pushed a thick slice into his mouth. Too much, really. The richness of flavour and the slipperiness of the butter made him smile; lovely stuff. For a moment he understood why Walter tended to gobble up his food. He called up the stairs: 'I've made tea. Paused a film.'

In the sitting room, waiting for Holly, he looked around as Terry had done, at the framed photos on the shelves, paintings and photographs on the walls, including one by Marvin of a pale, voluptuous woman sunbathing in a bikini in Regent's Park. There were vestigial handprints on every surface, other stains; for some reason the corners of the rug were curling up. On the mantelpiece he noticed an opened tampon packet, tampons emerging like oversized cigarettes. The twins still interrupted the pace of life so suddenly that a box of tampons could end up on the mantelpiece. He heard Holly moving upstairs, guiding a sleepy Pearl to the lavatory. He could picture Pearl sitting there, her feet not yet touching the floor, Holly standing in the doorway, ready to pass over the balled-up toilet paper in her hand. On the occasions he waited with Pearl himself, she tried to talk to him, wake herself up; but often she was so asleep he had to wipe her himself, a kind of cursory smudge of the paper. He liked taking her back to bed, placing both hands on her shoulders and manoeuvring her to the room, watching her arrange herself into a sleeping position, a little compact, plump Z, before he finally pulled the duvet over her. Before he kissed her, he gently swept away the hair that had fallen over her face, something he imagined she must want done, although she never seemed to care enough to do it herself.

Tonight Holly came down, wearing mismatched pyjamas, a bottle of cleanser and a cotton-wool pad in her hand, and a transparent sausage-shaped bag of pads hanging by a drawstring from her fingers. Her face looked bright, fresh, a little enlarged from the first wipes with cleanser. Her hairline was damp. She looked at her tea and said, 'Thank you.' Sitting on the sofa, she placed a large square cushion between herself and McCullough, which she used to tuck her bare feet under.

'What's the film?' He pressed a button that displayed a description. 'Great. Put it on.' She was always eager for films to start. It didn't matter that she might need to finish something, in this case dabbing cleanser on to her cheeks with a fresh pad. McCullough on the other hand needed a period of stillness, of readiness before a film began. He waited.

'Everything go OK?' He looked to the ceiling.

'Yes. They were lovely as usual.'

It was in her nature to forget that they'd ever been horrors when they were not being horrors.

'What were you reading to them?'

'Start the film.' She was close to finishing, a small pile of pads on the coffee table, the final one in her hand, folded in half, taking up the last of the cream. He pressed the button, fast-forwarding through a couple of ads, hitting play a second too late and necessitating a rewind, which despite an almost immediate press of play again seemed to take them back to where they'd been.

'Sorry.'

She smiled at him. What irritated him didn't irritate her. They reached for their tea and sipped, cradling the cups near their bodies. It was eight o'clock. Outside, in terms of activity, it was still very much day. Only the colour of the sky, its deepening shade of blue, made it feel like evening. McCullough tried not to be distracted by people passing by on the street, their shadowy presence against the shutters. There were times when the world beyond his house seemed a kind of anarchy, a place that was cold and hostile, and on some level in possession of a will of its own. Why he'd ever let his children go out into this world alone, he didn't know. Why did *he* ever go out into it? He looked over at Holly, who was watching the screen with her usual steady gaze, content to give herself over to the story. Was this how he was letting her down, by adding to the chaos . . . the fear of chaos? Did she worry that when he was down at the site he was on the outside, and when he returned he might bring something terrible with him?

He drew in a deep breath. Perhaps he should tell her about the post-apocalyptic world he'd described in the meeting at the Home Office two days before. It didn't look much different from the one outside now: there were no blasted landscapes, dead trees, hordes of scavengers, the weak and beautiful turned into catamites. But the psychic space would be new, and from that he wondered, if we looked deeply enough, we might see something blasted behind people's eyes. Was he right in what he predicted, in terms of the psychic fallout, the epochal change in our world view?

McCullough shook his head. Faced with such a future, steering the car off a road and over a cliff's edge seemed the only answer; obliteration the best option. Maybe they should have watched the documentary about the racing driver after all.

3

'I just worry it's never going to be the same again. I know on the surface you turn up and settle back in, but that's just because you have to. But you are changed. Sometimes I look at you and you look haunted. Maybe it's all the sleeping out, or maybe it's something else—how can I know? You've lost weight. You seem so disconnected, you might as well not be here. I'm frightened, Mac. You don't seem to care how much money this is costing. I don't know what you're prepared to risk. I feel panicked all the time. I can't pretend that I don't, or that I think it will be OK—I mean that we'll be all right in the end. If that were the case, everything would be fine. But that's always the case, isn't it?'

Holly looked at him. The argument had started as they stood either side of their big bed. Something had been said and then for ten minutes they discussed things openly, almost with relief, as if Edward's advice had been taken, and they now felt able to look at things objectively. But it didn't last long. The moment McCullough seemed too carefree about the impact of what he was doing, Holly felt like she'd given him permission to talk about a former lover and his eagerness to do so was selfish and hurtful, unthinking. How dare he?

He had stopped undressing: there was nothing in his tone that was carefree. What had she heard? What was she listening out for? Of course he was sensitive to her feelings, but she had asked him to explain what he was feeling and he was trying to do that.

She sat on the side of the bed and sighed; they were getting nowhere.

McCullough said, 'Then tell me how you feel?'

'I'm just so cross with myself. None of this is a shock. Not really. But I still can't handle it . . .' She looked down at her hands, ran a nail around the cuticle of her index finger.

'What I don't understand is why you're not prepared to accept this is all about you. It's all just *you*. And I don't mean that as a criticism, but as a fact. *You* are going through something. It's got nothing to do with God.' There was a shuffling noise outside on the landing; they both looked to the open door, but it was nothing: a breeze rustling the plant in the bathroom. Holly looked directly at McCullough and took a deep breath, as if in that moment she needed extra strength to look kindly on him, knowing that deep down this was what she believed and she must express it. 'If you want to know what I think . . . All this is about you being worried you're not a good person. You've always worried about why you're so easy to dislike—your words—even if you say you don't care. Maybe you didn't care before, but now you're a father you do, because it matters.

'It's taken us this long to get over the two years' lack of sleep, to feel normal again, and now you're asking yourself what it all means. Remember, before the twins were born, when you asked me whether bad people could be good parents? I'm not sure I took much notice because you're not a bad person. But now you're confronted with being a parent for the rest of your life, and it's not as though we have two easy children. Maybe your love for Walter has overwhelmed you and your difficulties with Pearl make you feel bad. Or maybe it's about how we've changed. But you're not going to find the answer *out there*. All that we can do is make choices and hope that they are the right ones and that as few people as possible get hurt . . .' She was aware she'd strayed into platitudes.

He smiled. 'You're right.' And she was. But it didn't mean that what was happening wasn't the case. It didn't cancel out the other thing.

She was emboldened by his agreement. 'What I don't understand . . . what I've never understood, is why everything can't begin and end with us, human beings. Why can't being moral, *being good*, be part of our evolution? I don't see these things as incompatible. I've never understood why evolution has to be selfish, or only selfish. Who decided that?

'But God . . . isn't that just us looking out there because it's much easier than looking at ourselves? We can give certainties to God that just aren't present in the world. Because that's all you're doing: looking for proof that to be good is to be Good. Or if you knew what was Good, you could just do that.' She paused; wasn't it that simple? Didn't he see that? 'One of the first things we're taught at law school is that rights are so much more efficient at protecting us—individuals, groups—than notions of the Good. If we have rights, it doesn't matter what someone thinks is good for us—they can't make us conform. Or dispose of us. And the reason we need this is because there is never going to be a moment when we all sign up for a single vision of what it means to be good. I know I am being simple-minded, but every day I see people who are the result of other people *deciding* to be bad—really bad . . . because they believe what they are doing is directed by God and therefore can't be wrong . . . because God is Good. People will inflict unimaginable harm on defenceless people in the service of the Good. I know you say that's religion, that's man, and not God, but I'm not sure that matters.'

She noticed he was looking down at his feet. He seemed sad, lost, as if she was somehow telling him off for something he knew couldn't be otherwise. But she needed to finish making her point; it might make a difference if he understood her. 'Mac, acts are decisions taken within a context. Monstrous acts, acts of goodness. There is no supreme evil or good. What does that even mean? How's it helpful?

'If we accept that we are dealing with people and what they can do, what they might be driven to do, or even do on a whim—it's something we can get at, make sense of, and perhaps change. We can create laws and institutions to protect us. Because that's really the only question we need to solve: how do we manage all the people on this earth? And we either decide human beings commit horrible acts because they choose to, and we do our best to manage that, or we decide a great Evil is acting through them which can only be fought by a great Good. And look where thinking that got us. Gets us.' She took a deep breath. 'I know you know this. But you don't see it day to day like I do. You don't see the extremes of life day to day. I don't want to be . . . I mean I don't want to say it . . . but it's easy to think about God and how to be good when you're not faced with this stuff. And when you are, well, you don't have the time.'

She was right, again, in a way. And he had no answer for her. He scratched his head. 'Calvin thought we were *all* totally depraved.'

'He was probably speaking mostly about himself. As most of us do when we make such harsh judgments. Look, Mac, even if someone were to come along and prove His existence—it wouldn't remedy anything. Look at the world. I'm never going to accept a God who has allowed all this suffering, whatever the grand plan. Because that's the argument, isn't it? We can't know what He has planned and therefore . . . what? I don't know. But I know what we're left with if we can't prove His existence—a kind of unregulated, free-for-all superstition, which is dangerous. Mac, trust me, you don't need God to be good. You just need to be good. Or to try harder to be good. That's enough. I'm so sorry, Mac—it all seems so . . . unnecessary.'

What could he say? It was in her nature to translate the world into a set of propositions that made sense. When he said things that were plainly ungraspable, she believed he was being deliberately obscure. Surely everything he wanted to understand could be explained using concrete terms, if only he were willing. But that wasn't what was at stake now. The incompatibility between how they saw the world was now so marked they feared not understanding each other on even the minor issues. Relationships couldn't be conducted like international diplomacy, where larger agreements could be built from small points of compromise. On some level, Holly had to accept that he might not be wrong: that our capacity for love comes from a bestowal by God, if only we look deep enough within ourselves. Was it really madness to wonder whether there might be an ultimate source to our love, a condition of possibility? He didn't require her wholesale acceptance, *her* conversion: just an openness to the notion that there might be something beyond the immanent, the material, known only by reason. But then she had trouble with this notion of 'acceptance' or 'openness'—it sounded like an ultimatum, a threat.

'Holly, I can't have you thinking I'm so totally wrong that I must be mad to think it. Which is, deep down, what it seems like. You should give me the benefit of the doubt. Isn't this at the heart of Pascal's Wager? Neither of us can be certain, but there is something profoundly hopeful in wagering one way and not the other.'

'Is that what you're doing—wagering?'

'It's not what it feels like, no.'

'But I'm supposed to?'

There was a pause. He adjusted his genitals. Holly noticed and raised her eyebrows. McCullough smiled wryly; we are physical selves as well, after all. 'Tell me, what do you tell other people? I mean those you can't discuss this with in quite the same way as with friends.'

'I don't know what you mean.'

'I was just wondering what language you use. What would you say if someone asks you if you believe in God, and then asked whether I do—what would you say?'

'I'd say I didn't and you did.'

'We could leave it at that.'

Holly looked at him. Was this a solution? No. 'It's not that simple. It isn't simply that you believe in God, is it? You're being disingenuous.'

'No, I'm not. I'm trying to find a way we can move on.'

'Mac, it's not about moving on. You're changed. I know you don't think so.'

'I do think so, but—'

'That's the thing: the "but" is OK for you. But not for me. It means you feel different. I don't feel close to you anymore—and I've always felt close to you before.' She paused. 'It's like you've been replaced by someone I can't connect to.'

He'd moved to the small sofa in the bay window of their bedroom and was sitting down, legs open, hands in his lap; he felt completely done in.

'Maybe you're right, in the sense that I must feel different because part of me is being taken up by all this, a part of me that has access to the whole, if that makes sense. And you're right, I'm disconnected because I feel that I'm being prepared somehow and I am on guard against that. But trust me when I say nothing bad will happen. I love you. I love the children.'

'You love everyone.'

'Really? That's what you've taken from all this? Have I ever said that?'

'Isn't that what you're supposed to feel—love thy neighbour as thyself?' She was so miserable. Pitiable.

'Maybe, maybe not. Maybe I'll receive a new instruction: "Love thy neighbour as thyself, but not as much as Holly and the twins." Would that be OK?'

Her misery was the kind of forlornness that could afford a brief and uncommitted smile. She shook her head. Would she accept a promise of priority, at least for tonight?

'I don't know what to say, Mac.'

'There is nothing to say. It's late.'

Pulling back her side of the duvet, she asked, 'Did you close the bathroom window?' The sill was low enough for a child to fall out. He went to check.

On his return, Holly was in bed, her book open on her lap. He lay down next to her, his book face down. 'Do you think we'll look back on this and laugh?'

'Cry, more like.'

'You mean with laughter?'

'Maybe *you* will.' She didn't smile.

He wanted her to be less hurt than she was, to be less sad, but he knew that wasn't up to him, and that he had no power over how she felt. If he had he could just commit to love her more, to show it more, prove it. But her hurt lay with her own self. He was to blame, yes, but it was she who was responsible for loving him less.

PART FOUR

Thou Shalt Not I

THE FOUR GOSPELS I

'Not I, not I, but the wind that blows through me!'

D. H. LAWRENCE,

SONG OF A MAN WHO HAS COME THROUGH

I

It was high summer. McCullough stood at the top of the bank under the oak in a rich warm shade. On the lowest branches, the small leaves were sparse and dull, an undistinguished green. Higher up they were denser, a muddle of darker shades. At the top, in the floating dimness, they were in silhouette, within which small broken shapes of sunlight sparkled. Where the sun found its way through unimpeded, the light was heavy, viscous, almost solid, and yet as it spread and pooled on the ground it seemed to darken from contact with the dampness that seeped up from the earth.

Marvin had said he'd be back, but it was Simon who had returned, keen to talk to Rebecca and Nathaniel about the finer points of Pascalian geometry. He'd called McCullough to update him on what was happening. Rich had announced his feelings to Rebecca, a side-on mumbling that finished with him standing with his back to her. She had been understanding, but the situation had become common knowledge around the site, and it wasn't just the four of them anymore; each day new workmen arrived, and Rich had found himself being teased and had retreated to the periphery of the work, confiding only in Nathaniel, who for some reason had convinced Rich that if he really loved Rebecca he shouldn't accept defeat. For a while, Nathaniel acted as love's envoy, and while he did his best to understand Rebecca's point of view ('forget it—it will never happen'), and relay it back with honesty and precision, he was more loyal to Rich and gave him more hope than perhaps he should have done. It seemed they were both optimists by nature and believed Rebecca could be won over (ground down) by true feeling, or at least an expression of it they had yet to find.

Terry had become impatient with them all. He had seen a doctor and had various tests, including a colonoscopy, the recounting of which lightened his mood, but nothing ('sinister'—doctor's word; 'ominous'—Rebecca's word) was found, except that Terry was now diagnosed as a clinical alcoholic and slightly anaemic. In general he set himself apart from the team and read his small Bible and other books he dragged around in his holdall. There were episodes of sudden belligerence, eruptions of aggression, but these were usually with subcontractors who it was agreed by all had been mouthy or cocky. Rebecca found her charms were usually enough to calm the situation down. Nathaniel, who had continued to be uncomfortable in direct conversation with Terry, at one point appeared to have stepped over an invisible line, and Rebecca had needed to send Terry home. More and more it had become Nathaniel and Rebecca's site. Terry insisted he was to be consulted on all important decisions, but was often absent, in too much pain, or, towards the end of the day, drunker (due to the painkillers) than he was able to handle, and slept next to the fire.

A small crane had been brought in; its caterpillar tracks, careless of the ancient grass, left their imprint everywhere. Huge panels of glazing were stacked and covered in plastic. Within the rectangle of the church walls there was now a twelve-metre-wide cylinder made out of thick white stone, the conic section into which the hexagon, tilted at a sixty-degree angle, would fit. The rough surface of the stone wall made it look like an ancient's approximation of a circle and because of this it seemed, at least to McCullough, more powerfully shaped than anything smoother.

Terry said its radius was millimetre-perfect. The only other thing in his holdall apart from books was the theodolite, a gift from Simon, and he'd become an adept. A large groove had been cut in the conic to take the sides of the hexagon, from which the extended lines would protrude. Then, emerging from the ground and finishing somewhere in the sky, the final intersecting beam would cross the three V shapes made by extensions of the hexagon's sides. What thrilled McCullough was that a space once meant to be sacred would now appear more like an artwork, but was really a geometrical theorem projected into three dimensions. That this had been suggested by his old friend Simon, and embraced by his new friends, moved him deeply. Yet he couldn't relax and felt an unplaceable worry. Gone were the pastoral setting, the team milling around, the semi-private language they'd created to get things done. It might have looked like a building site before, but this was of an altogether different order: there were men in hard hats and hi-vis jackets shouting into walkie-talkies, SUVs parked up, two vans, two skips, a crane with a yellow cabin turning on an invisible axis.

Rebecca was the first to see him, and called to Nathaniel, having cocked her head in his direction. Rich was sitting on the sheets of glass at the far end of the site, bandana and sunglasses on. Scanning everyone twice, McCullough couldn't see Terry.

After a brief chat to a man with a big beard, Nathaniel followed Rebecca up the ridge. He pulled drawings from his back pocket: basic sketches from a structural engineer, a friend of Simon's, with columns of calculations only he and the builders understood. McCullough tried to follow. 'It's simple, really,' Nathaniel assured him.

McCullough wanted to ask about Terry, but equally needed to know whether what was going on before him was madness, nonsensical, a great act of hubris. He turned to Rebecca.

'Does any of this make sense to you?'

'Of course.' She was in jeans, her hands pushed down in her pockets; it was the gesture of a builder confident of her work. Like her shoulders and her upper arms, her hips were brown and glistening. Poor Rich.

'How's Rich?'

'A pain.' It wasn't said meanly, but as a fact.

'It happens to us all. How else is a man to come in contact with his heart?'

'Why me?'

'I want to say because God places women like you around the world to do this very job.'

'I don't think so.'

'It's a theory that is more true in reality.' Then, 'Where's Terry?'

Nathaniel answered, although he knew the question was meant for Rebecca. 'Not here. He turns up now and again. He's become a bit of a liability, Mac.'

Rebecca explained, 'He's not eating at all now; he just drinks and smokes. And he's become obsessed in the way only Terry can by what is and isn't true in the Bible. You might want to take the blame for that.'

'I'll go and see him.'

Nathaniel said, 'He'll turn up,' clearly in no hurry for this to happen.

'Is there anything I can do, generally?'

'It's your project, Mac. Get your hands dirty, my son.' Nathaniel's working man's voice was full of wrong notes, part TV Dickens, part Dick Van Dyke.

'I wouldn't try that down there, Nat—you might get beaten up.'

Rebecca laughed. 'He does, and they kind of like it.'

2

McCullough sat alongside Rich on the thick plates of glass and said nothing for a while. When he opened the conversation, it was with a question about Terry. How did he look? How were his moods? But Rich had only one thought on his mind: how could Rebecca have gone out with Terry? It wasn't in Rich's nature to say anything specifically unkind, but he also felt others should be able to see what was plain to him.

McCullough had answers but knew none would help, and to reassure Rich that whatever pain he was feeling now would eventually go away was a banal truth, anathema to love. He also knew an offer of comradeship with a description of a comparable experience, with the opportunity to parse the shared feelings for general learning, would feel like a kind of mockery. Right now, Rich was focused on his own particular pain, a highly discrete set of feelings that he considered unique to him, and rightly so. What did he care about those things McCullough had learned after the breaking and partial mending of his own heart all those years ago? What was the use of being told that, irrespective of whatever happened with Rebecca, strength of feeling was important in itself—it was what made you a richer person, a fuller human being? One insight McCullough thought might be of some use was his own late acknowledgement that love and the erotic weren't indivisible, which meant Rich could settle for just loving Rebecca. Equally, if he was lucky enough to have an erotic encounter with Rebecca he could be content with that and not require her to love him back. Downgrading the erotic in favour of love was a disingenuous position. After all: love's own lust is to fuck.

So what could he say to help the boy? There was always suggest there was a similarity between unrequited love and a yearning for God to reveal Himself—both included an intransigent love-object. And both ended the same way: face-to-face with a blank, leaving us the choice to continue to love or resist it. It was extraordinary how few people chose the latter, even though what one imagined was supposed to feel bounteous, vivid, ecstatic, actually felt like a dull and plummeting emptiness where your heart or stomach or bowel were once located. He supposed he could argue that embracing the emptiness would transform it into a feeling of bounty. But it wouldn't be fair on the boy. It wasn't true.

In the end, after much thought and interruptions by workmen he didn't know, and who didn't introduce themselves, but nevertheless addressed him as Mac, he said, with a pat on the boy's knee, 'I feel for you, Rich. If you want to talk about anything, I'm here.'

There was no response.

3

Rebecca gave McCullough directions. She wasn't enthusiastic for him to go and suggested accompanying him. 'You know what he's like. It'll piss him off.' McCullough assured her everything would be fine—hadn't Terry turned up at his house unannounced?

It took him longer than he had anticipated. The estate of small houses was large and sprawling, and every street was the same as the next. The roads were narrow, the pavements wide, cars parked up on verges. The front gardens were small and square, mostly overgrown with thick grass; some had white goods left out in the centre, doors open or pulled off. Fences dividing the gardens were mostly broken down or rotten, occasionally replaced by iron rails. The skeletons of motorcycles were dumped against walls. Sunlight seemed to reach everywhere. Bare-chested men stood in doorways. They didn't recognize the sound of the car. The presence of an outsider was felt. When McCullough found the right road, he parked where there was a wide space.

Terry was sitting in the front garden, on a red, white and blue garden chair, the hollow metal frame leaning a little to the right. There was a large blue and white plastic cooler next to him. He was reading and didn't break his concentration until he sensed McCullough stop at the gate. When he glanced up, there was no surprise in his eyes. He took a breath and pushed himself out of the chair. There was a twinge of pain in his side.

'You found me.'

'Are you hiding?'

'It's all got a bit professional for me down there.'

'I know what you mean.'

'You coming in?'

McCullough unlatched the gate. Terry went inside the house. Another chair was brought out, unfolded without care for its obvious fragility, and plonked down. Terry tested it for basic stability on the grass. 'There you go. I'd introduce you to me old lady but she'd only think she'd forgotten you from somewhere—unnecessary stress for the old girl.'

McCullough looked down at the book on Terry's chair and read out the author's name. 'Géza Vermes . . .'

'Yeah. Deep shit. You want a beer?' Clutching his side, Terry leaned over and grabbed a can and handed it over to McCullough; it was warm. 'You fussy about warm beer?' There was a new, sharper edge to Terry's charm; his laughter had gone; the smile was genuine but somehow tighter, less generous. McCullough declined the beer. Terry placed it back in the cooler and sat back in his chair. He appeared to need to arrange himself, to distribute his weight so it didn't fall against or crush something in his stomach, as someone might who has a broken rib. He winced.

'I'm here to see if you're OK?'

'Just soaking in some rays.'

'You're still in pain.'

'Yeah. Need to improve me diet. I told the doc I was an ascetic. That I was going to sit on top of a pole—you heard of those people?'

'Yes.'

'Anything you don't know about?' The irritation showed in a flash—there, but quickly gone.

'You're missed.'

'I'm a natural leader, what can I say?'

'You seem grumpier than normal.'

'So would you be if your guts was playing up like mine.' He leaned forward gingerly and picked up his rollie pouch. 'They've even had a good look up me anus.'

'I've been told.'

'Journey through an arsehole via his arsehole. The nurse laughed at that one. I fucking loved the drugs they give you.'

'It seems to be in your side, like your kidney.'

'Displaced pain.'

'And that's the only reason you're so grumpy?'

'I don't appear to be filled with God's light. Not sure He approves of me.' For a moment he looked directly at McCullough, his hands finishing his roll-up. 'And don't tell me God loves us all.' He licked the adhesive strip.

'I'm interested in what you mean by "God".'

'"Course you are.'

'Well?'

'You were right about that shit—explaining what you mean.'

'It's impossible.'

'I wouldn't say that. It's just you've got to do a lot of graft.'

'Tell me.'

'You know me, always looking for who's doing the lying. Who's hiding what. I reckon they've been lying about God and doing a good job of it.'

'Who's "they"?'

'All of them. Any cunt who opens his mouth about God. You sure you don't want a beer? Weather for it.'

'Sure.'

'How's the family?'

'Good.'

'Missus?'

'Well . . .'

A rare laugh.

'Come back to the site.'

'You're all right.'

There was a long silence. 'I'm worried about you, Terry.'

'Why's that, then?'

'You were out of sorts when I was last down, and the others, they say—'

'What is it *they* say?'

McCullough knew he'd been caught out. He had just admitted they'd talked about him (a mistake), so he couldn't now deny it, but knew if he tried to hide it, he'd be sneered at: too easily intimidated. Terry didn't like to be appeased. Was this how he started fights?

'You're in pain, keeping yourself to yourself, getting a little . . . *lairy*.'

'That's about right. None of your business, though, is it?'

'Yes and no.'

'I'm a moody bugger. Ask me old girl. Ask Rebs. I deserve a slap, but no one wants to give it to me. How about you? You fancy it?' The eye contact was not broken until Terry pulled back and laughed. 'You don't want to take me on, Mac . . .'

'Come down to the site.'

'You think the work will be good for me? Take me out of myself? I'll just end up punching someone. Best to leave me alone. Let the drugs do their work. Besides, I'm reading a couple of books a day.'

'A couple?'

'Not getting much sleep.'

'Terry, you need better help than you're getting. Let me sort something out.'

'I don't mind people poking about, but I'm not shifting from here.'

'I'll drive you to London.'

'Now?'

'No—when I can get you an appointment with someone.'

'You're all right. I've got God on my side. Actually, I'm not sure I have. Maybe I'm an agent for the other side.'

'There is no other side.'

Hee-hee.

Terry finished his beer by rocking the fragile chair back and tipping the can up vertically. McCullough saw the last drops of beer drip onto Terry's tongue.

'I'm on the old incapacity benefit now, and she gets disability benefit. Keeps me in lager.'

'Terry, this is fucked up.'

'Just winding you up. I'm a good carer. Good son. I have a real sense of duty.'

There it was, this new drunkenness Rebecca had mentioned, playful and sarcastic yet alert for disagreement or overeager agreement, for condescension.

'Can I make you some food, Terry?'

'You hungry?'

'Are *you*?'

'I'm not a big eater.'

McCullough stood. 'Is there anything in there you'll eat?'

'You can't go in. You'll scare the old girl.'

'Then take me in, introduce me, and let me make you something to eat.'

'I'd have to get up to do that and I don't want to get up. I like it here. Who wouldn't?'

What could McCullough say? 'You're depressed, Terry. You don't even want to get out of your chair.' He looked down at him. 'What meds are you on?'

'All sorts.'

'Any antidepressants?'

'I reckon so.'

Terry needed to shield his eyes to see McCullough. 'Sit down, will you. Look, I'll tell you what, if I ever go back in, I'll eat an apple. How about that?' He opened another can of beer.

'You have to go back in—what about your mother?'

'You speak the truth. When I go back in.'

'How bad is she?'

'If I let her have a feel of me old chin beads, she remembers who I am.'

'It must be hard.'

'She was never exciting company at the best of times.'

'What did she do?'

'Dinner lady. Always a bit embarrassing when your son never turns up to school.'

'And your father?'

'You'll never believe it, he was a drunken sailor. I mean, what are you going to do?'

McCullough sat down and was content to be silent. Terry lit his cigarette, fingers dark from sun, dirt, nicotine; the blackness under his nails was packed in. Around his wrist a loose weave of some material had matted and hardened. His feet were bare and the same colour as his fingers, darker even, his soles black. Above his ankles his skin was pale and hairless.

'Come back.'

'You keep saying that but I'm afraid I don't think I'm getting out of this chair. There is as much chance of me getting out of this chair as of me being able to convert base metal into gold.'

'What about when the beer runs out?'

'Ah—you see, is that really getting out of me seat? I mean it is, but then again it isn't, if I return to me seat.'

McCullough regarded Terry softly, with heartfelt concern, but was careful to hide it, knowing he would interpret it as pity, which it was. But then he realized it didn't matter how he looked at Terry: the boy wasn't really there, he was deep inside the satisfaction he was giving himself by offering up his own kind of clarity on the big questions. He was more drugged than McCullough had realized.

There was nothing left to say. He could suggest he throw the chair and cooler in the boot, set Terry up down at the site just as he was, where he could be content that he hadn't left his chair but was just located somewhere else. Try and convince him that the site needed his presence. It wasn't true, of course, and Terry was too smart and unsentimental to believe him. He'd scoff, knowing full well it was McCullough who needed him. He and Rebecca both knew they were lightning rods for him, attracting versions of truth that kept him sane, like high-tension cables pulling at each side of his body to keep him upright.

'Do it for me, Terry. As a favour.' Why did he persist? Did he feel responsible for Terry's state of mind? He knew enough about general health to recognize an organic condition. But organic conditions had triggers, and it was naïve to deny that Terry's involvement in the project might have been a trigger of some kind. What particularly troubled McCullough was that he was making judgments about Terry in the same way as his own friends were judging him. Indeed, the only difference between Terry right now and himself, at least from his friends' perspective, was that he slept and ate reasonably well, and wasn't an alcoholic.

'Perhaps we're going through something similar, Terry.' It didn't feel like an admission of an organic mental illness of his own.

'Yeah, Mac, you're building a church; I want to sit in my chair. You want to spread the love; I feel like killing someone.'

'Fine lines, Terry.'

'Lines nonetheless, my friend.'

'I want to help you.'

'Of course you do. Maybe God sent me—to test you.'

'I don't believe that . . . in that.'

'Do you reckon . . . you know . . . do you believe a revelation, you know like you've had . . . can make you do something? I mean the fucking shock of it? That He overwhelms you so much, you think: fuck it, I'll kill someone—that'll be a test. The only test.

Take a fucking chainsaw and cut some fucker's head off. I mean that would test His love, wouldn't it? I mean, if you felt God's love after that—that would be it, wouldn't it? Proof.' Terry laughed to himself and took a slurp out of his beer can, his tongue hanging out.

'You remind me of a character out of Dostoevsky.'

'Which one?'

'Maybe all of them.'

Terry's stare was fierce—was this man taking the piss? Then he burped. Finally laughed. 'I'll have to read the fucker now.'

'You might want to start with *The Brothers Karamazov*.'

McCullough stood and looked up at the bedroom windows, dirty with smears. Someone had made an effort to clean them, but it looked as though a hand had just rubbed away an arc to see out.

'I'll be back tomorrow, Terry.'

'You know where to find me.' He didn't look up; it was said to the empty chair. His gaze was glassy, laughter hollow.

'Look at me, Terry.'

An upward glance required a painful swivel of his head, as if his neck was weak and his head heavy, not unlike the way Edward moved these days. 'Yes, Proctor McCullough, what is it?'

'Don't do anything stupid.'

'I promise. I'll be here tomorrow. I'll be awaiting your visit. You're a man I can trust and I've not said that about many men. I wish you well.'

'And I wish you well, Terry.'

He watched Terry's head swing back down to his chest. There was a pause, another burp, and then, churned up from his throat, a pained and angry: 'Now, fuck off.'

4

At the cliff's edge, McCullough and Nathaniel were joined by Pete, a youngish man with a halo of soft frizzy curls of an enviable rust colour. His skin was pale and freckled. He held his hard hat under his arm like a soldier might his cap before an officer. Nathaniel had pointed him out moments ago: he was project-managing the local teams; it was useless one of *them* trying to explain stuff to trades-people. Pete was a stonemason.

A photocopy of the original drawings from the structural engi-neer were produced. Pete smoothed it open and snapped out what he could of the folds. There was something that needed signing off. While McCullough was away boreholes had been made into the ground to reassure building control that the subsoil was indeed sand—which it was *in most places*—but they'd also found chalk. Chalk wouldn't hold the structure. Pete traced the hexagon, the extended lines and the angled beam, with his forefinger. It was 'no biggie', he assured McCullough, but it would require an increase in the size of the steels that made up the hexagon and *maybe* a decrease in the long beam, to be on the super-safe side. What did he think?

'All we found was sand.'

Pete laughed.

McCullough stared at the piece of paper without really seeing anything. 'I don't want the building to fall down.'

'Just go for the larger steels.'

'Is there any way I can see what it might look like, in terms of the change to the dimensions?'

''Course. I'll mock it up. You'll hardly notice the difference.'

McCullough stood for a moment looking out over the calm sea, a uniform bright blue except for darker patches where currents created small waves of tension.

He turned to Nathaniel. 'Let's walk down to the water.'

The rent in the cliff was jagged and the geology of the land vis-ible—sand, chalk, layers of limestone. Nat wore thick work gloves of a suede-type material. He took them off and shoved them deep into his pockets.

'How are things at home, Nat?'

'Fine. Good. Stephen's back in London, so everyone's a little more relaxed.'

'He was a piece of work.'

'Nasty piece of work, I think the saying goes.' Nathaniel was relaxed, his body language easy.

'You seem very content on the site. Project-managing the project manager.'

'It's cool.'

'You sound like Rich.'

He laughed.

'You haven't fallen for Rebecca, then?'

Nathaniel laughed again. 'She's cool.'

'It seems you're the cool one.'

There was a pause.

'Mac?'

'Yes?'

'If I didn't want to go back to university. Or be an actor . . . If I wanted to do this . . . do what Pete does. Something like that. Something like I'm doing now. Would you speak to my parents about it?'

McCullough laughed. 'Rebecca said Rich had asked you to talk to her, to make his case?'

'I didn't do very well.'

'Don't you think you should talk to your parents yourself first— see what happens? Just in case. They might be more defensive if I'm there as well.'

'I wasn't thinking of being there at all.'

'You'd have to be there; it'd be weird otherwise.'

'Not if it was somehow an accident you were with them alone. You could come to lunch. I'd get Rebecca to call me. Reception is really bad in the dining room so I'd have to leave . . .'

'So you have a plan?'

'They'd listen to you.'

'You'd be surprised how unconvincing I am to a certain type of person.'

He sensed Nathaniel's disappointment: he'd been let down again. It was a gift, in its own way, this ability to show his feelings without shame or embarrassment. Whether or not it was passive-aggressive (McCullough couldn't help but feel it was), it was also a kind of

emotional honesty, a willingness to show vulnerability, disappointment, even irritation, at not getting his own way, in a manner few
adults were able or willing to do.

'Are you sure it's what you want?'

'Totally. Isn't it obvious?'

'Yes. But they're going to be worried about things right now that
you don't care about.'

'And never will.'

'Hold on. Let's make sure of that. They have a vision for you. Of
you. And my guess is it's fairly narrow, but not unattractive to many
people. Most of them would be envious of your opportunities. That's
how they will see it. And they will want you to be happy.'

'I am happy. Doing this.'

'Now.'

McCullough sensed this was a greater disappointment because
it was exactly what his parents would say. The muscles in Nathaniel's
jaw tensed; his mouth went tight; he frowned. It was a neat trick—it
made McCullough somehow feel like an imposter, as if he'd promised
something that he was unable to deliver.

'Hold on, Nat. Let's not get all sulky about this. You think the
win here is your parents going, "Oh, yes, well, of course that's fine,
darling." But that's not going to happen—the win here is them just
not saying "no" and seeing some sense in it. We have to get them to
slightly refocus their vision.'

'So you will talk to them?'

'Isn't it better if you do it?'

'I don't understand why you won't help me.'

'What am I doing now?'

'Saying you won't help me.'

'Nat—give me a break. We're talking it through. That's helping you.'

'Maybe.' He picked up a pebble and disconsolately skimmed it
into the water.

Was it worth making clear to Nathaniel that he possessed aspects
of obstinacy and self-belief—what was traditionally called a thick
skin—that probably meant he would succeed in whatever it was he
wanted to do?

'I do sense, Nat, you will do what you want. In the end. And you will be fine.'

Nathaniel didn't want to hear this—it sounded like he was being fobbed off.

McCullough went on. 'You have abilities, a certain charm— you'll be an asset anywhere.'

Did Nathaniel shrug? McCullough recognized that frustrating paradox that comes with an certain kind of conceitedness: Nathaniel demanded positive endorsements of his character, and yet when they were offered, dismissed them as if they were a given. McCullough was beginning to feel worn down.

'What would you want me to say? If I did ...'

This was seized on with the unembarrassed happiness of a child; Nathaniel had no conception that McCullough might just be humouring him now—in his view, he had what he wanted.

'Just ... you know.'

'I'll need a little more than that.'

Again, the slight air of disappointment. Why wasn't McCullough willing to work a bit harder for him?

'I feel I'm being a little manipulated here, Nat, if I'm honest. You're asking me for a big favour. Something very difficult. I'm trying to discuss it with you, but I feel that not only do you want me just to agree to do it, but be happy about it and full of great things to say about you.'

'Don't you like me?'

'This is too much.'

'You'd do it for the others.'

'I'll do it for you, if I think it's what's best, but I'm not convinced.'

'You went to see Terry.'

'He's suffering. Really suffering.'

'He's a loser.'

'I'm unlikely ever to help you if you say things like that.'

'He always picks on me.'

'He's unhappy. But he's wrong to make you a target. Look, let me think about what I might say.'

'So you will talk to them?'

'Yes.'

Ah—the victory. The rightness of it. Nathaniel's body, bulky and strong, wide at the hips, filled with it. After a brief silence, he bent down and picked up another stone and launched it as far as he could. Did McCullough hear him mumble 'Result!'?

5

'You're doing the rounds,' Rebecca said. 'Checking on the flock.'

McCullough had joined her at the top of the bank, in the sun. She sat with her legs out, hands on her knees, back slightly rounded, the position of a ballet dancer doing light stretches after class. Next to her was a book on Pascal and probability, a short monograph, ordered online and printed singly. She saw him spot it. 'Thought I'd have a read. What's more interesting than the laws of chance?'

McCullough sat down and rested himself back on his forearms, chin on his chest, while he looked over what was meant to be his home one day. He knew it never would be, not for any reason in particular, but because it wasn't just his decision and that was fair.

'How was Terry? I bet he was infuriating.'

'He was. What about you?'

'You don't have to worry about me. I'm not smitten with anyone, still planning on going to college. I like it here, but it hasn't been life-changing.'

He looked at her. Was it possible to ask her: what's it like to be so devastating? He'd want her to focus on 'devastating'. Parse it. To devastate. To lay waste; to stun. He'd switch the two definitions around. Stun would come first. Then, to lay waste. But that wasn't right. When it came to this kind of beauty, to devastate was to clarify, to make a clearing, in the sense that when faced with such devastating beauty, he felt his inner world cleared out and something clarified, although quite what he was less sure of. But that was the effect of it, not how it felt to be the cause.

'My mum had a fun time with you. It was a bit weird, didn't you think?'

'At first.'

She was still sitting curled forward.

'Is something wrong with your back?'

'Just aching.'

'Maybe you should ask Rich for a massage.'

'And I thought *I* was cruel. The other day I cut my hand and got blood all over a white T-shirt. I changed in front of him. For a moment I was standing there in a bra. I didn't give it any thought. He's like a little brother.'

She rocked forward a little from the small of her back.

'How *is* your mother?'

'Good. Annoying. What did you think of her? Did you think she was sexy?'

'No comment.'

'I mean, I know she is in that elegant, matching underwear sort of way.'

'I couldn't possibly know.'

'You'd be surprised what we know about each other. I mean, we're practically the same age.'

'You seemed very much mother and daughter to me.'

'*A* mother and *a* daughter, unrelated. What time did you leave?'

'You saw me.'

'Oh, yeah.'

'Can you see Rich? Is he working?'

'Yes. He's being shown the brackets for the glazing; they have to be fixed to the stone. Simon has developed a polymer to fill in the gaps.'

'Simon is one of the good people. I mean not leavened by anything not good.'

'Your friend Marvin is the other way, I'd say.'

'You saw him at his most joyous.'

The sun was burning his face, his nose. He was beginning to sweat. He picked away the shoulders of his shirt and flapped open the collar. He felt a faint clogging at the back of his nose. 'There's a lot of pollen in the air. It gets me late afternoon.'

They sat in silence awhile, Rebecca kneading her lower back, then sitting very straight, shoulders back, arms out wide, slowly bringing them up until they crossed at the wrists. McCullough felt no shame watching her. She then flopped forward, her chest on her knees, her wrists crossed at her ankles. They were ballet positions. Even with so many people performing yoga or martial arts in public these days it was oddly disconcerting; after all, positions that expressed human drama were more arresting than those that were meant only to align our spiritual selves. Few people went to see performances of yoga. From under her arms, Rebecca appeared to look at him, not quite making eye contact.

'Do you want me to tell my mum you're here? She'll ask you to dinner again.'

What to say? Both 'yes' and 'no' would lead to further questions. Teasing.

'Do you want me to be your dad, Rebecca?'

'Yeah, right.' And then, 'Well?'

A pause. 'I don't know how long I'll be down here.'

'Smooth.' She leaned back, forearms along the ground, shoulders spiked up. 'I've stopped smoking.'

'Good, I wouldn't want you to die early.'

Close by, a bumblebee, a black heavy spot in the air, jagged around, just above the long grass; it seemed lost. A powerful drill started up, grinding at stone, the downward pressure and force of an arm and shoulder audible in the sound of the stone's resistance. The noise sharpened the air; somehow made it unfriendly, mean. Each time the drill was released, the bit whirring to stillness, it was if the air was cleared of something solid. There were hundreds of bolts to be drilled in.

Starting in a crouch, arms out before her at shoulder height, Rebecca rose slowly—a Z into an I.

She turned to McCullough. 'I better go back down. Pitch in. Are you coming?' She unguardedly offered her hand to help him up, a kindness.

'Thank you.'

They looked over to where Rich and Nat were being shown how

to lift the glass panels off the pile. Both had thick gloves on and held the handles of large black suckers.

McCullough said, 'That looks fun.'

Rebecca put her fingers into her hair, pitching it back and clearing it from her neck. 'Mother'll be upset if she misses you.'

CONFESSION

I

'I have had naive certainties all my life. I was in my mid-thirties before I realized historical context was important. Same with the notion of objectivity. Up until then I just thought greatness was some kind of incontrovertible quality that certain people or things possessed . . . and it was recognizable by anyone willing to look. I thought the world, as I saw it, was pretty much—objectively speaking—what it was. It was just about levels of engagement. I had no political beliefs at all, really. I thought art was the world's balm. More than that. When Dostoevsky said art would save the world, I thought he was stating the obvious. It was my mantra for twenty-odd years. The fact that my Marxist friends saw him as a reactionary was meaningless to me. I didn't even really understand. He was Dostoevsky, a genius—what more was there to say? Art was ahistorical or it wasn't art. Actually, I didn't even formulate things that far. I only now realize that this was what I thought.

'A girlfriend once said, amid all that solipsistic claptrap young people tell one another, that I was a *new* person. She actually said "new soul", but I'll go with "person". It didn't seem far off the mark. I mean: you don't grow into earnestness, do you? The "old soul"— which I *will* allow—won't have a trace of it. No one can deny life is attritional and to have lived once is to be a worn-out thing. Optimism is a thin top layer, and trust is not that deep a stratum. That said, I'm unusual of course—in that I possess at least a modicum of irony. They are strange bedfellows, earnestness and irony. Seldom found together. Don't you think?' He smiled.

'Go on.' Judith drank from her glass of whisky and pulled her feet up under her. Between them were areas of cold light; the sun was setting and entered the room obliquely, like a shard of golden glass angled at forty-five degrees. To either side lay shadow. Behind her a lamp was on, the pale orange light forced upward by a cone-shaped shade. There was a pool of light from the kitchen that reached McCullough's chair.

He felt a little shaky. The day had been hot and he'd worked hard. On the armrest his hand showed a tremor. It had been years since he'd shaken like this, his nerves playing out across his skin. Back then there had always been a girl, sitting cross-legged on the floor, looking up, with a different kind of earnestness. He remembered sitting in armchairs just like this. He was going to talk the girl across the room. Not seduce her. In his own way, he was going to bore her, outstay the time allotted to be interesting and perceptive, and then keep going. She would have to come to him . . . to shut him up. Any mystery he might create was conferred upon him by his remaining in the armchair, his legs crossed with a certain poise, and not joining her on the floor, whatever signals she might be sending. His great trick—but of course it wasn't a trick—was to bestow upon the woman the same ahistorical significance he attributed to artists, musicians, poets. It worked. They believed, briefly, because he believed wholly. He was a smoker then, which increased the shakes, or at least their visibility.

But Judith had said, 'Go on', and smiled and tucked her feet up and sipped her whisky.

He looked at his watch.

'You're doing fine.' Her American accent was delicious, liquid and teasing; she knew how seductive it was. She also saw through his shtick and yet was enjoying it for what it was.

Over dinner she had seemed happy to talk about herself, stopping only when their plates were empty, as if she'd planned it that way. They moved into the sitting room, where she poured two glasses of whisky and directed him to the chair he was in now. On reflection she had given little away, although he detected sincerity when she referred to herself as an orphan child. When Rebecca came in, 'bursting out' of a black shirt, her mother was amused, warm, patient and loving. The argument that followed was about washing machines, spin dryers, favourite pieces of clothing shrunk to *this size*, and who was to blame? When Rebecca had gone back to her room to finish getting ready, Judith was candid: 'Mine were never so—"wow", and she arched her back a little to exaggerate her own smaller bust. He didn't know what to say; she had her daughter's flawless, golden skin. She was also in a black blouse, two buttons opened.

When he arrived, she stood before him, a little on her toes. Her smile was fabulous. It announced the beginning of something. He was handed white wine and they clinked and drank. She was pleased to see him, she said. He asked about her book. It was fine. Where did she work? He was shown a small room next to the sitting room, the blind down. Pictures on the walls of Rebecca as a child, childhood paintings mounted and framed, and photos of the two of them going back almost twenty years. Rebecca seemed to have had a great flourishing of hair all her life. At three or four years old it was Afro-shaped, startling. McCullough studied each photo, looking with equal intent at mother and daughter. In one they were both in black bikinis, sitting on an otherwise deserted beach, smiling up at the camera. On the desk there was an Apple laptop, closed. Against the back wall was a bookcase with glass-panelled doors, all titles on Wallace Stevens.

'Yes, I'm adding to the great unread.' Judith switched on a lamp and leaned against the desk. 'What can I say? He moves me. I never tire of reading him. I think the world is as he says it is. In here, out there.'

He agreed, based on the little he'd read, although it felt like a betrayal. To confess to seeing the world as Judith did . . . It was then he began to tremble.

She led him back into the sitting room. They heard Rebecca, upstairs, put a record on. There was a slight skip and skid of sound.

'Shall I tell her you're here?'

'I don't think there's any need.'

The music was Marvin Gaye.

'She has all my vinyl up there. When she listens to Van Morrison, I can't bear it. I loved him so much, but I can't listen to him now.'

For a while they stood at the window looking over the road to the village green. The baby grand was a heavy dull presence next to him, its deep black gleam solid, implacable; the sheet music had been tided away.

'I still don't quite get why you live here.'

'Why do you want to build your church here?'

'I was possessed by an irrational impulse. I was obedient to inarticulate orders.'

'Well, I wanted to live away from the university, close to the ocean, and I fell in love with this apartment.'

'Can you have an "apartment" in a village? And I'm not sure what's over there is exactly "the ocean".'

She laughed and glanced up at him. 'I know what I like.'

He sensed she knew her own mind in ways that were enviable, like her daughter.

'How is it going down there on our beautiful clifftops?'

'Doesn't Rebecca give you updates?'

'Yes and no. She's quite besotted by the guy helping out . . .'

He went cold at this, and felt sick, almost panicked. On site he had taken it for granted that no intimacy outstripped theirs.

Judith continued, 'A scientist friend of yours.'

Ah—the warmth; veins flooded with relief. 'Simon.'

'Yes. She thinks he's a genius.'

Poor Simon. Heroic Simon. His date with Jane had not been a success. It had rained depressingly, which became a sign neither of them could ignore. They'd gone to see an exhibition of Edvard Munch (her choice), but due to the weather it had been busy. The gallery was warm and damp and Jane had felt hot and claustrophobic and wanted to leave after ten minutes. Simon had bought tickets for a jazz concert, based on information from Holly that Jane didn't like Kew but did like jazz. They had five hours to kill before it started and then it turned out to be a Louis Armstrong tribute band. Jane was generous enough not to be embarrassed on Simon's behalf and in the end had enjoyed it. But she was not generous enough not to think he should have known better, and, having made up her mind not to see him again, had helped him out with advice for future dates.

'He's a brilliant and good man.'

Changing the subject, Judith said, 'Poor Rich. He's been out on the front steps as predicted. Rebecca feels aggrieved when friends do this. Suddenly they're not friends. Or they don't behave like it.'

'It's Terry I'm most worried about. He's going through a very strange stage.'

'He's been fighting a lot again, Rebecca says.'

'It's not that he's manic, but there is a surge of confidence in him that seems unconnected to anything real. Of course, that is exactly the kind of judgment being levelled at me.'

Across the village green a man walked with a small black and tan dog. Between the road and the grass was overflowing; beer cans and newspaper lay on the ground, an empty packet of popcorn. There was music from the pub.

'How's your family?' Like her daughter, Judith had a delicious lower lip.

She was either playing with him or she understood life could be conducted on many levels, and believed she was permitted to ask him this without any interruption of an underlying narrative to the evening. But then she wasn't betraying anyone. The question was bewildering in its emotional complexity, at least in terms of what he was willing to say.

'The twins are too young to know what's going on.' He stopped. He sensed she was no longer listening; she was the single parent of a grown-up child and wasn't interested in other people's children. There was a long pause. Her eyes were marvellously teasing. He'd never been good at decoding expressions of seduction, what was required of him in return; there was always too much to disentangle, so much ambiguity, and he feared humiliation, mutual embarrassment. His eyes watered. He looked out of the window. 'Let's be honest—I'm betraying my partner.'

'Yet you're still here.'

'Yet I'm still here.' He'd toughened up over the decades: 'If this is merely a diversion for you, it's your duty to tell me.'

'Duty? Really? I'm not so sure.'

McCullough felt foolish. For a moment, despised. It was in the nature of a certain kind of scholar to spot sloppy thinking and to display their lack of surprise at being in the presence of fools. But he hadn't been sloppy, merely naïve: he'd supposed she would consent to a set of rules. Or one rule: that they were to make certain things clear. Not by a look or glance, or messages sent by ambiguous eyes, but more straightforwardly, openly. Because people might be hurt.

She soon forgave him. She had to. She wanted him to stay for dinner, to talk, perhaps go to bed with her. The question had been there since their first meeting: did she want him to spend the night? Could she imagine him fucking her? She liked him. But there was her daughter, this extraordinary girl she'd produced, who talked about this man with a mixture of suspicion, sarcasm and genuine affection. The morning after his first visit, Rebecca had laughed, reading in her mother's eyes that she too had taken to him, and said, 'No shagging my friends.' Adding, 'Not in the house anyway.' And here he was again, this strange man with a family in London, in her home. So it could only be sex. While he was here, building his church. It wasn't much of an example to Rebecca. Yet when was the last time she had been to bed with a man? Over a year ago. A dull Larkin scholar at a conference on twentieth-century English language poets. She'd been mean to him, horrible in fact. Asked how it was for her, she'd said like having a pencil stuck up her nose; a joke, of sorts. Nothing more was added to this assessment as he gathered his clothes off the floor and made his way across the room and into the bathroom, in a slightly crouched posture, a beaten man. She still had her bra on. What did that say? Was this going to be any different?

The day after her first encounter with McCullough she'd spent all morning in her office, sitting back in her chair, thinking about him, mostly in regard to herself. She was a Professor of Modern Poetry on sabbatical, struggling with the book she'd wanted to write for fifteen years, finding she had nothing new to say. Surely a man with a young family, who might bring God into her house, was a distraction she didn't need. Stevens seldom referenced God, at least not the Christian God, and whatever spiritual life Stevens might have aspired to was transmuted into poetry and the impermanence of reality. But she'd realized that morning she had no real idea how to think through what this man claimed was happening to him. She was so used to attending to everything as 'structures of feeling' rather than feeling itself, or, to go back to Stevens, as a 'supreme fiction', rather than accepting, at least on some level, that a category of truth existed, irrespective of what she might place in there. She remembered thanking God for Rebecca, a joyous, spontaneous gratitude, blurry-eyed and ecstatic, the dark little creature in her arms. Then when Rebecca was little and had come home from school with questions about Jesus, she had been liberal, responsible, open-minded. Many people believed many different things and must be free to do so. Had Rebecca asked her what she herself believed? She couldn't remember. And since then? It never seemed to come up. Not until three weeks ago.

'Sorry,' she added after a moment. 'That was mean.'

McCullough cleared a line of dust from the lid of the piano.

'This is a betrayal. Of course it is.' He wanted to make this clear but not mean anything by it.

'It's not for me to argue.' Briefly she gripped his hand.

Dinner was a light coq au vin, her favourite local cheese, then the whisky, from Islay, full of smoke, the beach. Rebecca came in to say goodbye, her evening not yet begun. 'Don't wait up.' She glared at her mother; promises had been made and were expected to be kept; and then she glared at McCullough, reserving for him a more amused glint, her smile cautionary. He was to be on the lookout.

How did he feel about Rebecca leaving? She had become, miraculously, the only steady presence in his life. She kissed them both on the cheeks.

The front door closed, a minute later a car door slammed, and an engine was revved too hard for a road next to a village green in the quiet of the night.

The whisky warmed him. The aftertaste was like iodine, child-hood. Judith asked him a very straightforward question: 'You're not a straightforward man, are you?'

He knew to pause. She qualified her question: 'Whatever the truth is about what is happening to you . . . can you draw a line from what you were like when you were younger . . . to now?'

He hadn't meant to give such a full answer, but then Judith hadn't known him back then, so he could be honest and explain himself in a way that Holly, Marvin, Lucien, others, would regard as self-aggrandizing, because what to him seemed naïve and foolish might also, given his general manner, be easily cast as arrogance. Lucien had once said he'd never felt so ambivalent about some-one before. Holly had been standing close by and agreed, but then decided McCullough would like that too much—to be so loved and hated at the same time. He remembered how Lucien had looked at Holly at that moment. How clear-thinking we both are, he seemed to be saying—how unsentimental.

Judith, knees drawn up in the chair, whisky glass balanced on the arm, could listen without prejudice, only commenting: 'So it would be true to say you have a predisposition—'

He interrupted, laughing, 'Or that I'm an appropriate vessel.'

It wasn't late. The night felt open, encouraging, as if it might never become truly dark.

'You haven't been down to the site, have you?' he asked.

'No.'

'Should we go?'

She arranged herself more comfortably in her chair. It was as if she was saying she had him where she wanted him.

'Rebecca tells me all about it. I hear people talk.'

'But . . .'

'I'm intrigued by different things.'

If he took a final sip of whisky and stood up, what would she do? The bottle was in the kitchen, on the table, with the mess of dinner. It had been a mistake on her part, leaving it there. He looked over at her glass; the liquid was like an Olympic bronze medal at the bottom. She'd hardly touched it.

'I'm just going to get a little more.'

She seemed happy for him to do so, without comment. To watch him. She was alone most of the day; it was her flat—apartment.

In the kitchen, his hand on the bottle, he looked at his watch. It was 10.15. Was that early, late? He seldom lasted past midnight these days. It was an embarrassment. What stamina he'd once had was gone. The first two years of the twins had taken something elemental from him. Holly was the same. Sleeping outside or in the tent, he was now used to the cycle of the sun. In the past, it had always been a particular kind of delight to go to bed as it was getting light, especially with a woman whose body was new to him.

He returned to the sitting room, poured himself an inch of whisky and set the bottle down on the floor.

'What shall we talk about?' He smiled at Judith.

'Whatever you like.' She drew her shoulders back, straightened them.

'What were *you* like, in your twenties?'

'A contrarian. Clever.'

'A nightmare?'

'Yes. But when you're not hideous . . .'

'And you had Rebecca.'

'I was twenty-four then.'

'Was it an easy decision?'

'No decision is easy.' Then, 'It was fairly easy.'

'How was the father . . . about it?'

'Magnanimous. Patrician. He was . . . is . . . completely without a moral compass. He has other children in the same situation. I suspect it's an evolutionary thing. They are spectacular genes. Look at the daughter he produced.'

'Are you not going to take any credit?' It sounded as if he was pandering to her and had missed the point of the conversation; it wasn't about her. She looked bored having to deal with his non-sequiturs.

'Do you speak, you and Rebecca's father?'

'I try to avoid it. He's sixty-one. He treats us both as daughters. I feel sorry for his sons. Brilliant people shouldn't have children. Or their children should be taken away from them.'

'What does Rebecca think?'

'You might have noticed she's a no-nonsense girl.'

'But he's her father. She must—'

'What? I have no real idea how they are together. He takes her to functions. I suppose he must either trust her to behave or not care.'

'How is she when she . . . ?'

'Withdrawn. A little.'

McCullough looked across at the window. There was nothing to see. The rest of the world, beyond the trees, might as well have been in a different dimension. The church, a few miles away, undeniably a real thing, perhaps even a material object with meaning, seemed little more than a drawing by Piranesi—an intricate cross-hatching of shadow and light, with nothing of the landscape, the cliff's edge, the sea to animate it.

'I should go.' There, it was said, although he made no effort to move, to finish his whisky.

'You can stay.'

In the second it was said he understood her meaning, but the following moment he realized he might have imagined it.

'Are your students scared of you?'

'Not at all.' She smiled, took a sip of her whisky; the glass in her hand seemed large. The disc of whisky listed and then settled as she set it back down on the side of her chair.

'I want to tell you that I have thought about God . . . in the broadest sense . . . for the first time, I realize, in twenty years. I'm the daughter of tragic church people. Did they send you?'

What should he say?

She continued, 'It's meaningful, no? To have discarded the central element of your parents' lives. And then forgotten about it.' She paused and looked at him. 'The awful part is, I can only think of banal things to say.'

'Is that not the trouble with pretty much everything in our world? We are no longer allowed the infinite regress into nothingness that might lead to real meaning. I actually blame Freud for most things.'

'Not Nietzsche?'

'For me it goes St Paul then Nietzsche, no one in between, or after. Nietzsche's breakdown in Turin is defining, I think. Like Paul's conversion. We are the children of St Paul and Nietzsche, even if we don't know it.'

She stared at him. 'And where do you fit in?'

'Me?'

'Yes.'

'I have nothing to say on that matter.'

She laughed. 'Nothing?'

'Or everything—that's the problem.'

She laughed again.

'I don't feel a compulsion to justify myself.' He paused. 'In any kind of Pentecostal manner, that is.' He offered a brief wave of jazz hands.

'But you're building a church?'

'A misconceived, ill-judged expression . . . Let's face it, it's unimaginative and grandiose. Whilst I don't think it says anything about what I feel, it says everything about *me*. It's embarrassing, if looked at from a certain angle.'

'Yet you persist.'

'I do.'

'Because?'

'There is a chance, I suppose, of creating something that . . .' What was it? 'I don't know . . . allows a little of the metaphysical back into our lives. Something that when encountered is so strange it reveals the world around it—in this instance, the ground, the cliff, the sea and sky, as being radically familiar, which is to say, worth contemplating again, and from that to wonder what it was that made us look again, and then to see a building that is both familiar and strange.' He laughed. 'If it works, it's a kind of phenomenological/ spiritual win-win—the real and other. Pretty much only achievable by great art or that great trickster, the erotic.'

He felt bad. He'd introduced the subject. He couldn't think of Holly.

Judith sipped her whisky; a drop escaped her lips, and she needed the back of her finger to draw it back up into her mouth. 'I confess, I'm attracted to you.'

2

He stood in Judith's bedroom as she sat on the bed and slipped off her shoes. He remembered saying something like, 'Well then', as she presented herself to him, looking up and smiling. The sudden change of height, the tilting back of her head, the shiver in her body as she adjusted her position, was in itself a kind of nakedness. She took his hands to the buttons of her blouse: she was in charge and he would do the work. The light from the half-pulled shade was colourless; it was neither day nor night. Her bed cover was white, dully bright; her pillows were European, large fat squares. As he opened one button, she pulled off her earrings into her fist, and, bending sideways from her hips, reached over to dump them on top of a chest of drawers. Her no-nonsense efficiency was erotic in itself. He wasn't drunk; he was past that. The world beyond them was small, and between the long blinks of his tired eyes it receded; there was nowhere but this room. It had been thirteen years since he'd been in the bedroom of a woman he didn't know. He felt marvellously displaced. Rich in self. Everything else was duty, sacrifice, work, linearity, where time ran away like water. But not here: here he felt connected to a richer vein of time, where life might be lived differently, passed through upwards and downwards, like the angels of Jacob's ladder. It was not a trivial matter what happened next. He paused to speak. To break or create a spell.

'I'm going to kiss your neck.'

She had shaken her hair off her shoulders and pulled it back. His fingertips were on her upper arms, gently holding her there; her fingertips moved up to his jawline, her slender arms between his. At that moment he realized he wanted the capacity for betrayal, to go hard against himself, whatever he believed, whoever he was; there was no law anywhere that couldn't be broken.

She kissed him and kept him there with her fingertips. Then their mouths parted a little. She spoke, in slightly more than a whisper, to make herself clear: 'It's your choice.' They both laughed; it was said almost into his mouth and was muffled and echoey.

He moved his hands down to her hips and gripped them. She took in a breath, reflexively, as if she'd been given her answer, and then steadied herself and calmed her breathing.

'Take off my clothes.'

Four garments: skirt, blouse, underwear, and she was naked and close to him. She stepped back, opened her arms, as if to curtsy, showing herself—this is what you've got to play with—and then stepped forward again, her body against his. Leaning back, she unbuttoned his shirt, opened it and laid her palms on his chest.

'You're very warm. What's burning inside you?'

'Right now—you.' He paused. 'But not only you.'

Looking down, she unbuckled his belt. 'We're grown-ups.'

Perhaps he wasn't quite in the moment, because he thought of Kierkegaard and Socrates. If there wasn't great wisdom gained by lust, by love, its consummation—the aesthetics of all this—then you were doing it wrong.

'Kiss me again.'

The kiss was an order and a disguise. She pushed her hand into his jeans and felt for his cock. She was experienced enough to prepare for disappointment. Her tongue sought out his tongue and whipped around it, teasing it out. There was the taste of whisky, the fresh basil from the salad. Both knew that from where they were standing, getting to the bed would be awkward; he still had his boots on.

She liked being naked in front of a man. But to lie down and wait meant having to contrive a flattering position; there were bulges and off-colour patches of flesh. She was not as perfect as she had once been, as her daughter was now.

She said, 'We should get into bed.'

His jeans were on his hips, his shirt open. His cock had grown in her hand.

'And if I can't?'

She felt herself close up, dry up. Become old. A crone. She reached to the back of door and lifted a silk dressing gown off a hook.

'You're free to go anytime.'

'Judith.'

'If you don't want to fuck me.'

What was there to say—I do?

'I want to do everything to you.' He looked at her; paused. 'I want to fuck you in every way I can.'

'You bastard.' With the side of her small fist she lightly pounded on his chest, but she laughed and repeated, 'You bastard.'

He took in a deep breath and then went on, 'I want to grab you, hook you up around my hips and enter you as you cling on to me, and then for us to stagger back and fall on to the bed. For me to struggle out of my clothes, madly, while you lie waiting, your legs fallen open. And then ...' She had placed her arms around him, her ear to his chest. 'And then I'd fuck you—you underneath me, my hand grabbing you, lifting you so I can get deeper.'

'Yes ...'

'As deep as I can go ... hard inside you ...'

'Yes ...'

'Then I stop ...' He heard her laugh. 'And pull out.' He paused. 'Do you want me to go on?' He felt her nod. He knew what he was doing; the moment was overwhelming.

'I look down at you. My tongue circles each nipple, teasing it up. I catch one in my teeth. Then, after drawing a little circle on your belly, on the inside of each of your thighs, I find you open and warm, melting, and within moments you will have to bite your lip to stop yourself coming. But don't worry, I can feel you, hear you, sense the tension in your body; I'm in control. So I stop again. My cock is as hard as it's ever going to be. It wants to be in your mouth. You know this and get up on to your knees and for a moment you are ravenous, but I slow you down because your lack of control is the sexiest thing ever and I don't want to come, because that's what's going to happen.' She was clutching him, one hand between her legs. He could feel the slow vibration of her body against his. 'So instead I turn you over, hitch you into position, arrange you so I can enter you completely, as slowly as it's possible to go and as deeply as it's possible to go ... you are really melting now, you are doing nothing but letting the sensation of being fucked take over you, reach through you, fill you up.

There are two sensations you love, the pressing in and then to have me fully inside you. I hear you say "fuck" to yourself because it's no longer pure pleasure, it's something more central, abiding. Terrifying.

'But then you notice that I'm still, deep in you, a great hard rod, and it's your turn. You must take over. You begin to move back and forth, the pleasure for you is now my anonymity, that you're in control. The sensations are dirtier. You want to transgress something. You know what I can see.

'And then we change again. I lie down and you sit astride me. (Yes, I am aware you're doing a lot of the work.) I thrust my hips up, so you can roll yourself against me. You are bent over and your nipples are near my mouth, and my tongue catches them and I suck and bite. And then, just as you need it, I place my thumb between your legs and press up.'

'I'm going to come.'

'And you start to come. With gentle revolutions of your hips, my cock inside. It's happening to both of us. I try to hold off, but as you come, that's it—nothing can hold me back.' He felt her fingernails in his chest. 'I tell you I'm coming', and that increases the charge in you . . . I am just this great pulse . . . while you . . .'

She came, holding on to him with one hand, her head against his chest, her dressing gown fallen off her shoulders. He waited, holding her, while her body convulsed, and the fluttering inside her stomach subsided.

Only after a full minute did she say, 'Now what about you?'

SIN

'It is usual at this day to speak as if Faith were simply of a moral nature, and depended and followed upon a distinct act of Reason beforehand'

JOHN HENRY NEWMAN

I

'You need to come back. I'm being called in almost every day. I just sit there, and after about three hours I'm told to leave. It's a kind of torture. These very plain men watch me. Sometimes they just stand there, sometimes they sit down. They call me Mr Pollock and smile—a tender, somewhat sad smile. It's fucking scary. It's like they are mind readers, and the smile is there to show me I cannot hide. No one seems to care that you're not around, which suggests to me that they think I'm the weak one. That's a kind of torture as well—not knowing what you're supposed to know but knowing you've been chosen to tell them; that you're the soft target. So come back and sort this out.

'Actually, I do know one thing. We've freaked them out. You planted a scenario in their heads they can't get rid of. At first I thought it was just your dystopian vision of a post-apocalyptic Blighty, a kind of general alarm at that outcome, but that's not it—they fear it's going to happen under their watch, making them unelectable. For-ev-er. Do you see: we presented them with a scenario that will destroy the party in power. You predicted a total re-evaluation of the nature in which society is structured. You called this re-evaluation epochal! "This time there will be no disconfirmation"!

'Please, you've got to come back. I don't care what shit you come up with, but we need to convince them that it's all data-driven, hard analysis, evidence-based, and not just made up in your head.

And—*and*—that we're not going to go to the media, or going to undermine them somehow. They think we're a loose cannon. You know me, Mac—I like my life. I have a good life.'

'Jim. Sorry. I'll be back in a few hours. But don't think you're being singled out. They must know where I am. And what I'm doing. Perhaps it's more to do with that. They'd be remiss if they didn't make some kind of connection between what we said and what I'm doing. Even if it's irrelevant.'

'Right. So you need to explain that.'

'There is nothing to explain. There is no connection. It's correlation, not causation.'

'I don't buy that, Mac. There is an intrinsic millenarianism in—you know—any pseudo-religious shit.'

'I can only speak for myself, and if anything, it's no more than a moral millenarianism. I don't think that's controversial.'

'I think you'll find it is.'

'No—the language is a little grand, perhaps. The end point, not.'

'I don't even understand what that means.'

'And atheists blame theists for thinking so small, so local.'

'Great. Let's use that. Don't worry, Sir Neville—we're not thinking local here, but something more . . . what? Oh, I forgot *epochal*. Fuck, Mac, I look forward to seeing you on the news—holed up in your church, surrounded by firearms.'

'I think we've strayed off the point. Are you due in today?'

'See, you have no idea. They just turn up wherever I am. First time I was in the pub. "We are here to escort you to the Ministry," they said. And I said, "What, the Ministry of Fear?" AND THEY DIDN'T LAUGH. You know I don't like to leave an unfinished pint, but swilling it back somehow didn't seem right.'

'But you did.'

'As I said, I don't like to leave an unfinished pint.'

'And you've never seen the Secretary of State again?'

'It's someone different each time. You don't know how unsettling it is for someone merely to say "Ah, Mr Pollock" and smile. I now know the English upper classes can do more with an "Ah" than other nations can do with all their hand gestures and face-pulling.'

'I'm sorry.'

'Well, you've got until you get here to think of something.'

'I will.'

'Can you at least give me an idea of what it will be?'

'No.'

'Then we're fucked.'

'No, we're not. Let's get it in proportion. All we've done is suggest how people might behave if there is a major chemical or biological attack, and the possible collective psychological fallout, especially if the army has to turn on the people, which is likely, given what we learned. We've done nothing more than show due diligence, given the brief. And as you know, we always like to give a little extra, and we did: we said—and I think I made it clear it was interpretation—that the nation will have irrevocably altered, and we will have entered a new epoch, which, for a while at least, will be ungovernable. The problem is that we seem to have set their imaginations alight. They didn't expect that. They expected one thing and got another. They're just panicking.'

'Well, I'm re-evaluating stuff, that's for sure.'

'I don't blame you. Let's talk when I get back. I'll stop by home first and then come straight to the office.'

'If I'm not here, you'll know where I'll be.'

'I will find you.'

'Try Room 101.'

Driving home at midday, motorway traffic was light, and the sun streamed into the car in a shifting mist of white and gold light. For most of the journey he needed his sunglasses on and the visor down. He listened to Ligeti's orchestral works, the highest notes of the *Cello Concerto* a glittering of sound that gave a kind of dispersing substance to the sunlight, something that might be felt in the hand, if only for a moment.

He felt no guilt. He'd left Judith sober and elated. The walk back to the site was without incident. He slept for an hour or so on the sandy part of the beach, wrapped in a thick blanket, the residue of the whisky keeping his blood warm. Tiredness robbed him of any desire to analyze. He felt purified, emptied out, all excitability of mind and body becalmed.

In the morning, still wrapped in his blanket, he reminded himself what he'd done and tried to gaze beyond the facts. What had really happened? He'd talked Judith into an orgasm and then she'd talked him, with slightly fewer details, into the same, putting her mouth around him at the final moment. She was content for him to leave almost immediately, tying up her silk dressing gown to stand by an open door, to see him out into the night. In the hallway, they'd kissed on both cheeks, depleted, their smiles vague, then wry; both knew it represented little more than the afterglow of intimacy.

Holly would leave him if she knew. She'd kick him out, her heart broken. There would be no argument or appeal to reason that might fix this. To think that was possible was somehow *more* morally wrong than the act itself.

He had understood the consequences of what he was doing, in the moment, and at no point feared the world would be fundamentally changed. Holly remained his partner and the woman he loved. But that didn't mean that aspects of world wouldn't be differently tilted when he emerged. *He* would be different. And he was. He felt as if he'd proved something he'd long believed to be true: we are defined by our flaws and it is only through our flaws that we meet life head-on. We can only know ourselves by what we find irresistible. Holly would laugh in his face, scorn him, if he tried to excuse himself with such casuistry. How many men have defended themselves in such a way? So-called religious or spiritually inclined men declaring this kind of behaviour, especially when it is discovered, to be part of a journey that takes them nearer to God? Didn't Jesus love the sinner more deeply?

Holly would regard this as little more than a pathetic continuation of his revelations: to him it meant one thing (positive); to her, another (negative). Yet he was sure that he hadn't counterfeited himself (the only way he could think to express it); he hadn't acted in bad faith. He was never going to resist Judith. It was a part of him to fall for her in that moment. In a way he could never explain, it was written. Whether it was finally weakness (fallenness) or strength (an existential choice)—it was fully him that he would do this: his deepest self was at work. The terrible truth for Holly was that if she really loved him—loved him at his deepest—she would understand that he was always going to have done this, he would never have not done this; the choice was indivisible from the person she loved. And not because of some psychological flaw or hard determinism, or even a superficial erotic vulnerability; but because it was him, over and over. The only real question then . . . was whether he truly believed it required Judith—Judith in her particularity—for his behaviour to be inevitable. Because without that being true, wasn't everything else false? He needed to establish that this slim, ironic, dazzling woman, this orphan/academic, presented something to him that it would have been against himself to deny. Of course, any serviceable psychologist would argue that there was a version of this narrative with Judith as a proxy Rebecca. But he didn't believe that. Judith was no less devastating than her daughter. To think she was a proxy was to believe that youth must trump age when it came to sex. He didn't buy that. Simply, in that moment Life had become greater than he was able to manage morally, and as such had subsumed him, and as a consequence he wasn't able to behave other than as himself—to behave freely as himself—as he always would if he were to act freely in this situation, a choice so shockingly free and deterministic at the same time that in its own way it was a perfect example of free will bestowed upon us by an omniscient God.

At this conclusion McCullough laughed so hard that snot blew out of his nose and into his lap. The surprise caused his hands to jerk the steering wheel and the car to swerve to the right, almost sideswiping a Mercedes doing over a hundred in the fast lane. That was also funny. Sudden death after such clarity.

But there was another difficult question. How do you take responsibility for yourself in a shared life? He accepted that most of the time life was a series of semi-blind tests where we try to balance what is right while hedging outcomes that suit us. Maybe this was following the same pattern. But how could he tell? Wasn't that the genius in each of us—our capacity to invent grand narratives when all we are doing is tinkering with the truth? In this instance, he had to ask himself whether the act was performed for itself, without meaning being derived by others, without it being a reaction to others in some way. In this sense, Holly was not betrayed because she wasn't being used as a means to an end. The difficulties he and Holly were going through played no part. What happened would have happened whatever the state of their relationship. Of course, Holly wouldn't see it that way. The act was betrayal at its simplest. It was adultery. Against a commandment, if a scriptural reference was needed. Hadn't they both promised each other time and again not to do this one thing, not to hurt each other this way?

But it would be worse than that for Holly. What had happened between him and Judith meant he'd experienced an intensity of feeling with another woman that was no longer available to them as a couple of thirteen years—all the erotic adventure for the most part played out. Even though that was not why he had done it (he was too wise on that score), all Holly would see—feel?—was the physical act, and she would recall the intoxication that went with sleeping with someone new, and know that this was how he'd felt with another woman. She would hate him for this, yes, but more hurtful, more unforgivable still, would be knowing that on the night in question, as on most nights recently, she had sat alone feeling nothing but a dull, withering sadness. So even if he were to persuade Holly that he still loved her, that he didn't love Judith, how would she not regard this act as deeply selfish, blindly selfish to another's feeling at their most vulnerable—the one thing real love was supposed to prevent? She might not even blame him alone, just recognize it as the final failure of their shared love to protect him from himself, that their shared love was no longer strong enough to shield him. It would be for this reason and this reason alone that she would ask him to leave.

2

The house was empty when he arrived. He phoned Holly and announced he was back. She said she was at Jane's and would be home in an hour; the children were playing with Jane's children, playing nicely, she said without prompting. She sounded distracted. The call ended abruptly, as if by mistake. He unpacked his things and had a shower. Lying on the bed, a towel around his waist, he opened a book but was quickly asleep. He dreamed of Terry. He was sitting outside the front of his house, on the same metal and plastic chair, the grass around him thick and green, a summer's growth. He looked like an artwork, an installation, or a man who'd capture the nation's attention for taking a stand on something. There was a small crowd at the fence, watching him. Had Terry made the nation believe in some impending miracle or was he sitting there, another Enoch, expecting to be taken up by the Lord? The mood of the crowd was fickle, at times angry and disbelieving, yet jostling for a good view, just in case; no one wanted to miss anything. Someone confirmed it was to be an ascension. McCullough found himself explaining calmly, with earnest care, that if his friend were to ascend, everyone would see it, so not to worry about where they were standing. Those at the front were reluctant to move: they knew it would begin on the ground, with a sudden trembling of the chair's legs, a shaky parting from the earth, the most basic rule of the universe contravened, and they wanted to be the ones to witness it first, to send word back that it was happening. Many claimed to have already seen something, but they were false starts. Each time this caused a surge forward. Sitting on the chair, legs out and fallen apart, with the occasional, absent slurp of beer or burp, Terry was oblivious. McCullough could see his pocket Bible, fatted with loose, handwritten notes. From where he was standing, gripped in Terry's nicotine-stained fingers, the book looked the size of a postage stamp, a Penny Black.

Then it started to rain. Some people left. There was an assumption that something as wondrous as this was unlikely to happen in bad weather. Someone pointed out that it was always dry over Terry. A person nearer to him said it only looked like that: it was the eaves of the house keeping him sheltered. Another said that miracles were only true if you were open to them. McCullough wanted to explain: it wasn't a time of miracles, that time had passed, faith now was hard work. He found himself at the front, although he hadn't made any special effort to get there. Unaccountably, the crowd behind him was now vast, like a great mass pressing to enter narrow gates. Their pushing forward bent McCullough over the fence a little. He didn't understand why Terry didn't invite him in, find that other chair— weren't they in this together? Yet there was little proof, apart from the odd glance, that Terry realized he was present.

Next to McCullough a boy was asking whether the man would shoot up into the sky like a rocket. He pulled at McCullough's sleeve. McCullough explained that if it happened at all, it would be slow and terrifying, worse than any thunderstorm, because the universe—not just the clouds or the sky—would have to break open to receive him. It was then that he started to wonder whether he'd misread the situation and they weren't waiting on Terry, but on him, that *he* was expected to do something. Was that the reason for Terry's sly glances; he too was waiting? But what was McCullough supposed to do? He had a vague sense that something had been agreed but couldn't remember what. Was there some marvellous hoax he'd forgotten he was a part of, or was he really possessed of a power he didn't know how to use? Had people been told that he would raise up Terry himself? They'd come here to watch him perform a miracle?

He turned against the fence, his back to Terry. He needed to address the crowd and make it clear: there would be no expression of unearthly power today. Not from him. Whatever they had heard, whatever they were expecting—it had all been a misunderstanding. He started shouting: 'Please, listen to me. There will be no proof.' There was jeering, a little heckling. Disappointment. People felt let down. 'Please—listen. That doesn't mean there is nothing. But you'll have to work harder. So much harder. Please, if you'll only calm down, I'll explain . . .'

He was waking up, rising into consciousness, a slow, pressing upward out of sleep. On the bed beside him, he felt Holly holding his hand.

'Explain what?' She was round-shouldered, pale. She'd been crying. She held his hand as if he were a dying man.

'Sorry. I was dreaming.' The words sounded heavy, ill-formed, as if he were partially paralysed. For a moment he feared he'd had a stroke. His eyes were unfocused: was it him that was crying? 'Where are the children?' He sensed Holly wiping her eyes. 'What's the matter?'

'I left them with Jane.'

He tried to pull himself up onto the pillows, digging his elbows in; he was weak. Holly released his hand.

He asked again, 'What's the matter?'

'Everything is ruined.'

Sleep still held a part of him back, as if he had left much of his life behind in the dream, and was now required to adjust to the real world with only a fragment of himself.

Holly's hands were now in her lap. She was wearing a skirt and her knees were pale. Her hair was thinner than when they'd met. So much had fallen out post-pregnancy that for a year she'd looked as if she were just starting chemotherapy. Over time it had thickened up a little, but it had once been as abundant as Rebecca's.

'I want to blame you. I do blame you.'

Her face was haggard, dry, deeply lined, as if she had aged years. How long had she looked like this?

He elbowed himself further up. The geographical coordinates of his dream were still with him: outside the window there was the thick summer grass, a crowd, Terry vibrating in his chair. 'I need a cup of tea.'

'You're not listening.'

'I am. Please. It's just—'

'You don't even care.' She was incredulous.

Of course he cared, her tears moved him, pained him, worried him, but she was so far away, and between them was the great depthless transparency. 'I'm sorry.'

'What are *you* sorry for?' For a moment she was simply cross—he wasn't concentrating. She wiped her nose with a tissue, a tidying up of her emotional position: she didn't believe in hysteria; only the death of one of the children would lead to that.

The night before, Judith had been this close to him, but there had been no confusion, no shift at the heart of his emotional world. He had not stopped loving Holly.

'You don't know, do you?' She laughed; it was scornful. It was if his ignorance was staggering. Her body tightened up. 'Lucien stayed here while you were gone. He begged to.'

McCullough glanced around their bedroom, decorated a year ago: new paint, new blinds, new soft-close doors on the wardrobes that had never really worked. But beyond that it was the same as it had been for the six years they'd lived in this house, a set of dimensions he'd looked at on the floor plans before they'd decided to view the property. It was a house like other houses. This was obviously the 'master' bedroom—a large bay window, a great volume of space, slightly irregular corner angles that he'd never liked. Details changed: the small sofa with clothes on it, dumped or folded; family clutter on all surfaces, just visible from where he was if he craned up a little. None of the photos of the twins were framed but were stuck in the side of the mirror or leaning against books or in piles of two or three on shelves, where now and again he looked at them absently. So just a bedroom then, untidier than most, but different only in superficial ways to the bedrooms of most people they knew.

'Say something. Or don't you care?'

What was there to say? He could feel her misery. He couldn't blame her. It was Lucien's fault. Who else would have contrived such an opportunity, given her situation? From the beginning it would have been tactical, unfeeling and objective-driven. Willed. But worse than that, it would have been contaminated with other motives. It didn't matter what Lucien felt for Holly, the sincerity of his feelings (which McCullough had always rather respected), after that evening in the pub McCullough knew that whatever pleasure might have been derived from the act itself, his betrayal of their friendship would have added piquancy for Lucien. He could hear Lucien claim, with a perverse generosity, 'Well, Proctor—you were with us in spirit. Isn't that something?'

And on some level this was also going to be the case with Holly. He didn't believe she had wanted to sleep with Lucien, that she desired him, but she had done so because of the state she was in, a state he, McCullough, had placed her in, making her vulnerable to Lucien making his move.

'Say something.' Holly looked at him; he was tanned, unshaven, his chest naked, skin white below the V of his shirts; a new mole had appeared that at other times she might have scrutinized more closely.

What was he to do? If he showed understanding, if he *forgave* her in that instance because he understood, she would hate him. Her tears, her guilt were for herself, her own stupidity, the irrevocable damage she felt *she'd* done; they were not a plea for gentleness or generosity of feeling. Simply, it wasn't about him, despite its being all his fault. All she wanted was for him to witness her wretchedness.

Perhaps he was in shock, McCullough thought. Lucien's long pale limbs wrapped around Holly. His soiled cock inside her.

He began to feel sick, as if Holly's confession was only now reaching him. He sat further up and drew in his legs. Holly needed to shift a little.

'In this bed?'

'No.' Pause. 'Downstairs.'

What did that mean? Anything . . . nothing? He thought of the sofa, the floor—the table must have been moved to make room.

'Once?'

'No.'

'Ah.'

How wrong was it to keep silent about Judith? But to confess now would mean the end. Just like that: you did this; I did this. What could survive that, at least in the short term?

'Last night?'

'No.'

Holly searched for his hand. He wasn't going to withdraw it, but he felt it was cold to her touch.

'You're always gone. He turned up.' It was that matter-of-fact, although of course that wasn't how it happened. She didn't pull him in over the threshold of the front door. She wanted to say more, to explain, but everything else involved details, her complicity.

Would it be easier to tell her about Judith and have her hate him? Was it a superseding betrayal?

'Does anyone else know?'

'Of course not. No one knows.'

'Lucien knows.' He smiled reflexively. This fact would have to be dealt with. 'I'm taking it for granted that you're not leaving me for him?'

'No.'

Both knew this was hardly the point. There were five minutes of silence. Cars passed on the road, parked, cars doors opened and closed, boots slammed shut, children were called and corralled and shouted at.

'It's an ugly image.' He felt no need to be kind.

'You're a bastard.'

But she didn't get up, and he didn't move. He was wearing only a towel.

'One of us needs to pick up the children.'

The banality. A confession of adultery, if that was what it was, then the children. He supposed it would be the same if he now told her the truth: someone would still need to pick up the children. Although he imagined it might be postponed for a while longer. Holly would need time to laugh in his face, not viciously or even mockingly, but laugh all the same. Hadn't she said for months that he was withdrawing from her, even if she'd stopped short of saying that this was the likely outcome? He'd have to follow her from room to room, trying to explain why it was not what she thought, or how it was different in degree to what she had done, because of the plain fact that they didn't fuck. Not even *once*. Then she really would laugh in his face; if he believed that made a difference he was mocking himself. Maybe this new church of his should be a place for such erotic encounters: he could have women masturbate in the pews while he sermonized a dirty story. More sickened laughter.

But there was a profounder difference. The difference between inevitability and reaction. In the short time he'd had to process what Holly was telling him, all he could think was that the act had been a reaction to her loneliness, abandonment, her anger at him. That she'd been taken advantage of. But what about what he'd done? What claim was he making? Did he really believe that something purer had occurred with Judith? That in its purity some meaning was available that transcended the body, its drives, our psychology at its most base? Might sex, however it is enacted, offer something else: ordinary life interrupted, in its intensity a simulacrum of numinosity, the experience of an excess of life beyond our bodies . . . and with the avowal of such a thing . . . a step to the possibility of God?

Holly's laughter would stop then; her pain would exceed anything she had previously experienced, because she would need to defend herself against pitying him. To pity him would be the end. To laugh at him, then pity him . . . love didn't survive this. It would fall away into nothing, cold and irretrievable; it would die.

But none of that was going to happen because he wasn't going to tell her.

Holly stood up and went to the window. 'What are we going to do, Mac?'

He paused. 'One of us is going to pick up the twins.'

She put her hands into the front pockets of her skirt. 'You just feel so far away. Even now. Why aren't you angrier? More upset?'

Should he say something about the great transparency?

'I don't know.'

She rocked forward a little on her toes, her hands still in her pockets. 'Maybe you don't love me.'

'My love for you is not in doubt. What about how you feel?'

'I love you. I want to love you. But I can't pretend there isn't a problem. Not now.' She paused and turned to face him. 'I don't feel valued. Your life seems to be elsewhere. What you care about is elsewhere. That's not fair. We were such a happy family. We're never going to get that back now. Oh, my God, Mac. What have I done?'

To say nothing now was an act of moral cowardice.

He remained silent.

APOCALYPSE

'The dismal situation waste and wild:
A dungeon horrible on all sides around
As one great furnace flamed yet from those flames
No light but rather a darkness visible'

MILTON,
PARADISE LOST, BOOK 1

'Naturally . . .' a pale hand was placed on a large, fat manila file on the desk ' . . . you make us uncomfortable. It's a very sensitive and complex issue. Indeed we have you to thank for that insight.' He paused. 'What did you think we were going to do?'

'You have nothing to be concerned about. I take my work seriously. My responsibilities.' McCullough was in a shirt and tie; he'd combed his hair. He worried in case there was a kind of perceived insolence in this concession to conformity.

'You used very apocalyptic language. It seems you are building a church on land once owned by a radical religious sect. You claim—what? To be the receiver of . . . how might you describe it?'

'I wouldn't.'

'But you don't deny—'

'All I can say . . . all I can tell you . . . is what I tell everyone: if I look to my everyday experience, I am unconvinced that the human being is no more than a survival vehicle for the selfish gene. And as soon as you arrive at that point . . .'

'Quite. But few if any who agree with you would choose to build a church.'

'It was a misunderstanding.'

'Over what?'

'What it all means.'

'Yet you persist.'

'Part of me believes that it might serve some purpose.'

'Is that not rather an arrogant . . . assumption?'

'I am not what people look for in a leader, apparently.'

'Have you not converted anyone?' His tone was measured and clear; he didn't want to be lied to.

'Converted to what?'

'Your evasiveness does you no favours.'

'If I told you . . . if I actually described to you what I believe, you'd laugh, not because of its preposterousness, but at how simple and unthreatening it is.'

'Indeed. But while you are keeping this from us, you are a . . . worry.'

'I've always been a worry: ask my mother.'

'I'm going to speak plainly. You could easily be taken for someone with extreme religious views whom the government invited to advise on behaviour in the event of something . . . apocalyptic. Do you see?' The man's nose wrinkled a little.

'I see.'

'None of us here thinks there will be an apocalypse.'

'Neither do I.'

'But you were persuasive. And so we've—what's the phrase?—reframed our view on what it would mean for the nation if one of these particular acts of terror were to take place and the fallout is as you say.'

'I'm not sure how I—'

'You look tired, Mr McCullough.'

Perhaps he should explain why. He'd spent the night on the sofa, having drunk two bottles of wine, after an argument that had woken Pearl and made her cry, and that made Holly cry, and for a moment everything had been desperate in a way that seemed ridiculous, almost theatrical, and yet made him reassess what it was possible for a family to endure before it must break apart. He'd also wondered how often this could be repeated. But this was only a passing thought, a weakness; he was committed to Holly, to the family, its love. He'd followed Holly up the stairs, echoing her reassurances to

Pearl: 'Mummy and Daddy love each other', adding, 'It's just that Daddy has been away a lot and it's been hard on Mummy.' They had been at the top of the stairs and Holly's look—a brief turn and glare—had made him flare with anger, shake his head and leave them to it.

His explanation was not meant to be sarcastic or trivializing, but Holly's reaction, her inability to see it as something helpful, ignited a fear in him he didn't want to confront: that they had become a couple for whom nothing was not misunderstood; everything was a provocation. Holly didn't come down. He heard the electric toothbrush. The bathroom light. The creaking of floorboards above him. That the night was still warm and only just dark seemed a punishment, as if time had allowed itself to be opened up so it might be filled with loneliness and desolation. For the next five hours he listened to music at the lowest volume and drank wine. When he fell asleep it was dawn.

The man waited for a response.

McCullough sat forward. 'You are clearly concerned about me. Please be assured I am not going to go to the media.'

'We don't believe you will. But you remain a liability in two ways. If there is a leak, the media will come to you, and you do not have to say anything for them to build a story on the same foundation as your church . . . misunderstanding.' He smiled.

'And the second way?'

'As I said, you are persuasive. And you now possess information. That combination makes us uncomfortable.'

'I've signed the Official Secrets Act.'

'Yes.'

McCullough laughed. 'Did you read my proposal? I so wanted this work. This was my way to contribute. I thought whatever abilities I might possess . . . they were perfect for this project.'

'Again, you were very persuasive. Even the PM wanted to meet you. Politicians like people who really understand people. It's a gift they often don't possess themselves.'

'I'm not some kind of double agent.'

'Oh, that you were: we have plenty of experience with them.'

'I really don't understand what you're worried about. I don't believe there will be an apocalypse. I do not think that I am any kind of messiah. I have no wish to convert anyone to anything.'

'And yet you are building a church.'

'You can't get around that one, can you?'

'It's hard to. Given the circumstances.'

'Please just tell me what risk you think I pose and what I can do to set your mind at rest.'

'You see, Mr McCullough, that's just it. We don't know what risk you pose—perhaps none—and therefore neither we nor you can do anything about it.'

The conversation continued for another twenty minutes and McCullough emerged from the office feeling weary, with a cramping in his stomach, his skin hot. Jim was sitting on a sofa, knees wide open, reading a newspaper spread out before him on a low table. He looked up. 'Good?'

'OK.'

'Only OK?'

'Good.'

Jim stood. 'We need to talk.'

Little was said until they were out of the building and standing in a small piazza with moulded concrete benches, ornamental trees in cubical timber tubs. To one side a small three-wheeled van painted the colours of the Italian flag was selling coffee. There was a long queue. McCullough and Jim lined up, facing each other; Jim had his hand in his hair.

'I didn't think civil servants could be such scary bastards,' he said. 'I don't reckon that fucker's pulse ever goes above fifty.'

'It's fine.'

'He enjoys torturing me. He's clever: he's worked out I have trouble taking things seriously, so he's making me take this really seriously. But I don't have the ... facility. You're the serious one. That was the deal. I'm the clever, ridiculous one; you're the earnest, serious one.'

'Nothing's changed.'

'Everything's changed. You're never here. You're also supposed to be the reliable one. I can't be reliable.'

'Don't worry. We've come to an agreement. I am going to make myself available should they ever need to discuss this area again, and you are no longer involved, unless they want purely statistics based analysis.'

'You talked me into this. I don't know why I ever listen to you.'

'Apparently, I'm very persuasive.'

Unaccountably, Jim spun on his toes, his frustration given motion. 'Look, Mac, I can't run this business with you never here. You've got enough money. You can keep ten per cent. Let me run it into the ground my own way.'

'I will do whatever you want me to. I'm already distracted enough. Holly's unhappy. I miss the children.'

Jim breathed out, bent over, supporting himself with his hands on his knees; it had been a long mental run to this point and he was exhausted.

'Plus, how do I know everyone isn't right and that I'm not having some kind of breakdown?'

'Is that what you think?'

Someone in the coffee queue had ordered eight drinks, complicated ones.

'No.' McCullough's mind was like mush; his stomach felt dry and crispy from lack of sleep.

For five minutes they watched coffee being made. When their turn arrived, Jim ordered two double espressos.

'OK, Mac—this is my one big speech. Whatever you're doing—stop. Nothing you do will change anything—.'

'Is that it?'

'I meant "big" in the amount that I believe in what I'm saying. Not long. I've known you for twenty-odd years. You've always reckoned yourself a great historical figure, deep down. You'll deny it, but it's true.'

'I'm not sure it *is* true.'

'You're building a church! You're not spending your time in the British Library. And you're not Socrates.'

'I look terrible in sandals.'

'Please, go about your business. But don't start thinking you're going to change the world.'

'Do you agree it needs to change?'

'Of course, but if Barack Obama couldn't manage it when he was the most powerful man in the world, intellectually brilliant, with a lovely smile . . . what can you do?'

A young woman in a dark-green apron gave them two small paper cups of espresso. From the deep pockets of her apron she handed over sachets of sugar and long thin stirrers of wood. Both men were dexterous enough to tear sachets, pour and stir without setting anything down on the ground. But they couldn't talk at the same time. Jim managed to spill a drip of the thick black coffee on his shirt. He tried to flick it off with his finger. 'What does Holly think?'

'You know what? Is it so mad that I want people to think more deeply about the levels of kindness and love they are capable of if they look within themselves, or, perhaps more importantly, beyond themselves? That there is a relationship with God in which our capacity for love and kindness is increased?' He paused. 'And as for Holly—she's got other worries.'

'You're going to become very unhappy, Mac. Human nature is a gross thing. What we're dealing with here is a will to power. Nothing else. Certainly not a will to kindness. That's a luxury. And our will to love? Boy—the most dubious of all. What we'll do for love rather undermines love, don't you think? I'm sorry, Mac—it's just plain ugliness out there.'

'I fear for the business without me.'

'You should.'

They caught a cab back to the office and spoke separately to accountants and lawyers. After a brief exchange of emails, a call to the Home Office, McCullough was no longer a director of the business, and was now an independent consultant on atrocity for Her Majesty's Government.

'This morning I thought they'd brought me in to apologize about having to have me "disappeared" . . . and now I work for them.'

'What are you going to tell Holly?'

'That you dethroned me.'

Mournfully, Jim intoned, '"For God's sake, let us sit upon the ground.

And tell sad stories of the death of kings."'

'That's a bit how I feel.'

'You do know I remember what you were like as a younger man? Only me and Marvin know.'

'I know.'

'Then be careful.'

'Or you could read it this way: I was right then, and I'm just trying to find my way back.'

'Only Jesus and Napoleon had fewer ego boundaries.'

'Certain mystics would think that that was a good thing; it means you're wide open to the plenitude.'

McCullough stole a look out of the office window, to the tops of the surrounding buildings, the blue sky, and then down to the vast building site. He didn't feel desperate, which he supposed he should, given the enormity of what was happening to him. But then neither did he feel full of hope, which he supposed he should, given the message he'd just claimed to Jim was guiding him. For the most part he looked distracted and lost, as though what he believed was like a beam of light shining from a clifftop, disappearing into the nothingness of the night sky. The light was there, but what did it reveal? Was this possible: to get a glimmer, a seemingly infinite glimmer, of something ineluctable and abiding, and then after a breath is taken or a word is said, discover it's gone? If you're lucky maybe there is an afterglow, a retinal image that lasts a few seconds longer. But within hours you begin to doubt even that, and wonder whether it was all an act of the imagination, a fantasy. At best, you hold on to it as an intimation of something sacred; not the thing in itself. But after a while you begin to realize that every time you speak of it, when you were once solemn and demanded seriousness from your audience, you are now laughing at the clichés, the obvious metaphors and tropes. Finally, years later, it is no more than a dinner-party anecdote, your funny story, told with great timing and aplomb, about the moment God passed by.

THE ACCUSER

'A grief without a pang, void, dark, and drear,
A stifled, drowsy, unimpassioned grief,
Which finds no natural outlet, no relief,
In a word, or sigh, or tear—.'

SAMUEL TAYLOR COLERIDGE,
DEJECTION: AN ODE

They had dinner outside in the garden. Holly served fish that the children refused to eat, green beans that they were happy to dangle into their mouths like spaghetti, and a green salad. She'd opened a bottle of white wine. There was condensation on the glass. She wore a dark blue dress of light cotton; it stopped above her knees. The soles of her feet were dusty from the decking. The sun was behind the chimneys and there was shade from the lime tree. The twins had wanted McCullough to chase them with a water pistol, but as they badgered him in the garden, they began to look too small for such things, and their demands seemed ridiculous, and as Holly swept the tablecloth over the table and set out jugs of water and juice, he'd lost his temper and made them both cry.

For the first half an hour on his return home from work he and Holly had said little to each other but hadn't avoided being in the same space. She asked him to look at the fish and he'd poked it with a fork. He enquired about the small contraption she was using to slice the green beans into long thin strands. He was careful not to read the label on the back of the wine bottle, to be seen to make a judgment. It seemed wrong that Holly didn't know where he had been, the seriousness of it, and that he felt unable to tell her he'd quit the business and was now ostensibly unemployed, or at least until the government required his so-called expertise. Walking home from the Tube he'd felt as though he'd been released from something binding, and imagined all the things he might do. Jim hadn't known the full picture when he assumed money wasn't going to be an issue but there was enough for at least a year.

At the end of dinner the children were given yoghurts, which they finished, leaving smears around their mouths, the pots falling to the side under the weight of the small spoons. They both shot from the table, neither parent caring they hadn't asked to leave or that they somehow knew that going to watch TV wasn't going to be prevented. They just sat there, occasionally sipping wine, weary, sick, and cold of feeling.

'You should know, I've resigned from the business. It wasn't fair on Jim.'

Holly turned to him. What could she say? In terms of their emotional lives it was a minor event. Even so, was it right to let this go? Wasn't it another sign of him losing all sense of responsibility? But to probe his reasons was to risk him reminding her of what she'd done. Any talk about responsibility might just as well be about her now. That was what she hated most. Her stupid behaviour had displaced his stupid behaviour. Compared to what she had done, his behaviour over the last few months now seemed just ridiculous, clownish, silly. She, on the other hand, was marked forever. She was Lady Macbeth to his . . . who? Hamlet? No, he'd like that too much. Was there a *Carry On, Vicar?* He'd hate that. Either way, it now seemed to her that everything that was happening to him, the so-called visions, the church, the instructions, however absurd . . . none of them crossed a line that couldn't be uncrossed. It didn't matter that she believed his emotional withdrawal was a similar betrayal. It couldn't be pointed to; it was a felt thing only. But what she'd done . . . the line was like a score in hardened concrete, indelible, and then built on, and she was on the other side. There was no chance of turning away and then looking back and what separated them being erased, even by the wildest of winds. But if he gave up this mad enterprise now and came back to her, the gentlest of winds would sweep away any evidence he'd once abandoned her.

She looked at him, sitting a little hunched over the dinner table. He looked older and unhappier than she'd ever seen him.

His hair was more than a quarter grey now. Making dinner, he'd followed her instructions, but kept physical space between them. Had the children noticed? Of course they had, Pearl's eyes darting between them, watching, assessing. What Walter felt, it was impossible to tell—these days he talked only about how lava was made, its great heat and destroying power, invoking Krakatoa and Stromboli as if they were mighty gods. All day she tried to show interest in what both children talked about, but the moment she thought she was absorbed in what they were saying, she realized she was thinking about what had happened with Lucien, asking herself over and over: why had she let him in the first place; how had it happened?

Half a glass of wine and he'd moved to kiss her and she'd let him, and after that the physical sensations just took over and she alternated between passivity and an erotic charge that would ruin everything if McCullough knew of its strength. What he imagined had happened, she could only guess: he'd asked for no details. But it didn't matter—she knew. She could see it all, as if it had taken place in the daytime, in a room without shadow or glare. Whilst it had ceased to feel real, it had somehow become clearer, truer. She feared that over time this room would be stripped of detail and all she would be left with was the act itself, taking place in a white box, a bare depiction of fucking. And it was this reduction of the act, this distillation down to its physical sensations, that meant no matter how hard she tried to disassociate herself, it was as if Lucien was still present, his hands on her, his cock inside her. She was never going to forget what happened because he was crawling over her body like an incurable skin disease.

She found herself praying: she'd take back her life just as it was the moment before Lucien knocked on the door, even if it meant at times feeling like her heart would break. She'd been so stupid. Lucien! How predictable. Someone who'd flirted with her for years, someone so clear about his feelings, his *admiration*. He'd walked straight in and through to the sitting room, candidly explaining how he hated McCullough right at that moment, and proceeded to open a bottle of wine held between his thighs.

It went unsaid, but it was obvious they had found themselves together to prove once and for all what narrow, vulgar people they were compared to the saintly McCullough ... so spiritually impoverished with their lawyerly, commonsensical ways. It wasn't even an excuse, after the fact. The only subject they discussed *after the fact* was how McCullough would be insufferable if/when he found out. Which Holly now realized was a deeper betrayal of her love than the sex, because it was so much more unkind. This was partly the reason she hadn't told Lucien to leave in the first instance: a shared understanding that McCullough had moved so far away from them that they both imagined him forgiving them for what neither had yet done. So it had all been about him. To test him. What had Lucien said when he was about to leave? 'We couldn't have done it to a nicer man.' It was flippant, yes, mean-spirited, of course, but it was, in its own way, the case, and they both knew it. As she shut the door on him she feared she was changed irrevocably and might stand there forever, or at least until one of the children called her. But after ten minutes she'd found herself looking up at the clock and realizing they'd be awake soon and there were packed lunches to make.

She stood up, dishes in her hand. 'Do you want a yoghurt?' How flat her voice sounded, so drained of love.

McCullough looked up and studied her. Her hair had lightened in places from the summer sun. There was no grey as of yet. She looked as if she'd lost weight since last night. Anyone who knew her well would know she was hurting in ways that were new to her. There had been moments over the day when he'd forgotten what had happened, not just instants but whole stretches of time when he was occupied with business, then it had come back to him and he felt like he'd woken up after an operation only to be told what had been found was terminal. Was this how she was feeling at the moment? He supposed that in the split second she'd asked him if he wanted a yoghurt, she'd set it all aside. Was this how they were going to get through? The minutiae of life interrupting waves of pain? His mouth appeared to decide he did want a yoghurt, and his mind wondered whether he really did, because he almost never said yes to pudding. Was he just trying to make a point? If so, what? It didn't feel like a coded reproach. He continued to study Holly. She looked away, dishes in her hands.

'Pearl's been itching. She might have nits. We should de-nit them both.'

'I'll do it if you want.' He said this without reflection. After all, it was something to do. It would require concentration and forgetting.

The twins in bed, Comedy Central on the TV, they sat at either end of the sofa, two glasses of wine before them on the table. Neither was concentrating, each could feel the other was distracted and unsettled. Holly had spent an hour calming Pearl down; the little girl knew something was wrong and was not prepared to be ignored or fobbed off with easy assurances—she had friends whose mummy and daddy didn't live together. She didn't possess the language skills to explain that she sensed this was where her mummy and daddy were heading, but her mood was articulate enough. McCullough accepted that the atmosphere in the house must feel like he and Holly were already separated. Even when they were in the same room, a cold space existed between them that neither would cross. Could Pearl feel this cold when she approached them? She was as directly sensitive to their world as Walter was indirectly sensitive to it. Where he would skirt around their coldness, Pearl needed to test it, feel it for herself, react to it. Her nature was to find within herself an emotional equivalence to the world around her; in this instance, her own kind of heartbreak.

Finally Holly lay in bed with her, whispering, describing all the lovely things they would do as a family, even promising her they would go and see the house and church Daddy was building. It was a mistake. Pearl perked up and wanted to discuss it with Walter. Holly was too weary and fed up to insist it was a promise contingent on her going to sleep; she just wanted her daughter to accept the emotional comfort and be done with it.

Walter's only noticeable response that evening was a look of worry when McCullough announced he'd sold his business. Both parents caught a flicker of something behind his steady eyes and sensed him retreat into himself. McCullough found him in the bedroom and asked him to sit on the bed and talk. The boy reluctantly agreed, but couldn't sit still, wanting to be free to build Lego over by the window and shut himself off from the explanation his daddy was giving him; he preferred it the other way around, explaining things himself, without interruption. McCullough seldom insisted he sit still. Walter repeated himself: he wanted to build Lego. After a pause, he did ask how he was to act when he saw his dad at home when he was supposed to be at work. What should he do? McCullough wanted to cry. Would he ever be able to guess his son's worries? Before he could decide what to say in response, Walter seemed to have a moment of illumination. He turned to his father and spoke in a calm, matter-of-fact way.

'You and Mummy always say to others that I don't like change, and I don't—not at all. But more than that, I don't like to worry about how to behave. That's why I don't like new places. I try to copy others but I'm not good at following. I'm not good at mimicking like Pearl. I am getting better. I know now to smile when someone is taking my photograph. I pull my mouth wide. Like this.'

It wasn't a smile; it was a kind of gurn. Thick-lipped. Expressionless. Idiotic. This time, McCullough couldn't stop himself from crying, and Walter was released to the window. It was hard to tell if anything had been accomplished. All the wriggling to get away suggested deep resistance, yet in his articulate response there was a kind of comprehension, even if it wasn't entirely relevant. On one level, McCullough worried that clinging on to Walter was a way to provide himself with some comfort and security. But the boy was now standing at the window, his tower of plastic IKEA drawers open, tipping the whole stack forward with thousands of Lego bricks ramped at the front. It was a marvel to watch, the blind rummaging as he looked for a piece, and its sudden appearance in his hand. A miracle even—given the number of bricks it defied basic laws of probability. If there was ever a time Walter let others into his world it was when he allowed them to observe his acts of concentration with Lego; watching him was a directly *feelable* experience, as few things are that take place in another's world.

It was at these times McCullough felt that the bubble around Walter—self-created or not—was so much thinner and more flexible than his own wall of transparency, and that Walter's world might occasionally include others, whereas he feared his own had no such permeability.

What he loved in his son, loved to watch for the vicarious pleasure it gave him, was Walter's fascination with cause and effect, the mind's emergent relationship with the physical world as a mystery of observable and invisible agency. It had started when he was two years old, with hours spent pouring liquid in and out of containers. He then moved on to elaborate mixing. After that came velocity and trajectory from thrown objects, to his all-time favourite— waves on a beach pushing up and withdrawing from his dancing feet. McCullough wondered whether on some level it was this that he himself was waiting for—this simplicity of experience but on a cosmic scale.

So they'd both spent the early evening reassuring their children that nothing was wrong, nothing would change, and were now sitting on the sofa as if nothing had changed, except it seemed an impossibility that their bodies would ever touch again.

The TV remained on Comedy Central because to discuss what to watch was something they would have done *before*, and they were in some other place now, and to normalize this with habits of old was a perversity. Even the recordings on the TV planner, if they weren't for the children, were a mutual choice—something watched and enjoyed together; the ends of films that neither could stay awake to finish; unseen episodes of long-running comedies and dramas; the occasional arts documentary they'd committed to watch at some point. How could either scroll down and ask the question, 'What do you feel like?'

After twenty minutes of silence, Holly stood up and said, 'I'm going to bed.' There was no inflection, just a proposition describing an action, the most basic of announcements, although she knew to say it was to make a statement of intent that changed everything. They seldom went to bed separately, especially not two evenings in a row. It wasn't even dark outside, so it seemed doubly like an act of defiance, a resetting of how things were done now, in this house, in this new world. McCullough knew that accompanying her was out of the question: to lie in bed, awake, in daylight, after only one glass of wine would be unendurable.

He said 'good night' but it was a reflex, politeness, and both judged the other harshly for not saying what was on their minds. What did it mean, all this silence and politeness? That they were giving up or just setting aside the emotional fallout for another time? Or somehow did they both hope that if they were lucky and they continued to interact through the needs of the children, over time, the silence, the uninflected language, changes of routine, the cold space, would all crumble away, and the ugliness would die a natural death, and they'd find themselves on the other side without having to go through all the rancour and recriminations? It was tempting to believe it was possible. But he knew there was another, more probable, outcome. The risk was that silence, although meant to be respectful of the enormity of what had happened, would accidentally kill everything good between them, as if the obvious and right consequence of emotional shock was emotional stasis, and rather than addressing the shock they were mistaking the stasis for a plan—just let this terrible thing fall away, and what had been constant over thirteen years must surely remain.

No part of him had thought of returning to Judith, in the belief that a new and better, more emotionally rewarding life was available down there. He wasn't that stupid. At that moment, sitting on the sofa in London, he wasn't sure Judith really existed. It was difficult enough to apprehend Holly as real—the woman he'd loved for years. Of course, that was another fear: without Holly being herself—fun, happy, easy to love—would she become someone he didn't recognize, not the woman he loved? It was important for both their sakes, for the relationship, that she remained herself. But that didn't involve leaving him in the sitting room as if this was somehow all his fault. That wasn't fair; and she *was* fair, usually. It was cold and unfeeling and she was neither of these things. He didn't want to hate her, even for a moment. To feel anger; to blame her. But she was abandoning him. The world was in error.

'Are you going to sleep down here again?' What answer did she want?

'I don't know. Last night I was drunk; I drifted off.'

'Suit yourself.' He knew not to judge her from her expression; her face hardened in ways she wasn't aware of when she was emotionally withdrawn. She added, 'If you come up, try not to wake me. Can you use your iPad to read?'

She left the room. McCullough pulled his mobile phone out of his pocket and sat hunched up looking at the screen. It took a while for new emails to download. He stared at the list. Did he want communication from the outside world? It was something to do. He deleted what it was unnecessary to keep. Scrolling through his texts, he stopped when he saw Lucien's name. Mail from two weeks ago. *They won't decant the bottle!* Nothing else. He tapped 'reply'. Was there anything to say, really? He supposed Holly had informed Lucien that he now knew. It was irritating, imagining that conversation: 'He's back. I told him.' And so on.

He put the phone down on the table and picked up his wine. It tasted of little; there was just the minor hit—mostly psychological— of its being alcoholic. He leaned over to pick up Holly's almost-full glass and poured it into his own. The rest of the bottle was in the kitchen, a long way away. It was all such a mess. Such a fucking mess. And he'd been the cause of it. If one looked at the chronology of events, there was no denying it: whether it was a midlife crisis or an authentic spiritual encounter, the mess started with him. Of course, there was no way of knowing if this hadn't happened whether or not something else would have. But to think they might have made it through life together without an event of this magnitude was to believe some more contented version of their life was possible and wish for it, or to wish that life had been otherwise.

He was back to where Nietzsche and God intersected. Your life was your life, and to wish for another was an act of bad faith (Nietzsche), or required intervention (God), if we weren't to act out what had been preordained for us from the beginning of time. Not that he believed God involved Himself that way: God neither knows the trajectory and destination of our lives because it was set before the beginning of time, nor can He intervene and change it if He so wishes. However, right now, he would take an old-fashioned interventionist God—a dispenser of justice and punishment. Working through all the blame and guilt himself was too much. There were times during the day when he felt as if some kind of trial was going on his head and he was listening to an endless loop of evidence and argument. It made sense: Holly and Lucien were lawyers, and he'd witnessed both of them argue cases in court. He could hear Lucien defend himself, the mitigation he might offer, and he heard his own testimony in defence of Lucien, recalling visits to Lucien's parents, astonished by his father's habit of referring to his son as 'the younger one', because the 'older one' was his primary concern—title, house, fortune. It was well within McCullough's nature to allow this simple fact to exonerate Lucien, without anyone introducing the damning testimony of Lucien the school bully, the humiliation he dished out at Oxford, his general disregard for others' feelings, especially those of women. But in the end, it didn't matter what was said, no one would ever know why Lucien had done what he'd done. The most that could be asked was how Lucien felt at the time, and now, three days on, sitting at home with Maria, or wherever he was. Maybe only feelings count when dealing with the unfathomable. McCullough asked himself: was there any chance Lucien was in pain? He supposed he didn't really mean pain, not as it was usually understood. But Lucien must have felt *something*, be feeling *something*, and it wasn't likely to be joyous, life-loving delight. Maybe what he was feeling was the cost of his denial of the pain he caused around him, the desperate struggle to live above the high crashing waves, or to be seen to be aware of the peril at all. Either way, deep feelings must be at play inside him, and what deep feeling other than love was ever good?

McCullough took a deep breath. The full wine glass was untouched. He looked at the phone on the table. Would it ring? Was there going to be something to tear him away from himself? The only person he could face speaking to was Rebecca; she was smart, sensible and seemed to care about him in her own way. What had her mother told her? Hadn't they both said they 'shared' most things, as mothers and daughters usually do? He doubted Judith would volunteer any information, so it was a matter of whether Rebecca wanted or cared to know, and whether she was willing to persist after her mother refused to tell her straightaway. He was fairly certain Rebecca would remain unchanged towards him, whatever she learned. Judith had given him a strong sense of Rebecca's father, and McCullough now recognized in her character the innate distancing from emotional mess that a particular kind of brilliance possessed. Did Rebecca even have his number? There had never been any need to exchange numbers. They just shouted at one another across the cliffs.

He tried to picture the site. It would be empty now, the Portland stone glowing palely orange from the fading sun, the steel beams casting long shadows across the grass. Approached from over the ridge, or up between the cliffs, it might appear either beautiful or a ruin. To earn its place it probably needed to be seen, in a single glimpse, as both—Pascal's mystical hexagon breaking out of an attempt to build something more traditional, abandoned as not fit for purpose. He didn't expect approval from anyone, whatever its success as a building. Perhaps the real confirmation of success could only come from Holly. If she were moved when she saw it, at least she might turn to him and smile, appreciate his efforts as she did the children's when they attempted something ambitious.

He stood and stretched and scratched the back of his hand. When would he be able to go back down? It needed to be finished by the end of the summer, before the weather changed, at least that's what all the tradesmen told him. But to abandon Holly now would be worse than anything he'd yet done. And yet to stay, lonely and bored, helpless—how long would he be able to resist? Maybe he should judge himself from what he eventually decided. Wasn't that how it always was? In the end we do what we want to do? He looked across to the TV. *Friends* was on.

He switched it off and dropped the remote onto the sofa. He picked up the full glass of wine, went into the kitchen and grabbed the bottle. On the landing upstairs, Holly's bedside light was visible.

He looked in on the twins. Still, silent shapes under duvets. Only Pearl's hair visible across her pillow. Where was he going to sleep? There was the spare room; the sofabed in his office. The spare room was characterless: a small double bed, a wardrobe and chest of drawers. No bedside table or light. The bulb of the ceiling light was without a shade. Blinds had been bought but never put up.

He gulped at his wine. It tasted rancid, metallic; his throat wanted to reject it. Pearl sneezed, a lovely compact *tchun*. He paused. Sometimes they came in twos and threes. It was a delightful sound.

The daybed in his office was piled with books, mostly of theology. He moved them onto the floor and sat down. It was hot in the loft, even with the window wide open. He needed something to read. Something engrossing. At the top of one pile was Augustine's *The City of God*—a book he didn't think he'd ever finish. There was an abridged version of Aquinas's *Summa Theologiae*—same likely outcome. Underneath it was Paul Tillich's *The Courage to Be*, which felt a little too on the nose right now.

He went to the shelves behind the door, as if something might be hidden there, and scanned without really focusing. There was a recent Faber edition of Wallace Stevens' *Harmonium*, a gift from someone. He tweezered it out with the tips of his thumb and forefinger. He flicked through, then back, let pages fall open. There was a hair on a page which he flicked away. He read 'The Emperor of Ice-Cream' and then 'Metaphors of a Magnifico', which he intuitively agreed was probably a sensible way to regard the world, and then 'Sunday Morning', one of the few Stevens poems he was familiar with. A woman sitting alone, before a big window. Was this the start of Judith's love of Stevens, or was that too obvious? Either way she must have at some point identified with the woman in the poem. The light from the big window, the death of her parents, the Fauvist colours on the walls.

> She says, 'But in contentment I still feel
> The need of some imperishable bliss.'

You and me both. He turned the page and read:

Supple and turbulent, a ring of men
Shall chant in orgy on a summer morn
Their boisterous devotion to the sun,
Not as a god, but as a god might be,
Naked among them, like a savage source.

Maybe there was no more to what he was doing than this. After all, the shape of steels might easily be mistaken for an enormous sundial. How much easier it would be to explain: 'I feel like building something in honour of the sun.' He would be thought mad, yes. But there was no argument that we are here because of its bounty, and will go with its burning out. Creator. Sustainer. Destroyer.

He slipped the book back, wiggling it in to make room; he could feel the densities of the books along the shelf; the immaterial content pressed into the finite space. There was nothing he really wanted to read. What could possibly be right for this moment? He returned to the sofabed and lay down. The glass of wine had been placed on a facsimile edition of the Geneva Bible. Perhaps it was true about the Bible: in its vast and often impersonal story a particular solace might be found. He felt like a salesman in a hotel, bereft of love, turning to the only book available to him. For an hour he sipped warm wine and read the Wisdom Books.

Morning. Everyone was around the table eating cereal, Walter humming.

Breakfast tended to start well and then became a tiresome canon of cajoling and censure: that's too much cereal; sit nearer the table; don't *look* at your sister, then; just one more spoonful; *pick* the cup up *off* the table, you're not a dog!

It was Walter who asked his father what he was going to do if he didn't have a job. There didn't seem to be any great anxiety behind the question this morning. McCullough said, 'Today, I'm going to see Grandpa,' something both twins understood was a good thing, a nice thing to do, but they couldn't quite understand why it was ever said, as it sometimes was, with a degree of excitement, as a fun thing.

Holly asked, 'Shall we do him a card?'

There was a growl from Walter and then a slow building 'No', lasting as long as his breath would allow. He wasn't angry; he was just making sure everyone knew it was an unacceptable request. If they'd asked why, he'd be clear and firm: it wasn't Grandpa's birthday and there had been no warning. Pearl, however, was keen, and it was agreed she would make a card straight after breakfast and Walter could sign it. McCullough ducked down to try and meet Walter's eyes: 'All you have to do is write your name.' There was no response, but McCullough could tell that having this in his future was a disturbance Walter would carry around with him until he was called to sign the card, at which point it would become a double disturbance: that he'd been required to do it in the first place and that he now had to pull himself away from whatever he was doing. McCullough closed his hand around his son's. He felt a need to reward Walter in advance (extra computer time, TV time, playing outside with the hose) just for contemplating it. But how was that fair when his sister had agreed to do everything, and keenly? She was already describing the picture she was going to draw.

'It's only your name, darling,' Holly said, and she held his other hand.

'I hate writing; you know I hate writing.' It was said simply, but with anger at himself. Six months ago he wouldn't have cared but more recently he'd become embarrassed when he struggled with activities he thought others found easy, and he didn't like to get things wrong. If he signed the card and made a mistake, he'd decide the card was spoiled, and if they weren't watching, rip it up, and this would cause a scene with his sister. Pearl would be justified in her anger; yet Walter's decision to tear or scrunch the card because he'd made a mistake that he didn't want the world to see, would move both parents beyond the more reasonable upset of his sister. That both parents said 'We'll be right here' at the same time made Walter laugh, momentarily halting the ever-deepening frustration.

Neither parent found it funny. Holly steadied her chin and found a false smile, which was little more than a folding in of her lips and a little added brightness to her eyes. McCullough looked away, and said under his breath, 'This is ridiculous. Jesus!' Walter started to laugh more hysterically and wriggle around on his seat, after which he dipped his head into what remained of his cereal. It would have been usual for Pearl to mimic this, to push the play further, but she had sensed her mother's distress and reverted to a baby voice: 'Mama . . . what's wrong, Mama?'

'I'm fine, darling,' Holly assured her, one hand over her daughter's. 'Everything is fine.'

For that moment they were an unbroken chain around the table.

Walter emerged from his cereal, face patched with milk, grey on his skin, Froot Loops stuck to his cheeks and on his forehead. He laughed each time one slid off, his tongue squirming about to catch it. This was enough to distract Pearl, and she tried to stick Froot Loops onto her own cheeks and forehead. Hands let go of hands. There were now two planes of existence around the table: the children having fun, and McCullough and Holly tired beyond recovery.

Holly made to stand up. 'Mac?'

'Yes?'

'Do you think I should arrange sleepovers for the children?'

Whether it was a good idea in terms of time they might spend together they would never know, because as fast as Pearl's hand went up, as if it were a choice which of the two of them might be allowed to go, Walter looked around and, wearing his most fearsome expression, screamed, 'NO SLEEPOVER FOR ME FUCKING HELL!'

THE FOUR GOSPELS II

'Let us go then, you and I,
When the evening is spread out against the sky
Like a patient etherized upon a table.'

T. S. ELIOT,
THE LOVE SONG OF J. ALFRED PRUFROCK

I

McCullough left home, saying he was going straight to Edward's office. But instead, he crossed two junctions to the main road and hailed a cab and directed the driver to the opposite side of town. During the night he'd decided on a surprise visit to Lucien's chambers, to force a confrontation, a scrap. If he was lucky it might result in Lucien being fired. His chambers, after all, was a gentlemanly place, where business was conducted with an old-world sense of dignity. What people did in their private lives was one thing, but at chambers a certain 'parade', as Lucien had once put it, was required. Which was why walking in and shouting 'You fucked my wife', whilst it might not do McCullough any material good, would certainly ruin Lucien, at least in terms of his current chambers; a man of his talents would find another position easily enough, but it would be at one of those places for which *parade* meant little more than the swish of their gowns, revealing Gucci loafers, anathema to Lucien, and a humiliation. The imagined scene was delicious, every eventuality played out, each one culminating in a grand stand-off, where for once in his life Lucien had nothing to say. After all, many of his colleagues knew McCullough was an old friend, and it was taken for granted you didn't do such things to old friends.

But after a damp, grey, lustreless dawn, breakfast with Holly and the twins, McCullough felt incapable of carrying out his plan. Advice was needed, and there was only one person with whom he might discuss these things without engendering emotion, unnecessary drama or unfair judgment. But that would be his second stop.

From the cab, he called Edward and asked if he might arrive a little late. Edward laughed: writing policy documents, staring out of the window while listening to Handel, was no urgent task—he could come whenever was convenient. McCullough thanked him.

At the black door, he knocked lightly. He had nothing rehearsed: it wasn't going to be that kind of conversation. His presence there was little more than an instinct to do something right. If he wasn't to become maladjusted somehow, he needed to be kind to someone.

Maria answered the door and looked as surprised as he'd anticipated. She gathered herself and said, 'What's he done?'

There was as ever only one answer: 'Nothing.'

'Then why are you here?'

'To see you.'

'Why?'

'Are you going to let me in?'

She smiled and stepped out of the way. 'I've made coffee.'

The kitchen was like his own, messy from a family breakfast and bright and warm from the morning sun. On the stove top the frying pan was still warm; Lucien always made himself something for breakfast. When both families had gone away together for the weekend, he had cooked them all his favourite breakfast of fried kidneys on toast, sprinkled with a little orange zest. He was comfortable at a stove preparing small dishes he enjoyed. He never cooked for the children.

Maria leaned against the counter; McCullough sat on a high stool opposite her.

'Where are the boys?'

'Sports clubs, Arty-Party. Who knows?'

McCullough smiled. 'How are you feeling, Maria?'

'Please, not with me, Mac.'

'It's just a question.'

'And you know the answer.'

'But I'm not sure I do. That's why I'm here. Last time we met was on the doorstep.'

'What's that got to do with anything?'

'I suggested you get medication.'

'You're checking up—seeing whether I followed your advice?' She was seldom shrill, she was too naturally ironic for that, but her voice could rise quickly and vibrate, warning against any contradiction.

'Not at all. That was flippant of me. But you're unhappy, I can see. And we were once good friends.'

'Were we? I remember there was a group of us and you never really spoke to me. Although we did get off with each other once. But nothing much happened. You were a good kisser, I remember.'

'You were very sexy.'

'Clearly not to you.'

'To me.'

'Well, that boat's sailed.' Coffee from a pot was poured into bowl-shaped cups. It was lukewarm. 'I still don't know why you're here.'

'I've quit my business—I'm a free man.'

'You're going to become a lady who lunches.'

'Quite possibly.'

She sipped her coffee. 'So what are we going to talk about? Your family, my family? Schools? I don't want to talk about your stupid church.' She smiled. 'How's Holly?'

'She's fine. No, not fine. You might say we're at a crisis point.'

'The perfect couple?'

'Not right now.'

'But you always thought you were, didn't you? That you'd chosen right.'

'I did choose right.'

'And everyone else didn't?'

'There are a lot of unhappy couples.'

'You're unhappy.'

'We're one of them.'

'I don't know what we're talking about.'

Much of the kitchen was white, the timber floor painted a soft blue—a bohemian touch. There was enough space for the mess of

a family of five to look manageable. The garden was little more than
a courtyard; at its centre, an iron table with a mosaic top and four
ironwork chairs.

'I want you to be happier, Maria. That's what I've come here
for. Nothing else.'

'I peaked early. It's all been downhill for some time. If you want
to try and push me back up—go ahead.'

'What is it about me that annoys you?'

'Why—do you think that's a clue? Isn't that rather arrogant,
Mac? Thinking you're the key to my happiness.'

'Got to start somewhere.'

'You don't think I'm jealous, do you?'

'Not for a second.'

'Then what? What do you think makes me so unhappy, given
that I have so much? Or is that part of it—having so much?'

'I don't think that's part of it.'

'We're not doing very well.'

'No. You seemed more receptive the other night.'

'I was drunk.'

She refilled both cups. The coffee was now cold.

'How are the twins?'

'Fine. The boys?'

'Fine . . . I think. How could I possibly know? They keep everything from me. They think I'm a loser. If only they knew what a shit
their father is.'

'Is he a shit?'

'You know he is. Don't be disingenuous.'

'You could leave him?'

'Could I? How helpful.'

'Sorry.'

She smiled wearily. She was getting tired of being so defensive.
'Look, Mac. It was a nice thought, coming round here. I do appreciate it. And my day will feel a little better for it. But there's nothing
to be done. I made bad choices, as they keep saying today about
naughty children. I should never have left my job, married Lucien,
had kids. It wasn't for me. But I did all three, and now I'm doing my

best to live with the result. Except I'm not very good at doing that. Which is a shame. That probably makes me seem like a cold person, but I'm not. I try and be the best mother I can. I organize, sort out, and pretty well manage three boys—and Lucien. We spend the weekends together and everyone gets on. Luckily the children have all inherited their father's ability not to show any extreme emotion. In that way, I'm a bit of an embarrassment to them. Does it matter? The feminist in me says yes—women get a raw deal in this family. We're idiots apparently. And because I'm regarded as an idiot, the boys will grow up thinking the same as Lucien, and Lucien's father— and that will be my fault. But I'm not sure what I can do about it now. And it's not a crime, is it?'

McCullough was quick to answer her, but softly. 'No.'

'See what a big help you've been.' She poured herself the dregs of the coffee—drips. There was a blush on her cheeks.

'Maybe I should keep you secret. Not tell Lucien you've been here.'

He smiled.

'Holly's happy in her job, isn't she?'

'Very.'

'Lucien thinks she's the bee's knees.'

'I know.'

'Everyone thinks that.'

'Right now, I'm not sure I do.'

Maria stood up, empty cup in both hands. 'Do you want more coffee?'

'No, thanks.'

'Wine?'

'It's not even ten o'clock.'

'You're right. What am I thinking?' Her laughter had a self-conscious buoyancy, but beneath it she seemed lighter-spirited than she had in a long time.

'Thank you, Mac.'

'I've done nothing.'

'First step to recovery is admitting that someone else who thinks you have a problem might be right.'

'Clever.'

'I got a first, remember? I was brilliant. Remember?'

'I do.'

'So what are you going to do with the rest of your day?'

'I have a few people I need to see.'

'Sounds ominous.'

'Yes and no.'

She leaned back down on the counter. 'Are you going to have a grand opening, when you're finished?'

'Finished my "stupid church"?' He smiled.

'Now don't be like that, Mac. Otherwise I'll go back to goading and generally disliking you.'

'Marvin thinks we're secretly a bit in love with each other.'

'You think all women are secretly a bit in love with you. You think it's a sign of . . . not so much good taste . . . as profound taste. You're so much deeper than other men.'

'Are you goading me?'

'Yes and no. You might be right.'

'I like women.'

'And they like you.'

'A certain type.'

'I'm afraid I'm not one of them.'

'I'll let Marvin know.'

'You're a sweetheart.'

Whether the warmth between them had a short half-life or Maria was just bored, she now made it clear it was time for him to leave. Her smile was suddenly rictus-like, a hardened version of Walter's heart-breaking photo face.

'I'll send Marvin your love.'

'Do.' She opened and shut the front door as if he was a tradesman with whom she'd made no connection.

McCullough stood on the pavement, looking around the empty street for a taxi. He couldn't help but feel there was something a little tragic about Maria. She had been brilliant and sexy; she'd been 'fun'. And now she was unfulfilled and miserable. Was she right, she'd peaked early? Maybe. It was certainly the case that she lived with a man who was always peaking, as if he were walking in a mountain range that just kept providing steeper, higher climbs, and yet each new ascent was effortless; even the thinness of the air had no impact on him.

Perhaps it was McCullough's job to find him up there on the peak and knock him off.

2

Marvin wasn't up—he seldom rose before eleven o'clock—and suggested in a hoarse tone via the intercom that McCullough go and get them an espresso each from a place far, far away and return in half an hour *or more.*

There was a cafe across the road with two aluminium tables outside and three chairs. Cigarette butts, flicked from the tables, were building up in the gutter. McCullough sat at one of the tables and ordered an espresso. Was much of his life going to be like this now, sitting in cafes with little to do? There had been many times when he'd wished it were the case. Finally his metabolism, the coffee notwithstanding, dropping into a lower gear, and with that the prospect of reading poetry again, something that he'd not been able to do for years. As if a book had miraculously appeared, he looked down at his hands. His veins were thick and distended. He recognized them, from his past, from his father. The pores on his skin, especially where hair extruded, were visible. To look closely was to see the signs of ageing, of irreversible change in colour, texture, a slackening of tension—it was all rather depressing.

The day was heating up. The sun flashed in the lower corners of Marvin's windows. The white, pink, yellow stucco façades of the townhouses were bright and flawless, almost with the promise of flavour. It was now a neighbourhood of great wealth. In each drive there were two cars, mostly German.

Across the junction, beyond a shiny black iron railing, was a mid-sized church, built from grey stone, its lower half obscured by a large rhododendron. Its noticeboard was dark red with gold lettering, freshly painted. A list of services, names of clergy, perhaps a website. Just another church, then—another Anglican church on a snug patch of land in London, neither grand nor modest, and certainly, from McCullough's point of view, without any promise of surprise, or a warm welcome. There were times when he passed Pentecostal services, usually taking place in an anonymous room above a parade of shops, and felt a vicarious joy at the *congregating*, as if the service really had been spontaneous and full of passers-by who'd experienced a physical pull to join in and come together. Surely it didn't matter where people met, the consecration of the space, its history or tradition—God would find them. Or more precisely, He was already present, which McCullough believed was probably closer to the Pentecostal perception of God's general whereabouts. He wondered what he would do if he came across one of these celebrations in an open space; would he join them and participate in his own way— something that would never happen if it meant opening a door? Perhaps this was what he should have done himself: accepted the pull of the location, but have built nothing, just marked out a spot. Maybe not even that. Just planted a signpost with an arrow on it. He laughed. Whatever people thought of his mental state now, that would seem madder still, sitting on a clifftop, a sign pointing to him.

A small espresso cup was placed on the table for him, together with packets of sugar and a spoon. He looked over to the church again. Beyond picturing a few (old) people standing in the pews and a vicar moving about before them, he wasn't sure he could imagine what went on inside, at least not when the daily and weekly services were not being performed. His last visit to a church had resulted in his gentle eviction. Wasn't the basic requirement of any Anglican minister these days, to offer to accompany you on your 'journey'? He'd just been sent on his way. Maybe he should try again, this time opening with more orthodox lines of enquiry. Even so, he supposed there would come a moment when, struggling to make his point, or infuriated by some dogma, he'd declare, 'Actually, I'm building a church of my own.' He almost choked on his coffee. *I'm building my own church!* My God, was that what he was doing? *'I* know a way you'll listen to me: *I'll build my own bloody church, then we'll see!'*

He pictured himself in a pulpit extemporizing a sermon, full of sincerity and passion, glancing up and finding no one present. Was that his destiny: obsession, affliction, madness? He knew nothing that happened down there would lead to that. However, if he and Holly were to split up . . . that was different . . . She was central to everything he believed to be good and worthwhile. Even his capacity to love her was somehow her doing. The only test he knew he would fail was how he'd cope if she stopped loving him. Not that he believed in being tested. But then not believing in things didn't mean such things weren't true. Hadn't he made that point precisely when announcing the possibility of the truth of his original visions? In his recurring dream, it was the impossibility of Holly not loving him and yet not doing so that was the trigger for madness. God's shocking gift was that, despite our capacity to love, Holly was free not to love him.

It would be interesting to hear the minister's thoughts on that. Free will was everyone's favourite subject, especially these days when every newspaper published articles informing us that we were as blindly determinate as beasts, or, as he'd recently read, thermometers. He'd take any advice that might help keep their love alive. No doubt prayer would be kindly offered, but as ever with no guarantee of intercession. We would have to know God's plan to promise that. How could he resist arguing: doesn't that mean God will intervene or not, prayer or not? Which means if God is seen to intervene, it's not really intervention but just part of His plan—prayer has had no impact. Or are we saying: He's open to listening, to intervening, and if you don't pray, you miss your opportunity? Because that means some things aren't fixed; they require us to act or not act. So no overall plan.

Not that he wouldn't pray his heart out if Holly stopped loving him, even without a fundamental acceptance of its efficacy, because that is the nature of despair: to finally turn to the impossible. And it wouldn't be the first time he'd cried out into the dark. It was only a month ago he'd pleaded on his knees for release. It didn't matter whether God was listening or not, or even existed or not, appealing into such openness was in itself mind-expanding, the whole universe out there to call into. Even if the universe itself was deaf, it still carried your call. Wasn't there some kind of infinite or eternal reciprocity built into quantum mechanics? And what human activity created more energy than the despairing prayer? It was probably this that was the felt proof of its power, the answering proof, whatever its actual success.

Well, he might know someday soon. He looked at his watch. Twenty minutes had passed. He went into the cafe and ordered two espressos to take away. He watched distractedly as the woman ground the beans and tamped them down in the stainless-steel cup, before slotting it and locking it into place in the machine. The little takeaway espresso cups looked like the paper thimbles handed out with pills in a hospital. The aroma of the ground coffee, much like the aroma of the dregs of wine in a glass, promised complex layers of flavour not present when actually drinking it. In a large bin next to the machine there was a great landfall of used grounds; it looked like the most fertile brown earth, as if it would be wonderfully soft underfoot. Whilst he didn't believe there was any meaning to be found in the differing proportions of labour to volume to pleasure in the 'espresso experience', it *was* a large volume of beans, and a great deal of labour, to create such a small amount of liquid that was finished in one or two gulps—so it felt right to dwell on it, just in case.

He paid with coins from different pockets and left a tip in the saucer on the counter.

Across the road, Marvin was on his doorstep, clutching closed a long dark raw silk kimono. He was sure to be naked underneath and a lot less modest in his own home. On the threshold, he took a cup from McCullough, drank it down and returned it into McCullough's hands.

'I know why you're here.'

McCullough followed him in. 'How?'

'It cannot possibly shock you that the first person Lucien would tell is me.'

'It does shock me.' McCullough began to tremble. 'Jesus, Marvin, what's happening? Why did they . . . ?' The tears in his eyes were heavy, irresistible. Sometime sadness was worse than desperation.

Marvin shut the door and guided him to a chair. 'Sit down.' With a little yank of the curtains he shut out any light. A lamp was on. Marvin made room for himself on his sofa, pushing away newspapers and contact sheets. He sat in the centre, legs crossed, and tucked the fabric of his kimono over his knees. He lit a cigarette.

'It was a confession. He fears you, Mac. He wanted my advice. Well, not advice. He wanted my reaction. To gauge the extent of his betrayal. He thinks I'm capable of far worse. Or he thinks my motives are ... darker, whatever my behaviour.'

McCullough put his head in his hands. He was soon crying without shame, without control; there was snot and saliva on his hands. *Holly, Holly, you stupid fucking stupid bitch. Lucien, you cunt.*

'He was contrite. He giggled. He called—God knows—eight times.'

A minute passed before McCullough emerged from behind his hands and looked around for something to wipe his hands and nose on. He needed to go into the kitchen for some kitchen roll.

'When were you going to tell me? Did you know I knew?'

'Yes. Holly told Lucien she told you. He spoke to me before and after that.'

'So you knew before I did?'

'I did.' Marvin smoothed the fabric over his knees. 'And I would have told you. But I had to see if Holly did first. And she did, and in good time.' He skewed his mouth into a rueful smile, adding, 'Order of knowledge is irrelevant.' And then, 'All will be fine.'

They could be so alike, Marvin and Lucien, and never more so than when talking about the other.

McCullough wiped his nose. 'You want to know something?'
'What?'
'The night Holly was fucking Lucien ...'
'You were fucking someone?'

McCullough snorted and a bubble of snot grew from his nose; he burst it with the heel of his hand; they both chose to ignore the mess it caused. 'No. If only. No, not if only, but ...'
'What?'
'You know that girl? Rebecca?'

Marvin laughed.

'No, not her. Her mother, actually.'

'Like mother, like daughter?'

'Not at all. But she's very seductive—like Rebecca. Nothing much happened. It was an erotic encounter, shall we say?'

McCullough looked directly at his friend. He wanted to remind himself that Marvin could be relied upon, that the laconic delivery wasn't a pose—wasn't, as it was with Lucien, a meanness of demeanour that was finally a narrowness of emotion. That Marvin entertained himself had to be acknowledged, but it was one of his gifts, being amused whilst also showing acts of kindness, although McCullough had never been quite sure how this was possible. Perhaps it was Marvin's lack of interest in judgment, believing as he did that we are all victims of broad genetic predispositions and early damage. This was only half true: for those who had hurt Marvin his condemnation was eternal. It wasn't that he was thin-skinned, but that his thin skin was also sore to the touch. In many ways he was monstrous; in others ways he was pitiable, a small animal carrying an unhealable wound.

McCullough wiped his nose again and went back into the kitchen to dump the ball of tissues into the bin under the sink.

'Can I have a glass of water?' He opened the fridge and poured himself some San Pellegrino. 'Want some?' There was no response.

Marvin called, 'So what are you going to do?'

'Nothing.'

Emerging from the kitchen with the glass of water, more kitchen roll, McCullough sat on the edge of Marvin's desk. 'What can I do?'

'You will do what you'll do.'

'Helpful.'

'I don't think the question is really what you do about Holly or about Lucien, but—and sorry for being so prosaic—what you do about what led up to this. Lucien's a chancer, but Holly . . . think what state *she* had to be in to do something like this. From where I'm sitting, I can't see anything other than what's been happening to you as the one and only cause.'

'There's the rub.' McCullough smiled.

'I'm sure she's re-evaluating her reaction and feels very bad indeed, but part of her is going to blame you. Will she ever love you again, quite like the old days? It's hard to see how. Camelot is over.'

McCullough tipped his head back to prevent himself from crying again; his cheeks felt hot.

'And my guess is you are not finished, knowing you as I do, Proctor McCullough.' Addressing him by his full name, Marvin hoped to bring his friend back to himself. 'This drama is not played out.'

McCullough dropped his head. 'What do you think will happen?' The angle of his head was that of a drunk unable to lift it off his chest.

Marvin was absently scratching at his bare chest with manicured nails.

'Me? You know what I think. People do what they want to do. Find out what someone wants and then you know what they will do.'

'Chastening.'

'It is.'

'What do you think Holly wants?'

'A family, you—the old you. Maybe even the new you—who knows? It would seem to me that's the problem—no one knows where *you* will end up.'

It was true. Nothing about him was fixed anymore, there was no established thereness that Holly might approach, gather up and embrace, and, perhaps more importantly, return to and find him similarly configured. She had no sense of him as a continuous self. He'd tried to provide it, despite his absences, but he knew he hadn't succeeded. And he'd always been reliable. Not entirely stable, but reliable. This hadn't changed, not fundamentally. But there must be a point where instability had a negative effect on reliability, and Holly should be forgiven for thinking she was now living with a man adrift, increasingly unable, as he imagined she saw it, to keep a firm hold of the mooring of their family, in some ways his final job. For months now she'd regarded him as more proximal to the horizon than her, and disappearing beyond it. You couldn't be reliable *in absentia*.

'May I ask, Mac? How do *you* feel about all this? What do you think is happening to you? Are you scared, excited—what?'

'It's oddly dislocating. Although it feels intensely personal. But maybe that's not right either. Certainly, whatever it is ... it's intensely happening *to* me. What can I say? It's just there, looming. Walter once said in one of his moments of genius that we don't remember anything from when we're babies because we didn't know the words for things *at the time*. Right or wrong, it's like that. I don't know the words for this. Language has run out for me.'

'Just thought I'd ask.' Marvin smiled and stood up, his robe falling open, his phallus long between his legs, a little brighter than the rest of him. As he passed by McCullough he patted him on the shoulder.

For the next five minutes they were silent. Marvin moved about, cleaning his teeth, taking full ashtrays into the kitchen, checking something on his phone, held close to his face—his eyes were bad.

'I worry Holly isn't going to feel loved because I'm not exhibiting obvious reactions to having been betrayed.'

'Maybe that is something you might do, then.' One knee on the sofa, Marvin opened the curtains a little and looked out. 'These things happen and not because people don't love each other, but because the love they feel doesn't feel right to the other—it's the wrong love. Or displayed wrongly. Or something. Holly wants a happy family and your love is part of the bond that holds you all together. She wants to feel these bonds, see them. She wants picnics, trips to places, weekends spent together as a family. You passing through, singing "I love you, darling, see you in three weeks", is meaningless to her. To her, your love is your presence.'

'I'm not even present to myself.'

'It's a fugue state. That's all. You'll return.' Marvin paused; smiled. 'Or you won't.'

'Comforting.'

'Isn't it?'

McCullough reached behind him for the glass of water, took a sip and placed it back on the desk. 'What should I do, Marvin? Tell me.'

'I know what I'd do. Make her tell me exactly what happened with Lucien, every detail, every disgusting little detail, and make us both sick. Nothing like a bit of shame and humiliation, disgust and shock, to cleanse the soul. You both need to shed some tears together, like those big balloon tears from earlier, but the refreshing ones. The big relief tears. But you'll need to go to some horrible places first.'

Like Maria, it was not unusual for Marvin to make it obvious when he wanted someone to leave, and given the circumstances he decided to make it extra obvious, knowing that those with broken hearts tend to linger. So he opened the door and stood by it. McCullough looked at his watch; they'd been talking for just under an hour. Marvin would have things to do. What they might be had been a source of mystery and amusement to his friends for almost two decades; it was seldom actual work.

By the door, he drew McCullough in for a hug, the folds of his robe open, the bed-warmth of his body still present. 'Call me if you want.'

In the sun, McCullough felt a little shaky, like a morning after no sleep or a night of drug-taking, of intense fucking, a man physically and emotionally spent. His stomach felt weighed down, like he was carrying an extra organ, something large and slippery, exuding a thick deadening poison. That was the point of going to see Marvin: to face the dark stuff in all its ugliness and have it stirred up so he might smell the putridity. It was Marvin's great gift to transform modern emotions back into medieval humours, substances more or less foul-smelling, and finding in this foulness a more reliable measure of our natures than anything we have to say about ourselves. In this instance, if the behaviour between McCullough and Holly remained blindly civilized, the deepest bonds between them would fall away and rot, and the nothingness would become uncrossable due to the stink. And, of course, without facing up to this, they wouldn't recognize what was happening. After all, civility meant politely holding their noses.

Walking up the road with little sense of what was going on around him, McCullough stopped at a junction. On the kerb, big black rubbish bags were piled up next to a lamppost, other bits of rubbish balanced on top. The lamppost was finely pebble-dashed with what looked like grit and glass fragments. It made him pause. The lamp was still on, a pale lemon bloom in the mid-morning sun, a sherbet sweet sucked of its colour. He stroked the rough surface. Someone passing dipped down and pushed an empty drink can into the rubbish, muttering 'Sorry, mate', recognizing an invasion of space, that a man scratching a lamppost had important things on his mind.

3

In his office on the Strand, Edward was dozing, head slung low. Under the ceiling light his hair looked thin, his scalp pink and flaky. His knees were fallen inward and his fly was open. It was a side effect of his condition to appear pitiable, a mix of fatigue and illness-induced decrepitude. There were times when he appeared to be dead, sitting there, slumped and still.

'Ah, Proctor. Come in, come in.' He didn't raise his head, but there was a slight movement in his shuddering crab-shaped hand.

'How are you, Edward?'

'Last day. Working life is over. I've done pretty well. Lasted longer than expected.'

He'd decided to keep the news from Holly, and by extension McCullough, and the effort had taken something out of him. Everyone's fear, including his own, was the standard one: without work, why carry on?

'I spoke to Holly this morning,' he said. 'Gave her the news. She said she would come down on Sunday.'

McCullough knew what he was asking: could he, McCullough, keep the children so he might have his daughter all to himself?

'I'll take them swimming.'

No movement. 'They'll enjoy that.'

'Did Holly mention I've sold the rest of the business?'

It was a jolt in slow motion: the surprise was evident, but the movement across his shoulders was laboured. Edward brought his head up painfully. There was fierceness in his eyes. A man with a family to provide for should not give up work. It was perhaps the only instance in which he believed there was a transcendental 'ought'.

'Don't look at me like that, Edward. I still have work. I'm now on a government retainer. I'm their Atrocity Czar. Very hush-hush.' McCullough's laughter was false and dwindled to a sigh.

'What does Holly make of this?'

'Things aren't . . . how shall we say? The home environment is not conducive to understanding at the moment.'

It had always been the case that Edward was a kind of vector for McCullough's and Holly's love. That her father liked and approved of him was important to Holly, and meant she'd been more lenient with his eccentricities, at least at the beginning. For McCullough, it was being witness to the love between father and daughter that helped him understand what he'd once felt was Holly's complacency about love. It came from an implicit trust in its free-flowing nature. Love wasn't supposed to be hard work.

'And you're still building this church?'

'I'm not building so much now. It has a life of its own.'

Edward regarded him, eyes narrowed. 'Can't say I approve of so much upheaval. And you've got Walter to look out for as well.' Had his patience run out?

'Outwardly I'm being very selfish, I know. What can't be known is whether that's the case beyond what I'm doing—'

'You're a fool if you think you can have some effect on the big picture. That's politics and business.'

'I'm a holy fool.' It was meant as a joke, of sorts. But he was glared at. There was a brief pause. Silence was not abnormal between them, and McCullough didn't feel obliged to speak.

Edward looked up. 'Do you want coffee? I've stopped drinking it. Makes the muscle spasms worse. But I'm allowed red wine. Advised to drink a glass a day. I use a small glass so I can have two. You'd be surprised how such things can make you feel as if some decisions are still your own.'

'You should buy one of those glasses that can take a whole bottle.'

There was no response from Edward; he had a gift for filtering out the irrelevant, a selective deafness.

'Holly didn't sound very happy.'

'As I said . . .'

The crab-hand rose up and dumped itself down on the joystick of his chair, the black plastic knob moved by the centre of his palm. The adjustment of his position was small, but he was now facing McCullough straight on. He lifted his head up. 'Could you sort my feet out, please, Proctor?'

McCullough had seen his right foot slip off and was waiting to be asked. He crossed the room. Setting it back required a kind of classic genuflection, down on one knee, head lowered. Edward's catheter bag was a third full.

Back in his seat, McCullough wiped his hands clean of the grit from the soles of Edward's shoes—shoes that never touched the ground.

'I've been offered this treatment, a procedure. To paralyse my legs.'

'Isn't that what the Multiple Sclerosis does?'

'Ironic, isn't it? It will help with a number of things. All the stiffness will go. The spasms. Some of the pain, I suspect, although they were a little cagey about that.'

'Why do you need it?'

'I've become impossible to move around. It's like I have rigor mortis in my legs.'

'Is it reversible?'

'It's not. I suspect I'll have it done. Seems wrong somehow. Self-inflicted paralysis. I've been aware that fighting the disease is probably not the best use of my energy, but this seems like collaboration somehow. Bad thing to do for my generation.' He laughed.

'Maybe see it as pragmatism.'

'Not very heroic, though, is it?'

'Have you talked about it with Holly?'

'This is why she's coming down. I need her to write down all the questions I should ask the consultant.'

'Good idea.'

Again they sat silently. McCullough couldn't help but wonder how much he himself had contributed to Edward's exhaustion. Holly's tone on the phone and his own news about his business, each would have had its effect. There had been a slow falling away of Edward's mental strength since he'd been trapped in his chair, unable to pace around and gesture. Maybe it was an essential part of being an embodied human, the fact we can cast ourselves about beyond our central mass, extend into space. Wasn't the act of pointing where our original existential intuition came from? McCullough was aware that he was projecting an imagined frustration, but it didn't seem a fantasy; he was a breaker of things, his body reacting strongly to events he felt deeply about. He looked over at the older man, heavy-shouldered, head slumped, his legs looking flaccid and pathetic even though they were intractable.

McCullough's way of determining whether Edward was asleep was to shift in his seat. On this level his senses had become sharper.

'You go, Proctor. It was good to see you, old boy.' The term of endearment was important: it was warm-heartedly ironic; they'd do better next time.

'It was good to see you too, Edward.'

The hand shuddered up, and then fell back to his lap. 'I'll see you soon.'

At the door, McCullough stopped and looked over at the old man. He wanted to tell him that he loved him, something he'd never done before, but he knew Edward wouldn't think it appropriate or understand why it was being said. In the end McCullough left in silence, not even waving. Edward's head slumped lower on his chest.

The street was hot and busy. Heat was added by workmen at the side of the road going hard at the pavement with pneumatic tools, their body temperatures seemingly having an impact on the humidity, creating a vicarious stickiness for passers-by. Oblivious to the direct sun, the youngest were stripped to the waist, filthy jeans low on their hips, boxer shorts pulled high to their waists, the tight elastic giving their bodies almost an hourglass figure. Tattoos covered their shoulders and their backs—women, Celtic symbols, words in cursive script. They concentrated on their objectives, but there was still something preening about their manner—they were there to be looked at, hard at work.

Two of the men were laying bright yellow cables alongside old rusting pipework. Centuries of man's intervention were visible in the strata of earth: broken brick, timber, bits of claywork. Protruding from the mud, the roots of trees resembled the limbs of large creatures, dead for millennia, yet when hacked away, the flesh was the brightest colour anywhere, pure and pale, glistening with the sap of life.

McCullough was hungry but didn't feel like eating; he had no taste for food. He couldn't face more coffee. He entered Jubilee Gardens. Office workers were having lunch on the grass. It was Friday, after all. Packaging was spread out, gleaming white against the green. Piles of it were pushed down into rubbish bins, the angles of the packaging still hard and jutting, with smears of avocado, mustard, rocket leaves stuck in the folds of cardboard. A few men had cans of beer. Chilled bottles of white wine were poured into the blue plastic cups from water coolers. The men leaned back on their elbows and smoked or vaped, or sat cross-legged, stubbing cigarettes out in the grass and dropping the butts into the cans. Women moved about on their knees, never quite finding the right position to keep their skirts from riding up, constantly pulling at hems. Most had slipped their shoes off.

He sat on the free corner of a bench, squinting while he searched for his sunglasses. He drew some gazes as always, but not for long. He was facing away from the river. Tilting his head back, he looked up at the buildings above the tops of the trees, a mix of pre- and mid-twentieth-century architecture, no two alike. The ornamentation around the windows, below the rooflines, was the consummate example of man's capacity to waste effort on the merely decorative; a wonderful, if ultimately unconvincing, argument against those who believed fitness for survival was our sole aim.

He walked down to the Thames. Across the river, to the right of the South Bank, there was large building site over which loomed the narrow frames of cranes. He followed them upwards and along their arms to the long cables suspending loads that were obscured by the surrounding buildings. The cranes' delicate geometric yellow framework stood in relief against the blue sky. Their lack of perceptible movement was hypnotic. (Were all the operators at lunch?) What did it say about the modern world that McCullough found something creaturely in them, a dignity in their stillness, the aloofness that came with great height? He yearned for such a state of rest, of disinterest, whilst still maintaining an overall view of the world. Would it be the single most obvious symptom of madness if he declared: *I want to be a crane*?

He needed to decide what to do. There was the whole of the afternoon before him. He was too exhausted to confront Lucien, and Marvin had reoriented the fight. It was now inside him. Perhaps he should just go home. Holly was there. He'd walk back and clear his head. It was a journey he'd made before from many different points of central London. But this time something more essential was in play. He feared never finding his way home. It was an indulgent and sentimental thought. Not because of the impossibility; Holly and the children were too strong a force. But there was also the attracting force of his other family, two hundred miles away. Maybe he should walk there, enact a kind of pilgrimage. There were times when he was home that he didn't quite believe they really existed, they were a fantasy he created when he was down there: he parked in the lane, walked across the field, lay down on the grass, and out came the pixies. Why not? Was it madder than what he was actually doing? What he needed was some common sense.

4

Simon opened the door to McCullough wearing a lab coat and large plastic goggles, his hands in latex gloves. He was carrying an iPad as one would a clipboard.

'Do you know?'

'Know what, Mac?'

McCullough mimed moving goggles to his forehead.

'Oh, sorry. We're moving labs. I don't have an office. There aren't any chairs. Everyone's at a meeting with our "high-value donors". I have a paper to write.'

It was a large room with marks on the floor where benches had once been fixed. At one end there was a workstation, and what appeared to be a large cabinet freezer, on top of which there was an espresso machine. Simon gesticulated. 'They've taken all the—you know—pods.'

'I hear your date with Jane didn't go so well.'

'I don't think I thought it through. How's the build going?'

'I love the mystical hexagon. It's going to be perfect.'

'That's Pascal.'

At times, Simon had an expression that was baffling to a close reader of faces. McCullough couldn't work out whether he had forgotten it was his idea or was simply reminding his friend that Pascal was the inspiration.

'How's that girl?'

'Rebecca? Don't you talk to her?'

'She's very smart. Very pretty.'

'She is.'

'Does she play chess?'

'Why don't you ask her?'

They were by a window. The closest large building was Senate House, built from Portland stone. The rest were narrow dark brick terrace houses from the eighteenth century, mostly occupied by the University of London.

'What am I supposed to know? You asked—'

'Nothing. Well, if you count me quitting my job, nothing.'

'Wow. How does Jim feel about that?'

'A sense of freedom. Jim's one of these people who wants to be accommodating but needs to go his own way. I, on the other hand, look as if I always want my own way but am oddly accommodating.'

'What am I like?'

'What are you like?' McCullough looked around at Simon, which always meant casting his eyes up.

'You're one of the good guys.'

'Boring.'

'No one finds you boring.'

'Women do.'

'There are certain expectations these days. It would be true to say that you don't comport yourself in what might be termed a fashionable manner.'

'What's that?'

'Ironic, I suppose. Cheap jokes. Post-modern.'

'Do you have that . . . manner?'

'A little of it. But we know a couple of the masters.'

'Marvin.'

'Lucien.'

'Is that how I should have been with Jane?'

'I'd like to see that.' McCullough laughed. 'I know it's shit. You want a girlfriend.'

'I arranged everything the way I thought she liked.'

'You had bad weather. It makes a difference.'

'I've been hanging out with Marvin quite a lot since our trip.'

'And nothing's rubbing off?'

'I think he's a bit different with me. We have quite a laugh, though. He really hates Lucien. Says he'd like to have him killed. Jane wanted to know all about him.'

'That's unkind. I'm sorry. I think it shows how unhappy she is. It's selfish, but—'

'I never meet anyone here. There's barely anyone to talk to. I know you guys think I'm weird because I'm a scientist; but these scientists think I'm weird because I'm not like them, and I hang out with you guys. Inductive reasoning would say I'm weird.'

'Until someone finds you're not weird. Isn't that how it works?'

'It's not much to hold on to, Mac. My life relying on a Black Swan.'

'Isn't that a fundamental of science—falsifiability?'

'Something like that. Shall I put it on my *Guardian* Soulmates page? "Male, forty-two, looking for a woman to falsify current compelling evidence that said male is weird"?'

'Holly slept with Lucien.'

It was unfair to surprise Simon like that. How was he meant to react to such news? Bizarrely, he moved his goggles back down over his eyes.

'Do you want to get back to work?'

There was no response.

'Sorry, Simon—I shouldn't have said anything. You mustn't—'

Mustn't what? Blame Holly?

'It was . . . is . . . as much my fault. You know how it's been. If I'm honest . . . Rebecca's mother, she and I . . . we mean . . . nothing like . . . Fuck! I'm sorry.'

Simon stared at McCullough, his goggles still down. There were scratches on the plastic lens.

'Please get out, Mac.'

McCullough stepped back as Simon loomed over him. 'What?'

'I want you to leave.' His voice revealed agitation. 'You have to leave now.'

'Simon, what's the matter?'

'GET OUT!'

There was no contact, no threat of violence, but with Simon's height and the absurdity of the big goggles, McCullough felt a strange fear.

'No, Simon. Don't be ridiculous. What's going on?'

Simon screamed, 'GET OUT. I hate you! I hate you all. You're all horrible people. GET OUT!'

McCullough looked around the stripped-out lab. Had he missed something here? Why was Simon in his lab gear when there was nothing in the room except for a bench, an empty freezer, and an espresso machine with no pods?

'What's going on, Simon?'

'You have to leave, Mac. This is my lab. I don't want to hear about this stuff. You and Holly and Lucien and that girl's moth-er—I don't want to hear about it! It's sick. You people make me sick. You always have done. You think you know everything. Always yak-yak-yakking about it. Everything's either a joke or some kind of crisis, isn't it? Well, you're the joke. Now get out!'

'Why are you here, Simon?'

'Because this is where I work. I have a job. This is my lab. I'm just making sure everything has been taken.'

'But why the lab coat, the goggles, the gloves?'

'BECAUSE THIS IS WHAT I WEAR.'

'But there's nothing here, no work to do. Is everything all right?'

'I've asked you to leave, Mac. Can you please leave?'

'Only when you tell me what's going on.'

'Nothing's going on. Now, leave. Go back to your little drama. Go and talk to Marvin—he'll love this.' He paused. 'Oh, you have already. Of course. But he wasn't enough for you. Needed to talk about it a little more. Spread the bad feeling around. Contaminate us all. Good thing I'm prepared. Should be wearing a mask—'

'Simon, Simon—I'm not going. Not until you calm down and discuss this with me.'

It was comic and horrific, Simon still looming over him, breathless with anger, eyes wide inside the goggles. It was as though he was feeling morally outraged for the first time in his life, and having never expressed it before, had lost control of himself. Had they all taken this tall gentle sensible scientist for granted and decided that he was no more than a man of logic, data points and mathematical equations—knowledge that held up buildings, kept planes in the air, calculated unimaginable distances? McCullough couldn't recall the last time he had seen Simon display feelings beyond patience and curiosity, gentle amusement. It wasn't that he didn't think his friend was incapable of strong emotions, but he had simply not been present before when something destabilizing had occurred, a triggering event. So what was the trigger here? Simon didn't want to think of Holly in this way, or be part of McCullough's betrayal, or that taken together the world had just become too ugly, too quickly?

'It's not right—what you're thinking. And it's not fair. We're your friends, and we've fucked up. That's all. Really fucked up.'

'I don't like it.' Simon ran a finger under his nose. Inside his goggles his eyes were pale and shifting around; he didn't want to look at McCullough but didn't move away. 'You've got lovely children. Marvin doesn't have children.'

'You forget Von.'

'He's not here, is he? And that's not the point.'

Simon's eyes were angry and cold, and for the first time McCullough sensed he was wary of being patronized, as if he no longer trusted his friend to look out for his feelings, his *weirdness*. There was an awkward pause.

'I can't bear to think about it. It's all ruined.'

Was this an overreaction, or was Simon the only one who could see things as they really were?

'Nothing's ruined. Things have changed, that's all. But nothing's *ruined*, for God's sake.' McCullough stopped himself from adding 'You're being naïve', though he felt it was true. He needed to make Simon understand that nice caring people were allowed to fuck up, even to this degree. But then he had to accept that up until five minutes ago, he and Holly were Simon's model couple, loving and caring towards each other, often extending that love and care to him, so a *felt* thing, rather than just something he witnessed at the dinner table, at their home with the children. It was an unspoken fact that Simon had been relying on finding someone like Holly. Did this mean what he couldn't bear was twofold: what Holly had done and with whom she'd done it? Was Simon having the reaction that he, McCullough, should have had two days ago? McCullough's dalliance was irrelevant. But Holly with Lucien? It didn't compute. It was the world turned upside down.

Was it worth McCullough explaining to him that it actually did make sense, more so than if it had happened with, say, him, a better man? In the current scenario Lucien and Holly had used each other—a negative collusion. Horrible stuff, yes, but recognizably human, and as such, forgivable. If Holly had sought out Simon, if she'd fucked him, that would have been an act of . . . nihilism. She'd have destroyed something of value, of meaning, full of love. But McCullough doubted whether explaining this would make it any better; it would probably make things worse—Simon had already said he'd had enough of his friends' psychological sophistry. Explanations were diversions from what was the case—the observable case. It was in that moment McCullough realized what he'd missed. Holly's state of crisis, stripped of cause or reaction. He'd not allowed himself to pause long enough to rest his gaze on her, even though just to look at her revealed the depth of her pain. He'd been too distracted. His own crisis was distracting. This was the terrible irony: he had been facing the possibility that there was more at play, so much more at stake than any one individual's pain that he'd been unable to see what was happening to Holly. It was as if his mission had become to understand how we feel anything at all, whether it be love, pain, mercy, hate, pity; he'd turned feelings into abstractions. Hadn't he promised her only weeks ago that this wouldn't happen? He promised more love for everyone. He shook his head and laughed softly. How stupid he'd been.

Simon turned away and moved over to the freezer cabinet. He stood there, shuffling papers into a file, which he placed in a box. He took off his plastic goggles and dropped them in on top and folded the flaps of the lid together.

'What you don't understand, Mac, is that all this just makes me feel pathetic. That I'm pathetic. It makes me realize, no wonder that day with Jane was such a failure.'

'I can see how it seems that way. I really can. But it's not like that. It's not all ugly and horrible. And certainly you don't have to be like that. No one finds love that way. But it does become like that now and again, and feel like that. I'm sorry—I shouldn't have involved you.'

There was a pause before Simon turned around. His hands were in the pockets of his lab coat; his face still displayed the anger of earlier. 'Thanks, Mac. I'm not a child. I'm not yours and Holly's kid.'

'Kid' sounded wrong, coming from him, cold, heartless.

'Please, I didn't mean I should have protected you . . .'

'Yes, you did.'

McCullough sighed. 'OK—in a way I did.'

There was a standoff, McCullough unwilling to leave, and Simon, now with the box in his arms, looking like a man who had been asked to clear his desk.

From somewhere in the room there was a buzzing sound, followed by a 'Flight of the Bumblebee' ringtone.

Simon hoisted up his leg to take a little of the weight of the box and pulled his phone out of his trouser pocket. He didn't look at the number, just accepted the call and said hello, glancing over at McCullough, who was rocking on his heels, arms folded, happy to wait.

'It's for you.'

McCullough paused mid-rock and regarded Simon, who held the phone out. 'Me?'

'Yes.'

He took the phone. 'Hello?'

'It's Rebecca.' Her voice was flat, grown-up.

'What's the matter?'

'It's Terry. He's gone. He was in the pub the other day . . . really looking for trouble. Nat and Rich got him away. He punched Nat. I went to his house yesterday, but he wasn't there, and his mother . . . she didn't . . . I mean . . . no one's seen him.'

McCullough looked out of the window. Roofs and chimneys, slate tiles and lead flashing, old and bent many-pronged aerials, dirty white satellite dishes. He didn't want to hear this. What could he do from here? Fucking Terry.

'Are you there? Mac?'

'Yes.'

'It was my mum who said to call you.' Rebecca sounded grown-up, yes, but she had consulted her mother.

'What can I do? He isn't *here*.' Was that why she was calling? 'I mean, not at my house or anything. Or at least I don't think so. Don't you have any idea where he might be?'

'It's not so much that he's gone off. It's the state he's in. He looks terrible and he's so angry. He's going to get himself into trouble.'

'What can I do . . . if you don't know where he is?' His voice sounded harsh. He feared caring. Going straight down there, attending to another crisis.

'When are you coming back?' Then her tone changed, inexplicably: 'Things are going well. You should see it.'

He saw nothing.

'Mac?'

'Yes.'

'You should be here. Why don't we have your number? That's crazy.'

'Nat does. Things are difficult for me right now. I'm sorry.'

'What's that supposed to mean?'

'Please, Rebecca. I will come down . . . soon. But I can't right now.' There was no pleading in his tone. He wanted to be left alone. Yet he accepted he had responsibilities, perhaps to Terry most of all. 'Look, keep me informed. I'll get Simon to text you my number. Sorry, I have to go.' He hung up and handed the phone back. 'Can you text her my number, please?'

Simon rested the box on the floor. 'What's wrong?'

'Terry is missing. She's worried. I don't blame her—if anyone's capable of a destructive fugue state, it's him.'

'What's a fugue state?'

'What everyone thinks I'm suffering from. When you separate from yourself. Escape from reality. Disassociate.'

'You can't go down there.'

'I know I can't go . . . for fuck's sake.'

Simon worked at his phone, looking down at the screen. 'It's done.'

He picked up the box. 'I'm leaving now.'

McCullough only half-heard him. Hadn't Terry insisted he was going to stay sitting in his chair? On some level, McCullough had taken him at his word. He held open the lab door for Simon and his box.

At the lift, his friend again rested the box on a raised knee and pressed the 'down' button. 'What are you going to do about Terry?'

'What can I do—if he's gone missing?'

The lift doors opened and they stepped in. McCullough pressed the button for the ground floor. Simon stared ahead, as if he was in a lift with a stranger.

McCullough looked down at his shoes. 'I couldn't bear anything to happen to Terry. He's always seemed to me to be possessed of something most of us might wish for, and yet none us would want to be him. I know it sounds fanciful but I sometimes think of Walter as an angel, as some kind of mysterious guide who's been sent to me. And I've thought the same of Terry. Although I do appreciate that no man gets sent two angels. Or even one. Especially when he doesn't believe in angels. And I know Walter and Terry are no more precious to the world than you or me or anyone else. Every person is of equal value. Yet at the same time I am certain the world loses more when it loses an angel.'

5

It was now late afternoon. In two hours it would be the time of day when the atrocity scenario took place. McCullough wondered whether he was acting out a version of this right now, in a minor scale, wandering the city, looking for a way to be reunited with loved ones, those who loved him.

Around Russell Square, people packed the pubs, sitting at tables on the pavements in the sun. Picnic to pub—who said it wasn't fun living and working in London these days? At a busy junction with a long wait at the lights, McCullough looked at his mobile phone: three missed calls from Holly. If he continued not to answer what would she do? Call Lucien: 'Mac's not answering his phone. Has he made contact with you . . . do you think he will?' There was now a sordid kind of intimacy between them. Because that's what fucking of any kind did: it created intimacy, and add to that adultery and betrayal, it must surely create a kind of collusion that if the circumstances were right would lead to another fuck—a more intense, self-abasing fuck. Whilst the thought of this caused his insides to drop away, what really made his stomach burn and gut muscles spasm was the idea of Holly turning to Lucien for acts of kindness, when McCullough knew that Lucien would regard any panic he heard in her voice as no more than an irritation, and if she cried down the phone all he'd hear was the snot and the saliva and do his best to hide his amusement.

So far the day had offered up no new plan for confronting Lucien, no practical alternative to his sleepless fantasies, but there was no denying he was moving closer to Lucien's chambers and further from home. If he maintained this was mere coincidence, a serendipitous outcome of wandering in a part of the city that was random in design, he was kidding himself—the destination had been set and every other visit had been a delaying tactic, justified in their way, but they were never going to prevent some kind of confrontation.

The various scenarios came back to him. His imagination allowed for a burst of violence, smashing Lucien's face with his fist, to feel the hard unremitting impact of punch after punch on those fine bones. He allowed also for a gun he didn't possess, and an execution scene.

On the corner of Middle Temple Lane, a woman he recognized was getting ready to cross; she smiled and waved at him with a little flutter of her fingers. He didn't know her name; a colleague of Lucien's, a junior barrister he'd met a couple of times. As she passed she said, 'They're going to the pub.' Of course they were. And he knew which pub. On Friday nights so packed you had to stand straight-backed, drink to your chest. Lucien loved it: a glass of red wine in his hand, a head above everyone else, never rowdy, and yet with something of the clubhouse about it, a safe place in which to be male and uncaring about the rest of life. The general air of arrogance came from the adversarial system, where success required the best of the English character—reason and imperturbability and a dandyish contempt for weakness; in short, any show of emotion. McCullough tended to feel irritated, threatened and competitive all at the same time. No one had ever thought he'd make a good barrister.

He was standing next to a postbox. The red enamel paint was bright and chipped. Cigarettes had been stubbed out on top of it. His phone showed another missed call from Holly, this time with a message. He listened. She just wanted to know when he'd be home. There was also a message from Jim, mostly the white noise of an empty room and then, 'It's eerie here without you.'

He wanted to switch his phone off, but realized with Terry missing he couldn't. The boy's flight was a failure. The church was supposed to be a city of refuge; it was meant for people like Terry.

The only mobile number he had was Nathaniel's, and McCullough couldn't face speaking to him. If he'd been attacked by Terry, it would be a difficult conversation. To Nathaniel, Terry's whereabouts would be irrelevant. McCullough knew that if Lucien were to meet Terry, his first impression would be the same as Nathaniel's: a loser, a waste of space, worse even than the potato heads who were drafted in to make up a jury. Poor Terry. Lucky Nathaniel. Set them level at birth and there would still be no contest. It was why a surplus of love was needed to deal with people like Terry, to deal with those who were harder work to love, when work was needed to grind down their edges or shear away the spikes, or just stare deeper and take on whatever strain that loving brought on oneself.

A postman approached, plonked his large grey plastic sack down and unlocked and opened the postbox door. He guided and corralled the slippery bank of letters into the sack, and then shook it, creating a heavy bulk at the bottom that looked as if it had been made up of thin layers of slate. The postman looked up at McCullough. 'You hovering?'

'Yes.'

'Nice day for it.'

'Yes.'

'You a barrister?'

'No.' Pause. 'Atrociologist.'

'Expert witness?'

'I wish.'

'They love themselves, don't they?'

McCullough presumed he meant barristers rather than expert witnesses.

'They do.'

'I think they should have to wear the same uniform as us . . . shorts in the summer . . . then see how they swan around. Ha!' He was pleased with this thought.

It was profound in its own way. Take away their gowns and all that swish was gone, and without the air billowing beneath them they'd be more earthbound, which was where the law should be.

The postman was diligent, having one last look inside the postbox before locking up the heavy cast-iron door. Ready to move on, he paused and looked up at the sun then patted McCullough on the bottom. 'Have a good 'un, son.' He was ten years younger at least.

McCullough waited another few minutes and then crossed the road. Lucien's chambers were at the end of the street, the small pub standing opposite. He half expected to see a single file of barristers, dressed in their gowns, crossing the road towards their local, like the members of some dark cult. It was how he imagined them now, through the vector of Lucien's evil. Having spent many hours in this particular pub, he knew many of Lucien's colleagues by sight, some by name, and when he was feeling generous enough to forgive them their rounded vowel sounds, the affected slurring of words, a certain bored breathiness of diction, they were remarkably ordinary—just people with jobs and families.

He passed the chambers and crossed over to the pub. By the time he reached the entrance he was trembling and sweating. The plan was to walk straight in, without breaking stride, push open the door as if he were in a Western. At least that way he'd have the element of surprise. From that moment, there was little chance they'd remain in the pub; if it wasn't busy now it would be soon, and Lucien would not want a scene in such a public space. He'd likely guide McCullough to his office, to the large wood-panelled room, the heavy velvet curtains kept half-closed, swish around his desk and sit back in his chair. That was to be avoided. It would set the tone. The street was the place, even if most of Lucien's colleagues would regard it as vulgar to step out of the pub and watch. The street was where McCullough would have the upper hand. Of the two of them, he was the more natural brawler. But that had been years ago. When was the last time he had faced someone down based on his willingness to take blows, to ignore pain? That was Terry now. Wherever he was.

The glass door of the pub was opaque and etched with a detailed pattern of a lion and unicorn. All McCullough could make out inside were semi-abstract body shapes, flashes of movement. Despite his determination to walk straight in, he stopped and rose on his toes to peer through a small area of clear glass. The pub fittings were generations old; the wood had the smoothness and gleam of a century of use, and the large mirrors were silver-backed, giving reflections of customers a pale and rosy-cheeked, gaslit look.

Lucien was at the bar, an almost-finished glass of red wine at his lips; he was laughing, with his hand on the shoulder of a man who was clearly the object of some good-natured teasing. The man's expression was ambiguously wry: he was being mocked, and while not particularly enjoying it, he had decided it was acceptable. McCullough rocked back on to his heels. Momentum had been lost, and his light-headedness and trembling prevented him from taking any decisive action. He began to regret turning up here. What was to be achieved by confronting this monster, when what he really needed to do was to make things right with Holly? He accepted that if Lucien were to step outside now he'd find a beaten man, someone he could ignore and push aside.

He opened the door.

If it is an instinct in some people to turn when a person enters a room who might do them harm, either Lucien didn't possess this gift, or else he possessed an even subtler instinct that had detected McCullough's presence, and in assessing the threat, found no reason for fear. With a nod of his head, a colleague alerted him to McCullough's presence. Lucien had been brought up not to react to surprises and McCullough watched his long body slowly turn, while his hand blindly placed the wine glass on the bar.

McCullough stepped forward, and with a stiff left-to-right flap of his hand indicated to the crowd that he intended to get through to Lucien unimpeded. The crowd obeyed and parted. Was Lucien's hand trembling on the edge of the bar? McCullough didn't find it difficult to read him: they had known each other for over twenty years. The slight stretch of the neck, the little outward jut of the chin, had been observed by McCullough many times at the Spry family dinner table, especially in front of his father and elder brother when Lucien had spoken out of turn or said something foolish—the only place in the world where he was regarded as a dolt. If there had been a tremor, however, it was just for a moment. It was followed by a big smile.

'You all know my friend Proctor McCullough. He does the Lord's work now.'

McCullough shook a few hands. Declined a drink. He wasn't staying long. Lucien's colleagues looked at one another. This was no usual encounter.

'You fucker, Lucien—you vile selfish fuck.'

Pause. Pout. Smile. Bit more neck; bit more chin; visible trembling of the hand on the bar. 'Yes. Indeed. Of course you're right.'

There were a few barely hidden smirks: some for McCullough— he was about to embarrass himself; but some were for Lucien—after all, the description fitted.

McCullough went on, 'I should hit you very fucking hard right now.'

He expected a side-on intervention, a plummy 'Now, look here ... just wait a moment', but everyone was silent.

The bartender, a woman in her fifties, without make-up, her hair a green-blonde, shook her head (these posh boys were incapable of making real trouble) and looked to the other end of the bar for a customer to serve.

Lucien pulled at his nose with thumb and forefinger; he was becoming conscious that without some swift thinking, he was unlikely to come out of this well.

Standing before Lucien, McCullough suddenly realized what his objective had been all along. There would be no violence, however much he wished for it; grown-ups like them didn't fight. He was there to work his way past this man's parade, find an angle of gaze that would make clear his inner workings, what really went on inside him and try to understand why Lucien had willingly caused so much pain. For the last forty-eight hours, Lucien had been a product of the imagination, a narrative created out of fragments of behaviour, Lucien at his pretend and real worst. A monster is easily created out of only monstrous parts. But McCullough knew that face-to-face he would not find a monster. Whether he would find a sociopath, someone not quite fully human, was a notion he remained open to.

'I'm not sure here's the place, Proctor.'

'It's a pub—surely it's just the right place.' McCullough was tall but still needed to look up at Lucien. It was dizzying, given his light-headedness and sudden surge of adrenaline. Was there a flicker of fear on the taller man's face? Was Lucien really afraid McCullough might hit him? Surely not; these things either happen straightaway or not at all. But the threat of violence was seldom present in polite society, so maybe Lucien simply didn't know what to expect—a rare experience for him.

'Don't look so scared, Lucien.'

A couple of male colleagues muttered Lucien's name and asked what was going on; they were ignored.

'I'm sorry.' That smile, showing his big white teeth, was Lucien's most attractive feature. It was the pivot of his charm. Here it was: wide, disarming, almost lovely.

'What for? That's crucial, I think. What are you sorry for?'

'Everything.'

'Ah—but I know that's not true, so how can I believe you are sorry about anything?'

'What *am* I not sorry for?' Lucien glanced at the colleague nearest to him, whose collar and tie seemed so high and tight they were like a brace for a bad neck.

'I can set it out for you if you want . . .' McCullough paused. 'Make it quite clear.'

'I've always been open to you about my feelings for Holly.'

McCullough laughed. Really? This was going to be his angle?

'You don't think it's relevant, my affection for Holly? Well, I think it is.'

Most of the customers had moved back a little, or else pushed their way to other tight spaces in the pub.

'So you're not sorry about that?'

'Perhaps in hindsight.'

'Fuck you.'

'What can I say? I gave you fair warning.'

Did Lucien believe that on some level this was a mitigating factor? Either way, his confession was shocking.

Lucien went on, 'I don't feel good about it. And before you say anything: if I don't feel good, there is a reason—I know what I've done. I understand consequences.' The trembling persisted, quick and fine, at the very end of his fingertips.

McCullough felt surges and collapses of energy, and knew there was nothing he could do to control his own physical state.

'Holly is hurt most.'

Lucien appeared not to have realized this might be the case— surely the betrayed must be hurt most, because what was worse than being a cuckold? He started to rub his thick tongue around his big teeth. It wasn't a very subtle tell. He had no response, a very rare moment for him. He tried to look grave. 'Then you'll have to forgive me.'

Lucien turned and called to the bartender, a little more loudly than he'd meant to, and shook his head, as if to clear his mind. 'Two large whiskies, Sally.'

McCullough saw himself in the mirror at the back of the bar. He was surprised by how healthy and strong he appeared. Time in the sun and the long days of physical work had transformed him. If he'd been asked to describe himself, he'd have imagined a white-faced and weakened man, a country curate. But it was Lucien who looked like that. There had always been a version of Lucien that was over-delicate, a thin and stooping figure.

McCullough straightened up. 'Have you told anyone else? Apart from Marvin?'

A thin smile and some advantage regained. Did McCullough think what he'd done was somehow so special that he'd confess to Maria?

'And how are you going to explain why we never see each other again?'

'If it comes to that, I'll invent something you said about her.'

'Holly could tell her the truth.'

'She won't. Holly won't want to spread the hurt. She'll think of the boys.' He'd lost patience with being defensive, and needed to point out what he considered an absurdity—the protection at all costs of children's emotional well-being: it only made them more vulnerable later on in life. Everyone was weakened by it.

McCullough imagined the pleasure of a small sharp blade sliding into Lucien's belly, a quick thrust that he would not feel, only realizing something was wrong when he turned cold, unable to think, weirdly doom-laden. It was in that moment that McCullough understood that if he had to argue Lucien's intrinsic value as a human being it would be as an article of faith only, the intrinsic dignity of every life; the betterment of the world was not part of it.

'Do I test you, Proctor? I do, don't I?' The big smile was back; it was a reflex for him. To cause outrage had always been part of Lucien's nature, his charm. Like Marvin, he believed it widened the scope of what might be accepted as permissible, and in that way regarded it as a contribution to progress of sorts.

Lucien laughed out loud. Game over.

McCullough studied his friend and felt in that moment he could read him with a completeness he'd previously believed was impossible or only God's privilege. It was a miracle, of sorts. Lucien was unmoved and unrepentant. He'd fucked his poor friend's wife and was now accusing this friend of being too kind-hearted to make him pay for it. What a nerve he had. But he shouldn't go too far. He'd always rather liked having him and Holly around, although some of his desire for her had disappeared after they'd fucked. She'd cried in a way he hadn't foreseen, and been sharp with him, not unlike Maria. But Proctor, this fellow here, hadn't let him down. Impressive stuff, turning up like this. Pushing him too far now would mean not being around when the bugger finally broke and that was something he didn't want to miss. So what should he do?

He felt an urge to be honest. Yet what did that mean? The only other cuckolded man who had confronted him wanted all sorts of details. Apparently, it was going to help him decide whether his wife had confessed to *everything*. But Proctor hadn't really asked anything. Not even for him to explain himself, although there had been that 'What are you sorry for?', a question he remembered from childhood when he'd been too keen to apologize. The answer to

Proctor's question was so obvious he hadn't felt the need to actually say it: 'Well, for causing all this, surely?' But at the same time he couldn't quite see what 'all this' was, and didn't want to apologize for something which, on reflection, he didn't feel sorry for—he'd been told off for that too many times.

After all, could you be sorry for something you'd planned in advance? Was that honest? He'd known he was going to go over there the moment he heard from Maria that McCullough was away again. He'd planned it like any man would. Holly was likely to be angry, hurt and vulnerable, and he would get her drunk, when those states were likely to become exaggerated. She'd known he had wanted her for years, which always meant the potential was there. When she asked him what he was doing at the house, knowing Mac was away, he'd said nothing. He hadn't needed to. Deep down she knew.

The whiskies arrived and both men drank them down in one. The moment of access was over. Lucien was once again just another human being in all his sameness and separateness. McCullough almost retched, his throat and stomach burning; only in this pub would Lucien countenance drinking such cheap wine and whisky. The pain in McCullough's guts was debilitating. He wanted to play back to Lucien everything he'd just learned: show him that there was nowhere to hide. But instead he said, 'I haven't eaten all day.' It was pathetic but somehow fitting. What else was there to say to Lucien? He was a monster, after all.

'I *would* suggest dinner . . .' Big smile.

McCullough gripped the bar. 'If Holly and I break up over this . . .' He paused, adding almost gently: 'It's all a fucking mess.'

'Well, if you will go building churches.' Lucien was not being sarcastic—he was pointing out a fact, nothing more.

McCullough looked around. They were no longer being stared at, just the occasional glance turned on them by those who didn't want to miss anything if it kicked off again.

'Didn't we discuss this the other week, Proctor? It does seem our life options are limited if we're not to hurt anyone. I suppose I was just pushing at the boundaries.'

McCullough looked up at him. 'That's it? That's your excuse?'

'Go home, Proctor.'

'Fuck off, Lucien. *You* go home.' He sounded drunk. The light-headedness, the burning in his stomach, had become too much—he was on the point of collapse.

'Unfortunately, my home life has always been like your home life is now.'

Was that possible? Lucien was surrounded by this level of pain every day? McCullough supposed it shouldn't come as a shock: as you sow, so shall you reap, and all that. Maybe Lucien's behaviour was not that unusual: he was just obeying an impulse to create misery as a validation of himself—a negative quest for self-justification, a search for a kind of authenticity. Nietzsche again: the triumph of personhood the only real moral act. Or was it even simpler than that: it was in our nature to want the world to be the same for others as it was for ourselves? Wasn't this what McCullough himself was doing? Whatever he was building, it was a version of the world that represented some essential aspect of himself, except unlike most people he'd felt compelled to make it material and locate it in a place. McCullough couldn't remember if Nietzsche had a solution to someone who created more pain than love. He supposed rather than regret your life, you must choose not to be born at all. Was that what he wanted for his friend—not to have been born at all?

In grabbing Lucien and hugging him tightly, McCullough felt like a Mafia godfather, but there was no threat or irony implied by his embrace.

'So you forgive me, then?'

'Forgiveness is overrated. You are deserving of love, that's all.'

Lucien laughed. 'I'll leave that up to you.' He felt himself instantly off the hook.

The evening sun pooled into the pub, a pale bright mist. It was difficult to see individual faces, and since the hit of whisky McCullough had had trouble focusing. Perhaps his surge of love came from this feeling of drunkenness. Nothing more than emotionalism. It was definitely time to leave. To go home. Not to walk or wander, but as he'd done many times from this part of town, hail a cab, give his home address, and, depending on the time of day, offer advice on the best bridge to cross, keeping his front door in mind and what he might be greeted with when it opened—chaos or love, or both. Tonight it would be different, of course. The false smiles and forced kindness between him and Holly would affect the children, which would make them demand more attention than normal, causing him to lose his patience, however generous he felt when walking in. This would inevitably lead to Holly staring at him, grim-faced and hurting. He'd resist saying anything aloud, it would get said anyway via the clairvoyant lines of communications they'd built up over the years. *This is your fault—you sort it out.* And so it would go on, until the children were in bed, miserable and confused, and he and Holly were in the sitting room, miserable and angry, the evening ending as the last two had done, Holly abandoning him before dusk, and another night spent in his office, lying wide awake, staring into the darkness, and listening out for any noise, for someone, anyone, calling for him.

Book Two

OLD TESTAMENT

God is a verb.

PART ONE

Thou Shalt Not II

TETRAGRAMMATON

'There is; it gives.'

MARTIN HEIDEGGER,
'LETTER ON HUMANISM'

I

He was found by Rich on the beach, waves at his feet, cut and bruised and delirious. When the boy first saw him, he didn't know what to do. He thought McCullough was dead, and wandered down as he might do to any dead thing, to give it a poke with his foot. But the body had groaned and rolled over and vomited.

The first person Rich called was Nathaniel, but it went to voice-mail. He then tried Rebecca, who was having breakfast. For the next thirty minutes he sat next to McCullough like a young child might his dying father. The tide was going out, the drawing away of the waves over the pebbles was all that could be heard. Now and again Rich whispered, 'The others'll be here soon.'

Rebecca came with Judith. It took all their strength to move him, to drag his body over the stones and shale, through the rent in the cliffs, up the bank, and to make him comfortable on the cold dewy ground.

In the morning sun, against the deep damp green of the grass, they saw just how pale and bloody he was. There was no sign of attack, but the wounds did not appear to have come from slipping over or a fall. Judith wanted to take him to hospital but Rebecca said no: they would look after him here. Mother glared at daughter. Daughter shrugged. During a short period of lucidity he was asked what he wanted and said not to be moved. With clothes found in the boot of his car, Judith changed him. Propping him up on her lap, she insisted he take sips of water. He did as he was told. There were periods when he lost consciousness and needed reviving with slaps to his cheeks. Some distance away Rebecca stood, watching, biting at her nails. Beyond the oak, Rich tried Nathaniel again. He was sent off to the village for bottled water, fruit, paracetamol.

The morning was clear and warm, the sky pale blue. Judith looked around at this place where her daughter had come each morning for months. She recognized it from the descriptions. There were two almost complete buildings, only roofs missing, some glazing. She'd imagined more disruption, more scarring of the land, and, in the first instance at least, an offence to the eyes. But the setting was beautiful, and the buildings, although unexpected, felt strangely familiar, as if they had grown out of the land as a surprise to itself. She was not hypnotized as such, but felt a compulsion to dwell on what she was looking at.

The edges of the church were precise, and yet the narrow palette of natural colours created a gentle bloom that softened and made hazy what was straight. She also felt that she could see aspects of the building that weren't possible from her angle of sight, as if all elevations were available to her at once. Wasn't this what Stevens meant by 'transparencies': a *seeing through* without any opening up of what was solid? In her own book she'd called it 'invisible permeability', as if solids became open fields of form and colour which we pass up against and drift into without any disturbance of the thing itself, no taking apart, no deconstruction. She seldom experienced this outside his poems, but she accepted it was happening here with these two unfinished buildings.

She looked down at McCullough. He was sleeping, an intense, saving sleep; on his face, behind his eyes, the struggle to restore himself.

To the left a forty-metre steel beam was laid out on heavy black plastic sheeting. She sought out her daughter, pointing and asked what it was for.

Rebecca was rolling a cigarette, her back to the oak, one knee up as she placed the tobacco in the paper. When she was finished, she walked out into the sunlight, and with her dark and slender hands demonstrated to her mother how everything would eventually fit together.

'It will lie across the intersection of three sets of two beams that will protrude from the sides of a hexagon inside the church. Can you see that low circular wall there? Inside there is an angled hexagon. It's called Pascal's line. From Pascal's mystical hexagon. I think it's meant to be—you know—the steeple. It's my responsibility.'

She had told her mother all this before, over dinner, with similar gestures of her hands, but in those moments Judith had chosen to think of McCullough as a dream, and as with those aspects of a dream that leak into waking life, paid little attention. But now he needed real attention, and in a way she'd seldom shown a man before. She felt panicked. Seeing him on the beach she'd wanted to walk away, and even now part of her wanted Rebecca to take responsibility—after all, this man was her friend, a man who had given her a new confidence by somehow not being the mystery she found most people to be. Hadn't Rebecca even given her permission to marry him? It was a joke, of course, but nothing was ever really a joke with Rebecca.

By mid-afternoon, McCullough was conscious. He couldn't speak, and didn't struggle to do so. At one point he felt his hand being held and looked up to see Rich there, gazing into the distance. It was impossible to signal his appreciation; a contraction of his fingers was all he could manage, after which Rich let go. Occasionally he was propped up and given pills, a drink of water. Once he heard Rebecca whisper close to his ear: 'It was me who said you wouldn't want to go to hospital; you'd want to stay here.'

For an hour it was just the two of them. Like Rich, she held his hand. At one point she said, 'Well, here we are, holding hands. Who da thunk it?'

It was then he spoke his first words, indistinct and broken, as if he were being powered by an intermittent electric current. 'I came to help you look for Terry.'

Rebecca squeezed his hand: Terry still hadn't been found, but he wasn't to worry.

When he awoke in the late afternoon, his mouth and lips were dry, but his body felt as if it might permit movement—there was energy that hours ago he'd been certain was permanently gone.

The others sat nearby. Judith was laughing, and in her soft ironic accent teased Rich about his feelings for Rebecca. Rich explained that over the last month he'd come to a new understanding: if he couldn't express his love fully, and that meant physically, it was still good to be honest about it—after all, what else better justified us as human beings than our willingness to be open about love, to give it gratuitously? McCullough wanted to call out 'Hear, hear. Good for you, Rich', except he realized he'd just imagined this exchange. The boy had said nothing.

How long had he spent on the beach, alone and bleeding? At no point during the long night had he doubted he would live, yet still he worried about leaving his children fatherless, the children of a man gone crazy and found dead on a beach. He knew that they were at an age when it would only be a couple of years before they began to forget him, and over time their felt experience of his love would dissipate to nothing. Holly would remind them, of course, as she would have to remind herself, given how hard it had been. But life would crowd him out. Did that prove the contingent nature of human love? His family would go on, his love unnecessary to their existence, even their happiness. He felt a great sadness and found himself calling their names. There was no strength in his voice, but from what little sound he managed, the cliff face created the gentlest of echoes. It was a good test of life, that rebounding sound, and he hoped that on some infinitesimal level, rather than die away, it might spread and carry on some mysterious quantum level, and make its way over the two hundred miles between him and his home, and into the dreams of whatever it was his six-year-olds dreamed of. But he wanted more than that: for the reverberation to softly penetrate their hearts and embed itself there, so he might send along the oscillations, of what he now imagined as a vibrating cord, messages of love, from his heart to theirs. The thought made him cry, and his body, cut and torn, caused him great pain.

Dawn was like death. It had the light of death, an immaterial greyness, without hope. The tide had come and gone and he was wet to the waist, shivering, physically depleted from the loss of blood and no food in twenty-four hours. For a time his body felt as if it was made of stone. To recover he retreated deep inside himself, knowing there was a risk of not returning. Despite what he now knew about the world, there was no chance he'd be saved a second time. That it had happened once, as he'd fallen from the cliff, his body suspended in mid-air—a sudden halting of time and motion—was in itself an impossibility, but without it he would have died, his body crushed on the rocks below. Not that he'd been laid down gently, cradled by great arms. But his fall had been broken, a few metres from the ground, so when he landed the damage was not fatal. Still, he screamed. Skin torn, bones chipped, the pain so strong that within a second he lost consciousness. When he came to, he was paralysed with cold, body heavy with seawater, and an ache tore at his heart. His short-term memory was faulty, pieces of it missing. It was simplest to think that it had been a dream. He'd walked across the clifftop and fallen, only to imagine later the sudden arresting of time. How, otherwise, might he explain what had happened? But then, that was not all that had happened.

He remembered Rich, a toe of his Dr Martens at his shoulder, prod, prod. He wanted to explain: 'I fell asleep in my car and then . . .', but could not go on. He sensed Rich sitting there by him, folding his bandana into different shapes, trying them on; but with no mirror to check the effect, selfies were taken.

With the arrival of Rebecca and Judith he felt safe because they were mother and daughter and would look after him. To move him they all adopted the postures of labourers ready to drag or carry a large bag of cement. McCullough knew from manoeuvring Edward that the weight of a man is great when he can do nothing to lighten himself. And Judith was so slight, delicate, a seeker of comfort. They needed Nathaniel. The boy would think nothing of hauling McCullough over his shoulder. In the end, he was dragged and carried up the beach, along the sand path and to the fire, which Rebecca got going quickly, following the instructions given to all of them by Terry at the beginning of the summer.

Beneath his body, heavy and inert, he felt the grass as a home to insects, scurrying life. Judith wanted to call Holly, but they were unable to find his phone. There were moments of disagreement, and at one point Judith panicked when he vomited down himself. He heard her explain that he might die, from shock, from exposure, how were they to know the extent of any internal bleeding? Rebecca was right to argue with her: he wouldn't die and he wanted to stay where they'd placed him, exactly there.

Later, Judith too clasped his hand, and in a whisper that felt warm against his ear, said wryly, mock wryly, 'You come into our lives . . .' It was meant kindly. She wanted him to feel safe, accepted.

Rebecca talked to him as if he were more conscious than he was, as if he'd asked to be kept up-to-date. 'Everyone's really concerned about Terry. Social Services are looking after his mum.'

Half asleep, he heard Judith explain: 'Rebecca has gone to get sleeping bags. So has Rich. Poor boy.'

At some point, his eyes open for a brief time, he caught Judith searching for split ends in her hair just like her daughter on those first days, when it seemed that she'd just turned up to taunt and needle him. Somehow Judith knew he was awake and talked to him from behind a soft, fine curtain of hair.

'For a long time I used to treat men appallingly if they weren't in love with me. At least Rebecca hasn't inherited that. She's more like her father. The truly superior rely on contempt to manage the world; no one gets near. Rebecca spoke to him on the phone a couple of nights ago and told him all about you. She made him jealous, which was more than I ever could. I could see her working at it. It gave me real pleasure to think of him discomfited in that way. Rebecca was upset afterwards. To have to do that, to get your father's attention.'

It was dusk when he was able to sit up and speak, the stars visible in the dark blue sky, perfect unthinking silver dots. The site lamps pooled even cones of light around the buildings, seeming, in their own way, to possess concentration.

Rebecca and Rich returned with rucksacks, like brother and sister arriving home after a holiday taken together.

He was given dry chicken breast pulled apart, more sips of water, thin slices of cucumber. He chewed methodically, creating moisture in his mouth. He wasn't sure whether he could taste it or not. Its texture was the most evident feature. To swallow he had to crane his neck. Working the food down felt softly mechanical. After a few bites, energy flowed through him like small flames being lit, warming his veins and muscles.

As soon as he could speak, explanations were demanded. He found he had nothing to say, at least not then. When he could listen, without falling asleep, Rebecca, Judith and Rich described possible scenarios to him, waiting for nods of agreement. Had he fallen? If so, he was lucky to have survived. Was he attacked? Did he remember anyone hanging around? Counterfactual narratives of doom followed. What if the tide had come further up the beach? What if Rich hadn't thought to look down there? Rebecca and Judith both looked at the boy. What made him do it? He shrugged.

It was Rebecca who knew there was more to it. She'd spent weeks trying to read him, and now she didn't even need to look at him to sense he was keeping something back. Yet she refused to ask what it was. She didn't dare, fearing he might say something that would put a stop to how she now felt about him. It was nothing to do with faith or belief, but she had finally accepted that she liked him, and wanted perhaps to love him, and bring him into her home and keep him there. She had even interrogated her mother on the possibility, at first unaware of what she was saying. When her mother ignored her, she'd become furious. Do you want to live alone all your life? Wasn't it simple: Holly didn't love him; he was perfect for her; what other man had met with her 'difficult' daughter's approval? Her mother—sleek, precise, so infuriatingly calm—had smiled and said, 'He'd cause us nothing but trouble. In the end.' Rebecca didn't believe this, and felt let down, and reminded herself that this woman was an academic because she didn't possess the emotional depth to be a poet. Later she found her mother crying at her desk, a display of emotion she could only remember from her distant childhood. Cool enquiry met with calm confession: yes, she was lonely. But it would always be thus. Standing in the doorway, Rebecca said she would instruct McCullough to visit regularly; it was impossible that they wouldn't fall in love. Judith wondered why her daughter didn't come and comfort her, instead of standing there, and for a moment hated her.

2

It was the middle of the night when he was able to stand, to shake himself free from stiffness, to blink clear his cloudy eyes, the watery blur. He examined his chest and stomach, and what he could see of his shoulders, sides and back. The others watched him pull at his skin for a closer view, wince in pain, and run his index finger over the ridges of scabbing blood. For a whole minute he looked at his palms, studying them close to his face in the dim light.

When he sat down, he reached for a bottle of water. The lid was tight. He passed it to Rebecca to undo. They watched him as he drank. When he finished he placed the bottle in the grass, making a little well for it so that it might stand up. The cap was replaced loosely.

'I want to tell you what happened. But please let me finish before you say anything. Of course, you are permitted not to believe a word of it.'

He sensed no alarm in them; whatever he was about to say would be leavened by their relief over his recovery.

'I don't know what time it was. I was asleep in my car. I'd driven down from London, arriving about midnight. I woke up and looked out of the window, and over here by the oak tree . . . there was a great pillar of fire. It was taller than the tree, although it didn't reach the sky. Its circumference was . . . I don't know . . . ten metres—maybe wider. It was just there. Not twisting or travelling across the ground. I checked I wasn't dreaming. I *wasn't* dreaming, but I checked anyway: turning the radio on and off, then the lights of the car, basic things that would possess a certain strangeness in a dream. Everything was normal. I knew I was tired and hungry but I wasn't hallucinating. Everything else was the same—just like now.

'I knew what it was, of course. I didn't need to wait until dawn to watch it become a pillar of cloud. In that sense it wasn't a shock. Or not a great shock. A moment of wonder, I suppose. How could it not be?

'I didn't get out of the car. I feared it was there for me, that it might take me up . . . burn me up. What you guys don't know is that it has become increasingly clear to me . . . that something like this was going to happen, although I always imagined it would happen inside me . . . that I might be engulfed from within by light or what I've been thinking of as . . . uncreated light. So it was a shock to see Him there, if you can forgive the pronoun, as a pillar of fire.

'Eventually I got out. What else could I do? The first thing I noticed was that there was no sound, no combustion, no great generation of energy—nothing was being eaten up in this fire. It was self-sustaining.

'I walked along the edge of the ridge, skirting it. I knew it was waiting. I sensed its patience. When I got closer, as close as we are now, there wasn't any heat, not as we understand it, but I knew I was in the presence of a force more powerful than . . . comparison is irrelevant . . . All I knew was that I was being permitted to withstand it.

'I hadn't said anything by this point. I mean out loud. I'm not sure I'd even said to myself "What is this?" or "What the fuck?" I was just there, mute. I supposed I'd been prepared. As I said, it wasn't really a great surprise. But then I was thrown back. Thrown through the air and smashed against the trunk of the tree. The force should have shattered me, broken my back, my neck, emptied me of life. But all I felt was my shirt rip and the ridges of bark cut into me as I slipped to the ground.

'As I lay on the ground, the pillar moved towards me and into the tree and burned there, right above me. It was no longer a column of fire; the whole canopy of the tree was in flames. The trunk was at the centre of the blaze, as if the roots of the tree were a source of some kind of energy coming up from the earth. The force was fierce, as if it was burning up everything. Except, as you can see, the tree is unchanged. It was unchanged as it burned. Still I said nothing. I didn't cry out. If anything, I laughed. I thought, if I'd had trouble convincing people I wasn't mad before, now what? I remember the pain in my gut from laughing. The first thing I said out aloud, the first thing I said to Him—yes, to God, or I suppose more correctly, Yahweh—was a sarcastic, "Thanks".

'And then the fire was gone. It didn't withdraw or burn down. It was just gone. I don't think it took even the smallest division of time to disappear. It was as if time went back to the moment before it appeared, or what had happened had occurred in a fold in time and the fold was snapped straight, and so that moment of time was gone. And then there was nothing, just the oak tree above me, the ground, the darkness around, and my body aching, and blood soaking through my shirt. I asked myself whether it really had been a dream after all. I'd walked across to the tree in my sleep, tripped on a root or something, bashed my head. I can't tell you how ordinary it all was. How it was impossible to believe that it had happened because there was no evidence. Nothing at all. How could there be?

'And then He was there. I mean He wasn't there, except I knew His presence was being made apparent to me. I was to understand that sitting—yes, sitting—behind the tree was God. I know it sounds ridiculous, but all I can do is describe what happened, what I saw, what I felt, what I know to be the case. I mean . . . I knew that the conception of Him was mine, that His material presence came from me. But I also knew He was there to give material form to, that this was being permitted by Him, it was what He wanted. Why, after the pillar of fire, the burning tree, this adoption of personhood? I knew I would never actually see Him, not like I can see you, but He had form, and in the rags that I'd given him, the torn and dirty cloak and hood that I'd given him, He sat there. I would be lying if I said I didn't sense that I had chosen well. That He was comfortable.

'It was a while before I said anything. I couldn't find a position painless enough to let me draw a deep breath. I was like a man who'd dragged his broken body to this tree, thinking: Here I will find safety. It seemed facile to ask for the pain to be taken away; I knew no such thing would be granted, had ever been granted. But after . . . I don't know . . . after a while . . . this was how it went.

'There were questions from me, sometimes spoken aloud, sometimes only to myself. It's funny, but imagine: what would you ask if you could sit down with God? What I learned is that there are no answers. Not really. There is just . . . access to Him. That's what I was being given . . . access to where everything resides. You don't interrogate God. He gives. And I felt, in being given access, in reaching in—because I had to strive beyond myself, to throw myself in—I passed through a veil of great sadness. Of grief. And it was only then I realized that I was bearing witness to a fundamental truth: all judgment falls on Him. Despite what we think, what others think . . . what is written. He judges only Himself.

'There was also instruction. Wordless, silent instruction. God doesn't speak English or Hebrew or Arabic. But He gives, as I said. At times, I felt I should be writing stuff down. Don't laugh. It felt like that. Although there was nothing to write down. That was clear. But there is a difference between instruction and understanding. I've had a lot of time to think about it . . . how to express it.

'It's simple. God is complete in Himself, uncreated, self-sustaining, without need, and yet we have the universe, which was an act of pure giving, and unnecessary to Him. First we must accept this. We are unnecessary to Him. And yet He still created us. And in doing so He reduced himself. For an act of creation to be a pure gift, it must come with complete freedom. But to allow complete freedom beyond Himself is necessarily a reduction of His complete-ness. Our freedom takes from Him—it must. And yet how can we even talk of a reduction in the infinite, the eternal? It doesn't make sense. But we must set that aside. Clearly we're way past what makes sense. Let's just say God will never run out of Himself. So we must concentrate on that first act. What does it mean? In that first act, God created *creation*. What was brought into being *first* was creation. If you want to go to Scripture, that's what it means to be created in His image. Like Him, we are capable of creation, gratuitous crea-tion, which is the free giving of ourselves, or the unnecessary giving of ourselves . . . the act we have chosen to call love. We might only have a tiny capacity in comparison; but we have it. And, of course, we also have the freedom to use it, or not. As He did. We are like Him in that way, too.

'And yet . . . there is a problem. Of course there is. We haven't chosen to do as He did. We chose the opposite. Instead of love we chose power, that other residuum of Him that abides in us. Maybe the first act was not possible, if we can use such a term, without some of His power finding its way into us. And so in the same way we carry with us a small parcel of love, we also carry a small parcel of power. But whereas love cannot be degraded or it ceases to be love, corrupted power is still power.

'Please, you must remember . . . all I had was access . . . no commandments, no narrative. Just Him there . . . to make sense of, if I could.

'So what did I sense? His great act of love was the end of something. That in a way . . . in a way we can't comprehend, He was harmed by that act. For the act to be truly giving, not to be some meaningless act of power, of majesty . . . harm must be a possibility. Without harm there is no risk, and without risk, what has been given . . . has no meaning. Maybe this is new.

'As I said, I didn't learn this; I wasn't told; but maybe this is how we must think about God now, if we are to be honest with ourselves. If we are to grow up.

'I know this all sounds simple-minded: that we share two elements with Him, love and power. But the consequences are not simple, if we've forgotten one—if we have set one aside, as we have . . . to the extent that we recognize it for what it is, its nature and possibility. We catch glimpses when we first fall in love; more rarely these days, in our acts of pity. Power is ascendant. Of course it is . . . it requires nothing of us—it's a self-animating force. Certainly, we don't need to search ourselves for it. Nor do we need to seek it elsewhere. Not like love. Love feels precious, our own and others'. Which is not how we think about power. We don't really think about power. We seldom notice how we use it. Looked at like this . . . it's limitless, unlike love. Whether that's the case or not, what's certain is that degraded power is like energy—perhaps they are the same things . . . entropic, unmanageable, becoming chaos.

'Love is different. It requires our attention. And when it does receive our attention, it gathers up and brings together . . . It binds and holds. Of all the things I've said that He made clear . . . this is the easiest to believe, I think. If we look at our behaviour, who amongst us believes we possess a surfeit of love? Maybe a few. Most of us . . . struggle. We yearn to love, but it's still a struggle. To be generous and patient, to be forgiving. And never more so when we need to offer it freely to those we don't care for or don't like.

'This is what I learned. This is what I would have written, if I thought He would permit it. He is the source of love, the source of our love, and only that. We are fools to believe He possesses other attributes. Anger, vengeance, judgment—what are they but our interest in power? Our nonsense. And we know this because if we turn to Him, He will transform our small parcel of love, that precious amount we feel we must use so sparingly, that we think some might not be deserving of . . . into a kind of grace, which is to love unsparingly. We ask Him for more love and it is given, and it becomes ours. Nothing more can be asked of Him. Of course, we don't even have to ask. It is not a question of prayer. There is nothing in the way of this; no barrier. No law or dogma, no book. Our sins have no impact. It can never be withheld. He gives. That is His nature.

'Eventually, I asked why I was being . . . why I was . . . Why me? I think I said this aloud. It was silly, really. It was met with silence, of course.

'I felt Him rise, ready to leave. I tried to stand up. It was difficult, but I managed, and made my way around the tree, holding tightly on to the trunk. How many paces around is it—nine or ten? I thought surely I was permitted to see what I had imagined for Him? His ragged cloak and hood? Remember, there was only moonlight and starlight. And as you can see, it is dark under this tree at night. I began to walk around, accepting that if I were to see Him it would require more than one revolution. And I was right. On my . . . I don't know . . . seventh time around . . . I caught a glimpse. The tail of His rags, the back of Him, disappearing into the darkness, and then He was gone. Just like before with the pillar of fire, a fold in time snapped straight.

'As much as my body would allow, I walked in His direction. I had no objective. And yet I went. But He was gone, and I had to accept that whatever joined us for that short time was no more. He and I existed separately now. What was weird . . . actually seeing Him, the back of Him, hurrying away like that, brought the first and only doubt, as if the glimpse I had didn't make sense, given what I knew. The most concrete element of all . . . that part didn't seem possible.

'And yet I walked on as if I might find Him, or discover . . . I don't know, something. What else could I do, return to my car and sleep? That's when I fell. I just stepped over the edge of the cliff. It's a law of physics, right, that if we step off a cliff we fall? The most basic law: gravity. And that if the cliff is high enough, and we step off and fall, we will die. And yet . . . close to the bottom, I stopped. *Everything* stopped, and I was held there. I could see the rocks below, the waves breaking over them as the tide came in. I was able to look around. At the cliff face; out to sea. I don't know how long it lasted, probably less than a second, and yet long enough for me to know what was happening, to accept that time had been suspended, motion had been arrested. Whether this had happened just for me, or just in this world, or in all of space and time, I don't know. Perhaps only a falling man would have noticed. Others might have felt something, but just thought they'd tuned out for a second. It's a thing that happens—a loss of concentration and time goes astray for a second or two. Perhaps it happens all the time. But in this instance, it meant that when I fell again, I only dropped ten feet. Then I was at the bottom of the cliff, broken and in pain. There was to be no alleviation of my suffering.

'The tide moved up over my body, then away again. I thought of my family, of you, knowing that I'd been visited by God, in the guise of Yahweh, and learned, if only I could process it . . . that all that is necessary, all that is true, and that everything else, the dogma and kerygma of all religions . . . the commandments, our sin, His judgment . . . in all this man is trying to evade the simple truth, or, more generously, is just missing it. Perhaps the heaviest irony of all is that His creative gift within us is what enables us to do this . . . to be distracted from the simple truth as we construct the supremely complex arguments for His existence, that extraordinary combination we've created: unknowable, impassible, transcendent, and yet still biddable to our local prayers. It's quite a feat. Of course, we could say that all that is beautiful about religion, all its irrational transcendent beauty, is His gift, and everything else is merely a corruption by us, our sinfulness, our depravity. We are human, after all. And yet . . . perhaps there is some other way to think about this.

Some acceptance we must come to. Our power is sufficient unto this world but our love is not. Maybe the truly powerful already know this. But the answer is simple. The solution is clear. We must ask for more love. Each one of us must turn to Him when we think we need it, and ask for just a little more love.'

He'd talked for ten minutes and was exhausted. He smiled; shrugged. Not much of an ending: *turn to Him for just a little more love.* But it would have to do. Why, after what he'd been through, add a rhetorical device to make it more persuasive, more convincing?

He looked at Rich, Rebecca, Judith. They had listened patiently, sometimes with their heads bowed. At times he'd sensed held breaths. Early on, a snigger or two. He had no sense whether they believed him or not, but he suspected they did not. Before he'd uttered a word, he accepted that they were going to think him mad, finally mad, and they had every right. What might he say that would distinguish him from a madman, what tone of voice, what language might he use that would make them understand—it all happened just as he said? All he could say was that it was the case: a God of sorts existed because he had talked with Him, up on the ridge, sitting under a tree. A small thing, really, if you thought about it. The encounter was short, the message simple. It made no difference that, close by, a church would stand. He couldn't claim the encounter as foundational. For that to happen he would have to share with others the story he'd just told to those sitting around him. He would need to make a proclamation. He supposed some people would find enough in the detail to want to turn the church into a kind of shrine. For others, the church would be irrelevant, the tree was the thing. Hadn't God first burned there and then sat like a peasant against its trunk? The tree wouldn't survive long, it would be broken up and taken to other parts of the world, each fragment a charged object, a relic, for those who needed the presence of God in such a way. But he wouldn't say anything because he didn't believe God required it. There was nothing to prophesy. No mission to undertake. The gift of miracle was not now his. He was unchanged. The church was still a folly.

He looked around. 'Thank you for listening. You've been very patient. I think I need to sleep now.' He lay down on the grass, making a pillow of his hands under his cheek. Closing his eyes, he added, 'At least you now know that if you think I'm mad, you won't be punished if I'm not!'

Judith laughed and Rebecca covered him with the blanket.

Rich stood up. 'All the way through that my mobile was vibrating. I didn't dare answer it.'

TERRY

'Is he his own strength?
What is its signature?
Or is he a key, cold-feeling
To the fingers of prayer?'

TED HUGHES, CROW FROWNS

I

'Terry has been found.' It was all Rich said, but he repeated it. 'Terry has been found.'

McCullough's first thought was that he was dead, taken at the same time as his own fall was broken—in exchange. It took him a moment to shake himself free of that and ask, 'What else?'

Rich looked at Rebecca. 'It was Dave from the pub. He heard Terry was at the police station.'

'At least he's alive.' This was Judith, stepping forward and rubbing her daughter's arm.

McCullough was silent for a moment. 'You should go, Rebecca. And you, Rich. But come straight back. Please.' He looked at Judith: did she want to leave with them?

'He'll be fine.' Rebecca smiled at McCullough. 'It's his second home.'

This hadn't occurred to him; he felt muscles in his stomach relax. 'But someone should go.'

Rich seemed nervous, twitchy. Eyes to the ground.

'What is it, Rich?'

'Dave said there were a lot of police about.'

'You said that all you knew was that he was at the police station.'

'That is all I know.'

Rebecca stepped forward. 'Rich . . . Just tell us what Dave said.'

'He said he thinks Terry's at the police station and there are cops swarming around. Loads of them.'

McCullough was unsteady on his feet. 'Please, Rebecca. You go with Rich—find out what's happening.'

Judith spoke softly, 'Please, Rich, go with Rebecca.'

She offered him her hand. 'Come on. Escort me.'

Her calm had an effect on all of them: she knew Terry best, understood him, and was the least worried. Knowing where he was seemed to be all the information she needed. What was happening to him now she didn't much care about.

'He'll need a drink and some baccy, right?' She said this to Rich so that he might understand that their shared knowledge of him was important.

The shortest route was decided on, which meant broken stiles, crawling under a hedge. Within moments they were silhouettes receding into the earth. It would take fifteen minutes to reach the village, then however long to find out what was going on; after that McCullough hoped Rich, at least, would be back with news.

He sat down on the ground. It was a minute or so before Judith joined him, a blanket around her shoulders. Neither of them said anything. Along with the food she'd ordered, she had also insisted a bottle of wine was bought, and had written exactly what she wanted on a piece of paper. McCullough asked for some and she poured him a glass, in the dark, holding the top of the bottle against the edge of the cup. As the gentle warmth, wonderfully familiar, moved through his body, McCullough closed his eyes and let the sensations gather him in and bring together all those aspects of himself that had been fragmented and discarded, in his car, by the oak, at the clifftop, on the beach below. Judith sat cross-legged, staring idly ahead.

McCullough nudged her. 'You must be tired.'

She said 'no' with a weariness that made them both smile and then laugh a little.

'You must think I'm insane. Properly. Certifiable, as they say.'

Another weary, if slightly more uncertain, 'no'. Another laugh.

'A fantasist, then?'

'Who am I to say it didn't all happen just like you said?' She sipped her wine.

He needed to find her with his eyes and draw her round. 'But you don't believe me as such?'

'Don't ask me that.'

She was right.

After a minute, he said, 'Holly slept with a friend of mine.' The laugh that followed was neither bitter nor sardonic, just expressing a different level of weariness—one that might never be recovered from.

'I'm sorry.'

'Thank you.'

After that neither of them felt the impulse to speak and together looked up at the moon, large in the sky, bright silver and pock-marked, appealingly present as its recognizable self, pure in its lack of meaning. McCullough contemplated its appearance of flatness; Judith felt she could see just how dusty it was up there.

The night grew cooler and he shivered.

Judith shuffled nearer to him. 'Do you want to share the blanket?' Without waiting for a response, she draped it across his shoulders and drew herself into him.

Beyond the cliffs, above the sea, the night was a lightless black, without horizon. It was this that he'd walked into, willingly, wilfully. Despite what he'd said earlier, did he possess some sense that if he walked beyond the edge he would be supported? As if he were setting some kind of test? No. It was much simpler: he'd forgotten that the cliff's edge was there. The moment he fell there was no belief God might save him, only a sense of having made a terrible mistake, a stupid mistake that would end in his death; it was a fall like any other. A coroner would be right to determine the circumstances as 'accidental' or 'misadventure'. What others might think, given the last few months—that was up to them. Only Holly would be certain that it wasn't suicide. She'd never express it openly, but she knew he'd never leave Walter. The boy was his final responsibility.

But he hadn't died. And that needed thinking about. Had it been a miracle? Rational interpretations were easy. A ledge or branch broke his fall, the evidence swept away by the tide; or some anomaly of the wind, an up-draught of some kind had held him aloft. Did it matter that he knew neither of these things had happened? But arguing his case meant contradicting everything he believed in, even now. God wasn't present in our lives in this way. He didn't meddle. Any defence of what had happened meant singling himself out. Because in this instance, God was present. God had meddled. But there was another reason to keep this to himself, to make no proclamation. What if someone believed him, someone of genius? It only took one, and over time a brilliant edifice of thought would be constructed, a million words to make sense of the simplest of truths, a new thing created to be believed and obeyed. It wouldn't matter that the simple truth would have been lost the moment the first sentence was written, the first blank page filled with words and marked with crossings out. It wouldn't make any difference if he warned against such an attempt—someone would feel compelled. If he criticized what they had written, he would be asked more questions, interrogated more deeply, so fresh attempts might be made, for greater accuracy. Perhaps the greatest of all human ironies is that man's most fundamental yearning, to make things intelligible to himself, pushes God into ever deeper obscurity.

Next to McCullough, Judith's warmth was present on his skin, her slender arm pressing into him. He leaned a little closer, sending a message he hoped she would understand: if you want to rest your head on my shoulder . . . And she did, after clearing her hair away from her eyes.

'They should be back soon,' she whispered, knowing neither of them had the energy to turn around to see if one, or two, or perhaps three dark forms were moving towards them over the fields. In that moment both recognized that they found it easy to offer an uncomplicated comfort to each other, to wish for the other that worry and weariness might fall away.

Eventually Judith slept, moving her head from his shoulder to his lap, content to have her hair softly stroked. She seemed a fragile thing, but who knew what reserves of strength there were in her body.

Leaning over her, he managed to refill his cup of wine. In London, Holly would be asleep, and he sensed that even in her dreams she felt alone. He hadn't called her from the car or when he'd arrived and now his mobile was lost. What must she think? That he was gone forever? Would she seek comfort in Lucien? He supposed if that happened their relationship was over. It would be Holly's way to make sure of it. The thought made his stomach turn cold. Yet if she knew about Judith, if she could see them together now . . . the sexual element from a week ago would be the smallest part of her hurt. What would break her was the tenderness he and Judith had shown each other moments ago. The uncomplicated kindness towards each other's needs. If she had witnessed that it would be pointless to ask her to forgive him, to find in herself more love for him. Love was human stuff as well, and it had its limits.

Judith stirred, pulled herself more tightly in, and palms together, placed her hands between her thighs for warmth.

McCullough tilted his head back and listened out for the approach of the others. There was nothing to hear. Soon he would have to sleep and that meant taking Judith in his arms and lying down next to her. He whispered what he was doing, and gently laid her down and rested her head on his chest. She breathed deeply and 'mmm-ed' when her body was finally able to relax against his. He had to pick away a few strands of her hair that had found their way across his face. At the bottom of his spine he felt a stone cut into his back. He arched a little and dislodged it. The hard comfort of the ground was all he needed for sleep.

2

McCullough and Judith awoke on instinct, Rebecca standing over them. She was shaking, crying, her face tear-stained, eyes small and red. They scrambled up. Neither had a moment to say anything before she collapsed. McCullough caught her and Judith screamed. Mother clasped daughter's face. 'What is it, darling? What is it?'

Rebecca looked up at them both and the large tears in her eyes were bright with the stars' reflection. 'It's Terry. It's Terry . . . He's killed Nat! Mac—he's killed Nat!' She stared up at McCullough; did he understand what she was saying?

To keep her on her feet, to take in what she'd said, McCullough needed strength that only a minute before he didn't believe he'd possess again. Two days ago he'd called Terry an angel and a possessor of truth. What had he done? And Nat. Poor Nat . . . poor, pathetic Nat.

He helped Judith take Rebecca into her arms, a full but flaccid thing, melting, giving herself over to a weaker body, but the body of love. Judith stroked her hair. Slowly both women buckled and kneeled on the ground together.

'Where's Rich?' The other member of this other family.

'The vicar guy sent him home. He wanted to kill Terry. Oh, Mac—it's horrible. Horrible. He chopped his head off! Terry chopped Nat's head off.'

Judith looked up, scared, in need of guidance. There was only wilderness and darkness around them.

McCullough wiped away the tears forming in the corners of his eyes with the back of his wrist. He prayed that none of this was true, that a mistake had been made. In a few hours everyone would be back at work, laughing, bickering, sneering, grumpy, silent, teasing—every combination of mood that the five of them had managed. But that was impossible. Even before he went missing, Terry had abandoned them. That didn't matter anymore, what he now needed was Nathaniel not to be lost to them as well. For a moment McCullough granted himself powers. The possibility of a miracle. He would bring back the dead; forgive the sinner. Hadn't he been witness to folds in time straightened out? What had happened to have unhappened. Might he do that himself? Then everything really could return to normal.

'I need to go. Maybe there's been some kind of mistake.' He said this as much to himself as Judith and Rebecca. Over the last twenty-four hours he'd lost weight and needed to hitch up his jeans. He felt like Terry, the body of an ascetic no jeans would fit. He thought of Nathaniel with his big hips, trousers pulled waist-high, tightly belted, that crude bulge. It was all a mistake. It could be sorted out.

'You need to get Rebecca home.' Looking out across the dark fields, he wondered whether he had the strength to make it to the village.

Judith helped Rebecca off her knees; she seemed without substance in her mother's arms. Halfway up, her legs gave way and she
collapsed again.

'You need to help me, Mac.'

He bent down and threaded an arm underneath Rebecca's legs
and lifted her up into his arms. She was the weight of a distraught
and wretched daughter. She was no weight at all.

They crossed to the cars, stumbling, in shock, moving as fast as
any parents might if they were carrying a dying child.

McCullough placed Rebecca into the passenger seat of her
mother's car; she was pliable, willing to be folded in. He crouched
down and held her hand in his. 'You mustn't worry. I will sort this
out. It's probably all a misunderstanding.'

She wasn't listening. She was fixated on what it must have
looked like, Terry attacking Nathaniel and doing *that*. She was
unable to stop the image looping in her mind. He only now smelled
the odour of vomit on her; she'd thrown up on hearing what had
happened and it had dried on her clothes as she'd made her way back.

He stood and looked down at her. She was like the survivor of
a road accident. The only survivor.

In his own car, he couldn't locate the ignition and his hands
fell into his lap, the keys to the floor. It was too much. He was too
weak, too limited; too foolish. Terry had beaten him. He'd beaten
him by rejecting him. By refusing to get out of his chair. By doing
this. Whatever had actually happened . . . whether it was it an
accident . . . the result of an argument, or had Terry sought out
Nathaniel with this in mind? But what could Nathaniel have said
or done that meant Terry thought he deserved this? Of course,
nothing he might have said or done deserved this, and Terry didn't
need a reason. Perhaps they really had argued and Nathaniel didn't
sense the danger or thought he was protected somehow . . . that
whatever he said or did he'd get away with it, because this was how
the world worked. McCullough knew Nathaniel regarded Terry as
no more than an irritation, dispensable to the real world, a criminal
type. And there was an element of jealousy there. Nathaniel felt he
preferred Terry. Someone he despised placed ahead of him. But none

of this mattered now. Terry had decapitated him . . . and whatever the circumstances, that was no mistake, no accident. It was for show. Or to prove something. The world had to know he was capable of such rage . . . or such calculation. Any charge of aggravated manslaughter would be wrong. A beating and unintended death was the work of a thug. Terry was no thug. McCullough took a deep breath. Poor, poor Nathaniel. A ridiculous man-boy. Even in his hard work there was something ridiculous about him. What was for Nathaniel nothing more than earnest, uninflected toil, to the others was comical, an absurdity.

In the darkness of the car, his hands cold and shaking, McCullough rested his forehead on the steering wheel. He closed his eyes. All he wanted was that Nathaniel's death and Terry's ruin were not somehow in exchange for his own life. He prayed to be reassured of this impossibility. He heard nothing.

3

Terry wasn't at the police station. He'd been moved to Exeter ten minutes earlier. Nathaniel's body had been taken to a hospital there. It was all true. There was no other version, no half-true version, no counter-narrative. Extraneous details, meaningless compared to the enormity of the outcome, were relayed to him by Geoffrey Guffie, who was sitting on a bench a few metres from the police station, ready to offer comfort as the news spread. He was dressed as he had been when he came to the site: old black trousers fallen in the seat, a creased white shirt unbuttoned top and bottom. Unlike the first meeting, there were slippers on his feet. He'd had a haircut and around his hairline his reddish skin looked sore for it. When he greeted McCullough, his voice was calm but the hand he offered in greeting trembled.

'I'm not new to this sort of thing. I had a parish in Manchester in the sixties. But it's the first time I've known both boys.'

McCullough was unable to take in anything: he wanted to ask questions and be given answers. He could see the police station over

Geoffrey's shoulder, and while the old man talked, he focused his attention on the lighted windows as if he might discern something, even though Terry was no longer there.

Geoffrey explained that Terry had presented himself at the police station around eleven o'clock and confessed what he'd done and where the body was to be found. He was not immediately believed, until they realized it might be dried blood on his jeans, and after he was asked to remove his hands from his pockets it was observed that they were covered with dried blood. His shoes were black with blood. It was in his hair.

'So it happened tonight?'

Geoffrey looked at him. 'I don't know; I presume so.'

'But the blood was dry, you say?'

A man in his fifties, dressed like a farmer, but with the manner of an army officer, approached. He called Geoffrey by name but without warmth. It wasn't Nathaniel's father. McCullough was ignored.

'I'm told he's been taken away?'

Geoffrey nodded.

'Do we know any more?'

'Not since we last spoke, Peter.'

'Nothing?'

'No.'

'I suppose you're praying for them both?'

'I am.'

'He's been a menace ever since he came here. My property has been broken into twice.'

McCullough took this in, eyes narrowing. Something didn't make sense. 'Sorry?'

The man now acknowledged him.

'My property. It's been broken into twice since he came here. He was a troublemaker from the start.' He paused. 'Do I know you?'

'No.'

'Then it's none of your business.'

McCullough stepped forward: he liked this kind of battle, with this kind of man.

'Listen, *friend*. I just want to point out that you're mistaking correlation with causation. And it is *my* business because I know both boys. So, please, for all our sakes . . . fuck off!'

A muscle in the man's jaw was visibly in spasm. He was tough, proud.

'Go home, Peter.' Geoffrey's gentleness was not supported by his expression, which said: There are things here you do not understand—things beyond you. McCullough watched as this subtly communicated message began to trouble the man. He was being told the world around him was mysterious in ways he'd never before considered. There was a wobble in confidence. His response was shriller than he'd planned. 'That's not for you to say!'

Geoffrey placed a hand on his shoulder. 'It's late, Peter. And nothing is happening here.' It was not in his nature to frighten anyone.

Over the next hour, Geoffrey waited with McCullough, who refused to leave, even when invited to stay close by at the vicarage. Each time Geoffrey went over to the police station, mostly on McCullough's urging, he returned shaking his head—nothing new had been learned. McCullough then interrogated him. What did he sense? What about their expressions? Are the phones going?

'Maybe *I* should try . . . be a bit more insistent.' McCullough was frustrated, not ungrateful.

'They tend to be fairly open with a man of the cloth.'

'I have my own church.'

They both snorted. It wasn't really laughter, but a chuffing noise made through the nose; a little of their pent-up tension was released.

At three o'clock, McCullough insisted Geoffrey go home: he would be needed in the morning—tomorrow was Sunday. The two men stood, shook hands and then hugged.

'I will pray for him. And Nat, of course. His parents. They are Catholic, you know.'

'Yes.'

There was a pause. 'His mother is very devout.'

'I know.'

'Anyway, Mr McCullough—you know where to find me.'

'Call me Proctor. Or Mac. Whichever.'

'Please, promise to get some sleep yourself.'

Before Geoffrey walked away, an attempt was made to tuck his shirttails into his low-slung trousers, but there wasn't quite enough fabric and they released themselves as his hand withdrew. 'This is my usual bedtime. A man becomes a night owl when he gets older.'

The dawn air was cold, in its own way merciless; the dying would know to give in at this hour. It was too cold to be stationary. McCullough stood up, rubbed his upper arms and looked around the village. The only light visible was in the ground floor of the police station, and then that went off. He turned around and looked down the road. He could see the village green, and across from that, Judith and Rebecca's flat. He'd been invited to spend the night there. There was a sofa, Judith's bed. After a couple of hours' sleep, a shower, some food, he could share what little he knew and the three of them would support each other, a loving family.

But that was to seek warmth and comfort, an escape. Terry's mother was at the other end of the village, alone in her house, as she would be now for years, perhaps until her death. Within hours, the small house would be the focus of police, neighbours, local journalists, and as the news spread, others would assemble, speculation would become fact, and the worst of her son would become all that he ever was.

The street was not easy to find. The first time, Terry had been sitting outside his house. Now in the dawn light all the houses looked alike, small and grey, strangely insubstantial. Most of the street lights were smashed. McCullough only recognized the house because the two plastic garden chairs and blue cooler were still there, as if Terry had just gone inside for more beer. There was no sense that the police had already been around; this wasn't a community likely to go back to bed after such an event.

McCullough paused at the front door. Wasn't he about to become what he feared most for her: a stranger making demands she wouldn't understand? Yet what choice did he have? Who else was going to help her make sense of what was going to happen?

The gentle knock reverberated in the still dawn as if he'd pounded at the door. Everyone on the estate would be woken by the sound. He looked around. The lights of the houses stayed off. He wondered whether his presence among them might be felt at some instinctive level, given his reason for being there. It didn't matter how deeply everyone was asleep, they would be stirred by this new negatively charged energy, this strange creature bringing news of harm to their midst. He knocked again, just one knuckle, close to the thick uPVC door. The sound was more vibration than noise. He placed his ear close. There was no movement inside. The next knock was a single rap, with a conscious sharpness to create a sound that might carry up the stairs and penetrate sleep. He stepped back into the garden. No windows were open. Finally, on his knees, he opened the letterbox and looked in. The hallway was narrow, and at the end, through a half-opened opaque glass door, there was a kitchen in shadow. He called in a half-tone, a carrying whisper, 'Hello.' It would wake no one. He tried the door handle; of course the door was open.

The house had a strong smell. Stagnant air, pans burned dry, and higher up, urine. In the kitchen, unopened letters were stacked on a sideboard. A big black bin was overflowing with beer cans, like a park bin in the summer. He opened the fridge and reared away. Cardboard milk cartons were fat with expanding mould. An open margarine container was empty but for smears of mould and something darker—Marmite? There was a rotting cucumber, soft and collapsed, covered in grey fur. A crumpled packet of bread, the slices a dull green. On the drainer, opposite, there was one dish and a fork, a mug in the sink.

At the bottom of the stairs, he flicked light switches. Nothing. All the bulbs had blown. The stairs were narrow, the carpet worn away and frayed from use; two spindles of the banister were broken. At the top there was a pile of laundry in a blue plastic basket. It was the source of the strongest smell and he had to cover his nose and mouth. There was no landing, just a square of space and three doors.

What must be Terry's bedroom was almost empty, a sleeping bag on the bed, no sheet, no pillow. His holdall of books was missing. On the walls, patches of paint had come away where there had once been posters stuck up at the corners with tape. In the bathroom, underwear was hanging over the side of the bath. The toilet bowl was soiled. The top of the cistern was missing. There was only one toothbrush, splayed from overuse, no toothpaste.

The door to Terry's mother's bedroom was open. She was in bed, on her side, facing away from him, a sheet pulled up to her waist. She wore a faded black T-shirt. The curtains were half open; the nets had a big brown stain in the centre, as if coffee had been thrown there. The dawn light was grey, deathly—what kind of day was born from this? She didn't stir when he stepped in. No instinct registered a strange man in her room.

She was younger than he'd imagined, late forties, a year or two older than himself. She looked like Terry: preternaturally thin, washed out. Her hair was long and colourless, dirty; hair of the unwell, the dying. He whispered, 'It's all right. I'm a friend. A friend of Terry's. I need you to wake up.'

Her sleep was deep. On the bedside table there were bottles of pills, an inch of water in a glass. Did she dose herself through the night, through the day? Was this how Terry managed her? The room was heavy with sleep, of a life weighted down by illness, drugs, loneliness. The bedclothes looked clean, but a high burn of urine still came off the bed.

What should he do? Maybe just stand there and explain and hope that in some way the meaning of what he was saying reached her.

He cleared his throat. 'I need to tell you something. Terry has done something very bad, and the police will come here soon, and will probably want to search the house. There might be journalists, too. People will be very angry.'

She remained motionless. What did he expect? He should have thought this through, waited a couple of hours and spoken to a neighbour, found someone who might be able to help, willing to shield her from the wider world, from the inevitable impression she would give: the vacancy caused by her dementia, the state of her dress, and, if anyone got close, her smell. Inevitably, she would be judged a contributing factor in her son's behaviour. She might even be blamed. What other kind of home do boys come from who murder and cut the head off their victims? He couldn't help but think she would do well to take the rest of her pills and avoid the anguish. Maybe it was the kindest thing he could do—assist her in this. Without her son to look after her what hope did she have? With no son to love, no son to love her . . . in whatever way this might have been communicated—what was the point of living? All he needed to do was sit next to her, feed her the pills, hold the glass of water to her lips as she drank, and comfort her as she drifted away. She might even mistake him for Terry, and then her last experience of life would be . . . of being cared for by her son. It was the right thing to do. It was merciful and loving.

But he couldn't do it.

He walked around the bed, kneeled down and placed his hand gently on her cheek. Her face was sweaty, the pores on her nose open and pitted with dirt; like her son's, her teeth were brown and rotting. Through her slack mouth he saw her tongue was pierced. His touch made her shudder, and as she moved, the sheet shifted, and the stench of a urine-soaked mattress rose on the displaced air. On her arms were track marks, collapsed veins. Her wrists were tiny, like a child's. Around the left there was a tattoo of one word: *Terence* in looping script.

'Please listen to me. A lot of people are going to come here. They are going to ask you questions. Don't be scared. No matter what they ask you, I want you to say this . . . just this: "I love my son." Do you understand? "I love my son." If you can hear me, please say it.'

He leaned in. The smell and heat from her skin made him break out in perspiration. 'Just try it. Whisper: "I love my son."'

His ear was close to her mouth. There was nothing. She was too far away. He turned the pill bottles into the dull light to read. He recognized antidepressants, tranquillizers, others specific to her condition. Might it be that whatever was demanded of her, she would never be present enough to understand? He hoped so.

After picking away the strands of hair stuck to her forehead, he leaned over and kissed her. 'I will arrange for someone to look after you. I will look after Terry.'

4

Rebecca was asleep. As if to prove it, Judith showed him, opening her the bedroom door a little, letting light in from the hallway. A young girl, with too much hair, body splayed under a duvet.

'*You* need sleep.' They said it together, to each other, and for a second they were both free from everything and laughed.

Judith held his wrist. 'Take my bed.'

'I can't.'

He had a plan. Not so much a plan as just being sure what he needed to do. Drive to Exeter to see both boys, make a final confirmation. Whether he'd be allowed to see either of them he didn't know. He'd wait days if he had to.

'You need coffee at least. Something to eat.'

There was a cordless phone on the kitchen table. He ought to call Holly, leave a message explaining that he'd lost his mobile. To say more would be to horrify her, and have himself judged as finding another excuse to stay away, choosing to be with people he hardly knew over being with his family. She would be right to feel this. Except these people were also his family. His other family. He knew it was unfair, and she would find it incomprehensible, but that didn't make it untrue. He pushed the phone away.

'Rebecca will want to go . . . when she wakes up.' Judith put a cup of black coffee before him.

'Let her. Bring her. I'll be there.'

Judith stood across the table from him. 'Why did he do it, Mac?'

'I don't know. He was in a terrible state when I last saw him. In pain, angry. Unreachable.'

'Poor Nat.' She paused. 'You don't think it could ever have been Rebecca?'

How long had she been thinking this? Had it been a question of chance? Might it have been her daughter, someone who in her strange way loved Terry?

'No. Nor Rich. And I hope not me. But Nat I understand, inasmuch as I understand it at all. Nat just thought Terry was a thug. What's the word today—a pikey? Something must have happened between them. Terry was looking for an excuse.'

'He killed him.' She wanted more sense than vague understanding, conjecture. Hadn't he spent the night in the presence of God?

The clock on the wall chimed and McCullough looked at his watch. Outside, the sky was brightening. There were no clouds. The occasional lorry drove past, a grinding gear change audible before the junction fifty metres away.

'Journalists may find their way here if anyone says Rebecca was his girlfriend. And if they see her, that's a story in itself. Who knows who's got a photo of them together?'

Judith shrugged at this and added milk to her coffee. 'They will discover that he was helping build a church. Maybe you will be blamed. Somehow.'

He knew this.

He moved the sugar bowl over to his side of the table. 'I hope they do.' Why deny he wanted a chance to defend Terry, make clear the boy was not to be judged by this one act.

The coffee felt bitter in his stomach, acidic, damaging, but adding milk would only make his insides churn. 'I should go.'

'Please come back and sleep.'

On the threshold of the door, they hugged. As he stretched to hold Judith, the cuts on his back opened, the scabs broke away from his skin. He felt blood running down his spine.

5

As he approached the police station, McCullough wondered what he might look like, what impression he would give—he hadn't cleaned himself up or looked into a mirror for two days. He peered at his reflection in a car door window. He recognized himself, but his image in the glass was too indistinct to show much more than the pallor of his complexion, its bloodlessness. Closer to the station, where people were gathered, he was scrutinized. Whatever he might look like, he was always an unexpected presence, different from others. It was the effect of possessing even a little charisma—it drew attention, exaggerated details, gave people pause.

The policemen on the steps to the station looked at each other as he stood before them. As plainly as he could, he stated his case: 'I am a friend of the boy ... who murdered ... his friend.' They regarded him as if he was shorter than they were and not right in front of them, eyes wary. He wasn't saying anything of interest. 'His mother has advanced early onset Alzheimer's. He has no other family and knows no one else.'

He asked nothing of them. After scratching behind his ear and tipping his cap forward as a cowboy might, one of the policemen decided that others inside could determine what to do. The door was held open.

The lobby was small, the reception desk was a cubby hole with a half-open sliding pane of opaque glass, an electric bell fixed to the sill. The office beyond was a large wood-panelled room, with free-standing desks, hard-backed chairs. The computers were old, screens large and deep, taking up much of the space on each desk. Policemen and women worked with files to one side, using two fingers to type. It was clerical, administrative work. Data entry. High on the back wall a large clock with an analogue dial and a red second hand said 8.04; the date—15 August—displayed in large black numerals.

The duty officer saw McCullough and stood up. He opened the window to its widest and leaned on the counter. McCullough used the same statement of facts as he had outside. The officer was unmoved. He wanted more. McCullough added that he would also be arranging the boy's legal representation; at present Terry had no one to call but him and he'd misplaced his phone. He was studied as if something he'd said needed mulling over. It was a lingering, tired expression.

'Wait here.'

To one side of the lobby, two wooden benches were fixed to the wall, the name 'Morgan' gouged into one of the arms. That took some nerve. Public service notices were pinned to a corkboard on the wall. Car security. Mobile phone security. A new local number to replace 999. McCullough sat down. His body was sticky with the sweat of tiredness, and he placed his hands, palms up and fingers curled, on his thighs. He felt brittle. As if his bones had been hollowed out, the marrow withdrawn. Blood had seeped through his T-shirt and dried. He pulled at the fabric and studied it. Should it be this pink, this weak? Under his T-shirt, he felt the cuts. The blood on his fingertips revealed the skin pattern. He supposed there would be a pad or something behind the desk on which he might dab these and be forever identified.

His breathing sounded more like a series of sighs, as if between times he forgot to inhale or was holding his breath for some reason. He needed sleep. Nothing more. Even if they let him see Terry, he doubted that he'd have the energy to deal with whatever he was confronted with. What *might* he be confronted with? Terry's clothes, stiff with Nathaniel's blood, would have been stripped from him; he'd then have been moved from cell to police van to cell and kept up all night answering questions. Would Terry finally be broken? Little more than two months had passed since they'd first met, and for half that time Terry had withdrawn into himself, using the Bible, as so many had done before him, to escape into another world, as complex and inconstant as our own, but richer with possible meanings. Whether Terry had found God in some unfathomable way, McCullough had no idea. There had certainly been no conventional conversion experience. He'd just become more distant, his perception darker, more conflicted. What might be discovered if the boy was subjected to psychiatric assessments? Would he be declared insane? It wasn't a given that such a killing was a symptom of psychosis. Maybe less so than a claim to have encountered God. But surely any act so far from the norm was in itself proof of something deviant? Perhaps to a psychiatrist murder wasn't that far from the norm, if you removed what fragile constraints might prevent us from killing. Maybe it was closer to primal human behaviour than to follow God off a cliff. After all, there were more murderers than prophets.

The duty officer returned and leaned on the counter. There was another long pause, as if everything he did was discretionary and he had to work himself up to a final decision. 'Guv says if he'll see you, you can see him. But right now he's sleeping.'

CELL

'It is only for the sake of those without hope that hope is given'

WALTER BENJAMIN

I

There was little left of Terry to recognize; he was collapsed and withered, one pale hand resting on his knees, a normal cigarette burning close to the tender skin between his fingers. His other hand was held awkwardly palm up, occasionally jerking as if he were asleep. He was wearing thick grey tracksuit bottoms and an oversized white T-shirt. There were no laces in his trainers. He'd always been slight, thinned out by nervous energy, but he was now reduced to a weak and deathly transparency. Where the neck of his T-shirt collar sagged open, his clavicle protruded, and the skin seemed stretched and pulled tight. It was like he'd become an alien version of himself, made of a different substance, lighter, almost weightless. His thick dull dreads fell forward, hanging before his eyes like matted vines. His posture was that of a stupefied drunk, a fully stoned teenager. But there was a greater sense of absence, of separation, as if he'd chosen to disembody himself.

The room had no table. There was nothing except a plastic cup of water on the floor. Ash from the cigarette floated down. The walls were whitewashed brick. There was no window.

All this McCullough could see through the spyhole of the cell door.

The policewoman knocked and then turned the key in the lock. The door was not heavy.

'Terry. A visitor.'

She refused to look directly at either of them. She didn't want to be involved. Terry made no movement.

McCullough stepped in, his breathing shallow. He wasn't afraid, but his skin prickled hotly, new sweat sticky under his clothes. He did fear if he closed his eyes for any length of time he might fall asleep, partly from exhaustion, partly from a deep reluctance to face his friend.

There was a chair against the right-hand wall. It would need moving to the centre of the room, seemingly an impossible thing to do. Where would he find the energy? What manoeuvres were needed? It felt like a puzzle he'd been set, and it panicked him. Wasn't there supposed to be a table? He'd expected a table. He looked around at the policewoman.

'There's no table.'

'No.'

The door closed. It wasn't locked.

McCullough tried to straighten himself, find confidence in his bearing. 'Terry . . .' He leaned forward, to peer beyond the dreads. Without Terry's participation nothing would happen; after all, it had been he who had brought them both to this place. Of course, Terry would disagree. McCullough had turned up without being asked. What did Terry care if he wanted to understand what had happened and offer himself as a refuge of love? When had Terry ever accepted refuge?

McCullough stepped forward and entwined his fingers, hands turned outward. It was reflexive . . . a preparation, readying himself for a difficult task. He felt like a child asked to solve the most adult of problems, and he was mimicking what he'd seen a parent do. But there was no tension in his limbs, no muscular control, as if he was afflicted with a kind of palsy. His presence here was pointless. What might he offer Terry? He could think of nothing. He felt deprived of ordinary human capabilities.

Beyond the room, all noise and activity were buffered by thick walls, and McCullough felt as if he were in a soundless world, of impossible stillness, with energy not so much at rest as suspended, awaiting instruction, ready to collapse or expand. If anything filled the room, it was the truth of the act that had brought them both here. But that was just him.

Was Terry even aware of him standing there? If he had escaped into a fugue state, he would be far away, in a time and place where none of this had happened. But Terry didn't run away; it wasn't in his nature. This knowledge gave McCullough strength; he did at least partly understand this boy. In that moment, Terry became like his own child. The horrendous nature of the act didn't matter; it was McCullough's job to relieve any suffering he might be feeling, take it upon himself, even just for a moment. He needed to reach Terry and convince him that he could be relied upon. It didn't matter what he'd done; not when it came to this. Hadn't he read somewhere that Judas's great sin was not to have betrayed Jesus but to believe himself abandoned by God? The sin of reason before God's love. But Terry wasn't Judas; and he wasn't God. There was a limit to the suffering he might take upon himself. After all, Nathaniel was dead; he couldn't forget that. What suffering needed to be alleviated there?

But he was before Terry now. He'd made his choice, and he consciously wished the boy released from whatever he was feeling, released of all the knots and darkness and poison. He pictured it all, falling from Terry's belly like the innards of a cow, cut free and dropping out of its stomach. Of course, there was nothing physical to be rid of. Yet it didn't seem impossible that some of the pain might be shared, that there were metaphysical channels that might be opened up between them and some of the pain transferred over. In a way he didn't fully understand, McCullough believed Terry's suffering wasn't just an individual experience, but part of an older, more ancient suffering. It was a ridiculous notion, of course, but that didn't mean it wasn't true. All that was required was to accept individuals are not completely bound and shelled in by their own bodies and that time is not straightforwardly linear. After that, sharing the suffering of others was possible. Wasn't that what was being asked when Christians were instructed to be open to the suffering of Christ? It was more than an act of the imagination.

But didn't that require some redemptive possibility within the act? What if Terry's murder of Nathaniel had been just an act of rage, of drunken, vicious, even joyful rage, and Terry felt nothing at all? There was no suffering to share because Terry wasn't suffering;

he didn't care whether he was abandoned or not. He'd done what he'd done and that was it.

It was possible, of course.

'Terry?' It was a whisper, but his whole body vibrated with it.

'Sit down, Mac.'

The voice was gentle. There was humour in it, and affection. He'd always been polite, and because of this he'd forced himself through the silence to greet McCullough, a guest. Through the heavy dread-locks, his eyes flashed towards the chair.

McCullough dragged the chair to the middle of the room and sat down; it was easily done after all, with permission. Terry dropped his cigarette on the floor; it had burned down to his knuckles without him taking a single drag. There were pale and weeping blisters around the base of his fingers, the webbing, white flesh, liquefying.

'Terry. Look at me.'

The boy peered up, his eyes only, just another flash.

'I don't know how long they will let me stay . . .' There was no inflection in McCullough's voice, just an echo-y declaration, as if he were hearing himself played back on a recording, someone he didn't recognize, hollow-voiced and insincere. He added, 'We don't have much time.' The frustration in his voice now sounded self-conscious, acted out.

Was there a flash of a smile? From wherever Terry had withdrawn to, that cheesy appeal had reached him and been recognized for what it was.

Perhaps this was the best McCullough might hope for: that Terry would accept this as a drama he was forced to participate in, if only to get rid of the man before him and be left alone.

'Are you going to tell me what happened?'

Terry didn't look up. Then, after a pause: 'I killed Nat.'

'Why?'

'I don't know.' It was the answer of a child.

'You disappeared. Where did you go?' The moment he asked it, the question seemed irrelevant—stupid. He reached over to clasp one of Terry's hands. Its withdrawal was a clear signal that he didn't want to be touched; a cross child's hand snatched away.

'Terry, I want to understand.'

'There's nothing to understand. I thought, what the fuck? Cut off his head.'

'I don't believe that.'

'No? How do you think it happened, then?'

'I don't know. Please, look at me, Terry.'

His heavy matted hair was splayed, the scalp beneath it dark. His neck to his T-shirt collar was dirty, then cold white where the dirt stopped.

'I just did it, Mac. It wasn't hard.' Looking up, he rested his narrow, watery eyes on McCullough, seeking comprehension of this fact.

'How do you feel? Now?'

He recalled Terry sitting like this in the pub, becoming drunker, slowly more bent over, face angled up, ready for an insult, searching it out—all that was needed was a single gesture, a look. Was it now just weakness or was he still being watchful?

'Nat was a pathetic, lonely, unloved boy.'

'You'd prefer it if I'd picked someone else?'

McCullough felt stupid. 'No. Of course not. Why did it have to be anyone?'

'It just did. I knew it weeks ago. I had to find out.'

'Find out what?'

'Whether I had the strength. How it would feel.' He paused. 'What would happen to me.'

'It was a test?'

'Isn't everything?'

'I want to know how you feel.'

'Go home, Mac. Go home to your family. They need you; I don't.'

There was no answer to that. No argument. As always, in his own way, Terry was right.

'I want to help you.'

'Do what? Repent? I repent. I did that right after. That's easy. But I guess you'd have to try it yourself to know.'

He expected to hear Terry's chuckle.

'Have you asked yourself why, Terry?'

He leaned back and to one side, reaching into the tracksuit pocket for a crumpled packet of cigarettes, the sharp corners of the box dulled. He pushed open the top and withdrew a cigarette, tucked it into his palm and placed it between his lips. The tip of flame from the lighter made the tobacco crackle and glow. He leaned back to slide the lighter into his pocket. It was all done with slow deliberation, as if moving like this made a mockery of time. The smoke was let out smoothly, expelling more air than the intake of breath needed to draw on the cigarette, perhaps releasing other things—conscience, will, physical pain. He took only one drag and then placed his hand back onto his knee and let the cigarette burn down.

'It's going to be blamed on me temper. I like a scrap, but—'

'What?'

This time Terry's breath was deep and held fast, as if he wanted to keep something in, whatever he was feeling to be dispersed within himself. McCullough looked down at his own hands: fingers intertwined, turned against each other—not strongly, but producing tension. It was an appeal of sorts, but to whom, for what?

They sat in silence.

'You know the difference between attrition and contrition, Mac? Of course you do. Attrition is how you feel about something you've done because you're worried about how the Old Man might punish you. Contrition is the real sadness . . . that you've made Him sad by what you've done.'

'Is that how you feel, Terry?'

There was the chuckle, finally.

McCullough had been too quick, too willing to believe it could be that easy, a choice between attrition and contrition.

'Why should I feel anything? Maybe I think it's all a bit of a laugh. Maybe I did it and felt nothing—you know, beyond "Sorry, Nat". And now I think—fuck: what a laugh.'

'I don't believe that.'

'But you've got to accept it as a possibility, haven't you? Without having done it yourself?'

'I don't accept it as a possibility. I have too much information. Just a few days ago I described you to a friend as an angel.'

'You're going to look pretty stupid, then.'

How could he not laugh? 'I still believe it.'

'Your honour.' The cigarette fell from Terry's knuckles, leaving the raw white flesh softened, like cooking fat. It was torture to burn away a section of skin and never let it heal; soon it would be translucent white pulp.

'Tell me something about how you feel. Anything. Anything at all.'

There was an infinitesimal pause. 'Sometimes I feel . . . vast. No, like a speck of dust. No, hold on. I feel just like always.' He shook his head. 'I'd like a drink.'

Hadn't McCullough felt like this himself over the last few months—turned inside out, first large, then small? Or was Terry really saying that nothing had changed?

He continued, 'I suppose I feel pretty shitty. But that's nothing new.'

'Do you want me to do anything? Do you want me to help you?'

Terry dropped his head. He accepted there were practical matters. 'If you have any spare dough, the old girl's going to need some help.'

'I'll see to it.'

'Then your work is done.' His head dropped lower still, as if he couldn't resist sleep.

'Terry?'

'You'd better go, Mac.'

'I'll come back soon.'

'Suit yourself. But it's not necessary. I done what I done.' It was said through thick, numb lips, a loose mouth. Had he been given medication, only now taking effect? There had been no straining away from his persistent gut pain, no digging into it with his hand.

McCullough reached over and placed his hand on Terry's shoulder. When he wasn't shrugged off, he gripped it. 'For what it's worth, I love you, Terry.'

It sounded hollow and arch, more bad acting, the work of a ham. But it needed saying. It didn't matter what Terry thought.

2

Nathaniel's parents' house was two miles out of the village in grounds bordered by a high rough stone wall and tall trees. The iron gates were closed. McCullough pressed the intercom from the car, leaning out of the window. There was no response, just white noise. He tried again, and then a third time. The voice that finally answered was young, haughty, impatient. McCullough asked if he might express his condolences. He needed to lean further out of the car window to be heard. He felt foolish. The gates dragged along the gravel as they opened. The long driveway was a slender S-shape, the grounds plotted with large English trees.

Three cars were parked in front of the house. He couldn't help but judge: Range Rover, Porsche, Peugeot.

Before he climbed out, he studied himself in the rear-view mirror and saw a man who might be related to Terry, thin and pale and lost. No tidying up was possible. His body odour had gone from strong to salty, acrid.

The front door opened as he stepped onto the stone threshold. Nathaniel's father. He was smaller than McCullough had imagined, frail, delicately boned. Not at all like his sons. He wore a yellow checked shirt, brown wool tie, burgundy cardigan. The skin of his face was covered in broken veins, wine-red hairline fissures. What was left of his hair had an oily gleam. His eyes were red and watery. No inner life was declared by them. Whether he took in McCullough's presence was unclear. He said nothing.

'I am sorry for your loss, Mr Price.'

It was met with silence. McCullough continued, 'I didn't know Nathaniel well, not really . . . but I know he was decent and loving and hard-working. I cannot believe what has happened. I'm so sorry.'

The reply was matter-of-fact, the condemnation in it absolute. 'I know who you are. People like you are a menace. If he hadn't met you, he'd still be alive.'

It was true.

'You know the one who murdered him, don't you?'

'Yes.'

'He terrorized this village.'

'I don't want to argue with you—not at this time.'

'He killed our son. Do you know what he did—how he did it?'

'I do.'

'He's a monster.'

'He did a monstrous thing, yes.'

'He killed our son.'

'Yes.'

'Murdered him.'

'Yes.'

'I want you to leave us alone.'

'I will, of course.' He paused on the doorstep and looked behind Nathaniel's father into the large square hallway, empty but for a hard-backed chair and—was this possible?—a suit of armour.

'Thank you for seeing me. My thoughts are with you.' He went to turn away.

'You've been to see him, haven't you? The other one.'

'Yes.'

There was a pause; McCullough's directness was a surprise to the older man, as if he'd expected to hear a lie.

The older man's voice trembled. 'You're the monster.'

'No. But it must seem like that to you.'

'If you had never come down here, he'd still be alive.' In repeating this, part of him believed that there might be a way of altering the outcome: no outsider, no church-building, no murder of his son. The old man hated himself for it. He understood the obstinacy of death. It was pathetic to think otherwise.

McCullough's impulse was to repeat the statement back, replacing 'he'd' with 'Nathaniel'—it was in him to win this point, knowing what he knew. But he let it go. It would never matter now that Nathaniel had wanted a different kind of family. They'd never understand it anyway. McCullough hadn't liked to admit it, but he knew that after their fight on the ridge Nathaniel had felt doubly orphaned, and that he hadn't done enough to convince the boy it wasn't the case—that he was loved for who he was. But was it really true, to the extent that he loved Terry, Rebecca, Rich?

'Please allow me to come to any service you might have.'

The large door was shut on him.

3

After a shower, McCullough was given Judith's room and ordered to sleep. He watched her tidy as he stood beside the bed, a towel around his waist. He couldn't deny he wanted her to get into the bed with him. Her body would cleanse him in ways he knew were only possible with a naked woman. To fuck would take him away from everything and he yearned for that. He rearranged the evidence of arousal under the towel. Judith averted her eyes.

Three hours later, he was in the kitchen, a bathrobe on, his clothes washed and drying on hangers next to the window. He ate what was put in front of him, grilled chicken and green beans, and drank a glass of red wine. The wine would enrich his blood, give it colour. Around his eyes, his skin was dry. There was a cold sore beginning on his lip.

He'd called Holly and explained that Terry—yes, that boy—had killed someone. Murdered him. Another boy who was helping out.

Holly's shock was tempered by a need for answers to other questions—questions that she'd been preparing; she had nowhere left to process new information. She confessed to calling Lucien; McCullough had left her no choice. It was said firmly: he wasn't to interrogate her. Lucien had told her what had happened at the pub and that he'd assumed McCullough went home afterwards.

'Are you ever coming home?' she asked.

He was silent. Of course he would come home.

'Mac—it's close to being over, do you understand that? Please tell me you realize that.'

Sitting on the side of the bed, naked, hunched up, his hand in his hair, he didn't know what to say. 'Of course I realize that. And I want to come home, but right now I can't. You have to be patient.'

'The children don't miss you. I don't want to sound harsh, but it's normal now for you to be away.'

'I know. But I'm needed here.'

'You're needed *here*.'

'I know.'

'I don't think you do. I think you just hope we'll stick around. For when you're ready to come back.'

'I think I know what the risks are. You've made them very clear.'

'Don't punish me for that.'

'I'm not.'

She was bitter. 'Are you sure? Really? How much thought have you given it? It seems you have a hectic life down there.' Then, 'Where are you ringing from?'

'Rebecca's. Her mother's. Rebecca knew Terry and Nat well.'

He swallowed, looking down at his naked thighs, his genitals lost between them. What would she think if she could see him, sitting on a bed, in another woman's bedroom? Distantly he thought he could hear Judith and Rebecca talking.

'Mac?'

'I'm here.'

'It's over. You know it. I know it. It would have been over months ago if it weren't for the children.'

'I don't believe that. I don't accept it. It's not over and it hasn't got anything to do with the children. We love each other.'

'I don't think you do love me.'

'You're not in a position to know that, are you? Do you still love me?'

She paused. She was also sitting on the side of the bed, naked under a dressing gown. She'd been in the bath, used oils sent by her mother. 'I don't know, Mac. Nothing feels like love, nothing in me feels like anything. I'm numb.'

'You have to let me see this through.'

'But I don't know what you're doing. If I thought sooner or later you'd get bored with it, I'd . . . I don't know. But that's not what you want from me, is it? You want support. You want me to understand. You want patience. But you may never come back. And I'm not going to come down there. You're holding on to us as an option.' She paused. 'What you've taken on, whatever it is . . . it's you now. You're someone different and I either have to accept that or not. But we're not a family anymore. I live up here with the children and you live down there and come and visit them. Walter has moved into his own room. You missed that. It was a big moment for them. They both wanted to know why you weren't here. I called you but you never answer your phone now—we're not even important enough for you to talk to on the phone.' She started to cry. 'What happened with Lucien . . . it was nothing. We both know that. Although I suppose I should thank you for behaving as if you cared for a couple of days. But then you disappeared again. You went there. Your new home.' She didn't have the strength to sound sarcastic.

There was no argument: that was what he'd done. Except she wasn't being abandoned, not indefinitely; it had never felt like that to him. He was sacrificing something in their relationship to make room for others. It might feel like an impoverishment to her now, but he believed by trying to do what he felt was right he would grow larger, and so that element of himself that would eventually be given back would be of similar size to before. He knew this to be true, but also understood that this wasn't something you could say of yourself. All he could ask was that for now she trusted in the content of his heart. He heard her laugh; it had all been said before. Another excuse to do what he wanted to do. What did it mean to trust in the content of someone's heart, anyway? Maybe he did still love her, he probably did, and maybe as much as before—how was she to know? And she still loved him, of course she did—so what? How unhappy was she supposed to feel for the sake of that love? 'Come on, tell me.'

To him it had seemed such a short time. When had all this started: the end of May? It was now August. But he knew that was not how Holly experienced it. Every hour was heavy with misery. In the evenings, time was so slow it felt like it turned in on itself, refusing to move on, as if the pain she felt wasn't content enough with its depth, but wanted to add an altered experience of duration; the feeling that it would never end. He knew this because he'd felt it once himself. He'd been stunned by the magnitude of unhappiness he was able to endure and still be present in the world. He couldn't understand why someone didn't do something. Why he wasn't hospitalized.

With the phone still at his ear, he shook his head. He looked down at his knees. The hairs on his legs were thick and dark.

'I'm sorry, Holly. But I don't know what to say anymore. What to promise. I'm not coming back today, or tonight. Or tomorrow. I'm needed here.'

'Are you? Really? Have you asked?'

'A boy is dead. Murdered by someone I felt close to. I cared for.'

'And what are you going to do—bring the boy back from the dead?'

'What if Walter did something terrible and there was no one there to comfort him?'

Holly started to sob now. 'You bastard, you fucking bastard. You evil fucking bastard.'

'I'm sorry, but it's the truth. He doesn't have anyone. His mother has dementia. There is no one else.'

'I hate you. I hate you.'

He listened to her crying. At times she wailed, as if she'd broken through to a future sadness, even more terrible than what she was feeling now, to a time when their son was alone and needed them. She couldn't bear to think that there might be a moment in Walter's life when he would look around, desperate for them, and not find them there. Hadn't she looked at that boy and seen a version of Walter? With his unwashed hair and brown teeth, so easily her son in twenty years. It had saddened her, but it wasn't so terrible, there were worse outcomes. But now he'd killed someone. That gentle and polite boy. Gentle and polite as Walter was now soft and loving. Of course she needed to give McCullough permission to stay, and to show the boy love if that was what he needed. It's what she'd want for Walter. She'd want someone like McCullough to be there.

All her anger was gone; she was no longer set against him. It didn't matter that she was still saying 'I hate you', in her mind he'd won—he could do whatever he liked. She was weak when he called, but she had found strength enough to resist him, to make her case. Now she felt purposeless, filled with nothing but sadness. Destroyed.

Pearl was in the bedroom doorway. 'Mummy, are you all right?'

Holly heard her daughter but couldn't stop sobbing, one hand cupping her mouth to manage the noise. With a flick of her other hand she directed her daughter to leave the room, to leave her alone, to understand—*not now*.

Pearl ventured into the room. 'Mummy, is it Daddy?' She took the phone from her mother's weak grip and held it in front of her face. 'Daddy. Is that you? My mummy's very upset.' She then placed the phone in her mother's lap. 'I think Daddy's crying, too.'

4

In the kitchen, Judith and Rebecca probed him for details about Terry; asked questions to which he had no answers. Both sat across the table from him while he ate. Rebecca put her feet up on a chair until they were gently pushed off by her mother. Eventually she left them together, saying, 'I'd better call Rich.'

'Mac, you can stay here as long as you need to.' Judith had paused before saying it, bracing herself, formulating her words. There was a sofa, her bed.

'Holly thinks I've left her. She doesn't think I realize yet. I think she thinks I love everyone but her.'

Judith had a dishcloth in her lap. 'Where does she think you are?'

'I don't think she cares.'

'What are you going to do?'

Was there really the option to escape here, to Judith, if he wanted? To become a visiting father to his children? Over time just a friend to Holly? Even to think of it made his stomach fall away; it wasn't possible. So many broken hearts. Surely he would be punished for that one day. No, of course not. He was free to make that choice, any choice, with God's unalterable love. As Terry was free to end Nathaniel's life. Not that they were the same thing, or even on a continuum, but people were equal in their freedom. The difference—the meaningful difference—was the world after the fact, the material change. What Terry had done was to reduce the sum of earthly good. Whatever McCullough did about his own situation, whatever the level of pain he caused, he was doing no more than adding another unhappy home to the world. It was selfish and irresponsible, but it didn't compare to what Terry had done. In taking Nathaniel's life, Terry had created an absence that could never be filled, never adjusted to. Terry took away life and created misery. It was like the addition of minus numbers: the amounts created were increases in nothingness or greater densities of nothingness. How might such a wilfully created deficit be redeemed?

Perhaps it was time to go home. If he went now, he'd be back in three to four hours, and if Holly was willing, something might be rescued. Her sobbing on the phone hadn't just been an expression of her sadness, but something more profound, a purge of feeling, a reconciliation of feeling, and once she had recovered she would finally recognize she had choices. To carry on her life as it was in all its misery and yet preserving the love that still existed between them. Or . . . to swerve away into a new life, mostly the same, but leaving him to go his own way. Why would she choose the former? For the children? Because of their shared past? Or for no other reason than that she still loved him? He was reminded of a story: a seventeenth-century priest offering advice to a congregant on how to think about predestination. If it really were the case that before the world was created God had decided who was to be saved and who was to be damned, why would you not think of yourself as chosen? What was to be gained from the other choice? And it wasn't a false choice. Even if it transpired you were one of the damned, at least you would have lived a good, loving life. At the time he'd laughed out loud; it was so wonderfully, beautifully right. It finally made sense of Pascal's Wager. Why we should bet on God rather than nothing. And following on from that: why we must choose love over power. The opposite was unthinkable. But this didn't mean Holly would ultimately choose him. Human love had its limits—as it should do.

Judith had set aside the dishcloth and poured him some more wine. 'Mac?'

'I don't know what to do. I can't abandon Terry. He doesn't have anyone.'

'He has Rebecca.'

'She's a child.'

'Yes and no.'

'What do you think I should do?'

'I don't know.'

He brought the glass of wine inside the circle of his arms on the table; the aroma under his nose was a kind of comfort. There was coffee on the stove.

'You can define the words "sacred" and "secular" to mean "out of time" and "in time". To believe in the sacred you merely have to accept that certain things can take place out of time. I think the deepest Christians understand that Christ is perpetually being crucified, perpetually resurrected. Because if that is not the case, they have to accept it as a local event, in time and place, and there-fore with no great meaning.' He paused and took a sip of wine. 'I know you know all this, but it's quite something. But I don't think the sacred has to be a purely spiritual notion . . . the preserve of spiritual thinking. There is music and poetry. Our experience of art can make us feel like we exist out of time . . . as if the music was composed yesterday, or the poem is precise to a moment in our life, hundreds of years on from when it was written. In this way we are time travellers. Or more weirdly than that—we can live in and out of time.'

He stopped for a moment to formulate his thoughts. 'But what we *cannot* do is be in two places at once, and that's what I need to do right now. No metaphysics permits that.' He snorted at the absurdity of a memory. 'I remember when I met Rebecca and Nat and Rich and Terry. They were badgering me about what I believed. I said there was no such thing as a necessary truth. I said we don't have to accept and live by necessary truth just because on the face of it things only make sense that way. But one truth I can't escape . . . is that I cannot be in two different places at once. It's obvious, I know. But for a while back there, I think I believed it was possible. We just had to think about what it might mean to be present differently, and on some level, I really could be down here and up there with my family at the same time.' He looked up at Judith. 'Poor Holly.'

Judith had angled her chair out from the table, turned her body a little away from him. He saw her glance at his shirt on a hanger by the open window.

'Then go back to her. Terry is not really your problem.' It was coolly said, its lack of warmth meaningful.

She stood to make coffee, her breath held in. She wanted to cry. She convinced herself she didn't want him; but it was still rejection.

McCullough sat with his head in his hands.

'Nat's father would disagree. He thinks if I hadn't been around none of this would have happened. And he's right, of course. Terry took the most from me, despite what he might think. When he came up to my house hauling all those books, I should have realized. When I saw him in the pub two weeks later with what can only be described as a "darkened countenance", I should have realized. Then over these past weeks, seeing him in terrible physical pain, as if he were wrestling with something inside, something happening in him, irresistibly . . . I should have realized.'

Judith turned around. 'Realized he would kill someone? That's ridiculous. Even if you thought it was a possibility, what could you have done: followed him around? I know—knew—Terry: this behaviour wasn't abnormal for him, not really. I've bandaged him up more than a few times. He had dark moods. Frightening dark moods. He is an alcoholic.'

'I gave him the moral conundrum. A thought game.'

'How so?'

'I spoke of God, and freedom, and God's unalterable love and no necessary truth.'

'He wasn't stupid. He didn't think, Oh, now I can kill someone.'

'But it infected him. And it infected him because I didn't know what I was talking about. All I did was offer him the freedom to go to more extreme places. Then there was the Bible, that terrible fucking book, full of killing and suffering, love and redemption. It's dangerous stuff. Plenty of people have done terrible things with the Bible in their hand. It's as simple as that.'

'The one thing you can't do is stay here to redeem yourself for something that you're not to blame for. If that's what you're after— go back to your family.'

He laughed, a broken, ironic laugh. She didn't get it. He didn't believe he was responsible, and he wasn't looking to redeem himself. But it would be an act of bad faith not to accept he'd played his part, and he owed Nathaniel and his family that honesty. Beyond that, out of time, Terry's suffering, to the extent he was suffering . . . there was only one thing left he might do. Love the boy, fully, gratuitously, *in time*.

MUTINY

'The primary word *I-Thou* can only
be spoken with the whole being.'

MARTIN BUBER,
I AND THOU

I

Another small room. This time the door was locked behind
him. Terry was sitting on a low bench, his back against the
wall. He was in a suit and tie, the tie's big knot slung low;
there were no laces in his cheap black shoes. He was not wearing
socks and his ankles were clean. At some point in the last twelve
hours he'd had a shower. He looked workhouse-scrubbed. Between
his knuckles, there was scabbing and a build-up of pus beneath small
brown blisters. Every now and then he tensed a little in his stomach,
as if a dull pain he was usually capable of ignoring grabbed at him.
There were small groans.

'It will be over soon, Terry.' There was nowhere for McCullough
to sit down.

'His parents in there?'

'Yes.'

'Copper went and got me a suit.' Along the far wall there was a
small window. 'They've run out of painkillers.'

'You're still in pain?'

'I should say.'

'You were pretty out of it when I came to see you yesterday. How
are you feeling today?'

The question coincided with a grab of pain in Terry's stomach
that needed an extra dodge of his body to stop it taking hold.

'Not great.'

'Have you seen a doctor since I saw you?'

'I'm an alcoholic, Mac—without a drink.'

There was movement outside the door. A sharp rap. Ten minutes was called.

'Are you prepared?'

'Not my first time.'

'You're pleading guilty?'

'Of course.' He paused. 'People'll be looking at me trying to figure out why I done it.'

'Yes.'

'Thinking they know . . . You must have your opinion, Mac.' It was the first time Terry had seemed unsure how McCullough might answer.

'I don't know.'

'Guess.' He wasn't going to be open-minded for long.

'You had the impulse, you felt compelled. I don't know. You were testing yourself. God told you. I really don't know.'

'Well, the Old Man's been on my mind, as you know.'

'So you were testing *Him?*'

He chuckled; it was cynical, weary. 'There is no God, Mac. Haven't I just proved that? Isn't Nat's body proof?'

'I expect more from you than that, Terry. Sorry.'

'You weren't there.' Terry raised his eyebrows: don't try and imagine what you can't possibly imagine.

He wanted to sit down next to Terry as he would do with his own son. But instead he stayed by the door. 'Then tell me.'

'What? What it's like? It's killing someone. It's not *like* anything.'

McCullough had read once that as death has lordship over life, to kill someone is an act of lordship. Except that it wasn't—that would be to overcome death.

'How did it feel?'

Terry looked up at Mac, moved a dreadlock out of his eyes. 'Like tossing babies up in the air to catch on bayonets.'

'You didn't do that.'

'What do you say, Mac? Different in kind rather than degree? It's not.'

The boy had paid attention: his habits of language, Dostoevsky. Had he believed Terry was impervious to influence, or that Terry had mostly influenced him? Either way he hadn't been careful enough.

'Tell me, Terry—what did it feel like?'

'That I was doing something so terrible I almost became joyful, ecstatic. That I had broken through. I don't know . . . that I could do anything. I felt . . . what's the word? Exalted.'

From outside, 'Five minutes.'

'I believe you. I believe that's what it felt like.'

Terry shrugged. 'It doesn't matter now.'

He was right. Whatever he'd felt at the time, it was short-lived, hours at most, a chemical thing. There was no devil inside him: he wasn't changed in any fundamental way, at least not elevated to a freedom that was unavailable to the rest of us. In minutes he'd be in front of a magistrate, Nathaniel's parents: a pathetic, unprepossessing young man in a cheap suit, a shirt and tie, scrubbed clean, no socks. A kind of nakedness to those who knew him. McCullough thought of Jesus presented to the elders, to Pilate, knowing that their questions were based on category mistakes, that their judgments were narrow because their perceptions were narrow and business must go on. Only Jesus knew he wasn't there to interrupt their business, to plead his case.

'Rebecca is very upset. She doesn't know what to think. You were the prodigal brother.'

Under his shirt, Terry's muscles were in spasm, his mouth jarred, and a groan was caught at the back of his throat. He pressed the heel of his hand deep into his stomach, hard into the muscles; his speech was strained. 'You know something, Mac? I'm twenty-three, or thereabouts. I'll be out before I'm your age. That's funny, right? Before I'm forty. Everyone's used to doing the numbers. He'll get twenty, probably do fifteen. I done it straight away. I mean even before I took myself down the cop shop. Pleading guilty, spares everyone the trouble of a trial. Then it's just about the numbers.' The pain slipped away. There was perspiration on his forehead.

'You're disconnected. You're disassociating . . .' McCullough had no way of knowing this, but assumed it must be the case.

'Maybe.' He looked up. 'Why are you still here, Mac?'

'In case . . . Just in case you need me.'

'I'm a resourceful guy. Maybe you're worried how you'll feel if you turn away?'

'Interesting phrase. Do you have anything to read?'

Terry looked around himself.

'At the police station, I mean.'

'Mags. By the end of today I'll be on remand—"custodial" remand. There'll be a library. Maybe there'll be a copy of *The Brothers Karamazov*. I started it—you know—before. I'm only at the babies and bayonets.' He sniffed.

'Do you want me to bring you a copy?'

'Cut out the pages and stick a file in there, will you?' Hee-hee.

Was he seeking to return to that time, earlier in the summer, when they had riffed together, digging up the earth, sanding and hammering in the pegs that secured the great oak beams. Or was this angel really a psychopath?

There was another flash of pain.

'You didn't answer my question. Has a doctor seen you?'

'Yes, Mac. Got to improve my diet.'

'I'm not sure I've ever seen you eat.'

'I believe there was a carrot at your gaff.'

McCullough stared hard at Terry: a thinned-out boy, flesh translucent, the dreads dead. 'It's extraordinary how much the body can take.'

'Punish the body to release the soul.'

'Where's that from?'

'An old northern soul record. Used to listen to it with Rebs.' Then: 'I know I done a terrible thing.' His head dropped down from the neck and he scratched deeply at his scalp, at the roots of the dreads. He then raised his eyes and pointed at his temple, two fingers shaped like a barrel of a gun. 'It's all in here—what I done. All jammed in. I took it in as it was happening. It was as if I sucked it all up, bit by bit. I wouldn't have been surprised if I'd looked around and there was nothing there. Nat gone, the blood gone, the knife, all sucked up inside me. Just hoovered up. I've always felt I was a bit inside out. It could easily all be in here, if you know what I mean.'

'Why did you do it, Terry?'

'Because there was room for it. It was possible.'

'I don't under—' McCullough stopped himself: did he really not understand? 'Explain it to me.'

'I can't. It's what I said: I felt exalted and I took it all in. And I don't mean accepted it. But I could do it—and I proved it. Nothing got in me way. And now it's in me, like a big expanding balloon. I don't know about your God . . . '

'My God?'

Terry laughed. 'Mac . . . you're an über-fucking-normal Christian, mate—just admit it. Do everyone a favour. Join the regular church. They'll love you.'

'Maybe; maybe not.'

'Trust me. I'm right. I know you think God wants you to soak up all the suffering. Except you can't, because I've got it all. I sucked it all up. It's me our friend has had His eye on all this time—not you. Go home.'

'No.'

'Suit yourself.'

Terry started to cough. There was a gurgling in his throat, something brought up and then swallowed back down. It was followed by a gripping pain that made him sit up straight, arch his back and stiffen.

'Wow. That was a bad one.' Then, 'Don't everyone wonder why you're not consoling Nat's people?'

'I suspect they do.'

'You seen them?'

'Yes.'

More beads of perspiration on Terry's forehead, round and clear, as if pressed out into perfect little domes from his pores. He expelled some air and wiped the perspiration away. His teeth were clenched hard; the level of pain was a surprise, even to him. It took him a minute to relax.

'How's your missus? The kids?'

'Fine. Good. Holly wants me to do what I can.'

'Good thing I came up, then, otherwise I'd just be another murderer.' His jaw muscles were tight; a smile was impossible, but his eyes flashed, just.

The door was unlocked and opened. A uniformed officer came in, handcuffs ready. 'Just until you get into the dock.'

McCullough straightened up. 'I'll go now.'

Terry offered his wrists and looked directly at Mac. 'You'll be up there?'

'Of course.'

'And I'll see you later?'

'As soon as it's possible.'

'My insides are fucking killing me.'

'We'll sort that out.'

'See you in a minute, then?'

'I'm not going anywhere.'

2

When McCullough found his way to the courtroom, Rebecca stood and indicated a saved seat beside her. They had no chance to speak before a door was opened and Terry was led up to the dock. Rebecca leaned against McCullough. It took him a moment before he realized she needed his arm around her. Two seats away Nathaniel's father sat with both hands over the handle of a hospital-issue walking stick, his three sons beside him. If Nathaniel's mother was there she wasn't sitting with her family. Terry was guided to a seat behind a large Perspex screen. Court protocol was mumbled through, tonelessly, then Terry was instructed to stand. He turned towards the magistrate. He was asked for his name, address and date of birth. Starting in half-tones, he gave his name, then cleared his throat and repeated himself, making an effort to project for the court. He was asked how he pleaded. This time he cleared his throat first. 'Guilty.' The magistrate informed the court that the accused was to be remanded in custody until a date was set for a further hearing at the Crown Court. Terry was tapped on the shoulder and led out.

In the lobby, close to the exit, McCullough and Rebecca paused and waited for Nathaniel's family to pass. His father stopped; his sons arrayed themselves behind him. Stephen acknowledged Rebecca with a nod of his head.

'We can't even bury my son. Did you know that?' He paused to lick his lips as if his mouth was dry. 'He thought you . . . you . . . were the bee's knees. Mac this, Mac that. I don't think I have to ask what he said about us.' He dropped his head, and then after a few seconds of silence, looked up. 'It's our job to keep them safe. That's all.'

McCullough wanted to say 'He's safe now', but feared it would be misconstrued as a religious platitude, which he supposed it was. But what he wanted to convey was that Nathaniel was free from the world, and that it might be argued, as many had, that that was no bad thing. Not that it ever gave much solace to those left behind. So instead he said what he believed, wholeheartedly, unchanged from when he visited their home: 'Nathaniel was a gentle, hard-working boy.'

The old man kept his eyes on McCullough, neither consciously reading him nor distracted by his own thoughts. It was a taking stock from a lifetime of relying on instinct about people—who was this man before him? It was Stephen who broke the moment, saying, 'Daddy, let's go,' and laying a hand on his father's shoulder.

McCullough noticed Rebecca's hand had found its way into his and their fingers were entwined. She was impassive at his side, almost in a daze, like a daughter patiently waiting for her father to finish an adult conversation.

Nathaniel's father transferred the walking stick from one hand to the other. 'The boy's mother spends all her time in church—what good will that do her?'

There was no irony intended. In his grief he'd chosen not to remember that the last few weeks of his son's life were spent building a church or some approximation of one. McCullough hoped that at some point this ageing man would come to appreciate his son's contribution, his earnest application, working every day, never in doubt of the honesty of physical labour. Would it ever mean anything to his family that each one of those monumental beams contained the pressure and push of Nathaniel's shoulder, and that the building's solidity—perhaps even its longevity—came from Nathaniel's will and strength? It needed to be explained, to be shown: Nat did this here, and this here, but McCullough doubted that moment would ever come.

The father was led away and helped through the revolving door. McCullough didn't move or speak, watching in his mind's eye Nathaniel at work, his body bearing the heaviest load, driving his brogues into the mud, those big thighs cranked and pushed upwards, a load-bearing and driving creature. McCullough had joked that Nathaniel had helped build Stonehenge, or such men as he. Nathaniel said 'no way'. He was no-nonsense like that.

Rebecca pulled at his hand. 'We said we'd meet Rich.'

They met in a cafe and ordered lunch, where they discovered they had bigger appetites than expected, the food tasting large and round and full in their mouths.

Rich wanted explanations. Why had McCullough said that what happened was more complicated than just Terry having murdered Nathaniel? He appealed to Rebecca: did she think this? Rebecca stared out of the window, using a napkin to wipe her eyes. Rich was upset and angry. It was simple. Terry murdered Nat. And he wanted it to be simple for others. Otherwise they were taking sides. He struggled not to cry. When Rebecca tried to grab his hand, he pulled it away and shoved it in his lap. McCullough explained what had happened at the hearing, and said as far as he knew there would now be assessments, reports to the court, then another hearing of some kind, then sentencing.

'So he'll just go to prison for life?'

'For a long time.'

'No matter what?'

'No matter what.'

It seemed enough for Rich that at least in this aspect what he expected to happen would happen.

After lunch, Rich suggested visiting the site. As they walked to the car, they all recognized this as a unifying act, and as a way of thanking Rich for the idea, McCullough offered him the car keys. This lightened the boy's mood, although he confessed he didn't have a licence. Yet. Rebecca insisted on going in the back.

In the driver's seat, Rich looked around the dashboard. 'Does it have sport mode?' McCullough leaned across and pressed the button. 'Awesome.'

The bends of the country lanes were taken along the racing line, with an instinct for the approach of other cars, gears smoothly and quickly lowered. Along straights the car reached dangerous speeds. Rebecca, unlike McCullough, factored in the swerves without being jolted, most of the time picking at her nails or looking abstractedly out of the window. Rich didn't take the shortest route, and at one point they found themselves on the road bordered by the stone wall of Nathaniel's house.

At the site, work continued. Contractors were fitting windows into the house, laying cables between the buildings, installing a septic tank. But this was trivial stuff: two of the six projecting steels were in place, revealing one of the points that marked the line of intersection.

McCullough shook his head to clear away the tears in his eyes. Rich knew most of the new contractors by name. With Nathaniel gone, when Rich wasn't on site, there was no one from the original team to coordinate anything. The rusty-haired young man wasn't around.

'Who's making all the decisions, Rich?'

'I think everyone knows what they're doing.'

It appeared to be the case: certain trades didn't need supervision. At one point, in the house, he asked someone where the bathroom would be, and the answer was confident, as if the guy was working off detailed plans. But there had never been any plans. Decisions had been made based on previous decisions, the materials chosen, manufacturers' instructions, the dimensions they had to work with, at best a pencil drawing on a wall, but most often a notion passed along from person to person. That these original decisions had been arbitrary, and the new ones had no overall vision to conform to, meant that both buildings looked like palimpsests, as if they had been up for centuries and endlessly reconfigured in accord with the prevailing style of the times, the spiritual needs of the people. But it was the opposite of that. They had gone up in a matter of weeks.

McCullough found himself taking photos on his iPad and emailing them to Holly, to Simon and Marvin. It was impossible not to feel proud, to be made dizzy by what was there. It was partly the stage of construction, the activity, but he also had the ineluctable feeling that something miraculous was being completed. Rebecca followed him around. When ordinarily she would have become bored and broken away or been distracted and left behind, she remained by him. McCullough stopped outside the nave end of the church where the largest of the vertical oak beams stood slightly in relief, not quite flush to the stone. He called Rich over. 'We need a carpenter or someone to inscribe Nathaniel's name here, his dates.'

'It'll look like someone's just carved it in, like on a tree.' Rich ran his hand down the grain of the timber.

'It won't. Not if done properly. We need to ask around. There will be someone.'

'Will all our names?' Rich asked. It wasn't an unfeeling demand.

'Why not—in the four corners. The four of you.'

It took a moment before Rich realized this would include Terry. 'You've got to be joking.'

After two hours together, it was only then that McCullough realized Rich wasn't wearing his bandana and his black hair was freshly washed, reddish highlights picked out by the sun.

'Let's leave it until it's finished.'

Standing behind McCullough, Rebecca said, 'I don't want my name here. Just Nat's.'

'I want mine.' Rich stared at them both. 'Well, I do.'

It was silly, all of it, but McCullough had started it, from a moment of genuine sentiment, by pointing out a place for Nathaniel's name, the great beam he'd made sure they raised.

Late afternoon, they sat on the ridge and watched over the works. At one point a man in clean overalls called up and asked innocently,

'What is it—this one?' Meaning: not the house. McCullough called down, 'A barn.' Rebecca added, 'An arty-farty barn.' The question was trusting and didn't deserve ridicule. The man called back, 'Heard it was some kind of church.' McCullough was happy to concede: 'It's that as well.' Could it not be both?

Rich started to pace along the top of the ridge, as he had sometimes used to do when he was first in love. Rebecca leaned her shoulder against McCullough and said, 'It was here you saw God.'

She had once been unable to speak without an inflection of irony, without some kind of criticism of him, often correct in its insight, at least superficially; but she now sounded tired and needed to test how stable he was, how reliable.

He glanced over at the oak tree, to where he had been sitting when He made Himself present. A week on, it didn't seem possible. He thought back to when it had happened. There had been no alerting difference in the quiddity of the world, no phenomenological shift that might permit it to happen. McCullough had been asleep and he awoke and He was there: first as a pillar of fire, then as . . . what? No matter how much he told himself that it was probably an interior experience projected outwards, the whole world turned into his subjective world for a moment, he knew this wasn't the case. Now, as then, he believed it had been an authentic encounter with God. He was happy to concede that the choice in how His appearance was made manifest was his own, and that his imagination had played a part, but that didn't undermine the truth of the encounter—a shape was needed because an essence was present.

So he answered Rebecca, 'Indeed.'

'If all this hadn't happened, would you have left Holly for my mum?'

It was a strange question, and seemed to conflate a number of things, but it was not without sense.

'Setting aside whether or not your mother deems me anything more than a nuisance, if I was going to leave Holly for anyone, it would be for your mother.'

'I think you are in love with each other.'

'That's no great achievement.'

'So you agree?'

'I wouldn't disagree. But I speak only for myself.'

'She's fickle. You should know that. I don't think she can really love anyone—not really. Because of her parents.'

'She loves you.'

'Yes. Maybe. In her own way.'

'She loves you.'

'Neither of us is emotionally—you know—a big giver.'

'I don't know. You go your own way, but that doesn't mean you don't give—in your own way. To my mind, you've been a bit of rock.'

'Yeah. Big-time.' She glanced over her shoulder to where boots stomped through the long grass. 'Poor Rich.'

Without discussion or signal they both got to their feet and brushed the dead grass from their rears and turned to Rich.

He took his hands out of his pockets. 'You ready to go?' Had he been waiting for them?

'I should be paying you more to come here, to keep an eye on things. Both of you.' Did he mean because there were only two of them now?

'Are you going back to London?' In asking this Rich suddenly realized he didn't want McCullough to go, even though a minute before, looking down at their backs, he had hoped both of them would disappear and leave him alone.

'Yes. No. I don't know.' Did he have a reason to stay? He wanted to see Terry after his first night in prison, but he accepted that this was not Terry's first night in prison. There was a difference, of course, but McCullough was mainly projecting again—imagining what his own first night might be like. And he would need to go home soon. The thought of seeing the twins created a lightness in his chest, a brightness in his blood, its movement through him swifter. It really was time to go; these were metabolic signals not to be ignored. And when he was there he needed to make an extra effort to be properly present, as they always were for him. He would use the drive back to reconstitute himself, to become a better father, uncontaminated by what he'd left behind.

Standing next to him, Rebecca put her arm in his and they made their way down the bank. Rich walked with them, but took a curving line a few metres away.

Between the two buildings, where three months ago he'd marked off the large rectangle of grass, there was now only mud. Gone were the tussocks and ankle-turning divots; instead, wheels and caterpillar tracks had flattened it out and given it the texture of man. He looked across from the door of the house to the door of the church. The slanting line was perfect. Made to be crossed. Whether the grass would return or would have to be newly laid he didn't know. On the air was the sharpness he remembered from the first day, an edge to the breeze, salty. He doubted very much he'd ever live here, or that anyone would, but he was certain that for someone who encountered this place in search of something, if he or she were willing to attune themselves to what was present, what he had wanted to achieve was accomplished.

PART TWO

Forgiveness

HOME

'This institution,
perhaps one should say enterprise
out of respect for which
one says one need not change one's mind
about a thing one has believed in'

MARIANNE MOORE,
MARRIAGE

I

Holly looked tired and ill, thinner, paler; her face had changed shape, lost any bloom of happiness. The children, especially Pearl, clung to him. He sensed a performance, her playing a role to make things better for Mummy. Walter gripped onto his father's cuff and led him to the computer to look at the Lego website, and then to his room to see some trading cards he'd started to collect, and then to his bed to look through a book of black-and-white photos of volcanoes he'd found in the second-hand bookshop. What McCullough noticed was how his son's grip remained locked on his sleeve throughout, as if that small amount of purchase might keep his daddy there.

Hours later, McCullough and Holly sat on the bed, their backs to each other. It was not the posture of defeat but of weariness—the end of a long day. When he'd arrived home they'd talked openly about Terry, then of Nathaniel, and what his parents must be going through. Grimly, they'd used it as a topic of conversation to deflect the more immediate issues, yet allow them still to speak of serious things.

Before bed they'd resumed old habits, positions on the sofa, choice of television shows, the timing of herbal tea—McCullough always a beat behind, looking to Holly for instruction, permission, as if it were no longer his house. He wanted her to relax, confident of his presence, because he himself felt good and strong, as if an aspect of his old self had returned, at least in part. She hadn't asked him when he was leaving again; she didn't want to state for the family record the temporary nature of his existence at home. It gave him hope.

But, sitting on their bed, it all seemed too much. Something more than habit was required to bring them together again. Neither knew what it was, and Holly had no energy left to discuss it. McCullough had returned looking well, as he usually did, despite claiming he'd hardly slept and was worn out. This doubly upset her: this healthy look combined with the warning—as she saw it—that he was without sufficient strength to work through what needed to be settled between them. He made no excuses. He did apologize. At one point, when they passed on the landing, he'd stopped and embraced her, but there was no pliancy in their bodies. It upset them both that they couldn't even manage a hug. He said sorry as she walked away and into the bedroom.

In his office there were letters, packages, magazines to which he subscribed. For an hour he answered emails. A request from the Home Office for a meeting was answered with a short apology: a family matter needed his attention. A later email from Casper asked him to respond to the set of queries bullet-pointed below. Ironically—was it ironic?—he was asked whether as a nation we might meet the challenges as outlined in the original brief, and 'brought to life' so vividly in his report, if religion/the Church played a more active role in people's lives? Casper didn't make clear whether they were interested in the Church as an instrument of order, or they really did think it might have a genuine role in healing, given its fundamental notions of forgiveness and love. McCullough wrote back that in his view—for what it was worth, and with his very real ambivalence towards all religions notwithstanding—one major gain would be a greater sense of corporate identity, and that this might offer an alternative to the zeitgeist of individualism and the somewhat engorged sense of personal rights most people had these days. He wasn't sure 'engorged' was right, but he left it in. He added: perhaps, also, governments shouldn't be so keen to claim the rightness of a purely secular society and regard the marginalization of the sacred, and its removal from the public square, as unequivocally a good thing. Might it not be the case that to encourage a wide range of religious expression in the public square would create a space for exchange of ideas, openness to dialogue (most humans thought and believed similarly, despite the details), and therefore potential unity? Certainly, in the event of an atrocity no appeal to reason was going to work, and whether it was via the Church or some other kind of community-building initiative, any government that tried to move in this direction *after the fact* would be regarded as cynical and opportunistic. He signed off that he hoped he'd been useful and not to hesitate to contact him if something wasn't clear, his standard final message to a client, on the assumption that he'd been useful and everything was clear, though this time he doubted both.

He and Holly had changed into their pyjamas self-consciously, aware of their brief nakedness, but neither wanted to create an extra perception of conspicuous difference by going into the bathroom clothed and emerging ready for bed.

Finally, Holly said, 'This so boring. So boring. It's like everything is just dead between us. Why are we even trying? What are we trying to do? It's over.'

McCullough stared out beyond the window. It was late, the night dark, just a bloom of light over the house opposite as if they were having a party in their back garden.

'Is that what you want?'

'I don't want to feel this unhappy, to feel this miserable.'

'No.' But emotional states were temporary, he felt. 'Things will get better.'

'But there's nothing between us anymore. You have this whole other life. You don't need us.'

'I need you *and* the children. Do you think when I leave the house you all cease to exist, that there isn't something sustaining me, that is *in* me?'

She paused before answering. 'Sometimes everything you say sounds so slick. You always have an answer. But I'm not sure I can believe you anymore. Not if I don't feel it. Whatever is going on down there—it doesn't include us. You went there because we weren't enough.'

'That's not true. But you refused to trust me.'

This angered her. 'Trust what, Mac? Trust what?'

'OK. You didn't back me.'

'If you'd chucked in your business to become a . . . I don't know . . . a baker.'

'Cliché.' The analogy irritated him.

'OK. I don't know . . . opened a bookshop—whatever . . . I would have backed you. Of course I would. But that's not what happened. You are asking me to believe that you have been picked out by God for some mission.'

'I never said that.'

'Isn't that what it was? Isn't that what you think?'

He had to lie. 'No. I don't know.'

'I think you do. I think that's exactly what you think, and it's madness, Mac. Pure and simple. But let's say I support you, or back you. Think what that means: "Oh, didn't I say? Mac's been given a special mission by God—we're all very pleased. We're moving to a clifftop. It's terribly exciting." Because that's what I'm left with.'

He laughed. How could he not? Holly continued, 'Believe me when I say I've tried to work out a way I might make sense of it. But I can't.'

'What does your dad think?' Quite why he asked that, he didn't know. After all, he knew the answer: if presented with all the facts Edward would fear that McCullough was about to flee the family home just like his wife.

'I don't care what my dad thinks.'

'Stupid question. Sorry.'

'What are we going to do?'

'We could do nothing. Or we could do something.' He wasn't being facetious; he was trying to think what that something might be.

'I can't carry on like this.'

'You won't come down—see the site?' Did he really believe it would make a difference if she saw it?

'I'm not moving down there, so what's the point? What's it going to prove? That you haven't been wasting your time? I know that—I'd be shocked if you had. It's got nothing to do with down there. I'm amazed you don't see that, don't know that.'

'You're right. I'm sorry.'

'God, I'm tired.'

His mind drifted to the bedrooms of the twins, to the quiet and calm of their sleep.

'Maybe we should all take a holiday.' It was an idea he'd punted before and it had been rejected as a sop. But this time he added, 'As a family. A family holiday, with activities. Lot of things to do together. Walking, biking, swimming.'

He heard her pause and find a seam of warmth within herself. 'I'd like that.'

'Then let's do it.'

Holly turned away and got into bed. He stayed where he was for a moment and then lay down. Neither of them spoke again or dared read the other's face for fear of finding doubt. A way had been found to enable a night's sleep together in the same bed, and that was something.

2

Holly decided it wasn't a good idea to tell the children about the holiday. Not just like that. Not without more thought. She hadn't slept, she said, for thinking about it.

The back doors stood open, sunlight on the threshold. The children had been allowed to squeeze oranges to make juice and there was a strong scent of citrus in the air. They were now watching television with bowls of grapes in their laps. McCullough did not respond. She was right, in as much as that was the sensible approach, but it didn't achieve anything to wait, to look for reasons not to go—they were too easy to find.

He made coffee and stayed at the kitchen table turning the pages of the newspaper. Between articles, he asked after Holly's friends, people they both knew but he hadn't seen for a long time. Both recognized that none might be considered happy. Lack of money, boring jobs, dull relationships—life-satisfaction scores were not high. Of McCullough's friends, his London friends (Holly asked after them out of politeness), he could report nothing; he didn't feel able to talk about what had happened when he saw Simon. Holly admitted to avoiding Maria's calls. This produced a laugh from them both. Maria's reaction to what had happened (if indeed she knew) would be of an entirely different emotional order from everyone else's. Considerations of love, of feelings, wouldn't come into it. There would be no discussion of pain. Certainly not of heart-break. Morality was even less likely. Yet she would want to discuss something. Possibly—and this occurred to them at the same time, and may have been the reason for the laugh—to suggest a straight swap. She was aware of Lucien's feelings for Holly, and perhaps had reconsidered her own feelings towards McCullough after their coffee together.

He rose from the table.

'Where are you going?'

He didn't know. He sat back down. It was impossible to settle. For a while he stared outside, chin resting on the heel of his hand. The morning sun created a bright and vivid haze in the air, and with a narrowing of his eyes he found he could slip into a contented inter-zone between himself and the world. The lawn looked particularly clear and bright.

He'd always liked grass, especially in the morning; it promised softness and warmth, yet always felt enlivening, quickening, full of other promises. It was the only reason to go camping, those first naked footfalls in the morning. He remembered being ten or eleven years of age, sitting cross-legged in a circle of friends, aimlessly pulling up small tufts of grass, learning that if you placed a leaf between both thumbs and blew there was an ugly but somehow pleasing sound. He remembered feeling very grown-up, perhaps because to be a child largely meant running around, and so the first time you sat down and talked, life had fundamentally changed, fun had a new quality. Then there was that holiday in Brittany, just before the children started school, when he lay down at the edge of an orchard, the grass short and spiky, a strong breeze blowing over him, and felt he was a part of the earth. Sleepily, he had decided he might lie there forever, enfolded. The sound of the twins playing was carried to him on the breeze; at times they seemed to be right beside him, almost inside his ear, even though he knew they were deep in the orchard. Their chuckling became one with the breeze, a cooling sound carried on the warm thermals passing over his face. Finally, he heard them approach, distant giants trundling, then looming shadows, before becoming—suddenly—two bodies on top of him, weights of enormous pressure, like two heavy pillows dropped from a great height. For a while the breeze enfolded all three of them as they rolled over the soft, solid ground.

He pulled himself out of his reverie and looked at Holly. 'Let me just book us a holiday.'

'Do you promise . . .' She stopped herself, realizing how harsh her expression must seem to him: a kind of reprimand before the fact.

'We'll go for a week. It can only be good. I'll look and then we can decide.'

In his office, he searched broadly for family activity holidays.

After half an hour, Holly appeared behind him and watched over his shoulder: Italy, the French Alps, all-in deals in Greece, Turkey.

'They like water—they need water. And Walter likes history.'

'Sicily?'

'Can you go up Etna?'

'I think so.'

'He would like that.' She drew up a chair and sat next to him, leaning forward, elbows on her knees, her hands in the prayer position in front of her mouth.

'Or there's Vesuvius? Then we've got Pompeii.'

'Pearl needs other children.'

'There'll be . . . I don't know . . .' He clicked. 'What do *you* want?'

'Happy children. Nice food. For us to be together as a family.' It had always been this simple for Holly; she loved her work when she was there.

A place was found. An apartment in a villa with a pool in Sorrento, 'perfect for families'—a week available in two weeks' time.

'Shall I book?'

'Do you think we'll find something sooner?'

'You're keen now?' The sarcasm was tenderly expressed.

'I don't want anything to go wrong.' She laid a hand on his knee. 'Mac, you have to promise me. I can't take any more. You have to understand that.'

He stared at the screen, absently scrolling through the photos. There was a lemon grove around the pool; outside the apartment was a large square balcony with terracotta tiles. 'It'll be very hot.'

On the shelf above his desk his credit-card details were written on a piece of paper. He reached up and got them. 'Let me book it . . . We'll have a lovely time.'

That night they made love. There was a decision to cuddle, then to be naked, and then the unexpected strangeness of their bodies created reflexive movements, to stroke, to press themselves against each other. To go any further required provisos: that they could stop at any time, and they weren't to make judgments if it wasn't a success. They did their best to enjoy it, as if the pleasure was more spontaneous, deeper, and they were more lost within the moment than they were. Afterwards they both agreed that it went fine. 'It lasted longer than I expected and we saw it through to the end,' was how McCullough summed it up encouragingly. Holly laughed. They waited a few minutes in the dark before bedside lights went on and books were picked up.

In the morning he phoned Judith and asked after Rebecca. Rebecca took the phone to her room. She wanted to see Terry but not without McCullough. Could he come today? He said it wasn't possible, but in a few days—besides, arrangements needed to be made: you can't just turn up at a prison. He would look into it. Sort it out for Thursday. He explained that he needed to be at home as much as possible, and in two weeks he was going on holiday with Holly and the twins. There was silence at the end of the line. He tried to reassure her: we'll set up regular visits. He made certain she understood that she could call him at any time, even when he was away. Before they finished the call, Rebecca said that Rich had come round and sat at her kitchen table for a long time without saying anything. 'I think my mother might have liked a son—she was really sweet to him.'

'It's easy to be sweet to Rich.'

There was a pause. 'I'm supposed to be going to Cambridge at the end of September. I don't want to. I can't bear the thought of it.'

'It might be a good thing.' He'd done it again, after weeks of not doing it. However sensible and possibly right he was, it was also a disappointment to her to hear him say it. 'Sorry—I know you hate me stating the bleeding obvious.'

'It doesn't suit you.'

'I'm now going to ask what your mum thinks.'

'Call her Judith.'

'What does Judith think?'

'I could be fooled into thinking she's happy to have me around.' He laughed.

'Can I come and work for you?'

He didn't know what to say; he wanted to cry. In all this time she'd asked for nothing, at least not openly, so vulnerably.

'I don't know what to say. You mean in London?'

'Maybe . . .' She didn't really know what she meant. She would never plead or cry; it wasn't within her.

'I still don't know what to say. I don't really have a business anymore.'

There was a pause. 'It's fine.' Then, 'Just thought I'd ask.' Her old toneless self.

'Rebecca. Listen—of course I can help you get a job, but you said "work for" me.'

'Do you want to speak to my mum again?' She was built to tough things out. She didn't wait for an answer. He listened as she walked out of her room, down the hallway and called, 'Mum.'

It was clear Judith didn't expect to speak to him again, that Rebecca was to finish the call. In her own way, Judith had moved on; there was little warmth in her voice, as if she didn't really know why he was speaking to her. Wasn't he Rebecca's friend? He felt unfairly abandoned.

It took him an hour to recover, but a coldness remained in his gut.

He phoned the prison to ask about visiting and was told Terry had been moved to the hospital. He asked 'Which hospital?' and was told '*The* hospital'. He called the nearest hospital and pretended to be Terry's father, but no information was offered. It wasn't even clear that Terry was there, although the receptionist confirmed the hospital admitted prisoners too sick for the prison infirmary. McCullough's stomach now felt like frozen sheets of metal. After two more calls to the prison he was told Terry was in his cell; it was lockdown. He knew it was a stupid question but he asked it anyway: 'Any idea what's wrong with him? Can you tell me how he is?' The laughter was pitiless. The frozen sheets now burned hot. He went into the bathroom and vomited.

When he heard Holly go out with the children, he went to the bedroom and masturbated. He thought of last night with her; of Judith; Rebecca; he couldn't help it. Orgasm released him to a dull sleep.

Dinner was tortillas. McCullough pretended to sneeze the guacamole onto his plate. He then dared Pearl to touch the end of a chilli with the tip of her tongue, and she spent most of the rest of dinner with her tongue in a glass of cold milk. Walter ate standing up, humming a little.

The iPad was brought out to look at photos of the villa in Sorrento. Holly stood behind McCullough, her hand on his shoulder.

After dinner, they all watched a film together. There was a lot of fidgeting from Walter and strolling around in front of the screen. Getting both children to clean their teeth properly was so much harder than it should have been.

At nine o'clock. McCullough opened a second bottle of white wine and finished it all himself. He didn't feel drunk until he got into bed and found he couldn't read. He rolled onto his side and looked up at Holly, reading with her spectacles perched on the end of her nose. 'We—I mean human beings, not just you and me—have to turn to God for more love. What is needed to create a better world isn't to be found within us. The current world is our evidence for that. We need God.' He smiled. 'It's what I believe.'

Holly looked down at him, at his eyes locked vaguely on her. 'You're drunk.'

'I know. But it'll still be true in the morning.'

He believed this. Of course he did—it would be the same in the morning and for all time. But what did he mean—really? All he'd said was that God was the source of our love. Similar claims were being made around the world every hour. In what way was his utterance any different? Without something more persuasive, it was just a drunk, febrile whisper. It didn't matter that silence might be the only honest expression of God: no one listens to a man who puts a finger to his lips; no one learns anything. Mystics speak only to other mystics in the echo chamber of silence, contemplation, separation. No love is enacted alone on a mountaintop. He had to face it: something must be said. But what? What might he say that could be made sense of when confronted by the real world? He knew that belief doesn't change anything, not in that sense. The world remains the same, which somehow becomes the proof of the failure of belief ... as if belief itself was divine action. What he needed to explain was not the truth value of 'God is the source of our love', but why believing it didn't produce immediate effect. Explain that the statement possessed both a truth about us and God ... and the human truth was a responsibility to discover God's truth ... and that required hard work, and was unlikely to yield much. Did it make it less true because of that ... because work was required? Was it a contradiction that the utterance was simple, the work difficult? Did we want God to do all the work for us? As if we are children. Infants.

He knew that any final success would be as elusive as the truth was ungraspable, and yet that didn't invalidate either the work or the truth. To his mind it was evidence of its ... ultimate truth. If a flood of love was easily won, our gaze would be acquisitive, greedy, turned inward on ourselves, our own needs. But he also knew that if we turn our gaze outward, as we should, we are so easily distracted. And trying to look both ways at the same time produces little more than giddiness, or a kind of flashing transparency that is somehow impossible to see through. That was where the work came in, our need to focus and concentrate. Our soul—was there a better word?—had to be like a wide-angle lens spinning on a pivot, neither lingering on our inner selves nor distracted by the world. But instead trying to make out, in all the vague and kaleidoscopic flickering, those in despair and in need of us, and then to recognize and accept that our own narrow selves lack what we need to provide ... what it is they need ... and we must ask for help to be there for them as much as if possible. It was a pragmatic theology. There were certainly less useful ones.

In his semi-drunken state he wondered whether he should confess all this to Holly; differing truth-values, the hard work and spinning lens. He sensed, from the triteness of his confession only moments ago, that she believed he'd given in—even she would have found little to argue with in what he'd said. A gentle summation; easy to dismiss. Compared to what had happened under the tree—it was nothing. What if he now told her about that? Would she listen? There was a woman, a family elsewhere, that had been willing to listen, at least at the time, when he was broken and in need. What they'd thought, he had no idea, but they were open, patient and loving. Perhaps it was because there was no jeopardy. Whatever he said, however insane, it was just a story told by someone they'd grown fond of. They could afford to be generous, because one day, probably soon, he'd be gone.

He felt himself laugh silently, a chuckle deep in his belly. Across the bed he heard Holly ask, with a lightness in her voice he'd missed, 'What's so funny?'

He rolled over and looked at her. 'What's so funny?' There were so many possible answers.

VISITING

'Yield violence to violence: no end yet
In pain's finale.'

GEOFFREY HILL,
THE ORCHARDS OF SYON, XXXI

McCullough had never before visited a prison and yet there was a disquieting feeling of recognition when he arrived there. The small, compact visitors' building was early Victorian, but had recently been modernized to offer a more convenient space and better facilities for the families. The prisoners' experience could only be guessed at, although the walk across an external quadrangle allowed glimpses through the small, barred ground-floor windows. McCullough sensed something thick and dumb about the walls, as if life bounced off them. He could imagine the interior surface, the cool slick industrial paint over old brick refusing to yield when struck by the heel of the hand, the knuckle, the head. The walls weren't permeable to distress, to despair, states that the material world can sometimes find irresistible. He tried not to peer in. Prison life was easily imagined from television dramas and documentaries, photographs in the newspaper. Maybe the disquiet he felt was because of this— walking through a prison was like passing a famous actor and for a moment thinking it was someone you knew but couldn't quite place.

He was with Rebecca. When he had pulled up outside her building she was sitting by the bus stop. He felt like he was picking up a teenage daughter from school or friends. The ease with which she got in the passenger seat, fastened her seat belt and silently stared ahead, moved him. As they drove along, she said little, deflecting his questions with short answers, making one joke about being kept behind in the prison when they left.

Was she guilty of 'prisonable offences'?

'Sadly, no.'

The small prison car park was full, but this hadn't stopped other cars parking in all the turning space, on the pavement, the grass verges. McCullough tucked his car on the verge just in from the entrance; he would have to leave before a section of other cars could move.

Rebecca asked, 'Is this wise? Don't want to piss off the crims.'

'Aren't the crims locked up?'

'You ever seen their families?' She smiled.

'Have you?'

'On TV.'

Rebecca leaned over for a hug. It was awkward, while sitting in the front seats, necessitating quarter turns of their bodies, but he felt she wanted him to convey something to her and he tried.

At the reception desk, they were relieved of phones, keys, wallets, and scanned for other metal items. In the anteroom there were posters warning visitors not to pass anything over the tables. Along the far side there was a table with a small tea and coffee machine, jugs of water, plastic cups. McCullough and Rebecca arrived as the doors to the main room were opening. It was impossible to see over the crowd and no one seemed in any rush to go in. What McCullough and Rebecca felt neither could have expressed, although they knew it was similar, and for that reason didn't look at each other for fear of seeing it expressed; to have it reflected back would be to feel it more deeply and they didn't want that: both of them feared crying. At that moment shuffling forward was enough.

It took a short scan of the room to find Terry at a table in the right-hand far corner, next to an opaque window strengthened with grey metallic mesh. The moment Rebecca saw him she began to cry; McCullough felt sick, without hope. Could it have been only a week since the hearing? Terry was slumped against the wall, head back, mouth open, eyes slitted, staring up, seeing nothing. Their approach became a looming over him, then a shadow over his eyes. He responded only after McCullough said his name. He tried to stand, but was unable to, moving was too much. His skin was almost green, and underneath, where there should have been flesh, some subcutaneous give, there was nothing but thin bones and pale blue veins.

The two visitors sat down, eyes fixed on a person they only vaguely recognized.

'You're dying, Terry.' McCullough knew this, and knew the reason must be some kind of aggressive cancer—that all along the pain wasn't alcoholism, diet, the soul in distress; it was organic, a disease.

Rebecca looked at McCullough. 'What do you mean?'

'Terry?'

Before he could speak, Terry was seized by a spasm in his stomach. He did his best to contain it, to make no sound; his forehead broke out in what seemed like miraculously large balls of perspiration. He reached for a handkerchief in his pocket, yanking it out by its corner, and wiped his face.

'Roll me a fag, Rebs?'

'What's wrong, Terry?'

'I need a fag.'

'No one else is smoking.' She turned in her chair.

'It's banned.' He lifted the sleeve of his T-shirt to reveal a nicotine patch. 'Fucking useless.'

'Might improve your teeth.' This was McCullough.

Terry did his best to hee-hee. 'Not much point now.'

Rebecca looked again at McCullough; she refused to follow what was being said.

'How long?' McCullough asked.

'The old doc says weeks.'

'*Weeks?* What is it?'

'They reckon it started in me pancreas. Big organ, deep in the body. Lot of dense shit around it. But it's pretty much everywhere now.'

'I'm sorry, Terry.'

'Yeah. It's shit.'

Rebecca wiped her cheeks with the tops of her arms, to display bravery, the meaninglessness of her tears. 'Can't they do anything?' There was something false in her voice: she knew they couldn't, but what else was she to say?

'Manage the pain. Hard-core drugs. Always an upside.'

Under the table McCullough and Rebecca had taken hold of each other's hand. They would have reached over for Terry's, but he was sitting too far away, leaning against the wall, his hands limp in his lap.

'How come you're still here?'

'I'm a confessed murderer, Mac. Prison is the only place for me.'

'You should be in hospital.'

'That time'll come. Soon.'

McCullough stared at the boy and tried to imagine what was inside him. How long had it been there? He'd seen posters on the Tube: pancreatic cancer killed in months, especially in the young. 'Is there any way that this had anything to do . . . I don't know . . . ?' It was a pointless enquiry, but it was in his nature to ask, to think through what it might mean if this was the case: how might it have affected Terry's behaviour?

'It's not in me brain. Well, not yet.' He turned to Rebecca. 'How's Judy? Still in love with our great leader?'

McCullough answered for her, embarrassed. 'I doubt that was ever the case.'

'She always rather fancied me, didn't she, Rebs?' Terry was beginning to relax, and whatever pain he was in lessened. He wiped his forehead.

Rebecca stared at him. 'She will be so upset.'

'What about your mother?' McCullough remembered her like a ghost from a film.

'They tell me she's being looked after. I take it that's you.'

'Carers. Not me personally.'

'Still, your dosh.'

'Someone needs to tell her about this.'

'She just needs her tea and pills. Don't worry her about any of this shit. Hardly going to have a big send-off. I might make some notes on that, actually. There is fuck all to do here.'

Rebecca stood up and walked away. The room went quiet and eyes followed her out. With just enough volume for people around him to hear, Terry called out: 'My bird, yeah. My bird.' He laughed. He wanted everyone to look at her and at him. He tried to sit forward, but there was something in his stomach restricting his movements. 'Do you want to see if she's OK?'

'She'll be fine.'

First one hand then the other were flopped up onto the table, and Terry pulled himself in, as if something serious was now going to be discussed. Always the conspirator.

'What is it, Terry?'

'Look, Mac. I don't have to die in here. It's like compassionate leave or something, except you don't come back. The hospital said a normal patient would either go to a hospice or home, depending.'

'What do you want to do? Where do you want to go?'

The boy's hands were like dead chicken's feet. 'I ain't dyin' in here. But not the old girl's place, either. Maybe the hospital. How's the build going?'

'You can't die there.'

'Why not?'

'How would we look after you?'

'Can't deny a dying man his last wish.'

'It's really weeks, Terry?'

'Look at me. I'm young—fast metabolism. It's a fuck-off cancer.'

'I'm sorry.'

'Yeah. It's shit.' It was what he'd said before, an automatic response. Maybe he didn't even think this. 'How's the family?' It wasn't so much bravery as his inexhaustible self doing its thing.

'Good. We're going on a holiday, which is a positive.'

'So you didn't fancy Judy then?'

'Of course I did.'

'Yeah, she's hot. Skinny, though.'

'Slender.'

'You're so gay.' Hee-hee.

'Really? That's your response?'

A wave of pain, of hot pain, returned. It was a thing growing, spreading, and eating away at him, metastasizing in every organ, generating energy.

Terry leaned back and tried to get a small bottle of pills out of his pocket, but it became caught in the material.

'Help us out, mate.'

McCullough leaned over the table; Terry leaned further back.

'I'll need some water.'

Across the room there was a long bench with another, bigger, hot drinks machine, plastic cups, two-litre bottles of milk and a jug of water.

McCullough had to weave between tables to get there, and chairs were deliberately moved out to impede him. He looked to the prison officers for help but they just laughed to themselves.

As he poured water into the plastic cup his hands shook. The first attempt tipped the cup over with the force of the water. There was no kitchen roll. He held the mouth of the jug to the rim of the cup and poured in only a small amount, an inch.

Back at the table three pills were in Terry's open hand.

'Opiates. They fuck with your stomach. I haven't had a shit in days.' He did his best to slam them into the back of his mouth, but one dropped into his lap which he couldn't find.

'Where is it, Mac?'

McCullough picked the white pill out of a fold in Terry's white T-shirt. 'Here.' He placed it in Terry's hand.

'Cheers.'

Swallowing the sip of water was a struggle for him and produced a new wave of perspiration.

'Can I ask what you do all day?'

Terry's eyes closed. It seemed to cool him, as if the light in the room was too bright, creating a corresponding heat in his head. 'Have a think.'

'Are you able to read?'

'There's a library. Got a copy of *The Brothers Karamazov*. Picked up where I left off. Just got to where old Zosima is dead and starting to stink. That's clever. Imagine the pong you'll get from me.'

McCullough tried to laugh, but there was truth in what Terry said—the colour of his skin, the perspiration. At his death, all that would be left was something rotting, the cancer eating its way out. He looked into Terry's pale, weak eyes. 'What do you think about? In your cell.'

He didn't need to reflect. 'Nat.' Then, smiling, 'Me dad, wherever the old fucker is.'

What Terry thought about Nathaniel, McCullough couldn't bear to hear. The beads of perspiration on Terry's forehead, on the backs of his hands, seemed to be pure water, spring water; against his hot skin they looked cool. McCullough had read somewhere that body heat was entropic; dying must increase that transformation, degrading life into the lowest form of energy.

'Tell me about your dad.'

'Nothing to say. A boozer, like me. Fucking useless. Reckons he knows everything. Like me.'

'Where is he now?'

'Southend, I expect. He doesn't move around much. With some woman. A real charmer.'

'Like you.'

'You bet.'

Terry glanced over McCullough's shoulder. Rebecca was in the doorway. Her face was discoloured by tears, almost like a birthmark or a burn down her cheeks. She came in and sat back down, saying 'sorry'. She leaned forward, clutching her stomach, as if in her own kind of pain.

Terry rested his head back against the wall and closed his eyes, and for a moment seemed to doze. He was in profile to Rebecca; three-quarters profile to McCullough. After a minute, his eyes opened again, squinting in the light.

'There's a prison chaplain.'

'What does he say?'

'That he's around.'

'You haven't talked?'

'You know me, always up for a bit of chat. Remember what I told you ages ago, in the boozer? History's written by the winners. I told him Jesus was a loser. He misunderstood what I was saying. Thought I was saying Jesus was like a "loo-*zer*". He made a faint L-shape with his thumb and forefinger. 'Probably gets a lot of that.' There was a snort of laughter. 'We agreed Jesus won in the end. He went a bit further—Jesus's final victory is in our death, when we come to know God through him. God is the ultimate reality, apparently.'

McCullough sensed some acceptance of the possibility. Weakened by illness, Terry wasn't going to fight the genuinely unknowable.

It was Rebecca's time to try and understand, and she leaned further forward.

Without altering his position, Terry's eyes shunted left and found her. 'Rebs?'

'You went to the doctor, you went to the hospital—how come they didn't find it?'

He shrugged. It had never been Terry's style to think about such things; he was never really concerned with himself, at least not with his body—he was just interested in responding to the world as it appeared before him.

'My body was a wreck, Rebs. It's a miracle the cancer bothered.' There was no laughter. Before them was the evidence, the diminishing evidence, that it had bothered.

'Do you need anything?' McCullough pulled at the collar of his shirt, then pinched at his nose—it had started to itch. The room was airless and full of bodies. He felt dirt building up in his nostrils; his groin was hot.

Rebecca was on a separate tack. 'Terry—are they just going to keep you in here?'

His slitted eyes moved from Rebecca to McCullough. He'd made his request; he didn't want to talk about it again. McCullough took hold of her hand. 'We'll sort it out.'

Elsewhere in the room people were preparing for the end of the session.

Terry muttered, 'It's longer at the weekend.'

'We'll be back tomorrow.' This was Rebecca, nodding, promising, searching for the clearest demonstration of her feelings. She looked for a reaction from Terry, that he was comforted, or at least accepted that he wasn't going to go through this alone. But she got nothing back. She began to cry.

Terry wasn't cruel. He smiled at her. 'Mac's got a young family. Been neglecting them. I can wait. If you know what I mean.' There was a pause, and then a wave of something passed through him; not so much pain as a kind of lassitude, as if he were in the middle of a desert and the burning sun had taken away all his strength. Perspiration broke out again and his skin seemed to turn pale and tighten, like a shroud wrapped around him. It made dying seem more like suffocation, as if he couldn't draw in any air. Even his pores seemed to narrow and close. McCullough recognized this: he'd felt something similar when trapped behind the translucent wall that had started all this, but at least there had been air, a breathable space. For Terry, the only air was outside this film, and he was sucking at it and getting nowhere. It was horrific to watch.

'I'm taking you back to your cell.' McCullough stood up and moved around the table. A guard stepped away from the wall.

McCullough laughed. 'Really? Really? Look at me. At him. What do you think we're going to do, for fuck's sake? Break out? Have a little dance?' A couple of the other inmates laughed. Around the room other officers straightened up.

He heard a whisper, a gently lengthening, 'Maaaac . . .', and when he looked down, Terry was smiling.

'Sit down, you old cunt. They'll handle it. They'll bring in a wheelchair. All mod cons here.'

McCullough's impotent rage had given Terry a shot of energy: cancer wasn't going to deprive him of a chance to mock. That was his job.

As predicted a wheelchair appeared, pushed over the threshold of a door leading to a long corridor. It was brought by two guards.

McCullough and Rebecca wanted to help, but were warned away, explicitly this time: *no hands on the prisoner*. Terry seemed unperturbed by the way he was grabbed and dropped down into the chair, further evidence that his body had never been important to him and he'd switched off a part of himself. Rebecca and McCullough

watched, powerless and transfixed. The folding of a body too weak
to manage itself was impossible not to witness.

Terry looked up. 'Just so you know, after Rebs here, you're second
on me list of permitted visitors. Or last. Depends how you want to
look at it.'

Somehow they failed to say goodbye, or say it aloud. There
seemed to be no opportunity. Terry was wheeled around in a small
circle, and before they thought to run around in front of him,
was pushed off into the corridor. The other prisoners stood up
at the sound of a buzzer and turned away from their visitors, a
few not unhappy to return to their cells for some peace and quiet.
As McCullough and Rebecca lined up to leave, they were openly
assessed, sneers on a few faces. After all, their visit was to a confessed
killer, a brutal killer, a killer of someone local.

In the car Rebecca cried into her hands. McCullough dropped the
lid of the glove compartment and found some wet wipes.

'Here.'

He looked at himself in the rear-view mirror. What might be
visible behind his eyes interested him. But there was nothing to see,
except that he was alive and healthy.

'I'll take you home.'

'No!' She sounded panic-stricken. She didn't want any decisions
taken for her. She feared everything now had some sort of meaning
and the wrong decision could only lead somewhere dreadful. He
was unprepared for this.

She looked at him imploringly, 'Don't go. We can't just go.'

'Of course not. Sorry.'

She was angry. 'I bet you think God did this. That Terry deserves
it.' She rocked her head back against the headrest.

'Not at all. And you know that.'

'Then how do you explain it? You. I want to know.' There were
tears on her cheeks.

'I don't.'

'So Terry just dies?'

'Yes. He dies and we feel a terrible loss.'

She kept her breathing steady, ignored the wet wipes and used her sleeve as a tissue. 'But you think you've met God. You said it.' She was beyond judgment, irony. It was just a fact: he'd said this.

'What can I say? We are free creatures, imperfectly created by nature. The sequence—Nat's murder and then Terry's death—is random, the working of chance. Wrong place, wrong time. That's it. None of this is in contradiction to the existence of God.' But that wasn't what she was asking.

'I don't want him to die.' It was said plainly. She turned to him, her head still against the headrest.

'No,' he said.

'He's the only one who ever understood me.'

'You mean ignored you?' He smiled.

'Didn't stare at my tits all the time.' It was a statement of fact.

'You went out?'

'Sort of.'

'Tell me about it.'

'Nothing much happened. He wasn't really interested. He wasn't bad in bed, just ... I don't know ...'

'Rather drink a warm can of beer?'

'Never really there.'

'When he came to my home, he was like a child. Ate what the other children ate, watched what the children watched. He was very polite.'

They smiled at each other and returned their heads to the headrests, a place of repose. Both felt they could stay there, looking out into nothing, forever. But eventually McCullough had to move the car after someone flicked the bonnet with a finger.

They drove in half-silence, Rebecca pointing out briefly where her mum might be at this time of day.

McCullough suggested they go to the site, to speak to Rich, keep him involved. Rebecca refused; she just wanted to drive around. But when she recognized that they were nearby, she told McCullough to go if he wanted.

—

Rich was up on the roof of the house hanging larch shingles. He saw them from a distance as if inwardly alerted to their presence; he spanned his hands above his eyes to make sure. His descent was that of a young boy who'd only just stopped climbing trees, nimble and hazardous.

Both buildings were close to being finished. All the glazing was in and the midday sun produced in each pane a squarish reflection of light, as if the church was covered in brightly shining armour or the semi-opaque carapace of a translucent animal. All that was needed was the great steel, craned into position, fixed and welded on, a soaring hard line held high in the sky.

Rebecca kept hold of McCullough's hand as they walked down the ridge; she was careful of her footing in a way she'd never been before. There were the usual introductions to new people: electricians, plumbers—men who for the most part worked inside the buildings. McCullough wandered through the house, scanning detailing, the finish—timber floorboards flush against skirting, the position of light switches, choice of door handles. Had this been Rich's work or had someone else made these decisions? He found no fault.

In the nave of the church, McCullough positioned large stones for them all to sit on. Rich chose to stand, foot up on his stone. He reminded McCullough of Nathaniel, seldom at rest.

After a pause, Rich said, 'What is it?'

McCullough scratched his head. 'It's Terry. We've been to see him. He's very ill. He's been ill for a long time—we've all known that. But they've worked out what it is, and it's something they can't do anything about. Cancer of the pancreas. And it's spread. He will die soon.' The words sounded empty, like an echo without a primary sound.

There was a difference of a year between Rebecca and Rich and yet it seemed to McCullough that it was a deeper wrong that Rich should have to experience this at his age, two friends dying so terribly.

'I don't care. I just want to get . . . this done.' He didn't move beyond placing his hands in his pockets; he wasn't wearing his bandana and his dark hair glistened in the light.

Rebecca looked up at him. 'You should have seen him, Rich.'

'I don't care. He wasn't ever really my friend. That was Nat. There was you lot and me and Nat.'

McCullough stood up. 'I don't think it was ever like that.'

'It was. I spent a lot of time with Nat. More than any of you.'

Rich took his foot off the stone and straightened himself. Rebecca glanced at McCullough, to seek agreement on what she was about to do, and after getting a nod, stood up and hugged Rich. 'Don't be angry. This is terrible for us all.'

Rich's body began to shudder, the tears a small element of his grief; he remained standing, hands in pockets, letting himself vibrate inside Rebecca's arms. She held him with the flat of her hand on his back, with patience, saying nothing.

McCullough took this moment to walk out of the church, his phone ringing in his pocket. It was Holly, asking when he'd be home. Her tone was efficient; things were back to normal; it was safe to ask.

He said, 'Later than expected. I will explain.' He felt her silence. 'I'm sorry.'

Back in the church, Rebecca and Rich were standing apart. There were fine beads of perspiration on Rebecca's suntanned skin. There was no shade; the light streamed in. He thought of a southern church, of languishing in the heat during a long sermon. But this wasn't a church anymore, in the same way the building next to it would never be a home. They were relics of a particular summer, and for as long as they remained up, at least for him, monuments to his friends. For others—because there would be others here—Nathaniel's murder and Terry's death would be irrelevant, perhaps something dimly remembered or read about. Most people would encounter the two buildings by chance, walking over the clifftops, and would descend the slope or cross the field to investigate more closely. But the primary work would have been done, the shock of finding such buildings on a clifftop. Once inside the building, there would be no great surprise; it would function as such buildings are supposed to, as a place of reflection, solitude—a nice place to be.

He walked over to Rich. 'If you need me, just call. And I'll be back soon. And visit me if you want.'

It took a moment, but Rich found a way to ask, 'What about Terry?'

'Do you want to visit him?'

'Not on my own.'

'Then come with me in two days.'

Rich brushed dust off his knees.

'What is it, Rich?'

'Am I in charge here?'

McCullough glanced at Rebecca. 'Yes.'

After a short silence, the boy left, and was quickly . . . visibly . . . back on the roof of the house, a basket of shingles beside him.

'Terry said if he had to die anywhere . . . he'd choose here.'

'Here?' Rebecca looked around as if the building had never had pretensions to be a sacred place.

'Yes. But I think he was just searching for somewhere. Anywhere but prison or hospital.'

'It's a building site.'

'And it still will be.'

'It's going to be that soon?'

'I don't know. In my experience the young hang on and then decline quickly.'

'You know someone this has happened to?'

'Yes. A little older. Ovarian cancer. She was as brave as . . . I don't know. I can't contemplate it. I think about her often. She had a little boy, a year old.'

'That's terrible. Awful.' She began to cry again. 'Did you love her?'

He smiled. 'I didn't know her that well, Rebecca. Just over a long time. Which is what happens when you get older: You don't know people well, for a long time. But something about her death was transforming. At least for me.'

'I think you loved her.' She laughed, relieved to talk of death so openly.

'I promise you, I didn't.'

'Was she beautiful?'

'Not sure how that is relevant.'

'Told you.'

He laughed. 'I need to go. I'll be back down in two days. Do you want me to drive you home?'

'I'll keep Rich company. Make sure he's OK. It's me who's really in charge, right?'

'No—Rich.'

'You're joking.'

'You're officially Rich's underling.'

'You think I should have fucked him, don't you?'

McCullough really laughed at this. 'If I was Rich, I'd say yes. But I know that kind of mercy is no mercy at all.'

'You never tried it on.'

'You're eighteen.'

'Girls mature faster.'

'And I'm finally mature.'

'You didn't even think about it?'

'Every man would think about it.'

Rebecca regarded him. For the first time he found her easy to read. She had thought about it, too. But this was all behind them.

'And there's nothing between you and my mum?'

'No.'

'We Ash girls aren't up to much, are we?'

'Nah—amateurs.'

'Your wife must be really something.'

'Partner.'

'Does it matter?'

'Not really.'

They kissed each other on the lips, lightly, with a brief pause to celebrate the new openness in their friendship, an uncomplicated love.

FAMILY OF LOVE

'You are accepted.'

PAUL TILLICH,
SHAKING THE FOUNDATIONS

I

Terry was taken by ambulance from the prison to the hospital, then to McCullough's house in London, where the spare room had been prepared and the local hospice at home team notified. McCullough had taken the decision himself, insisted on it to Terry, and then shared it with Holly. It meant postponing their holiday. There was an argument that neither was proud of. A struggle in a doorway. Both children cried. Holly claimed it was over. McCullough ignored this. What else could he do?

Over a two-day period there were negotiations with the Prison Service and the Crown Prosecution Service, who required that two clinicians submit medical reports confirming the expected length of life for a patient with stage 4 pancreatic cancer. McCullough hired a private ambulance, which proved more complicated than he had expected, and two specialist nurses, who were employed at a daily rate to ride with Terry. At first the CPS refused to permit non-custodial remand, and a petition to the court to release Terry into McCullough's care was required. Holly's help was essential, the gifts of a good solicitor, her experience in this sector. For two days she refused. She looked around their home and pictured it in a week's time, a murderer dying there. She pleaded for understanding. It was wrong for the children. It would be too traumatic. She hated McCullough's resoluteness.

'I want him to die where he's loved.'

'He's not loved here.'

'He is by me. By Rebecca.' She was travelling up with Terry.

'You said he wanted to die—you know—down there.'

It would have been impossible; the buildings were only complete on the outside. Spitefully, Holly suggested there must be some intrinsic failure in what he'd built.

'He needs round-the-clock attention. It won't be for long.' He'd said this before.

'But you don't know how long.'

'No. But not months. You'll see.'

'I don't *want* to see. I don't want the children to *see*.'

'I know.'

There was no solution. They had also argued about Rebecca, *another* person in the house. He joked—what else was there to do?—'You wait until you see her.'

What he did with the children was to sit them down after their bath and talk to them about the man who had come to see them, the one with beads in his beard and cat tails in his hair. He would be coming to stay with them because he was very ill. An illness for which there was no medicine. He would stay in bed in the spare room and a proper nurse would look after him, and sometimes Daddy and a girl.

Walter asked, 'Is he going to die?'

'Yes.'

It was all the information Walter needed and he asked if he could leave. He stepped away from an embrace.

Pearl wanted more. 'Will he cry a lot, the boy?'

'No.'

'Where are his mummy and daddy?'

'They can't help him like we can.'

'Mummy doesn't want him to come here, does she?'

'No, but only because she cares about you and Walter, and doesn't want you to be upset. He will look very ill.'

'Can I help?'

'Yes—of course you can. Terry would like that.'

Holly said she would never forgive him; he'd promised they would speak to the children together.

Each day before Terry arrived, McCullough spent hours on the phone. Between times, he read emails from Casper, each a request for something minor that wouldn't make any difference to what he'd predicted, as if they were seeking a loose thread that if pulled might prove he'd made some terrible error of judgment and everything could go back to normal. The latest email read: *We'd like a series of pen portraits. To put some flesh on the findings. Not too many—say, eight.*

McCullough wrote back, jauntily. *Hi, Casper. Just to be clear: you'd like about eight pen portraits of psychological behaviour during a major biological attack? Let me know. Cheers, Proctor.*

Casper replied in an instant: *Definitely not more than ten. About a page of Word each.*

Holding for an insurance quote for the equipment he'd hired, McCullough typed with one finger: *Hi, Casper. About eight, but not more than ten, pen portraits of psychological behaviour during a major biological attack, about a page long in Word?*

Yes. Also, if you can—I think most people are very visual—you could choose a picture, maybe off Google Images, to represent them. I think that would really work.

Is that to be included in the page of Word?

Just insert it at the top. It doesn't have to be hi res or anything.

Thank you, Casper. I'll get on to it.

A hospital bed with a pressure-relief mattress was delivered. Holly opened the front door. She refused to let it in and began to cry. McCullough asked the delivery men to wait.

'This is not right, Mac. This isn't a hospital.'

'I understand. But it's necessary. To prevent bedsores.'

'You just don't get it. I know what it's for—that's not the problem. The children have gone through enough. I don't know why you can't see that.'

The shadows of the two men could be seen through the opaque front-door glass. They were sitting on the wall, smoking.

'Children are resilient. I don't see what lasting damage it will do. Best they find out now it's part of life.'

'I'll never forgive you for this.'

'That's your choice.'

'You really are a selfish bastard.' She left and went into the garden where the twins had assembled all Walter's Lego minifigures in the grass and were forming complex communities.

The spare room now had a blind, a shade for the light, an arm-chair moved from his office, but it still looked like a room in a provincial B&B. The hospital bed wasn't going to add to the ambience.

The nurse that had been assigned by the hospice was Polish, young, small, with sweet crooked teeth that she covered with her hand if her smile was prolonged. Her name was Agnes. What kind of life she had left in Poland McCullough didn't feel he could ask, but her voice was that of a Russian countess: deep, husky, each word appealingly slurred, although everything she said was helpful and caring. On the phone she sounded like a lover. She was Catholic, and even in the hot weather wore tights.

They talked in the spare room, although he had only intended to give her a glimpse of it through the open door. After a few minutes they both sat down on the bed. Agnes said usually the sick person's room was on the ground floor; it made things easier. McCullough explained that would be impossible, because of the children. She then outlined what she would do, and what to expect, covering her smiles with her hand when he made inappropriate jokes. He apologized; said it was a way of coping. Very British. Agnes said in Poland everyone cried. He said she might find Terry was an unusual patient. She should also know that he was coming from prison because he'd killed someone. A friend. Murdered him. For no reason.

'There must have been reason.'

It was true, there must have been.

She asked, 'Is he your brother?'

'No—just a friend.'

'He has no family?'

'No.'

'We will make him comfortable.'

At the front door, rather than go around McCullough, she ducked under the arm that held the door open, already at ease with him. She drove a VW Polo.

The night before Terry arrived, McCullough arranged a babysitter so he and Holly could go out to eat. At first she refused, asking what was the point? But she didn't want to embarrass the babysitter when she arrived, so agreed to go somewhere nearby. For an hour.

The evening was warm. It had rained earlier, fiercely for about twenty minutes, and the leaves of bushes and trees were glossy and dripping. Water pooled around drains, and in places spread to the middle of the road. Litter was soaked and smudged under foot.

The restaurant was Lebanese, eight tightly crammed tables, open to the kitchen over the small cramped bar. It was the nearest restaurant to the house, but they might have chosen it on any night. The owner said that every table was reserved; but it was early and McCullough promised they'd be out within an hour. The seats were benches with small cushions. They sat by the window, McCullough with his back to it. People they knew would pass, mothers and fathers of children from school coming home from work.

McCullough ordered a bottle of beer. When it arrived Holly took a sip, as if testing it, and then ordered one herself.

'It's the same thing all over again. Everything you ask . . . refusing you makes me look bad.'

'I'm sorry. But what option do I have? He has nowhere else.'

'But that's not why you offered. You *wanted* him to come to us.'

'I want to look after him.'

'But he killed that boy. Just killed him. No provocation. You don't seem to understand that. You don't think that matters.'

'I *knew* Nat. That boy. Of course it matters.'

'But you care more about . . . Terry.'

'Now—yes. Because I can *do* something about it.' He paused. 'There is a passage in the Old Testament. David pleading with God not to take his dying son. But once the boy dies, it's as if David moves on immediately. It seems cold, and somehow suggests his original pain was not authentic, but that's not true: he understood the nature of his power, its limits. Just because Nat went to his death in such a horrific way, does that mean Terry should be abandoned, or that because I can do something *now* I don't feel the loss of Nat?'

'I don't see how that's the same thing.'

'Maybe it's not . . . I don't know. There is also Jesus's instruction to let the dead bury the dead. I can only be useful to the living.'

'That's twice you've invoked the Bible.'

'It has its uses.'

Holly sighed. 'What's going to be next?'

'Nothing, I promise. Nothing like this.'

'You're not going to go off to Africa?'

He couldn't help but laugh. 'No. But you're right. There will be something.'

'And you don't know what?'

'I have abilities. I will put them to use.'

'Doing what?'

'I don't know.'

'But you've never just worked, have you? You're not going to join a charity, are you? Not that I disapprove of that. And from what I can see, you're not going to join the normal Church. Even that would be something. More stable.'

Wasn't that why he'd built his own church, or whatever it was now? Wasn't that why churches were built in the first place, for the reification of the spirit, to give stability to that dizzy feeling of the infinite contained within us? That, and the weather.

'I feel more stable now. At the beginning of the summer . . . at times I thought I might disappear . . . be absorbed out of this world. I felt I was . . . I don't know . . . atomizing. All that space in atoms—I sensed all that space in me, in all things.'

Their food arrived: grilled lamb's kidneys, tabbouleh, flatbread burned at the edges.

McCullough's appetite was strong. He ate nearer the plate than Holly, with more use of his hands. Strength was needed if he was going to wrestle with death. Holly picked at the tabbouleh, removed a whole parsley leaf from between her teeth.

'I think Pearl will try and get involved, and she's too young. And Walter—it's hard to know how he's taking it. He's quieter because he's worried having a guest will change things. He uses the spare room.'

Had she given in? He supposed she had. She needed to be responsible for the children now.

'I know. I've noticed it. But life is going to intrude on his routines. He needs to—'

'But this is someone dying in the room next to his.'

'I know, I know.'

It was wrong, mad; a stupid thing to do. But it wouldn't feel so intense, so condensed, when Terry was here. They wouldn't all be pressed in the spare room standing over the bed of a dying man. It would mostly be hours of silence, of nothing happening. The district nurse said Terry would sleep most of the time and then die. Medication would manage the pain. There would be no screaming in the night. And school was starting in a few days; the children would spend a third of the day outside the home; more time would be spent asleep.

'I will manage it so they are not exposed to anything upsetting. Agnes—the nurse—understands.'

'I know who Agnes is.' Holly hated herself, but having two young women in her house . . . 'I suppose Marvin thinks it's fine? I'm sure he's loving this.'

'My concern is Terry, getting him here and making him as comfortable as possible.'

'You're still talking about him as a normal person. He isn't. He killed someone—someone's son. Think about someone killing one of our children.'

'I've thought about that.'

'You'd want to kill them. I know you.'

'And I would, if I came across them doing it—how could I stop myself? And for days and weeks after, I'm sure. But this is not like that. And there must be a difference between how we act in the moment, and . . . Do you not think—ultimately—you have to forgive someone, even if they did something that terrible to you?'

'Don't ask me that.'

'I'm trying my best to do what I believe is right. That we should stand close to those in most despair, even those who commit the most terrible crimes. We must love them—I don't see what other option we have.'

'I heard you saying something similar to Pearl about Sorcha at school.'

'Because it's the same thing. She wanted to know what to do when someone is being horrible to her. I said you can retaliate, ignore them or love them. Retaliating is no good. To ignore them . . . how does that change anything? To love them is the only option. She looked a bit stunned, but I think she understood.'

'She's still having trouble there.'

'Of course. It's the answer, not the solution. There is no solution. It's the will to love that counts. Like Pascal's Wager. Making the decision is important. Even if at first we don't believe in it. To wager on it is the beginning. We are embarked.'

'I thought it was betting on God exists, because if He doesn't, it doesn't matter; but if He does—well, you're OK.'

'A common misreading. Popular nowadays because it makes God out to be obtuse. And believers to be craven.' He finished his bottle of beer and mopped up the sauce from the kidneys with the rough side of the flatbread. 'What can possibly go wrong if we make the decision to love more those whom we resent or dislike, even despise?'

'Is this what God is telling you?'

'Yes, it comes directly from Him. And supersedes anything written in scripture that contradicts it.'

'You frighten me when you say things like that.'

McCullough reached for her hand and smiled. 'Imagine how *I* feel.'

2

The first thing Terry said when he awoke in the spare room, his eyes still closed, sensing McCullough there, was, 'These are some dear sheets.'

They were Egyptian cotton, new, from John Lewis. McCullough had bought three sets, one for the bed, one in the wash, a spare set. And big square pillows. Terry was in a white hospital gown.

Without opening his eyes, he asked, 'Who's going to wipe my arse?'

Agnes replied, 'Me.'

Half an eye opened.

He'd been too weak to walk unaided from the ambulance, but had refused to be carried on a stretcher through the garden gate and into the house. He was content to be supported by McCullough and Rebecca; and, once on the stairs, to use the banisters to pull himself up one step at a time. The house was empty of other people. It was five o'clock. Holly had taken the children to McDonald's, as a treat. Terry stopped three times, but didn't sit down, just leaned over, one hand on the banister, one flat on the nearest step, and waited until he could breathe. McCullough noticed Rebecca look around the hallway and into the sitting room. She had a full backpack with her. A daughter home from university.

'You're in the loft. My office. There's a daybed. It's mid-century Danish.'

Rebecca had spent the last few days with Terry at the hospital. She'd been allowed to stay over and had slept in a chair until the last night when a mattress was provided. In the early morning she went to his house and packed a bag. His mother was in bed. The kitchen was clean; the carer had been in. Her only response to Rebecca explaining why she was there was to mutter her son's name and look around, as if he might be somewhere in the house. 'God, it was depressing,' she said.

'How was the journey?'

'He slept most of the way. I think they gave him something.'

An hour later, Terry was asleep again. Sitting in the armchair to the left of the bed, Agnes read his notes. Rebecca could be heard moving around on the floor above. McCullough hovered in the hallway waiting for Holly and the children to return, to make introductions. He'd been shocked by how bad Terry looked. As he helped him onto the bed, the gown rose up, and while his torso was just thin ribs and plasticky flesh, around his stomach there were visible lumps, like hard knuckles pressing out. It scared McCullough, this physical declaration of what was depriving Terry of life. There was no mystery; it wasn't killing by stealth; they were there: hard, demanding growths. The beads in his wisps of beard were gone. There was now a patch of baldness where the large dread had been, and the rest of his hair was mostly dying. Asked to make a prognosis based on what Terry looked like, he might have given the boy hours.

Standing in the hallway, he was almost pleased to receive an email on his phone from Casper.

How are things coming along? There is no real deadline but the end of the week would be great.

He was tempted to answer: *A self-confessed murderer dying of cancer has just been made as comfortable as possible in my spare room; I don't really know what to do with myself—please advise.* In that instance he trusted only Casper for unbiased advice.

Rebecca appeared before him, wearing a dress, smoothing down the front as if awaiting presentation. 'Where's your wife?'

'Let's just call her Holly. She'll be here soon. With the children. A not so rare treat to McDonald's. Do you want anything to eat?'

'In a minute. I'll just see Terry.'

Agnes came out, and Rebecca went in, as if shifts had already been worked out.

'Your friend is funny. He would like to see you.'

It was only a couple of metres down the hall, taking a matter of seconds, but Terry was asleep when they entered, mouth open. Rebecca was sitting on the corner of the bed, gently holding his foot over the sheet, her legs crossed, bare knees golden-brown from months of sun. Downstairs the door opened and the children charged in together, into the sitting room, racing to the TV.

'I should go down. Rebecca—do you want to come down in a couple of minutes?'

In the kitchen, Holly was unpacking a large salmon, two big bags of spinach, new potatoes, wine. She didn't look up when McCullough entered.

'He's here. Asleep.' They were either side of the worktop. 'I'm going to need your support.' He felt like crying. It was too much.

'I'll do my best.' Her smile was weak but honest.

'Rebecca's here.'

'You said she would be. I bought enough for everyone. It will be ready in about forty-five minutes. Agnes must feel welcome to eat with us.'

'I'll tell her.'

He heard Rebecca coming down the stairs, slowly, sometimes both feet stopping on the same step before she proceeded. There was a pause as she passed by the sitting-room door and he heard her say hello to the children. Their response was distracted, toneless. He called, 'We're in here—at the back.'

Holly came out from behind the counter and prepared herself. McCullough said, 'This is Rebecca Ash. Terry's oldest friend.'

Both women said hello and Holly offered her hand.

'Mac put me in the attic.'

'I'm only thankful that's not where he put me.'

What might that mean? he wondered.

Rebecca smiled, 'Like Mrs Rochester.'

It was Holly's first natural laugh for a long time.

While McCullough opened the wine, Rebecca said, 'I'm not really sure how to be a guest under these circumstances.'

Holly smiled again. 'Just do as you please. Really.'

'Can I have a cigarette outside?'

'Of course.'

McCullough and Holly watched as Rebecca worked out the locking system on the folding doors, and then drew them open. On the deck she pulled up a seat and sat down, kicking her suede desert boots off her feet.

'She's more beautiful in real life.'

'When have you seen her?'

'On your phone. Pearl showed me.'

'I'm not going to deny it.'

'Have you tried to sleep with her?'

'Not for an instant.'

'I don't believe you.'

'It's true.'

'But you would have done, if she'd been willing.'

'She wasn't, and I wasn't. Counterfactuals do no one any good.'

'Just remember you've spent more time with her than me this summer.'

'And others.'

What really annoyed Holly was that once again he'd trapped her, this time in her own home. She couldn't wander into the garden because an impossibly beautiful young woman was out there, and upstairs, down the landing from her bedroom, a nurse was sitting with a dying man. She wanted to punish McCullough, rightfully punish him, for bringing a beautiful woman and a dying man into her home—who else did that? What other home in the world at that moment was like this? It wasn't fair: the only alternative she was left with was the sitting room with the children while they watched cartoons, and she'd done that all summer.

She unwrapped the salmon and turned it over. It had been prepared. All she needed to do was slice some lemon, chop up some dill, and grind salt and pepper inside and over the skin.

'Will Terry eat anything?'

'I don't know. Last time I think all he ate was a carrot.'

'You need to ask him.'

'I will.'

'And you need to take the children in there. They can't think of that room as having something strange or mysterious in it. Pearl will explore, you know she will.'

'I need to do it when Terry's awake, and he sleeps a lot.'

'It might be better if he's asleep. If they see Agnes there, they'll see he's being looked after. That's what I want them to understand. That everything's OK. Can you do it now for me?'

He pushed at the door to Terry's room, holding it open with his palm. Agnes welcomed the twins in with a finger to her lips, and they obeyed, shuffling in shyly, behaving not unlike the way they did with Edward. Illness wasn't new to them. Terry was asleep, propped up on the pillows, his head to one side. There was light behind his eyelids, a soft and bruised light, and a little flutter, as if they were a membrane with the stirrings of new life beneath them.

'Is he dead?' This was Pearl whispering.

'No, just sleeping. Dozing, really. He's very tired.'

'He's had a bath.' This was Walter, drawing something from his memory, the thing that stood out, from seeing Terry at the beginning of the summer.

'Yes.'

McCullough turned to Agnes. 'How is he? Holly is cooking: salmon, spinach, new potatoes. You must join us.'

She nodded.

Part of the hospice equipment was an intravenous morphine drip with a plastic remote with a small blue button; a single click and a catheter opened, and drugs flooded into Terry's veins. There was another remote, with a red button to call Agnes, or whoever was on duty. A button for each hand. Both had fallen out of Terry's palms and onto the bed. McCullough pointed out the red button to the children. 'This is how he tells us he needs help.'

From her belt, Agnes unclipped a small monitor. 'This beeps.'

'Can I wear it?' Pearl wanted to be part of the action and she glanced at the button on the bed and then back to the monitor and looked up her dad. 'Please . . .'

'It's really for Agnes and me, and sometimes Rebecca.'

'Not Mummy?'

'We'll see.'

He noticed again that, despite the warm weather, Agnes was in thick flesh-coloured tights. Her dress was sleeveless, blue with small white birds in flight across the front, diagonally, like a sash. It was made from cheap material. The hem had fallen.

'Let's leave Terry and Agnes alone.'

'Can we visit?' Pearl was rigid as he tried to move them both out.

'It's your home. But you need to ask whoever's in here and do what you're told.'

Still she wouldn't move. 'Can I stay now?'

Walter was pulling on him, wanting to leave. McCullough stepped out of the way and the boy slid past and went into his own room and shut the door.

'You should go now too, Pearl.'

'I can be quiet.'

It annoyed him: it was just stubbornness. And the novelty. And that she liked Agnes. And Terry intrigued her. Lots of reasons then. He knew he judged her harshly sometimes.

'OK. Two minutes.'

'Five.'

She was impossible to defeat. 'Until I come back or Agnes asks you to leave.'

From the bed came a groan, then a swallowing sound that caught in the throat. The convulsions, as Terry's lungs tried to find a breath, were like the death throes of an animal, its throat ripped open. From his mouth a pink-red foam bubbled out and became pink dribble down his chin. His whole body jerked forward, as if he was in a fit, or wanted to cough his lungs up, or rid himself of something hard and resistant, caught in his chest. He had no strength to fight and just let it happen; it was like a possession. McCullough saw blood vessels burst in his eyes. Agnes was quick, her hand behind his neck, a tissue held under his mouth, while at the same time straightening his back a little. It lasted only seconds. McCullough covered his daughter's eyes and moved her out of the room. What he saw scared him. Holly had been right—this was no place for a dying man.

After ordering Pearl downstairs, McCullough waited on the landing. His daughter looked shocked but not deeply, maybe less than he was. Perhaps she'd taken him at his word: there would be a very sick man coming to stay.

Walter opened his door. 'Is he OK?'

'Yes. He just needed to catch his breath.'

'Did Pearl see?'

'It's like a very bad cough.'

'I'm going to shut the door now.'

'Yes. Build me something nice. Something super-complicated. We can show it to Terry; he'll appreciate it. That's his thing: how stuff fits together.'

'Like Lego?'

'Exactly like Lego. I bet he loved Lego as a child.'

'Will he want to play with my Lego?'

'No, darling.'

'Will he move it?'

'No.'

'Susannah moves it.'

'She's just tidying up so she can clean.'

'I can't find pieces. Important pieces.'

'Do you eventually find them?'

'I do.'

'So that's OK.'

'I'm not sure.'

'It is. I promise you. How was McDonald's?'

'None of your beeswax.'

'Thanks for that.'

They both laughed and Walter withdrew.

Back in the spare room, Terry was propped up, eyes open, chin cleaned. On his forehead the perspiration was bright and hot. He looked wretched, as if his body had been wrung out, twisted in gigantic hands, and dumped down, a remnant of a man.

'All right, Mac.'

'Hey, Terry.'

It was all that was said before Terry's eyes closed and he drifted off. McCullough stepped out of the room. Agnes followed him and gripped his hand.

'It is normal. It is nothing. Don't worry. He's very tired from the journey. Very tired. He needs lots of rest. Tomorrow he will be better. A little.'

'Thank you. Should we offer him food? I don't know what's best.' He heard the panic in his voice.

'I give him all the nutrients he needs. What does he like?'

'Warm lager and cigarettes.' He smiled.

'He can have a little of both, if he wish.'

'Wishes.'

'Wishes. Thank you.'

'Really?'

'Of course. Why not?'

'Because he's dying.'

'What would you want?'

He paused. 'My children.'

'To eat?' They both laughed. Maybe he could handle this.

Agnes's free hand pointed back into the room, and she let go of McCullough's with the other. 'I go back in.'

He sat at the top of the stairs and lay back. Through the floor-boards, he heard Holly and Rebecca talking. Rebecca was describing the conic section of Pascal's mystical hexagon, probably making shapes with her hands, as they all did now. She mentioned Simon, calling him a genius, and said yes when asked whether or not she had met Marvin. There was the clink of a wine bottle against thin glass, and he could see, feel, hear and taste the chilled white wine being poured. Was that what he'd want if he were dying, the cold minerality of good white wine? He preferred red, but not as a dying man—at least that was how it felt at the moment. He imagined Terry's face, the perspira-tion, the heat of aggressive growth within him. If he pressed a glass to Terry's lips, what would he do? Surely any kind of alcohol hit would give him pleasure. It was what McCullough himself wanted now, but he couldn't push himself off the stairs. He would wait to be called.

Dinner was easy, quiet, polite; there were no alerts from upstairs. Agnes was persuaded to drink a small glass of wine. On this, her first day, she planned to stay until nine o'clock; her usual hours would be 7 a.m. to 5 p.m. She made sure that they understood she was only twenty minutes away if they needed her. Rebecca asked her if this was what she did all time, you know . . . with people dying?

It was. Holly then asked, 'How is he? In your experience.'

'His blood pressure is very low. He's weak.'

Pearl looked back and forth between speakers. Walter wrapped each piece of potato in a spinach leaf, squeezed lemon over the dark green balls and ate them. The two of them hadn't argued since their return from McDonald's.

At the end of the meal, McCullough went upstairs with Agnes to look in on Terry; it was the longest he had been left alone since he'd arrived. McCullough feared they might find him dead. But he was in exactly the same position as when they'd left him, propped up, head slung to one side, mouth open, a soft gurgling sound in his throat.

McCullough laid his hand on Agnes's sleeve. 'Why don't you go now? Give me the monitor.'

'No, no. I stay longer. You go back down, and be normal—it's important.'

He looked over at Terry. His breathing was shallow, the minimum possible to keep him alive. A quick glance would suggest he was at rest, fully asleep, not intruded upon by a dull pain. But it soon became clear that his breathing was laboured, each shallow breath caught at the top of his lungs, as if it reached something and became entangled, after which there was a slight sound of strain, of friction. It didn't seem to disturb him.

Normality was abnormal: sitting watching *The Daily Show* with Holly and Rebecca, a small monitor in his lap. It had five lights and a small speaker; if Terry felt too weak to press the button or couldn't find the handset, there was a microphone. It meant, as it had done with the baby monitor for the twins, hearing every rustle, cough and miscellaneous noise from the bedroom. Agnes had advised turning it off: they were not yet at that time when noises were meaningful, or all Terry was capable of. McCullough kept it on.

Before he went to bed he stood in the doorway of the spare room; Rebecca sat in the armchair. Pale yellow light came in from the window: the next-door neighbour's bathroom light. Whether or not Terry opened his eyes, they heard him press the pain-relief button, and a slight change in his breathing followed. Agnes said she advised her patients to sedate themselves at night and especially at dawn. To try and wake with the house.

Rebecca left the room, obeying Agnes's one order: a good night's sleep for everyone.

Too tired to undress, McCullough lay on top of the bedclothes, a book across his chest. Next to him Holly was on her side, looking at him, palm supporting her head, elbow dug into the pillow.

'Are you OK?'

'Don't know. A little freaked out.' He stared at the ceiling. 'It's a lot to take on.'

'I'm glad you did this. I'm sorry.'

'It's not over yet. I'm sorry. I wasn't prepared.'

'What weren't you prepared for?'

'Not feeling anything. I feel completely detached.'

'You're asking too much of yourself.'

'To *feel* something?'

'Rebecca said the same thing. She thinks she's got used to it and somehow that's wrong.'

'I feel responsible for her.'

'That's feeling something. And that's in your control.'

'I also feel exhausted.'

'As you should.'

'There is no way I'm going to be able to sleep.'

'Just read.'

He looked down at the book, his thumb between the pages. *The Rainbow*. A novel with *a lot* of feeling; overwhelmingly so. Why had he picked this? It was a comfort, he supposed.

'I can't read this.'

'I'm not surprised. Give yourself a break—read something light.'

He placed the book on the bedside table next to the monitor, turned on his side and put his hands under his face, palms together, and brought up his knees. The first green light flickered. It could have been from the ambient sound of the room, or a noise from outside the house coming in through the open window, or perhaps his son turning in his sleep, a little elbow hitting and resounding through the wall. He planned to check on Terry every two hours; the boy would never press the alert button unless it was serious, and even then McCullough was uncertain whether he would do it, which was why he'd insisted the audio was turned on. What McCullough feared most was Terry dying alone. It was another of his many projections, a sentimental one, but it remained true that few people would want to go through this alone, and it was in his power to be there. And yet here he was, only a few metres away, lying on his own bed. Should he not go and sit by Terry all night? No. It would be oppressive for both of them. And Agnes had ordered them all to sleep, and he trusted her. Oh, how he trusted her. Had he found another angel? His son, Terry, Agnes?

Nathaniel had been discussed at dinner when the children left the table. Rebecca hadn't shown great warmth, but then she seldom did for anyone except Terry. McCullough said he'd failed Nathaniel. All the boy wanted was demonstrations of friendship, loyalty, love, but he was often a strain to be with. Insufficiently loved by his family, he had become selfish, needy, somehow vain. How Terry had been brought up it was almost impossible to imagine: absent father, addict mother, benefits, truancy, prison. McCullough supposed this was worse. But Terry was battle-hardened, a survivor, as ironic as that was now. Nathaniel had been thin-skinned, vulnerable, a victim. He had needed love so that he might become easier to love—lovable. But the truth was McCullough just hadn't found Nathaniel interesting enough. What he'd given to the site in physical labour was in direct proportion to what he lacked in emotional intelligence, generosity of spirit. Then there was the nasty side, the snobbishness. He hadn't been easy to love; and he hadn't always been easy to like. The question of whether Nathaniel might have changed if McCullough had given him more attention was now unanswerable. But what was knowable was that he hadn't tried hard enough when he'd had the chance. His heart had been open, but not fully. Not without prejudice.

It was too much to think about, too overwhelming, and there was a deep pain in his heart. His balls ached. His thighs ached most of all, as if the thick veins and arteries were filled with something hard and sluggish. Next to him, Holly's light went off. It was good he hadn't turned his bedside light on, because he would have felt obliged to turn it off, and he was unable to move, paralysed by tiredness.

The green lights of the monitor flicked upwards. For a split second they reached the red light at the top, and then dropped to nothing. It might have been just the movement of a finger. It might have been Terry dying.

3

Terry said he'd slept well until Pearl had come in, in her pyjamas, at seven o'clock. She'd sat on the corner of his bed and asked gravely how he was feeling. Did he like Agnes? What about his room? She said her room was bigger.

'She wanted to know where the old beads were. I wished I'd saved them for her now. Don't have much to leave behind.' It was all said breathlessly, weakly, head slung back on the pillows, no strength in his neck. Yet he wanted to talk.

'What day is it?'

'Tuesday.'

'Could be my last Tuesday. Now there's something I couldn't give a shit about.'

Downstairs Agnes was making herself coffee; Rebecca was still asleep.

'I've always imagined that if I was in your position, Terry, all I'd do is listen to Bach.'

'Put some on if it'll make you happy.'

'Funny.'

There was a pause. Terry pushed himself up. The tendons in the pits of his elbows strained. There was more perspiration, more coughing, a shake of the head and a 'fucking hell' under his breath. There was nothing else in the world but this straightening movement, negotiating the weak spots in his body, thinking about the minimum exertion of energy required to achieve his goal. He looked like a paraplegic manoeuvring himself across a bed to his chair.

When he'd settled, he looked over at McCullough. 'It's funny. I hear every creak in the house. All the conversations going on. Not the words, just—you know—the chat. *And* everything outside. How many cunts are there out there using power tools on a Tuesday morning?' His meagre laughter was for himself. 'Go and tell them some cunt is in here dying.'

McCullough sat on the arm of the chair. 'You're remarkably ... serene. I know that's not the right word, but it's a kind of serenity.'

'You don't think if I could stand up and fight I would? Nah, I was always good at picking my fights.'

'Not with Nat. That was a bad fight. You know that, don't you?'

There was no response. Instead Terry's eyes narrowed and looked to the window. Whether he was thinking about what had just been said or deliberately rejecting it, McCullough couldn't tell.

'Terry?'

'I could've told you ten years ago this would happen. What I did to Nat. It wouldn't have stopped it, mind. They don't lock you up for saying things like that. Maybe sectioned, for a while.'

'What did you know? What did you think would happen?'

'That there was only one way to release the tension. Simple as that.'

'I don't believe you.'

'It's how it feels. Like if I don't kill someone, I'll go mad.'

'But you didn't, for all that time, and then you did. Why?'

There was a click and what seemed to be a dizzying warmth moved into Terry's veins. His gaze receded, eyelids lowered, and his hand slowly opened. It was an escape. But also a kind of practice, for an easeful death.

McCullough watched the sleeping boy for ten minutes and then went downstairs. He and Agnes smiled at each other as they passed in the kitchen. There was no sign of Rebecca.

In the garden, he sat in a lawn chair with his feet in the damp grass. 'All flesh is like grass.' He knew this from Brahms' *Requiem* rather than scripture. Either way it wasn't true. There was a freshness to grass that flesh never had—not even a baby's—that was like silk. Was there a successful simile for dying? There was nothing that he could recall that described what Terry was going through, in all its boredom and awkward suffering, although he supposed there were diaries and memoirs he'd never read.

What he was witnessing was a sweaty, dragged-out affair, Terry shuffling step by step towards something. It was commonplace to think that life represented the perfect middle, a short length of time as a pivot between two infinitely stretching periods of nothingness, not-being and no-more, the same state either side. Yet he wasn't entirely sure he really believed this. The second infinity must be different. If the laws of thermodynamics were right, surely that meant that dying and death involved the transformation and not the reduction of energy. But did that mean that each person's life, based on how it was lived, might alter the quality of this unchanging sum, and if so did this qualitative change unbalance the *nothing*;

something; nothing equation? Was it possible that there was *something* in the second *nothing*? You didn't need Eastern mysticism or mysticism in general to believe this; it was written into the universe. It was just about how much personhood you wanted to allow as residuum in the ongoing energy. He supposed if he wanted more proof that Terry might live on in some other state, there was quantum entanglement—the positive electrons that comprised Terry in life would switch to a negative condition on his death, and the negative partner electrons out in the universe would switch to positive. Of course, the probability that a replica Terry might be configured elsewhere was low to impossible, but there was no reason why on some level he might not continue to exist as an infinitely fragmented self spanning the universe. Again, it wasn't a mystical notion—the principle was in the genuine spookiness of these quantum relationships.

He sat for an hour undisturbed. The sound of the fridge opening brought him back to himself and he turned in his seat. It was Rebecca wearing a dressing gown.

'Can I have some juice?'

'Of course.'

She poured herself a glass and joined him in the garden, tobacco and cigarette papers in her hand. Her dressing gown was knee-length, a thin silky material. As she sat down she drew together the lapels. He knew her feet and ankles well, like those of a grown-up daughter or a young wife. She smoked sitting forward, efficiently, as if it were a medicine she must get through.

'I thought you were quitting smoking?'

'Changed my mind. I was bored within an hour.'

'Think how Terry must feel.'

McCullough realized he'd been dreaming of a plan to bring Terry down into the garden. He asked Rebecca what she thought.

'I think *I* could probably carry him.' She stared into the middle distance. She was barely awake.

'How did you sleep?'

'It's very hot up there.'

'I know. Sorry.'

'It's all right.'

'Have you called your mother?'

'I spoke to her. She's a bit of an out-of-sight, out-of-mind type.' The girl yawned. 'I noticed a few years back most people . . . when they call their parents, say "It's me". I've always had to say "It's Rebecca". You know. To remind her.'

'So we do share something. My father often used to say, "Oh, it's you."'

'Are you an only child?'

'Sort of. Only living one. And if the other had lived, no me. I was the disappointing replacement.'

'Wow.'

'The Lord giveth and the Lord taketh away.'

'Except it was the other way round.'

'Yes, the Lord gave and took away and then gave again and sort of took away again by not giving quite what was wanted.'

'Does the Lord do that?'

'Isn't that what He does all the time? That's the point of the Lord, if we're talking in these terms—He's a mystery.'

'A bit like a Secret Santa.'

They both laughed. 'You should switch from maths to theology.'

'It starts in five weeks. Still don't know whether I'm going to go.' Her eyes moved away from McCullough, as if to look up to the room Terry was in, but then her gaze returned to the ground, to a hangnail on one of her toes.

'Agnes seems to think it could be days or weeks.' He wanted her to be informed, prepared.

'I can't leave him.'

'Do you want me to speak to the university? I'm told nothing much happens in the first couple of weeks.'

'I don't know. I really can't see the point of studying maths just because I'm good at it. And I can't stand all that "elegance" stuff. It's a closed system. Isn't that finally a big bore?'

'Can you switch courses these days? I mean this late on?'

She shrugged. 'Do you think we should check on Terry?'

'Agnes is with him.'

In a garden nearby there was a mother and a baby and small child; an inflatable swimming pool was being filled with water. It was a glittering sound.

'Where are your children?'

'I don't know. With Holly. With friends. It's school in a couple of days.'

'They seem nice.'

'Only "seem"?'

'I don't think I'm very maternal.'

McCullough suggested they go out for lunch. He'd show her the neighbourhood, the Tube station—her route out if she ever needed to escape. Battersea Park was close. It had a small zoo with meerkats; a pagoda; then across the river was the Kings Road—clothes. Rebecca shrugged, pressed her lips together. She seemed to enjoy her second roll-up of the day.

Before heading out, they looked in on Terry. Agnes left the room carrying a bedpan under a white cloth. Terry was on his side, which was unusual. He looked at them out of one eye. There was spittle on his pillow, an enlarging damp patch. Evidence of life was not much more than this, and the occasional spasm under the sheet. In comparison, McCullough and Rebecca felt like they might do anything at that moment: run, dance, spin plates.

'We've decided, if you're strong enough, we might see if we can get you downstairs into the garden later, maybe give you a sip of warm lager . . .' It sounded pathetic, patronizing—the two of them standing there so full of options. 'Maybe give you a toke on a rollie, if Agnes permits it. A few of the old pleasures.'

Rebecca added, 'It's up to you.'

Terry's one open eye was that of a blackbird's. It studied them, but not beyond appearances. It certainly wasn't clear he'd heard them.

'We'll be back soon.'

They were pleased to withdraw and be on the landing.

Rebecca whispered, 'I don't even know whether he knew it was us.'

'He's very tired. Go and get ready.'

He waited, sitting at the top of the stairs, elbows on knees, knuckles pressed into his cheeks. From the open windows at the back of the house he could hear the sound of the young family in the next garden, splashing water, and the plashing of little feet in the sodden grass.

Rebecca came down, in jeans cut-off just above the knees, a black singlet, Birkenstocks. She was all shoulders, knees and elbows. It was another example of the ease of health, this time wonderfully combined with youth—the loveliness of joints easeful under the skin. Terry would soon become a body of spikes, of knots under thinning flesh. Nothing much would be easy.

They went down the stairs, quickly and in silence.

The sun was livid in the sky. It had been a summer of this pale sun, as if it had stepped forward, grown large and more intense, and more difficult to see. There was no shade on the street and the end of the road was a blur.

'Which way?'

He pointed.

At the corner they met Holly and the children. She had bought lunch: salami, Gruyère, good tomatoes heavy on the vine; artisan bread—sourdough. McCullough looked at Rebecca: did the girl understand the adult drama she was in?

'We were just going to get Terry some of his favourite lager, as a treat,' she said.

Of course she understood.

The twins looked at this young woman with their father. She wasn't ill or a nurse. She seemed to follow him around.

There was a brief pause, then smiles, before Holly nudged the children on towards home. McCullough felt exposed, as if he'd bumped into his old family with his new wife. There wasn't any truth to this, even as an indication of something that might one day be true, but that was how it felt. Holly had nothing to worry about, of course. If anything McCullough was most concerned what Pearl might think: did it seem to her that he now had another daughter to whom he was giving more time, a person he was less quick to judge?

Agnes joined them for lunch, and they talked of church, the Catholic Church in Poland, her local church here. She said she tried to go every Sunday but her job often didn't allow for that. She was certain God understood. Her accented English made everything sound tragic, fateful, full of sadness, even though what she was saying was no-nonsense and pragmatic. Pearl asked what a Catholic was and McCullough explained to both children what happened during the Reformation. Walter listened with great intensity, eyes averted, one ear cocked. He also made a formidable sandwich that he tore at with his small teeth without swallowing, the bread becoming a large bolus of dough in his mouth. Pearl had drawn her seat close to Agnes's and was watching what she was doing and tentatively copying. Agnes ate with her elbows in, her shoulders drawn up. She didn't want to take up space. Beside her was the monitor.

They discussed moving Terry downstairs for the afternoon. Shade was important; a place to recline. McCullough said everything needed was in the shed. Agnes warned him if he was going to carry Terry to prepare for some 'lumps and bumps'—a phrase he'd heard a GP use when he himself had gone for a check-up after extended stomach pains and was examined by a pressing of fingers. He was sure he'd seen photographs of cancers in books and on the internet, but nothing precise came to mind. He imagined organs, softly firm. As Agnes stood to return upstairs, he asked her again: was this an OK thing to do? She nodded and picked up the monitor. 'I will give him a wash and get him changed.'

The children were allowed TV while the lunch things were cleared away and things arranged outside. Rebecca spent time staring into the dishwasher, only to declare, mystified, that it didn't look the same as the one she was used to.

'You sit down.' This was Holly, lightly manoeuvring her away by the hips.

'I'd like to do my bit.'

'Sit down. Sit in the garden. It's fine.'

Rebecca stood there, uncertain, mouth askew. The back pockets of her cut-off jeans bulged with tobacco, papers, lighter.

McCullough was at the door. 'I think I should get him . . . settle him without an audience. What do you think?' It was his way of saying: you all need to leave. Holly was holding a tea towel, wiping her hands and wrists dry. On the sill was some hand cream, which she applied. Her smile was tight; it seemed her warmth extended either to him or to Rebecca, not both.

He went upstairs.

Terry was awake.

'So, we're going to try and get you downstairs and into the garden. It means lifting you up and carrying you down. What do you think?'

It was the first time since he'd met Terry that he felt no implacable resistance, no inviolable barrier to the potential of this kind of contact, to physical intimacy. Terry's character, tough and ironic, clear-minded and sarcastic, seemed put away, at least for the time being. He was just a dying body responding to surges of pain.

Picking him up required Terry to obey instructions: 'Lift your knees; arm around my neck.' As McCullough placed his arm around the young man's back, a hand under the hot, sinewy armpit, Terry croaked, 'No tickling.'

Before the actual lift, McCullough looked over at Agnes. She sent him a clear message with her eyes—be confident in your movements—and mimed what he should do. As he drew himself up with Terry in his arms, he overestimated Terry's weight and his own body suddenly felt hollow. Together, somehow, they weren't the sum of one man.

'Not much left of me.'

All McCullough felt were the boy's bones, as if he were struggling to hold a set of bagpipes. The top of Terry's hipbone and the bottom of his spine pressed in against his own stomach; the sharpness of Terry's shoulder dug in. It was all Terry could do to tuck his head into McCullough's neck, otherwise it would have fallen back, the head of the dead. McCullough could see them both, separated from their surroundings, as a symbolic expression of love. He'd stood before many *pietàs*, and didn't know whether he was now mimicking them or was in the middle of a similar act of love. But there was no other way to hold the boy, except in his arms, head tucked into his neck, cradled, finally without strength to fight, unable to do what he did best—separate himself, walk away, disappear.

'Let's get you downstairs.'

Agnes was at the door.

But the gentle twists of McCullough's body as he tried to manoeuvre past the bed, between the chair and the chest of drawers, were too much.

'I don't think this is going to happen, Mac.' It was whispered into his chest, as if Terry were talking directly to McCullough's heart.

'Are you sure?'

'Sorry to spoil the party.'

'No problem.'

He stood there with Terry, both of them almost weightless, while Agnes changed the bed. She had planned to do this once Terry was downstairs.

'Did you carry your missus over the threshold?'

'We're not married.'

'Oh, yeah, I forgot.'

Through the open window there were the sounds of someone working on a car. McCullough didn't know who they were. Most of his neighbours were a mystery to him. He wanted to call out: *just shut the fuck up*. It was from this sudden surge of anger that his own weight returned and he felt he might collapse. A shudder passed through Terry, a pulse of something, then the boy groaned.

'Are you OK?'

A pause.

'Maybe I'll die in your arms.'

Without either of them really thinking it . . . was this what they both wanted—to get it over with now, just like this?

Agnes smoothed down the white sheet and then billowed out another and tucked it in at the bottom of the bed. 'There.'

Stepping forward, first one knee, then the other, McCullough laid Terry down.

'I think I'll take a little of that lager now.' He managed a wink at Agnes.

McCullough called from the top of the stairs: 'We're staying up here. A can of warm strong lager is requested.' He tried to make it sound light-hearted, a joke, but was disappointed that they hadn't made it downstairs, as if he'd failed somehow. In advance of the attempt, he'd felt the sensations Terry would experience in the garden: the gentle breeze, the calm of the blue sky, his senses free from the constraints of the house, of the small room, the bed and sheet. It was what he would have wanted if he were dying during such a summer. It was partly why he'd slept outside all those nights down at the site: he wasn't dying, but he felt a need for something that might renew him.

Rebecca came in with the can of lager, opened it away from her body, and passed it to McCullough.

The can was too heavy for Terry to hold and he refused to have a small amount poured into a glass. Rebecca offered to hold the can for him, but he looked over at Agnes and said, 'Let the girl do her job.'

It took some time and an extra pillow to prop him up so he could drink more than a shallow sip.

'Not going to lie—I never could taste much. But it's a lovely feeling.'

'I'm glad.'

Rebecca sat on the corner of the bed, one knee up. 'Want me to roll you a ciggie?'

'Am I to be executed in the morning?'

It was a joke, of course. But then he added, 'I'd bring back the death penalty for cunts like me.'

At six o'clock there was a faint knock on the front door, which Pearl was instructed to open while Holly watched from the kitchen. She struggled for a moment with the latch, and then heaved the door open with both hands. It was a young man, more a boy, with a rucksack at his feet and a bandana in his hands.

Holly called, 'Hello? Can I . . . ?'

Pearl called back, 'It's a man from Daddy's phone.' At which point McCullough appeared at the top of the stairs.

'Rich!'

'Thought I'd come personally—you know—to say I think it's all finished, just a bit of snagging and landscaping to do.'

Rebecca was now looking over the banister. 'Hey, Rich.'

Pearl stayed by the door and backed herself against the wall to let her daddy through and bring in this boy, who, for some reason she didn't quite understand, she liked the look of. When Rich had passed her she called up to her brother, 'Walter. Walter! There's another one—another one's here.'

'I've got pictures, Mac.' It was a struggle for Rich to pull his phone from his front pocket with his hands full of the rucksack and the bandana wrapped around one fist.

'Show me in a minute.'

'I've also brought a tent. Just in case.'

'Of what? We might go camping?'

Rich looked a little confused and then laughed. 'Didn't know how much room you'd have.'

McCullough led him down into the kitchen.

'OK—so this place is massive. You could fit my house in this room.'

Rebecca joined them and ruffled Rich's hair. He smiled, but reared away a little.

'It's not that big. You might have to bunk with me.' She was cruel.

'We'll sort something out.' This was Holly, who then said: 'Hi, I'm Holly.' And then: 'This is Pearl. Her brother Walter is upstairs.'

'Do you want tea, Rich? Beer? How did you get here?' McCullough opened the fridge; he felt excitement, warmth, relief, a general flooding of feeling.

'Tea, please.'

Holly filled the kettle.

'I came by train.'

'Sensible.'

McCullough thought of Terry hitchhiking earlier in the summer and decided that having travelled by train meant nothing bad would ever happen to Rich.

Around the kitchen table, Rich's phone was passed from hand to hand, the screen brushed with variably nimble fingers, so each picture could be seen in order.

When it came to her turn, Holly reared back. 'Wow. It's extraordinary.'

McCullough sat with his hands jammed between his thighs, letting everyone else look first. He wasn't sure he wanted to see the pictures himself. For the last ten days he'd only thought about what was happening down there once or twice, and was unable to imagine what it looked like. In his mind it would always be an unfinished building, surrounded by mud, all the lush grass he'd slept on, all the long ancient grass he tried so hard to protect, tramped down and gone. Wasn't it supposed to have been a timber shack or an upturned boat, a temporary object that found permanence through use, an accretion of materials keeping it steady, rather than something with measured and approved foundations, steels that came from a foundry on the backs of flatbed lorries, made to calculations of weight and angle only achievable by computer? Would the final expression, on some level, be a disappointment?

'It's very good, Daddy.' Pearl flicked through the photos. 'Really good.'

McCullough took the phone from his daughter's hands. There it was, finished. The final steel was in, an abstract representation of a steeple, or even more abstractly, of yearning. In one photograph the sun was reflected along its length, at its highest point hot and bright, and then cooling as it passed the roof of the church, after which it faded away as it entered the hard elemental darkness of the earth. It was a beautiful thing if you liked such things. And he did. Others, he was sure, wouldn't. Maybe after all it was a matter of taste. Enactment, encounter, enchantment—all depended on whether you liked what you saw.

'We should show Terry. You should show Terry, Rich. He'll be . . .' McCullough got up. 'Come on—just say hello.'

Walter was sitting on the corner of Terry's bed, turning a small Lego model in his hand, taking him through the detail. There were various moving parts that Walter described without looking up to see if Terry was following. Agnes, smiling, made noises of appreciation.

'Wal-ter . . .' McCullough said gently. 'Terry's very tired.'

A pale hand rose from the bed, somehow saying with precision, It's OK. Let him.

'See.' Walter was determined to finish.

McCullough laughed. On most occasions it was difficult to make his son understand directions with even the boldest and most clear hand gestures—he often looked in the opposite direction to a pointed finger. McCullough didn't want to think his son had selective difficulties, but sometimes it seemed that way.

'There is someone here. Someone to see Terry.'

'Who?'

'A friend.'

There were still some moving parts undemonstrated and Walter needed to finish what he planned to show.

'OK, darling. You carry on. But be quick.'

McCullough had wanted Rich's appearance to be a surprise, but he could see Terry was now unsettled: who was it behind the door?

McCullough whispered, 'It's only Rich.'

Terry didn't move but it was clear the world had suddenly become too tiring: Agnes, a boy and his Lego, McCullough's almost aggressive sensitivity, and what felt like a crowd behind the door.

'OK, Walter, out, out.'

McCullough guided his son through the door. 'Terry needs to sleep.'

For some reason everyone was now at the bottom of the stairs, in the hallway, like they were all gathered to go out—a large, modular family only occasionally finding themselves together. Holly led the children into the sitting room and asked them if they'd like her to read to them. It was a risk. In the wrong mood Pearl would consider it a babyish thing to do. Walter always said yes. Rebecca led Rich into the garden and set up a chair for him.

Sitting at the kitchen table, McCullough found himself halfway between the two sets of people. Upright, stiff-backed, hands on his thighs, he felt like a Victorian father waiting for his dinner. But how else was there to sit? To slump forward would be to give in to an atrophy of the body that might never be reversed. He felt no pull from either part of the house: Rebecca would look after Rich; Holly, the twins. And directly above, sitting with a posture of almost equal stiffness, Agnes was watching over Terry.

This sudden lack of responsibility would have felt good if it didn't feel so bad. Something about his body felt out of kilter. It was like his middle, from chest to thigh, was misaligned, shunted a little to the left, as if he were made of three blocks and the central one was off-centre. He felt queasy, and the more he focused on it, the profounder the misalignment seemed to be. He feared its permanence, that he would never feel fully integrated again. Its cause was easy to determine: sympathy with Terry's eaten-up insides. He assumed Terry was experiencing a more intense version, his body becoming less his as the cancer encroached, readying himself for a point when the cancer required more life than it was possible to give without sacrificing its host. Was there anything to be done at this late stage? Was there a last chance?

He had always believed in the possibility of mind over matter. It was self-evident that the mind was more than physical material and that the body was intrinsic to its being—no separation was possible. There were many correlations between acts of will and sudden reversals of terminal illness. Was that still possible at this stage, just days from death, whatever the actual cause of recovery? At night he didn't so much pray for Terry as send messages of healing to the boy's body, as ridiculous as that seemed. But then he had to believe that if his contact with the divine had left some residue of energy within him, it would be a healing power. Only weeks ago he'd read that prior to Jesus, Jewish mystics were more like faith healers or shamans than miracle workers, using herbs and roots, incantations and rituals to exorcise and cure. What made Jesus different was that *he* was the healing, his embodied presence the source. This was why they flocked to him. It wasn't just the laying on of hands, Jesus's deliberate action; to touch him without his consent, on his blind side, worked just as well. He had no choice.

This was what McCullough wanted for himself now. Of course, he understood that if he suddenly found himself possessed of the gift of healing he should run to the nearest children's hospital and kiss the forehead of a dying child, and then on and on, until he was empty. But he also knew there were others less deserving who might need him. What did it mean to heal the sinner before the innocent?

The answer was clear to him. Those who had removed themselves so far from God's love were in the deepest pain, and to try and relieve this was to demonstrate the depth of compassion that was needed in this world, the choice that was required to transform it. In this sense saving a dying infant achieved so little.

But none of this had been gifted to him. Instead, he was sitting at his kitchen table experiencing a mild, vaguely geometric disassociation from his own middle. He wanted to call for help, for someone to come and push him back into alignment. He wondered whether his son might be the best person, given his own odd alignment with the rest of the world and his gift with Lego. Because that was how McCullough felt: as though a large brick was wrongly positioned and he needed disassembling and reassembling; he needed Walter's nimble, super-flexible fingers working with implicit speed to achieve the correct symmetry.

This image of simple blocks reminded him how he and the team had started to construct both home and church in those first weeks, little more than rudimentary geometric shapes slotted together, based on the basic notion that brick-shaped things, large or small, when placed together tended to produce building-shaped structures. It was work in which Nathaniel had summoned up more strength than any of the others put together, and Terry, when it was fitted together and flush, had seemed to appreciate it in ways not quite accessible to the others. Nathaniel and Terry. One dead. The other soon to die. He couldn't remember who'd arrived first; who came down off the ridge first. It had been in Nathaniel's nature to work, Terry's to observe, but that didn't mean it was that way around. All he could remember was that within hours Terry had ridiculed him, mocked him and entranced him. Angels had complex natures.

Of course, he now accepted Terry wasn't an angel. Not in any way that might make sense to others. But that didn't make Terry like others, someone who might be judged as others might. This was difficult territory. How do we make sense of someone who becomes so afflicted, so tormented, that for some inexplicable reason they think that they need to experience the senseless power of killing another human being—as if this might somehow give their life meaning, or explain something to them? How might this be reconciled using simple moral categories? Maybe this was at the heart of it. Drinking and fighting, and finally, murder, were Terry's way of ruining himself, dispelling any good . . . simplifying who he was. All he wanted to do was to commit some final act that tore up any chance of mistakenly being judged good. Except, of course, it would never be about others' judgements—not for Terry. The act was a mirror by which he might finally know himself, unalterably. But if that was the case, he'd miscalculated. There was nothing unalterable about human beings. Killing someone, killing Nathaniel, didn't make him irredeemable and damned. There was no equation of behaviour, no divine judgment, that condemns people to that outcome, whether they want it or not. People commit worse crimes and live full, happy lives. You can do a lot of terrible things and still go on living well—we are strong that way. Committing terrible acts is as compatible with living a happy life as devoting yourself to ministrations of mercy, pity, and love. But then McCullough wasn't comparing like with like. Terry had chosen an entirely different path: to commit an incomprehensible act, confess, and then live with it on his terms, in the face of it.

But how incomprehensible was what he'd done? Wasn't murder commonplace? It didn't take long to happen in the Bible, and it didn't take much to make it happen. Terry's act wasn't so shocking that it would force the world to turn away from him, uncomprehending. Neither did it represent something the world could not face about itself, as if Terry was exposing a terrible truth. But Terry had never said that was his intention. At this point he'd said nothing at all. Right now only Terry and God knew why he'd killed Nathaniel. In this way, Terry and God were alone in this together. It didn't matter whether Terry rejected God, every act of this enormity must require that we stand in front of God at some point. It didn't even matter whether God existed or not. That was the ineluctable truth about man and God. There comes a time when we must stand in front of Him awaiting ourselves—our final coherence. For Terry, a roving drinker, dispensing wisdom and picking fights, it was never going to be an easy encounter. God was too strong, too canny for those who wanted to take Him on, even in their fiercest denial.

Maybe Terry's objective was to try and remove himself from any confrontation, to swerve away from such an encounter. As if there were a choice of direction. Another miscalculation. There is no act which He won't confront. That was the final truth about an act of evil, even the *sum* of evil. It wasn't that there was so much of it; rather, neither act nor sum could be equal to Him. He can take it all. But that wasn't Terry's style, either—to avoid a fight. He liked contact. Maybe in his mind this was a way to force God to reveal Himself. He accepted that what he'd done required judgment, but he recognized only one authority.

There was one final possible explanation. Terry had committed this terrible act because God's absence or hiddenness was a torment to him. He couldn't go on without proof, without a revelation, and had tried to force an intervention. He'd killed Nathaniel as a cry into the silence, hoping in the final moment that God might stay his hand as He did with Abraham, a knife at the throat of his son. Was that why it was a beheading? It had started with that awful posture of ritual sacrifice, but with an expectation he'd be commanded to stop? Was Nathaniel murdered because God failed to intervene in a sacrifice He hadn't commanded?

So many explanations; perhaps one, perhaps none, was right. But that didn't matter. Terry had failed to understand: God's presence is revealed by love only, in that love exists at all. Terry had chosen to go against that, as he was free to do, as he was now free to suffer alone if he wished.

McCullough raised his eyes to the ceiling. The poor boy was up there, facing the end, probably days away. Watching Agnes, McCullough realized that she'd learned it was important to give the dying privacy, even if they needed round-the-clock attention. She seemed able to make a space around herself that didn't impinge on Terry. McCullough knew himself well enough to know he was unable to do that. He wanted to be as close as possible to the action. When he was in the room he sensed Terry feeling weirdly jostled by his presence, as if his personhood intruded, pushing itself into the invisible field that was Terry's dying, like a face pressed into a tightly held sheet. It wasn't simple nearness. It was a kind of neediness, a desperate energy that vibrated to all parts of the room, looking for feedback, charging up the particles and creating invisible weight and silent noise. He couldn't help himself; there was something to experience and he wanted to be there.

Holly called it plain and simple voyeurism. During their first argument about Terry coming to their house, she had predicted it: the more ill Terry became, the more McCullough's wish to be a witness would seem like a kind of death porn. She was wrong, of course, or at least partly. Who wouldn't be drawn to such an attritional death, to watch a body diminish from within, while the spirit, whatever that might be, remained the same? But that wasn't all. For as long was Terry was alive, Nathaniel's murder was also present in the room, complete unto itself, not as something past, but as an enduring fact, and this co-existence intrigued McCullough: the living truth of Terry's dying in the living truth of his murderous act. In the light of these two perpetually colliding states, he thought he might discern something. He'd insisted to Rebecca that he didn't believe in divine retribution, and of course Terry was ill before the murder. But he also understood that in orthodox theological terms, an omniscient and judgmental God would know in advance what Terry would do, and while punishing it with cancer, still allow it to happen. But any advance knowledge on God's part was the end of free will in its purest sense. Didn't he now know that God bestowed on us free will to His own loss, if those terms were even meaningful? He supposed it might be said: in choosing against Himself, God surpassed His own omniscience—He was possessed of a greater knowledge in our freedom.

Holly came into the kitchen and called out into the garden, 'Do you want some tea?'

The clock said four-ten. What McCullough really wanted was a drink, a cold Sauvignon Blanc, bottle on the table, condensation running down the sides, large wine glasses. And to read with his feet up. To read for pleasure. In an empty house. What he wanted was for everything but wine and the printed page to go away.

'I'll do it.' He needed the distraction. 'Does Agnes drink tea? I can't remember.'

'No, just coffee.'

'Should we make coffee as well?'

Holly touched his shoulder. 'I think we should let Agnes take care of herself—she's used to making herself at home.'

He stood at the counter, watching, while Holly put out the mugs and dropped teabags in them. She looked up at him. 'I feel like a stepmother. To your teenage children.'

McCullough snorted. 'I'll think of something to make for dinner. Rich eats a lot. He's still growing, I think.'

'The children don't seem too unsettled.'

'No.'

Throughout the exchange, neither felt that the other was looking for an angle for rebuke, and they smiled at each other as they picked up the four mugs of tea to take into the garden.

Rich explained what was left to do at the site. A gardener friend had said not to bother about seeding, just to let nature do its business, and he'd found someone—a local handyman—to sort the snagging. 'Oh, and we're still off-grid.'

Was that a good thing? Was that right?

McCullough asked to see the photos again and Rich handed him his phone. 'Any visitors? Comments?'

'The vicar guy's been down. I think he might have said a prayer, I don't know. A building inspector gave me a load of paperwork, stuff we need to provide. We really should have taken pictures of everything we did at the beginning. They've had to dig holes to check the depth of the foundations. *Again*.'

Rebecca was lying on her front. 'Our great leader is the only foundation we need.' It was said tonelessly, as if this truth had been inculcated in her but she still didn't quite believe it.

'It's true,' McCullough agreed, and laughed.

'Are you going to come down and see it?' Rich said.

'Not until after—' He didn't need to finish. Rich cut him off with a nod. But he was disappointed.

'I will, though.' McCullough didn't want to let the boy down; for a moment Rich's face, the need expressed in it, reminded him of Nathaniel's.

'Sorry, Rich, I need to ask: has there been a funeral for Nathaniel?'

The lawn offered up its detail to Rich, his fingers exploring grass roots. He lifted up his hand when a ladybird wandered onto his finger. 'Yeah. The church was pretty full. His brothers didn't exactly look pleased to see me. His mum cried all the way through.'

McCullough sat back. He failed to imagine anything precise. Little more than the pews taken up, a coffin brought in, a priest of indeterminate age. It would have been a requiem mass, he supposed. The homily would refer to Nathaniel's young age. The peace he had found. Any eulogy would have been short.

'It was good you went.'

'Some people asked where you were . . .' Rich glanced at Rebecca and then looked annoyed in the way Rich always looked annoyed, a conscious knitting of his brow, as if anger was against his nature. He wiped the ladybird into the grass.

Rebecca knocked away at the lighted end of her cigarette, putting it out, and threw the stub into a bush. 'What did you say?'

'I didn't know.'

'People asked whether it was true about Terry. As if they thought it might be—you know . . .'

People would think what people always think: that it was some kind of trick. A fast one being pulled. 'What did you say?'

'I said it was.'

Rebecca leaned forward and rubbed Rich's knee. 'You were brave for going.'

Before dinner Rich spent ten minutes alone with Terry, while Agnes was downstairs making a salad; she'd brought containers with her in the morning and made a space for them in the fridge.

It was difficult for McCullough to pull himself away from hovering outside the bedroom door, but he heard Rebecca on the phone to her mother and went and sat on the stairs to the loft and listened in. It was quick, efficient, with Rebecca answering 'fine' to most questions.

Dinner was fried halloumi, pitta bread, a tomato and cucumber salad, a parsley, chilli and caper dressing, and the much-needed Sauvignon Blanc. The children filled their pitta bread and wandered around the kitchen; neither Holly nor McCullough had the energy to insist they stay seated.

Rich asked about his work, and he answered honestly. 'My ex-partner has pretty much taken over. He's a prediction specialist. As for the government work I told you about, they're now trying to assess the likelihood of what I said might happen actually happening, and what to do about it. Unfortunately they are not really including what I said in their modelling because deep down they don't believe it will happen *as I said*, even though that's what they want to measure.

'It's not unusual. It's really hard to comprehend something that sits outside your general belief in how the world operates; in the same way you can't measure something for which you have no system of measurement. Right now they are using a system that requires a different order of analysis. Their data points are irrelevant because none is derived from a real person. Or rather they *are* derived from real people, but the structure of the survey, the inevitable language issues, the cognitive dissonance, produces an insight gap, and that means you are making construals out of data that has no intrinsic meaning. I try to keep respondents—people—at the heart of my analysis, however much data there is. You have more chance of being right if person X actually does Y than no one in data set X doing Y, but you find a statistical likelihood they just might based on—I don't know—regression analysis or something.

'Interestingly, I've said a dirty bomb is much more likely than a biological or chemical attack, which is what they're planning for here. I told them why, but they said I had no data for it—it was a hypothesis. I said, you don't need data for the bleeding obvious. Boys like building bombs. They like explosions. You don't need anything beyond a thought game to get to that.'

McCullough realized he was speaking quickly, as if talking about work set him free from other worries.

'Don't tell me no one else has thought that—boys like exploding bombs?' It was a challenge from Holly.

'You'd be surprised how few people think that way. I said it and it silenced a room.'

'Because they thought you were mental?' This was Rebecca, of course.

'Because all the Excel sheets before them don't allow for that kind of gender preference, or the child in the man, or for vanity.'

'What about you, Mac—where does vanity fit in with you?' Another challenge from Holly.

'Big time.' He may as well admit it. 'But I built a church, not a bomb—which proves my point: vanity builds big showy things.'

'What about killing lots of people? The other stuff—the chemical stuff—might do that.' Rich wasn't sure he liked the caper dressing.

'Two things: terror isn't about numbers. It's about impact. And while chemical and biological weapons may be very frightening and kill more people, a dirty bomb going off in the centre of London will have more visible impact, and kill plenty of people. Hospital wards filled up with Ebola victims disappear off our TV screens. Eventually.'

Holly's eyes shunted to the twins. Walter was listening.

Rebecca said, 'Are you saying they don't have people working on this?' With her arm stretched over the table she was dipping her halloumi in Rich's dressing.

'I suspect they do, but there was no evidence of it when I went in. The reverse, in fact.' He poured more wine into each of the glasses.

There was pause, then Rebecca added, 'Maybe Nathaniel and Terry are well out of it.'

Holly took a breath. 'A lot of my clients have lived through these things, similar things. Most, I think, would still choose life.'

McCullough looked at his children, then at Rebecca and Rich. He saw them clearly, brightly, as if in exaggerated 3D. They all seemed indestructible. Immortal. What level of attrition would be needed to wear them down to the point where they would give up life, make dying an act of will?

'Holly's right. Let's not forget while I've been down there building—'

Rich interjected, '*I've* been building—'

'We've *all* been building at some point or other. Holly represents asylum seekers fleeing war, torture, political oppression. Some people do real jobs!' It was supposed to be self-mocking but it didn't quite sound right and seemed facetious, patronizing.

Holly collected up the plates, sliding one under another, piling up the cutlery, holding it down with her thumb. Rebecca moved to help but was told to sit.

'There are some raspberries and blueberries for pudding. There's also some mascarpone if anyone wants it.'

To McCullough it sounded like something he'd want to eat if he was upstairs, dying. Berries, white wine, Bach; a list was being compiled. He made sure a few berries were set aside for Terry.

The twins started to squabble over the amount of mascarpone each had. Brought up with considerably less than he and Holly were providing for their children, McCullough heard the complaint, 'He's got more mascarpone than me,' with mixed emotions. 'The horrors of being a middle-class child,' he said. 'I'm surprised they don't say "mascarpone" with an Italian accent.'

Walter laughed at this and tried it out, the whole statement: 'She'sa gotta more-a mascarpone than me-a.' It was a decent attempt and funny at first. But it was clear to both parents that it wasn't going to stop after one or two tries, and a rush of adrenaline was on its way, especially as Pearl would want to exploit this fun for all it was worth. The first thing she did was to laugh loudly, to make sure Walter continued, despite McCullough's firm 'Enough now'. When Walter went to repeat it, Pearl stole a raspberry from his plate. He only had raspberries. While she was being told off, her tongue came out, unsubtle by her standards, but that level of operations could wait until everyone was near-hysterical. Rebecca giggled and continued eating; Rich looked embarrassed and stopped.

The first clunk came unexpectedly from a straight-armed fist, as if Walter had suddenly learned to punch rather than lash out. This shocked Holly, who was unable in the moment to accept it was instinct rather than a willed attempt to knock his sister out. The fullest impact had been curtailed by Walter's arm needing to thrust past McCullough's back, although there remained a sharpness to the contact, which after a shocked pause caused Pearl to scream and struggle for a counter-attack, before deciding to hold back and think about her next move. By this time Walter was screaming that it was Pearl's fault for stealing his raspberry *and* sticking out her tongue, an accusation that was interrupted only when he noticed his sister looking at him with a sly grin, enough of a provocation for him to try and climb over McCullough to get to her, crying out, 'She's giving me a face! She's giving me a face!'

Holly shouted, 'OK, OK—enough.'

Walter repeated it again and again. 'She's giving me a face!' He was broken by the unfairness of it.

What came next McCullough should have foreseen. Pearl started saying 'He's-a gotta more mascarpone' in a perfect Italian accent, distracting them all. It was genius, instantly turning Walter's flooding tears, his red-blotched face, into a mask of reluctant, pained laughter. She laughed too, to provide momentum. Rebecca's eyes were now wide. Glancing at Rich, she mouthed a 'wow'.

'OK, Walter. Computer time.'

In that instant everything stopped, as if Walter's mood was the dominant one, responsible for the electrical charge in the room, and with this act of misdirection McCullough had withdrawn all energy down to a single exchange.

'With you?'

'Yes, with me.'

But it wasn't over; Pearl had spotted an angle. 'You never play computer with me.'

It was true, in part. He did sit with her and watch her use the computer and listen to her explain what she was collecting, buying, growing on various websites. It was a different experience watching Walter, who liked simple—and not so simple—challenge games where the rules might be understood in a few moments. While McCullough never felt the compulsion to play himself, he was content for ten minutes or so to enjoy the on-screen mayhem as Walter bashed away at the arrow keys and made sharks, penguins, cavemen eat, swim and bonk on the head various obstacles in their way. Ten minutes of having his daddy next to him was usually enough, after which he was happy to be left alone to work his way up the levels. It wasn't clear to McCullough whether his son was any good at these games, but he presumed he was because it seemed that Walter was good at anything he wanted to do; his interests were narrow, or at least didn't tend to run concurrently, so he tended to be very good at only one thing at a time.

This time they spent fifteen minutes lying on McCullough's bed playing Crossy Road on an iPad—a source of endless fun for them both. When distracted like this, and both looking in the same direction, Walter would sometimes talk about himself without prompting, seldom expressing a real worry but nevertheless opening up about something in his world that required a little working through. This evening he said his sister was interested in Terry and kept going into his bedroom.

'Are you interested in him?'

'I'm not.'

('No' would never suffice for Walter.)

'You were showing him your Lego today.'

'He said he liked Lego.'

'You asked him?'

'I did.' (Neither would 'yes'.)

'When?'

'When he came.'

'And he said he liked Lego?'

'He did.'

'Have you shown him other models, more than the one this morning?'

'He can't hold them.'

'No.'

'Do you talk?' McCullough rephrased this. 'What do you talk about?'

'He likes to talk about you.'

'What does he say?'

Pause. 'None of your beeswax.'

'Come on, tell me.'

The iPad rested on Walter's knees, his spindly fingers spreading raspberry juice across the screen, which McCullough wiped away with his sleeve.

'He's funny.'

'Yes, I know. What does he say?'

'Funny things.'

'He's very ill.'

'He's going to die. I know.'

Was it unfair to ask more of him? 'What funny things does he say?'

'The worms that eat him will be no good for catching fish.'

'Ah. Anything else?'

'He says you're funny.'

'Does he now?'

'He does.' A small laugh. There were incidences of subtle humour that Walter seemed to get, as if he were more aware than they realized of his own semantic eccentricities.

McCullough sat up and shunted himself to the bottom of the bed. 'You carry on here, if you want.'

Before going downstairs, he looked in on Terry. Agnes wasn't in her chair. Terry was asleep, mouth open; his black and rotting teeth looked like the keys of a broken typewriter. For some reason McCullough peeked into Walter's bedroom. The floor was covered in green and orange plastic IKEA boxes full of Lego bricks, and his table was covered with children's encyclopaedias and instruction booklets, half-assembled models, abandoned ideas—the workbench of an inventor.

McCullough paused at the kitchen door. Every part of the house seemed to have a threshold that required a conscious instruction from mind to body for him to cross. It was easy enough, but he found that tonight, with everyone around the table, his stomach needed a little bracing, as if not to do so might risk his bowels opening. Holly glanced at him and then returned to her conversation with Rebecca.

He went in and picked up his wine. It was tepid now and tasted like the after-burn of vomit at the back of his throat. He addressed Rebecca and Rich: 'Why don't you two go out? There's a cinema a short walk away. Dare I say a club?'

'Good idea.' Holly was keen for them to take the opportunity.

'Trying to get rid of us?' Rebecca smiled.

In his broadest East London accent McCullough coaxed her, 'Come on, girl, 'ave a night Up West.' It didn't really sound as he had wanted it to and lacked timing. More than his body was misaligned.

Rich didn't want to make a decision.

Holly said, 'Please don't feel you have to do anything.' Noticing Rich's averted gaze, she glanced at McCullough, eyes asking, Is he OK?

'Rich? Want to walk down to the shop and get some beer?'

The request was straightforward and Rich got up from the table automatically—he'd done a lot of the fetching at the site.

The street was quiet. No power tools being used; no cars being fixed. McCullough had always felt comfortable with Rich away from the site, wandering in silence; he was a boy without an angle, who asked for very little. Without a doubt, the easiest to love.

'Thank you for looking after everything. Sorry for abandoning you.'

Rich was fixing his bandana. 'Do people wear these here?'

'Yes, some do.'

'Are you pleased—with the work?'

'It looks great. It really does.' He felt unconvincing, addressing Rich's need rather than what he himself felt; he had no idea how to express that. But in principle the answer would have been the same.

They walked on, crossed a main road and went into a shop. 'You choose.'

At the large refrigerator, Rich scanned the cans, the bottles, the deals. 'What do you want?'

'I'll stick to wine. Choose for yourself and Rebecca; we've got a couple of cans of Terry's favourite.'

Rich pulled a four-pack of Stella from the refrigerator.

'You don't want that—it'll be horrible. Go for 1664, or maybe Red Stripe. Or you could try a local artisan beer—a pale ale.'

'We have those, Mac—down there.'

'Of course.'

'Should I get cider as well?'

'Why not?'

Cradling four cans of lager and two bottles of cider, Rich moved past McCullough—who was picking out chocolate—and dumped them on the counter.

'Do you want anything?' McCullough asked him, placing a bar of chocolate flecked with sea salt on top of the cans of beer.

'Can I have some wine gums?'

'You may. What about Rebecca?'

'She likes gum. Just get that.' He picked out a blue sparkly packet.

McCullough paid with a card. The owner double bagged the alcohol and handed it to Rich.

Back on the street, they paused at the kerb, two buses before them, stationary at the junction. The engines were heavy with heat, their parts toiling.

Rich took a breath and swapped the bags over to the other hand; there was a red line across his palm.

'So how long's Terry got?'

'A week. Maybe two. I don't know. The doctors are quite good at predicting—so a week.'

'He looks terrible.'

'Even for Terry.'

A small laugh from Rich. 'Yeah, even for Terry.' Then, 'At Nat's funeral, I felt so sad, I wanted to kill him. And I hated you and Rebecca—I really did.'

'I understand.'

'You should have been there, Mac. I don't understand why you weren't.'

'I'm not sure I would have been welcome.'

'You didn't try, did you?'

'No, I didn't—you're right. I picked sides.'

'How could you pick a murderer?' He was toeing at gum stuck flat to the pavement.

'Because . . . I don't believe Terry wanted to do what he did. Not like some psychopath without feeling. And because of that I believe he is suffering.'

'He's not. He doesn't care.'

'You don't know that.'

'Do you?'

'It's a choice I have to make. The other choice is unthinkable.'

The buses moved on; people brushed past them, taking their chance in the traffic. A teenager with a bike wanted them out of the way and knocked McCullough with his front wheel. There was a short staring competition. Rich brought his concentration back to Terry.

'I wish he'd die.' It wasn't said unkindly.

'He will. And it will get easier.'

'Do you wish he'd die?'

'Rather than what—get better? No, I wish he'd get better. I wish he'd go to prison and come out in fifteen years and somehow be changed. You might find this difficult to understand, but I'd like him to come out changed and be happy. Of course, it's easy to wish that, because it's not going to happen. But if the question is: do I wish he'd die soon? I can't even say that I do.' He needed to change the subject; he didn't know what he felt. Perhaps he did want it over—to walk in the door and be told: he's dead.

'How are you feeling about Rebecca? You don't have to share a room—you can sleep on the sofa.' McCullough managed to ask it casually, and with warmth. For the first time that evening his timing wasn't off. He waited out the embarrassed pause.

'Everyone thought I was more into her than I was.'

The road cleared and they walked across.

'You may be right, Rich. But I'm not going to give you the benefit of the doubt here. I'm a great believer in love, in broken hearts. You're only half-human if you haven't had your heart properly ripped out of your chest, torn in half, stamped on, and kicked into an oily puddle.' Once again, he wanted to be jokey, wise and jokey, but had succeeded in neither.

'Only Rebecca understands what you go on about.'

By the gate to the house McCullough went through his pockets for keys. In the end, they had to knock.

The evening was spent outside in the garden, Agnes staying late with Terry. It was an act of kindness on her part. A new friend had arrived in the house and she wanted to help.

Rebecca and Rich played Go Fish with the twins, after which Holly insisted that anyone under sixteen go to bed. After three 'last' games, Rebecca took Pearl and Walter up with Holly. When Rebecca returned she said, 'It's amazing—they don't do anything they're told. Is that normal?'

McCullough laughed, 'I say no; Holly says yes.'

'I think I must have been a good girl.'

Rebecca then pressed Rich into learning Texas Hold 'Em. They both needed a little tutoring from McCullough, who eventually got himself down on the grass and played.

Holly was gone an hour. Before returning to the garden she made herself some herbal tea. The chocolate was brought out and shared.

Sometimes their talk was directed to the open window at the side of the house, an acute angle of flight, relying on reverberation from the next house to reach Terry.

When Agnes came down she said, 'I think he's listening but he's very weak. Hearing goes last.' It was 10.45. She handed over the monitor to McCullough. 'His blood pressure is very low,' she said quietly. 'And I think he's got an infection of some kind. I call Carol now and I pick up the prescription in the morning. But antibiotics will make him feel bad. He says he does not want any medicine. The doctor will say go back to hospital.'

McCullough put the monitor in the grass, steadying it; he felt a new autumn coolness in the ground. He stood up. 'Really? I thought he'd stay here until he . . .'

'It is possible.'

'Have you told him?'

'Only that he needs antibiotics.'

Rebecca stayed sitting on the grass, glancing up, as if the information wasn't really meant for her.

McCullough craned his head around to the window. 'So we'll just see where we are tomorrow, is that right?'

'Yes. I'll be here at seven.'

'It's almost eleven now. We can manage in the morning.'

Holly put her herbal tea on the grass and stood up. 'Mac, we need to make sure Agnes goes when she's meant to leave.'

Agnes placed her hand on her chest. 'It's OK.'

With mock sternness, Holly glared at her. 'It's not OK. I'll convince you by the time we're at the front door. I'm a lawyer, you know.'

Agnes's teeth flashed, and were quickly covered up. McCullough kissed her on the cheek. 'Do as Holly says.'

'I will.'

He remained standing. 'Are you two OK?'

They both nodded. Rich took a sip of his beer, slurping off the top, much like Terry used to do.

After a moment Rebecca looked directly at McCullough and said, 'What must he be feeling?'

McCullough shook his head. Every guess would be a presumption.

'Mac?'

The lack of an answer, a quick answer—something he'd always been good at—created an isolating silence between them all. It was his nature to reassure, and they had become used to this, including him. But he had nothing. How could anyone know what Terry was going through?

Rebecca's hand reached for his. Only the ends of their fingers touched. Somehow he could feel the pattern on her fingertips.

She said his name again. 'Mac?'

Hot tears came into the corners of his eyes. 'I don't know, my darling. I really don't know.'

APOCRYPHA

'Logic is neither science nor art but a fudge.'

BENJAMIN JOWETT

Earlier in the day, Rebecca had handed McCullough a copy of *The Brothers Karamazov* from the bottom of her rucksack. Taken by Terry from prison to hospital, he had demanded she read it to him when she was at his bedside and then insisted she pack it when they left for McCullough's. It was an old copy, the spine broken. Whether this was from multiple readings in prison, or it had arrived in the library in this condition, he couldn't tell. Was it fanciful to imagine that some prisoners turned to Dostoevsky in their despair? There were worse choices. McCullough had flicked though it. No passages were underlined, no pages turned over. He remembered Terry's small Bible, almost rabbinically full of annotations. Where was that now?

He was sitting in Agnes's chair, the novel open in his hands. Terry was asleep, mouth open, breathing shallow, jaw slack from weakness. The collar of his T-shirt was skewed. It looked uncomfortable, as if it might be pulling somewhere. The boy's legs had fallen apart under the sheet. Only his hands retained the appearance of life, the pain button in his palm, fingers twitching. McCullough closed the book, although a thumb remained within its pages.

'I once read a story about the Dalai Lama. He was asked by a Westerner how he, the Westerner, might become a Buddhist. The Dalai Lama said, "Why do you want to become a Buddhist when you have a perfectly good religion of your own?" Those weren't his exact words, but you get the point. I have no idea what the Westerner replied, but I'm sure his expression was one of disappointment, and certainly he had no intention of returning to Europe and exploring boring old Christianity. Because that would have been his perception of this 'perfectly good religion'. And I understand that. Of course I do. Even the Catholic Church with its bells and smells, its saints and miracles, is still mainly old white men in cassocks showing very little outward evidence of great wisdom. Then there are the churches. A particular interest of mine, as you know. Compared to all those jungle temples and hilltop retreats, your average church is just not that conducive to spiritual awakening. There is nothing extrinsic in the setting that makes one confident that contemplating the Divine is going to yield much. Then there is the Bible. A book that requires you to have read very few books or an awful lot of books to appreciate it. Because without a lot of context, these days it promises more than it delivers. Which means, in the end, few people of my generation, your generation, would disagree that Western Christianity seems a little—I don't know ... dullsville. Where is the sense of real mystery, the promise of transcendence and/or inner peace? I know the Catholics bang on about mystery, but they're so controlling about how it is expressed, it ceases to be mysterious. But then in my view it shouldn't really be about these things anyway. If we reduce religion to a bit of mystery and inner peace—which is what most people are after when they think of spirituality—what have we got? That story about people sitting down to a great feast but only being given very long spoons. The search for inner peace is the version where everyone is trying to feed themselves. The long spoons are there to feed others.

'It's one of the reasons I've never really been drawn to mysticism in any of its forms. There is a real moral problem concentrating on one's own transcendence—or indeed one's own relationship with God; it seems to me to be missing the point of anything that we might construe as religious or God-decreed. But if we set that aside and look at the promise of mysticism, especially when as Westerners we look East, then—wow! I can't pretend to know much about the lived experience of Eastern religions, but I've been around enough Western converts to know what the attraction is. Mindfulness, transcendence, renunciation. Silence.

'Of course, that's perception rather than reality. I don't suppose half a billion Buddhists are spending their days under trees trying to release themselves from samsara; they are more likely to be

plumbers, engineers, shopkeepers, dinner ladies, going about their
business in the same desperate rush as ourselves. I suspect only very
few practitioners of Zen are trying to solve the koan 'Why has that
bearded man got no beard?', at least full-time. But as spiritual exer-
cises from five thousand miles away, added to our own disillusion-
ment with consumerism and religion . . . how can it not have appeal?

'But if we return to the Dalai Lama: he was merely saying
Buddhism isn't more fit for purpose than any other religion. He
was saying, at the deepest level, all religions are the same. But for
many people these days it seems authentic spiritual life can only be
found in geographic otherness, the "exotic". What we're after must
feel different to what we know. Because what we're after can't reside
at the end of our street, ministered by someone who grew up in the
same town, with the same life, quoting from that boring old book.
Perhaps the heaviest irony is that Western Christianity is *us*, but that
weirds us out because whilst it's true, it's us behaving at our most
odd, and not in a cool or mysterious or otherworldly way—more
in a pallid, toothy, slightly suspicious way. So how are we to walk
towards this? We don't; we walk away.

'And then there's its message, or the language of the message.
It's not mysterious or gnomic, it's just baffling. Let's take the central doctrine of the Trinity. There is a lovely moment in the *Book
of Common Prayer* . . . a passage I've read many times because I *do*
get it on some level. It's a description of the Trinity. For most of
the passage the three persons God, Christ, the Holy Ghost are
the same: one, indivisible. And then suddenly we have the Holy
Ghost's difference. It's not "unbegotten" but "proceeding". Don't get
me wrong, it's both beautiful and right . . . and yet . . . so obviously
a work-around. On the face of it, the Trinity should be profoundly
mysterious, and as challenging as any Zen Koan in its incompre-
hensibility, but somehow it's not. It's just baffling, as I said. Partly
because it's so obviously a fudge. I mean think about it: I'm not even
sure if you're a Christian whether you're even allowed to love God
directly or it must be through Jesus Christ, or whether we can do it
alone, without help, or we require the Holy Ghost to get us there.
And I've done *a lot* of reading.

'And then we have Original Sin. Quite frankly, I'm not surprised people want to reject a religion where you have to chant "it's my fault", or accept without argument that we're all born into depravity, capable only of evil, and that any good we do is God working through us. Actually, I do have some sympathy with Original Sin. It's not hard to argue that we're a faulty lot and it's good to be reminded of our imperfection, it's an important corrective to all those utopian ideologies that have human perfectibility written into their mission statement. Which I might add is something that can also be said about a lot of Eastern mystic traditions. Purity, perfectibility; it's a distraction. I suppose what I'm trying to say is . . . it's very easy to talk oneself out of Christianity. There is too much over-thinking, which, as you know, I believe is our great burden.

'Actually, Islam is interesting here. It's long been my opinion that Islam's success is based on learning from the mistakes of Judaism and Christianity—all the scriptural inconsistencies, the endless conflicting interpretations, the working out of meaning after the fact by rabbis and theologians. Rejecting all this allowed Islam, as much as possible, to create a more watertight case, one less vulnerable to clever dicks having their say. All the strong stuff was included; all the more problematic stuff sorted out. You have one God, but don't make him exclusive to one set of people. In fact, if there really is One God and no chosen people, there can only be one religion, so everyone is a Muslim, even if we don't know it yet. That's smart. I know Paul tried to argue something similar, but he swerved from the One God stuff.

'Islam is very simple. They have a great prophet, but they didn't spend centuries arguing over his essence. Honouring him sufficiently is enough. Finally, make sure the book—because you've got to have a book—is non-linear, ahistorical, and one-tone, so its authorship can be attributed to God without the clear evidence of many writers. To my mind, Muhammad was even more of a theological genius than Paul, and I do think Paul is extraordinary. Paradoxically, because of the coherence of Islam, it creates its own kind of otherness. Human beings are messy and argumentative. The Quran allows Allah to exist deep in mystery. Harold Bloom has Yahweh as a great *character* in Jewish Scripture, which I'm not sure is quite right, but He certainly has many attributes of personhood, and hence we feel he is somehow knowable. And Jesus's *"Abba,* Father"—again, way too familiar, and easy to dismiss or misappropriate because of that. Then there is Jesus himself; in many ways an ordinary man, and because of that recognizable and relatable. If anything he is special rather than mysterious. It's only when the Church Fathers get hold of him that the mystery is constructed. But it's too late, because with the exception of John, the mystery is not really in the Gospels, which is where most of us get to know Jesus. Christ's beautiful mystery is a beautiful afterword. It's for those who care to read on, or for those who pay attention when the minister starts talking in incomprehensible sentences. Who has the time or energy for that? And beyond that—what's the promise? No one in Islam "walks with us" or is interested in "our journey". It's a religion of submission and obedience. The reward and judgment is clear. Not so Christianity; at least not these days. Of course, I approve—to be sketchy on the detail is honest. But we still have this structure, and it doesn't really allow for a great deal of wriggle room. It's the big contradiction. Deep down the most devout know this, which is why—ironically—they continue to build and make safe the structure, because in essence the Christian proclamation is too vague, too non-specific . . . too impossible to follow without guidance. For me at least, this vagueness, this lack of structure, is Christianity's great mystery. The existential nature of Jesus is a mystery. In Matthew's Gospel alone he's inexhaustible. But again, apart from scholars, who wants an inexhaustible text? For most of us it needs managing. As humans we fear chaos, and too much freedom of thought carries the risk of chaos. This is at the heart of "The Grand Inquisitor" section of *The Brothers Karamazov.* So what did the Church do? They replaced the words and actions of Jesus with structure—a governing interpretation, with ritual. It doesn't matter where you look, however egalitarian or open-minded the structure is, a certain dogma must be adhered to. You simply can't go it alone with Jesus. But the one thing Jesus asks us to do . . . is to look deeply into ourselves, something we can only do alone. He knows it is only when we look deeply enough into ourselves that we will make the right choice, his choice, to be compassionate, kind and forgiving. But man's nature when confronted with this level of self-scrutiny is to be scared, evasive, lazy. And we know fear is the first foundation of control. That's another irony. Jesus's radical stance will fail because of man's weakness, man's fear. But it's only in accepting his radical stance that we lose our fear and are able to act with more love, more self-sacrifice. It's only in our weakness that we can act at all from the heart. That's a complicated dynamic to make sense of. There is no promise through meditation like Buddhism, no straightforward strength or clarity like Islam. To be a Christian is to work hard on ourselves and then be unsure as to what the right thing to do is. Yes, at its best, Jesus's hand is in our hand, but he doesn't lead us, whatever the Church says. And then there is always the chance of a miserable and pitiable death like his. Who wants that? I'm certain that those who think deeply about Jesus's story find a profound beauty in it, an inexhaustible mystery, as I do. But the Church as we understand it now—it's just commoditized faith.

'I suppose what I'm saying, Terry, is that you were both right and wrong when you said I was just a regular old Christian and should just accept it and join the Church. But in the end I think you were more wrong. I don't believe much of what goes for basic Christianity. It might be that everything I believe would be rejected as heresy. Actually, there is no "might". Without a deep acceptance of Jesus as the Son of God, as the Incarnation, without a belief in the resurrection, I can't call myself a Christian at all. And yet what if all that is just the human stuff, coming from our nature to create and invent, to order and impose? What if it's just a diversion, a swerve from the message—the noise and not the signal? As you know, I've been exposed to the signal for some months now. And there are things that have happened that you don't know about. Whether they are more or less meaningful or just part of the discernment process—of getting closer to the signal—I don't know. But I suppose the most desperate difference between real Christians and me is that I think Jesus's teaching will fail, that love will fail, and that makes what I believe incompatible with two thousand years of Christian dogma. It's taken me a long while to admit this. In many ways I've had to go against my nature. But in my heart, I know it's true.

'But what does that make me, then? I would like to call myself a tragic Christian. Which, I suppose, many would consider a contradiction in terms. But it's a fair interpretation, I think, of the central event. I remember us discussing this months ago. To me, the Crucifixion is the central event; the signal. It's what we should be listening to. What we should attune ourselves to. Love, in its strongest ever expression, fails. Of course, Christians will say the Resurrection is the central event. Everyone dies; no one else is resurrected. But Jesus is. That's the signal. That's the "sign". No matter how strong the power on earth, there is greater hope in God in heaven. The tomb was empty etc. But this is the noise, I'm afraid. Us creating a whole lot of noise because we're unable to live with the central event: that Jesus died on the cross. Jesus as a redeeming force, as eternal hope, as embodied love, died. He tried and failed. We failed him. And it is in this failure, confronting his death as our failure, letting ourselves be a daily witness to his death, that we're one with Jesus. But I don't think any part of the Christian communion will accept that. But who's to say I'm not right? Who's to say that the tragic version of the Jesus story, one that acknowledges our own hopelessness, is not the correct one? I mean, doesn't the real freedom come in not believing in the Resurrection, but in facing Jesus on the cross, being with him there, over and over, and through this, whatever else might be true, becoming, as much as we can, more loving, more compassionate human beings? It doesn't change the outcome. It doesn't change the truth. But it might change us.'

McCullough looked over at Terry. His breathing was shallow. His eyes were not quite closed. His open mouth produced a soft gurgling sound, life as its most basic, percolating.

Why had he said all this? Was it a confession of some kind, safe in the presence of a dying man? He supposed he knew that even just lying there, dozing, strong opiates in his veins, Terry would still hear a false note and somehow reflect it back, and with that he would learn something. It remained the case that he trusted Terry to know him in a way he didn't know himself. It was as if Terry possessed a gift that was a positive for others but a torment to himself. Whatever honesty he demanded from others, he demanded something more elemental from himself. But the quest for undiluted truth is pain. There can only be failure, despair.

McCullough glanced down at the novel with the photograph of Dostoevsky on its cover. It had been designed to make the ageing writer look like a saint in a mediaeval icon. It was this that had kicked off his train of thought. It reminded him that Dostoevsky was a member of the Russian Orthodox Church, a very different institution from the Western Church. No Augustine for one. And then he'd remembered an English composer who had converted to the Russian Orthodox Church, and recalled wondering at the time—cynically, he now supposed—if the conversion was in fact the search for a kind of spiritual glamour, if such a thing were possible. And this had led him to the story about Dalai Lama. So, not a confession then, at least not at the start, just his musings turned outward, as if the two of them were back at the site and working together.

'Hey, Mac.' It was a whisper, a struggle, but the determination to be heard was there.

'Hey, Terry.'

'Won't be long.'

McCullough pulled his chair close to the bed and leaned in to hear.

'I say that to her—Aggie. She doesn't laugh.'

Terry cleared his throat. The strain on his body was painful to watch, chin pushed up, neck arching, anything to get rid of what was clogging him up. His breathing sounded hollow, like a waterless pipe. He started to convulse. It was the violent thrashing of his first day, but as if something solid was rolling around inside his chest, a separate entity in its own death throes, unwilling to give up, wanting out of the body containing it. McCullough held his hand, as if he might offer a steadying force—something to connect Terry's body to the world. His hand was hot, dry, weak. It took ten minutes for his breathing to steady. The sheet was soaked. Terry withdrew his hand; found the medicine button, but did not press it.

After another ten minutes, his eyes opened again. 'Mac?'

'If you talk, you're going to cough, and it's too much. You need to rest.'

'Move the pillow.'

With the back of Terry's head held in the palm of his hand, McCullough inched the pillow up. He tried to loosen the collar of the T-shirt as well, or at least free the fabric from around Terry's neck.

'Agnes says your blood pressure is very low. And you've got an infection.'

It wasn't interesting information and was ignored. Terry then tried to clear his throat again; it was easier this time, as if some kink in his neck had been straightened.

'Not long.' It was still a whisper, a rasping, as if the sound was being made by friction at the back of his throat, no air required.

'You've said that.'

'Just testing.' Then, 'Take the book off the bed.'

The thick novel was spine up, pages spread on the sheet; it was as if Terry could feel the strain on the spine, a downward pressure, and the content weighing heavily. McCullough placed it on the floor.

'So . . . Mac . . . Which brother do you reckon I am?'

There was a drinker, ironist, angel, and murderer.

'Why?'

'Just making conversation?'

'I'm tempted to say you're like them all. Maybe not the illegitimate one. No, not him.' He paused. 'But then maybe you're not like any of them.'

'So who killed the old man?'

McCullough looked down at the book. He couldn't remember where in the story the killer was revealed.

'Who do you think?'

It didn't matter. It was just a novel, after all. A whodunnit. Terry closed his eyes. McCullough felt the distance between them, as if Terry wasn't just dozing or even asleep, but somewhere else entirely. He pictured a ledge on a mountainside. A narrow shelf on a sheer face of rock. A place of isolation. Restful in its absence of life and colour.

It was now McCullough's turn to feel the pressure of the novel. At his feet, it was inert and silent, yet compared to this room it was full of life: of argument, rancour, kindness, desperation and stupidity. There was not much love in there; not really. He picked it up; something to hold onto.

There was silence for a few minutes. Somewhere along the back gardens a dog was let out and barked at something before being called in by its owner.

'Mac?'

'Yes.'

Pause.

'You know I came looking for you?'

McCullough looked at him. 'What? Sorry—I didn't hear what you said.' He moved the chair closer.

'You, Mac. I came looking for you. Before Nat.'

It wasn't a surprise. McCullough had wondered about it. Seriously; idly. Then dismissed it like a man ignoring a boy's opinion on serious matters. But now it was true. At least the idea was true. The unaccomplished fact. He felt sick, in the instant imagining . . . in the split-second imagining of the two of them . . . under the tree. A fight. The stupid, messy, thrashing of a fight.

But it hadn't happened. And it didn't matter now.

'What do you want me to say?'

Did Terry want McCullough to confirm that he understood what was being said and accept it as true, as if the act had taken place in some way?

'Just know I'd've done it.'

McCullough gripped Terry's hand and didn't allow the boy to withdraw it.

'Maybe you would have killed me, Terry; maybe I would have killed you. What I want to know is . . . why are you telling me this now? Surely you don't think you need to confess this to save your soul? Of course you don't. So what then?'

'It should've been you, not Nat.'

'Maybe.'

'You know it's true. You're just a fucking con artist.' There was a smile. But no laughter; no *hee-hee*.

There was nothing more to say. It didn't matter whether Terry believed what he'd just said or not—it still would have made more sense: his death; his murder.

He let go of Terry's hand and watched the chicken-foot fingers close around the remote and find enough grip for the button to be depressed. In seconds the dying boy was asleep, mouth hanging open, the air making fluttering sounds in his nose, in his throat, as if it were passing through gills. It was steady but not peaceful, like a complex engine set going a long time ago but now running at its simplest level, just producing a little internal light. McCullough was content to think in such mechanistic terms. It didn't mean that the light produced was the sum total of the workings. Terry was still there. But that's the stage they were at.

He opened the novel. Saw the names of Ivan and Aloysha. Terry hadn't turned the question on him. Which one of the brothers was he, if indeed he was any of them? Perhaps the most that could be said now was that he wasn't the murdered father.

MIRACLE

'Give me the world if Thou wilt,
but grant me an asylum for my affections.'

Josef Tulka /W.B. Yeats,
"The Wanderings of Oisin"

It was like a hiccup of electricity, a tiny snap of light above the bed. If you drew a line from the centre of Terry to the geometric middle of the room, it happened there, a sudden brightness turning inward, as if there had been an infinitesimal blossoming of light that flashed out in an instant, or like a tiny diamond snatched away into the palm of a hand.

Whether McCullough saw this or not, he knew something like it had happened because he replayed it to himself based on something he was sure he'd witnessed, even if it was only vaguely, out of the tail of his eye. It was too quick for his senses to dwell on and comprehend, to muster into definite shape, but phenomena could still be caught this way, at least in essence. It wasn't that he'd only half-seen it or half-missed it—part of him had seen it fully and yet at the same time he understood it hadn't happened at all.

While he would have said that it occurred in the centre of the room, just above Terry, he wasn't sure that was correct either, or it was a simplification—instinct told him that it took place in the whole of the room, perhaps even beyond, happening everywhere— the universe itself turning inside out, like a coin, dull on one side, bright on the other, and for a second the bright side was turned outwards.

McCullough chose to believe this was how Terry died, that he'd witnessed the enfolding of his soul into the universe. It wasn't an event that required an acceptance of spiritual matters; it was an observable physical phenomenon, the capturing of energy, or transference of energy. God wasn't needed.

His watch said 12.33. He wanted to provide an accurate time of death if he was asked. He subtracted three minutes, aware he was rounding down.

When he stood he found himself caught a little between the chair and the bed and *The Brothers Karamazov* at his feet. Terry's face looked loose, his cheek dragging to the pillow in a soft rictus. His eyelids were pale and his hands open like an old woman asleep, something small fallen from her hand. In the diffuse night light, the white sheet over his body looked like marble, no tremors beneath it, spasms, the body's pulses. There was a stillness, but also a tidiness, in death.

He called Agnes as instructed. A TV was on in the background. A Polish channel. McCullough whispered and then listened, looking at Terry without intensity, without emotion. Was that normal? Was he, when it came down to it, a man without feeling? It had been a worry all his life. To feel things deeply was really just to feel them to your capacity, and was no indication of great volume, of absolutes. Agnes said she was sorry. She had feared it might happen; the infection. Arrangements could all wait until morning if he wanted. He wondered whether her dropping of the definite article was idiomatic English or a mistake. He replied that he wanted to do what was best. 'Wait until morning'. She'd done it again.

To reach Rebecca, he had to step over Rich, deep in his sleeping bag, snoring. Lying on her front, Rebecca had one arm above her head, the other hanging off the side on the day bed. He crouched down and whispered her name, tentatively touched her shoulder.

Her waking was quick. He sensed she didn't know it was him, not immediately. She sat up, feet on the floor, and grabbing the front of her singlet, stretched it down over her knees.

'Mac . . . ?' Blindly her hand searched under the sheet for something, finally drawing out, bunched in her fist, knickers.

There was no need to explain. She knew. It was the only reason he'd wake her.

'Turn around.'

Rich rolled over inside his sleeping bag, twisting the material. A snore was disturbed. Then finished.

Rebecca followed McCullough down the stairs and to the back of the house. The bedroom door stood open. He stepped out of the way to let her through. She stood, as he had only minutes ago, at the end of the bed.

'I've called Agnes.' It was meant to reassure her: she was not to worry about anything.

Her tears were few, brushed away with a finger across her cheek, then reflexively wiped off down her singlet.

'Were you here?'

'Yes. We talked a bit. He went for the pain button and then . . .'

'So he was in pain?'

'I think he just wanted to sleep.'

'What did he say?'

'Nothing.'

'No last words?'

'Not really.'

'I'm glad you were here.' She looked at him. 'Should we wake Rich?'

'I don't think so.'

He stood next to her and put his arm around her waist. He felt the warmth of her sleep, her hot skin.

'So no miracle then?'

'I suppose not.'

'I don't want to think he's in hell or anything, for what he did.'

'If there is any accountability it's in facing God's sadness. Just that instance before we feel God's everlasting love.'

'You don't really believe that, do you?'

'Yes and no.'

He supposed he did believe it. At least more so than not. But it was really an answer to a human question.

'I should call my mum.'

'If you want.' Then, when she didn't move, he said, 'Do you want to be left alone?'

She threaded her arm around his waist to keep him there, laid her head against his shoulder.

'No. I'm a little bit scared.'

'Do you want a cup of tea?'

He felt her laugh; tightened his grip. 'I think we should have a cup of tea. He's not going anywhere.'

The French windows open, the night air seemingly warm and cool at the same time, McCullough poured them both not tea but whisky. Rebecca sat on the table; he leaned against the counter. She raised her glass: 'To the end of an era.'

McCullough took a deep breath. 'I've never really liked whisky. I've tried to, but it all tastes the same to me.'

'I like rum.'

'I used to like rum.'

'Should we have rum?'

'Not sure there is any.'

Rebecca knocked her whisky back, pulled a pained face and offered her glass for a little more. 'I don't really like the taste, but I like the feeling.'

'Isn't that what Terry said about lager?'

'I don't think he could taste anything.' She sat with one leg idly hanging over the other, her foot bouncing a little. He'd never seen so much of her flesh. The whisky burned his throat and repeated on him.

'Holly will think it weird if I stay, won't she? Stay here, I mean.'

He didn't answer for a moment. 'You should go to Cambridge. Cause some trouble.'

'I really can't be arsed.'

'That's the spirit.' He finished his whisky and put the glass on the counter.

'I want a different life,' she added.

'Than what?'

'This stupid one.'

'I don't want to get all Nietzsche on you, but that's an act of bad faith. Whatever modicum of contentment that's possible requires you to will your life in all its particularity, even if given the choice to change it, which is impossible anyway. In fact, he says we should will it over and over again. To think anything else is an annihilation of self.'

'Did you say that to Terry? What about Nat's parents?' She was up, with hand outstretched, demanding the bottle of whisky. He poured her two fingers. Kept the bottle with him.

'It's worth thinking about.'

'Yes, O wise one.' It had been a long time since he'd seen her like this, sardonic, finding him laughable. But there was warmth in her response now.

'You should have a cigarette; don't worry about going outside.'

'I left them upstairs.'

'Do you want me to go and get them?'

She nodded.

When he returned the whisky bottle was on the table, Rebecca's glass empty. He dropped the packet and papers next to her. She grabbed his sleeve. 'Sit next to me.'

He did so; their hips touched.

'I'm a hateful person, aren't I?'

'No.'

'I'm selfish and dissatisfied.'

He laughed. 'And I'm an egotist know-it-all.'

She looked him and said, 'You're really not,' as if she was admitting it was a mistake about him that could easily be made. She was a little drunk. Her foot came up, toes stretched out; she found something invisible to his eye to pick away at.

'Did you have sex with my mother?'

'No.'

'Do you want to have sex with me?'

'You're drunk, Rebecca.'

'Just answer.'

'I'm not going to answer. I don't recognize the question.'

'It's simple, Mac: do you want to fuck me?'

'No.'

'I think you do.' She was nudging him with her shoulder. It was more joking than flirtatious.

'Please, Rebecca—Holly might hear.'

She stopped and slumped a little. 'Isn't death supposed to be a turn-on?'

'I'm not sure a "turn-on" is right.'

She took a slug from the bottle. 'Oh, well, you lost your chance now.'

He couldn't deny that there was a falling away within himself, but it passed, and he realized that despite the desire he felt, he would always have turned her down, and there was no regret—in the same way he felt no guilt for imagining what it would be like.

He stood up and went to the counter and lifted the kettle off the stove top. 'Do you want that tea now?'

She let out a long sigh. 'Poor Terry.' She began to cry fully, with big tears, too big for her hands to contain them, and only able to stem the snot pouring from her nose by pulling up her singlet to wipe it away. Her cries brought down Holly, who immediately sat where McCullough had been and held Rebecca in her arms.

She looked up at McCullough. 'Is it Terry?'

'Yes. About half an hour ago.'

'I'm sorry.'

Holly then concentrated on Rebecca, gripping her more tightly, whispering, 'You poor thing. You poor, poor thing.'

He wanted mint tea, and went out into the garden for fresh leaves. The surface of the leaves felt pleasantly rough and thick to his fingertips, recognizable in the darkness, low to the ground. In the next garden a fox crossed the lawn and stopped under a line of washing to watch him. In the half-light and stillness it was like a coloured pencil drawing of a fox; even its colouring was as though only partially filled in. It moved off on the tips of its paws. McCullough liked its stealth. The night was long.

He looked up into the night sky. It wasn't an ancient or a wondrous sky, but a distant, semi-dark firmament, capping off infinity. Was Terry out there now, a scattered version of himself, a new configuration of energy? Did it matter? He recalled standing in the garden at night, a week after the twins were first home from hospital, one baby in each arm, their faces smudged into his shirt, saliva soaking through to his skin. It felt like the natural thing to do: shuffle them up and turn their faces so they might look upwards and be introduced to the moonlit night. It was their first encounter with how it felt to be a tiny spot beneath the vastness, yet somehow able to take it all in, contain it with one cursory glance. At a week old they were mostly blind, and beyond the ends of their flexing fingers and crinkly toes, experience was meagre. It was for him he was doing this. Between their smallness and the great universe, he was claiming the space he would occupy to protect them. In a whisper he explained how long it had all been there and what he knew of its movement, its speed and expansion, and where they were in relation to it all. It was enjoyable, configuring the universe in his own way, drawing it down to two new points of existence, two new witnesses.

Mint leaves in hand, he went inside and dropped them into the cups and poured over the water. Rebecca was tidying up her face with tissues, laughing in little desperate bursts as Holly made feeble jokes about what McCullough was like when they first met.

'He was a little insane, basically.'

He stirred the leaves in the cups. 'I'm here, you know.'

'We know.' They said this together and there was more laughter. A pause followed.

'There was a lovely fox outside.'

But they weren't listening. Holly had taken a tissue from Rebecca's hand and was dabbing it under the younger woman's eyes.

'Do I look all red and puffed up?'

'I'm afraid you do.'

More laughter.

The three cups of mint tea were set on the table. McCullough scratched at his growth of beard. He felt sweaty. In need of a shower.

'I know this is going to sound weird . . .'

They both turned to him and said a sceptical, elongated 'Yes?', so perfectly in sync that they could have been mother and teenage daughter ganging up against him.

'But I'm going to go and check on Terry.'

It took them only a microsecond to regard each other, to find the same look in each other's eyes, and laugh again.

He left them to it: a sensible man with things to do.

It was a little darker in the room, the light from the window a little colder. He picked up the novel and placed it on the chest of drawers.

If there was any change in Terry, it was that he was no longer ill. The illness had been like an assault, something active that required resistance in the body, and in death that fight had ceased. He now looked just hollowed out and starved, a body in need of work and preparation. If the sheet were removed he would look like Holbein's painting of Christ in the Tomb: a long, emaciated figure, a body forever dead. He then remembered Terry in court, in a suit too big for him even then. Now, on this body, its fit would be clownish. How conventional he was, imagining Terry in a suit, as if this was how the dead must be buried. Couldn't he be wrapped in a sheet? Or would it appear too much like a shroud? Decisions would need to be made. Were they his to make, with Rebecca and Rich? If not them—who else? He supposed some sort of service was required. The site was finished; it was the obvious place. No doubt a few locals—the bikers and hippies—would turn up; they tended to be sentimental over their own. But who else? Rebecca would know. What might be expected from his poor, afflicted mother? She needed to be offered an opportunity to say goodbye.

He looked over at Terry. Should he cover his face? If the children came in they might be frightened, knowing he was dead, but if he were left uncovered they'd just think he was asleep. But then Pearl might try and wake him, and then what?

He moved around to the side of the bed and leaned over and kissed the boy's cooling forehead. He tasted the saltiness of the perspiration dried on his skin. He paused, lips resting on Terry's forehead, and even though there really was no point, he sent messages of comfort that he hoped might still get through.

PART THREE

Love III

DEATH

'They say eyes clear with age.'

PHILIP LARKIN,
'LONG SIGHT IN AGE'

He was surprised at the lack of bureaucracy when it came to disposing of the body. Legal requirements were straightforward: if it was to be buried, he needed a certificate of death from one doctor; for a cremation he needed certificates from two doctors. It made sense. You can't exhume ashes cast into the wind, and ashes in an urn didn't yield much, even with DNA testing. In this instance, it was accepted that Terry wouldn't have cared what they did with his body, and so their deliberations were mainly for themselves. Rich couldn't believe even a coffin was optional.

After the second doctor had left at nine o'clock, Agnes cleaned Terry and washed his hair. Rich, Rebecca and McCullough sat at the kitchen table, imagining such a job. Rich yawned.

'It needs to be quickish,' was how McCullough started the discussion. 'The body decays. Degrades.'

'Rots,' Rebecca clarified; then asked, 'What day is it anyway?', as though she needed this information for a meaningful timeline to be set out.

'Monday.'

'Really?' Her hand occasionally moved to squeeze Rich's, who seemed distracted, fidgety.

There was no evidence of how upset Rebecca had been in the middle of the night; her skin was bright and warm, her limbs as supple as always. She laughed a lot, which he supposed was unusual.

Together they agreed a 'regular' funeral wasn't quite right. Some kind of service down at the site was a good idea. And it was agreed that whoever wanted to attend was free to do so. What to ask of

Holly, and by extension the twins, he hadn't decided. The twins vaguely remembered the funeral of a great-grandmother two years before and had asked him what was going to happen to Terry, to which he'd replied: 'Good question.'

McCullough then asked Rebecca and Rich what thought they should do with the body. There was a brief pause, after which the usual ideas of disposing of a body 'ceremonially' were proffered: buried at sea, burned on a boat at sea, burned on a pyre on the beach, buried on the site, burned at the site.

'If we buried him we should plant something on top.' Rebecca was doodling 'Terry' across the top of a newspaper, turning it into a lightly filigreed work of curling ivy, then something stronger— baroque ironwork; then all filled in to nothing.

'I quite like that there is only one tree there—an oak. We could bury him next to it.' McCullough turned the paper around and looked at the blue rectangle she'd made, paper torn through. 'What would Freud say?'

'Who cares?'

'Can I make tea?' Rich pushed himself up slowly.

At the counter he put on his bandana, tying it at the back of his neck and positioning it across his forehead; tea-making was the work of a samurai. The whereabouts of everything was pointed out by McCullough from the table; cupboards were opened and closed.

'So what are we going to do?' Rebecca sat back.

'First I hire a van.'

'And just chuck him in the back?'

McCullough needed to stand, to think, work out the stages, and connect them up. 'This is why you call undertakers. They undertake all this stuff. And the grieving family sit in the kitchen drinking tea.'

'How are we going to get down there? Don't the family sit in a car together?' Rich again; he didn't seem to be aware that he'd explicitly referred to them as a family.

Was there a vehicle that could take them all down to the site? Six people, one body, without the undignified and frankly comic outcome of Terry having to travel in a sitting position? He saw no problem in wrapping Terry up in a sheet and folding him in the back, if that was what it took, but they'd need a closed boot. It would be foolish to have a wrapped body visible through the back window; if the twins came along, they were certain to stop a number of times on the way. What he needed was a people carrier for the number of passengers, a closed boot for the body, and an SUV-type vehicle to get across the fields.

'Do you want me to sort out the transport?' Rich dropped teabags into the three mugs. The kettle was clicked on.

'Yes. Then we get a coffin or we wrap Terry up in a sheet. We drive down to the site. It's not a big deal.'

'A coffin will rattle.' Rich was good with such details. Both relevant and irrelevant.

Rebecca sat forward. 'If I had my choice, I'd do the pyre on the beach thing.' She shrugged; she didn't like to be definitive.

'I don't feel strongly.' McCullough looked at Rich, but quickly added, 'It's more what we say. And the music.'

Rebecca sat back and scratched her upper arm. 'He didn't really like music that much. He was strange like that. A bit of in-your-face Hip hop maybe.'

'I'll think of something.'

'We'd never hear it at the beach. We'd have to drag the generator down there. Even then I'm not sure. Depends which way the wind is blowing. And it might be very echoey.' It was said seriously—clearly acoustics was one of Rich's things.

'I'll text a few people. When shall we say?' Rebecca directed this at Rich, now pouring the hot water into the cups.

He shrugged. A quick rattle of a spoon in the cups and then a look around for where to dump the sodden tea bags.

'Under the sink.'

It might not have been noticeable to the others, but McCullough felt slightly panicked by all this, troubled by something essential that he couldn't quite explain—a slippage of material certainty around him, especially the ground, onto which he pressed his feet firmly to feel any new give that might be there; but it was a floating walnut floor, it was meant to allow for movement. He hadn't really slept after Rebecca had gone back up to bed, and when he'd finally dropped into a semi-conscious state his dreams had been full of dread and he awoke sweating. At dawn he'd checked Terry and felt himself in the presence of a ghost. Not the ghost of Terry exactly, just something hovering in the room. It was a combination of the dull light, Terry's pallor lifting off his face, his own immense tiredness. When he'd touched Terry's face, his skin had been cold, and he could feel the body hardening beneath his fingertips; the jaw was already rigid.

Around six o'clock he slept deeply for an hour and then the alarm had gone off, at which point he'd felt like he could sleep for days, but Holly had said he needed to take the twins to see Terry, before they wandered in themselves.

There were no surprises: Pearl refused to go in until she found the right expression and pitch of grief; Walter, at the end of the bed, asked a basic question: 'He's stopped breathing, hasn't he?'

After a shower, McCullough had sat in Agnes's chair dozing, until he was called down for breakfast. On the threshold of the kitchen he stopped. Why were the children in their school uniform? He spotted the chocolate-covered cereal on the table. First day back at school.

'Sorry.'

Holly turned to look at him. 'What for?'

'I had no idea they were back at school today.'

'They start at eleven.'

'I should have remembered.'

'You've had your friend here.'

It wasn't the first time he'd felt like a mysterious visitor, looking in on a family to which he felt connected only in that they recognized him, didn't regard him as mysterious, and yet were at the same time surprised to see him relaxed and willing to fully participate in what was going on. This was something he assumed many fathers and some mothers must experience, and nothing to do with him in any special way, including having been away most of the summer. He didn't question their love for him. He felt loved, matter-of-factly, which he assumed was the best kind of love. Yet he still felt separated. If he was honest he was more connected to the dead boy upstairs, clearer in his friendship with Rebecca, easier in his manner with Rich. This was why he'd forgotten another important day in the lives of his children. Holly recognized this, but had decided to ignore it. Yesterday she had said she rather liked having a full house. But it was more than a full house for him. There were more than people present; God and death were also guests, and that was too much. Was it really only six months ago when the mention of God was something to be politely or not so politely ignored, and death in the house unthinkable in a family with young children? Now both would have to be reconciled if he were to be properly present for both families, to be committed to them all.

Death was most pressing. It was upstairs, stubbornly inside the body of a boy who had remained baffling to the end. He supposed 'inside' was right, at least as a superficial description. Not that it felt like an occupying force. But when he was sitting there reading, listening to Terry's breathing, and then heard the sudden choke, the sound of the small heart attack that killed him, it was as if the boy's internal world was cancelled and absence had moved in. For some this was a description of God—the presence of absence. Well, it was certainly true of death. How had Terry experienced it? Had there been any awareness that this was his last moment in time? Was it experienced as qualitatively different, as a half moment—the other half (perhaps this was the great mystery: there wasn't another half) happening outside of time, not in the sacred sense, for there was no reason to believe time persisted on the other side? If Wittgenstein was right and death wasn't an event in life, in some curious way it might be said to not happen at all. Except few would argue that was really the case. So in the end, death was a known event that couldn't in itself be known. What an awful conundrum for creatures desperate for knowledge, for answers. If he compared death to the birth of the twins—now there were two knowable events, graspable and nuzzle-able. Worlds in his hands. But that didn't mean he wasn't equally baffled when presented with them, minutes after they arrived, and for days, weeks, months after—still. Death didn't have that privilege alone. Nor God. The least that might be said of death was that it created problems to solve. In this case, transport, notifying the Crown Prosecution Service, the Prison Service, deciding what to do about Terry's mother, how to manage a dead body during a hot summer. Events in life.

Rebecca had finally insisted Terry would have liked that idea of being thrown on a fire: wasn't that how they all remembered him, squatting there, poking away at the small flames of their campfire? McCullough wondered how quickly Terry would burn, so stripped of flesh and fat. But in the end they agreed that Terry would have approved of such a straightforward and honest approach. A body, devoid of self and soul, thrown on a fire, burned down into ashes, and left to be blown away on the breeze, and depending on its direction, either dispersed among the grey rocks or dissolved in the waves.

In the kitchen doorway, standing loosely in his own clothes, McCullough felt that he would soon be similarly reduced to the weight of Terry's dying body. In a few days he'd have the body/mass index of a mystic, as if he'd actively chosen to dull the grosser senses with abstinence. What had Terry said: punish the body to release the soul? McCullough doubted he himself would be able to withstand such punishment, abandoned in the desert, eating only locusts, resisting temptations, open to further influxes of questionable visions. The only emptying out he could make sense of needed to happen in the presence of others, as an example, or as a resource, to show that even as finite repositories of love we must still give. If he was ever to become so thinned out, it must be because he was used up; others had used him up. He realized (and if he didn't, Holly would remind him) that there were plenty of reasons to be suspicious of this: he was not without a desire to be well thought of, admired, even adored. But this was all part of it. To go out into the world with his weaknesses, to be as widely human as possible, and yet always trying to tilt for the good . . .

Pearl swivelled in her seat. 'Are you going to have Coco Pops for breakfast, Daddy?'

Daddy. That was his name. For his children he was the definition of the word. As the children grew up that definition would change, as they extended over time and space their feelings would become more complex, reflective, judgmental. There was little chance his relationship with Pearl was going to be without issues later in life. But that was good: it was going to be *their* life together. It would never be short of love, and, on McCullough's side, astonishment. And then there was Walter, who needed him, relied on him, and yet required of him only one thing: constancy of behaviour when it was asked for. That Walter was content to be alone and was happily self-sustaining for most of the time was a blessing. It promised happiness where McCullough had feared loneliness. But he also needed to accept that his role as an unconditional giver of attention was essential to Walter's trust in the world. In that way, the days and weeks when he had been away were no more of a problem to Walter than when he was at work. Walter didn't regard him as much absent as hidden. The constancy of presence was felt.

So it should be easy to step into the room and be with them as much as was possible, engaged, interested, a hands-on father, pourer of milk, mopper-up of spills; tidier of hair, collars, shirt-tails. Most importantly, maker of jokes Mummy wouldn't approve of. All three were there, turned from the table, looking at him, waiting.

But what then? Didn't he also need to offer this unconditional love beyond this threshold? What if he didn't have enough for both families? He no longer felt full or abundant as he surely must if he was to be there for all those who needed him. He no longer felt the intimation of a great inflowing. The reverse: he felt depleted, used up. But then it wasn't really about love. That was taken for granted, by them all, Rebecca and Rich included, as it should be. It was about more than his presence in the room. It was his mood, his attentiveness. No one required he declare his love every day, to somehow prove it. But then neither did they want him just to be there as an administrator of life. And inevitably this was what would happen—he would turn to the problems that needed solving. And that meant whilst he would always be there, he would be distracted, frustrated, his feelings for everyone a beat behind. He would be a broken and fragmented self, pretending continuity. Even now he was split, listening for movement upstairs, as he did in the evening with the twins, but this time for the stirrings of two teenagers, a son and daughter who were on his mind for very different reasons.

After Holly left with the children for school, he lay on his bed with his laptop and searched car-hire websites. He was too tired to make a decision and called Rebecca, who descended from the loft with a quick and unaccountably heavy tread. To see what he was doing, she lay down next to him.

'I went to see Terry and he's all stiff.'

'Rigor mortis.'

'I know. How long does it last?'

'Doctor said a day in this weather.'

'That would look funny, carrying him out of the house.'

'I should alert the neighbours.'

'Or not.'

They both laughed.

'Me and Rich are going into London. On the Tube. Rich is a bit freaked out. He hasn't been in the room yet. He's back in his sleeping bag. Do you want to come?'

'No, thank you. But thanks for asking. What are you going to do?'

'He's agreed to the Tate Modern.'

'Did he have any choice?'

'Not really.'

'Look after him.'

'I'll hold his hand.'

'You don't have to hurry back. Do you want some money?' He pointed to where his wallet was on the chest of drawers. 'Just take it as a fallback.' She hopped up and handed it to him. He gave her everything in it.

'Thanks, Dad.' She kissed his cheek; it was a nuanced performance. It made him feel pleasantly old, his age.

For the rest of the afternoon, with everyone out, and before school ended, the children charging in noisy with tiredness, McCullough sat with Terry and read more of *The Brothers Karamazov*. Terry's stillness was not unsettling and he allowed himself to inwardly address the boy, content to think of him existing elsewhere, although he didn't believe that was the case. Banally, he said to himself that

Terry lived on inside him and Rebecca, and that was enough. Terry had never been a great conversationalist, his gifts had been different.

When the children returned home and were given their screen time, he sat with them watching a Pixar film. Midway through he dozed off. He was vaguely aware of the film ending and Holly summoning the children out of the room, and of being covered with a throw. His body contracted in the warmth and he succumbed to a deep sleep. He dreamed he was lying on his back in an empty landscape, eyes open staring up at a blazing sun. He felt himself to be finally free from all the chaos of the world, slowly distilled to his essence, both creaturely and transcendent, his soul seeping through the atomic structures of his body. Like a conductor's hand over a musical score, a floating presence gently coaxed him to release more of himself, to give in and become one with the universe, its abiding and sustaining force. When this had happened before, he had believed it wasn't in his power to hold back; it had been more like a smash and grab, or a tearing apart, like he was mozzarella stretched between two slices of pizza. But now as he slept, he felt that he was being offered the supreme choice: to join with God and be infinitely restored or stay put and carry on as he was. It wasn't a zero-sum game—what he had already been given would remain with him. And yet as always, he resisted, because he feared being taken fully. He didn't want Holly to call him, and then when she came to look for him to be found missing, the blanket fluttering flat. But then he asked himself, 'Why take me and not bring me back?' He listened for a moment, but there was no answer. Of course, there would never be an answer. But that didn't matter. So he breathed in and filled his lungs full of air and released himself.

DEATH IN LIFE

'The two worlds are asleep, are sleeping, now.
A dumb sense possesses them in a kind of solemnity.'

WALLACE STEVENS,
AN OLD MAN ASLEEP

I

The twins immediately rolled down the bank, arms clasped tightly at their sides, hands flat to their thighs, bodies as stiff as instinct would allow. It was thick, soft mud at the bottom, but Holly didn't mind, saying, 'I've brought a change of clothes.'

McCullough held Holly's hand as she was taken over the field and presented with what had been built. It scared her, moved her; it seemed unreal. Nothing about the two buildings fitted the landscape, except that they were there and the landscape surrounded them. No matter what McCullough had said about it being a barn, or an artwork, a municipal sculpture, the main building was no other thing than a church. The house was recognizably a house. It seemed disproportionately small, a miniature dwelling, although there was no real difference in size. As for the church, the others—Rebecca, Rich—talked about it as if it were nothing more than a big shed or greenhouse, just something difficult to erect, always referring to the place generally as 'the site', never intimating its strangeness. Had she not been paying attention, had she not seen the photographs on his phone? She vaguely remembered McCullough saying the idea for the beams had come from Simon, and that Rebecca had made it work, and that if they were lucky it might redefine what was thought of as a church, but at other times he had also seemed bored and spoken of the entire enterprise as a mistake, a knee-jerk reaction, a cliché. Was this some sort of double bluff or reverse psychology? She didn't think so. Yet did he know what he'd built on this clifftop? Again, the others joked: at least it'll keep the rain out—maybe. On the drive down, McCullough had wondered aloud what it might look like a thousand years from now. But she realized that even with all the glass smashed and the stone gone the way of stone over many years, it would be unaltered.

'It's what you get when a bunch of amateurs set out and actually finish.' This was Rebecca passing by.

'Yes,' was all she could say.

McCullough watched the children, mud pressed into their clothes, knees, hair. Walter stopped in front of him and asked one of his odder questions: 'Did you bring us here?'

'Yes.'

'Thanks, Daddy.'

They loved to roll and would only usually stop if ordered, but the cliff's edge offered fascination and fear, and they were told that if they wanted to look over it they would have to lie on their stomachs. Then there was the beach and the sea below. For Walter, this was the moment when he'd remember the wonder of the waves.

As far as being interested in what their daddy had built, the buildings were no more fun, or different from, other weird buildings they'd been taken to.

Without much discussion, Rich had taken Terry from the car, on to his shoulder, and brought him down to be placed in the church. If Nathaniel were alive it would have been he who would have carried Terry.

McCullough led Holly across the ridge and down the bank. The earth between the two buildings had been turned and churned; there were ruts elbow-deep. Nature would need help to heal them.

'I cordoned this off originally. To protect the thick grass. I loved the grass here. It was like moorland. Like up there.' He pointed to the horizon.

'Mac—what do you see when you look at this?'

He gazed at the two buildings, one either side. 'I don't know. But I appreciate the church is more sculpture now than a building. I don't know what that means—whether it's a failure or not.'

'Do you like it?'

He followed the six steels that projected above their heads, spreading in different directions, the great intersecting beam emerging from the earth and finishing abruptly in the air and yet in his mind somehow continuing on into the sky.

'What do I think? I don't know. It's been instrumental, I suppose. Rather than anything else. What do you think?'

'It's like I don't know you, Mac. And I don't mean that—you know—in the way we've been . . . How did you . . . ?'

'Don't give me any of the credit. I just bankrolled it. We just bankrolled it. And let's not forget, it's been like building the pyramids—it's cost lives.' He paused. 'The original vision was for something more modest, a shack, or a timber and stone house, a small meeting place. Really quite old-fashioned and conservative.'

'Well, this is certainly not a *church* church.'

'It's got a kind of steeple.'

'A fallen steeple.'

It did look like that, if you had a predisposition to see something tipping over rather than righting itself. Holly was the latter way in most things. He noticed her angling her head to see what a different perspective might bring, and narrowing her eyes as if trying to make out an obscured image. As for him, this was the first time he'd seen the building 'finished', workers gone, most of the large items of machinery removed. What *did* he think? It seemed as if the stone, timber and glass fitted together, which was good, and the great steels, if looked at a certain way might be deemed a deconstructed steeple, whatever that might mean, or looked at another way—upside down, as Holly was doing—as an anchor of sorts, which he supposed was also good. Whether the buildings were in accord with the landscape, or by some creative tension revealed something not intrinsically present in either, he didn't know. At least not yet. Whether or not they might create accord or tension in those who encountered them, he doubted he'd ever know.

Holly squeezed his hand. 'You are a mysterious person, Mac.'

It was decided that Rebecca and Rich would go into the village and try and get some sense of the numbers planning to come, which meant, as Rebecca pointed out, going round the pubs.

McCullough asked them also to listen out for what other people were saying—this wasn't going to be without insult to those who knew Nathaniel, and some might think such an unorthodox send-off was a celebration.

'What do we say?' Rich needed guidance.

'They should speak to me.'

'I'll handle it, Rich.' Rebecca would never be shy of an answer in any confrontation; in this way she was like Terry. In only that way.

When they were at the top of the ridge, McCullough called, 'And go and see your mother, Rebecca.'

Holly asked, 'What's her mother like—as beautiful?'

'Different. Attractive, yes.'

It would be time soon to go and see Terry's mother; he didn't want to. What would he find?

Holly had laid out a picnic. The twins, finally bored of rolling down the ridge, of staring over the cliff, were now playing in the house, treating it as their own, mostly pretending disasters—volcanoes, air raids, a zombie apocalypse. They each played many parts. It was a rare moment of shared endeavour, as they consciously enjoyed getting on, being generous to one another: Pearl, the great maker of rules—being flexible; Walter, the great insister on rule-following—giving way to changes of plan.

Holly opened wine. 'Don't say it.'

'Say what?'

'Look how happy they'd be down here.'

'I hadn't planned to, but look how happy they'd be down here.'

There were tubs with the contents for sandwiches—Serrano ham, Manchego cheese, thick slices of tomato, rocket, and olive oil and balsamic vinegar mixed in an old jar of olives.

The children were called, and arrived interested only in what there was to drink, which they quickly consumed. Running back down the slope they picked up speed and momentum, but managed to stay upright.

Holly was a patient sandwich-maker. 'OK. I admit it. It's lovely.'

Half an hour later, they all walked down to the beach. There was a light breeze that seemed to undulate with differing temperatures, gentle strokes of cool and warm against their arms. The twins were sent off to collect quartz and search for ammonites, and given permission to paddle in their Crocs.

Holly looked up at the cliffs, their obstinate and unadorned height. 'It seems dangerous. For children.' Under their feet were the grey and cold pebbles on which he'd lain for hours after he'd fallen. He remembered their give as he had tried to move, a grinding rearrangement against one another, a collapsing of space.

'No one has fallen.'

'Not yet.'

'Children walk with their parents all the time across the clifftops. But don't worry, I'm not going to suggest we live here.'

They sat down and tossed pebbles, awkwardly underhand, into the shallow waves, watching the splashes.

'So it's going to be here? On this beach you'll do it?'

'It's what I'd imagined.'

'You do realize that we'll be bringing up children who've seen a man cremated on a funeral pyre on a beach.'

'It's called modern parenting.'

'I'm not sure it's that modern. Some people would think of it as abuse.'

'Some people think our children's limited screen time is abuse. Others that it's abuse that they get so much.'

'Maybe this would unite them.'

The night before, the children between them, they'd explained what was going to happen. When someone was cremated, usually, at least these days, in this country, a coffin was put on a conveyor belt and went through a door. But it would be slightly different for Terry: they were going to build a bonfire. ('Great—can we help?') Then, wrapped nicely in a sheet, Terry would be placed on the fire, like they still did in some other countries. ('Will there be fireworks?' 'No, darling.') Then they would all think quietly about who had died. ('Terry?') And then they'd go and stay in a little hotel.

The children had been keen to get away, bored as only seriousness bored them, but McCullough kept them back for a moment and asked whether they understood. They nodded. Then fled.

Holly put her hand on his knee. 'I still want life to go back to normal, Mac. After this.'

He knew she worried that Terry's illness and death were an intermission, a tragic diversion, and that tomorrow or the next day he would be faced with nothing to do, no work, no project, and perhaps even the depression that followed such emotional exertion. But now was not the time.

The children had moved along the bottom of the cliffs and Walter had found driftwood to smash on the rocks and throw into the sea and watch float back in. The results required repetition; he was a natural experimenter. Pearl returned alone with a splinter in her palm, which she brought to her father, knowing he had the patience, the concentration and the knack for removal. One end poked out; the rest was shallowly visible under the skin, and looked like a tiny insect in its cocoon. To remove it required pressing and pinching and a story to distract her, which involved telling her that he might have to push it in and hope it came out in her poo, then commanding her attention with the grim details of horrible worms that humans sometimes ingested and which burrowed out through the skin, often at the ankles, or even the corner of people's eyes. Holly suggested getting tweezers from the car, but he was certain his nails could ease it out.

Producing a high echo from the cliff face, Walter cried out, 'Crab!' Pearl spun round on her bottom. Crabs had always been important creatures in their beach-roving. 'Hurry up, Daddy.'

'It'll wait.'

'But it might scuttle off.'

Her urgency, the right verb of motion, moved him. He remembered teaching them the sounds of animals, but no one had taught them the verbs of motion. He'd noticed when they had first said 'scurrying' for ants: 'They're scurrying everywhere, Daddy.' They were on the decking outside the kitchen doors. It was the day he'd first placed his finger over the end of a hose and created a great fan of water. His easy ability to produce this had seemed a miracle to the children, and because their small garden provided nowhere to hide, for them or the ants, it meant everyone was drenched. It was one of those moments when he realized the twins took it for granted that he possessed great powers.

The splinter was out, and was peered at and shown to Holly, and then placed in a tissue to show Walter later. Over by the rock pool the children both stared down at the crab, Pearl listening to Walter explain whatever he'd learned about crabs; she always liked to defer to his knowledge—it gave her pleasure to be good in this way.

McCullough leaned back on his elbows, pushing away at the stones to get comfortable, and looked out over the sea, his chin on his chest. 'I'm sorry. I never wanted to put our family at risk.'

'I know.' Holly was leaning forward, all sloping back and breezy hair; from the waist of her jeans bulged full firm flesh.

'What I don't understand, Mac, is how you've been allowed to do this, build this?' She looked around at him, resting her chin on her shoulder.

'It's not mysterious. The land has a covenant allowing for church-building. This goes back to the 1650s. And then there is will. My will. Or perhaps more relevantly: faith. For a few days I believed this would be built more than anyone else believed it wouldn't. Only a few days. At the beginning.'

'You know I don't believe any of that. It's not how things operate. You're either legally allowed or not allowed to build on a piece of land.'

'Clearly I was allowed. So no mystery.'

The twins appeared before them, Pearl with a dead crab in her palm the size of a shrimp. 'It's a baby,' she explained.

'Was,' McCullough couldn't help but correct her.

'Still is. A dead baby crab.' Walter didn't like inaccuracy from an adult.

'Is either of you hungry?' Holly asked.

Both of them nodded, and mother and father stood up and turned towards the break in the cliffs.

Rich and Rebecca had returned and were collecting small piles of timber offcuts from around the site. They sorted them as if some bits of wood were not fit for burning. Rich had a plan so the fire would light easily and then burn strongly. According to Rebecca twenty people might turn up, maybe more. But not loads. She'd said eight o'clock—was that right?

'What about your mum?'

'She'll be here, I think.'

Away from Rebecca, Holly said, 'You seem very keen for her mother to come.'

2

At the door of Terry's house, he paused as he had done the night of the murder, but this time it felt worse because he had just been with his own family and was not beside himself with exhaustion and shock, doing what he believed was the right thing, automatically. Now he was anticipating Terry's mother's condition: the dullness in her eyes, the old signs of a desperate life, the uncertainty of what she might understand. His impulse to turn and leave felt cowardly. It was cowardly. It was selfish. The action was back at the site and that was where he wanted to be.

It required an act of will to knock. He heard a noise from inside almost immediately and footsteps coming to the door.

The woman smiled and explained that she was Debs's carer, Jackie. Behind her, the house was clean, the former strong smell gone. A radio was on in the kitchen. She invited him in before he'd said anything more than his name. Was she expecting him?

'Debs is upstairs sleeping. She came down for her lunch. I insist on that. But she does like a nap in the afternoon. I'm just putting the kettle on.'

She led him into the kitchen. 'She sometimes talks about her son, Terry, but I'd stay away from that. I don't think she knows. She thinks he's still a little boy.'

'He's why I'm here.'

Jackie stiffened at this. Had he tricked her? He didn't think so.

'You're not the doctor?'

'No. I'm sorry—I should have said. I'm a friend . . . of her son's.'

Should he also inform this woman that he'd commissioned the agency that employed her?

She was watchful now, eager to defend herself against assumed judgments. 'She won't go outside. I've tried. She just won't. It's not my business why. If you don't believe me, ask her yourself.' The former warmth towards her patient had gone.

'It's OK. I'm not here to snoop or to judge you. I just want to talk to her. It's Terry's funeral today.'

'Suit yourself.' Jackie was struggling; it was in her nature to be helpful. But she didn't like surprises.

'Maybe you should wake her. She doesn't know me.'

'I expect you want me to bring her down?'

'No. Unless you think it's best. I'll speak to her wherever she is most comfortable.'

'She never gets out of bed unless I insist. Sometimes not even for the toilet. I've got a plastic sheet under there now. I do laundry every day.'

'I'm sure it's not easy.'

'I'm used to it.' She didn't want her competency, readiness to work, disputed.

'Please, I don't have much time. I just need to know whether she understands what's happening, and if so, if she wants to attend.'

'You're wasting your time, but it's up to you. She doesn't have any lucid days.' Jackie was getting used to him, and judged him to be less of a threat.

'I just need to check. It would be wrong to exclude her if . . .'

The kettle was turned off. There would be no tea.

'I did wonder about a funeral.'

'You knew he died?'

'I heard.' Then, 'Are you the man from London?'

They were around the same age. 'Yes. Terry has been with me.'

There was a gleam of curiosity in her eyes. It wasn't so much an opportunity to extract details for gossip, more that the son of the woman she looked after had chopped off the head of a local boy, and Jackie was therefore involved, and entitled to be kept informed.

'Sorry—I need to go up, if that's OK? I have to get back.'

'You'll get nothing.'

'I'm sure you're right.'

Jackie looked disappointed.

From the bottom of the stairs, she called up, 'Debs darling, the man from London is here.' Then to McCullough, more warmly, as if she wanted to keep him where he was: 'My old mum had it. But she was in her eighties. This one—she's not forty-five. I found photos. She was pretty. But you could see she hung out with the wrong sort.'

'She's been very unlucky.'

Agreement didn't sit comfortably; Jackie liked her opinions to stand without comment, and repeated herself: 'You'll not get anything from her.'

'I know. Thank you.'

The windows were open, nets billowing, the room being aired. The bedside table had a crocheted doily spread over the top. Medicines were grouped into bottles and packets. The tumbler of water was clean. Terry's mother was on top of the bed, on her side, turned away from him, her knees drawn up. Her hair had a shine to it, the black T-shirt and stonewashed jeans were clean. Her bone-white skin seemed scrubbed. Had Jackie, on her first day, sat her in the bath and showered her down? He could picture this: the temperature of the water never right, a struggle, a stranger making demands on her—arm up, lean back, close your eyes. Jackie would have been thorough. It must have been painful and distressing, but she would at least have felt free of the dried sweat, her own heavy, sticky smell. He imagined before being washed her body must have felt as if it adhered to her clothes like a larva within its casing. It was because of this change in her appearance that McCullough sensed her sleep was a choice, that she really was taking a nap and not hiding in a deep medicated slumber from which she was unable, or unwilling, to wake.

Now he knew her name he thought he should call her from the doorway. But it didn't feel right. Instead he whispered a cautious, hesitant 'hello'.

She didn't stir. He tried her name. 'Debs?' Nothing. He'd been mistaken: the fresh air, clean sheets, the shine of her hair—he'd read them as signs of a new kind of life, that she might be inwardly refreshed, the paths to reach her cleared away. Yet nothing within her registered this strange man was present. No instincts were at play.

The upward movement of the nets distracted him. The billowing had a lateral movement, like a Mexican wave. He moved to the end of the bed. A hard shudder passed through the sleeping woman, a throb. But it was muscular, reflexive. A sign of nothing.

He walked around to the side of the bed and kneeled down. He'd been mistaken again: up close her face was no different from last time—pale, sweating, pitted. He whispered her name and then laid his hand on her shoulder and gently shook her.

Her eyes opened. There was no fear or recoil, just incomprehension. She stared at him for a few seconds and then her eyelids dropped as if it were a strain to keep them open, like a child woken from a deep sleep. He'd seen this years ago in addicts when they were disturbed. Why choose real life?

McCullough moved his hand from her shoulder to her face, to her cheek. If she couldn't understand who he was or what he was going to say, he hoped at least she might sense the tenderness he felt for her, as Terry's mother.

'Please don't be scared. I'm a friend. I want to talk to you about Terry.'

Was there the faintest tremor of recognition at the sound of her son's name, or was it his hand trembling on her cheek? Maybe this was the only way they might communicate, via the tiniest vibrations of feeling. He needed to assume she was like her son and open to him in ways that were not explicit. But there was no reason to believe this was the case. It had been a mistake to come. He was here out of a misplaced sense of duty, with no sense of what to expect or what to do. In the drive over, he'd tried to foresee the conversation, but in truth he'd only imagined his part, a consoling monologue, as if performing some kind of pastoral care.

He started to explain, falteringly, his mouth dry, hand still trembling on her cheek. 'Terry died three days ago. He was comfortable and looked after. He did a terrible thing, a really terrible thing, and nothing will make that right. But in his own way . . . he was a good person.' (Was that right? Did it matter now?) His legs ached, and he sat up a little. 'I'm here because it's his funeral today, and I want you to know, if you want . . . you must come. I will help you. You will be looked after. Rebecca will be there.'

He moved his thumb across her cheek, as he had often done to Walter when he had tonsillitis or Pearl an earache, and he wanted to send messages of safety and calm, and smooth away any resistance to a tranquil and restful sleep.

He sensed another shudder, this time just beneath her skin, a field of nerve endings repelling his touch. Had she understood what he'd said and now wanted him to leave? He had to ask himself: was this a kind of wish-fulfilment on his part? If she somehow indicated she want to come with him, how would he manage her? Even getting her from the bed to the car—it would be impossible. There were sure to be moments of panic.

He studied her face. It was in his nature to be alert to subtle signs of reaction; it had been his job for twenty years. He often had to remind clients: there is never nothing in a face; there is always something to discern. But in her stillness she seemed no different from the dead body of her son. And yet he had to believe that there must be something present, however hidden it might be—a field of consciousness, an emergent self: something. But he also knew that whatever he discerned might equally be a projection, an assumption of feeling. It was, after all, possible she wasn't feeling anything at all. What if she were now only governed by her biological self, an aspect of being that is only concerned with life at its basic? Maybe all that could be said of her behaviour presented to the woman downstairs was that it was muscle memory, habit, the body behaving as it must to survive; even her response to her son's name was now just a reflex.

So she would not be coming with him. All that was left to him was to say goodbye, as perhaps the last person to look on her tenderly. Few people would now think of her as a mother, or imagine what she might have been like with a little boy playing at her feet, held in her arms. It didn't matter what she'd done to herself to take away whatever pain she was in—there would have been moments of love, of wonder, surprise and laugher, of a little boy clambering onto his mother's lap and the warmth created there between them. But that was now at an end. She was in a slow, inexorable decline, waiting for some biological event to end her completely. No one would ever know what deep, unanswerable yearnings for her son remained within her, a mute love sent out into the world, and finding no love object, returned to her without explanation—a definition of hell by anyone's reckoning.

He kissed her on the temple. She tasted of death.

SERMON ON THE BEACH

'Begin, and cease, and then again begin,
With tremulous cadence slow, and bring
The eternal note of sadness in.'

MATTHEW ARNOLD,
DOVER BEACH

I

It took just over an hour to build the pyre, taking armfuls of timber down to the beach, the twins rushing back and forth with single pieces, often too big to hold, so that they were dragged over the earth and grass, leaving a scored line. Rich stayed on the beach and constructed a small airy wigwam inside the main frame and filled it full of wood shavings and kindling and newspaper. After the armature of planks was laid around the wigwam, Rich allowed wood to be thrown on by anyone, as long as it landed pretty much vertically. Once the structure was almost complete, he and McCullough created a small platform halfway up, two planks deep, where Terry would be laid. This wood had been soaked in seawater so it wouldn't burn before Terry was placed there. The pyre was so high and wide at its base, Rich and McCullough would need to step inside the outlying wood to set Terry up there. Rich cleared a little space.

Kicking pebbles up against the outermost wood for extra support, he asked McCullough, 'Is this what you had in mind?' It was a question McCullough had asked him many times over the last three months; in this case he'd been given no vision—it had been Rebecca's idea. He looked at his hands; he was trembling again. Driving back from Terry's mother's house, he knew that he had abandoned her. But he also knew that the only practical solution to her solitude was to take her back to London to be looked after in his home, and that was impossible. Of course, he might have taken her life, as an act of mercy, returning her to Terry, but that was beyond him, and a sentimental thought. At a bend in a narrow lane he'd almost hit two children running ahead of their parents.

'I need to see my family.'

Rich followed him up to the site, oblivious to the older man's mood. 'Are you going to say something, Mac? Some people who are coming knew Nat.'

'I knew Nat.'

'I know. But you seem to have forgotten him.'

McCullough stopped. How many of the dead must he contain?

'Of course I haven't. I think of him every day. I told you before . . . there was nothing I could do for Nat. Terry was suffering.' It had become as simple as that; there was no softer or fuller version: David and his son, Judas, other examples that might make what he believed clearer, more acceptable.

'He should have suffered. Nat was my friend.'

'Terry's need was greater.'

'How do you know that—you're not God. We all thought you were scared of him—Terry.'

Why was the boy trying to pick a fight now?

'"Scared" isn't the right word. He unsettled me. I thought he was some kind of angel. A possessor of truth.'

'I don't understand that, Mac. He killed Nat. You can't think he's an angel now, after he did that?' Rich didn't like to make eye contact when he asked such questions.

'I don't know. No, of course not. I don't know what I think anymore.'

'I want to understand. I really do.'

He clutched Rich by the upper arms and stared into the boy's gentle eyes. 'OK, Rich, if you really want to know what I think . . . try this. It's not my idea, so it's got nothing to do with Nat or Terry, and even though I'm going talk about Jesus, it's not even a religious idea, or maybe it is—I don't know.

'Before Jesus, love was a limited and narrow emotion binding together lovers and families, a kind of local emotion, perhaps even a fitness adaptation to make society function, a sublimation of order, power, obedience. But *after* Jesus, love became a way of being in the world, a new way of being, replacing power and obedience. After Jesus, love became a way to live, and that included loving sinners as well as saints. More so. That's the point.'

'You're not Jesus. And I don't understand what this has to do with Nat and Terry.'

You're not God; you're not Jesus. He knew this.

'I don't understand why he did it.'

Of course he didn't. Who could make that claim?

'No one does, Rich. Maybe Terry didn't know. Maybe even God doesn't know.'

Rich looked at the ground. 'So you don't think God gave him cancer?'

McCullough pictured Terry's mother. He brought Rich into his arms. 'No, Rich. Life would be simple, if that were the case.'

2

From the clifftop, the beach around the pyre looked desolate, the rocks without mercy or pity. The pyre might have been assembled by others and left there, a statement whose meaning it was impossible to discern. It was larger than he'd expected, perhaps more like the shack he'd originally thought to build. All the wood left over from the construction had been used. In that way, also, this was an ending.

People began to arrive, a varied bunch, mostly drinkers. They knew one another and moved between small groups, beer cans wedged in baggy pockets, or carried in double-bagged carrier bags, handles stretched from the weight. Everyone rolled their own ciga-rettes; joints were openly made. A disinterested onlooker would have formed the wrong impression of Terry, but McCullough wondered whether on some basic level they would have been right: these people did represent Terry, or at least the world in which he had lived much of his life—it was in the nature of these people to let him be himself, to drink and pontificate, to be smart, to be angry, to be left alone. Without consciously thinking it, McCullough wanted to be surprised by the composition of the crowd, and find people who, like him, had discovered something special in Terry, and then to look further and see hordes coming over the hills, because as a charismatic he had amassed followers everywhere he went, and news of his death had spread in ways that couldn't be explained. But this hadn't happened. There were fifteen or so standing on the ridge. Should they have tried to get the message out beyond the village? Would that have made a difference? Probably not.

Simon appeared, followed by Marvin, both dressed exactly as before. McCullough had called Marvin, to invite him down, with little expectation he would come. But as Marvin made clear: a burning body on a pyre on an ancient beach—nothing would keep him and his camera away.

Simon strode over to McCullough and hugged him; he was stronger than he looked and his embrace was powerful.

'Thank you for coming, Simon.'

'Marvin drove. He wanted to come.'

'You didn't?'

'I did.'

'I'm glad. How are you?'

'I went out with Jane again.'

'Really. That's good.'

'Another disaster.'

'I'm sorry.'

Simon shrugged.

Marvin shook McCullough's hand. 'I have no news. Good or bad. How are you?'

McCullough laughed. 'It's complicated.'

'I'll say. I've got Lucien tied up in the boot. We thought we'd throw him on the pyre as a starter. We *are* planning to eat the boy, right?'

Simon was examining a flint in the softening light. 'He hasn't got Lucien in the boot.' Good to get the facts straight.

Marvin walked down to the pyre, camera in his fist. Out of habit he still used a viewfinder and turned the lens in ways not often seen these days. He took contextualizing close-ups of pebbles, gently breaking waves, the grain of the timber. Even his photographs of the cliffs were more colour and texture than anything suggesting scale. When he passed people, he said 'Just ignore me', as if he were at a wedding. It was difficult. He was unlike anyone else there and brought with him a dark worldliness—it was clear he didn't live as others did. McCullough instantly thought of Judith. Of introducing them.

Geoffrey arrived, his short old legs struggling over the tussocks of grass, his huge stomach falling out of his white baggy shirt. The end of his walking stick had collected a hard plug of mud. His beard seemed longer, in a point at his chest, and his face pinker from the long summer sun and blotched with red from exertion. He wasn't too out of breath to talk.

'I've prepared something, old boy. A few words. Feel free to call upon me. But I really don't mind if you don't.'

McCullough placed his hand on the old man's shoulder, pleased he was there. 'Thank you for coming.'

'Ha—that's usually what I say! Good luck.'

'You went to Nat's funeral . . . ?'

'I did. Nice boy. Difficult family. But still.' Geoffrey paused and looked around. 'Have to say, this looks tremendous. You non-denominational chaps have a good eye for what will get noticed.'

McCullough drew in a big breath. 'I'm not sure that was my intention, and I'm not sure I can be called non-denominational. I might make the place a gift to "you chaps".'

'See if we can't plant something down here . . . If Holy Trinity Brompton get a whiff of it, they'll be here in a shot. But I guess you don't mean them. Actually I'm not really sure what I'm talking about. Bit out of my comfort zone. Anyway, it's a wonderful place you've built. But I do have to ask myself: who'll come?'

Attendance numbers preoccupied him, as they did other Anglicans: a church needs a congregation. McCullough wasn't sure he believed that was true. Hadn't he once been told that conducting services was essential even when performed to empty pews? You don't pack up and go just because no one is there; that is to misunderstand the nature of the sacred and ritual. Of course, the opposite is also true: just go wherever there is the need.

McCullough smiled. 'We should discuss it some other time.'

'Indeed. But as I said, I've prepared something. Do call on me if you want.' He looked around him, grinned amiably and then said, 'Rum bunch.'

McCullough laughed.

Across the field, Rebecca walked to meet her mother. Judith was in a patterned summer dress, sandals, satchel strap worn across her body, hair tied up. It seemed a kind of moral error to have her walk across fields, but he accepted that it merely didn't suit her—she was not built for uneven ground. He joined them when they reached the top of the ridge.

'Hello, Judith.'

He was allowed to kiss her; at least that was what it felt like—permission granted.

Rebecca left them, to walk over to the small group of drinkers and casually sip from an offered can.

'Thank you for looking after Rebecca. She's finally found a father. Maybe a mother as well.'

Judith's voice was a set of contradictions, somehow peremptory and yet warm and teasing, but also indifferent to its impact. Her expression was the same: her eyes flashed, her smile was loveliness, and then just like her daughter during those early days, she looked bored. He had to accept that her feelings for him might exist at both ends of the spectrum and everywhere in between, or perhaps nowhere. To confess that he loved her, or for a time had loved her, was certain to provoke laughter.

'It's nice to see you. Thank you for coming. How's the book going?'

'It's fine. I think. I hope. It's work.'

'Holly is here.'

'And your children.'

'Yes.'

'Do they know it is here that God chose to take form before you?'

Her voice betrayed nothing—neither belief nor incomprehension.

'No.'

She found his hand and held it for a moment and then moved away. Seen by Holly it would seem no more than a compassionate gesture, to wish him good luck for the rest of what would be a difficult evening. Perhaps that was all it was.

Rich came up to him. 'Do you think we should start the fire? It might take a while to get going.'

'Where is Terry?'

'I moved him to the doorway.' Rich pointed blindly behind him to the church. 'I think he might smell a bit.'

'He would have liked that.'

'So what are we going to do?'

McCullough looked up at the sky. The blue was losing its intensity, but true night wouldn't arrive for a couple of hours, and the stars later still. He imagined each star switching itself on, not in unison with others, but randomly, as a complicated set of old electrics behind the firmament did their thing. He could imagine the wiring, the valves and conductors, everything built haphazardly over time, and in its own way as beautiful as the stars it powered. He wasn't usually quite so fanciful, but he also considered the possibility of its truth, that above the night sky it was really like this and all the astronomers and astrophysicists had just made a huge mistake. In this instance, little was to be gained by recognizing the rest of the universe.

He looked back at Rich. 'We don't want people standing around as it catches, waiting . . . I don't think.'

There were now thirty or so people. Some were probably merely curious, drawn by word going round the pubs that a man was to be cremated on the beach. McCullough found himself searching for members of Nathaniel's family. Was it possible they'd come? He didn't think so. Rebecca was with her mother, talking to Holly. He stared at them for a moment. Holly was laughing; Judith's gaze was politely intense.

'Let's go and light it. But do so without attracting attention. Some of these fellas look as though lighting a fire might be their expertise.'

Rich laughed. 'That's my dad. He's just like that.'

By picking up a couple of crates as if work still needed to be done, they got to the beach without being followed. McCullough placed the crates a metre apart and found a plank of wood from the pyre to lie across them. 'For the Reverend Guffie.'

'He'll break it.'

McCullough tried it with his foot; pressed down. The crates settled into the stones.

Rich squirted lighter fluid in vertical zigzags around the pyre. The liquid was absorbed instantly into the wood, leaving dark damp lines up and down in a loose and looping pattern. He then squatted by the opening that led into the middle, leaned in and aimed the thick jet at the kindling and newspaper, giving it a good soak. 'This should work,' he said, craning his neck around and looking up at McCullough standing behind him.

'Be careful,' McCullough warned.

'If I've got it right—one match should do it. Stand back.'

A long box was pulled out of Rich's back pocket, and with a gesture that reminded McCullough of the playing of a small percussion instrument, there was a high-pitched scrape and a whisper of ignition. The match was then darted in. The lighter fluid was only gently combustible, not an accelerant, and it took a moment for the kindling to be fully alight, a bright rough-shaped heart at the centre of the pyre.

'Told you. I'm the master.'

It was Terry who always kept the fire going at the site. Had Rich coveted this job?

It took a few minutes before they were confident that the large pieces of timber were catching. It was time to collect Terry and carry him down.

3

Holly kept the children at a distance. Rebecca and Judith stood nearby. Most of the others moved nearer to the entrance to the church, although they didn't crowd around. There was no collective feeling of solemnity, but then there wasn't much to see that might create such a mood—everything looked more humdrum than expected: no bier, no robes for the carriers; Terry was not adorned with anything beyond a clean bed sheet.

'I don't think we want a procession,' McCullough said to everyone, to no one. 'I suspect there is no dignified way of doing this.'

To carry Terry in his arms, bound in a sheet, didn't feel right; even if no one else pictured Michelangelo's *Pietà*, he would. But Terry wasn't heavy enough to require two people; he'd just be this fallen shape between them, a dead man removed from a battlefield. He decided to take the boy over his shoulder, as Nathaniel might have done with something of similar size. At the pyre, Rich would help manoeuvre the body onto the narrow platform.

When he emerged with Terry's body, there was no reflexive gasp or movement backwards—he was watched as a man doing something vaguely interesting might be watched. Marvin took pictures, but without urgency; he didn't move like a photographer desperate to find a perfect angle, to capture a moment. McCullough heard Walter, in his full-toned voice, say to Holly: 'Is that Terry?'

The crowd chuckled.

McCullough raised his eyebrows at Holly, acknowledging that in years to come it might only be the two of them who would remember this in all its absurdity. He then looked at Rebecca and smiled grimly, before nodding at Rich to lead the way.

It was a procession only in that from a distance there was a line of people walking in the same direction. It wasn't the trudge of monks or pilgrims.

At the top of the beach, McCullough's foot slipped on a large stone and he lost his balance. Rebecca, legs awkwardly splayed, grabbed at him to keep him upright.

'Thank you.'

'You're welcome.'

The pyre was large and bright and tall, a pillar of fire, but this time the flames were at the mercy of the changeable breeze, and didn't reach to the sky. Even so, it was an impressive sight. From the clifftops, it would have seemed a permanent part of the landscape, fire escaping from the earth. Even its shape was just a smaller version of other shapes in nature, a fractal universe.

The crowd's reaction was one of collective shock, finally recognizing what was going to happen: they were going to see a body thrown onto this powerful thing.

McCullough turned to Rich. 'Are we actually going to get him up there?'

Rich didn't hear him. The roaring of the flames was loud. Tramping feet on the pebbles sounded like the noise of ancient warriors invading.

McCullough looked around at the crowd. Its number was more or less the inhabitants of a small village gathering around a Guy Fawkes Night bonfire. Somehow this diminished the power of the pyre, and he felt the silliness of what they were doing. He turned back to the fire. The strength of its heat was dangerous, forbidding.

The crowd split into small groups as people tried to get as close as possible and yet avoid the billowing and shifting smoke. Those nearest coughed and pulled up T-shirts over mouths and noses.

Judith was still with Holly and the twins.

All that was left to do was to heave Terry onto the platform. T-shirt hooked over his nose, Rich was there, hands spread to take one end of the body.

To get Terry in place they needed to raise him almost head-high and then reach over the inclining angle of the burning wood. Their feet were inside the outer layer of pyre, inches away from the heart of the fire. Finding the right approach was difficult, and neither could give the other instructions because of the smoke. But they'd worked together enough to anticipate each other's thinking. The idea was to lift Terry above the height of the platform, and then using the momentum, place him as far back as possible so his weight didn't tip the platform forward. They needed to avoid the body rolling off and lying pathetically at the foot of the pyre, like a sheet from a washing line blown against a fence.

As they heaved Terry on there was a small collapsing of the inner frame, and timber that had burned down gave way. Embers burst around them. McCullough pushed his foot further into the fire. He could feel the heat through the leather of his boot. When Rich moved away, McCullough kept Terry on the platform with his hand pressed against the boy's side. He then counted to five and let go. For a few seconds, he stood there, palms out, as if warming his hands. The body seemed stable.

There had been some gasps at the original cracking and splitting sound, but when he turned around, no one had moved. McCullough noticed Geoffrey stand and place his hands together in prayer, fingers entwined.

The fire was still not burning directly under the platform, and with no loose edges to catch the sheet was not yet alight.

McCullough turned to each of the disparate groups, beer and cider cans in their hands, plastic bags at their feet.

'Thank you.'

The twins, standing in front of Holly, held juice boxes. He gave them a quick wave and smiled. They waved back. It was then he noticed, standing alone below the cliff, an older man leaning on a stick, a cap pulled down over his eyes. He had aged, as if ten years had passed since they last met. McCullough wondered how to acknowledge him. Whether to acknowledge him. It was enough to meet his gaze and hold it.

It was time to say something. He'd rehearsed nothing. Not a word. Not even how he might begin. Every time he'd thought about it, something had come up, or his mind had been a blank. Some things were beyond preparation.

But he was here, others were here, and something needed to be said.

Before him everyone was a grey-blue blur, as if the crowd had taken on the colour of the smoke, the stones on the beach. He tried to look inward and hope, as people always said, everything would be fine if he spoke from the heart.

'Let's say it first, and say it plainly: Terry committed the most terrible act. He killed our friend. He killed someone's son. And let's also make it clear: Nat's murder was no different from an execution in all its horror. It was barbaric. Unspeakable. And it will always be so, to his family, his friends, to the world. There is no working through this, no finding good or right in it. Perhaps it was even worse than an execution. There was no historical or religious animus, no misguided sense of right.

'It is true that Nat and Terry were never really friends, but much of what is built on the cliffs behind you is their work—Nat's willingness to labour; Terry's care over every detail. If they were similar in another way it was that they both lacked generosity about the other.

'And yet as we face what Terry did to our friend, we also have to face that it was a friend who did it, and ask ourselves, does he cease to be our friend? I don't see how. It is no secret that I felt great warmth towards Terry. But I want to set that aside. I want to ask: faced with what he did, faced with a person who committed such a terrible act, what do we do? What is left for us to do?

'As I've said to some of you already, I believe Terry was tormented. I believe he was on some kind of a mission. I know this is difficult to hear and sounds like an excuse, but it remains the case: Terry was on some terrible and awful mission to prove that authenticity was only available to those who have the strength to offend man, to offend God. There is no freedom in being good; it's what God wants, after all. And perhaps you can never truly know why you are being good, or for whom. What drove him to think this, I do not know. Whether I am partly to blame, I don't know. But either way, Terry somehow found himself in a place where he believed negative authenticity was all that was available to him. And he took it. But we have also to set that aside.

'Now we have to ask ourselves, what happens when we set aside our friendship with Terry, when we set aside his motive—what are we left with? There are just two options: judgment or love. We either judge, or we realize, absurd as it is, that we must love. I suppose there is also indifference, but not to this. So it is not a false choice. We can, of course, hand over responsibility to others. But that is a kind of cowardice.

'There is also so-called natural justice. The opportunity to deliver the punishment that we ourselves, his friends and neighbours, all those affected, think fit. To take it upon ourselves to do what we deem is right. After all, Terry confessed. There was no uncertainty.

So what would have happened had that been permitted? Would Terry have lived through the night? Possibly not. But let's say he'd been allowed to live, just a day, what would we have done then? At some point a decision about what to do with him would have had to be made. There would probably be a trial of some sort, followed by a judgment, and then punishment. Death or imprisonment— who knows? But these are just practicalities, and for now we can set them aside.'

Behind McCullough the fire shifted, a series of small collapses, embers bursting high into the dusk. He turned to see whether Terry was stable, whether or not he was beginning to burn. Parts of the sheet nearest the inside of the fire were blackening, and flames were now finding their way along the underside of the platform, soon to lick the outward face. In a few minutes, Terry would be lying within a long cradle of fire. McCullough paused to watch and then turned back to the small crowd.

'So what else? Once the practicalities have been decided? We must decide what is best for us. To face our feelings and express them is important. There is no sin in feeling anger, hatred, the desire for vengeance. They are natural. And because we live in enlightened times, we might also want to think about why this happened on a more general level, what it tells us about society, our young people. But these are diversions.

'So I ask again, what else? What are we left with, after all practicalities, our feelings, the search for understanding, when we have judged and feel right in our judgment? Perhaps nothing is left. But that cannot be. No good can come of nothing. So I ask again: what are we left with? When we've set everything aside. What is left? Of course, the answer is clear. Love. And in this case impractical, nonsensical love, because we are asking of ourselves to love those that we rightfully hate, that we have judged and punished. To love those who behave as if they hate us, which they may do. Of course, there is indifference again, turning away. But what good will that do?'

McCullough paused, and looked to his left and right. Rebecca and Rich were now standing next to him. Rebecca was crying.

'Some will have noticed I have been slippery, asking, "What are we left with?", "What good will that do?", when these are not our concern. Those are questions for philosophers, jurists, politicians. So what is our concern? What, to quote a great theologian, is our utmost concern? It cannot be wealth or ambition—we know that. It cannot be hatred—we know that. And power is the worst of us. Perhaps our utmost concern should be to live a good life. A proposition that many claim is too vague to be meaningful. But for a moment let's look for meaning in it. Let's see where we arrive. Is it not obvious what is at the heart of the Good? Aren't we just asking what is at the heart of kindness, generosity, compassion? And isn't the answer to that easy? Love is at the heart of these things. Without love they are just empty concepts, and with love they are inexhaustible. And so now we know. To live a good life is to place love at the heart of life, and that is worthy of being our utmost concern. And now what was vague or meaningless is clear and precise. In an instance we know now what we must do. We must love Terry. Killer of our friend. Killer of our son. And in doing so we have just created a new world. A better world in an instant. Yes, it might only last that long, because inevitably there will be something else to which we must turn, to which our first emotions will be anger, misery, hatred. But at least we now know that at some point we can set these feelings aside, and that it will be easier this time because we know, no matter hard it might always be, it can be accomplished. Even if only for an instant.'

There was more cracking and spitting behind him and he turned again to look. The sheet was blackening, and beneath it Terry's body was contracting. There was a strong smell of burning, of cooking, charred flesh, and a pungency he found surprising, as if Terry had been basted with some exotic oil. He turned back to the small crowd and took in a deep breath; the back of his throat was dry and his lungs felt clogged with smoke.

'The night Terry died, he confessed he came looking for me first. That I was who he planned to kill.'

There was a cry from Holly and she buckled at the knees. Standing close by, Judith stepped over to her and clasped her around the waist. Pearl looked round and smiled. Then turned back.

'In a way, it would have made more sense had it been me. Without making grand claims for myself, and if I am right about why he did what he did, perhaps the negative authenticity he was after would have been more complete. Terry liked me as much as he liked anyone.

'So let's say he'd been successful and found and killed me. Let's look at the outcome for others. He would have deprived my partner Holly of . . . well, right now . . . that's not entirely clear. But certainly the act would have deprived my children of a father. My lovely children, standing there with their mother. The pain I feel when I contemplate this . . . I want to cry out, to vomit. I want time to collapse and to meet Terry on the ridge back there and kill him even for thinking it. Now, when he is already dead. But it didn't happen. It is only an act of the imagination. It is nothing compared to the real pain that is here among us—sorry, sir, but I have to acknowledge your presence.' He looked directly at Nathaniel's father. 'Please accept that anything I say is nothing compared to your loss. And yet I must hope that it is possible that the love you feel for your son, for your sons, is just a part of what you are capable of feeling, and although Terry is now dead, and that might afford you some peace, at some point you will find it in your heart to forgive him, and perhaps even to love him. To find in yourself the possibility of such a thing.'

As everyone sought out the person McCullough was addressing, the old man turned and made his way slowly up the beach; he hadn't removed his cap.

The fire was now shifting every minute or so and falling in on itself, the longest pieces of wood breaking and collapsing in like a stumbling horse. When Terry rolled off the platform and into the centre of the fire, the displacement of air created ash and glowing embers that spread like a great nest of fireflies dispersing into the night. There were gasps and 'wows'.

McCullough's throat was dry and clogged from the smoke and he tried to clear it, splitting out ash-grey phlegm. He had one more thing he needed to say.

'Sorry. I will be finished soon. You've been very patient. I know I can go on.' He paused and coughed; he could take ash in his mouth. 'Please believe me when I say there is no instruction in what I've said. There is no commandment to act this way. All I've tried to do is outline a choice that some of us have forgotten we are capable of making. It's easy to say, I know. And I don't expect many of us, least of all myself, to be successful—especially in the way we measure success these days. There will be no transformation. Each day will continue to contain more suffering than seems right by any measure, and because of this we will continue to ask the question: if there is a God, how can He permit this? And who can blame us if we reach the obvious answer—there is no God. But that is to misunderstand God. And not only in this moment, but God as He is whatever your conception of Him. God won't turn this world around. There is no grand plan that will make sense to those of us present at the end. There is no plan at all. There never was. There has only ever been God's gift . . . which is us in our freedom to love . . . our painful, confusing, and at times burdensome freedom to love.'

He began to cough again. He lifted his T-shirt over his mouth and nose and took in a deep breath. He stood up straight; he needed a minute more.

' . . . And because of this freedom, we must accept that we have been left to ourselves. We are the grown-ups in this world. We are not God's children and we are not God.' He had to stop and cough, empty his lungs, choke out the smoke; if he didn't do so, he feared he might vomit. 'But neither are we abandoned. Unless, that is, we abandon . . .'

It was no good. He couldn't breathe. For a few seconds he stood bent over, hands on his knees, struggling not to faint. The coughing was now a reflex and out of his control. Rebecca patted him on the back; the *thwack* echoed off the face of the cliffs. He straightened up and whispered, 'Thank you, Rebecca. It's OK. I'm OK.' He steadied himself. 'Unless that is we . . . abandon . . .' What? Did he really know? He'd assumed it was the coughing stopping him, but he wondered now whether it was because he had nothing left to say. He laughed and coughed; coughed and laughed. In the end, it seemed he'd achieved what he set out to do: he'd said nothing; but neither had he remained silent.

When it was clear that was it, he had finished, a few people clapped. One man said, 'See ya, Terry,' in a muted voice.

And then from the clifftop a strong voice shouted, 'Burn in hell, loser.'

The crowd turned around, and someone bellowed back, 'Fuck off, Simon.'

McCullough bent over, hands on his knees again.

From the back, rising from the makeshift bench, Geoffrey stood up and walked forward. 'I'd like to commend him to God, if I may?'

McCullough looked up from his bent position. 'Of course.'

Everyone waited, although many felt impatient while Geoffrey stood before the pyre, his hands close to his lips, and whispered words that no one could hear.

When he could straighten up and breathe without coughing, McCullough went over to Holly and the children. Judith stepped away, and looked around the crowd for her daughter. Rebecca saw her and waved, which was echoed by Judith with a slightly hidden command to join her.

Holly kissed McCullough. 'You must be very tired.'

'Exhausted.'

Pearl looked up. 'It was nice what you said, Daddy.'

'Thank you.'

She then asked, 'Who was that old man?'

'Someone Terry hurt in a very terrible way. It was very brave of him to come here.'

'Is he burned now?' This was Walter. He wanted to see. For the longest time the boy had been forced to watch in silence and now he wanted to examine. After a glance between his parents, he took his father's and sister's hands and led them down the beach as if walking them to a playground.

The pyre was now only waist-height, a ring of black wood around it. Now and again the breeze shifted and a gust of smoke drove them back, their feet slipping on the stones. Terry was now a hard-black thing, a hard curl of a body, at one end something of the shape of a skull and at the other something of the shape of feet. McCullough didn't imagine the children would be able to make out the body from all the charred wood surrounding it; it was more that he knew what to look for. He doubted there would only be ash left; the temperature required to burn up bones was never going to be reached—something he hadn't thought to consider. What would be left would be recognizable as a body, like the remains from Pompeii or Herculaneum, a charred shape, given form by a hardening of substances, whether it was the sheet or muscle and bone or some combination, he didn't know; but certainly at this point the folds of the sheet seemed part of the form lying there.

Squatting down, he retrieved a long thin piece of wood, only a little burned at one end, and gave it to Walter. 'Here. Be careful.'

It had been a kind of torture for the boy not to be able to poke and disturb the fire, to cause new flames to emerge.

Pearl stayed close to her father, holding his hand, her fingers fidgeting in his palm. She also demanded that her brother be careful, looking around for her mother, the only sensible one.

Within ten minutes the beach was mostly empty. Rich had sat down next to Geoffrey, who'd returned to the bench after his prayer. Judith and Rebecca were gone, although McCullough expected Rebecca to return. Holly, her bottom perched on a large rock, watched him and the children.

McCullough shouted, 'We'll only be a minute,' although he knew it would take some time before Walter would be content, with so many things to be discovered, reactions to cause. To see the boy's face at work, lit up by the light of the fire, prodding and scattering, calculating his next disturbance, moved McCullough, and he was forced to reflect that only weeks ago Terry had sought to deprive him of this, and with it deprive Walter of his father's loving protection. It didn't bear thinking about. But he was right in what he'd said. In that moment, faced with Terry, someone he loved . . . he would have killed him. It wasn't even a real dilemma.

He looked down at Terry's burned body, a blackened mass that if struck hard enough might break apart, something he and Rich would have to do at some point; he couldn't be left as he was. He turned his gaze to Walter, striking pieces of charred wood, revealing burning embers as they broke apart, and now and again, the sudden appearance of a new flame. In his hand, the ticklish fingers of his daughter could be felt. He looked around for Holly. She was walking across the beach towards them.

AUTHOR'S NOTE

There are many subjects in this novel that require technical knowledge—world religion, criminal law, construction. But as a novel is first and foremost an act of the imagination, oftentimes I've decided poetic licence is preferable to hard and intrusive research. But just in case anyone wonders: yes, you can build on sand! It's got something to do with kilo-newtons. Turning to God, I've chosen to capitalize the pronouns, although it seems there is a debate about whether that is correct or not. It has not been my intention to offend anyone who holds specific religious views, but I accept that my challenge to the Christian Communion in my discussion of the 'signal and not the noise' in the chapter 'Apocrypha', may do just that. I apologize in advance for any offence caused.

ACKNOWLEDGEMENTS

This book has taken years to write: one might argue most of my life, or at least the thirty-five years that have passed since my state-school teacher, Michael Stewart, gave me a copy of *Crime and Punishment* by Dostoevsky.

Undoubtedly Dostoevsky is the single strongest influence on *As a God Might Be*, followed by Wallace Stevens, the source of the novel's title. But many other writers, philosophers and theologians have influenced, inspired and challenged me during the writing of this novel. My debt to them is enormous. In no particular order they are: Rowan Williams, Keith Ward, John Bowker, N. T. Wright, Paul Tillich, Karl Barth, Terry Eagleton and Roger Scruton, Pascal, Kierkegaard, Heidegger, Nietzsche, Wittgenstein, George Steiner, Harold Bloom, Marilynne Robinson, Gavin Hyman, William James, Géza Vermes, Dietrich Bonhoeffer, Thomas Weinandy, David Bentley Hart, Peter van Inwagen, Christopher Hill, Raymond Tallis, Sara Maitland, Leszek Kołakowski, Francis Spufford, R.S. Thomas and Simon Critchley.

As will have been noted, short quotes have been used at the beginning of each chapter. It is my hope that where source material is still in copyright, 'fair use' will be accepted as a reason for permissions not sought.

Much of the first draft was written at Gladstone's Library, and to all of the staff: a big thank you for making me feel so at home. Damian Barr recommended the library when I was desperate for a place to write and a debt is owed to him for that timely suggestion. My colleagues at Blinc have allowed me time away from work responsibilities. My sanity has been managed by Dr Allswell Eno through kind words and the right choice of medication. No small feat. Thank you to the Newkey-Burden family for permission to use the artwork of Pen Furneaux.

More general thanks to Leo Hollis, Jim Poyser, Duncan McGuffie, Marcus Wright, Helen Pisano, Luke Meddings, Cambridge Jones, Fox White, Curtis Radclyffe, Becky Abrams, George Young, James Tookey, Eloise Millar, and the remarkably clairvoyant Special Angel K.

Particular thanks and love to Valarie Smith for being my first reader of this novel—her kindness, sensitivity and enthusiasm made all the difference as I approached the final revisions.

I have no doubt the road to publication would have been very much longer if not for a chance meeting at a small-press fair in Peckham with Sam Mills of Dodo Ink. The moment I said I'd written a 'theological' novel, she said she wanted to read it. And from that moment, its fate/plight has been in the most generous and loving hands. Thank you, Sam.

From the rest of the Dodo Ink team—Alex, Thom, Tomoé, Jess, Sorrel, Jayne—there has been nothing but deep understanding of what I wanted to achieve, and unwavering dedication to its success.

Thank you to Nicci Praça for all advice and support, but especially for suggesting the final version of the title.

The original title of this novel was *Family of Love*, and final thanks must go to my own family of love, Bridget, Wilder and Macleod. What they will make of this novel, I don't know. But it should be plain by now: without them, it would never have existed.

ABOUT DODO INK

At Dodo Ink, we're book lovers first and foremost. From finding a great manuscript to the moment it hits the bookshop shelves, that's how we approach the publishing process at every stage: excited about giving you something we hope you'll love. Good books aren't extinct, and we want to seek out the best literary fiction to bring to you. A great story shouldn't be kept from readers because it's considered difficult to sell or can't be put in a category. When a reader falls in love with something, they tell another reader, and that reader tells another. We think that's the best way of selling a book there is.

Dodo Ink was founded by book lovers, because we believe that it's time for publishing to pull itself back from the brink of extinction and get back to basics: by finding the best literary fiction for people who love to read. Books shouldn't be thought of in terms of sales figures, and neither should you. We approach every step of the process thinking of how we would want a book to be, as a reader, and give it the attention it deserves. When you see our Dodo logo, we'd like you to think of our books as recommendations from one book lover to another. After all, aren't those the ones that we take the greatest pleasure in?

At Dodo Ink, we know that true book lovers are interested in stories regardless of genre or categorization. That's how we think a publishing company should work, too: by giving the reader what they want to read, not what the industry thinks they should. We look for literary fiction that excites, challenges, and makes us want to share it with the world. From finding a manuscript to designing the cover, Dodo Ink books reflect our passion for reading. We hope that when you pick up one of our titles, you get the same thrill—that's the best thank you we can think of.